# Mallory Beck
# Cozy Culinary Capers
# Books 1-4

DENISE JADEN

# DEDICATION

To my wonderful readers! I love writing stories and having such
encouraging people to tell them to makes all the difference.

# Book One

# MURDER
## at Mile Marker 18

### DENISE JADEN

# JOIN MY MYSTERY READERS' NEWSLETTER TODAY!

Sign up now, and you'll get access to a special epilogue to accompany this series—an exclusive bonus for newsletter subscribers. In addition, you'll be the first to hear about new releases and sales, and receive special excerpts and behind-the-scenes bonuses.

Visit the link below to sign up and receive your bonus epilogue:

https://www.subscribepage.com/mysterysignup

# MURDER AT MILE MARKER 18

An unlucky amateur sleuth, an adorable cop, and a cat with a hunch…

If anyone had told Mallory Beck she would become Honeysuckle Grove's next unschooled detective, she would have thought they were ten noodles short of a lasagna. Her late husband had been the mystery novelist with a penchant for the suspicious. She was born for the Crock-Pot, not the magnifying glass, and yet here she is, elbow-deep in fettuccine, cat treats, and teenagers with an attitude, the combination of which lands her smack-dab in the middle of a murder investigation.

Maybe she should have thought twice about delivering a casserole to a grieving family. Maybe she should have avoided the ever-changing green eyes of her seventh-grade crush—now the most heart-stopping cop in town. Maybe she should have stopped listening to the insightful mewls of her antagonistic cat, Hunch, who most likely wants her to be the town's next murder victim.

Whatever the case, Mallory Beck got herself into this investigation, and she has a distraught teenage girl counting on her to deliver the truth.

# CHAPTER ONE

The wife of a war correspondent or a fighter pilot or even a venomous snake milker (yes, there is such a thing) might expect to be a widow at twenty-eight, but certainly not the wife of a novelist.

And yet here I was, learning how to live life in the oversized house, in a small West Virginia town we settled into only a year ago—alone. To be fair, I hadn't done much in the way of living in the last eight months since Cooper died, but after an offhand comment from my sister about me being under great threat of becoming a cat lady, I was determined to start today.

Being a cat lady wouldn't be so bad if the cat I'd inherited didn't loathe me.

I swung my legs out of Cooper's black Jeep and did a little hip shimmy to straighten my skirt as I stood. Picking out clothes this morning had been about as difficult as choosing between cake and pie (no one should ever have to make that choice). What does one wear that says, I'm fine, just fine, and I haven't been moping around my dark house for the last eight months, nope, not me, but nonetheless, please, keep your distance?

Even though it was the middle of August, I had settled on a black skirt with the tiniest of polka dots and a light cornflower blue blouse with matching pumps and a headband that pulled my in-need-of-a-trim bangs back. It didn't spell out the last eight months of my life, but it did the job in making me feel tidy and unapproachable. My coffee-brown hair fell halfway down my back now, full of split ends, but it actually didn't look half bad today for how many months it had been matted against my living room couch.

I strode for the church, the same one I hadn't stepped foot inside since

Cooper's memorial service. Church had always been Cooper's thing. I'd gone along to play the part of the good wife but didn't spend too much time considering how I felt about God or how He felt about me. At least I hadn't before He decided to snatch my husband from me.

Two greeters in their mid-forties stood at the closest open glass doors—a man in a gray suit and a woman in an apricot summer dress. Thankfully, I didn't recognize either of them. I'd chosen this as my first big public outing because, at more than three hundred people, I figured our church was the one place I might get in and out of completely unnoticed. As I approached the greeters, though, the woman leaned into the man and whispered something.

I gulped. Apparently, this was how it would go: People would recognize me, remember Cooper, and not know what to say. Why, again, had I gotten out of bed this morning? There had to be at least one Netflix series I hadn't binged yet.

The woman at the door pasted on a bright smile as she turned back to me, just in time to say, "Good morning."

"Good morning," I murmured back, but my voice came out hard and crusty, like bread out of a too-hot oven, or like I hadn't used it in more than a week. Come to think of it, other than talking on the phone with my sister, I probably hadn't. My tone, at least, had the desired effect, and the greeters let me pass without another word.

My next goal was to make it through the lobby and into the sanctuary without garnering any other stares or attention. This part was not easy. All eyes followed me as I entered the church lobby, and I was pretty sure I wasn't just imagining it.

My late husband, Cooper Beck, had been a well-known mystery writer, so I was used to recognition. After only five years, I hadn't been married long enough to get used to this feeling of notoriety, and I guess I had assumed it would have died with Cooper.

Apparently not so. And not only that, but every single person nearby was scanning my body, probably taking in my too-bright cornflower blouse and thinking it inappropriate for someone in mourning, or noticing the tiny polka dots on my skirt, or wondering why I still wore black after so many months, or…something.

While I was lost in my warring thoughts, Donna Mayberry spotted me, at first only giving me a glance, and I thought I might make it into the sanctuary before actually having to speak to her. But then she did a double take, quickly followed by the head tilt of pity. By this point, I knew that look well. That look was why I had taken to grocery shopping and running errands at midnight instead of during the day like a normal person. At midnight, I could safely avoid the head tilt of pity.

"Mallory Beck?" Donna called with an arm straight up in the air, so any stray person in the vicinity who hadn't yet set eyes on me might do so now. "It's so nice to see you out!" she said loudly, calling public attention to my self-imposed isolation in only two seconds.

Donna had the kind of long legs that would be impossible to outrun. In fact, I blinked, and she was right there beside me. Donna was long everywhere—from her fingers to the dark, shiny hair that fell past her waist. She wore a summery yellow dress that touched the floor, and I had to wonder what kind of a store made clothes that would look long on someone like nearly six-foot Donna. Whether it was her hair or her stature or her clothes, though, Donna Mayberry always seemed to have a way of making me feel frumpy and underdressed.

Then again, maybe all these people would finally look at her instead of me.

Donna and Marv were one of the first couples Cooper and I had met when we'd settled into Honeysuckle Grove a year ago, and while Marv worked about sixteen hours a day, Donna naturally excelled at everything from shrub carving to Michelangelo-inspired nail design, and seemed to have a little too much time on her hands—time to know everything about everyone.

"How are you doing, honey? Is this your first time back at church?" Again with the head tilt of pity. Even though I doubted Donna could know I hadn't left my house in thirteen days, somehow her tone confirmed she absolutely did.

"First time, yes," I replied. No point in denying it.

She angled me away from the imposing stares and nudged me toward an alcove as though she could sense how much the staring bothered me. A second later, a tall, potted plant concealed us in the corner of the lobby, and I had just let out a breath of relief when Donna suddenly started pulling at my skirt.

I grabbed for my skirt and looked down in horror. Was Donna trying to undress me? Was this a bad dream? Maybe I was still sleeping soundly—or as soundly as one could beside a hostile cat while dreaming about being undressed in public.

But as I blinked and then blinked again, Donna held up a pair of beige control-top pantyhose she had peeled off the outside of my skirt to show me. A second later, she tucked them into the outside pouch of my gray leather purse.

"Oh!" I let out a loud noise, something between a yelp and a laugh. "Thank you!"

As I peeked around the plant, it seemed everyone had lost interest in us, thank goodness.

"Well, you'll have to sit with us." Donna straightened her own dress and looked down as though something equally embarrassing might have happened to her, but I was pretty sure we both knew that wasn't how the universe worked. I doubted Marv was here, so "us" likely meant Donna's gossip posse—that was what Cooper and I used to call them—but as Donna tugged my arm toward the far side of the lobby, a jolt of panic shot through me.

"Oh, I can't," I said, pulling away from her eight-tone sunset nails. "I'm, um, meeting someone, and I said I'd be sitting on this side." The first lie I could think of launched off my tongue. I just couldn't imagine sitting with Donna's posse and having them all whisper, "Yes, but how are you really doing?" fifty times throughout the service.

Donna looked to either side of me as though she might regard this mysterious person I could be waiting for. I could have continued with the lie. Said my sister was in town or conjured an imaginary friend or something to put her mind at rest. But I was suddenly just so tired from all of this interaction—the most I'd endured in eight months—and so I simply stood there staring at Donna like my brain had taken an extended vacation.

Eventually, she said, "Oh. Okay then. If you're sure?"

I nodded as she backed away, leaving me to my social anxiety.

A few more head tilts greeted me as I took my seat near the back of the sanctuary on the right, nice and close to the door. Thankfully, my chosen outfit—sans the sticky pantyhose—did its duty of keeping me mostly unapproachable. The church had rarely filled to capacity when Cooper and I had attended, so I had some confidence I'd have the back bench to myself. The only time I'd actually seen this place full was at Cooper's memorial service, but most of those were mystery fans and people fascinated with death, not people who had actually known him.

Soon, the service started with singing and then the pastor's invitation for people to donate and volunteer in any area they were able. Nothing had changed in eight months, apparently. Honeysuckle Grove Community Church still didn't have enough money in the building fund or enough people to host small group Bible studies in their homes. It seemed so very odd that while my life had been turned on its head, leaving me without a husband or a profession, every person around me seemed like a walking robot, pre-programmed for a life that would remain constant until their pre-determined time of death.

As though Pastor Jeff could read my mind, he started his sermon with, "We are not robots."

That was one thing I'd forgotten about church. Pastor Jeff had a great gift for storytelling. He usually started one of his stories with a bold and unusual statement, and then went on a long rabbit trail about his son's first crack at baseball or about that time he lost his luggage in a Taiwanese airport, but then brought it back around to that first bold statement in a way that made the entire congregation think, Ah, I see what you did there!

4

But today, I feared I didn't have the brain capacity to follow his breadcrumbs. He chattered on about what it meant to be part of a family and body parts working together and covering a multitude of sins. At least I had been correct about getting the back bench to myself.

I tuned out for a minute, or maybe it was more than a minute, because the next thing I knew, Pastor Jeff closed his Bible and bowed his head to pray.

I'd done it! I'd made it through the entire service. Okay, maybe I hadn't taken much of it in, but I'd spoken to an actual person, I'd sat here and proved I could act normal, and I hadn't drawn a single bit of attention to myself. Well, besides the part where I wore my pantyhose on the outside of my skirt.

"I'm sorry to have to tell you there's been a recent death in the congregation," Pastor Jeff said. At first, I expected all eyes to once again turn to me, but then quickly realized "recent" in Pastor Jeff's books meant something during the last two seasons. "This past Friday, August the thirteenth, Dan Montrose met his death in an unfortunate accident."

Pastor Jeff resumed bowing his head to pray for the family and their loss. His deep voice boomed with emotion and instantly made me feel like I'd gone back in time eight months. I could physically feel grief for this family I'd never even met, like a two-hundred-pound anchor in my stomach. Pastor Jeff went on to talk about the shock of the death and the wife and children this man had left behind, and because I couldn't bear the weight of the extra grief, I kept my eyes open and focused on our authoritative, if somewhat frazzled, pastor.

Pastor Jeff wore jeans and a beige button-down today. His hair was more in need of a trim than mine, which was saying something, but in every bit of his countenance, he oozed compassion. I wondered how overworked Pastor Jeff must be to take care of such a large congregation. It must involve a lot of stress for someone who cared so much. After Cooper died, Pastor Jeff visited me three times at the house, until I'd finally donned a face that convinced him I was doing fine, just fine, and didn't need a fourth visit. In truth, I probably did need that fourth visit, but even then, in the midst of my grief, I had somehow inherently known that I would be doing our overworked pastor a great favor by letting him move on to some other hurting soul within the church.

"Anyone?" Pastor Jeff said, and it took me a second to realize he had finished praying and now gazed over the congregation with his eyes pleading, as he often did at the beginning of the service when asking for volunteers. I had tuned out again. "Can anyone be the arms of this church body and deliver a casserole to these hurting folks, to help out this part of our church family?" He scanned the entire congregation a second time. "It doesn't have to be anything fancy."

5

He looked to the far side of the sanctuary where Donna and her gossip posse huddled whispering, and then in front of them to where the rest of the church staff sat. The church secretary, Penny Lissmore, let out such a large breath of disappointment, I could see her chest heave from across the large worship center. Pastor Jeff sighed as though admitting defeat to her and explaining telepathically that they'd have to add Casserole Delivery to the long list of things someone on the staff would eventually have to get to.

After Cooper died, I'd had at least a couple of casseroles delivered to me. That time was a bit of a haze, and I definitely didn't ponder at the time how much cajoling it might have taken to get someone to pick up a casserole at the store—they were the store-bought variety, I remembered that much—and bring it over to my house.

I got it. Approaching a grieving widow was probably near the bottom of most people's lists of favorite things to do, right below getting a root canal or having a wardrobe malfunction on your first day back at church. But for the first time, I understood how comforting those little acts of kindness could be.

While I was lost in my thoughts again, I didn't immediately notice the church secretary and an associate pastor look my way, followed by Pastor Jeff. His face broke into a smile that looked as though heaven had just opened and angels were descending right here on this side of the sanctuary.

"Mallory Beck!" he said, and I startled at my name. "I knew I could count on you. Thank you so much, Mallory. The Montrose family will really appreciate this."

I blinked as I clued in to what he was saying. And that's when I realized my hand was high in the air.

☐

# CHAPTER TWO

Two hours later, I stumbled through my front door, carrying more groceries than one person should be able to manage. As if to prove my point, as I kicked the door shut behind me, the bottom fell out of one of the brown paper bags in my right arm, and dried noodles scattered everywhere.

Hunch peeked around the corner to investigate. Cooper's cat generally snubbed his nose in my direction. Once in a while, he greeted me with a hiss—usually when I was already having a particularly bad day. My sister, Leslie, thought I should really take Hunch down to the SPCA if we didn't get along, but I couldn't get rid of Cooper's beloved cat. Of course I couldn't.

But we also couldn't stand each other.

Now he looked up at me as if saying, "This is new," about not only the noodles on the floor, but also about my overloaded arms. Generally, when I made a trip to the grocery store, I returned with one bag, maybe two. It didn't take a lot to feed a single person, especially one who rarely remembered to eat. Or a single person and a mourning cat.

Yes, mourning. I should take a step back and explain. You see, Hunch was not a normal cat. Hunch's personality was more dog-like than feline in many ways, and he had been every bit the ideal mystery writer's companion. The cat had only ever seemed to enjoy Cooper's company, and I hadn't taken it personally when Cooper was alive because they clearly fit together. When Cooper paced, Hunch paced right alongside him. When Cooper came up with a great plot idea and snapped his fingers, Hunch perched on his haunches right at Cooper's side to high five his owner. I kid you not. Or in this case, would you call it a low five?

I still didn't take Hunch's bristly nature to heart. It just disappointed me that we both missed Cooper terribly and yet we couldn't comfort each other through our grief.

But I could never fill the void Cooper had left in Hunch's life. I couldn't possibly stir up the kind of creative energy that new mysteries and their solutions brought with them. I'd been reading Cooper's novels nonstop for six months to keep what little he'd left behind close to me, and all it had taught me was that I'd lost someone brilliant. No wonder he'd had such a large fan base.

I dropped the intact grocery bags onto the kitchen counter and returned to clean up my mess. Hunch was still investigating, sniffing every inch of my torn grocery bag and its contents like a squatty feline bloodhound. He looked up at me and I swear he raised his eye whiskers on one side as if to ask, "What, exactly, are you up to?"

"I wish I was up to something more exciting," I told Hunch. Cooper had often talked to his cat, but for me, it had always felt strange, at least before today. "Just cooking up a casserole for some nice people who recently experienced a death in the family."

Hunch's fur pricked up on the word "death" and even though there was no story here, no mystery about what I planned to concoct in the kitchen, I figured it wouldn't hurt to let Hunch think differently.

"I'll have to figure out what to do now that I've wasted my noodles," I said, pacing a few times back and forth in our entryway and drumming my fingers on my chin. Hunch watched me for a few seconds. And then he joined me.

The truth was, I knew exactly what to do. And, in fact, purchasing the dried pasta noodles had been a cop-out on my part—barely a step above buying a frozen lasagna.

I didn't blame anyone else for opting for store-bought, of course. Other people had busy lives, while I had absolutely nothing on my agenda, besides getting out of bed and pouring a bowl of cat kibble. Also, most other people didn't have a culinary degree.

Half an hour later, my oven pinged to let me know it was preheated, but I still hadn't decided on a recipe. I had all the ingredients for a basic pasta recipe, but basic seemed much too boring when I hadn't had the opportunity to cook for anyone in eight months. I'd bought tomatoes, so I could flavor the pasta that way, but it still didn't seem good enough. Why hadn't I picked up some spinach? Maybe some saffron?

It ended up being three days and four trips to the grocery store later when I finally decided on a recipe I was happy with. I'd fried sauces and taste-tested a dozen different cheeses. I knew beyond any doubt that I was putting far too much thought into this, and yet I couldn't seem to stop myself.

Besides, once the casserole was cooked, that meant I had to actually deliver it.

But by Wednesday, I had finally worked up the courage and got out of bed by seven in the morning to get started—a time of the day I hadn't seen in many months.

Once again, I preheated the oven, mixed eggs, flour, and salt, and separated my dough into three balls. I blended my first ball with a dough hook and a cup of pureed spinach, the second with crushed tomato, and the third with some olive oil and a touch of saffron. By the time I rolled them all out onto my counter and sliced them into thin fettuccine noodles, I was perfectly pleased with the bouquet of edible colors.

Hunch had been lying on his chair at the kitchen table, chin on his paws, since I started. His eyes followed me throughout the kitchen as I asked myself questions aloud about my recipe and then answered them as if each one were a clue in a grand mystery.

For the first time in eight months, Hunch and I seemed to enjoy each other's company, and all at once, something felt very right about this decision to make a meal for this grieving family. The truth was, I never needed to work again if I didn't want to. Cooper had excellent life insurance, plus a steady stream of royalties from his books. But therein lay the problem—I didn't want to go back to working in a bustling kitchen, and yet I terribly missed cooking, as it never seemed worth putting much effort into the process for only one person. It would be so much easier to stop sitting around my big, lonely house, moping all day every day, if I had somewhere to be.

And now for at least one afternoon, I did.

I continued to ask questions aloud, like, "I wonder how the man died," and "I wonder how his wife is dealing with her grief," as I heated some oil in a saucepan over medium heat, to keep Hunch's attention. I warmed my crushed garlic in the oil until fragrant, added more freshly boiled and crushed tomatoes, and salt. By the time the sauce thickened, I had some chopped basil ready to add.

I grated some cheddar and tried it with the sauce, but quickly decided it lacked richness and added some gorgonzola. Then I layered the casserole into my best white casserole dish—pasta in three different-flavored mounds, then the sauce, a little extra sea salt, and finally the mixture of grated cheeses. I decorated the top with chopped green and yellow peppers for color.

I popped it into the oven and set it to bake twenty-five minutes. And then I raced upstairs to choose an outfit for today's special outing.

# CHAPTER THREE

By eleven o'clock that morning, I stood on the doorstep of a sprawling cornstalk-yellow mansion in the upscale Hillcrest neighborhood of Honeysuckle Grove. Cooper had bought us a large house when we had moved to town—large enough, we'd thought, to fill with a boatload of children one day—but it was situated in the flats and nothing like this mountain of a house.

A four-car garage sat off to the left, with mature trees lining a walkway on either side of the expansive yard, but I headed for the ten-foot-wide marbled steps that led to the front door.

When I'd said goodbye to Hunch from our doorstep, he had been sitting on his haunches in the entryway, and I suspected he would be in that same exact position when I returned, eager to hear what I'd discovered during my outing.

The doorbell let out three long chimes when I pressed on it. A moment later, the heavy oak door creaked open, and a maid with flawless bronze skin stood on the other side. The maid wore an actual bonnet and one of those old-fashioned black dresses with a white apron, but her dress ended mid-thigh—shorter than I'd ever seen on any kind of uniform. With long, dark lashes and high cheekbones, the lady was very pretty and had great legs, so it wasn't surprising she'd want to show them off.

"Um, hi." I held out the casserole, hoping my gesture might say it all, as my casual conversational ability hadn't returned since Cooper's death. But the maid just stood there, staring at me with a blank expression. "I'm delivering a casserole on behalf of Honeysuckle Grove Community Church?" I asked it as a question because now that I thought about it, did these people need or even want my delicately prepared dish if they had a maid and probably a cook who could prepare anything at their whim?

Still, I reasoned, maybe the act of kindness would mean something, even to folks with an unlimited supply of money. You never knew.

I held out the casserole another inch toward the maid and said, "Is Mrs. Montrose at home?" All I'd gotten out of Pastor Jeff in the small amount of conversation I could endure Sunday morning was a last name and an address.

"You know the family?" Her blank stare persisted.

I shifted uncomfortably. "Um, no. Not exactly. I was just bringing this by…"

Quite suddenly, she spun and walked into the mansion, leaving the door wide open. As she strode off, she said, "I see if I find her. There is a velatorio—a wake on right now, you know."

I sucked in a breath. I hadn't known. From the sounds of the woman, a stranger delivering a casserole at this moment was about as inappropriate as bringing a carton of cigarettes to a cancer patient's first chemo treatment. I was torn between racing my casserole back to my vehicle or placing the dish somewhere just inside the doorway before escaping.

Before I'd known these people were wealthy, I'd decided to use a casserole dish Cooper and I had gotten as a wedding gift, figuring the gesture would force me on another outing to come and retrieve it. But I knew without a doubt that I would never show up on this doorstep again in search of my beloved casserole dish. When I tried to picture it, all I could envision was me, draped in rags, holding out my hands, and saying, "Please, ma'am? Alms for the poor?"

The image should have made the decision easy. Back away and save the casserole for yourself, Orphan Mallory. But I was having trouble doing that, and before I could force myself to retreat down the steps, another lady stood in the open doorway.

"Mrs. Montrose?" I asked. All this internal debating had made me breathless.

"Yes?" This lady's face bloomed into a bright smile, and again I doubted whether or not I had the right house, the right family. The lady wore her auburn hair in a big bouffant, like something out of the sixties, but her cream-colored, perfectly-tailored dress looked modern. The cream color made me pause again. Could this truly be the wife of the deceased?

But more than my curiosity, self-consciousness consumed me as I stood there in my khaki capris with a sleeveless floral blouse that was tied at the waist. My dress was more than inappropriate for a wake.

"I'm so sorry if this is poor timing," I said and, as hard as I fought it, found my head tilting at her. "I'm delivering a casserole on behalf of Honeysuckle Grove Community Church?" As I said the words, a familiarity developed. Had I seen this lady at church before? It had been so long since I'd been a regular attendee, I couldn't be sure.

11

"Oh, how lovely," the woman said, her smile brightening even more. "Please, do bring it in and put it on the dining table." She opened the door wider. As I stepped inside, she glanced down at the steam-obscured lid and asked, "Does it have gluten? Or dairy?"

I gulped and stopped in place. I stalled, slipping out of my ballet flats as Cooper and I had been in a habit of doing since buying our new home. "Oh. I'm afraid it has both," I finally said.

When I had worked in various restaurants in the city, they had always listed gluten- and dairy-free options on the menu. It helped with the awkwardness of having to revamp recipes. Allergies hadn't even occurred to me during this morning's cooking spree.

Mrs. Montrose moved deeper into the house. I glanced down and noticed she'd left her shoes on, which, now that I thought about it, was probably more common for a wake, wasn't it?

"No matter, the kids will eat it." Mrs. Montrose waved a casual hand back at me as I debated between putting my shoes back on or leaving them behind. I left them behind for fear she'd lose me in her massive house. I was already dressed completely wrong. What was the difference if I was barefoot? As she continued to lead the way, she murmured, "And if they don't eat it, the greedy, bloodsucking leeches will," so low that I didn't know if I was meant to hear it.

Mrs. Montrose led me through an open room filled with mourners—all dressed in black with either what looked like a mimosa or a fancy canapé in hand—and through to a dining room filled with more food than I had ever seen in one place—and I had worked in more than one restaurant!

The oversized dining room table didn't have an inch of free space. Mrs. Montrose surveyed it quickly, flashed another smile back at me, and said, "Not to worry, I'll call Lupe to help. Lupe?" She pushed through a swinging door and returned a second later with the short-skirted maid on her heels. "Please help Miss...?"

This seemed like an opportunity to be an ear of understanding to these people, so I took it. "Actually, it's Mrs.," I said. "Mrs. Mallory Beck. You see, I also lost my—"

"Do find a place for Mrs. Beck's lovely dish," Mrs. Montrose told her maid, already leaving the dining room to return to her guests.

By the time I had watched her go, I turned back to find that Lupe-the-maid had cleared the perfect spot for my casserole dish. She reached for it, potholders and all, placed it down, and removed the lid. Steam swirled up from within it, and I sighed happily at the cheesy aroma. But as I looked around at the dining room, empty of people other than the two of us, I wondered if it would even get to be enjoyed while it was still warm.

Before I could thank her, Lupe had whisked the lid and potholders toward the kitchen, and as soon as I was left alone, I felt more than awkward. Why on earth had Pastor Jeff thought these people needed a casserole? And delivered by someone who was actually in mourning, no less?

I looked over the table, filled with shrimp rolls and zucchini parmesan and slices of triple-layer tuxedo cake, and tried to decide if I was hungry. The least I could get out of this task was a decent meal, and it wasn't as though anyone was around to see me help myself.

But I sighed and decided against it. Even if I thought I was hungry now, one or two bites in, and I'd realize I wasn't.

I headed back for the foyer. Not a single black-clad person looked my way as I slunk through the front room, not even Mrs. Montrose, whose cream-colored dress stood out against the sea of black. She was currently being jabbered at by a skinny man with dark slicked-back hair in a three-piece dark suit. As I passed, I heard him say, "We need to hire somebody ourselves, find the car that hit him, and sue the pants off the guy."

The man winked twice at Mrs. Montrose. At first, I thought he was trying to send her some kind of a secret signal like Marty Sims, the protagonist in Cooper's mystery series might have done, but after he did it again, I realized I'd only been reading too many of Cooper's novels. It was clearly a tic.

I moved through the open room toward the foyer with my mind still on mystery novels. I hadn't heard how the man of the house—Dan Montrose—had died, but from the sounds of things, it was an accident where the other driver had fled the scene. If it had been a murder, who would be the culprit? The maid in the short skirt? The radiant and beaming wife of the deceased? Or the mysterious man in the three-piece-suit who had a tic?

Maybe I wouldn't be so bad at concocting my own mysteries, after all. At the very least, I could entertain Cooper's cat.

Just inside the foyer, I stopped in place. A lady stood in my path. She wore a simple black skirt with a matching billowy blouse and stood facing away, holding a photograph of what must have been Dan Montrose. I could immediately tell by her shoes—a JC Penny black pump with scuffs on the heels—that she wasn't as wealthy as most of this crowd.

I didn't want to retreat into the open room of people, but I also couldn't get to my own pair of lone coral flats I'd kicked off without asking this lady to move. I figured that was the lesser of the two uncomfortable options and cleared my throat. The woman turned to reveal her tear-streaked, familiar face.

"Beth?" I asked at the same time she said, "Mallory Beck?"

Beth Dawson had been our realtor when Cooper and I looked for our first house in Honeysuckle Grove.

I looked again from the photo in her hands to Beth's tear-streaked face.

"I'm so sorry," I said—the one phrase I swore I'd never say to a grieving person, as it didn't help one bit. I quickly covered with, "How did you know the, um, deceased?"

Beth nodded and placed the photo back onto the foyer's narrow oak table. "He was my sister's husband. It's just awful what happened."

"Oh? Your sister is Mrs. Montrose?" I could see the resemblance now. Beth wore her auburn hair closer to her head and donned a fair bit less makeup, although she clearly wore some, as it had streaked around her eyes.

"Yes, Helen is my sister," she said, and the statement seemed loaded with…something. Underlying emotion? Years of sisterly fights over shared clothes and competing for boys?

This thought made me immediately piece together the fact that Mrs. Helen Montrose seemed perfectly fine after her husband's very recent death—only five days ago—while her sister was quite broken up about it.

I had to comment. "It seems like your sister is holding herself together quite well."

Beth twisted her lips and tilted her head. I wasn't entirely sure what the look meant, but then she went on to say, "You know who's really hurting over Dan's death? The children. They haven't been eating, don't want to talk to me or to Helen, and haven't even come out of their rooms all day."

I put a hand to my chest, physically hurt from the thought of how much his children must be suffering. I glanced down at my lone pair of flats, which someone—probably Lupe—had aligned neatly beside a wooden coatrack. But now I didn't want to leave. Helen Montrose didn't want my help and comfort, but perhaps someone in this household did.

"Do you think it would be okay if I brought the kids a plate of food to their rooms?" I asked Beth. Being their aunt, she would know if this was inappropriate. "I just brought a fresh casserole."

Beth smiled. "You know, they'd probably love that. I think they're tired of everyone they know asking them if they're all right. I promised I'd give them their space today, but I hate knowing they're not getting anything to eat."

I smiled. "Where do I find their bedrooms?"

"Right up the stairs from the dining room. Come on, I'll show you."

Before she turned to lead the way, I said, "Wait," and dug into my purse for a tissue. I pulled one out of a package and handed it to her, motioning to her eyes.

She smiled her thanks, and a second later, Beth was tidied up and leading me back through the open room of people. Not a single person looked away from their conversations to us. Lupe wove around the room with a tray of canapés, which made it clear why the dining room was so deserted. Apparently, these people didn't retrieve their own food.

As we moved through to the dining room, I asked Beth, "I overheard

14

something earlier, and, well…Was your brother-in-law killed in a car accident, a hit-and-run?"

Beth let out a long sigh. "That's what they tell us, yes. Where did you hear that?"

A rush of heat traveled up my neck for having been caught eavesdropping. "Oh, well, I had just been about to say goodbye to your sister, and a man was telling her he wanted to find the car who hit Dan and sue him, or something like that."

Beth nodded and slipped a tendril of shoulder-length auburn hair behind her ear. "That would be Terrence Lane. He's another lawyer at the firm where Dan was a partner." She shook her head. "I'd heard there wasn't much chance of finding the person responsible. If Terrence can, I'm all for it."

If the person took off, it seemed as though there had to be a way to find the person so he or she could at least be held accountable for that.

But Beth sighed again. "I supposed it wouldn't bring Dan back, regardless. This family has enough money, and I'm sure the person already feels awful. So what's the point? Why not just let everyone get past their grief and move on with their lives."

She didn't ask it as a question, and so I didn't answer. I couldn't say I agreed with her. If Cooper's death hadn't so clearly been an accident, if there had been any mystery hanging over the fire at the bank, about why it had happened or who was at fault, I would not have been able to think about anything else.

Although, I guess that was true anyway.

"Oooh, that looks good," Beth said, taking my attention and pointing to my casserole. "Amber loves melted cheese."

I reached for one of the untouched plates and dug a heaping scoop out of the casserole dish. Then I decided I should really include a small mound of each type of pasta. It would mess up the appearance of the rest of the casserole, but it wasn't like that mattered too much in the empty dining room. "And Amber is the Montrose daughter, I assume?"

"Yes. She's fifteen and has been pretty upended about the whole thing."

"No doubt. Is she the oldest?"

Beth shook her head. "Danny Jr. Or I guess he's going by his middle name, Seth, lately. He's seventeen. He's been really angry. I don't know if he'd take any food, but you could try."

Her tone didn't sound hopeful, but nevertheless, I reached for another plate and filled it with an extra-large helping of pasta. I'd heard that teenage boys could eat. Soon I had two beautiful, appetizing tri-colored pasta plates ready for delivery.

"Right up there," Beth said, pointing up a set of stairs. "Danny's room is at the top of the stairs. Amber's is halfway along on the right."

"Okay, thanks. You're sure you don't want to come along?" Now that I was actually making a move toward the stairs, awkwardness consumed me. I didn't know these people, after all.

Beth lifted her flat palms up to face me. "No, no. I'm giving them their space. Oh, and I should warn you, if Danny's friend Cade is with him, you might just want to leave them be."

I was already on the second stair, but I turned back. "Yeah? Why's that?"

Beth shook her head as she headed for the kitchen. "When those two get together, they're never up to any good."

# CHAPTER FOUR

I'd barely made it to the top of the stairs when I made out two male voices through an almost closed door. Great. What had I gotten myself into? I certainly didn't want to insert myself into the middle of two troublemaking teens.

I paused on the top stair for a second, rethinking that. Or did I?

I didn't have children, although Cooper and I had been eager to have them, just as soon as he finished the last book in his latest series and I worked my way up to sous-chef, so I could forever have that title on my resume. It didn't happen, obviously, but I did understand troubled teens. In fact, I had been one.

Dad had moved us around a lot after Mom left. Six months here, two months there. I'd even lived in Honeysuckle Grove for a short stint in seventh grade. It was why the town had been on my radar and I'd suggested it to Cooper as a place to settle down. Here, more than anywhere, felt like home when I'd been a young girl. But Dad had said it didn't suit us, and after nearly a year, when I'd only just started to let out my breath, he told us we were moving again.

I'd been in high school when I realized he'd been lying about every single one of those moves. The towns had suited us just fine. He'd just been lazy and irresponsible and couldn't hold a job.

So out of anyone, I understood angry teenagers. And now, hovering on the top step, I recognized the tone one hundred percent.

"You're sure it's okay I'm here?" one voice asked. I had to guess it was Cade, as Danny Jr.—or Seth—lived here.

"Sure," the other voice said, his voice all gravel and spite. "My dad's dead, like you wanted. Who's going to stop you? My mom wouldn't care if we stayed in here and played Call of Duty for the next year."

Whoa. I took a step back on the stairs, nearly tripping when Cade said, "Dude, you wanted him dead as much as I did."

This was a whole new level of angry teenager. Sure, I had been mad at my dad, even hated him at times. But I never would have wished him dead.

"So you're not even going to college now that your dad's not around to make you?" Cade went on. "What about the deposit?"

"Ha. Who cares now?" the Montrose son replied. "Mom's going to get a huge insurance settlement and she won't care if I spend the next four years working on the 'Vette. It's Dad who was making me go, making me keep up my grades. Now that he's out of the picture, I can do what I want. Maybe I'll even become a mechanic."

I looked down at the two plates in my hands, deciding in an instant that I might be hungry after all. I'd just take one plate to Amber first.

I tiptoed past Danny's room and tried to remember the directions Beth Dawson had given me. Halfway down on the right?

Thankfully, a door down the hall was open a few inches. Through the gap, I could see a teenage girl stretched out on her bed. I balanced one plate on my arm and knocked with two knuckles.

"Yeah?"

I nudged the door open and extended the fuller plate of casserole toward her. "I brought you some food?"

Her eyebrows pulled together, distrust evident, but the girl was immediately familiar. I had definitely seen this girl at church, probably more than once by how familiar she seemed. She wore jeans and an oversized lime green sweatshirt that read I'M NOT ALWAYS SARCASTIC—SOMETIMES I'M SLEEPING. She had the same auburn hair as her mother and aunt, but hers was curly and cut short into a pixie cut.

"I'm from Honeysuckle Grove Community Church and was asked to bring by a casserole." The girl still didn't say a word or even beckon me and the food toward her, so I felt the need to fill the silence. "I lost my husband eight months ago. I guess that's why they asked me to deliver this."

This explanation was definitely stretching the truth, but Amber's look softened, and it sounded a lot better than I volunteered because no one else would, and I didn't want to see Pastor Jeff begging on his knees.

"Oh. Okay. Thanks." Amber had a soft, vulnerable face with rounder cheeks and fuller lips than her mom, but I could see how this young face might become hardened to look more like her mother's over time.

I brought her a plate of casserole. "No allergies?" I asked as I passed it over.

One side of Amber's lip turned up slightly as she shook her head. I was referring to her mother's probably long list of food intolerances, and thankfully she seemed to take my question as a lighthearted joke.

"I'm Mallory, by the way. Mallory Beck."

She finally reached for the plate and one of the forks I'd brought along from the dining room table. Without looking up, she took a bite. Then another. And then two more.

"This is really good," she said through a full mouth. Finally, she looked up, glanced at the plate in my other hand, and said, "There's a chair by my desk."

I opened my mouth to tell her the other plate had actually been for her brother, but then closed it quickly. If this grieving girl was inviting me to stick around, who was I to argue?

"So how did your husband die?" she asked when I'd just sat down and taken my first bite of melted cheese. It ended up going down the wrong way and causing me to sputter and choke. I put my plate on her nearby desk, which was neat as a pin with makeup and books so precisely lined up along each side, it looked like they had been measured with a ruler.

I coughed into my elbow, but then Amber said, "Hands up," and demonstrated, lifting her arms high in the air. I followed suit. I coughed just a couple more times, and she added, "Don't die on me now," which made me want to start choking all over again.

I'd somehow made it through the last eight months successfully avoiding talking to anyone about the details of Cooper's death. Of course that could have had something to do with the abandoned grocery carts I'd left in my wake upon seeing familiar faces at the grocery store or sitting in the most remote of church pews. But this young girl asking me about him now, as shocking as it was, also somehow felt…refreshing.

"Do you remember hearing about the snow that collapsed on some old wiring and started a fire at the bank on Fifth Street last winter?" Honeysuckle Grove was on the large side of being a small town. Even if I had lived here my entire life, I had doubts if I would be chummy with most people in town, and certainly not this affluent family. However, the bank fire had made headlines for weeks.

So it didn't surprise me when Amber's eyebrows pulled together and she drew out the word, "Yeah," as though hoping I wasn't going to say what came next.

"My husband, Cooper, had been at that bank. He'd been in the safety deposit vault and was one of three people who didn't make it out before the

19

whole thing went up in flames."

Amber's eyes went wide. I braced for her I'm sorry, but instead, she only nodded. After a long minute of nodding, she said, "I bet you had questions after it happened, huh?" I couldn't coax any words right away, so Amber went on. "Like why it had to happen while he was in there, why not half an hour before or half an hour after? Or why was he one of the people who didn't make it out alive?"

I had asked all of those questions countless times, along with many others. The police and building inspector had thoroughly explained the unfortunate combination of bad weather and ancient wiring that had caused the accident, and yet a loop of these questions kept swirling in my mind, even eight months later. Now, listening to Amber ask each question with such passion, as though she was asking them about her own dad, I realized maybe all of the questioning was simply human nature.

Because I still couldn't bring myself to speak on the subject, Amber went on. "Did you go there after? To the bank? Did you see it?"

With three pointed questions, I had no choice but to coax an answer. Either that or run out of here like a frazzled chicken. "I, um, yeah, I did. There wasn't much to see, but I had to look at where he died." It had been a mess of charred beams and gaping holes. I'd heard the bank had received a facelift since then, but I hadn't had any desire to see its new finish.

Amber's chin jutted out, and I instantly sucked in my bottom lip like I'd said something wrong. "See?" Her eyes widened. "Mom says it's morbid to want to go out to where it happened, that I'll have nightmares, and I need to just move on and forget about the horrible accident. Yeah, right. I'll just forget about Dad's death, pretend it never happened. Paste on a smile and say, 'Accident? What accident?'" There was the sarcasm her sweatshirt had promised. Amber's face implored me, begging me to see the similarity.

And although she was only fifteen and I truly had no place here in the midst of this family's decisions as they grieved their father and husband, I couldn't help myself. I understood Amber's viewpoint completely. What if I had been forbidden to visit the bank property where Cooper had died? What if I'd been too young to have a driver's license and get myself there?

"And he didn't just die anywhere," she went on, setting her half-full plate on her nightstand so she could add to the passion of what she was saying by holding out her hands. "It was on the Old Mission Highway, toward Maryland."

I shook my head slowly, wondering if that was supposed to mean something. If it did, I wasn't following. I'd heard of the Old Mission Highway, but I wasn't sure I'd ever driven on it.

Thankfully, Amber went on to explain. "It's this tiny old highway leading out of town. My parents got married along there, in a big green space right near Big Bear Lake Camplands. Then, because they got married

20

on May the fifth, they drove out to Mile Marker 5 and carved their initials into a tree on the side of the road. A few years ago on my birthday, Dad drove me out to Mile Marker 27 and helped me carve my initials there, because I was born on December twenty-seventh."

I was momentarily distracted, thinking how awful it would be as a kid to have a birthday so close to Christmas. But Amber stood, her arms out, imploring me to pay attention to what she was telling me.

"So he liked to mark the mile markers along that highway of important events?" I asked slowly, keeping my eyes on hers as though that might help me understand.

Then she finally said the sentence that made it all click into place. "You could say that. The most important event of his life—his death—happened right at Mile Marker 18, and no one will even talk about it!"

I squinted and tilted my head, wondering if this all could be true. Her eyes stayed locked on mine, serious, determined. Why would her mother be so tight-lipped about her dad dying in such a significant place?

And so even though I knew it was wrong if her mother had discouraged it, I placed my own pasta plate aside and asked Amber, "Do you want me to take you out there?"

Amber took two giant steps toward me and grabbed my hand. "Are you kidding me? Yes!"

If Helen Montrose found out, she had the money to make sure I got into big trouble over this, but even so, I stood and pulled out my keys to show her I wasn't kidding at all.

☐

# CHAPTER FIVE

Before we headed for the door, I insisted Amber leave a note for her mom. We switched places—she took the desk chair and I sat back on her plush cream-on-white bedspread, while we came up with a reasonable story about how she went for a walk to visit a neighborhood dog that she loved.

As Amber wrote, I surveyed her room. Even the tiniest of items were in their place. As a teenager, my room had usually contained mere glimpses of visible floor space beneath discarded clothes and schoolbooks, so we definitely were not alike in that regard. A pair of men's muddy shoes stood out, aligned just outside of her closet, along with a black garbage bag. Before I had a chance to ask about them, Amber started talking.

"Mom's allergic to cats, dogs, anything with dander," she explained while writing her note. Her voice had taken on a lightness I hadn't heard in it before, and I felt as though the opportunity to get some closure over her dad's death was definitely something she needed. "To tell you the truth, I think she just doesn't like animals. So she doesn't bother me when I need to get my fix with Tinkerbell down the street. And she would never, ever come looking for me while I was doing it."

Our next problem was getting out of the house without raising the attention of any of Amber's family or the wake-goers. Amber assured me she had done this many times.

"If you knew my parents' friends, you'd know they're pretty wrapped up in themselves. You'd have to spell out 'We're doing something wrong here' for them to even blink an eye."

Even though Amber tromped loudly and spoke in a normal tone as we passed her brother's room, I couldn't help but tiptoe.

Seth clearly wasn't as self-absorbed as his parents' friends. He swung his door open when we'd barely made it to the stairs. He looked between his sister and the twenty-eight-year-old woman tiptoeing toward the stairs behind her. "What's going on? Where are you going?"

Before I could stammer out an excuse, Amber spoke up in a perfectly calm and collected voice. "Don't you and Cade worry your pretty little heads about it."

Seth dropped his voice to a low hiss. "You're going down there? Into the pit of vipers?"

Amber continued her trek down the stairs and called over her shoulder, "Chill, Danny. I'm not going to the wake. Just taking Mom's friend to see Tinkerbell."

This seemed to satisfy Seth—or Danny. I didn't know what to call him now if his sister still called him Danny. But his outburst confused me. Why would her brother care if she went to the wake? Why did he consider his parents' friends to be "vipers," while Amber only saw them as self-absorbed?

"You're going with her?" Danny said to me, an edge to his voice. Much slower on my tiptoes, I had yet to make it past his door. "What do you want? Our money? Amber can't help you with that. Might as well go straight to our mother."

I stopped and turned to the angry boy. His reddish-brown hair stuck up on top and looked out of place with his dark slacks and white button-down. It wasn't as though I lacked compassion. Perhaps a revolving door of adults came in and out of his life, trying to leech onto his family's money. Perhaps this was the only way he knew to protect his sister.

But I had only delivered a casserole, for crying out loud! I didn't deserve the brunt of this.

"Listen, kid," I told him, skipping his name altogether. "I don't want anything from you or your family. I brought a casserole by and heard your sister hadn't been eating. I thought she could use a few minutes out of the house to clear her head." I took a step toward him. "Have you got a problem with that?"

In that second, Danny Jr.'s eyes widened, and he looked like a Danny Jr. He looked like somebody's little boy and not the angst-filled teenager who had been standing there only a second ago. He looked down at the floor and said, "No. 'Course not."

The bedroom door swung open wider behind Danny, and another boy about the same age stood in the doorway. This must be Cade. He, unlike Danny, was not dressed for the occasion in ratty sweatpants and a dirty T-shirt that looked out of place in this swanky mansion. His blond hair was equally unruly.

Cade looked at me with his jaw tight, and with eyes that lacked any emotion, he said, "The guy's dad just died. Cut him a break." He didn't give me a chance for any rebuttal. A second later, he yanked his friend back into his bedroom and slammed the door in my face.

Highly embarrassed for saying all the wrong things, I raced down the stairs and arrived in the dining room, now empty except for Amber. I looked back toward the entry, where I'd left my shoes, but Amber grabbed my hand and pulled me the other way, toward a swinging door.

It led to the kitchen where Lupe busily placed fresh hors d'oeuvres from the oven onto a serving tray. I supposed she was more of a housekeeper than a maid. A teenage boy with tan skin and black hair stood beside her at the counter, doing the same.

"Spread them out," Lupe told the boy, taking absolutely no notice of us. "Make them look fancy."

The boy scowled and murmured, "Gotta be some kinda pompous jerk to notice how spread out the roulettes are." He picked one up and popped it into his mouth.

"Stop it!" Lupe glared at him.

The boy laughed. "Why don't I go ask Helen if I can have some? She thinks I can do no wrong." It didn't seem like a serious suggestion as he resumed placing the roulettes onto the serving tray.

Lupe shook her head and whispered, "Only couple more days."

Unnoticed, Amber pulled me behind them and out through another door. A second later, we stood in a mudroom that was larger than my master bedroom.

"Who was the kid?" I asked, but then realized he was probably older than Amber. Teenagers never liked to be called kids. "I mean, the guy working with your housekeeper?"

Amber rolled her eyes. "That's Lupe's son, Nando. He must have done something wrong to deserve the punishment of helping her. She doesn't make him come here often. My dad never liked him hanging around."

But her mom did, I thought but didn't say. Apparently, Helen Montrose thought the housekeeper's son could do no wrong.

Amber shoved her feet into a pair of white sneakers, crushing the heels until she worked her feet all the way into them.

"Um," I said, looking between our feet.

She looked at me with raised eyebrows. "You're going to look cute out there on the road in bare feet."

I nibbled my lip. "My shoes are at the front entrance."

Amber took a sidelong look at my feet, reached into a shelf, and pulled off another pair of white sneakers. The things were pristine and looked like they had never been worn outside of the house.

I took the sneakers, and although they felt a little snug, at least I wouldn't be in them for long. I glanced back toward the kitchen, glad no one had discovered us. "Let's do this."

Amber led us through another door that opened into their four-car garage. Three bays contained a vehicle, and yet it still felt open and spacious, as though it could easily fit four or five more.

Amber ran a hand along the car closest to us, a maroon sedan. "This was dad's car."

I glanced down at the high-end pristine car, surprised it had been fixed so quickly and completely in five days after a fatal accident.

Before I could ask, she pointed to the second bay. "That's Mom's Tesla." My eyes lingered on the deep metallic blue vehicle. I wasn't much of a car person, but a Tesla would be my dream vehicle. "And that's Danny's." She pointed to an old bright blue Corvette. It had to be a 1970's or 80's model. The wheels had been removed, and it was up on blocks.

"Danny's a mechanic?" I asked, recalling the earlier conversation I'd overheard with Cade.

This made Amber laugh. "Maybe he wished he could be one, but if you ask me, he coulda bought a fully functioning Corvette four times over with the amount he's put into this thing."

Amber didn't give me a chance to ask any more about her dad's car or that beautiful Tesla as she led me out through the far garage door and down the side path toward the street. I glanced both ways, but thankfully, all the wake-goers had remained inside. I hurried down the street to my Jeep.

"Nice ride," Amber said.

Truthfully, I'd always been a small car type of person. My own vehicle was a white Prius. After Cooper died, I don't know what changed, but every time I went out to the driveway, I naturally gravitated toward his Jeep. It had been his baby when I'd first met him. I'd argued that he should trade it in for something a little more environmentally friendly. He'd argued about how driving it made him feel powerful, like he could endure anything that came into his path.

And now here I was, trying to find that feeling and not giving a single thought to the environment.

"Thanks," was all I said. "Now where's this Old Mission Highway?"

Amber directed me toward the outskirts of town, and even though the radio droned some top forty music, it seemed unbearably quiet in the Jeep.

"So you're, what, about sixteen?" I happened to know from her Aunt Beth that Amber was actually fifteen, but in my experience, teenagers always liked to be mistaken for being older.

"Fifteen," she said, a smile fighting at the edges of her lips.

"And so tenth grade?"

"Mmhmm. In September."

And then more silence.

"And your family goes to the community church?"

She snickered. "Only me and Mom—and only because I make her. Dad works—worked," she corrected, "seven days a week, and Danny wouldn't be caught dead in a church."

It made sense now why Amber was the most recognizable.

"What do you do?" Her voice, or maybe just her question, sounded abrupt.

"Oh, me?" Stupid question for the only other person in the vehicle. "I used to work in restaurants. Working my way up to chef."

"That's why that casserole was so good, huh?"

Now I fought a grin. "I'm glad you liked it."

"I always wanted to learn how to cook. Mom said she'd get our housekeeper, Lupe, to teach me, but…" Amber looked out the passenger window.

I much preferred the conversation focus on her future in cooking than on mine, so I pushed. "But?"

Amber shrugged. "Lupe's always treated me and Danny like entitled brats. Dad liked her too much to fire her, probably because she dresses like a tramp." Amber shrugged again, as though this side of her dad was old news. "I'm surprised Mom hasn't canned her yet. It's probably only because she's looking for a new BFF for Danny."

"Lupe's son, Nando?" I asked. I recalled what Lupe had whispered to her son, about only a couple of more days. I wondered if she would be "canned" by the end of the week.

"Yeah, Mom loves him, probably more than she loves us." She snickered, making clear she didn't truly believe this. "Nando just knows how to play adults. He puts on this fake politeness, like he's Mr. Manners or something. Different story when he's around me and Danny."

"So Danny doesn't like him, then?"

Amber shook her head vehemently. "No way."

The Jeep became quiet again. Too quiet. I adjusted my rearview mirror, pausing to make sure I really wanted to make an offer. But just as my hand had shot up in church without my express permission, it was already leaving my mouth. "Maybe sometime I could teach you to cook."

"Yeah?" she asked, and I could feel her eyes boring into the side of my face.

"Sure." I cleared my throat, trying to get my bearings back about having unwittingly planned another social occasion. "I don't think you're entitled. Or a brat." I flashed a smirk in her direction. "Then again, I just met you."

I expected some sort of sarcastic comment in return, but she came back with, "You said used to. What do you do now instead?"

I shifted and adjusted my rearview mirror again to avoid her question, but it only reverberated in the air around us. I didn't think moping in bed with a cat who wants to claw my eyes out was a satisfactory answer, so finally I settled on, "Not much."

"That's because of Cooper?" she asked, more bluntly than I expected.

I nodded toward the steering wheel, but thankfully, right then we came upon our destination. Amber pointed. "This is it. Mile Marker 18."

I pulled over and took in my surroundings for the first time. "This? This is where the accident occurred?"

We were at least fifteen miles out of town, and clearly eighteen miles to the state border. I didn't think there were any towns in between. Tall trees lined each side of the pavement with a small shoulder and then a drop-off down a steep bank. The straight road veered only slightly as far as the eye could see in either direction

"That's what the cop said." Amber pointed. "Mile marker 18. I eavesdropped on the whole conversation and made notes." She flashed me the screen of her phone to show me. Sure enough, a small green post with the number 18 indicated our location.

I put the Jeep into park and turned off the engine. No traffic, no dark unexpected corners. It hadn't even rained in the past two weeks. It just didn't look like the site of an accident.

Amber stepped out of the Jeep in an instant and stood in the middle of the road, surveying the location. I wanted to tell her to get off the road, but the truth was, we would see a car in either direction long before it had a chance to get close to her.

By the time I stood beside her, Amber had bent to her knees, inspecting the pavement. "No black tire marks."

I looked down the road in each direction. Perhaps the accident didn't occur exactly in this spot, but then again, the pavement appeared unmarked gray as far as the eye could see. "I don't even see any debris from the cars."

"Car," Amber said.

"What's that?"

"Only one car. There wouldn't be debris, but you'd think there would at least be skid marks."

"One car?" I tilted my head. Had Dan Montrose run into a tree? But, no. I'd heard hit-and-run.

"Yeah, Dad had gotten out of his car when he was hit."

"That's why his car hadn't been damaged?" I surmised.

Amber nodded, seemingly still deep in thought. "Why would he get out of his car way out here in the middle of nowhere?" She marched toward the roadside in front of my Jeep and bent down to study the green mile marker.

Why indeed? But the last thing I wanted to do was give Amber any extra ammunition to dwell on the details of her dad's death. We had come here so she could get some closure.

"Maybe there was something wrong with his car? I'm sure he was trying to hitch a ride back into town and the driver simply didn't see him." As I spoke the words, the explanation felt more plausible.

Amber, however, still didn't look convinced. She moved off the shoulder and ran her hand over the bark of a nearby tree. "But the police brought Mom out here and she drove his car home. There was nothing wrong with it."

"Cars can be unpredictable sometimes, making noises one minute, stopping the next." Even to my own ears, the excuse sounded weak.

But Amber looked like she wasn't even listening. She'd stopped at the second tree she had inspected. Squinting, she moved her face closer, tilting her head. She had both hands on the bark now. "What's FDS?"

"Huh?" I moved over to her side. Sure enough, FDS had been carved into the tree bark. From the darkened, almost black letters, it looked as though it had been carved some time ago—definitely not in the last week. Amber had gotten so quiet, I wondered if she was waiting for my answer.

"I have no idea—" I started to say.

"And why Mile Maker 18? What ever happened on the 18th?" She moved to the nearby trees almost frantically, pawing at all sides of them for more carvings. I searched in the other direction, trying to be of help. I had a feeling that what had been meant to help calm Amber's anxious questions was actually having the opposite effect.

I couldn't find any other carvings, and when I looked back, Amber had disappeared. I moved back to the mile marker and could see flashes of her lime green sweatshirt through the thick of trees and down the steep bank. "Hey, you probably shouldn't—"

"What about his shoes?" she said, in way of an answer.

"His shoes?" She had gone far enough that I had to yell.

"They were muddy when we got them back from the coroner. Even his pant legs were muddy."

I thought back to the muddy shoes that had looked out of place in Amber's pin-neat bedroom. I took in the dry gray road and the dusty shoulder, and it didn't compute. Then I moved a step into the thick knit of trees. From what I could tell, the ground sloped down for about twenty feet and then leveled off to a small creek. Or maybe it was more of a swamp.

"Do you think there's anything to find down...?" I started to ask Amber, but not loud enough that she could hear me. I began climbing down the steep bank, using tree branches for balance. "Careful," I called as I almost lost my balance. I was tempted to turn back, but I couldn't let a fifteen-year-old, who I'd brought out here, let's remember, tumble down the hill alone and injure herself. I had to at least go along.

A dozen steps down the steep bank, I remembered the sterling white shoes I'd borrowed. I looked down, but it was too late. Already stained brown beyond repair, they would be impossible to fully clean. Amber didn't seem to care about her own shoes, now more brown than white, and so I figured I shouldn't be too concerned either.

By the time I reached the swampy creek, Amber stood over a fresh mound of wet dirt. Beyond that, a foot-wide hole had been dug out of the earth.

"It looks like somebody dug something up here." Amber crouched and took some wet dirt into her hand. She felt it between her fingers, as though she'd be able to tell by the consistency who had done the digging and whether or not it was the same dirt that had been on her dad's shoes. If we were in a Cooper Beck novel, and she was Marty Sims, she'd probably be able to.

But Amber was right about one thing: It did look like something had been dug up here, and recently. What were the chances that some random person had been out here in the middle of nowhere at Mile Marker 18, digging up something during the same week that Dan Montrose got out of his car for some unknown reason and was struck to his death?

The chances had to be slim to none.

# CHAPTER SIX

The entire drive back to the Montrose mansion, I tried to keep my suspicions to myself and provide answers to all of Amber's burning questions.

But my answers weren't doing anything to put either of our minds to rest and we both knew it. I pulled over at the end of Amber's street, not wanting to get any closer for fear that a visitor of the wake might see me dropping her off, but Amber didn't get out.

"The cops will never listen to me if I go to them with this," she said, looking straight ahead. "They didn't even want me in the room when they came to talk to Mom about the accident."

Accident. The word suddenly rang out in my head as false. Was it an accident? What was Dan Montrose doing out of his car? Why the carved initials in the tree? Who had dug something up down the bank? Why were there no skid marks? The questions Amber had been asking for the last hour now plagued me as well.

"Would it put your mind at rest if I reported our findings to the police? At the very least, they could look into what might have been dug up, or when the ground might have been tampered with, and how close that was to the actual incident." Calling it an incident felt a little more accurate.

"Yes!" she said, turning toward me, her eyes hopeful and wide. "Let's go."

Oh. I hadn't meant right this second. I also hadn't meant for her to come along with me. But who was I kidding? I wouldn't be able to go home, kick up my feet in front of the TV, and put this out of my mind. I needed answers as much as Amber did.

Twenty minutes later, we pulled into the Honeysuckle Grove Police Department parking lot. We walked up the winding cement walkway, and Amber opened the glass door to the building and held it open for me.

30

Clearly, she appreciated me doing this and didn't think she'd make any headway on her own.

In truth, she probably had a pretty good grasp on her place in all of this. When I had been a teen, I remembered feeling invincible, until that one time when the rug was pulled out from underneath me. Dad grounded me from the car and the phone and then my boyfriend dumped me because I couldn't call him back.

Ahh, the façade of teenage invincibility.

At the busy police department reception desk, we waited for a full five minutes before the receptionist even acknowledged us. It gave me the feeling that even now, as an adult, I held no more power or invincibility than a fifteen-year-old in the greater world, despite driving a power-inducing Jeep for the last eight months.

Finally, the woman in wire-rimmed glasses and a tight bun greeted us. "Yes, can I help you?" She didn't actually sound as though she wanted to be of any help.

"Hi. We'd like to speak to the detective in charge of the Montrose incident, please."

The woman typed into her computer for several long moments, so long I wondered if I should repeat my request. But just as I opened my mouth to do so, she looked up.

"You can share any pertinent information with me, and I'll pass it along."

I'd only just met the woman, but somehow, I didn't believe her. "We'd really prefer to speak directly to the detective in charge." I motioned between Amber and me.

"Our detectives are very busy. Now, is there something else I can do for you?"

I squinted. I'd had very little personal interaction with police or authorities, but I had helped research police procedures for several of Cooper's novels. Back in our college days, when I used to hang out with him at the library, poring over computer logs and reference books, he explained to me that one solid tip would get Marty Sims, his lead detective, into action. The police department would have taken any informant seriously. I'd never had a chance to ask, "Well, what if the receptionist wouldn't allow your informant to get to Marty?"

"I just...can't we talk to someone in charge?" I asked.

The lady raised an eyebrow, and the motion looked painful with her tight bun. It was clear who had the upper hand in the room, and it was not the bumbling twenty-eight-year-old amateur sleuth who was supposed to be helping a young girl find closure.

"This is the daughter of the man who lost his life," I explained, motioning to Amber. Thankfully, she didn't look at all annoyed at me for dragging her into the conversation. If anything, she looked eager. "She really wanted to talk to the detective about the details of the…incident."

The lady's countenance softened. I had the distinct impression that Amber would have been much more successful on her own here. "I'm afraid Officer Martinez isn't in the office at the moment," she said to Amber. "But we have counselors in the office if you'd like to sit down with one of them?"

Amber's jaw tightened. "No. Thanks."

"When will Officer Martinez be back?" I asked. It wasn't lost on me that this receptionist had referred to him as an officer and not a detective. It made me wonder if the accident site had been investigated at all.

The lady looked back at me as though I was an annoying gnat she had already swatted out the door once. "I'm afraid I couldn't say."

"Well, can we leave a number so he can call us?" I crossed my arms, trying to find the upper hand, or at the very least a toe's worth of footing in this conversation.

The lady stared hard at me, and then turned to Amber. "What's your number, honey?"

Amber flinched at the endearment but rattled off her phone number in a monotone.

"I'll get one of the counselors to give you a call," the lady said and turned back to her computer as though dismissing us.

Amber flapped her arms up to the sides, and I felt exactly the same way.

"Come on," I said, grabbing her arm and directing her toward the door. "We'll figure something out."

"See? That's exactly what I thought would happen." She stomped down the cement path toward the parking lot, and I hurried to keep up. I wanted to offer some reassuring words, but an equal amount of frustration coursed through me.

Then, suddenly, Amber stopped in place, and her mouth gaped open. I followed her gaze to a man in a police uniform who had just stepped out of a police cruiser.

He started walking our way, his gaze locked on the building behind us, but Amber stopped him with, "Detective Martinez?"

I squinted as she said it, for a couple of reasons. First, because hadn't the receptionist called him Officer Martinez? And second, because I knew him.

"It's Officer Martinez," the man grumbled at Amber, as though he had just read my mind. "What can I help you with?"

"I…my dad… did you…?" It was the first time I'd heard Amber at a loss for words. I should have come to her rescue, but I was too stunned to do anything of the sort—stunned and fixated on Xander Martinez.

"I'm sorry?" he asked.

Amber turned to me with wide, pleading eyes. I had to say something, but all that came out of my mouth was, "Xander?"

The officer turned and squinted at me. He looked as handsome as I would have expected from the twelve-year-old Xander Martinez. I wanted to see under his police cap to see how short he kept his dark hair now. It used to be curly on the ends.

He tilted his head, but thankfully, this wasn't the head tilt of pity. "Mallory Vandewalker?"

"Actually, it's Beck now. Mallory Beck." Through all the times Dad moved us around the country, I didn't remember many of my classmates, but Xander stood out in my mind. I'd had a terrible crush on him in seventh grade. Of course, so had most of the girls in my class.

He smirked. "Right, well, actually it's Alex now."

It was my turn to say, "I'm sorry?"

"I haven't gone by Xander since I joined the academy. I've been—"

"If you two are done flirting..." Amber dug her fists into the sides of her waist. "Can we get back to my dad? You know, the one who was hit by a car and killed last week?"

My eyes darted to the cement path in front of me, humiliated for more reasons than I could count. Thankfully, Xander—er, Alex—came to the rescue.

"I'm so sorry. And what was your dad's name?"

Amber crossed her arms. "Dan. Daniel Montrose. You're the officer who investigated, so you should know all about it, right?"

"I wrote up the report on the accident, yes." He bowed his head and shook it. "I'm so sorry about you losing your dad." Alex truly did sound sorry.

I took a deep breath, steeled myself, and joined the conversation. "So there was no investigation?"

Alex turned to me. I remembered those expressive emerald eyes. The girls in seventh grade used to joke about wishing on a two-leaf clover. "Well, yes. A team was brought to the scene when I'd discovered the extent of the damage, but I'm afraid West Virginia has one of the highest accident rates in the country, and we only have a small police department. Being Friday the thirteenth, and a full moon to boot, that night was beyond crazy for us. I doubt they've gotten far on this investigation."

I pulled back, surprised. "So you didn't even look for the car that struck and killed a man?" Even though this clearly didn't fall under his personal job description, I couldn't help addressing the question directly at him.

Alex shifted uncomfortably. "It hasn't even been a week. I'm sure they've had a forensics team out there by now, and when they get a chance—"

"When they get a chance?" I had read and helped with enough of

Cooper's novels to know that if a crime scene wasn't investigated immediately, it would be of no use. "They haven't apprehended any possible drivers yet?"

"Where would you suggest we start, Mrs. Beck?" he asked in what sounded like a rhetorical tone. "Should we drop our other serious and pressing cases to check every vehicle in Honeysuckle Grove for traces of tissue in the event that the culprit hasn't already wiped the front of his or her vehicle with a rag and some bleach?" His words seemed to reverberate in the quiet air around us, and again he turned to Amber and said, "I apologize for being so blunt."

"Not every vehicle," I interrupted. "Only the ones with the right paint color and height. Forensics should have been able to secure some traces and identify how high off the ground the car was that struck him." Alex did a double take at me, which only spurred me on to say more. "They should have searched the roadside for clues as to what had gotten Dan Montrose out of his vehicle way out there, and if there was any significance behind it." I studied him as I said this, wondering if he had discovered anything in this regard. I certainly wasn't about to spill everything we had found to this unhelpful cop, no matter how attractive he might be. I'd much sooner speak to his superior.

Alex—or Officer Martinez, as I was trying to train myself to think of him since we were now using formalities—stared at me with his mouth open, as though at a loss of what to say.

"So there's nothing you can do to find out what really happened to my dad?" Amber asked.

He sighed and looked back at Amber. "Have you spoken to your mom about this? I've gone over the details with her."

Amber pulled her arms tighter across her chest. "The details like the fact that he was hit at Mile Marker 18?" Officer Martinez started to nod, but Amber had more to say. "Or the fact that there were no black skid marks on the ground near there, so the driver clearly didn't even try to stop? Or the fact that my dad had no reason to be out of his car, out in the middle of nowhere, and for some reason had mud on his shoes?" She let out a loud humorless laugh and then added, "Oh, right. None of those things were in your report, were they?"

I hadn't been ready to share all of that, but in an instant, I decided this was probably better. Let Officer Martinez give us some explanation for these things.

He took a step back from us, and then actually stepped into the flower bed lining the cement walkway to get around us. "If your mother has concerns with the case, have her call the department and talk to Captain Corbett. I was only the first officer on scene. I'm afraid there's nothing I can do."

A second later, Officer Martinez had raced up the path and disappeared into the police headquarters, not looking back once.

If that was one of Honeysuckle Grove's finest who we had to depend on to keep us safe, we were in big trouble.

# CHAPTER SEVEN

My plan to help Amber find closure had backfired in a big way. As I pulled up to the curb down the road from her family's mansion, not only did she not want to get out of the Jeep, she was now convinced her father had been murdered and the entire police force of Honeysuckle Grove was trying to cover it up.

"Yes, there are a few things that don't add up, but that doesn't mean this was intentional," I told her, despite my own strong reservations. The fact that Dan Montrose had been out of his car at a specific mile marker, along a significant highway, kept tingling my Spidey Senses. It likely had something to do with my binge reading of Cooper Beck novels over the last eight months, I kept telling myself. However, Amber continually raising my suspicions aloud didn't exactly help.

"It doesn't mean it wasn't," she retorted.

"Listen, if you're concerned, I think all you can do is talk to your mom about it." She heaved out a labored sigh, expressing how much good she thought that might do. When she still continued to sit there, for so long I actually did consider the environmental unfriendliness of the Jeep, I added, "Let me give you my phone number. If you think of anything else I can do to help, let me know."

This seemed to satisfy her, and she pulled out her phone so I could rattle off my number for her. A second later, I felt my phone vibrate in my pocket.

"There. You have mine now, too."

"Okay. Great." I wasn't sure I'd instigate contact with this fifteen-year-old I'd just met, but this seemed to satisfy her enough to get out of the vehicle. "Talk soon," I said before she shut the door, and I didn't even know why.

36

Twenty minutes later, I walked through my front door, and sure enough, Hunch was sitting back on his haunches exactly where I'd left him. The second I closed the door behind me, he launched forward and sniffed every inch of the now-brown sneakers I wore.

"Hey, buddy," I said as though we were BFFs. Staring at my feet and my cat, the realization hit that I was going to have to get a hold of Amber again after all if I ever wanted my own shoes back.

Hunch let out something between a mewl and a growl. I often wondered if my inherited cat thought he was a dog. He sniffed over every new smell that entered our house, he growled on a regular basis, and he loved to go for car rides—at least he used to when Cooper had been alive. Cooper would have been able to decipher the friendliness of the sound Hunch made now, but I didn't speak Ornery Cat well enough yet. Today, though, I suspected I had some news that might get him on my side.

"So interesting thing at the wake I attended today..." I kicked off the dirty sneakers and led the way toward the kitchen. I glanced back to see if he'd find my conversation topic more interesting than my dirty borrowed sneakers. Soon he moved into the hallway behind me and followed me all the way into the kitchen. I started with, "The guy who died..." because the word "death" in any of its grammatical expansions would certainly gain Hunch's attention. "It seemed this Dan Montrose was up to some strange stuff before his death."

I topped off Hunch's cat kibble in the kitchen. He just sat there, again on his haunches, staring up at me as though he couldn't care less about eating at a time like this. He wanted more of my story.

Fair enough. I wasn't lying about the strangeness. I went to the fridge to retrieve some sausages and peppers to cook up for dinner. Maybe I'd make a soup.

As I chopped vegetables and simmered onions with sausage chunks, I relayed the entire day's events to Hunch. The more I spoke out loud to the cat, the more normal it became, and I suspected the audible talking would do us both some good.

"I can't get over the fact that his death happened right at Mile Marker 18 on a highway that he'd been known to mark significant details. There were also some initials carved into a tree there, like at the other notable mile markers, but they weren't fresh, so he clearly hadn't just gotten out of his vehicle on the night of Friday the thirteenth to carve them out." I recounted the details of the missing skid marks, the muddy shoes, the freshly dug hole, but then returned to those initials. "What or who is F.D.S.?" I asked my cat.

Hunch looked up at me with his usual deadpan stare.

"Well, you're not much help, are you?" I winked to show him I was kidding—not that he would have understood my words. He took the odd bite of food while I described Amber, her brother and his friend, her mother and their housekeeper, as well as the rest of the wake-goers, but mostly he just lay on the floor, head on his front paws, staring up at me.

As I described each one of the people I'd come across today, I purposely played up his or her motive for murder, or at least covering up a murder, the way Cooper used to do when plotting a new novel. The embellishment was for Hunch's benefit, but as I finished with that skinny lawyer—Terrence somebody or other?—I wondered if I was exaggerating any of it.

"I guess the truth is, there could have been a lot of people who had a motive to murder Dan Montrose. He didn't seem all that well-liked, even by his own kids." I spoke the thought as it came to me.

Murder, even more than death, sparked Hunch's interest, and a second later, I looked down to find him rubbing his multi-shaded gray body against my legs. He had never done that before—not once in the half dozen years I'd known him.

"We even went to the police," I told him. I appreciated his affection and, to be quite honest, would have done almost anything in my power to make it continue. "But the cop on the case didn't seem to have the slightest interest in helping us figure out exactly what happened to Dan Montrose." I sighed, inwardly berating myself again for how I'd lost my focus because of a seventh-grade crush. "It seems like the police barely took the time to investigate it. If only that blockhead of a cop would've been willing to look into it, maybe I'd be able to stop the whole thing from rattling around in my mind."

I'd hoped calling Xander—Alex—Martinez a "blockhead" out loud would help me reset my attitude toward him, but the word still rang out as false, at least to my own ears.

Hunch paused and stood stock still against my capris and bare calves. I didn't think I imagined his fur prickle tautly against my skin. He let out another mewl/growl, but this time I could read the unfriendliness in it.

"I know," I said. "I wish he would've helped, too."

But Hunch only let out another mewl/growl, this one sounding even angrier.

That's when it occurred to me that Cooper's detective-assistant cat somehow wanted me to do something about this. As if to make his point clearer, he pad-padded down the hall toward the entryway, paused on his haunches, and let out another mewl.

I missed his softness and warmth against my legs—pretty much the extent of physical touch I'd received in the last eight months. At least that was the excuse I gave myself for following. I hadn't even gotten to the cat in the middle of the hallway, though, when he picked himself up and moved along with heavy footfalls, as if he were the one dragging a little mouse toy in front of me.

Not that Hunch had ever had the patience for toys.

I found him perched beside my dirty sneakers. "Yeah, they're a mess, aren't they?" I asked. "I suppose I should clean them, huh?"

Now my response was all growl—not a single bit of mewling.

This didn't surprise me. Deep down, I knew why I'd been summoned toward the front door. I just didn't know what in heaven's name Hunch expected me to do about it.

As if he realized I'd need direction, he started sniffing around, not only near my borrowed sneakers, but he covered every inch of the entryway.

"You think I should go back out to the site of the incident and look around?" I asked.

Hunch sat back on his haunches. If a cat could smile in satisfaction, that's exactly what I would have called the look on his little whiskered face.

I couldn't believe I was letting a cat push me around. But truth be told, I couldn't get the whole thing off my mind anyway. I hadn't taken a very thorough look around while we were out there earlier for fear of feeding into Amber's unrest.

Maybe it was a waste of time to drive back out to the site of the incident, but time was one thing I didn't lack. Maybe it would be a waste of gas, too. Then again, I could take the Prius.

I could only hope the trip would put both mine and Hunch's minds at rest.

# CHAPTER EIGHT

Apparently going back to the crash site wasn't as easy as walking out the door and jumping into my Prius. After putting my soup on hold on the stove, I pulled on the dirty borrowed sneakers, headed out the front door, turned to pull it shut behind me, and there was Hunch, nose nudged through the opening.

"Oh. You want to come?"

I swear he looked up at me like I was daft. And I must have been because a second later, I scooped up the cat and brought him along. After so much time spent alone over the last eight months, with Hunch and me most often keeping to ourselves, the little bit of camaraderie I'd enjoyed with him today was addictive.

I had to admit, after driving Cooper's Jeep for my last dozen outings, my Prius felt low and small, almost as if I were an insignificant particle of dust in the greater world. I kept trying to reassure myself of my environmental responsibility, but I still couldn't help regretting my car choice.

Hunch sat up straight on the passenger seat as though he were human— or at the very least, part hound—and I was tempted to put a seatbelt around him. I highly doubted he'd allow it, even if it would fit.

"You're not going to pee or anything, right?" I asked, even though he'd never once had an accident in Cooper's Jeep or anywhere else he shouldn't have.

He didn't even dignify my question with a glance. In fact, he turned to gaze out the passenger window.

I'd chosen the dirty borrowed sneakers, as I figured they couldn't get much worse if I decided to trek down near the swamp again. It was nearing sunset, though, and I definitely didn't want to find myself down there alone after dark. I had great doubts that Hunch could do anything to protect me from a killer on the loose or even my own klutziness on that steep incline.

As I drove, I reached over and popped open my glove compartment, checking for my emergency flashlight. I pulled it out and dropped it onto the passenger's seat beside Hunch, and he rested one paw on top to hold it in place. Caught up in my thoughts of my cat and flashlight and how fast the sun may go down, I wasn't paying any attention to the mile markers until, suddenly, I passed Mile Marker 27, and familiarity made me quickly swerve onto the shoulder and slam my brakes.

On instinct, I threw out a hand in front of Hunch, but with his enviable nervous system, he barely budged. I let out my breath, checked behind me on the empty highway, and then backed the Prius up to the mile marker.

"December 27th is Amber's birthday," I explained to Hunch as I reached for the door handle. "Apparently, her dad carved something here on a tree a few birthdays ago."

With that, I hopped out of the car and headed for the shoulder and the nearest tree to Mile Marker 27. Sure enough, it took no effort at all to find a carved heart with the initials A.A.M. inside it. The carved letters looked at least as worn and dark as the ones at Mile Marker 18.

I looked back at the car. Hunch was propped up with his front paws against the passenger window, apparently waiting to hear what I'd found. I snapped a quick photo with my phone and then quick-stepped around my car to get in and tell him.

I was so immersed in my excited explanation to Hunch, as well as my curiosity about whether the carved letters looked to be in the same style once I had a chance to compare, I didn't immediately notice the other vehicle parked on the far side of the shoulder as I pulled up to Mile Marker 18. It was an early 2000's model Toyota with a dented back fender. Rust had formed around the dent. It appeared to be empty, but its presence sent eerie shivers through my stomach.

"Why is there another car parked out here at Mile Marker 18, one that has clearly been in an accident?"

Hunch didn't answer, of course, but it still made me feel less alone to ask the question aloud.

The damage was on the back of the car, not on the front where it would be if it had struck a person on an empty road, and the damage appeared to have happened months or even years ago, I reasoned to make myself feel better.

But I hadn't yet turned off my engine, and I wasn't sure I wanted to. As if Hunch knew this, he let out a low growl.

Lost in my decision-making, I jumped in my seat when a knock sounded at my window.

I looked first at Hunch, who appeared perfectly calm, still resting back on his haunches. Turning slowly, I looked out my own window.

Xander—er, Alex… Officer Martinez had somehow snuck up along the back of my car without me seeing him. He had been home to change since we last spoke and now wore a gray hoodie with a pair of snug jeans riding low on his hips. Without his police cap, his dark hair, while trimmed short, still held the little bit of curl that reminded me of seventh-grade Xander. It almost had the effect of making me warm toward him.

Almost.

I lowered my window. "What are you doing here?" I asked in a forced monotone.

"The same thing as you, I imagine. Come and look at something," he told me, already walking away.

I sat there, staring after him for a long moment. First, trying to regulate my heart rate, and second, trying to get over what a jerk Xander Martinez had turned into. I wouldn't have expected it from the sweet boy I'd known in the seventh grade.

A sudden claw to my leg made me cry out. "Ow!"

Hunch held up his paw as though he had zero remorse and would happily do it again. At least it brought the added reminder of why we had come here: to look around for clues as to what had truly happened to Dan Montrose. And if Xander Martinez wanted to show me another clue, jerk or not, I should probably get out of the car.

I reached for the door handle and immediately heard something akin to a purr from the other side of the car. Maybe cats weren't so hard to read after all.

But as I turned to shut the door, Hunch was already outside, rubbing up against my leg.

"Oh, sweetie, you should wait in the car." I had barely reached down toward him when his growl started, only making more obvious how wrong my endearment toward him had sounded.

I sighed. When Hunch had first followed Cooper home, he'd been a cat that roamed freely, indoors and outdoors. In fact, my and Cooper's first house, just blocks from the university, used to have a little doggie door that the cat used. A few months into becoming cat owners, I showed Cooper an article about how cats lived up to twice as long if kept indoors. The very next day, he had nailed shut the doggie door. Hunch hadn't fought it too hard, as Cooper still took his laptop out on nice days and let Hunch hang out on his lap, and he took him along on car rides often, but since Cooper's death, I couldn't recall if Hunch had been out of the house even once.

Maybe that was why Hunch didn't like me.

Whatever the reason, Hunch wanted no part of being left in the car, and even though I worried about letting him roam outside, I also didn't mind the idea of having some company out here—company other than the brash Officer Martinez.

I walked toward where Officer Martinez—I was determined to refer to him formally from now on—crouched at the edge of the shoulder of the road, inspecting something. When Hunch and I moved closer, I asked, "So you finally decided this was worth investigating, I guess?"

He shrugged and looked up at me, and I swore for a second he looked like the sweet seventh-grade boy I'd once known. "I always wanted to look into it further. The captain told me to get down the road to another accident ASAP, and the investigative team was already here." He shrugged again. "I have to do what I'm told if I want to stay on the force."

"Except now?" I raised an eyebrow.

He shoved his hands into his hoodie pockets and stood. "I'm on my own time now. It just kept gnawing at me after I talked to you earlier."

You and me both, I thought but didn't say. "And so what have you found?" We were right beside the tree with the carved initials, but he had been crouching, so I wondered if he'd discovered something else.

He twisted his lips. "Not a lot to go on, huh?"

I stood there for a long moment, debating whether or not I should tell him about the hole Amber and I had found earlier, and about Dan Montrose's muddy shoes. He wasn't the friendliest or most helpful guy in the world, and he wasn't even here in any official capacity. Then again, he, at least, had some police training. What did I know about this stuff, beyond having helped Cooper with a little book research a handful of years ago?

Before I could make up my mind, Officer Martinez squatted again, but this time it definitely had nothing to do with the tree. "Here, kitty, kitty," he called.

Hunch had moved into the middle of the road and was feverishly sniffing the pavement. I looked in both directions. No cars were coming from either way, but I supposed it was a good idea to get him off the road just in case one appeared when we were distracted.

But before I could march over and pick him up, Officer Martinez told me, "They cleaned up the blood around there. I don't imagine the chemicals they used would be good for your cat."

Amber and I had been looking for black skid marks. We never would have noticed this slightly washed-out splotch of pavement. I was thankful, at least, that Officer Martinez was able to shed some light on the location of where Dan Montrose had been killed. Now that he'd pointed out, it would be easy to find again.

That's why Hunch seemed to be in a frenzy of sniffing. "Oh, you'll never get him back by calling him cutesy names," I said. Instead, I turned to the cat and said, "Hey, Hunch? Come and look at this clue over here."

Hunch paused but then padded over toward us. He sat back on his haunches and looked straight up at Officer Martinez. The cop looked at me with a strange expression, as though trying to ask me telepathically if we were really going to share our clues with the cat. I gave him one solid nod, and finally, he turned back to the slope right beyond the carved tree and pointed.

Hunch rounded my legs and busily sniffed around what looked like a skidded footprint a few feet into the trees and down the slope. I was surprised I hadn't seen it earlier. I thought this was the exact same path I'd traversed with Amber. Although, come to think of it, I'd been more concerned with catching up with Amber at the time. I moved closer and could make out the deep impression of a heel with a long strip of skidded fresh dirt below it.

Hunch sniffed at the outer rim of the print, which made me murmur a question toward him. "Is it the same as mine?" Hunch glanced at me, glanced briefly at my shoe, which I'd outstretched toward him, and then returned to sniffing. "Did someone else go down here?" I asked my cat rhetorically. The footprint, now that I looked closer, seemed to be wider than my small foot.

Officer Martinez, oblivious to my one-sided feline conversation, said, "It looks as though someone climbed down here, and recently."

"Is that right, Sherlock?" I mumbled.

Hunch moved farther down the steep hill, and while Alex stayed behind to snap a few photos of the footprint with his phone, I carefully climbed down after Hunch.

"Are you sure you should go in there?" he asked from behind me. "It looks pretty steep."

It did. And it was. I'd already traversed it once today, after all. Thankfully, these high-quality, never-been-worn sneakers had good grip on the bottom because when Hunch stopped only a few more steps down the bank, I was able to hold myself there to see what he'd found.

I could make out a tiny swatch of purple paper smashed into the dirt. It wasn't even two inches in length, but on that two inches, it appeared to have a loop of black—though not enough to even spell out one letter.

"It looks like a swatch of gift wrap," I observed.

Officer Martinez moved closer behind me. "Hmm, you might be right. Don't touch it though," he added unnecessarily. "And don't let your cat touch it, in case it's important." He snapped another couple of photos.

I laughed and raised an eyebrow. As if I had any say at all over what Hunch decided to do. "Why? Because a tiny piece of a wrapping paper is going to show us what really happened to Dan Montrose?" I shook my head, trying to ignore Cooper's voice in the back of my head citing how significant small clues could prove to be.

"And you're right," he went on, "the paper might be nothing. But I didn't see much else in the way of garbage on the roadside near here. If someone threw it out their window, wouldn't we have seen more traces of it near the road? It looks more to me like a piece of paper—perhaps gift wrap—that had gotten stuck on someone's shoe, probably the person who climbed down here, and as you so astutely pointed out, there's not much reason for a person to get out of his car way out here."

I wasn't sure if the astute comment was sarcastic, so I chose to ignore it. I figured I should probably mention that Amber and I had climbed down here earlier, especially when we found three more clear footprints that were so mashed into the mud they could have been either of ours.

I kept my mouth shut, leading the way to the swampy bottom where the hole Amber and I had found earlier...

Had been filled in.

"What on earth?" I stood, shaking my head, while Hunch crawled low to the ground in a renewed frenzy of sniffing. He also knew something was clearly wrong here.

"What?" Officer Martinez asked. "Are you seeing something I'm not?"

I heaved out a big breath. "Amber Montrose and I climbed down here earlier today. There had been mud on her dad's shoes when she got them back from the coroner and she wanted to know why. Not three hours ago, there had been an open hole here, with dirt piled to the side. Someone has been back recently to fill it in."

"Or to bury something," Officer Martinez said, snapping a few more photos. "I wonder if I could get Steve Reinhart out here to take a look."

"Who's Steve Reinhart?" I bent to get a closer look at the newly covered hole but was careful not to touch anything. Hunch was also making a wide arc around the fresh dirt. My smart investigative cat didn't need to be told about the importance of keeping a clean crime scene.

"He's a detective on the force—one I'm somewhat friendly with. He wasn't on the case last Friday night, and too bad he wasn't, because he wouldn't have missed all these bits of possible evidence we're finding."

"Are you sure the other team didn't find them?" I asked. I didn't think I imagined Alex avoiding my gaze and my question. I stood from the muddy earth to press him. "How do you know what the investigative team found?"

Now Alex definitely avoided my gaze, but at least he offered an answer. "I had a quick look at the file before I left the station today. Unfortunately, the detective in charge is not..." He trailed off, looking uncomfortable, like he didn't want to discredit anyone on the force.

But I couldn't help but ask. "Is not what? A good detective? The most astute? What?"

Alex shook his head. "He's been known to let things slip."

I furrowed my brow. "And so what did he let slip this time?"

Alex sighed and spread out his arms wide to the sides. "All of it. The hole you said you found, the bright paper, the footprints." He shook his head. "There wasn't even a note about the muddy shoes."

"You're kidding?" I said.

"I wasn't going to bother Steve until I came out here to see if anything truly didn't add up. But when your young friend—"

"Amber," I put in.

"When Amber mentioned her dad's muddy shoes, and then when I found no mention of them in the report, I had to at least look into it."

I took a deep breath and tried to let my frustration over this go. It was equally frustrating not being able to touch anything, not being able to dig in the dirt and see if someone had really buried something. "Do you really think someone would come back to bury something right at the site of the incident? Doesn't that seem odd to you?"

Officer Martinez shrugged. "I've heard of stranger things. Murderers leaving so-called calling cards and such."

"So that's what we're talking about here? Murder?"

Hunch let out a low mewl. I'd forgotten all about him. He sat on his haunches, licking his muddy paws.

"I didn't say that," Officer Martinez said, clearly backtracking. "And you know I'm not here in any official capacity, right? I'd appreciate it if you didn't go down to the station and mention I was out here digging around."

I squinted at him. "You'd get into trouble for that?"

What kind of a careless police department oversaw this town, anyway? Or was it a sneaky, underhanded police department? I crossed my arms and thought about this. I'd quickly taken the police's word on the details of Cooper's accident, the same as Helen Montrose probably had with the information about her husband, but now I had to question if that had been such a smart idea.

"The captain specifically told me this was an open and shut case. He told me to sign off on it that night and I did. There's protocol…" Even Officer Martinez sounded as though this wasn't a very strong argument.

"Even if there was a possible murder committed? The captain can't mean that. Or if he does, it seems to me like there's something suspicious going on at the police department. Am I wrong?"

Officer Martinez shook his head and looked down at his hands. "No, it just…it's probably not even about this case. It's about Captain Corbett's biases. He likes who he likes in the department, he hates who he hates. In my case, it has to do with my dad."

"Your dad?" I squinted.

"Two years ago, he was on the force and got on the captain's bad side. I mean, my dad has transferred out of town since then, but Corbett still likes to call the shots with me. I can never question him. He knows I want to work my way up to detective, and he's always putting roadblocks in the way of that. It's why I barely spent fifteen minutes at the scene last Friday. Just long enough for the investigative team to arrive."

"What? I don't understand. You have to be able to do something, to tell somebody. What about this detective friend of yours?"

Officer Martinez locked his leafy green eyes onto mine, and suddenly, he was Xander again. Or maybe Alex suited him even more. "I'd encourage you to go into the station and report what you've found to the captain, I really would. I'd just...please don't mention my name. I could get in a lot of trouble for this. But besides that, believe me, if you really want to get to the bottom of this, it's better that you don't." In this moment, he didn't look at all like the brash police officer I'd spoken to earlier today. He looked like a puppy who had been kicked. "And I will talk to Detective Reinhart about what we've found. I'll do everything I can on my end."

He pulled a flashlight from his pocket and shone it around the filled-in hole. I hadn't realized how dark it was getting. "So someone was out here just to fill in the empty hole," he surmised. "Why would they bother?"

I pressed my lips together and thought this over while Hunch took to sniffing around the dirt once more, as if he were the detective and we were simply his lackeys. "I wonder if Amber told anyone what we found earlier. I know I didn't." I looked at Alex, hoping I could trust him. I was pretty sure I could. "I told her if she was still worried, she should tell her mom."

Alex nodded. "Well, maybe that should be your first stop then." I looked at him in confusion. "If Amber has been in contact with anyone about this, or if someone may have even overheard her talking, well...Let me put it more plainly: If perhaps she's been loose-lipped with her discoveries around someone who could have intentionally killed Dan Montrose, I think you should check in on Amber as soon as possible."

# CHAPTER NINE

I didn't think I should show up at the Montrose mansion in my muddy state, after having muddied my second pair of capris today, so I headed home first, took a quick shower, and then started with a text to Amber.
<I wanted to come by and get my shoes. You around?>

I was certain not to add anything incriminating in case Alex had been correct and Amber was somehow now connected to a murderer. Only a second later, she returned my text, which put my mind at ease, at least a little.

<Yup. What about a cooking lesson? Or was that all talk?>

Hmm. I'd forgotten about my offer to teach her to cook. But that might give me the perfect excuse to talk to her alone.

<I'm up for it. You want to ask your mom if it's ok to come to my place? I can pick you up and drive you home after.>

Less than thirty seconds later, she texted back.

<Yup s'all good. Meet you at the corner.>

I doubted enough time had passed that she had actually asked permission, but at the same time, I was eager to get her out of there and probe her with a few questions.

Hunch seemed to know he wouldn't be coming along on the short car ride to pick up Amber. He'd been meticulously licking every inch of his fur since we walked in the door and he didn't stop now.

"Be back in fifteen," I told him on my way out, to which he responded by flipping a hind leg over his head to give himself a full bath.

Sure enough, Amber stood at the corner where I'd dropped her off earlier, my shoes in one of her hands and my clean casserole dish in the other.

"Thanks," I said when she passed it over. "I wasn't expecting the dish back so soon."

I wondered if it was Amber or their housekeeper, Lupe, who'd had the forethought to put the casserole into another dish and clean this one.

But then Amber told me, "Yeah, I had another helping and then I dropped it off at my brother's room. Danny and Cade inhaled the rest in about two seconds, so I figured I might as well return the dish."

I felt a wash of pride come over me as I turned the corner of Amber's street. When I had worked in restaurants, the chefs always received the praise, certainly not the prep cooks. Cooper had loved my cooking, but it had been a long time since I'd gotten any sort of compliment.

To cover for my flushed cheeks, I asked, "Your mom said it was okay to come to my place?" I still had my doubts. She didn't even know me.

Amber shrugged. "She didn't see my note from earlier, so I just left the same one."

"And your mom won't think it's strange that you've gone to see the neighbor's dog after dark?" I probed.

Amber laughed. "I doubt Mom would think it was strange if I went to the neighbor's house at three a.m. You know, as long as I was dressed appropriately and had some makeup on."

I thought back to how perfectly Helen Montrose's makeup had been applied, how perfectly put together she looked at her husband's wake, while her sister Beth had black mascara streaks under her eyes from crying.

"So then if you left the same note, you must not have told your mom what we found earlier? Where we went?" I pulled into my driveway and turned to her, but she looked back at me with one extremely raised eyebrow. "No?" I pushed. I needed an answer.

"Obviously." She let out a huff of a laugh. "She would have killed me. She would have killed you."

It seemed strange how easily Amber joked about her mom killing one of us under the circumstances. Or at least I hoped it was a joke.

She followed me up the steps to my front door and inside. We had barely stepped over the threshold when she dropped to her knees and squealed like a little kid. "Oooh, you have a kitty!"

Hunch had little patience for the "kitty" moniker, and he also had sharp claws and little tolerance for people touching him when it wasn't his idea, so as she moved toward him, I started to say, "Oh, Hunch isn't the friendliest of cats…" But I trailed off when, seconds later, Amber scooped him up into her arms and he nuzzled up to her neck. He was also purring.

"Well. He obviously likes you," I stated the obvious, trying not to feel the sting of his rejection toward me.

Come to think of it, one time almost two years ago, Cooper's dad came to visit. Cooper's mom had died after a long battle with cancer not long before that, and I recalled Hunch having the same reaction to Cooper's dad. He'd sat in his lap purring all afternoon.

Maybe I hadn't given Hunch enough credit. Maybe he was more than the novelist's ideal companion.

I led the way to the kitchen. "I should have asked on the way what you wanted to cook. I went grocery shopping yesterday…"—and the two days before that, I added silently—"but depending on what you want to make, we might need more supplies."

Amber followed me, Hunch still purring in her arms. She sniffed the air. "I was going to say we should make that same casserole, but whatever else you've got going on here smells pretty great, too."

I shrugged. "Just soup, but if you're hungry…?"

Amber placed Hunch down beside his food dish and nodded emphatically. Hadn't she just eaten my casserole for the second time today? But I served her up a bowl just the same. I also served myself some. I had left it to simmer as soon as I got home but hadn't actually felt hungry by the time it was ready. Maybe I could eat now that I had some company. It had worked earlier today in Amber's bedroom.

I sat across from her at the small, round kitchen table with my own bowl—a table I hadn't sat at in over eight months. Why eat in a kitchen by yourself when you could eat with your favorite TV characters?

"So you didn't tell anyone where we went today?" I wasn't sure if I should tell her that I'd been back out there with Alex, or that the hole had been filled in. She probably didn't need to hear anything that would feed her suspicions about her dad's death.

She took a slurp before answering. "Well, I told Danny, but he didn't care."

My spoon stilled in place. "You told your brother? What did he say?"

I thought back to how relieved Danny Jr. had been about not having to go to college and about the freedom he now felt about pursuing mechanics. I didn't think it was enough reason to kill his own father, but then again, I wasn't an angry teenager. At least not anymore.

Amber shrugged and continued eating. "He thinks I'm stupid for worrying about it since we can't bring Dad back from the dead or anything."

I took a small bite, mostly so I could keep an even voice. "And do you think your brother would want your dad back? If he could have him?" I kept my eyes on my soup, but then looked up when I sensed Amber's brooding silence. Again with the extremely raised eyebrow.

"Of course," she said finally. She placed her spoon down. "What are you saying?"

I waved a casual hand and took another bite, trying to erase the tension as well as the questions of why Danny Jr. had started going by his middle name and why he would tell his best friend about his relief to have his dad out of the picture. "I'm not saying anything. Just wondering if anyone could have overheard your conversation with Danny?"

Thankfully, Amber returned to her soup, unbothered. "Doubt it. I mean, if Cade was still there, he might have heard since we were right outside Danny's room. Come to think of it, Cade probably was still there because he came into the kitchen when I was washing your casserole dish."

Danny's voice came back to me. My dad's dead, like you wanted.

I nodded to Amber and made my voice as casual as possible. "Did you tell Danny about the hole we found down the bank?"

Amber shrugged. "Yeah, but he just thinks I go looking for trouble. He figured it was a dog or coyote or something that dug the hole."

It was possible, but would a coyote return to fill in his hole? I snapped my mouth shut before I could say this out loud, reminding myself I didn't want to share that part with Amber, at least not yet. Instead, I tried another tactic. "Did Cade know your dad very well?"

This made her snicker, and she showed me her empty bowl in request for more. I started to stand to get her some, but before I could, she was already up and across the room, helping herself. "Dad hated Cade. Kept telling Danny he should get some friends with some aspirations."

Odd, considering Cade had been the one surprised that Danny had no intention of going to college. But I decided not to mention that conversation either. "Do you happen to know Cade's last name?" I asked, again with forced casualness, but not much seemed to get by Amber.

"Why?" She dropped down into the chair across from me again with a fresh bowl of soup, looking me right in the eye.

I took a bite, stalling. Then another. Finally, I shrugged. "I was just thinking of going back to the cops, talking to the captain there, and if there's anyone who had anything against your dad, well, I thought maybe I should mention it."

Silence took over the room.

"If you don't want me to mention him, I won't," I said, even though I wasn't completely sure I meant it. Cade seemed to be the most likely suspect here of wanting Dan Montrose dead, at least if his son could be believed. And he also seemed to be suspect of overhearing about the hole out at Mile Marker 18. Then again, would Cade have had time to hear about the hole, drive out there to fill it in before Alex and I returned, and then get back to the house before Amber left? Perhaps just enough time.

I gnawed at my lip in disappointment as I wondered how close Alex and I might have been to catching Cade in the act.

Finally, Amber answered with a shrug. "I guess you might as well tell the cops anything that could be important, then hopefully they'll at least get off their butts and look into this. His last name is Peeters, with a double E."

I committed the name to memory and nodded. "Anyone else you think I should mention? Anyone who really disliked your dad or whom your dad disliked?"

Amber let out a humorless laugh. "How long have you got? Half the people at the wake probably thought Dad was greedy and corrupt and figured he needed to be taught a lesson. He called the cops or the city on neighbors almost weekly. He joked about defending people who had money, regardless of their guilt. He talked down to almost everyone. Half the lawyers at that backbiting firm would have done almost anything to clear the way to move up in the ranks."

"Anything? As in murder?" I asked.

Amber shrugged one shoulder, not offering a yes or a no.

"There was one lawyer at the wake named Terrence something?" I asked, hoping I at least had the first name correct.

Her forehead buckled. "Terrence Lane was there? I can't believe he'd show his face at our house again."

Terrence Lane sounded right. "What do you mean? Why wouldn't he?"

Amber shook her head. "Yeah, I'd definitely mention him to the cops. He's a real climber, has been trying to push anyone out of his way to make partner for as long as I've known him. Terrence was at that dinner party two weeks ago. I never stay for those things if I can help it, but my parents always wanted me to at least make an appearance. I remember I'd come down the stairs right when Dad had turned and knocked a drink out of Terrence's hand. I guess he'd been bringing it over for my dad, who'd already had one too many."

Amber looked up like she was picturing the whole scene, and I wondered how hard it must be for her to think of one of her dad's last moments like this. "After he hit the drink out of Terrence's hand, and Lupe rushed over to clean it up, he turned to Terrence, pointed a finger right in his face, and said, 'Stop following me around like some kind of mutt. We need smart lawyers at the firm, not sniveling idiots that are too principled to choose between a winner and a loser.'" Amber's eyes widened to demonstrate how awful the scene had been. "This was in front of everyone—every single lawyer and legal assistant at the firm. Then he added, 'You'll never make partner as long as I'm at the firm.' Terrence went beet red and then walked straight out our front door."

I made shorthand notes about the dinner party, already thinking about how I might be able to call into the firm and get someone else to corroborate the story. Terrence had seemed like he'd been looking for the person who had killed Dan Montrose at the wake, but perhaps that was only to cover up his own guilt.

"He had more motive than anybody, if you ask me." But Amber continued on, listing several other names of lawyers at the firm who had a grumbly attitude toward her dad at best, and she repeated each of their names and spelled them out so I could make a list. She went on to name extended family members who had never liked Dan and may have been after the Montrose fortune. I couldn't see how they'd think they'd have any right to it, but I made notes of their names all the same.

I would add her mother and brother's names to my list after Amber left. I couldn't shake my questions about Helen Montrose's unusual cheeriness at her husband's wake or the way his son had spoken so callously about his dad's death. I thought they at least warranted looking into, even if she didn't.

Amber didn't end up with anything in the way of a cooking lesson, but when I drove her home, I promised we'd get together again soon.

And hopefully by then, I'd have something more to explain the oddities surrounding her father's death.

# CHAPTER TEN

Apparently, it took a lot of convincing with just a touch of panic to get an appointment to meet with a police captain.

After nearly an hour on the phone the next morning, I'd finally tapped the long-suffering tendencies of the police department's receptionist. In the end, I'd had to stretch the truth and tell her that it wasn't a specific case I was concerned about, but rather a couple of officers and their incompetence. She had wanted the officers' names, but I insisted I would only give those to Captain Corbett directly.

I strode into the station just before eleven, cutting it closer than I would have liked. Hunch hadn't wanted to listen to reason when I told him animals were not allowed in police stations. I had practically heard him arguing aloud, "But what about police dogs, Mallory? What about them, huh?"

And so I'd argued along right back at him about how police dogs went through special training (to which I'd received some extremely raised eye whiskers) and how "each dog is assigned to a specific officer, and do you have a specific officer who would vouch for your presence because don't forget we're leaving Alex Martinez out of this."

In the end, I'd had to race out the door and pull it shut before he could follow me.

The police station reception was plastered with warnings of how to behave, wanted posters, and a bulletin board with a flyer advertising an upcoming police barbecue. The same receptionist who had dealt with us yesterday again greeted me with what I suspected was a suppressed eye roll. I felt somewhat smug as I told her, "I have an appointment with Police Captain Corbett at eleven a.m."

She looked me up and down, clearly less than impressed. Because of the summery weather, I'd chosen a coral dress for the day, complete with a matching headband, but under the receptionist's gaze, it suddenly felt unprofessional. I glanced down at the receptionist's nametag, which read "Hilary."

Hilary the receptionist made me wait fifteen minutes in the small, sterile waiting room. I considered texting Amber to let her know my whereabouts, but then decided I'd see if I could get some positive news to relay first.

"Miss…" Hilary looked down at her notes as though she couldn't quite remember the name of the sole person waiting for an appointment. "…Beck? Captain Corbett will see you now."

The receptionist spun on her heel and marched down a hallway. I guess I was expected to follow?

I jumped to my feet, suddenly concerned that this receptionist intended for me to miss my appointment after she lost me within the bowels of the police station. That wasn't going to happen if I had anything to say about it.

Hilary let out a loud sigh when I finally caught up to her outside an open office door.

"Captain Corbett, your eleven o'clock appointment is here. A Miss Mallory Beck."

"Mrs.," I said, not because I cared about the distinction, but only because I felt the need to correct her about something.

Hilary didn't dignify my correction with any kind of response, and instead turned and quick-stepped away. I couldn't believe her rudeness. Then again, I guess it seemed as though I'd gone over her head after she wouldn't book me in to see Officer Martinez yesterday. I only hoped she didn't recall the specific officer or the specific case I had been asking after when Amber and I had been at her desk. I was going to do my best to keep Alex out of this.

"Come in. Have a seat," Captain Corbett said, motioning to a chair across from where he sat behind a large mahogany desk.

He wore a very decorated-looking black long-sleeve police uniform with a gold badge on his left breast pocket attached to several other gold pins with chains. There were also gold stripes and stars on patches along his sleeve. I didn't know what any of them meant, only that he must be capable. Alex had some sort of personal problem with this man, or at least his dad had, but in only a second, my hope grew that once given all the facts, this man would surely be able to help. He had a bushy gray mustache that matched the gray hair remaining on the sides of his balding head and clearly wasn't new to police work.

"I understand you have a complaint about someone within the department?"

I sat up straight on the edge of my chair, choosing my words carefully. "Well, not exactly, no. It is, however, about one of the cases your department recently investigated, and I have reason to believe there was foul play involved."

Captain Corbett furrowed his brow and flipped through a few pages on a legal notepad as though he might find the case in question right there in his notes. He picked up a pair of black glasses and perched them onto the bridge of his nose and then looked over them at me.

"Foul play? Is that right?" He didn't leave me time to answer, and I was glad. The question didn't quite sound rhetorical, exactly, but more like he was jockeying for position in this conversation. "And which case are we talking about here, ma'am?" His voice had a twang that sounded more Texan than West Virginian.

"It's the Dan Montrose case. You see, I drove out to where the car struck him, and I found it interesting that he got out of his car so far outside of town where there seemed to be no reason to, and I understand his car was operating just fine, and when I looked around more closely—"

"Helen Montrose said there might be a few of y'all comin' down here and tryin' to stir up some kind of a story." As Captain Corbett cut me off, he leaned back in his seat and put his hands behind his head in an obvious power position.

I pulled back in disbelief. "Sir, I'm not trying to stir up anything. I'm simply a concerned citizen."

"Right." He drew out the word as if to highlight the falseness in it. "And so you have no vested interest in this family or their commodities?"

I shook my head. "Absolutely not. I didn't even know any of them until—"

At this, he actually laughed. "Oh, I see. And so this is simply a good Samaritan effort is it, Ms..." He looked down at his notes to find my last name, and I felt in no hurry to provide it to him.

The gall! No wonder Alex had such an awful time working under this man. If Alex's dad had transferred out of town to find a new boss, I wondered why Alex hadn't followed suit. Then again, one thing I remembered about my seventh grade in Honeysuckle Grove was that everyone else was in a hurry to grow up and get out of this small town. Not me. I had loved Honeysuckle Grove more than any of the other places my dad had moved us to. And Alex had loved it, too. Said he would retire here. I remembered that.

"...Beck." Captain Corbett snapped his fingers as if he deserved some kind of a medal for suddenly finding my name on his messy, paperwork-covered desk. "Hang on, isn't there some mystery writer in town by that name?"

"That was my late husband," I said through gritted teeth. I did not like his tone.

"This ain't one o' your husband's stories, Mrs. Beck. You think you're the first one who's come in here demanding we draw out an investigation or dish out some sort of dirt to go into someone's article?" He laughed again. "Why don't y'all tell me exactly what kind of vested interest you have in this case, Ms. Beck, and I'll be certain to pass it along to Dan Montrose's grieving widow."

Grieving? I wondered if he'd actually met Helen Montrose face to face, or perhaps the woman had put on more of a show of mourning at the police station than she had at her own husband's wake. In fact, this whole line of questioning—which Captain Corbett had somehow turned around on me—made me wonder if Helen Montrose and Captain Corbett had made some kind of a private agreement regarding the investigation of her husband's death. I hadn't wanted to think of Helen Montrose as a serious suspect in the killing of her own husband, but maybe I shouldn't be so quick to dismiss her.

"Mrs. Montrose will know you by name, I assume?" Captain Corbett pressed. The more he spoke, the more intimidating he became, as though he could sense that I truly was sticking my nose where it didn't belong, and he was going to keep pushing until I admitted it.

"You can tell her it was a concerned citizen," I told him, standing.

The longer I stayed here, the angrier I became, not just at Captain Corbett, but at Helen Montrose, Danny Jr., and his friend Cade Peeters. With Terrence Lane and with anyone who'd had odd behavior at the wake or motive to kill, and most definitely at whoever had actually driven their car into Dan Montrose.

I reached for the door. "Thank you for your time, Captain."

I definitely couldn't thank him for his help, now could I?

If Amber was right about her father being murdered, and everything I'd found at the scene of his death indicated she was, it was clearly up to me to figure out who was responsible.

# CHAPTER ELEVEN

That night, Amber, Alex, and I stood in my kitchen as I described my meeting with Captain Corbett in detail. This was our Dream Team, it seemed. I'd lured Amber over under the guise of another cooking lesson, and I'd had to look Alex up in Honeysuckle Grove's online phone directory to get a hold of him, but I didn't think I'd be able to figure this out without either of them.

"I can't say I'm surprised." Alex leaned back against the counter and shook his head when I got to the end about Captain Corbett threatening to go back to Mrs. Montrose with my name. "Corbett likes to throw his weight around, but I was still hoping that having the information come from an outsider might do some good."

"My mom likes to throw her weight around, too." Amber bent to pet Hunch, who had been rubbing affectionately against her legs since she arrived. "She's also overly concerned about anybody being into our business. She probably told the police captain to deflect any focus from this case as quickly and quietly as possible, and I'll bet she said it in a way that came close to sounding like a threat."

I peeked at my crab cakes in the oven. They weren't quite done. Strangely enough, the buzz of having all these unanswered questions gave me the same type of energy as a bustling kitchen once had. I hadn't stopped cooking since I'd gotten home at lunchtime. "I don't see Captain Corbett simply sitting back and taking a threat from random townsfolk."

To this, both Alex and Amber laughed. I raised my eyebrows at both of them until Amber explained.

"Oh, believe me, my parents have never been random townsfolk. They practically own the mayor of this town. Why do you think we have a downtown street named after us?"

I blinked once and then again. "Wait, Montrose Avenue is named after your family?"

Both Alex and Amber chuckled as if this were old news.

"Okay, well, I wish I would have known that." My mind raced with this new information. I grabbed the bag of flour from one of the bottom cupboards and plunked it onto the counter. "So all we have to do is talk our way into another appointment with Corbett. This one is for you," I told Amber. I wasn't sure what to make with the flour, but finally having a promising next step filled my hands with nervous energy again. I wanted to knead.

Amber stood, and Hunch resumed offering his full affection against her legs. "Wish it were that easy. My parents have clout. Or I guess only my mom does now. Nobody will listen to me, least of all the police captain." She turned to Alex. "You'd know that better than anyone." She turned to me to explain. "I'd been sleeping over at my friend Shayla's house, but I came home early the next morning as soon as Shayla's mom told me what had happened." She turned back to Alex. "You wouldn't even let me in the same room when you gave my mom the details of the accident."

"That's because your mom insisted." Alex took one of my kitchen chairs, flipped it around, and sat backward on it. He was in casual clothes again, jeans with a green plaid button-down that matched his eyes.

"See?" Amber said, arms splayed open.

"She has a point." Alex helped himself to one of the snickerdoodles I'd made earlier this afternoon. "So, listen, I convinced Steve Reinhart to drive out and take a look at the scene. He had the same concerns, seeing the footprints and the hole that had been filled in, and called Corbett to get permission to get a forensics team back out there. Corbett told him Detective Bradley would handle it."

My eyes widened with hope, but the look on Alex's face made that hope deflate. "Why? What's wrong with Detective Bradley?"

Alex shook his head, his gaze on my small table. "There are dozens of unsolved hit-and-run accidents on the books, and Bradley's the laziest guy on the force. I don't even know how he made detective, but somehow, he seems to be one of Corbett's favorites. In other words, if Corbett wanted this case swept under the carpet, written off as a simple hit-and-run with no motive or suspicious circumstances, Bradley's the guy to do it."

I rolled out my dough. I'd unthinkingly grabbed some yeast from the fridge, measured some warm water, and added sugar and salt all while Alex had been talking. I started mixing and slamming the dough down onto the counter, which immediately helped clear my head. "Okay, fine. So where do we start if it's up to us to find out the truth?"

"We haven't found any solid evidence that there's foul play involved, and I can't—" Alex started, but I had no patience for him trying to back out of this.

"Listen, you don't know everything, okay?" I glanced at Amber for the go-ahead. She gave me one single nod, so I turned back to Alex. "That wasn't just any highway that Dan Montrose died on. He had carved his and Helen's initials at Mile Marker 5 to commemorate their wedding day. He'd carved Amber's initials at a specific mile marker to commemorate her birthday." I paused for effect, and then added, "And we found FDS carved on the tree right behind Mile Marker 18."

I turned to Amber, letting that new information sit with Alex. "You said your dad had a lot of enemies, but who would have wanted him out of the picture the most?"

Amber shrugged. She took a seat across from Alex and helped herself to her own cookie. "Lawyers, relatives, neighbors. Like I said, it could have been anybody."

I blew a breath up toward my bangs, even though they were pulled back with my coral headband. "No one person in particular? No burning hatred?" I already had a couple of names in mind: Cade Peeters and Terrence Lane. But I wanted her to corroborate them.

She twisted her lips, thinking about it, but the passing seconds only served to frustrate me.

"Okay, let's start with this: Why might your mom want to curtail an investigation? I know she wanted to keep it quiet, but was that only because of local gossip?"

Amber's head snapped toward me. "I don't know, but she didn't kill my dad if that's what you're saying." I replayed my words, and it did sound as though that's what I had insinuated. I opened my mouth to backtrack, but Amber went on. "Believe me, it's not because she's some kind of saint. Mom suggested firing different people at the firm like she was throwing out yesterday's newspaper, but trust me, she isn't the type to do any kind of dirty work herself."

Huh. That did sound like Helen Montrose, at least the little I knew of her.

"Speaking of dirty, you took all your dad's shoes and clothes when they came back from the coroner. I'm curious as to why?"

Amber shrugged and reached for another cookie. "Mom actually left them for Lupe to clean, and then they were going to get given to a thrift store. I don't know what I thought I'd do with them, but I just couldn't handle that idea, not so soon at least, so I brought them to my room. I still haven't been able to bring myself to clean them." She looked down at the floor as though this embarrassed her.

"Well, if you hadn't mentioned the mud, we might not have found that hole yesterday," I told her.

Alex interrupted before I could think of anything else to say to make her feel better. "And was anything else on his person? Did anything else get returned from the coroner with his clothes, like a cell phone, perhaps?"

"Isn't that something the police should know?" I asked and regretted it the second it left my mouth. Alex's eyes flitted away. Now I'd made them both feel bad about their actions. "Never mind," I added quickly. "I get it. Bradley took over the case. Of course all the clothing and belongings would have ended up with the coroner, but why wouldn't they be in any kind of report? I can't believe that the whole coroner's department is that lazy."

Alex shook his head. "I can't get access to the coroner's report. Normally, it's copied to our main police report, but for some reason, it didn't make it to Detective Bradley's paperwork. There's simply a note that says, 'See coroner's report.' But there was one note from forensics."

I stared at him, waiting.

"Nothing major. Just that it had been a low-riding dark blue vehicle that had struck Dan Montrose. There were traces found at the scene." My hope started to rise again but was squashed only a second later when he added, "But not nearly as much detail as I would expect. There's no exact shade of blue, no metallic content, not even any idea of where the paint color was lifted from—on Dan Montrose's body or somewhere else at the scene. There would be thousands of vehicles that match that description in Honeysuckle Grove alone, not to mention the outlying towns."

I separated my dough, at a loss for where to go from here, with baking or with the case, but Amber's mind was still on other aspects.

"His cell phone came back to us, too," Amber said. Both Alex and I stared at her until she went on. "Mom's pretty much a technophobe, so I think she gave it to Danny to reformat it. I'm not sure where it went. Danny probably still has it."

I looked to Alex, wondering if he could do anything to find cell phone records—without his boss finding out. But I couldn't ask that of him.

I turned back to Amber. "Yesterday afternoon at your house, I overheard a conversation between your brother and Cade. I got the impression Danny wasn't planning to go to college, you know, now that your dad's not around to argue it." I figured this was no time for secrets, and I needed to get all the information out on the table. "I know Cade hated your dad, but how did Danny get along with him?" I kept my voice gentle, so this wouldn't be mistaken for an accusation again.

Amber shifted uncomfortably. It took her several long seconds to answer, but I waited her out. "Lately not great. He hasn't been listening to either of my parents much lately, and that night of their dinner party with the firm? Danny was supposed to make an appearance, too, but he ended up staying out all night with Cade. When Danny came in the next morning, Dad tore a strip off him and said he wasn't to spend another minute with Cade Peeters."

"But Cade was there at the wake. Your mom didn't care about that?"

Amber shrugged. "I don't think she didn't care, it's just…she just hasn't been able to concentrate on anything besides keeping up a strong front and the funeral arrangements."

I had to wonder if that was what made her appear so cheery and put together at the wake—staying singularly focused. "And when did your brother start calling himself Seth?"

"About a year ago." She looked down at the table. "I don't think it meant anything."

"You don't think changing his name away from that of his dad signaled anything serious?" I wanted to slap myself. Again with the thinly disguised accusations, Mallory! But thankfully Alex intercepted.

"In my experience, a name change isn't always about distancing yourself from someone or reinventing yourself as a different person."

I supposed Alex would know about name changes. If he'd wanted to distance himself from his dad's reputation within the police force, I would've thought he would have changed his last name.

"For me," he went on to explain, "it had to do with another guy in the academy, also named Zander—with a Z. Still, it got confusing, and he didn't have a great chance of graduating." Alex shrugged. "So often I think it can be for a really simple reason."

Amber crossed her arms over her chest, not letting my accusing suggestion go. "My brother didn't kill my dad either," she said, still clearly upset with my wording. But the waver to her voice told me she wasn't a hundred percent sure. Still, how difficult would such a thing be to process?

"Nobody's saying he did," I told her gently. "But don't you think Danny's anger at his dad warrants asking him a few questions?"

She furrowed her brow and looked down at Hunch, who still wound himself back and forth and around her legs.

She didn't answer, and so I added, "You don't even have to be a part of any questioning if you don't want to be, Amber. In fact, it's probably safer if you aren't."

Her head snapped up, and her furrowed brow deepened, but now it looked more determined than confused. "If my family members could have had any part in my dad's death, I need to know about it. No one's leaving me out of any more conversations." She balled her fists on the table.

"Fair enough," I told her. "So let's figure out how and where we can talk to your brother."

☐

# CHAPTER TWELVE

The next morning, I drove the Prius down the mile-long driveway to Honeysuckle Grove's only golf course with Amber and Hunch in my passenger seat.

"You're sure he's here this early?" I asked.

Amber shrugged. "Well, no. But Lupe told me he left the house wearing a polo shirt." She scratched Hunch under his chin, which he seemed to appreciate. "Danny is very good at dressing for occasions."

"And a person has to dress up to go golfing?" I had no idea. I'd never been golfing and had only dressed in a pair of white capris with a peach cardigan this morning, as it promised to be another warm sunny day. Even less dressy, Amber wore jean cut-offs and a purple hoodie that read: BONJOUR. G'DAY. ALOHA.

"Nah. But most people do, and if you want to go into the club, you have to."

I nodded and parked several spaces away from the nearest car, a Jaguar. Looking over the parking lot, I took in the other half dozen cars. Ever since Alex had mentioned the traces of blue paint found at the scene of Dan Montrose's death, I hadn't been able to stop thinking about Danny Jr.'s vehicle—a blue Corvette I'd seen with my own eyes.

But the Corvette was nowhere in sight.

"How would he have gotten here?" I asked Amber. I didn't want to feed into her suspicions of her brother until I had questioned him, but I had to suck in a breath when she shrugged and pointed to a maroon sedan. "He brought your dad's car?"

She shrugged again and nodded as if this was no big deal.

In an effort to regain my even keel voice, I turned and looked at Hunch. "Now I told you, you can't come along for this part, right?"

Hunch seemed smarter than the average cat, but I still could never tell how much he understood when it came to the English language. It hadn't hit seventy degrees yet this morning, but I cracked my window open, along with Amber's, and a second later, Hunch stretched on Amber's lap and then happily leaped into the backseat.

At least that was one problem off my mind.

"Danny doesn't get out of bed early unless he's either forced to for school or golfing."

I nodded. "Who do you think he's here with?"

She shrugged. "Who knows. Probably met up with some other guys from the club. He used to golf with Dad, back when they got along better, but lately, he goes at least once a week and doesn't talk about who he plays with."

"And you're sure Cade won't be here with him?" I'd asked this by text earlier and she'd only answered with a quick "NO", but now she expanded on her answer.

"I'm pretty sure Cade can't afford a membership. He definitely wouldn't be accepted into the country club."

The way she said it, so bluntly, seemed to add motive to Cade as a suspect. We got out of the car, and Hunch remained in the backseat, licking his paws.

"Have you golfed much?" I asked Amber.

She led the way across the parking lot, toward the Pro Shop. "Not really my thing. But Dad made me go once or twice a year."

"Can't we just go out onto the course and find your brother?" I asked, hesitating as we closed in on the Pro Shop. My skin itched at the thought of too many people knowing about us investigating Dan Montrose's death. If it got back to Helen Montrose that I was putting suspicious thoughts into her daughter's head, or back to the police captain about me sticking my nose into somewhere it didn't belong, it could mean trouble.

But Amber only laughed, unbothered by the concept. "You want to search an eighteen-hole golf course, be my guest." She held out a hand toward the miles of green grass that started at the edge of the pavement, and I understood her point.

Thankfully, she knew something about the procedures of a golf course, which was more than I could say for myself. It was just after eight a.m. on a Thursday, and even with the few cars scattered in the lot, the Pro Shop was empty, save for one man folding shirts at a display table. Amber marched straight for the counter, and the man stopped his folding and met her on the other side.

"What can I help you with?" The man's nametag read SCOTT. He wore white pants and a pink collared golf shirt so bright it made me wonder if it was Breast Cancer Awareness Month.

"I'm looking for my brother, Danny Montrose. Can I find out his tee time?"

Scott rattled his mouse to bring his computer screen to life and then scrolled through a short list of names. "I don't see a Danny— Oh, wait, there's a Seth Montrose. Could it be listed under a relative's name?"

Amber rolled her eyes at me and then turned back to Scott. "Yeah, that's them." As Scott ran his finger across the screen, Amber murmured to me, "My multiple personality brother."

"Not too many around yet. He was one of the first out at 7:16. You should find him around the sixth or seventh hole by now."

"Gotcha," Amber said, holding up a hand in thanks.

"Thank you," I called as I followed her out the door.

Even though Amber had only golfed a handful of times in her life, she thankfully seemed to know the course well enough to navigate to the sixth hole without a map. Two men were teeing off, but Danny wasn't either of them, so we continued on to the seventh hole. Even knowing where to look, it was still a lot of walking, and I heaved out a heavy breath when we stopped on the green and stared around at the vast empty hillside around us.

"It's usually busier in the summer," Amber said. "Although Dad and I never came this early. I guess it makes sense why he might be ahead."

We moved around a small grove of trees toward the eighth hole and saw Danny, just setting up his ball on a tee. He was alone.

"This couldn't have worked out better," I murmured quietly to Amber, but her forehead creased in confusion.

"Hey, Danny?" she called out before he could take his first shot.

His shoulders slumped at his name, but he didn't immediately look over to us. In fact, he stared off in the opposite direction. "Can't I go anywhere to get some time to myself?" he said to the far side of the golf course.

Now I felt bad. My solitude had meant everything to me in the early days after Cooper's death. No matter how angry Danny had been with his dad, he would still be grieving and probably needed some time on his own, too.

Amber clearly didn't clue into this line of thinking. She marched straight for her brother, crossed her arms, and said, "My friend here has some questions, and Lupe told us we could find you here."

Finally, Danny turned toward us, but his gaze stayed on the sky as he shook his head and murmured, "Stupid Lupe." He finally looked at his sister. "What does your friend want to ask me about?"

I was pretty sure Danny must own a sweatshirt about sarcasm as well. Or he should.

"I just think...we both do..." I motioned to Amber and myself. "That something's fishy about your dad's death. Maybe it's nothing, but we want to make sure." I carefully watched Danny for his reaction, but he only took in a big breath and let it out on a loud sigh, as though we had already exhausted him.

"Is this about that stupid hole Amber found? Has she gotten you all riled up about that, too?"

It seemed he wasn't going to be overly helpful, but because he also hadn't shut down the conversation so far, I forged ahead. "It's not only that. Where were you the night that your dad died?" I dropped my tone softer, again thinking about his possibly conflicting feelings.

Danny reached for his upright golf bag as though searching for a different club. At first, I thought he might ignore my question, ignore me, but then he said, "I was home. Playing video games with Cade."

"All evening?"

One solid nod.

"Just you and Cade?"

Another single nod.

"And I understand your mom was out at a charity event. Did she call you with the news?"

Danny shifted his shoulders as though the question made him uncomfortable. But at least he answered it. "Nah, she came through the door just after ten, crying and freaking out. I told Cade he should probably go out the back way. He did, and then I came down to find out what was wrong."

"And your mom told you what had happened?" I confirmed.

Danny let out a humorless laugh. "I guess you could call it that. Took quite a while to decipher her words." Danny slipped the club he was holding back into his bag and grabbed another. He turned it in his hands but didn't make any effort to resume playing.

"Your mom seemed much more composed by the time I saw her at the wake," I observed. Sure, it had been almost a week later, but I had still been a walking zombie a week after Cooper's death.

Danny scratched at his red-brown hair. The short ends turned up as though they would be curly like Amber's if he let it grow. His cheeks darkened, and he looked at his feet. I got the impression he didn't want to answer this, but I waited him out.

Finally, he looked me straight in the eye, and angry words erupted from his mouth. "Maybe she had a good reason to act like she had it all together. Maybe she's a good actress. I heard she held it together for a few hours at the wake, kept muttering something about the will and its stupid stipulations all morning. Who knows with her. We're just kids, right? No one ever tells us anything." An edge of bitterness leaked out in his voice, and he seemed as though he was pointedly avoiding Amber's eyes, but I wasn't sure how to pry about his feelings toward his parents.

Instead, I decided on a different line of questioning. "So Cade was there playing video games with you all night? The night of your dad's death? He would vouch for you?"

Danny's face darkened, and he gripped his golf club so hard his knuckles whitened around it. "What are you here for? What are you implying?" He looked between me and Amber, and thankfully, Amber stepped in.

"She's not accusing you of anything, Danny. I told her you're not behind this—that's why we came to you for help. She just wants to confirm your alibi before we start prying into other people's business, so no one can point the finger back at you." It was a good tact—to put this all under the guise of protecting him. Maybe Amber truly meant it that way. If I were being honest, I still wasn't completely convinced.

And then, to make matters worse, Danny shrugged and said, "Alibi? Pfft. Well, if you're looking for an alibi, truth is, I probably don't have one. Cade went out for snacks sometime after eight. I told him we had plenty downstairs, but he wanted some spicy Cheetos or something. I can't remember. Anyway, he ended up being gone for almost an hour. Came home just before Mom did."

An hour to get snacks seemed like a long time. "Did he have a car?" Before Danny could even answer, I added, "What kind and color is it?"

Danny screwed up his face, likely because I was pushing the blame toward his best friend now, but Amber answered me.

"He drives this bright green Ford Fiesta. He calls it his frog. The thing is so old and ugly, he always parks it down the block."

Old, ugly, and noticeable. Danny wasn't supposed to be hanging out with Cade, and yet there was an eyesore of a car clearly stating that he was on the very night of his dad's death. That had to mean something. But also, did his car's paint color clear Cade of suspicion?

"Could Cade have borrowed your Corvette to go to the store?" I blurted the thought the second it came to me.

But it only caused Danny to laugh, and this time, it sounded like something truly was funny. "Sure, if he'd wanted to replace the carburetor, weld the exhaust leaks, and slap the tires back on first." He laughed again.

I looked between Danny and Amber. "The Corvette doesn't run?" I hated to admit it, but relief washed over me at this new bit of information.

Danny jutted out his chin. "It will."

Amber openly rolled her eyes in a way that made me think this was an ongoing argument in the Montrose household.

"And your mom was driving her Tesla that night?" I asked, just to check, even though I couldn't in my wildest dreams imagine the hated friend, Cade Peeters, being permitted to drive that beautiful car.

Danny squinted. "Of course. Why?"

I looked at Amber, but her gaze remained squarely on her brother. "What about Lupe? Wasn't she there that night? Couldn't she confirm you were there?" Like a dog with a bone, Amber wasn't going to let this point go until she could find an alibi for her brother.

She had already told me she had been sleeping over at a friend's house the night her dad died, but Lupe usually worked until whenever her son, Nando, got off work and came back to pick her up. Most days she was there until ten or eleven at night.

Danny's hands relaxed around the golf club, and his eyes roamed back and forth over a patch of grass in front of him. "Oh. Yeah. I guess Lupe was somewhere in the house. She came to try and help calm Mom down after she came in freaking out, but I waved her away. I didn't see her again after that."

That made me feel better. At least Lupe would be able to verify he had been there. If Cade had left for over an hour, only to come back with a bag of spicy Cheetos, and if he overheard the conversation about the hole by mile marker 18, green car or not, he was beginning to look like the most likely suspect. He had motive—as Danny had clearly said, "My dad's dead, like you wanted."

He had opportunity, as he was gone from the Montrose house and alone when it happened. All I had to figure out was the means. Was it definitely a blue car that had struck Dan Montrose? Or could the traces of paint have been there from another accident? Could Cade Peeters have used someone else's car to strike down the man?

I had made some notes the night before, and I glanced at the notepad from my purse to go over them. "One more thing," I said to Danny, but just then the two men who had been playing their own game a couple of holes behind Danny appeared from around the grove of trees.

"Oh," one of them said, stopping in surprise. "Sorry."

Danny let out a low growl under his breath and glared at his sister. When he turned back to the men, his voice took on forced pleasantness. "Nope, my fault. Go ahead and play through. I'm going to be a few minutes, apparently." The last word was loaded with his frustration, even if it still sounded pleasant toward the strangers on the surface. His mom wasn't the only one who could act.

We followed Danny behind a nearby bench.

"What's this one more thing?" he gritted out, making his frustrations more than clear.

"When your dad's stuff came back from the coroner, I heard his cell phone went to you, to wipe it?"

He glanced at Amber so quickly I almost missed it. "I, uh, didn't get around to that yet."

"No? Can we have a look at it?"

68

Another glance at Amber. "Look, I don't think you want to, okay? I don't think she wants to." He motioned to his sister.

I had seen Amber get choked up more than once while talking about her dad, but no matter how much she didn't know about him, I suspected she already understood he wasn't a glowing example of humanity. She needed her unanswered questions put to rest.

She cleared this up for Danny. "You think I don't know what Dad was like? What, was he screwing someone out of their money again?" She slapped her cheeks and made an O with her mouth. "Oh, I'm so surprised. Or, what? He was sleeping around?"

"He was sleeping around with Auntie Beth!" Danny hissed, interrupting her.

They both stood there, stunned—Amber at the news, and Danny that he'd said it out loud. Clearly, Danny hadn't meant for it to come out so bluntly. Thankfully, the second gentleman who was playing through had taken his shot and the men had already started to wander away after their golf balls, leaving us alone for the moment.

"I...you're wrong..." Amber looked like someone had just kicked her dog-friend Tinkerbell. "I don't think she—"

Danny nodded. "I thought I was wrong for a long time, too. I hoped I was wrong, but ever since Mom gave me his phone and I hacked his password, I know I'm right."

Amber's gaze flitted back and forth over Danny's face. Slowly, it looked as though she was starting to believe him. Soon I would have two very upset teenagers on my hands.

"I understand if this is a sensitive topic for Amber, for both of you," I said. "But as someone who can see this whole thing objectively, would you be willing to let me see what's on the phone?"

I hadn't yet decided what I'd do if he said no, if they both said no, because I just knew there would be something on that phone that would lead us to the truth.

Danny let out a low humorless laugh. "Have at 'er. I turned off the security." He motioned to his sister. "Amber can do what she wants, but trust me on this one..." He met her eyes head-on. "You won't be able to unsee any of it."

☐

.

# CHAPTER THIRTEEN

I stopped down the road from the Montrose mansion so Amber could run in and retrieve her dad's phone from Danny's bedroom. He'd told her where to find it and had given her one last warning that she might not want to see the explicit texts between her dad and her aunt.

I had only gotten her to agree to let me look at it with her so far, but I'd continue working on convincing her to let me give her an overview.

From my vantage point, I could see the edge of the large Montrose property and all of its manicured shrubbery. A young gardener was busy clipping some of the slightly overgrown branches. I debated ducking down in my seat, but the gardener seemed oblivious to me.

The more I watched him, the more familiarity struck, though. I pulled out my phone and snapped a photo when I caught his profile. Zooming in, I could see I was right. It was the housekeeper's son—Nando, was it? I wondered if he regularly helped with the gardening around the mansion or if he was doing it as a favor to Helen Montrose—who Amber mentioned had taken a liking to the boy and his boundless manners.

The more I gazed at the zoomed-in photo, the more I could see an edge to the young teen. There was anger behind his clenched jaw, and so I suspected it was his mother who had roped him into helping with the gardening and not the matron of the house who appreciated him so much.

In my distraction, a dark blue Tesla sailed by me, snatching my attention. On instinct, I ducked. Helen Montrose drove a dark blue Tesla!

Soon, the Tesla turned into the Montrose driveway and moved out of sight. I let out my breath. It hadn't occurred to me until after Amber and I had left the golf course, but the new information we'd gotten about Dan Montrose's affair with Amber's Auntie Beth seemed to make her mom into the number one suspect. She owned a dark blue Tesla, a low-riding vehicle that matched the police report. Then again, I looked along the curb of the street and at least a half-dozen dark blue vehicles were in view just in this one block.

I shook my head, reminding myself she also had a strong motive. If Dan Montrose was having an affair with Helen's sister, and there was some sort of stipulation in the will that made her put on an act as though everything was fine when clearly it wasn't, it only shed more suspicion on her. It was strange. I'd only met Amber two days ago, and yet my heart ached for her as though I'd known her for years.

My heart stuttered when Amber hopped back into the passenger seat of the Prius and dropped a cell phone into the middle console. She had taken the route through the neighbor's yard and seemed to have missed seeing either her mother or Lupe's son, who had now disappeared out of sight somewhere in the Montrose's large yard. Hunch, who had been patiently waiting on the floor of the passenger side, hopped up onto her lap.

"You'd never know it, but that's not the friendliest cat in the world."

Hunch, as if on cue, immediately started purring like a race car, and Amber looked over at me with a raised eyebrow.

To get the subject off my traitorous cat, I asked, "Does Lupe's son always do your gardening?" I motioned my chin toward the yard, even though I couldn't see him at the moment.

"Nando?" She scrunched up her face, but soon after, it flattened to something more understanding. "I suppose it makes sense. Dad didn't like Nando, called him 'that Mexican kid' whenever he was hanging around. Mom loves him, though, and Lupe probably wants the help." She shrugged.

"Alex is meeting us at my place on his lunch break," I told her as I swung a U-turn toward my place. "Apparently, the case file had some new information, and he has something to tell us. I hope that means it's being investigated further."

"Huh. I wonder if it's about Cade."

"Cade?"

Amber nodded. "While I was inside, I called Danny to get Cade's email address. Danny thought I was just confirming his alibi so he gave it to me right away. But I figured if Cade's our most likely suspect, I could set up a time to meet him somewhere. I'll keep my phone recording in my pocket in case I can get him to admit to anything."

"Hmm. Let's talk to Alex more about that first." I tried to make my voice sound even and unconcerned, even as alarm bells went off all over the place inside my head. I was not about to let a fifteen-year-old go fishing for information from a possible killer by herself—even if I no longer thought of him as the most likely suspect.

Then again, letting her go home and sleep in the same house with her mother each night could just as easily involve danger.

I shook my head as I pulled into my driveway. I suspected my overactive, murder-mystery-binging mind inhibited my ability to think straight sometimes. Killing your husband in a heated rage over an affair was different than killing your own daughter.

Alex had already parked along the curb. Hopefully, he would put some perspective on the whole thing.

He met us at my front door. He wore his police uniform again and took off his hat as he met up with us. I braced myself for him to act brash like he had last time he'd been in uniform, but when he opened his mouth and motioned to Hunch, still in Amber's arms, his voice actually seemed playful. "You bring your cat everywhere you go?"

"Not if I can help it," I grumbled. I opened the door wide to let them go in ahead. Hunch jumped out of Amber's arms and trotted toward his food dish in the kitchen, human affection all but forgotten.

"I understand you found your dad's phone?" Alex asked Amber.

"Uh-huh."

"Was it wiped?"

Amber shook her head. "Danny said he hadn't gotten around to it. We haven't looked at it yet, though."

Tension edged her voice, so I redirected the conversation. "You said you found something of interest in the file, Alex? Did Captain Corbett decide it deserved another look?" We all headed for the kitchen.

"It might be nothing," Alex said. He and Amber took their usual seats at the table, and it seemed my fingers itched to cook again. I was making far too much food for one person these days. Far too much for all three of us, in fact. Even still, I pulled roasted chicken, bacon, Swiss cheese, and alfalfa sprouts from the fridge and then headed for my breadbox for a fresh loaf. I'd whip up a nice chipotle mayo to round it out. Alex added, "But there was a note tacked on today, indicating Captain Corbett would be in attendance at the will reading."

"Will reading?" I asked as I carved off six slices of pumpernickel. "I thought those only happened in the movies."

There hadn't been a public will reading for Cooper or his mom, nor for my grandmother a few years ago. In Cooper's case, I had been the one to dig out the will and deliver it to the law office, and as the sole beneficiary, it was dealt with in just one afternoon between me and my lawyer. We'd never seen Cooper's mom's will, and in my grandmother's case, I had received a copy in the mail, followed by some jewelry a month or so later. But what did I know about how these things worked? Maybe will readings were a popular event for the rich.

Alex went on to explain. "They don't have them often, no, but if any contention is expected, or if specific stipulations apply, then sometimes they do. What's truly odd, though, is that the police captain would be required at one."

My mind stuck on specific stipulations. "Danny said there were some stipulations in the will. He didn't sound like he knew what they were, though. How can we find out?"

"That's why I wanted to meet you at lunch today." Alex opened the sealed container from the middle of my table and helped himself to a pecan tart. Amber followed suit. I kept working on their sandwiches, keeping my motherly comments about ruining their appetites to myself. "The will reading is this afternoon," he said around a mouthful of tart.

"Today? Really? Where?"

"At this estate lawyer's office." Alex pulled a folded paper from his pocket and laid it onto the table. "I don't know how easy it would be to eavesdrop on this thing, but I figure if the police are invited, it could be a fairly large gathering."

"Well, obviously, I can't go," Amber said, but she didn't look as deflated by this realization as I expected. Her next words explained why. "While you're busy, I'll send that email to Cade, see if I can get somewhere on investigating him."

I turned to Alex. "Amber thinks her brother's friend Cade Peeters had something to do with the accident. We found out he and Danny were playing video games the night of Dan Montrose's death, but Cade needlessly went out for an hour to buy some snacks." Alex's eyebrows knit together, so he was definitely listening, but I enunciated the next part, as I wanted him to hear this section the most. "Amber thinks she should set up a meeting and dig for information from Cade, using her phone as a recording device."

Amber nodded, eagerness written all over her face and clearly not noticing my concern.

After a long minute of thinking this over, Alex said to Amber, "Hmm, a phone probably isn't the best recording equipment, especially with someone who might be nervous."

I widened my eyes at Alex. Was he seriously encouraging Amber in this?

He turned to me next. "You should probably get ready for the will reading. It starts in half an hour."

I looked down at myself. I'd worn capris and a cardigan out to the golf course, which I suspected wasn't exactly will-reading attire, but I couldn't leave the room while Alex egged Amber on about questioning Cade on her own.

But then he turned back to her and said, "How about I nose around the station and try and find a wire for you to wear? It just might take me a day or two." Amber lit up at this suggestion. "Go on," he said to me. "We'll be fine." As I started to leave the room, Alex threw me a quick wink. Ahhh, he was buying time. "Now why don't we figure out what's on your dad's phone."

He picked it up from the table as I left the room, and I hated to admit it, but I was glad they were figuring that part out without me. The more I thought about it, the more I knew Amber would absolutely not have let me keep anything on that phone from her. But I also didn't particularly want to be around when she set eyes on any incriminating messages from her Auntie Beth for the first time.

Funny, when Beth had shown Cooper and me houses around Honeysuckle Grove, I'd known she was single, but I could never have imagined her as someone's mistress. Even now, I felt like I needed to see some incriminating evidence to believe it.

Then again, I supposed it would be hard to believe that kind of deceit of most people. That was why they called them secret affairs. I only hoped Alex would clue into the fact that this made Helen Montrose our prime suspect for the murder of her husband without me having to outright say it. Or perhaps he already understood this. He had encouraged me to go sit in on this will reading, after all.

I pulled on a pair of pantyhose and made certain of no extra pairs riding along on the outside of my navy skirt before pulling that on, wondering what Helen Montrose would select for her wardrobe at a will reading. Would she be composed like at the wake, or a crying mess like Danny had described her?

Ten minutes later, I straightened my navy blazer on the most boring and drab outfit I owned as I walked back down the stairs. The key was to be unnoticeable, I reminded myself.

When I walked into the kitchen, my wardrobe became a distant memory. Amber held a crumpled Kleenex in her hand, and her eyes were red. Alex continued to scroll through Dan Montrose's cell phone, but it seemed Amber had seen enough.

"Was it true? What Danny said?" I asked softly. I didn't want to spell it out again.

Amber nodded into her lap.

Alex spoke in an equally soft voice. "I've skimmed through all of his texts from the last couple of weeks and a few of his emails, and the messages between him and Beth are the only things to raise any red flags so far. But Amber's going to let me keep the phone to go over it a little closer."

"Does this mean my mom killed him?" Amber burst out, and a new flood of tears erupted from her eyes.

I took a chair beside her and slid my arm around her. "No, sweetie, it doesn't mean that. We don't even know if your mom knew about what had been going on between your dad and her sister, and we haven't even asked her any questions yet." I had to admit I still had my strong suspicions that she knew very well what her husband had been up to, and therefore had a pretty strong motive, but I wanted to deliver that news to Amber in bite-size pieces.

Alex cleared his throat. "I have some work to do this afternoon around the grounds of the library, but I thought Amber could come along if she's up for it. Maybe she can confirm a few alibis from there." He raised his eyebrows in question toward Amber, and my knotted stomach loosened in gratefulness for him in that moment. I wondered if he had a little girl of his own at home. I also wondered if he was actually allowed to bring a teen civilian along to his job. Whatever the case, he sure knew how to brighten her up.

Once decided, we all stood and headed for the door.

"Should we meet back here after five?" Alex asked, again with the playful smirk. "It seems as though you've cooked up enough food to feed an army." They were both taking their sandwiches to go, but I no longer felt hungry. His smile flattened suddenly, and he added, "Oh, unless it's a problem with your husband?"

Alex looked around the entryway as though he might spot some of Cooper's shoes or coats lying around. It occurred to me in this moment that when I'd introduced myself as Mallory Beck at the police station. That came along with some assumptions.

But I still wasn't used to talking about it. "Oh. Um. No, it won't be a problem."

Thankfully, Amber rescued me from another difficult moment. "Come on, Officer Martinez." She opened the door for him. "I'll tell you all about it on the way."

I was grateful for that kid. In only two days of knowing her, she had brought a lot of good things into my world. I hoped I would be as much of a positive force in her life.

Or, at the very least, I hoped I could be a shoulder to cry on through some hard truths that might be on the horizon.

Twenty minutes later, I parked across town at the offices of Estate Lawyer Nelson Reed. The tall building housed at least two dozen businesses, but I easily located Mr. Reed's office on the wall directory near the elevator on the first floor. Several other people walked through the glass front doors and headed for the elevator, and when I stepped on and they pushed button 5, it seemed we all had the same destination.

Thankfully, I'd chosen well with my outfit. Most men wore dark suits, and the one woman on the elevator wore a black skirt and blazer similar to my navy one. I had added a matching wool fedora, and it seemed to do the trick of keeping people's interest away from my face.

When the elevator door opened, I blended with the crowd as they moved down the hallway toward office 518, but then they veered off suddenly at two wide-open doors.

They all headed inside a large boardroom with close to fifty seats, and I made a quick decision to follow. Perhaps large gatherings were held here instead of in the lawyer's actual office.

A dozen people were already seated, while others milled around talking. I spotted Helen Montrose right away—the sole person wearing a pink floral dress to this event. If she were a Jekyll and Hyde type, today was clearly one of her brighter Jekyll days.

She snapped her fingers high in the air and said, "Nando," loud enough that most people in the room looked her way. That's when I noticed Lupe and her son, Nando, at the perimeter of the room, offering up platters of cookies to guests.

Nando immediately grinned at Helen Montrose and wove his way over to her. She stood with a well-dressed couple I didn't recognize, and Nando seemed to know without being told why he had been summoned. He offered the cookie tray to the couple, and they both helped themselves to one.

Strange that Helen Montrose brought her own housekeeper and her son to a will reading. Wouldn't the law firm offer that sort of thing? Perhaps Mrs. Montrose simply liked to flaunt her wealth.

A lineup had formed near the coffee, so I decided against getting myself a cup. No need to put myself in a situation where someone might ask how I knew the deceased. Instead, I lingered just outside the doors and kept my eyes down on my phone.

Every couple of minutes, I peeked up from under the brim of my hat to take in more of the room and its occupants. Beth Dawson had arrived, but so far, I hadn't seen her anywhere near her sister. She didn't look as broken up today, and instead smiled and nodded as she greeted different folks around the room. Her somewhat glassy eyes and pasted-on smile made me wonder if she was medicated. I pulled my hat an inch lower, as she would be the most likely of the attendees to recognize me.

The only other familiar face was that of the lawyer from Dan Montrose's firm, Terrence Lane. In his same three-piece suit, he looked like a skinny giraffe, almost cartoon-like with his ultra long, thin legs and angular features. He moved through the room, talking to different attendees for only a few seconds each, but he had the air of someone on a mission.

As I took a step through the open doorway to follow Mr. Lane's progress around the room, out of my peripheral vision, I caught sight of a man in police uniform, striding down the hallway toward the boardroom.

Captain Corbett! Shoot, I had forgotten about him. I turned in the opposite direction to put my back to him and took quick steps back into the hallway.

By the time I turned back, a man in a pinstripe suit and glasses sat behind the table at the front of the room, flipping through a set of papers, and cleared his throat.

Most of the chairs in the room filled quickly with the lawyer's presence, and while a few open chairs remained near the front of the room, I would be far too obvious there. And, in fact, a second later, Captain Corbett helped himself to one of the front row seats. I wanted to sink into the floor or a wall to make myself invisible, but instead, my next best option was to inch my way behind one of the open doors. I took deep, steadying breaths as I moved, keeping one eye on all of the familiar people in the room to make sure they didn't look back at me.

A second later, I had made it to safety and let out a gust of air. Unfortunately, the lawyer in the pinstripe suit didn't have a terribly loud voice. I only made out bits and pieces as he announced the will reading and how it was being held at the request of Daniel Montrose. I'd have to ask Amber later why her dad might have requested a public will reading. I wondered if both he and his wife enjoyed flaunting their wealth—even after Mr. Montrose wasn't here to do it personally.

Then again, perhaps this would be his way of announcing his affair with Helen's sister.

Mr. Reed continued the spiel, asking that any contestations be made publicly today before submitting them formally in writing, and proof of stipulations was to be met today.

The more he spoke, the more I wondered if Dan Montrose had only suggested a public will reading for the drama of it.

The lawyer droned on, reading a lot of legalese from the actual will. I made notes on a small notepad from my purse, not sure how I'd make heads or tails of any of it. Maybe Alex could help me later, or I could meet with an independent lawyer. I only hoped I would understand enough to figure out what transpired during these proceedings.

Mr. Reed did most of the talking for at least half an hour. I tried not to tune out and kept popping candy from my purse to keep myself alert. He spoke of Dan's house, his vehicles, artwork, and personal belongings, all going to his wife, Helen Montrose.

"Any contestations?" Mr. Reed asked, to which there was no response.

Business holdings became more complicated, as Dan's law firm interest was assigned a value, which could be bought out among the partners. Several lawyers spoke up, arguing the amount, and I peered through the crack of the door to see if Terrence Lane added to the discussion.

He didn't. Then again, if he had been trying to make partner, I supposed he wouldn't have any kind of vested interest in Dan Montrose's holdings in the firm.

Mr. Reed knocked on his desk with a gavel. "If you would like to contest this point formally, you may proceed in writing. Until then, the value of Mrs. Montrose's assets in the firm stands."

Some grumbling throughout the room followed, and I made a note of the contention.

"If that's settled," Mr. Reed said, "let's move along."

He read several other points in the will, and almost every item seemed to be promised to Helen Montrose, so it confused me why all of these other people had gathered, if not simply for some kind of dramatic show. But soon smaller items cropped up, bequeathed to other people: An antique watch went to his son, Daniel Jr., a specific painting went to his brother, Ben Montrose, and a cabin at Cedar Lake went to Beth Dawson. Mr. Reed went on, and surprisingly, Helen Montrose did not contest this gift.

"The stipulation on cause of death," Mr. Reed announced. "In the case of suspicious cause of death or suicide, all allocations here within become null and void. In such a case, all properties named within shall go to the Clinton Foundation."

The Clinton Foundation? Huh. The Montrose Family wouldn't have struck me as Clinton supporters. But I clued back in when Mr. Reed spoke again.

"Do we have someone present who can verify this?"

"Yes, sir. Captain Corbett from the Honeysuckle Grove Police Department." Captain Corbett's voice boomed out much louder and more commanding than Mr. Reed's.

"And what has been declared the cause of death?" Mr. Reed asked.

"The death of Daniel Montrose was deemed an accident, without clear intent, by hit-and-run."

"Well, then," Mr. Reed said. "Thank you for your attendance, ladies and gentlemen. All points within the last will and testament of Daniel Montrose stand."

Immediately, a rush of activity erupted throughout the room. Seats shuffled on the floor, people grumbled to one another or chattered animatedly, and one person swept out into the hallway so quickly, I ducked into the tiny space behind the nearest door, so as not to look as though I had been lurking.

And good thing I did, as the person was Beth Dawson. I could only make out a small sliver of her, but she suddenly stopped within that small sliver of my vision only a foot from my hiding spot.

"I guess you'll leave us alone now," Helen Montrose's voice said, although I couldn't see her from behind the door. "Too bad you only got that stupid cottage. You obviously never meant much to Dan."

Beth Dawson let out a single huff of a laugh. "Dan knew I never wanted anything from him. If you want the cottage, you can have it. I just want Dan back!" Her words became louder at the end, as though she were physically chasing her sister. But I could still make out the small swatch of her in front of me.

After a couple of seconds, I clued in that Helen had returned to the boardroom. Beth Dawson stood alone, watching her sister's retreat, and if I played it right...

I quickly slipped away from around the back of the door while Beth was still focused on the other direction. "Beth?" I said as though surprised to see her.

She turned, and her face was a contorted mess. Tears streaked her face, but she forced a smile upon seeing me. "Oh, Mallory, hi. What are you doing here?" She swiped a hand at her tears.

I passed her a tissue from my purse and motioned further down the hall. "Just meeting with Cooper's estate lawyer about some unfinished business. These things take forever to wrap up." It hadn't been true in Cooper's case, but Beth wouldn't know that.

"Unless you have boatloads of money," Beth murmured under her breath, but I heard her fine. I just didn't know what I was supposed to say in response to it. Thankfully, Beth shook her head and added, "I'm sorry. I didn't mean anything by that."

"Are you here for something to do with Dan Montrose's death?" I asked, all wide-eyed and innocent.

Beth's face immediately crumpled, and she swiped away more tears. She nodded until she could get her voice back. In that moment, I felt like I could confidently say that Beth Dawson had truly loved Dan Montrose. I wondered if that would make Amber feel better or worse about the whole situation.

Finally, she said, "Yes. It was his will reading. But I should really go."

I nodded and gave her a quick hug before letting her hurry down the hall and into the elevator. I remained in the middle of the wide hallway. Dark-suited people trickled out of the room and also headed toward the exit.

I could certainly use my ruse again—simply here to see another lawyer—but was there anything else I could accomplish here? Maybe I should just go.

Just then, Terrence Lane made his way out of the boardroom. His face looked twitchier than the last time I had encountered him at the Montrose mansion, and his fingers trembled as though he'd had too much caffeine.

He headed down the hall in the opposite direction of everyone else, toward the lawyer's offices, and as he moved farther in that direction, I saw my opportunity to converse with him privately.

I raced ahead, rooting in my purse for my notepad and pen, an idea suddenly coming to me. "Mr. Lane? Mr. Lane? Can I please have a minute of your time?"

Terrence Lane stopped in place and immediately started wringing his hands. "Yes, miss? What can I help you with?" Again, he had the double wink to his eye, and I had to remind myself it was a twitch. This man wasn't hitting on me.

"I'm Mallory Vandewalker," I said, in an instant deciding on my maiden name, "from the Honeysuckle Grove Herald." Everything I knew about journalists I had learned either from TV or from when I'd helped research Cooper's novels. Still, I forged ahead. "I was hoping to talk to you at the wake. Helen Montrose indicated you were investigating the vehicle involved in the hit-and-run accident of Dan Montrose. Can you comment on that?"

Terrence Lane became even more jittery, if that were possible. He glanced toward the boardroom, and his face took on a mask of indecision. "Helen Montrose told you that? She told you to speak to me?"

I doubted I'd get by with a bald-faced lie on this one. "She indicated you'd had some leads."

"I...um...I'm afraid I can't speak on that." He flicked his thumb against a fingernail.

"Even off the record?" I asked, folding up my notepad. "You see, I've been assigned to this story, and I feel it in my bones that there's something more to it, someone who should have come forward, but I'm afraid with everyone being so tight-lipped about it, I've found myself at a standstill."

Terrence's dark eyes flitted back and forth over mine. Close up, his angular cheekbones gave his face a sunken appearance, and each of his expressions was starkly different from the one before. I could tell how much he wanted to open his mouth and say more to me.

I tucked my notepad into my purse and put on my most trustworthy face. "I honestly won't report anything you tell me. I just really hoped not to go back to my boss and tell him I couldn't find anything to go on here. Can you give me any kind of a hint of where else to look?"

Another glance toward the boardroom, and then, to my surprise, Terrence Lane grabbed me by the arm and tugged me farther down the hall and around a corner. I quelled the yelp that wanted to come out of my mouth.

Terrence leaned in and told me in a rushed whisper, "You can't tell a soul I told you this. Not a soul," he repeated, to which I quickly nodded, "but I found out from the Montrose's mechanic, Mel Stanley, that one of the Montrose vehicles was brought to him the day after the accident." Terrence glanced toward the corner, but everything remained quiet at this end of the hallway. "Actually, he didn't tell me that, so you may not want to barrel in there asking questions. He wouldn't tell me anything, but I saw it scrawled on his desk planner."

"And what was the make of the vehicle? What was the color?" I asked, quickly thinking through every Montrose vehicle: the un-drivable Corvette, the dark blue Tesla, and the maroon car Dan had been driving. Then again, there had been a Ben Montrose mentioned at the reading.

Terrence shook his head. "Didn't say. It just said, 'MONTROSE FIX FRONT FENDER ASAP.'"

I nodded, searching for my next question, but Terrence didn't let me ask it.

"Find out which Montrose vehicle it was, and I think you'll find out who did this to Dan."

My mind swirled, but Terrence Lane raced away from me before I could ask any other questions.

# CHAPTER FOURTEEN

Back at the house, I pulled together a stir-fry while I waited for Alex and Amber to arrive. Chopping broccoli, carrots, and sweet white onions seemed to be a good way of funneling my energy. I had only just started simmering my ginger and garlic when a knock sounded at the door.

Sure enough, Amber and Alex stood on the stoop, and when I opened the door for them, they walked inside, already talking.

"All I'm saying is that it's not a very effective place to patrol," Amber was telling him. "You woulda caught way more speeders on Selkirk. It runs beside the highway, so everyone wants to go faster."

"Right. I'll keep that in mind in case Corbett one day says, 'Hey, Martinez, why don't you choose your own patrol route today?'"

They had the sort of easy bickering about them that made me think of a brother and sister, or a teasing uncle. I suspected Amber had been trying to rattle Alex's cage all afternoon.

They followed me to the kitchen, barely taking the time to say hello. When they got through the kitchen door, though, their bickering finally came to a halt.

"What smells so freaking good?" Amber didn't leave me time to answer. She followed me over to the counter to survey my assembly line of preparations. "And when did you say you were going to teach me how to make some of these recipes?"

I smirked and passed her my knife. "You want to slice up these water chestnuts?" I showed her the size I wanted, and without another word, she got to work.

It gave me a moment to catch up with Alex. As soon as I met him at the table, he stood from where he had already plunked down into his usual chair and placed a hand on my arm.

"Hey, I was sorry to hear about your husband," he said softly. "I didn't know."

My eyes flitted to a piece of floral art on the wall to keep them from watering. "Right. Yeah. Well, now you know."

Thankfully, he seemed to understand that I didn't much want to talk about Cooper, not when I'd already had such an emotionally taxing day. "I'm eager to hear about the will reading, but let me tell you what we came up with first."

I sat across from him, glad to have the focus on the Dan Montrose case.

"While I was patrolling, Little Miss Smarty Pants over there spent some time at the library checking up on her mom's alibi."

Amber grinned over her shoulder, and then went back to chopping. She carefully worked at the water chestnuts, trying to get them all exactly the same size. I could have told her not to be so concerned, but I had the feeling she, like me, enjoyed having something else to focus on.

"First, she emailed Cade." Alex must have caught my concerned look because he quickly elaborated. "We agreed she shouldn't arrange a meeting just yet, so instead she just asked him where he buys his spicy Cheetos. She told him she was in the mood for some and the grocery store was sold out. Then she called Honeysuckle Grove Parks and Trees Foundation, for which Helen Montrose had been attending a meeting the night of the accident," Alex told me. "She pretended to be an employee from the meeting hall where they had gathered and asked to double-check the exact meeting time, as well as setup and tear down for her records."

I raised my eyebrows in Amber's direction, but she didn't turn to see the praise. Alex went on. "I, myself, can vouch for Mrs. Montrose's presence at the hall an hour after the incident, as my partner and I had delivered the news personally. But Amber checked in with a few Instagram accounts of women she knew were on the board of the foundation with her mom. Their photos showed her on the stage all evening. To be sure, she messaged these women and heard back that her mother had been on the stage throughout the entirety of the meeting. So Helen Montrose could not have been the one to strike her husband with her car," he said, spelling it out for me.

I thought through everything I had learned that day, including what Terrence Lane had told me about the Montrose vehicle that had been repaired. "Do we know if she was driving her blue Tesla that night?"

"Doubt it," Amber said over her shoulder. "Usually Molly Taylor picks her up for all those board meetings."

"Can we find out for sure?" Alex asked. He had obviously caught on to my line of thinking. Because if she hadn't been driving the Tesla, we were back to suspecting Danny again. His only alibi was their housekeeper, Lupe, and we hadn't spoken with her yet.

Amber's voice suggested she was oblivious to our thoughts. "Sure. I'll message her when I'm done with this."

My mind was a rattled mess. I didn't want to think Danny, a boy of only seventeen, might be capable of purposefully killing his dad. I stood and headed for the counter, deciding to get the sauce simmering. Maybe that would help me think.

As soy sauce and hoisin began to fill the kitchen with new sweet and salty aromas, I took a deep breath and told Alex and Amber all about the will reading.

When I got to the part about the Cedar Lake cabin going to Beth Dawson, Amber's chopping—now onto yellow peppers—became louder and faster. "She used to go there with us when we were little," she said, bitterness leaking out in her voice.

I couldn't think of a single response that would make Amber feel any better about that, so I moved onto the next point. "And I found out about the will stipulation your brother had spoken about," I told them. "Apparently, if his death was a suicide or suspicious in any way, all allocations in the will would be void, and all of Dan Montrose's fortune would instead go to The Clinton Foundation. It's in my notes," I told Alex. I had left my notepad on the table for him to look at, but I couldn't stop thinking about this point, because the death certainly was suspicious. So who had the most reason to cover that up?

"The Clinton Foundation?" Amber stopped chopping completely. "Are you sure it said that? My parents hate Hillary Clinton. Especially Mom."

Alex confirmed the fact. When he found the clause that I'd hurriedly scribbled, he read it aloud.

"Huh." Amber resumed chopping. "It sounds like some kind of a slap in the face to me."

I dropped some rice noodles into my pot of boiling water, wondering what that meant. Had Dan Montrose expected some sort of foul play in his death? Then again, if he was having a serious affair with Helen's sister, I wondered if the stipulation had been a recent addition to the paperwork.

I went on to tell them about the altercation between Helen and Beth that I'd overheard, and then what I'd found out about the car repair from Terrence Lane.

"He was really jumpy, so I wasn't sure what to make of that."

Amber dumped her peppers into the pan of already simmering veggies and then waved a casual hand. "He's always like that. Mom's told him more than once that he should lay off the coffee, but he never listens to her. She doesn't sign his checks." Amber smirked. Clearly, she didn't seriously suspect Terrence of wrongdoing, and to be honest, neither did I. "But what he says is true. Mel Stanley is our mechanic. He's the only person Mom'll let work on her Tesla."

"So if your mom was definitely at that board meeting, picked up by Molly Taylor, and couldn't have been out wrecking her own car—which she would take in as an emergency repair the next day—who could have driven a blue Montrose car out by Mile Marker 18 that night?"

Even though I suspected I knew who—at this point, it had to be Danny Jr.—I waited for Amber to come to the same conclusion.

But she only shrugged, looking unbothered as she used my wooden spoon to stir the vegetables. "Danny's Corvette's up on blocks, Dad was driving his car, and Mom's Tesla would have been in the garage."

I nodded. "Right, but who could have been driving it, if not your mom? Could Cade have borrowed her vehicle from the garage?"

Amber let out a loud cackle of a laugh. "No way, Dad specifically told Danny that Cade wasn't allowed to use any of our cars. Ever." I watched as this all started to piece together in Amber's mind. A swallow traveled down her throat. "It coulda been Lupe, I guess," she said, but her words didn't sound terribly convincing.

"Could it have been?" I pressed.

"She doesn't borrow our cars often, but Mom's told her to take the Tesla a couple of times for an errand when Nando had Lupe's car." The more Amber spoke, the quieter she became. She knew we had to check up on Danny Jr.'s alibi next.

But then Alex placed my notepad down on the table and said, "Did it have to be a Montrose vehicle?" I furrowed my brow and started to nod, but he added, "Couldn't it have been a vehicle that the Montrose family simply paid to have repaired?"

That brought us back to implicating Helen Montrose in some part of her husband's murder or, at the very least, its cover-up.

Still, I hoped this thread of new possibility wouldn't fall apart the moment we pulled at it.

☐

# CHAPTER FIFTEEN

The sun had set long ago. Amber and I organized a plan to spend the next morning questioning Lupe to see where that led us. Unfortunately, Alex had to be back on duty.

I wasn't crazy about the idea of Amber spending the night at home, but I hadn't come right out and said that. I'd asked her if she wanted to check with her mom if she could finish up a cooking lesson tonight and then stay over. I mentioned it under the guise that it just seemed easier than driving her home tonight only to meet back at her place in the morning. She'd texted her mom and simply received a response of : OK.

I wasn't sure what to make of that barely involved parenting but tried not to judge. The woman had just lost her husband, after all.

"Oh, and Cade emailed back," Amber said, still looking at her phone. "Says you can get spicy Cheetos anywhere, but he got some just last week at the little supermarket at the corner of 3rd and Hemlock."

"That's just down the hill from your house, right?" I asked.

Amber shrugged and twisted her mouth like the thought was distasteful. "Not really. It's all the way down in the flats. Plus, it's in an area where the lowlifes hang out. I suppose I shouldn't be surprised Cade went there."

"Why don't I look into the store first thing tomorrow," Alex said, standing from the table and heading for the front door. "I'll be done at five, so do we want to meet back here?" Alex opened the front door, but then turned back. "Or if you think you'll still be at Amber's place, maybe I should change into some casual clothes and meet you somewhere closer to there?"

"Here's fine," I told him, already excited about the prospect of making another dinner for more than just myself.

I followed him outside and took a few steps toward his patrol car. As he was about to step into the driver's side, he stopped and looked up at me.

"Oh, I almost forgot..." He held up a small purple item in a Ziploc bag. I walked closer so I could see it better. "It wasn't wrapping paper, after all. Forensics found traces of chocolate, so they're suspecting it's a chocolate bar wrapper." He held out the Ziploc bag with the tiny swatch of wrapper we'd found down the bank by Mile Marker 18.

"What are you two talking about?" Amber asked. She followed us outside to see. Even Hunch made his way out my open front door to sniff out any new evidence. She looked back and forth between our faces and then at the swatch of wrapper in the Ziploc. "Wait, that looks like a Frucao wrapper."

Alex and I both looked at her. Hunch sniffed the air up toward the Ziploc, and Alex dropped it down near his thigh so my cat could get a better whiff.

"What's a Frucao?" I asked.

Amber shrugged. "It's a chocolate bar Lupe's mom sends her from Mexico every once in a while. She usually gets a bunch at a time, so Mom makes her give one to me and one to Danny."

I could definitely see how Lupe may have seen the Montrose kids as entitled. I glanced at Alex, but he was already onto another question. "And these were delivered to your house?"

Amber shrugged again. "All Lupe's mail comes to our house. I don't know why, really. But come to think of it, she hasn't given us a Frucao in ages. I bet Nando's hogging them all for himself."

"Nando likes the Frucao chocolate bars as well?" I asked.

"Yeah. It's different than the chocolate bars you find here in the grocery store. Frucao's got this spicy—" Amber stopped when she seemed to clue in that we couldn't possibly be this interested in comparisons between national chocolate brands. "Wait, where did you get that?" She motioned to the Ziploc bag.

I nodded. "Out by Mile Marker 18. On the bank near the hole."

Amber's eyes widened. "Lupe." She drew out the whispered name.

"It's just a candy bar wrapper, or a piece of one," Alex said. "Certainly nothing to rest this case upon, and as you said, Amber, both you and your brother also like Frucao bars. Maybe your dad did, too."

"No, Dad never ate chocolate. He didn't even like sweets."

But I understood. Amber needed someone other than her mom and brother to look at as possible suspects.

"We'll get over there and talk to Lupe first thing tomorrow morning," I told Alex. Then I turned to Amber. "Are you going to be able to hold it together to ask a few questions without throwing blame around?"

"Pfft. I did fine with my brother, and with Mom's charity workers, didn't I?"

"She did that," Alex said, backing away toward his driver's door again.

"Amber's got this. Just ask a few probing questions and then we can put our heads together about it later."

Truthfully, I should probably be more concerned about my own ability to ask casual nonthreatening questions, as I seemed to keep messing that up, even only with Amber.

Throughout the rest of the evening, as I taught Amber to mix and bake an easy zucchini muffin recipe, I practiced a few casual leading conversation starters in my head.

Do you have any chocolate, Amber? I have a real craving. Maybe Lupe knows where some is?

Oh, hey, Lupe, I heard you were here when Mrs. Montrose came home and had to tell Danny about his dad being flattened like a pancake. That must have been awful!

Then again, maybe I'd better let Amber take the lead on this.

She'd also been deep in thought through most of our cooking class and later, as I got her settled into the guest room, but first thing the next morning, she let me in on her mental process.

"So if Lupe borrowed the Tesla and, for some reason, drove it out to Mile Marker 18, left a chocolate bar wrapper down the bank in the mud, and then ran over my dad, first of all, why would she do that? My dad was the one who paid her salary. He's the one who hired her. Twice!" she added.

"Twice?" I asked.

"Yeah, she used to be my parents' housekeeper years ago. When Mom got pregnant with Danny, she'd been on bed rest for most of it, so he'd hired a fulltime nurse that took over as housekeeper. I guess Lupe went back to Mexico and got married, but when that didn't work out, she came back asking my dad for a job again."

"And how long ago was this?" I asked, trying to get a full picture.

Amber looked up at the kitchen ceiling. "About four years ago, I think. Dad fired our other housekeeper, Emily, because he'd always liked Lupe."

I nodded, thinking this over, but Amber went right back to her train of thought on the night of the accident.

"Also, why would my mom or brother have taken the car into Mel Stanley, because I'm pretty sure Lupe wouldn't have been able to bring the car in and put it under my parents' name?"

"You're certain about that?" I asked. I grabbed two zucchini muffins for each of us, and we headed for the Prius. On the way there, I checked my phone and had a new text from Alex.

<Cade's alibi checks out. The manager at stu's convenience store knew him by name and said he was hanging around talking to friends outside the store last monday. He figured he was there for an hour or more. Was driving a bright green car.>

I quickly clicked my phone off before Amber could catch sight of the text. It might be better to have her continue thinking of her brother's friend as a suspect until we could at least confirm her brother's alibi. "What if Lupe came into the shop claiming that your mom had sent her to get a car fixed?"

Amber twisted her lips. "I guess it's possible, but I still don't get why Lupe would have wanted to kill or even hurt Dad. He was the nicest to her of anybody."

I backed out of my driveway, again with Hunch on Amber's lap, and headed up the hill toward her neighborhood.

"Hmm, well, maybe she didn't mean for it to happen. Maybe somehow she didn't see him, hopped out of her car to see if he was okay, and that's when a piece of chocolate bar wrapper swept out onto the road's shoulder?"

"And all the way down near the hole?" Amber shook her head. "It still doesn't explain why someone dug the hole, though, does it? Or why FDS was carved into the tree."

She was right about that. Right about all of it. When I couldn't fall asleep last night, I'd lain in bed, doodling in my notepad and going over all of the various clues and oddities we'd discovered regarding Dan Montrose's death. I had spent a lot of time deliberating on what FDS could possibly stand for. The closest I had come was with Danny's first two names—Daniel Seth. But what was the F for? Some kind of expletive?

"Well, we have a lot of things to ask Lupe about then, don't we?" I said. "Let's just take it slowly and try not to raise her suspicions of why we're asking." I reached for Hunch, and he let out a low growl, but I adopted my sternest voice to tell him, "Mrs. Montrose is allergic to you, buddy. This is one stop where you won't be able to help investigate."

But Hunch hissed at me, not having any of it. He didn't like being stuck in the car, and who would? But then Amber, his new BFF, came to my cat's rescue. "Mom'll never know if Hunch stays in the backyard for a bit." She held him up so she could look at him eye to eye, a dangerous feat with a regularly hissing cat if you asked me. "Only if you promise not to wander off?"

Hunch gave her a sweet little mewl in reply, and I supposed that settled it. We headed down the street to the Montrose mansion with Hunch in Amber's arms.

Amber led the way around the side of their yard, the same route we had taken when we snuck out during the wake. Once we made it into their yard, she let Hunch down near the back porch, and he immediately started sniffing every plant and blade of grass in the vicinity. With a good quarter acre of flower gardens, flawless green grass, and lawn furniture to investigate, I was fairly confident we'd find Hunch still nosing around by the time we returned. Besides, as it had been when Cooper had been alive, Hunch wouldn't wander far with an investigation afoot.

I tiptoed behind Amber into the mudroom, and it was a good thing we were quiet because the door to the kitchen was open a couple of inches, and we immediately heard voices. Amber silently crept forward, and I followed in her footsteps.

At first, I didn't recognize the lady in jeans and a black blouse that Helen Montrose was speaking to through the gap of the open doorway. But then the lady turned, and familiarity struck. Her legs didn't look quite as good in jeans, and her black hair seemed flat without the bonnet, but this was unmistakably the Montrose housekeeper, Lupe, in plain clothes today.

I furrowed my brow, thinking Amber surely would have told me if it had been Lupe's day off. But only a moment later, Lupe spoke, stealing my attention.

"We stay through the will reading like you tell us. Now give me my money and we leave town. You never see us again."

Helen Montrose let out a humorless laugh, but nonetheless poised a checkbook onto the kitchen island and started to write. "You act like you haven't done anything wrong. I can't believe I'm paying you. I didn't kill Dan."

Lupe dug her fists into her waist. "No, his son kill him."

I froze in place, and because I was crouched so close to Amber in the doorway, I could actually feel her breath catch.

"Now, where me and Nando passports? He keep them in a safe some place here?" Lupe directed her eyes all around the kitchen. In an instant, Amber and I both glued ourselves to the mudroom wall, out of sight.

"Ha!" Helen said loudly in a tone that almost sounded like it contained some humor. "Dan never kept a safe, never trusted it, in case the police showed up with a search warrant one day. Dan buried things. If you'd known him at all, you'd have known that. Good luck finding your passports." She laughed again.

"Nobody did right in all this. Nobody." Lupe snatched the check out of Helen's hand and started to turn away.

In an instant, I grabbed Amber's arm and yanked her toward the back door and outside. Thankfully, a giant shrub right beside the back steps made the perfect hiding spot. Seconds later, the door opened and closed with a bang.

Through the shrub, I could make out Lupe's form. She wore red shiny high heels with her jeans and looked quite stylish for a housekeeper on her day off. Or now that I thought about it, it wasn't simply a day off, was it? This was her day of termination.

Her heels clacked along the cement path until a moment later when they stopped in place. I peered closer into the shrub to see what she had stopped for, and then my breath stilled. Hunch, just off the path in the flower bed, was kicking up dirt.

"Pierdase!" Lupe hissed at Hunch and kicked one of her red shoes at him.

Hunch moved quickly away from her shoe and then skittered off to hide behind a nearby azalea bush. When I turned back, Lupe had crouched onto her knees and was digging with her hands in the dirt where Hunch had been.

It didn't take long for her to find something. Less than a minute later, she stood, brushed off her hands and then her jeans, and picked up a dirty Ziploc bag—this one had two navy objects inside. They looked like passports.

The eyeline through the shrub wasn't great, but nonetheless, the grin that spread across Lupe's face couldn't be missed.

☐

# CHAPTER SIXTEEN

As soon as Lupe had cleared the backyard, we gathered Hunch up, and Amber pulled me toward the neighbor's fence. "I think we should follow her," she said. "Come on, this is faster!"

Faster, true, but quite the obstacle course, with decorative rocks and shrubs to navigate around, and as we scaled a wooden fence, which Hunch and Amber both had a much easier time clearing than I did, it reminded me I wasn't fifteen anymore.

Even though I still wasn't certain of why we should follow Lupe, with so much to sort out from the last fifteen minutes, I was more than willing to let Amber call the shots for the moment.

By the time we reached my car, I figured we must have lost her, but Amber told me, "Don't worry, there's a long traffic light at the bottom of the hill. Takes forever to go green. We'll catch up."

And we did.

Once in clear view of Lupe's navy Ford Focus, Amber shook her head ruefully. "I should have had my voice recorder on."

But would she have wanted to have proof that it was actually her brother who killed her dad? Of course I didn't spell this out, but I probably should gently bring up Alex and how we eventually needed to be honest with him about everything.

"Wait, Lupe has a dark blue car?" I blurted, the thought suddenly coming to me. Even though Lupe had just stated the identity of the person who had struck down Dan Montrose, I couldn't help grasping for the rest of the truth. Had Danny taken his mom's Tesla that night? Or Lupe's car, to try and frame her for his dad's murder?

"Yeah, I don't know why I didn't think of it. Maybe because it's barely ever at our house. It used to be Danny's, but our dad hadn't wanted him to buy the Corvette and waste all his time trying to rebuild it. So when he went ahead and bought it anyway, Dad went ballistic and gave Danny's car to

Lupe. Danny's had to beg to borrow my parents' cars or take the bus ever since."

Motive. Nothing but motive.

"Where do you think she's going?" I asked because the direction Lupe turned made my stomach tighten for a whole other reason.

"If it were me and I'd just gotten some kind of huge check from my mom, I'd hit the nearest bank," Amber said. She didn't notice how the word "bank" shook me as she ran her fingers all the way from Hunch's neck to his tail. He lapped up the affection, both of them oblivious to my distress. She went on about Lupe. "She's lying, you know. There's no way Danny did this. She's just trying to pin it on him, and my mom's too out of it to realize the truth."

It made more sense now why Amber didn't seem to be a mess over this new information. I didn't know if I agreed, but all I could think of was the word "bank," coupled with the direction we were heading. The bank Cooper had died in was just around the corner from here. As the bank came into view, my breath caught. Lupe pulled into the parking lot of the strip mall where it was located.

I hadn't been back here in almost eight months. In fact, besides surveying the site shortly after his death, I'd made a concerted effort not to drive down this particular street.

The last time I'd set eyes on the structure, the façade of brick had been blackened, with half of the roof collapsed. Now the bank and the shops on either side of it were barely recognizable, with brand new stucco walls and much more modern-looking signage.

I swallowed. It made my insides turn that I hadn't been back again before they made the changes. I hadn't gotten one more look at where Cooper had spent his last moments.

"See, she's going inside," Amber said, breaking me from my thoughts.

I still wasn't exactly sure why we were following her. "Do you think we should follow her inside?" I asked, even though I couldn't imagine many places I'd less like to go.

Amber shook her head. "Nah, but let's see where she goes after this. See where she lives, just so we know."

Again it seemed odd—and maybe a tad entitled—that Amber had no clue where the housekeeper who had been working in her home for years lived. But I nodded. I didn't have another plan, and at this point, I needed any thoughts that might distract me.

I had just started to sort through my thoughts about why Lupe, Helen, and Danny might have been in on covering up Dan Montrose's murder together when Amber said, "That's where her son, Nando, works." She pointed across the strip mall parking lot to a small Mexican restaurant called La Cortina.

"Right. He'd had Lupe's car the night of the accident because he had to work." I'd reverted to calling it an accident with Amber. It seemed gentler than saying the night your dad died. Or worse, the night your dad was murdered. "So they must live far enough away from here that he wouldn't have been able to walk."

I was still piecing it all together, but at least I'd figured out that Danny must have used his mom's Tesla the night of the accident.

"Maybe you should go and check to make sure he was on shift last Monday night," Amber suggested. "To make sure he definitely had Lupe's car." She was clearly still pulling at any possible threads that could exonerate her brother. "If he's working now, it would seem weird if I did it."

But fruitless or not, the idea of going anywhere so I didn't have to sit here staring at the new face of the bank spurred me on, and I eagerly grabbed for my purse. "Did Nando have anything against your dad?" I reached for the door handle.

Amber shrugged. "Don't think he liked any of us, but he was hardly ever at our house. You know, at least before my dad died."

This didn't surprise me. Besides, if Lupe considered the Montrose kids entitled, it made sense that Nando would feel that way, too.

Amber said, "I'll give the horn three quick honks if Lupe comes back, though, because if she's spouting lies about Danny, it's probably more important to follow her."

Amber's brain processed all of this much quicker than mine. I had been used to that with Cooper, and it brought back a strange sort of nostalgia.

As I walked across the parking lot, I thought back to when I'd sat across from Cooper many times in our college library. I'd help to research specific murder weapons or police procedures for one of his new novels. I'd only have to read a small paragraph out loud for Cooper, and seconds later, his hands would fly into a frenzy over his laptop as though his mind had pieced together a hundred new plot ideas from the one paragraph.

The door to La Cortina opened with a middle-aged couple leaving as I arrived. They held the door open, and I walked inside to see bright blue walls with orange leather booths. A number of velvet, gold-adorned sombreros hung on the walls, as well as an upright beaded decorative iguana. The place was nearly empty, not surprising considering the time, barely eleven in the morning. One man sat alone at a booth, reading a newspaper and sipping a coffee. Otherwise, I was the only customer.

As I headed for the counter, I prepared my story. A bronze-skinned boy met me on the other side. This boy was taller and had fuller cheeks than Nando. "Can I help you?"

I glanced down and his nametag read: MATEO. "Um, yeah." I looked at the backlit menu above him. "A week ago, on Friday the thirteenth, I came in and had a great platter that the guy who took my order recommended, but I can't remember which one it was. Were you working last Friday?"

The boy looked up, searching his memory. "Yeah, but I don't remember recommending anything." He stared at me, not offering to help beyond that.

"Was there anyone else who you know was working last Friday?" I asked. "It was in the evening."

The guy raised an eyebrow, seemingly in disbelief that I would push this issue and not just order. Finally, he turned and yelled through the food warmers into the back kitchen prep area. "Anyone know if they were working last Friday night?"

He didn't wait for an answer, but instead grabbed a clipboard from the wall, flipped through it toward the back, and as he did, glimpses of different pages indicated it was daily listings of who had been staffing the place. The oldest ones seemed to be at the back of the clipboard.

Thank goodness for places that weren't as technologically advanced as they could be.

When the boy returned to meet me at his till, he said, "Don't think so. I was the only one here. So, uh, did you want to order something?"

I ordered a platter #4, barely paying attention to what it contained. I kept glancing at that clipboard, which the boy had hung back on the wall. He gave me the total, and I had just enough cash to pay for it. As he gave me my small amount of change, I had an idea.

"Oh, but I'm allergic to paprika, so can you make sure they don't use any spice blends with paprika in them? And I'd also like some jalapenos, but on the side, and only cheddar for the cheese, if you wouldn't mind." When he didn't immediately move, I added, "But the paprika is the most important thing. No paprika anywhere near my dish, please. I'm anaphylactic."

I could sense the boy's eye roll, even if he didn't offer one outright. Thankfully, though, my annoying requests had the desired effect, and he headed back toward the kitchen to have a conversation with the cooks. I glanced quickly at the man with the newspaper, but his gaze stayed on the article he was reading.

I took two stealthy steps sideways and pulled the clipboard from the wall in one fluid motion. There wouldn't be much time, so I didn't look up again until I found last Friday's date. The pages were all looped around two giant rings at the top, and I decided in an instant that I wouldn't have time to either take the page off properly or snap a photo. Instead, I ripped it quickly from the two rings.

I was shoving the page into my purse with one hand while replacing the clipboard with the other when Mateo's voice sounded, coming back around the warming units. "All our spice mixes have paprika, so it might be kind of flavorless."

I let out my breath. Thankfully, he hadn't noticed me with the clipboard or my new position at the counter. "Oh, that's okay!" I let out a loud laugh to cover my nervous voice. "I'm used to flavorless food."

The boy headed back to the kitchen to tell the cooks to go ahead with my order, but that's when three quick honks sounded from across the parking lot.

It looked like I wouldn't be having flavorless tacos after all.

☐

# CHAPTER SEVENTEEN

It hadn't been a mistake to steal the La Cortina schedule. I double-checked the date, Friday, August 13th, but Nando Sanchez could not be found anywhere on the page for the date of Dan Montrose's death.

I made a quick right as Amber relayed this information. We had almost lost Lupe by the time I had raced across the parking lot and started up the Prius, but now I caught sight of her dark blue car with its signal on, two traffic lights ahead.

"You're sure he didn't have another job anywhere else?" I asked Amber.

"Pretty sure. Whenever Lupe talked to her mom on the phone, she always bragged about how Nando was working his way up to assistant manager at the Mexican restaurant." She let out a low chuckle and added, "I don't think Nando was nearly as proud of his mom and her job. I heard him more than once telling her she shouldn't be working as someone's maid—she was better than that." Amber shook her head. "Ridiculous. My dad paid her really well to take care of our house."

"Like, how well?" I asked. Lupe's jeans and shiny red heels had looked like designer brands. I turned another corner to follow Lupe, and she surprisingly started climbing back into the hills again—into a different wealthy neighborhood. This wasn't near the Montrose mansion, but these places were larger than my big house and seemed to have equally nice views.

Amber shrugged. "I dunno, but probably several thousand. And it's not like she had expenses. She ate at our house. She did her laundry and got her mail there." Amber looked ahead of us up at the large houses. "Although, I guess if she lives up here, that might be her problem." Amber crinkled her forehead like she didn't understand why Lupe and Nando would live up the hill in this ritzy neighborhood on a housekeeper's income.

"We don't know that she's going home," I said, weaving around a corner to keep Lupe in my sights, without getting too close. "Maybe she's visiting someone."

Amber smirked. "Ha. Maybe Lupe has some hot, rich man on the side."

If that were the case, I suspected this would be a goodbye visit. Lupe, after all, had just promised Helen Montrose she would soon be leaving town. "I should have asked if Nando gave his notice at La Cortina," I said.

Just then, Lupe made a sharp right into a driveway. I sailed by her in order not to draw her attention. Once around the next bend and out of sight, I stopped and took a breath. Thankfully, there was no one behind me. I looked around for somewhere to park, but in this part of the neighborhood, there weren't a lot of shoulder options. It seemed you'd have to know someone to park in one of these giant driveways.

I headed up the hill farther and eventually found a shoulder spot I could fit my Prius into. Once parked, I turned to Amber. "Now what?"

She shrugged. "Want to go back and sneak around a little?"

I didn't, really. I'd never had much ability to stay calm in these high-stress type of situations, but if Amber was willing and eager, I supposed I should be, too. I certainly wasn't about to let her snoop around alone.

Hunch, again, growled at the idea of holding down the fort in my car. He followed us, creeping low to the ground as we wound our way back down the hill toward the driveway we'd seen Lupe pull into. Her car wasn't in the main driveway, it turned out, but instead off to the side on a gravel patch. There were no other cars in the driveway.

"Maybe she cooks or cleans for someone else?" I suggested.

"Doubt it," Amber said. "She's usually at our house from eight in the morning until ten at night, six days a week."

I looked up at the large house in front of us. It had to be three stories, covered in stucco. Even though not as large as the Montrose mansion, it was far bigger than the house I found too big to live in alone.

Amber stepped forward, eager to investigate, but I held her back behind a nearby neighbor's motorhome for a minute. "I'm going to text Alex what we've found so far and where we're at. You know, just in case."

Amber anxiously tapped her fingers on the motorhome as it took me several minutes to update Alex on the conversation we'd overheard between Helen Montrose and her former housekeeper, Nando's alibi with his mom's car that hadn't checked out, and the address of where we had followed Lupe to.

When I slipped my phone away, Amber said, "So soon?" in her usual sarcastic tone.

I rolled my eyes at her, and we moved stealthily onto the next house. We ducked beside Lupe's blue Ford for a minute to take in the house a little better. It was even bigger close up, with wide stairs leading up to large double oak front doors. I peeked through the windows of Lupe's car while Amber surveyed the exterior.

"It's a nice car for a housekeeper," I whispered to Amber, but then remembered it had been Danny Jr.'s. It was probably a few years old, but now that I looked inside, it came with a navigation system and smartphone hookups. I hadn't opted for those options in my Prius because of the price hike. Apparently, Amber hadn't been kidding about her parents paying their housekeeper well, not to mention these kinds of perks. Which begged the question of why on earth this lady would want to literally kill the hand that had been feeding her.

I tiptoed around to the front of the car. Even though whichever vehicle had hit Dan Montrose had likely been into Mel Stanley's repair shop the very next day, I wondered if there might still be any evidence to the fact.

Amber crouched behind me and ran a thumb over where the fender met the headlight. "Does this paint look different to you than the paint on the hood?"

I squinted and studied it closer. It was certainly possible, but then again, it could have been the glare of the sun that made the fender paint look shinier. I peeked at the undercarriage and closer at the windshield. Even though I'd read about how to check if a car had been in an accident—more research for Cooper's novels—I didn't know enough about cars to actually decipher any of it myself.

Out of the corner of my eye, movement caught my attention, but it was only Hunch. He was creeping along the side of the big house as though he had found something, or at the very least, he was searching for something specific.

I tiptoed between Lupe's car and the side of the house, following my cat deeper toward the backyard. Hunch had, after all, led Lupe to the exact spot in the Montrose garden to find a buried baggie of passports.

"Where are we going?" Amber whispered from behind me.

I shrugged and pointed to Hunch, who barreled ahead in a way that only a cat without any fear of trespassing could.

The house appeared even bigger from the side than it had from the front. While the Montrose mansion had been on a large plot of land, complete with mature trees and sculpted shrubs, this house only had room for a small cement walkway along the side of the house before a neighbor's fence. There would be no hiding if someone appeared at either end of the walkway and caught us here.

Thankfully, we made it to the other end quickly. The backside of the house contained a small patch of grass, and my eyes quickly surveyed it, looking for my cat.

Amber tapped me on the shoulder and pointed, and that's when I saw him, halfway up a set of wooden back stairs. I looked back at Amber, and in silent agreement, we moved forward after Hunch.

We had almost made it to the top of the stairs when voices came through a screen door.

"I don't care how many millions you got out of that two-faced corrupt family," a young male voice said. "This is my home. Go to Mexico if you want. Now that I have my passport, I don't have to work for some stupid distant uncle anymore. I can get my own job. I'm staying right here."

I looked back at Amber with wide eyes. She mouthed the name, "Nando."

I let Amber squeeze closest to the door while I backed down one stair and silently pulled out my phone. I shot Alex a quick text:

<I think you should get over here ASAP!>

Lupe's voice came next. "Here? How you think you're going to stay here, hijo? You think Mr. Montrose is going to keep paying our rent from his grave? You know how much a place like these cost in the real world when somebody isn't taking care of you?"

Thanks to Amber's earlier suggestion, I fumbled over my phone to find my voice recording app. And just in time, too, as Nando really let loose all of his thoughts to his mom.

"Pfft! Taking care of us? You think that man cared at all about us, Mamá? It was hush money for your little secret that you kept with him. You acted like we'd come live in America and start our own life, our own business like Uncle Carlos—"

"I try—" Lupe started to say, but Nando wouldn't let her.

"But that was never what you planned on, was it, Mamá? I'm tired of keeping secrets, and I'm tired of living like we need some rich bolillo treating us like slaves. I never needed no fancy house. I never needed him to admit to being my papá. That was all you."

His…papa? I looked at Amber, but her attention remained rapt on the screen door.

"Fernando Daniel Sanchez!" Lupe dropped her voice, and it turned to begging. "Please!"

I couldn't make out the rest of her words through the screen door as she went on, and neither could Amber apparently because she slowly depressed the thumb pad on the door and inched it open. I held my breath, but I was pleased with how silently she managed it. I caught a few more of Lupe's hushed words now: "No tell anyone" and "policía" and "Abuela in Querétaro."

But Nando's name kept echoing in my head. Fernando Daniel Sanchez. Fernando Daniel Sanchez. And suddenly it hit me—FDS!

While I concentrated on hearing and deciphering, I didn't notice Hunch sneak by me, and then by Amber, through the open door, and into Lupe and Nando's kitchen, until I saw a last flick of his tail.

"Shoot!" Amber whispered back to me. She ducked onto her hands and knees, inched the door open wider, and crawled forward to retrieve my nosy, rule-breaking cat. She had made it all the way into the kitchen, with only one foot still in the gap of the screen door, when suddenly Nando's loud callous laugh made me freeze in place.

"Well, well. What do we have here? If it isn't sweet and innocent Amber Montrose. What? Is she breaking and entering into my home? That couldn't possibly be true, could it?" He let out another laugh, this one closer to maniacal. "Should I call the police to come and get her?"

My first instinct was to launch forward toward the screen door and somehow get in between Amber and what sounded like a mentally unstable brother she hadn't known she had, but as I took a step forward, Amber pulled her foot from out of the screen door, and it slammed shut.

The loud sound stopped me in place, and I took a breath, quickly rethinking my plan. If Nando truly was off his rocker, and if he had killed Dan Montrose in cold blood, maybe I should go for help.

As if to prove my point, Nando said, "I have a better idea. I killed one Montrose. No skin off my back to kill another. And don't worry, I'll make it look like an accident—or no, better yet, a suicide!" His voice sounded self-congratulatory. "Poor little rich girl couldn't handle her daddy's death…"

"Fernando, no!" Lupe hissed from farther away. I still couldn't hear her voice well, and I suspected she was keeping her distance from both Amber and her crazy son. "You can't do this! Not again! I cannot fix this time!"

"Shut up and get me the zip ties from the toolkit," he snapped at his mom.

I tiptoed down one stair and then another, hoping my voice recorder was still doing its job. But when I stepped onto the third stair, it let out a creak, and I froze in place.

"What? Who's there?" Nando asked sharply. "Did you bring someone with you?"

Two thudding steps sounded in the kitchen above me toward the door. I held my breath and raced down another six steps two by two, knowing I wouldn't make it around the corner before he got outside and caught me.

But then a loud "Mrrreeooowww!" overtook all of my noisy steps, and as I raced to the bottom and around the corner, all I heard was Nando yelling, "Owwww! Get this thing off me!"

I waited around the corner, thankful for Hunch's distraction. I hoped his diversion had given Amber a chance to get away. But Hunch let out a loud yelp and then, seconds later, a loud whining sound from much closer.

Ten seconds passed. Then twenty. Only the ongoing whining of my poor cat. No Amber.

I moved farther down the side of the house until I was out of hearing range. I stopped my voice recorder, forwarded the recording to Alex, and then hit dial on his contact.

He had barely said hello when my words barreled over one another to get out of my mouth. "It's him! Nando Sanchez killed Dan Montrose, and now he's got Amber! He wants to kill her, too!"

"Wait, what? Okay, Mallory, breathe. Tell me where you are. Are you at the same address you texted me?"

I nodded, even though he couldn't see it, and eventually got a "Yes" through my dry, parched mouth.

"And he has Amber in the house? And he threatened to kill her?"

I nodded again. "Their suite is hidden away, up a back stairway of this house. I think he zip-tied her arms and maybe her legs. I sent you the voice recording, but I have to get back in there. What if he's doing it now?"

"No, Mallory, no. If that's his home and he has her tied up, he's probably not in a hurry to do anything right there, especially if others live in another part of the house. You need to stay out of sight. Find a place to hide. I'm on my way."

☐

# CHAPTER EIGHTEEN

The next five minutes were the longest of my life. I found a shed in the backyard to hide behind, and from there, I caught flashes of Nando and Lupe arguing through an upper kitchen window, but I had no idea if they had Amber tied up on their kitchen floor—or if she was even still okay.

And Hunch was most definitely not okay. After his diversion, Nando had seemingly kicked my cat out the screen door and down the twelve stairs onto the grass. He'd been yowling in pain ever since, and his left leg lay at an odd angle. Cats were known for landing on their feet, and if any cat had more cat skills than all the rest, it was Hunch. For him to have been injured in a fall, I had to guess that Nando had kicked him really hard.

I wanted so badly to go and check on him, to pull him back behind the shed with me to safety, but I knew better.

The sound of the screen door whipping open took my attention from my yowling, pained cat. Nando stood in a wide-set power stance in the doorway, feet braced apart with hands on his hips, surveying the cat and then the otherwise quiet yard. I stayed perfectly still, and he didn't look my way. "I'll take care of this, Mamá. You just call Abuela and tell her our home is here and we have every right to stay. I'm making sure of it."

He yanked Amber through the screen door and down the stairs. She had duct tape over her mouth and her hands were bound behind her back with zip ties, but relief washed over me to see her still living and breathing.

But that thought vanished quickly when he shoved her around the side of the house toward Lupe's car.

I had no idea where he was taking her!

I raced out from behind the shed, along the side of the house, and made it to the front yard what felt like an instant later, but only caught the exhaust of Lupe's car as Nando had already backed out and rounded the closest corner. Still no sirens, no sign of Alex. Then again, the police station was all the way on the other side of Honeysuckle Grove.

I splayed my hands out, at a loss of what to do. Only a second later, it came to me: Lupe!

I raced around the house and up the back stairs and found Lupe still in her kitchen, a small room considering the size of the house, weeping and speaking Spanish into her phone. My tenth-grade understanding of the language was no match for the speed that her words tripped out of her mouth.

"Hang up!" I told her. "Now!"

She was hunched over the kitchen counter and looked up at me in stunned silence. I took two giant steps toward her, grabbed her phone, and hung it up myself.

"You can't do anything about what your son did to Dan Montrose, but you can stop what he's about to do to his daughter." I didn't give her time to argue or even think about it. I hoped her mothering heart would be enough to lead her to do the right thing here. I yanked her toward the door and down the stairs, and thankfully, she didn't fight me.

At the bottom of the back stairs, I bent to check on Hunch. I gently prodded his back, and his yowling became louder as I touched his stomach. When I got to his hind leg, he made a low guttural growling sound. I lifted him from the ground, trying to keep that hind leg as still as possible, and cradled him in my arms.

"Don't worry," I said over his noises. "I'm going to take care of you, buddy. We just have to take care of Amber first."

As I pulled Lupe up the hill toward my car with my other arm, I asked her, "Where was Nando taking her? What were his plans?"

A fresh round of tears flooded her face. "I don't know! He don't say!"

My hope started to dwindle, but I tried to intercept its plunge. "We'll figure it out. Call him."

I motioned to her cell phone, and she hit a number to dial, but it rang and rang endlessly as we made our way to my car. While she focused on getting through to Nando, I pressed the call button on my phone in my pocket. The last person I'd dialed was Alex, so I hoped it would get through to him so he could overhear that we were on the move, without Lupe knowing.

As we got into my Prius, she finally hung up her phone, and I said, "As I drive, you tell me every single thing Nando said to you."

I propped my phone upside down in my cupholder. If Alex had said anything on the other end, it must have been while the phone was in my pocket. Thankfully, he stayed silent now. As I drove us down the hill where I'd seen Lupe's car disappear, Lupe rattled off frantic clips of sentences, whatever she could remember from her son. I kept reminding her that she was saving her son's well-being as much as she was saving Amber.

As she talked, I pieced together the details of Nando's anger. Nando had only just found out that Dan Montrose was his father last Friday. He'd threatened to go public, to which Dan threatened to reveal a police file he had on Lupe.

"What police file?" I asked.

"I think he getting work visas for us, but he only steal our passports and then plant drugs on me to get caught. I not use drugs ever, but Dan make it look like I do and call the police, then once I arrested, he pay off police to let me out. He say he have to bribe them not to put me in jail. But he keep file on me. He say if I keep my mouth shut that he Fernando's father, he find us place to stay and give me police file and passports back when Nando turn eighteen so we go back to Mexico."

Mile Marker 18. That was the significance.

Lupe went on to describe the night Dan had died. He usually never came home before dark, so Nando had been watching a movie in the Montrose's theatre room. When Dan returned earlier than expected, he was already in some kind of a bad mood. Then he lit into Lupe about keeping "her Mexican kid" out of his house and she'd better not have told anyone he was Nando's father. Apparently, Nando heard it all.

Then when Nando threatened to go public about Dan being his father, Dan rushed off to dig up the police file, saying he was going to have her and her Mexican kid deported once and for all.

"Nando follow him, and after he dig up the file, Nando drive into him." Lupe let out a fresh round of tears into her hands. "He come back, and at first, he tell me he hit a deer, so I fix the car."

It wasn't until Nando, who could read English a lot better than Lupe, looked at the so-called police file after he'd killed Dan that they realized it had all been a ruse to scare Lupe. The file was just a bunch of papers with her name on them. The police officers who'd pulled her over had been in plain clothes and in a dark unmarked car, likely not real cops.

Once I had that part figured out, I grilled her about the earlier details. "I don't get it. How did you have a baby so close in age to Danny Jr. without anyone knowing?"

She shook her head and looked into her lap. "Years ago, I think I love Dan Montrose. He act like he love me, too, but then I get pregnant and I about to tell him when he say Helen is pregnant with a precious son but she have to be on bed rest. He hire a new nurse and fire me that same day. I return to Mexico and try to raise Nando with another man, but he beat us, so finally I come back to tell Dan about his son. He never want to accept it."

I shook my head, taking all of this in. Amber knew her dad hadn't been an upstanding guy, but I had a feeling she would be pretty shocked at the extent of his secrets and lies.

Providing I found her in time to tell her.

"He always threaten me if I ever mention what really happen, he have me arrested and deported for good. I could never come back to see my brother, Carlos, again."

I shook my head, wondering what all that information would have done to a seventeen-year-old boy. But even though Nando had killed Dan Montrose in a fit of rage after he found out what must have been some pretty shocking news, Lupe could still prevent him from becoming a serial killer without a conscience. Or his anger could completely consume him.

"Where would he take Amber Montrose?" I asked in as calm of a voice as I could manage.

"He say he would take care of her. Is all he say!" Lupe cried.

"Think! Where could he have taken her in the middle of the day where no one would see or hear what he was doing?" I glanced at my phone in the cupholder. "Would he have taken Amber out to the same place? To Mile Marker 18?"

She shook her head. "I no think so. Fernando is a smart boy. He say he make it look like an accident."

Suicide was the word I remembered, but I needed to keep her talking.

"Where did he hang out when he wasn't at home or working? Where might he go to be alone?"

She shook her head, but then stopped mid-shake. "We used to go to bridge off old closed-down highway. He used to say it was our spot because no one else knew about it."

"Old highway? Where? Not the Old Mission Highway?" I didn't know Honeysuckle Grove well enough to know these details. Lupe directed me, and I could only hope she was being truthful with me and not leading me off the trail so Nando could get away with killing Amber.

As I turned the Prius away from town and the roads became more and more deserted, I also became concerned for my own safety. The truth was, if Lupe and Nando got rid of both me and Amber, neither of them would have to be responsible for anything they had done.

Of course they didn't know about Alex listening in.

Hunch let out a low yowl that made me wonder if he had the same concerns. I glanced over the seat and said, "It's going to be okay, Hunch. We're going to find her."

Lupe instructed me to turn again at a faded wooden sign that read: HISTORIC HIGHWAY – OPEN TO FOOT TRAFFIC ONLY.

I ignored the instruction and forged ahead in my Prius on a bumpy road in great need of repair. "How far is the bridge?"

"Not far," she told me. Her brow furrowed, and she moved her head from side to side as though trying to see around corners before we turned them. "We usually walk. Is just around the next turn, I think."

In a split second, I pulled over to the edge of the unused road, hit the brakes, and stopped the car. We weren't going to surprise Nando if we pulled right up to the bridge in a vehicle.

But only a second later, Lupe launched out of the passenger door and ran ahead. I jumped out on my own side and ran after her, catching up and yanking her back by one arm just as she reached her own car, parked around the next bend at an angle in the middle of the road.

When I'd dragged her out of her kitchen, she had opted for some slip-on shoes, rather than the red heels, but I wore sneakers so it was unlikely she'd be able to outrun me even if she got away again. Besides, the farther we moved along the road, the more potholed it became.

Just as I had started to let out a breath of relief that we'd found their car and I'd caught Lupe, she opened her mouth and started yelling. "Fernando! Is us! She make me bring—"

I yanked Lupe's arm to shut her up, but it was too late. We'd no longer be able to sneak up on Nando. As Lupe's echoing words faded, it became eerily silent. He had said he'd make it look like a suicide. Had he already done it? Had he planned to throw Amber off the bridge?

I patted my pockets for my phone, but realized I'd left it in the cupholder of my car when I raced out after Lupe. It was up to me to do something to save Amber, and fast.

But as we moved in front of Lupe's car and farther around the corner, Amber was nowhere in sight on the pot-holed road or on the large wooden bridge in front of us. The flow of the current was thick and fast and headed back into town. Rocks protruded here and there, creating white water. This explained how Nando planned to make it look like a suicide if he threw her in here. She'd get tossed in every direction until someone spotted her ravaged, rock-beaten body closer to town.

Or didn't.

Although her bound arms would have to tip someone off that she hadn't done it herself.

I kept moving forward, onto the bridge, checking the rafters below, eying the expansive river underneath for a bobbing head, but there was nothing.

I gulped down a cry and kept moving forward, onto the slats of the bridge to get a closer look. I was so busy frantically scanning the water looking for Amber, it didn't occur to me that I hadn't seen Nando until he grabbed me around my neck from behind.

I shrieked, but he gripped me tighter to silence me. "I don't know who you are or what you want with me, but you are in the wrong place at the wrong time, senorita."

"No, Fernando, no!" Lupe said, crying, but she also wasn't fighting Nando in any way. She was going to let him do whatever he wanted to us.

I turned to her and pleaded, "You have to stop him, Lupe! Our blood is on your hands, too!"

"Shut up!" Nando snapped, but instead of pushing me farther onto the bridge, he yanked me away from it.

I fought him, swinging my arms and kicking my feet, but within seconds, he had me pushed up against a tree face-first, practically kissing the bark. I stopped fighting for a second and reached up to protect my face, but that seemed to be his plan because a moment later, he had both of my hands wrenched behind my back. Before I could blink, he had my hands secured tightly and painfully.

"Ow!" I winced. "You don't want to do this, Nando!"

Lupe was a crying mess and clearly not going to be of any help.

Nando, on a mission, didn't stop. He grabbed both of my legs and pinned both my ankles together to secure them with a zip tie, too. No matter how I struggled, he was stronger than me.

Thankfully, he hadn't seemed to bring any duct tape along, and so I kept talking. My voice might be my only weapon, and I intended to use it. "You may think you'll be able to live with this, but you won't. This will haunt you for the rest of your life." I turned to Lupe. "It'll haunt you both."

"Don't listen to her," Nando gritted out to his mother, "and stop your crying. These two aren't worth it."

Lupe, sadly, did as she was told, and her cries, or at least the volume of them, subsided. But then I heard a muffled sound, like a girl with her mouth covered, trying to call out.

"Amber?" My hope soared as the muffled sound became louder. The leaves shifted nearby. He hadn't thrown Amber into the water!

Nando motioned his chin into the trees and told his mother, "Go get her. These two obviously like to be together, so let's have them take one last swim together." Nando laughed—actually laughed—as though this were funny.

Lupe disappeared into the trees, leaving me with Nando. I watched his eyes as he checked over my ties and added a second zip tie to my wrists for good measure. Again, I wondered what it would do to a seventeen-year-old kid to realize your mom had been lying to you your entire life because your dad felt as if she was good enough to sleep with and clean his house, but not good enough to admit he'd impregnated her.

"What Dan Montrose did to your mom was wrong. Unforgiveable," I told Nando, trying a new tack. "There's no mistaking that he should have been arrested."

Nando laughed again. "Who cares? People like that don't get punished. Not unless people like me punish them." He shrugged as though this was everyday business. "I took care of it. Now I'm taking care of his nosy daughter, too. And I'll make sure she dies knowing what kind of person her daddy really was. Sorry you stuck your nose in and got in the way."

He didn't sound sorry in the least.

Lupe pulled Amber along behind her through the trees, still crying. Amber's mouth was still taped, so I suspected she hadn't been able to talk any sense into Lupe, and her wrists had scratches and streaks of blood from fighting against the zip ties.

"You've known Amber for years," I said, pleading with Lupe now. "Can you really let Nando—"

Nando yanked me away from the tree and pushed me toward the bridge, effectively shutting me up. I had to hop since my ankles were bound, and Lupe pulled Amber along behind us, without even being told to. She clearly felt she couldn't do anything to stop her out-of-control son.

I may not have had arms or legs, but I still had my voice, and I planned to use it until I no longer could. "You already killed the man who wronged you! Amber did nothing wrong. Let's make her understand why you had to do what you did, and then—"

"I said, shut up!" Nando pushed me so hard, I fell onto my knees on the bridge. They stung and then immediately ached in pain.

As he yanked me to my feet again, I said, "I'm not going to shut up because what you're doing is wrong and you know it."

He pushed me forward. "Talk all you want. No one can hear you out here!" He yelled the words as if to prove his point. "You're still going into the water, and so is Amber." He looked back to where Lupe pulled Amber along, but with much less force. Nando and I were almost in the middle of the bridge already, while Lupe and Amber had barely gotten a foot onto it. "Come on. Hurry it up, Mamá."

I shook my head at their strange mother-son relationship and had to wonder if it had been off-balance even before he found out about the lies. Nando pushed me up against the waist-high railing of the old rickety bridge. The one rotting wooden rail was all that kept me from falling into the tumbling river twenty feet below.

Could I at least somehow pull him in with me so he couldn't do this to anyone else?

But even if I could, his arms and legs weren't bound. There was a chance he'd be able to fight the current and swim to shore.

Nando turned back to his mother and had just growled in frustration when suddenly his growl stopped and his eyes widened. I followed his gaze to see Alex and his detective friend, both in uniform, sneaking silently from the nearest bush toward the bridge.

"Hold it right there!" Alex called. "Fernando Sanchez, get your hands in the air!"

He was about to comply with the order, or at least we all thought he was. But before Nando decided to oblige and get his hands into the air, he used them to give me one strong shove that knocked me up over the railing and headfirst into the water below.

☐

# CHAPTER NINETEEN

So this was how I was going to die.

I tried to take in a huge breath and hold it, but it got knocked out of me the second I hit the water. As the ice-cold water enveloped me and the current pulled me under, I thought about the fact that Amber was safe, barely onto the edge of the bridge. I had at least managed that much. It might not get me into heaven, but it had to give me some credit with a God I rarely spoke to. I wondered absently if Hunch would make it through this day, too, or if we would both soon be reunited with Cooper in some kind of an afterlife.

The current tossed me around and continued to pull me under. My leg struck a sharp rock and stung, but only a second later, I couldn't feel it for the pressure engulfing my chest. Opening my mouth to the currents pulling me under would mean the end of me, but my chest and body ached with the effort of keeping it closed. My body's automatic response of trying to take a breath, even when there wasn't one to be had, seemed to take over.

I thrashed my bound arms and legs, trying to swim like a mermaid to get to the surface, but I no longer knew which direction was up. I opened my eyes, but they didn't help me one bit. The sparkly lights that had been behind my eyes a second ago morphed into something more like flashbulbs going off in my head, each one like a knife through my skull.

All I wanted, all I needed, was for this to end somehow. Blackness instead of lightbulbs, weightlessness instead of all this pressure.

I let my body take over. I had to, gasping for the breath that wasn't there.

And, finally, the blackness was exactly what I got.

My afterlife, as it turned out, didn't involve Cooper or Hunch. It only involved a lot of dark numbness. An endless amount of stillness.

It seemed like such a shame that I'd just started living again only to die. God, why? I asked inwardly. In that one prayer, I was asking Him about several things: How could He let Nando get away with this? Why had He taken Cooper from me so soon, when Cooper had been my only real link to spirituality? Why was He taking my life right at the moment when I finally had friends?

But then the stillness was interrupted some poking and prodding. Muffled voices. My weightless body felt as though it was rocking, back and forth, back and forth, back and...

All at once, fire ignited in my throat as a tsunami launched out of it.

"That's it," a deep male voice said. "Get it out."

I didn't want to get any more out, but my body was clearly listening to this man's instructions and not my own because a second later, another tidal wave of bile and water erupted from within me.

"Come on, open your eyes, Mallory!" the male voice said.

The thought wouldn't have occurred to me, but I tried it, and then regretted it immediately. The bright flashbulbs were back. But then something masochistic within me made me open my eyes again anyway, for as long as I could stand it, and slowly, the brightness became more manageable.

"It's all going to be okay now," the male voice that belonged to Officer Alex Martinez said from above me. He wiped my sopping wet hair from my face, and that's when I noticed he was just as wet. His hair was curlier than usual from the water, and even though I knew I shouldn't focus on that part, I couldn't seem to help myself.

Had Alex jumped into the river to save me?

"I guess swim club was a good idea after all," he said, as if in answer to my silent question.

Even though I suspected Alex's ability to save my life had more to do with rigorous police training than with seventh-grade swim club, the faint memory of sneaking into the bleachers at the local pool to watch twelve-year-old Alex swim laps brought with it the best kind of nostalgia.

Alex was in great shape. Swim club or no swim club, I had no doubt he would be capable of battling a raging river. I guess I just felt humbled and surprised that he'd do it for me.

"Amber?" I croaked out. "Is she okay?"

Alex smiled. "She's going to be just fine. Detective Reinhart is taking her down to the station to ask her a few questions. Lupe and Fernando are both in custody."

I started to let out my breath, but then it caught in my aching throat. "Hunch?"

Alex squinted down at me, but then surveyed the riverbank around us as though he fully expected to find my cat roaming somewhere nearby.

"In the backseat of my car," I told him. "He's hurt."

Alex nodded and stood. "I'll take care of it."

Before I could ask him anything else, or even thank him for saving my life, two paramedics appeared on either side of me. They checked my eyes, ears, and throat, which all felt like they'd recently been tossed into somebody's bonfire.

"We should take her in," one of them said.

"I'm fine," I argued, attempting to sit up. But I clearly wasn't, as the movement made my vision wobble and my head boom. I lay back down and let them move me to a stretcher.

It's all going to be okay now. I repeated Alex's words in my head, but I felt like it was going to take a long time before I'd believe them.

☐

# CHAPTER TWENTY

They kept me overnight in the hospital, which didn't seem so bad, really. I kind of enjoyed having nurses come in and out of my room to check on me, all of them so kind and friendly, and even now I dreaded going back to my lonely house.

When Alex arrived later the next morning, I practically leaped for joy at his familiar face. He had changed into dry jeans and a blue button-down since yesterday, but even without the uniform, I could tell in an instant that this was all business.

"How's Hunch?" I asked, partly to soften the mood, but also because I was truly concerned.

Alex nodded. "His hip joint had to be reset and he's being fit for a cast on his back leg, but his stomach didn't suffer any permanent damage. He'll heal just fine."

"He's going to love dragging a cast around," I said sarcastically. Hunch had never had much patience for anything or anyone that slowed him down or got in his way.

"Regardless, you can pick him up at the vet as soon as you're released. The police department is picking up the bill." Alex handed me a business card with the vet's information and cleared his throat. "I have a few questions to round out Reinhart's report."

"Reinhart's report? Isn't it your report?" I raised my eyebrows, but Alex looked down at the floor as he took a seat on the only chair in my small hospital room.

"Corbett says because I already signed off on this case, I can't put my name to any of this."

"Or get the credit," I added, already piecing together why Alex seemed so down when he should have been elated at proving himself as a competent detective. He didn't confirm or deny this, and because I didn't want to rub salt in the wound, I decided not to push the issue.

"So far, Fernando Sanchez hasn't been talking much. We've been able to make some sense of the situation from overhearing your conversation with his mother, Lupe, but we'd love your perception concerning the night Dan Montrose died."

I had been thinking of this nonstop since I was brought into the hospital. It gave me something to concentrate on while being poked and prodded. I thought I had most of it figured out.

"Nando overheard an argument with his mom and found out Dan Montrose was his father. Apparently, there was a contract, plus a police file on Lupe, keeping her quiet until Nando turned eighteen, and in exchange, he paid Lupe well and took care of all of their expenses. When Nando found out about everything and threatened to go public, Dan went out to dig up the police file at Mile Marker 18. I suspected he buried it there as a marker of Nando's eighteenth birthday—as Dan liked to commemorate dates along that highway. But Nando couldn't wait that long and followed him out there. He didn't even have to get his hands dirty to get the file—or at least he didn't at first. He stayed in his car until Dan climbed back up the hill and then ran into him and snatched the file out of his dead hands. When Lupe overheard Amber telling her brother about finding a hole out at Mile Marker 18, she called Nando, and he got right back out there to cover up the suspicious hole."

Alex nodded, writing it all down. "And do you figure he repaired the damage to his mom's car himself?"

I shook my head. "You may need a warrant, but if you check with a mechanic named Mel Stanley, I think you'll find that he completed the repairs. It looked like there could have been some mismatch in the paint on the front fender of Lupe's car. You could also check the code on the windshield, as well as the radiator and cooling lines to see if there had been any recent repairs to them."

Alex raised his eyebrows at me. "You know a lot about cars."

I felt a blush rise up my neck, but I had to admit the truth. "Actually, no. Nothing. I wouldn't know how to actually find any of those things myself, but I used to help with research on my husband's novels."

Alex shifted uncomfortably in his seat at the mention of my late husband. "Ah. Yes, well. I'm thankful for the insight, regardless."

In an instant, it felt like we had lost any comfortable camaraderie that had ever been between us. It reminded me that we had only known each other as adults for about three days. The saying easy come, easy go came to mind. Would Alex and I even continue our friendship now that I didn't need his help on an investigation? Not only that, but as he confirmed everything I had gone through at Lupe's house and then at the old highway bridge, our conversation became more and more a matter of business. It felt as though our whole reason for talking was quickly coming to an end.

In fact, my whole reason for being around other people quickly seemed to be coming to an end.

It wasn't as though I had enjoyed helping a fifteen-year-old through her grief, all while trying to solve the murder of her father, but something about it being over and done left me feeling lonely and purposeless already.

"All right, well, I think that's all I need." Alex flipped his book shut and stood, confirming my thoughts.

"You know where I am if there's anything else." I forced a smile up at him.

He headed for my hospital room door, but then stopped in the threshold of it. "You really were a huge help to me, Mallory. I can't thank you enough."

I nodded but couldn't bring myself to say anything for fear of crying. By tomorrow, I'd be back in my house, alone, with no reason to reach out to anyone.

But then he added, "If I ever come across anything else suspicious in Honeysuckle Grove, I know who I'd want to bring in as a special consultant." He winked, and just before he let the door fall shut behind him, he said, "You'll let me know when Hunch is feeling better and ready to work, huh?"

☐

# CHAPTER TWENTY-ONE

A week later, as expected, I was back on my couch, covered in blankets, Netflix on my screen, and feeling about as lonely as I had in my whole life. Not only was Hunch annoyed with his cast, but he was also clearly annoyed with me. He pretty much spent his days across the room glaring in my direction.

I was tempted to call Amber and invite her over just to make my cat happy, but after all she'd been through with her family, all she had learned about them, I didn't want to be a reminder of that horrible time. I hoped she would somehow get past all of it and move on.

As I reached for the remote control from the coffee table, my phone lit up beside it with a new text. Odd. My sister and dad almost always phoned and rarely texted. I picked it up to look closer, and for a second, I was sure I must have somehow wished Amber back into existence in my life.

<So what about this cooking thing?>

I nibbled my lip, and tears of thankfulness filled my eyes. I hedged my hope, though, as I texted back.

<Your mom ok with that?>

A second later, an eye roll emoticon appeared on my screen. I wasn't sure I felt completely justified in corralling a fifteen-year-old for my own selfish reasons without her mom's knowledge or permission. Then again, her mom had just been an accessory in covering up her dad's murder to protect her inheritance. Maybe Amber needed a different adult figure in her life for a while.

But my fingers flew over the keys of my phone as if still determined to keep my hope at bay.

<I don't have much to work with at the moment.>

Thankfully, determination was a word Amber was familiar with.

<Meet you at the farmer's market in 20>

I smiled. It wasn't a question.

My smile flattened, though, as I looked down at myself. I hadn't showered in three days, and twenty minutes was most definitely not long enough to make me look presentable. However, I also didn't trust my texting fingers to ask for more time without pushing Amber away again. I hit two letters: OK. And then I raced up the stairs, likely making Hunch think I had lost my mind.

Twenty-two minutes later, I found Amber at the farmer's market's cheese counter looking over the array of options with a creased forehead. My wet hair stuck to my head, and my jeans hung loosely from forgetting to eat for the week, but at least I had checked for any errant pantyhose or other wardrobe malfunction before leaving the house.

"How do you choose from so many types?" Amber said in way of a hello. It reminded me of how good teenagers could be at skirting around any too-heavy emotional topics. I didn't know how badly I needed someone with that skill until right that second.

I pointed. "Well, start with the ones you know. What's the difference between cheddar and mozzarella, for instance?"

Amber shrugged. "Mozzarella's kind of flavorless."

Ahh, the girl had so much to learn about cheese. And I was exactly the person to teach her.

"Excuse me," I said to the clerk behind the cheese counter. And then I proceeded to order small amounts of a dozen different cheeses.

"What are we making?" Amber asked as we walked away with our cheese purchase.

I waved a finger in front of Amber's face. "Ahh, young Skywalker. Not make. Learn, you must."

Amber raised an eyebrow at my dorkiness, but she smiled just the same.

"We need a handful of other ingredients to make the cheeses pop," I told her, leading her toward a vegetable stand.

She stayed quiet as I picked out some bell peppers, a couple of habaneros, a yellow zucchini squash, and an eggplant. Even as we moved along to the fish market, the bakery counter, and then to pick up a few pieces of fruit, she remained silent.

It wasn't until we headed back to the Jeep, arms loaded with fresh groceries, that she finally opened her mouth again to speak. "Terrence Lane made partner at the firm. I guess the other partners didn't feel the same way my dad did about him. He's representing Mom and keeping us updated on what to expect. He figures it'll be several months before anyone goes to trial, but he says Lupe will definitely do jail time."

I couldn't read the mix of emotions leaking out in her voice. Satisfaction? Sadness? Relief?

"Just Lupe?" I asked. Had she somehow tried to take the blame for her off-kilter son?

"Thankfully, we get to keep the house since it was in Mom's name. We don't have boatloads of money or a housekeeper anymore, though, which is kind of annoying because Danny never learned to clean up a single thing after himself."

"Oh yeah?" I said. I wasn't sure if I should ask more about her mom, but hoped she felt free to keep talking.

"Terrence says the longer Nando's case takes to get to trial, the better it will work out. If he turns eighteen, they'll try him as an adult. Still, he'll probably try and plead down to voluntary manslaughter and get off with only a few years." Any fifteen-year-old who hadn't grown up with a lawyer for a father likely wouldn't have such a strong grasp on all of this. She blew out some air as I started to drive toward my house. She shrugged as though she'd already come to terms with the injustice of it and went on. "I mean, I know my dad wasn't a good guy, and maybe he deserved some kind of payback, but he didn't deserve to die." She sighed, and I was glad she could get some of this out. I suspected it was the first time she had. "I suppose I should be happy Nando was caught and will be punished at all."

"Well, that's thanks to you," I told her. "You'd make a pretty good detective one day."

She raised an eyebrow. "You think so?"

"I know so." I wouldn't actually wish for her to work under Captain Corbett's leadership, especially because he'd somehow made the lack of investigation of the Montrose case the fault of the detective originally assigned to it. After seeing Captain Corbett's lack of initiative with the case firsthand, I didn't believe it for one minute. I still didn't trust something about the man. For as long as I lived in Honeysuckle Grove, I'd be keeping an eye out for the police captain.

As Amber and I loaded the groceries into my kitchen, Hunch surprisingly didn't immediately come to greet us. Then again, it took him a lot more time and effort to move around with his cast.

"Why don't you go find Hunch," I told Amber. "Believe me, he'll be glad to see you."

I felt slightly embarrassed about my messy house. I hadn't bothered to pick up much after myself in the last week and had been too rushed to do anything on my way out the door, but I was so glad to have Amber here that I could push some of the embarrassment aside. And she didn't seem to notice or care.

Less than a minute later, she returned with Hunch awkwardly in her arms with his cast sticking out, but he purred in her arms. I went over and scrunched the fur on Hunch's head, hoping he would realize in his oversized cat brain that I was the one who went out and brought his best friend back.

Then again, Hunch was so intuitive, he likely knew that all the credit actually went to Amber.

As I laid out the cheeses and corresponding food items to help their flavors come alive, Amber sat at the kitchen table in her usual chair and kept Hunch happy. She opened the cookie container, but today it was empty. Later Amber could help me remedy that.

"Hey, are you going to the church picnic on Sunday?" she asked as I brought over the first pairing—a red pepper with warmed mozzarella.

After my debacle with the pantyhose and then that out-of-body volunteering episode, I hadn't been planning on going back to church for quite some time. "I hadn't thought about it. Why?"

She shrugged. "I kinda wanted to go, but I doubt my mom will want to." She took a bite, and her eyes widened at the taste.

"That's mozzarella," I told her. She squinted as though she didn't believe me. I was buying time as I thought over her request. If Amber wasn't bitter toward God and church after all she'd been through, why was I? Especially since I had so many questions for Him that still needed answers. "So…your mom? She's not going? To the picnic?" As usual, my prying questions came out as anything but casual and non-invasive.

But Amber, the intuitive girl I'd gotten to know pretty well in a short amount of time, answered what I was really asking. "She's spending her time doing community service because Terrence told her to, but to be honest, I think she loves it. It keeps her busy, and now that she's not getting anything from Dad's will, she's going to have to get a job sooner or later, so I'll bet she's trying not to think about that. But I doubt she'll want people at church finding out about it."

"Hmm," I said. It sounded as though perhaps Mrs. Montrose received the worst punishment of all—a life-long sentence of working like a commoner. "I suppose I could go," I said before I rethought it. "Sunday. To the church picnic," I added.

Amber's whole countenance brightened. "Good. We should make something. It's a potluck."

I nodded, my mind already reeling with ideas of what we could prepare, not only for Sunday, but the day after that, when I hoped to invite Amber over for another cooking lesson. And the day after that.

She'd be back in school in September, but my hope was high at the moment that I could make a habit out of being a little more social in the next couple of weeks before that happened.

A church picnic didn't sound like the most exciting afternoon in the world, but then again, delivering a casserole to a grieving family shouldn't have been nearly as exciting as it had been either.

I returned to the counter to retrieve a plate of sliced gruyere with French bread, pink lady apple, and some slivered chives. I looked over my shoulder at Amber and Hunch, who watched me, eagerly awaiting my return.

I supposed you never knew where you might find some sort of injustice to give you purpose.

And I supposed you never knew where you were going to find a new friend.

# END OF BOOK 1

# UP NEXT: MURDER AT THE CHURCH PICNIC...

*Murder has such a sting!*

If anyone had told Mallory Beck she would become Honeysuckle Grove's next amateur sleuth, she would have thought they were ten walnuts short of a brownie. Her late husband had been the mystery novelist with a penchant for the suspicious. She was born for the rotisserie, not the binoculars, and yet here she was, having just solved her first murder case. It had all started with delivering a casserole to a grieving family and finished with the help of a sarcastic teenager, a cop with kind green eyes, and a cat with a hunch.

Maybe she should have thought twice about delivering another casserole, but this one was for the potluck at the annual church picnic, and what could possibly go wrong at a picnic?

READ ON IN THE SERIES NOW...

☐

# Book Two

# MURDER

## at the Church Picnic

DENISE JADEN

# CHAPTER ONE

Almost nine months and I still felt like a flake of eggshell in a bowl of yolks every time I attended a social gathering alone. At least today I'd made an extra effort to avoid any wardrobe malfunctions. Even if I did something brainless like leave the house without brushing my hair or putting on pants, I'd be meeting Amber, my new fifteen-year-old BFF, who, with any hope, wouldn't let me traipse through a public park in my underwear.

I collected the cheesy bacon and potato casserole from my kitchen and then said goodbye to Hunch, a cat with an attitude if I'd ever met one. He had recently broken his leg and dislocated his hip, so I was trying to have some grace for his bristly attitude. I compensated for his growls with my perkiest voice.

"I'll only be gone a couple of hours," I singsonged to him.

Cooper, my late husband and Hunch's true owner, used to talk to him aloud constantly. In fact, with Cooper, it had usually been less like talking to a cat and more like some kind of intelligent three-point discussion. I hadn't quite gotten comfortable with having conversations with my feline roommate yet, but then again, I didn't need his help in plotting my next mystery novel like Cooper had.

"Maybe I'll even bring Amber back with me," I told Hunch, and this earned me an uptick of his whiskers.

Amber had been visiting me almost every day since we'd solved the murder of her dad together and brought the guilty parties to justice. She always came around under the guise of a cooking lesson—I'd promised to teach her how to prepare everything from baked sourdough to ratatouille, and in fact, she'd assembled today's casserole pretty much on her own with only my instructions from the kitchen table. I'd simply popped it into the oven this morning to warm it up, filling my kitchen with the scents of savory sharp cheddar and apple-smoked bacon. Amber had wanted to make a casserole with bacon in it, and while I was as big of a fan of crispy pork as the next girl, we'd had to play around a little with the recipe so the salty flavor hadn't overpowered the rest. We'd started with nugget potatoes, but in the end, I'd suggested adding a couple of Yukon gold and Vitelotte purple potatoes to round out the flavors and add some vibrant color.

In truth, Amber probably did only show up for the cooking lessons. Me? I'd do almost anything for the company, and Hunch, I was fairly certain, would do almost anything to have someone other than me in his lair.

I left my cantankerous cat in my wake and headed for Cooper's Jeep with Amber's casserole in hand. After my husband's death, I'd driven his Jeep for months, trying to find the powerful feeling he'd claimed to have gotten from driving it, but today I chose it because of the FOR SALE sign posted prominently in the back window. I didn't often spend much of the daytime out in public, but today at the park would be the perfect opportunity to get lots of eyes on it. Surprisingly, posting the FOR SALE sign in the vehicle had made me feel the strongest I had felt in the last eight and a half months since I lost my true strength—Cooper.

I took deep breaths to steady myself on my ten-minute drive to Bateman Park. I kept telling myself it shouldn't take this much bravery to simply leave my house. It would certainly have been easy—too easy—to back out on attending the annual church picnic if I hadn't made a commitment to Amber. She had originally asked me to go with her because she didn't think her mom would be up for it. As of last night, though, it turned out her mom wanted to go, and so that left me still feeling committed, but meeting her there instead of picking her up. I hoped these solo outings would eventually get easier with time and practice

I turned the corner onto Bateman Road and discovered my next problem. Finding parking might prove as difficult as interpreting my cat's growls. The picnic was supposed to start at eleven, in lieu of today's church service, and it was already five to. I didn't like to be late, especially with someone meeting me, but nevertheless, I turned the corner and drove farther from the park in search of a space big enough for this giant gas guzzler.

I should have expected as much on such a beautiful day, but most of the time, my brain still wasn't as quick on the uptake about normal life situations as it used to be. As I wove around various back streets, I passed plenty of people walking toward the park, arms loaded with lawn chairs, blankets, and food. I recognized one couple—Marv and Donna Mayberry—which only served to increase my already racing heart. Chatting with couples after losing your spouse felt a little like driving a three-wheeled car. Marv worked long hours, so it was more common to have one-on-one time with Donna, but apparently not today. Some people strolling toward the park wore dresses and suits, and I looked down at my peach T-shirt and denim capris, wondering if there was some kind of church picnic dress code I wasn't aware of.

At least Amber would be here somewhere, and I couldn't in my wildest dreams imagine her showing up to the park in a fancy dress. I'd yet to see her in something more formal than a hoodie and cut-offs. It was just a matter of finding her. Up the next block, I finally found a space big enough for the Jeep.

Cooper had kept a couple of lawn chairs in the back of his Jeep for as long as he'd owned it. They hadn't been used in over a year, but it was time to get the creaks out of at least one of them. I'd come back for the other if Amber hadn't brought her own. Thankfully, they had backpack straps on them, so I grabbed the red one on top and slung it onto my back. Then I reached for my purse, complete with suntan lotion and bug spray, and finally for the warm casserole. The scent of salty goodness wafted up toward me as I adjusted the lid. Now that it was fresh out of the oven, the flavors had baked into one another, the melted cheese had rounded it out, and it smelled amazing.

Foot traffic thickened as I strode closer toward Bateman Park, and I kept my eyes peeled for Amber and her mom. They both had auburn hair and were both striking in different ways—Amber with her big-eyed attitude and her mom with her bouffant hairstyle—so they shouldn't be hard to spot.

Before I could find them, I rounded a small hill to get into the park, and a flurry of activity captured my attention. Tables were being assembled with food under one of the two giant park shelters, kids chased each other around the playground, and at least a dozen carnival games were being erected between the food shelter and a big open field. I'd been happy when Amber told me our contribution to the day would be food because that sounded much more up my alley than setting up and manning a ring toss or a kiddie pool fishing pond.

I surveyed the nearly one hundred heads of those either helping set up or involved in clustered conversations, but Amber and her mom weren't among them. The giant shelter on my left consisted of a large wooden gazebo with a cement floor and a half dozen picnic tables under the overhang. The tables wouldn't have nearly enough seating for our congregation, but other church members busily set up oblong tables and chairs from the church basement all around the perimeter of the shelter.

The one other shelter in the park stood about fifty feet away, and this one had rows of white chairs lined up in front of the cement area and white tulle decorating the front rafters of the shelter. A nearby table overflowed with wrapped gifts. It looked like preparations for a wedding. Two men in suits straightened the twenty-or-so rows of chairs, and many of the formally-dressed folks I'd seen on the sidewalk milled around that side of the park. I let out a breath, glad I hadn't dressed inappropriately for the picnic after all.

As I headed for the church's picnic shelter where the hot food had been placed, a nearby commotion caught my eye. Pastor Jeff was in the midst of a hushed argument with a lady I didn't recognize. She couldn't have been more than five feet tall, but what she lacked in height, she made up for with her large pregnant belly, stretched tight under a pale pink dress.

She flapped her arms to the sides, and as I moved closer, I started to make out the problem. "The bride and groom expected to have the whole park to themselves. It's their special day and they'll be here any minute! I'm their wedding planner. How do you think this is going to look for me?"

Pastor Jeff pushed his hands toward the ground and spoke in his usual calming and authoritative tone. "I understand your concern, Mrs. Winters, and I have no idea where the mix-up happened, but let's just take a deep breath and see what we can do." Pastor Jeff angled away from the pregnant lady, toward where the carnival games were being assembled. He quickly located his wife and called, "Emily? Let's try to keep all the games closer to the playground, all right?"

Between Pastor Jeff and his wife stood Marv and Donna Mayberry. They were one of the first couples Cooper and I had met at Honeysuckle Grove Community Church. Donna leaned into her husband and whispered something, likely an embellished rumor. And just like that, the giant game of telephone that always seemed to start with gossiping Donna Mayberry had begun.

"I don't care how much you move those games," the pregnant wedding planner said in an exasperated tone to Pastor Jeff. "The Bankses and the Albrights are still not going to appreciate kids running through their ceremony, and all the noise a church picnic will generate. They're not going to want these people they don't know hanging around their wedding!" She flapped her arms again. Pastor Jeff took a breath, about to speak, but she interrupted him. "Look, I don't know how the municipal office could think this park is big enough for both a wedding and a church picnic, but it's just not. I'm calling them right this second to sort this out."

I couldn't imagine the municipal office being open on a Sunday, but she pulled out a cell phone and marched away with it, not giving Pastor Jeff a chance to respond. That left our pastor staring straight at me, the only other person in the immediate vicinity. The deep grooves of his face told me he wanted to find a solution as much as the wedding planner did.

And like the last time I'd seen Pastor Jeff looking helpless, I wanted to do what I could to take that pained look off of his face.

"What can I do to help?" I asked.

Pastor Jeff wore a lavender dress shirt and khaki shorts that looked lovely together. I attributed his tidy and coordinated appearance to his wife,

4

Emily, being here helping, instead of at her usual Sunday morning job in the church nursery. But in only one second, Pastor Jeff ran a hand through his sandy brown hair, and it stuck up in all directions, effectively ruining the put-together effect.

He shook his head. "I need to get the games moved as far away from the wedding as possible." He turned, and I took a step to follow him, but then he swung back around and said, "Actually, could you ask Sasha to gather some parents and corral the kids to keep them near the playground? That would help."

I looked to where he pointed to a lady in a long purple paisley dress. I knew the woman, or at least I had known her many years ago. She'd been my seventh-grade English teacher, back when I'd lived in Honeysuckle Grove, West Virginia, with my dad and sister more than fifteen years ago. Her hair had grown from shoulder-length to halfway down her back, and it was grayer than it had been back then, but she still clearly wore the same paisley dresses.

"You mean Ms. Mills?" I asked.

Pastor Jeff nodded, but he looked eager to rush off and speak with his secretary and the rest of the church staff to figure this out. "Yes. She takes care of our children's ministry."

If I'd had kids, perhaps I would have known that. Cooper and I had wanted kids, lots of them, but sadly, he'd been killed in a fire at one of the local banks shortly after we settled into town.

I nodded to Pastor Jeff, but still had my casserole dish in my hands, so I followed him toward his church secretary, near the food shelter, saying, "Yes, right away. I'll just put this down first."

Pastor Jeff was too concerned about his current problem to worry about me and spoke to his secretary from several feet away as he approached. "Did we not book both shelters for the picnic, Penny? Their wedding planner, Mrs. Winters, insists she has the park booked for a wedding today." He motioned to where Mrs. Winters stood angrily punching something into her phone's keyboard.

"Oh, I, um, I'm afraid I don't know." Penny Lismore was in her early twenties with bright naturally-orange hair and big blue naïve eyes. She had been the church secretary for a little less than a year. I only knew this because she had been new on the job when Cooper died, and she had made many apologies to me about not understanding procedures in booking a memorial service. Today she looked equally clueless as she picked at the side seam of her navy shorts. "Troy said he was going to book it."

I placed my casserole dish on a nearby table and looked up to where both Penny and Pastor Jeff had moved their gazes. Near the carnival games, with a clipboard in hand, stood Troy Offenbach, the treasurer of Honeysuckle Grove Community Church. He had trim blond hair, statuesque posture, and a stoic face that meant business, even at a picnic. My knowledge of Troy Offenbach was about as limited as my knowledge of Penny Lismore. He had printed off a detailed bill for Cooper's memorial service, and I had paid it.

Troy hadn't been particularly compassionate about the fact that I'd only just lost my husband a week prior, but I hadn't expected him to be. He was a numbers guy. If Cooper had taught me one thing from when I'd helped him research his mystery novels, it was that if you wanted to get a better handle on the cast of people surrounding your story, they could all quickly be reduced to certain stereotypes. Troy was all about the accounting, Penny was an employee who could follow simple instructions but wasn't much of a self-starter, and Pastor Jeff gave from the depths of such a big heart every time he came across a problem, no matter how large or small. I feared it might be the thing to break him.

"Troy!" Pastor Jeff held up an arm and beckoned his church treasurer toward him.

I took a breath and remembered the job I'd been given. Besides, did I really want to get in the middle of this situation with no easy answers? As I quick-stepped toward the kids' play park and my seventh-grade English teacher, the pregnant wedding planner moved back toward the trio of church workers looking exasperated.

"The municipal office is closed on Sundays…" was the last thing I heard as I strode away quickly.

Sasha Mills, the children's ministry coordinator, seemed no less frazzled. There had to be twenty-five kids under ten in her care, and her eyes darted from place to place as she called out short phrases such as, "Ethan, stop hitting her!" and "Amy and Zara, you're going to have to share!" and "Dominic, get down from there!" to the boy up high in the oak tree. Their parents, it seemed, were all busy helping with the picnic preparations.

"Excuse me? Ms. Mills?" I said, already feeling bad for interrupting this very busy lady. Ms. Mills had always been a bit of a softie, and if I were honest, it surprised me to see her still working with young children, ones I expected would know how to railroad over her instructions without a problem. After a couple of other called instructions, she turned to me.

"Yes?" She looked me up and down. Again, I doubted my capris and peach T-shirt. But when her gaze settled on my face, I suspected the look had more to do with a grown woman calling her Ms. Mills. It just seemed too strange to call my former teacher by her first name.

"I'm Mallory Beck—er, Vandewalker," I added, realizing she wouldn't know me by my married name. But I wanted to take up as little of her time as possible, as, out of the corner of my eye, I could tell that the little boy she'd called Ethan had started hitting the girl again. It wouldn't be long until screams ensued. "I'm not sure if you remember me…" I waved a hand. That part wasn't important. "Anyway, Pastor Jeff has come across quite an issue. Apparently, the park has been double-booked. He asked me to see if you could enlist the help of a few parents and corral the children into the playground area?"

As I said the words, Ms. Mills raised an eyebrow at me, and I realized that even if the consequences were a bomb that was about to go off or the impending end of the world, corralling this group of children was easier said than done.

"How can I help?" I asked, so at least she'd know she wasn't facing this problem on her own.

Ms. Mills took about three seconds to survey the situation, and then she pointed to a large red Rubbermaid bin near the food shelter. "Why don't you get the bin of Nerf guns? I have an idea."

As I raced to grab the bin, Ms. Mills called out the names of a few nearby parents. They came right over, and she stepped onto the wood chips of the kids' playground area and called out, "Children, listen up! The grass and the trees are lava!"

There was maybe a one-second delay, and then all of the kids who were outside of the square of the wood-chipped area looked down at their feet and raced toward the playground as Ms. Mills called out, "Three, two, one!" She pointed the mothers who had joined her around the perimeter of the playground, and they spread out.

Kids pointed and laughed at the few stragglers who hadn't made it onto the wood chips in time, but I had to hand it to Ms. Mills. She had a much better grasp on how to handle these young kids than I would have.

Most of the church men and teens followed Pastor Jeff's directions and dragged tables and games away from the wedding shelter. Other than the young kids, nobody hesitated to pitch in and help.

The Nerf gun bin was heavy, so I dragged it behind me, but only a second later, it lightened. I looked over my shoulder. Amber Montrose had grabbed the other end.

"Thank goodness you're here!" I said, now much more glad about her presence as a helper than simply so I wouldn't be standing at a social gathering alone. "The park was double-booked with a wedding. Pastor Jeff is trying to figure it out and asked that we keep the kids corralled over here."

Amber smirked—her usual reaction to most problems. Today she wore a sleeveless black T-shirt with her cut-offs that read: BUT DID YOU DIE? Her auburn curls were held back with a matching black headband. It may have been her personal style of mourning, as her dad had died less than two weeks ago.

"That should be easy," she said sarcastically.

As we arrived at the playground, Ms. Mills was already in the midst of discussing "rules" for a new game with the kids. "Nerf guns are only to be used in the wood chip area," she said. "The grass is still lava, and if I catch you with a Nerf gun on the lava, you'll lose all weapons for the rest of the day. Got it?"

The kids barely listened. At seeing the bin, all twenty-five of them barreled toward Amber and me, and only a second later, the hoard had elbowed us away from the bin so they could get in closer. Nerf guns swung up and out of the bin, and I could immediately tell this could be another accident waiting to happen.

Ms. Mills joined Amber and me near the edge of the wood chips. "This isn't going to last long, but it was all I could think of on short notice. Can you find out what's happening from Pastor Jeff?" She turned to Amber. "Can you hang out on the far side of the playground and help keep them within the boundaries, Amber?"

Amber nodded and headed that direction. I wasn't sure if Amber knew Ms. Mills from children's church or if she'd also had her as a teacher at school, but I didn't have time to ask. I turned and raced back toward the food shelter.

More guests had arrived since I'd been focused on corralling the kids, and there was a stark difference between those who were clearly here for a church picnic—in shorts and T-shirts and carrying lawn furniture—and those in dresses and suits, here for a wedding celebration.

As I skirted around picnic-goers and wedding guests to get back to the pastor and his two assistants, the pregnant wedding planner shook her head at Troy and then strode away with fists balled at her sides. I followed her eye line to three limousines that had just pulled up to the curb of the parking lot.

As if there wasn't enough to stress about, apparently the bride and groom and their entourage had arrived.

☐

# CHAPTER TWO

The church staff quickly formed a huddle.

"Penny hadn't organized the picnic before, so I stepped in to help," Troy Offenbach told Pastor Jeff. I was still a couple of feet away from them, but stopped in place, not knowing if I should interrupt.

"And you booked the entire park? Both shelters?" Pastor Jeff asked him.

Troy glanced away toward where the carnival games were now at a standstill of being set up without him there to direct the process. When he looked back to Pastor Jeff, he seemed almost out of breath as he said, "I'm sure I told them to book it the same as last year and every year before that. I don't know what went wrong, but I'll have to call the municipal office on Monday and sort this out. They'll have to give us a refund."

Pastor Jeff shook his head. "Monday is not good enough, and I'm not concerned about a refund. These people are getting married here today!"

"Right," Troy said, blinking fast a few times. "But it's a big park. We'll just keep to our side, and they can keep to theirs."

Even I knew that wasn't going to work. The two shelters were too close to one another. The hubbub of activity and current noise level only highlighted the fact that the bride and groom would need a pretty serious microphone system to overcome this cacophony.

And as if this thought was their cue, at that moment, the children with their Nerf guns decided the grass was no longer lava, chased one another outside of the square wood-chipped playground plot, and ran in figure eights around both shelters. A half dozen mothers chased and tried to discipline their children, but it seemed Nerf guns were akin to a shot of straight sugar to these kids.

"Ms. Mills doesn't know how she'll keep the kids corralled," I said needlessly to Pastor Jeff, simply to highlight the problem for Troy-the-treasurer's benefit. Even though it was ninety degrees out, he wore a yellow dress shirt and full-length slacks.

"She's going to have to, at least until the ceremony is over. Then I'm sure everyone will relax a little." Troy pushed his wire-rimmed glasses up his nose.

Before I had time to argue this, the pregnant wedding planner marched toward us with an entourage following behind her, including a very young-looking bride and the groom. I was surprised that not only was the groom allowed to see the bride before their wedding, but he was sticking so close to her, it almost seemed like they were attached by an invisible string. The wedding planner's light brown hair had come almost entirely loose from her ponytail. At least fifteen people trailed behind her, some clearly involved in the bridal party in pastel pink dresses and tuxes with pink bow ties, and others, I guessed by their ages, included the parents of the marrying couple. A photographer with a large camera hovered nearby, already taking photos.

But all I could focus on was the very beautiful—and very angry—bride.

Maybe just into her twenties, she wore a princess-style dress, with a ten-foot train that dragged on the grass behind her. She seemed unconcerned about dirtying her cream-colored satin as she dug her fists into her waist and glared at me, Pastor Jeff, and then pointedly at Troy Offenbach, as though Mrs. Winters had already informed her that this was all the church treasurer's fault.

"You'd better believe that no one is going to ruin my wedding day!"

One of her bridesmaids, a curvy girl in her late teens in a pale pink satin gown, moved up behind the bride to tidy her blonde cascading curls, which seemed perfectly in place to me. The photographer moved in closer and got a shot of the two girls before the bride reached back, annoyed, and swatted her bridesmaid away.

"Stop it! Do you think I care about my hair right now, Lacey?" The bride's high-pitched nasal voice made her seem a little less pretty.

The barely-twenty man in the tuxedo beside her grabbed for her hand. "Sweetie, let's figure this out. We could just move the ceremony over to the far end—"

The bride snapped her hand away. "We're not moving our wedding ceremony, David. In fact, I'm calling the cops!" She held out an open hand, and only a second later, her wedding planner placed a cell phone into it.

"Candi," the groom tried again, and I didn't know if that was her actual name or a pet name, but she just shook her head at him and continued to dial.

The photographer, as if doing his own part to break the tension, said, "Mr. and Mrs. Banks?" to a well-dressed couple in their late forties. "Can I just get a shot of you over by the flower garden?"

The woman held up an index finger to him and then turned to the bride.

"Honey, this is your day. If everything's not perfect, we'll figure something else out."

"We will not figure something else out!" the bride practically exploded, but the older couple was already following the photographer toward a lovely patch of New England Aster and purple great laurel.

Pastor Jeff and Troy backed away. "We have to come up with a contingency plan. Maybe move things back to the church?" Pastor Jeff said in a hushed voice, so as not to be heard by the wedding party. "Or delay until next Sunday?"

Troy shook his head and furrowed his brow, the first sign I'd seen of him having any real emotion. "I don't think we can assign another Sunday to this. Do you know what we'd lose in offerings? And if we move the whole picnic at this point, how many people do you think would really come?" Troy crossed his arms over his chest, looking like a child that didn't want to do what he'd been told. "We have every right to be here, and I say we're staying." He didn't wait for Pastor Jeff's argument. He swung around and marched for the carnival games, barking orders at all of those who had paused their setup duties before he was even close to them. "Let's get that ring toss up! The kids are getting bored…"

Pastor Jeff turned back to the wedding party group. Now that I looked them over, the three bridesmaids in satiny pink dresses and groomsmen in tuxedos stood out like royalty among the peasants. I pegged Mr. and Mrs. Banks, who were posing so naturally for the photographer near the flower bed that they could likely do it in their sleep, as the mother and father of the bride. The blonde lady wore a floral dress and looked very much like her angry cream-clad younger version. The father of the bride wore a tuxedo that appeared to have been perfectly tailored to his svelte frame. The bride was still ranting into a cell phone, pacing back and forth on the lawn nearby, with her groom less than a foot away, nibbling his lip and not doing a thing to help.

"See?" the wedding planner said to Pastor Jeff. "David and Candi are not going to stand for this."

So Candi was her real name. David, the groom, didn't seem nearly as motivated by this turn of events as his bride-to-be, and I thought he probably would stand for this, along with anything else that stood in his way.

As if he'd heard my thought, just then he said, "Oh, it'll still happen," loud enough that even I could hear him. "Candi will figure out a way to fix this." He followed Candi back and forth with his eyes as she paced, as if willing this statement into being.

As I surveyed the group of bridal party and family members standing around, listening to the altercation, in various stages of upset over the shared park, several things became apparent. First, the bride's supporters and the groom's supporters were quite literally divided down the middle with a good three feet of lawn between them. Second, there was a noticeable class difference between the two groups. The bride, her bridesmaids, and her family all dressed as though they had money, made obvious by their designer dresses and suits, up-dos that could only be the result of a professional stylist, and an air about them as if they had all been severely displaced, even though they'd been standing here for less than five minutes.

The groom's side of the lawn, in contrast, while not as fancily dressed by a longshot, looked as though they were in no hurry to lend a hand or try and solve this predicament. They placed baskets and shopping bags of wedding supplies down at their feet, as though they suspected they would be standing here for quite some time waiting for the double-booking to get worked out. A few of them had already taken a seat on the grass.

The photographer returned and said, "Mr. and Mrs. Albright?" surveying the crowd as though he had no idea who they might be.

A shaggy-haired, fortysomething man in a slightly tattered navy suit that looked a couple of decades old and his wife in a loose-fitting beige dress raised their hands.

"Parents of the groom?" the photographer asked in confirmation. I didn't blame him. These two didn't look dressed for any wedding, certainly not their son's.

Mr. Albright picked up a huge oblong bag from at his feet. It was big enough to store a small person and filled with at least a dozen bottles of red wine in clear bottles, which stuck out at all angles. The stocky man didn't seem to struggle with the bag's weight as he moved with his wife toward the flower garden at the photographer's direction.

As they walked, I overheard the photographer say, "I'm from the Honeysuckle Grove Herald. I'd just like to get one quick shot of you folks if that's okay."

Wow, the local paper. I just assumed he had been a hired wedding photographer, but apparently, this union was newsworthy. I suspected the photographer was underplaying the process because he'd taken at least a dozen shots of the parents of the bride.

But I'd barely blinked, and sure enough, he was done with them. Mrs. Albright, with braids down either side of her head, wrung her hands, looking anxious as she made her way back to the gathering of people, while Mr. Albright took his bag filled with wine and sidled up near his son. I wondered if he'd gotten permission to uncork wine in a local park, or if perhaps it was non-alcoholic.

But my questions very quickly turned back to the other glaring questions of the day when Mr. Albright said, "Maybe it's not meant to happen today, son," to the groom.

David Albright visibly flinched away from his father and moved closer to Candi, who was still ranting into her cellphone.

David looked a lot like his mother as he started to wring his hands against one another. "Candi will get her way. You just wait."

Pastor Jeff had left my side to move over to where his wife had her attention divided between setting up carnival games and the bride on her cell phone. Penny Lismore, the church secretary, had also wandered off. That left me as the closest church representation with all of these wedding folks staring straight at me. I most definitely didn't want anyone to start challenging me to fix this, so I sidestepped a dozen feet away, probably looking like a klutzy showgirl, to find Amber near the playground.

"None of them will stay put," Amber said with a shrug, not looking nearly as exasperated about it as Ms. Mills or the other mothers clearly were. Kids had scattered around every corner of the wide-open park. Some chased each other with Nerf guns between the rows of white chairs set up for the wedding, even knocking a couple of the chairs over. I wondered if all this excitement was a result of the Nerf guns—a backfire on Ms. Mills' part, to say the least—or if someone had tried to bribe them back to the playground with candy. Two kids raced right in between Candi, the bride who had apparently finished her phone call, and Troy, the church treasurer, who in the last thirty seconds had erupted into a raging argument about who had more right to the park for the afternoon.

David remained nearby, watching the argument ping-pong back and forth, but didn't come to his bride's aid.

Candi waved her hands at the church treasurer, while her bridesmaid had reappeared behind her to tidy up her hair once again. The bridesmaid grinned from ear to ear, paying little attention to the hair she was tidying. I followed her gaze to where the photographer crouched nearby. The bridesmaid changed her angle and tilt of her head several times as the photographer clicked away on his camera.

As the bridesmaid turned to a new angle, Candi actually swatted the girl's hand away so hard I heard a smack. "I told you, I don't care about my hair right now, Lacey," she barked at the girl, oblivious to the photographer. "I let you into my wedding party. Isn't that enough for you? Now get out of my way!"

Lacey's face flushed as she pulled away from the bride, but then a second later, she squared her shoulders and marched toward the photographer. I sidled a little closer to hear her spelling her name for him— L-A-C-E-Y—while the photographer noted it. She followed it with her last name. B-A-N-K-S.

Candi and Lacey, I mused to myself. Now that I looked a little closer, I could see the sisterly resemblance. Candi was clearly older, but not by much. I couldn't help checking out her belly for half a second, but the satin bodice appeared smooth and flat.

Candi's parents stood nearby, involved in their own argument.

"Just go make sure Hector's behaving himself," Mrs. Banks told her husband. "All we need is him causing a problem after everything else today."

Maybe it wasn't so much an argument as an instruction because Candi's father simply nodded and started to obey, but not before Candi could turn from where she'd been talking a blue streak at Troy to add her two cents. "I told you this wasn't going to work with Uncle Hector here! Is this going to be a problem? Like I don't have enough to deal with today."

Candi scanned the park, and when her eyes settled, I followed her gaze to where a man near the church's food shelter, only a dozen feet from me, waved her off with a hand. He stood close enough to have heard her remark, and he looked straight in her direction, but he only started chuckling at it. Apparently, Uncle Hector had a sense of humor.

"Look, Hector," Candi's dad said as he made his way over. "Either stay in the white chairs or we're going to have to ask you to go."

"You're gonna send me away? Why don't you just take care of Ella? It's my niece's wedding day, for crying out loud!" he slurred and accented his words with a smirk. While the rest of the bride's family were dressed to the nines, this man wore jeans and a green plaid shirt. His eyes were glassy, like he'd been drinking even though it wasn't even noon.

"Nobody's sending you away. We just hoped you could stay in your seat for today, Hector." I could see why Candi's dad got pushed around by his wife. He didn't seem to have a commanding bone in his whole body.

"You just keep Ella in check." Hector pointed at the father of the bride, almost hitting him in the eye, then turned and stumbled toward the white chairs.

Mr. Banks moved back toward his wife, but my attention was rapt on Candi's Uncle Hector because as soon as Mr. Banks had moved away, he stopped in place and looked around conspiratorially. When helping research Cooper's mystery novels, he used to explain to me how little ticks, like darting eyes or excessive licking of lips, could often lead his main character, Marty Sims, to the guilty parties.

Hector didn't move toward the white chairs, as instructed, and something about his darting eyes told me he was just as guilty about something as a villain in a Cooper Beck novel. It seemed while all the adults from the church were either trying to corral their children, working on moving and setting up the games area, or following the argument between the bride and church treasurer with interest, the church's food shelter had been left unattended.

I pulled out my phone, pretending to take a photo of the chaos in the park, while I watched Hector out of my peripheral vision. He looked both ways and then quietly slipped under the church's food shelter. I glanced around to find Pastor Jeff or Emily, but they were dragging a games table out past the playground and were out of earshot.

When I turned back, Hector was closing the lid on a big blue Rubbermaid container stashed under one of the shelter's picnic tables.

He moved away quickly, and I felt unsure about confronting the drunk man, so instead, I raced forward toward the Rubbermaid container, wondering if it contained a float of money or some other valuable item. Uncle Hector appeared, of anyone on the bride's side, like he could use a few extra bucks. But I didn't get there because right at that moment, Candi let out the loudest shriek I'd ever heard.

As I looked over, she slapped at her shoulder, stumbled forward a few feet, and collapsed to the ground.

Both Troy and David swatted at the air around them as Candi's parents raced to her side.

"Oh, no! Was there a bee?" Candi's mom looked up at the groom and church treasurer from where she knelt beside her daughter. Candi gripped her neck as though desperately gasping for air. Even from my distance away, I could see that her hands were covered in red hives.

David nodded. "She arched her back like she'd been stung between the shoulders." He looked around and called out loudly to no one in particular, "Does she have her EpiPen?"

Candi's dad bent and stroked his daughter's hair. "It's going to be okay, honey. You're going to be fine!"

Candi's eyes appeared glazed over, like she couldn't take in anything happening around her, including her dad's voice.

The wedding planner rushed over with a white sparkly handbag tight between her hands. "I have Candi's purse. Let me see if she packed an EpiPen." As she rooted through Candi's small bag, she called out, "Does anyone have an EpiPen?" Before anyone could volunteer one, she added, "Wait! I found it!"

Seconds later, she struggled to bend down around her big belly beside Candi on the ground, fumbling over the package. The wedding planner seemed skilled at many things, but bending to the ground wasn't her strong suit in her current state, and she clearly didn't have a clue how to use an EpiPen.

David stood by, dumbfounded, while Troy snatched the package from the wedding planner, bent at Candi's legs, pulled up her dress just enough to reveal a pink garter, and a second later jabbed one side of the tube into her thigh.

I turned my attention to Candi's face and waited for what felt like an eternity. Her eyes flickered and then closed, her hands fell from her neck, and seconds later, she lay perfectly still.

I moved out of the church's food shelter to get a closer look. Lacey Banks was jabbering away to the newspaper photographer nearby. "I don't have any allergies," she said as I passed. "I can't even imagine having an allergy to something like bees. I mean, you wouldn't even want to leave the house!"

Everyone surrounding the bride had clearly been through this before with her, and I was sure they knew what to look for. The setup for the church picnic had paused, and everyone stood watching from their own vantage point. It felt like the whole park was holding its breath.

I had no idea what to expect from a severe allergic reaction. How long did an EpiPen usually take to kick in? I figured I must be overreacting, and yet I couldn't fight the feeling I should call for an ambulance.

I sidled back from the large circle that had gathered around Candi's still body and pulled out my phone. As the 911 operator answered and I relayed the information of where we were and what had happened, a police car pulled up along the curb behind the line of limousines.

Officer Alex Martinez stepped out, and I had never been so happy to see a familiar face.

# CHAPTER THREE

"I just called 911," I told Alex as I rushed over to meet him just outside his police car.

"Because of a park rental dispute?" He raised an eyebrow like I'd lost my mind.

I shook my head, quickly putting together that he had arrived because of Candi's call, not due to my emergency call only seconds ago. Alex's eyebrows deepened into a furrow. I had known him in seventh grade when he'd been my number one crush, and I had learned way back then how to read his expressions. His green eyes darkened. He had a way of looking angry when he was actually worried or confused.

"No, there was a wedding double-booked in the park and the bride collapsed. She was stung by a bee, and they've administered an EpiPen, but last I saw, she didn't seem to be responding."

We both looked across the grass to where the crowd surrounding Candi had grown considerably. Mr. Banks had his daughter hanging limply in his arms. He walked quickly toward the parking lot with Mrs. Banks on one side and David on the other.

Alex marched to meet him. As I kept pace, he asked me, "And you called 911? How long ago?"

I had to jog to keep up. "Not more than a couple of minutes."

"Sir," he called out to Mr. Banks, "there's an ambulance on route. I'm going to call in and see how far they are away, but I suggest you place her down and wait at the grass near the edge of the parking lot. If she still doesn't revive on her own, they can treat her on the way to the hospital."

"But the EpiPen always works!" Mrs. Banks said. The words came out so strong, they almost sounded as though she were blaming Alex for this.

"I understand." Alex nodded, and I was impressed at his aura of calm, even though I could tell by the way his fingers rubbed at the seam of his dark police pants that he was anything but. "Let me just check on the ambulance's arrival."

He hurried toward his police car, and Mr. Banks started to bend to place his daughter down, but neither of them got very far before the ambulance siren could be heard. Seconds later, it turned the corner onto Bateman and pulled alongside the first limousine.

Paramedics emerged from the two front doors, and Alex raced over to meet the first one. I couldn't hear him from where I stood, but by the speed of his lips, I could see he was relaying the situation to them efficiently while the paramedic opened the back door to the ambulance and removed a portable stretcher.

Mr. and Mrs. Banks spoke frantically to the other paramedic near the rear of the ambulance. Much of the crowd had followed the Banks family to the parking lot. The paramedics instructed Mr. Banks to place his daughter down on the stretcher, then proceeded to check her pulse, pupils, and blood pressure. I couldn't hear what was said between the two paramedics, but a seriousness filled the air as they loaded Candi into the back of the ambulance.

Alex moved away, holding up his hands to the growing crowd. "Folks, please move back from the parking lot so the ambulance can get moving as quickly as possible."

People listened, murmuring worriedly to each other. The back ambulance door closed with Candi, Mrs. Banks, and one of the paramedics inside, while Mr. Banks and David rushed toward the closest limousine.

Mere seconds later, both vehicles were gone. Others who must have been close to the family followed suit, quickly getting into vehicles and driving off in a hurry.

While I stood in place, stunned at everything that had just transpired, Pastor Jeff approached Alex. "Did they tell you anything, officer? Is she going to be okay?" Concern leaked out in Pastor Jeff's voice, and worry etched lines into his face.

The people around the park—both picnic-goers and wedding guests— were all at a standstill, their eyes squarely on Alex and Pastor Jeff. Even many of the kids had stopped racing around, understanding that something serious had happened.

"They were going to treat her on route to the hospital. Her family is with her," Alex said in way of comfort because there didn't seem to be too much else to be said. I watched Alex's eyes carefully to see if he held any expertise in this area or might have gotten any extra insight from the paramedic he spoke to, but he looked just as clueless as I was.

Pastor Jeff nodded at least ten times, his eyes steady on Alex, and I could see him trying to come up with anything that could make this situation better. Then he turned to face the church picnic side of the park. "Folks, I hate to do this, but I'm calling the church picnic for today. We'll talk about whether or not something can be done to reschedule, but under the circumstances, I feel this will be the only thing we, as a church, can do to help. If any of you would like to remain and join a prayer circle, I'd like to see us do what we can to support the wedding celebration that was planned to happen here today."

He seemed to be choosing his words carefully. I quickly scanned the crowd for Troy to see how angered he was at this new information, but I couldn't see him anywhere on either side of the park.

Pastor Jeff clapped his hands together, and that seemed to set all of the church-going folks into the motion of packing up.

When I turned back to Alex, he had his cell phone to his ear. I couldn't make out what he said quietly into his phone, but only a second later, he shoved it into his pocket and asked me, "Do you know the bride's name?"

"Candi. Candi Banks." As I spoke, Alex pulled out his notepad and scribbled some notes. "Her parents, Mr. and Mrs. Banks, went with her to the hospital, along with her groom, David…" I snapped my fingers, and the name came to me. "David Albright." I looked around for young David's hippie parents, but they were nowhere to be seen in the crowd. "Mr. and Mrs. Albright must have followed them to the hospital."

Alex nodded as he made notes. "Anyone else from the wedding group that might know the bride and her family well, from your estimation?"

I surveyed the wedding side of the park. Many people had moved into somber-looking groupings. Several of the white chairs had been rearranged haphazardly, and a few were occupied, but not in a way like they were waiting for a wedding, more like they were settling into a campsite for the weekend.

I spotted the pregnant wedding planner near the wedding shelter, arranging bouquets, probably at a loss of what else to do.

"It looks like the bride and groom's family, as well as the wedding party, have gone along to the hospital," I said, and then pointed. "That's the wedding planner. Mrs. Winters, I think her name is. I'm sure she could figure out who in the crowd is connected to the bride."

It had been difficult to tell how many were here for the wedding earlier when the park had been filled with a mix of well over a hundred picnic-goers and wedding attendees, but in the couple of minutes that I had been talking to Alex, it seemed many had either followed the family of the bride to the hospital or gathered their children and rushed them out of a scene of so much excitement. There was now a clear separation between the picnic-goers, who were busy packing up, and the wedding guests, who seemed to be waiting to be told what to do.

"I should probably help clean up." I looked from Ms. Mills, trying to connect kids with their parents, to where the meek pastor's wife was trying to organize packing up the games. Troy was still nowhere in sight. Pastor Jeff stood near the food shelter, organizing a prayer circle, which already included almost a dozen people.

Alex nodded. "I have to check in with the station." He motioned to his police cruiser behind him, and then glanced at his notes. "But I'll check in with Mrs. Winters and find you before I go."

I nodded and headed off toward Ms. Mills. In truth, I was torn between joining the prayer group and staying nearby to see if I could help either Alex or Emily Hawthorne. Ms. Mills only had four kids under her care now, and two of them were the pastor's twin boys. She didn't need my help, but I headed there anyway, trying to push away my instincts to join the prayer circle. Candi Banks had been so unresponsive when they took her away, and I couldn't get the image out of my head.

It wasn't that I didn't believe in prayer, but I'd had a shaky relationship with God since Cooper died. I still didn't understand why He would have taken someone so young, so good. Amber and her mom had already joined the prayer group, and I wondered why I couldn't get past my nine-month-old tragedy to pray for another family if they could get past their much fresher one.

"What can I do to help?" I asked Ms. Mills.

She smiled, much more relaxed than she had been fifteen minutes ago. "I'm fine. Why don't you join the prayer circle?" She motioned in that direction.

I took in a breath and angled in that direction, but just then, Alex crossed from his cruiser, making a beeline for the wedding planner. His buckled forehead told me that something had changed in the last two minutes.

I intercepted him. "Is everything okay?"

He kept his eyes on the wedding planner, and his mouth formed a frown as he shook his head. "They couldn't revive Candi Banks."

"I—what?" Alex finally met my eyes, and I said the words so he wouldn't have to. "She's dead?"

One solid nod, and then Alex pushed on toward Mrs. Winters. I sucked in a breath and held it. Ever since Cooper's death, I couldn't watch people being given tragic news, even on TV. Plus, after so recently helping Amber through her dad's death and confronting a murderer, my first inclination was to protect myself and my new best friend. And so, finally, I headed for the prayer circle and nudged my way in beside Amber.

About twenty people had their heads bowed while Pastor Jeff continued praying for the bride's health, her family, and the various stresses of the day.

He prayed that somehow the bride and groom could still have the wedding of their dreams.

I swallowed against my parched throat, knowing I should probably open my mouth and inform Pastor Jeff of the severity of the situation, but I just couldn't do it.

"What? No!" My thoughts were interrupted by a loud cry from across the park. I followed the sound to see Mrs. Winters with arms splayed open, a look of shock on her face. "She can't be dead! Candi can't be dead!"

Alex had a hand on her shoulder and was pushing his other one toward the ground, clearly trying to calm her down.

But she swatted his hands away and started pacing with her hands out. It looked like she was asking Alex questions, either that or murmuring to herself, but I couldn't hear anything else from my place across the park.

"I can't do this." The emotional words from close by snatched my attention. Mrs. Montrose shook her head at Amber. She had the same pasted-on smile as she'd worn at her husband's wake only a little over a week ago, but her quiet voice was shaky. "I have to get out of here."

Amber nodded, looking pretty shaken up herself, but ever the strong daughter, she took her mom's hand and led her out of the prayer circle. As she left my side, she murmured, "I'll call you later."

"Of course," I said. She was being the strength her mom needed, but who was being her strength? I hoped as I got stronger, I could be there for her more.

Pastor Jeff had been stunned a moment ago, but he quickly seemed to gather his wits about him. "Folks, listen up! The Banks family needs our prayers now more than ever."

# CHAPTER FOUR

By the time I looked up from praying, Alex had calmed down Mrs. Winters some, and most of the wedding décor had been packed up. Men in suits with somber faces hauled white chairs toward a large van in the parking lot, while Mrs. Winters stood nearby, dabbing at her eyes and talking into her phone.

The church games had been packed up as well, and the crowd had thinned considerably. Emily Hawthorne was packing up food supplies under the nearby shelter. I went to help.

"Several people forgot to take their dishes home," she said either to me or herself.

"That one's mine." I pointed to my white casserole dish with the orange and blue flower emblem on the side.

She sighed. "I guess I'll have to call around about the others."

"Why don't you let me do that?" I said. I glanced at two large coolers nearby. "If I can borrow those coolers, I can take all the food and dishes and return them to their owners. You and Pastor Jeff have enough to worry about."

Emily looked up at me with a sad smile. "Thank you, Mallory. I'd sure appreciate that."

I was surprised she remembered my name. We'd had a short conversation at Cooper's memorial service, but the community church had several hundred members and had hosted several memorial services since then. Plus, Emily Hawthorne was usually needed in the church nursery.

As I organized the remaining six casseroles to fit into the coolers, Emily instructed a couple of men from the church to move other supplies to her vehicle. When one of the men picked up a blue Rubbermaid container, it

22

jarred my memory.

But it wasn't the same Rubbermaid container Hector had been digging into. That one, at twice the height of all of those left, seemed to have already been packed away and into a vehicle.

Emily was headed toward the parking lot with an armful of paper plates and cups, but I stopped her. "Hey, I know this isn't too important at the moment, but when you unpack the bins, if you find anything missing, let me know. I saw someone suspiciously digging into one of them earlier."

Emily paused and furrowed her brow. Then she nodded. "I'll let you know," she said before continuing her trek toward the parking lot.

Pastor Jeff and Emily probably erred on the side of being too trusting. Even if the church had brought a large float of money, and it had been absconded by Candi Banks's Uncle Hector, I doubted Emily Hawthorne would ever mention it again. Especially after everything that had happened today.

By the time I had retrieved my Jeep and loaded up the leftover food, it seemed almost everyone had cleared out of the park.

Another police car arrived and two officers got out on either side. One I recognized as Detective Reinhart, the handsome sandy-haired detective who had been willing to help Alex with Amber's dad's murder case, even though neither of them had been authorized to investigate. I had only seen Detective Reinhart from a distance before, but he reminded me of a Ken doll who was likely married to a beautiful Barbie. The other cop wasn't bad-looking either, and I had to wonder if the Honeysuckle Grove Police Department only hired the most attractive men in town. Although, I supposed that didn't hold true for the sixtysomething overweight and grumpy Captain Corbett.

The officer I didn't know headed for Pastor Jeff, who was chatting with a couple of the only church-goers still left at the park. The officer pulled him aside to speak with him, and the couple waved goodbye as they started to head for the parking lot, but the officer held up an index finger, and they remained in place a few feet away.

Alex stood near where the wedding setup had been, having a serious-looking conversation with Detective Reinhart. Alex held a roll of yellow crime scene tape, and Detective Reinhart took notes down in a notepad.

I hurried over toward them.

"Albright," Alex was telling Detective Reinhart. "A-L-B-R-I-G-H-T."

Detective Reinhart paused his notetaking, turned, and flashed an easy smile at me, as though they weren't in the midst of a life-and-death crisis. "What can we help you with, Mrs. Beck?" His voice was much deeper than I'd imagined it, and I felt a silly school-girl flutter at the fact that he had remembered my name. But thankfully, only a second later, my brain came back online, reminding me of why I'd really come over.

"Is there something wrong?" I looked down at the roll of crime scene tape and then over to the detective. It seemed like an odd question, as clearly a lot had gone wrong in the last hour. But this was a detective on the force. Why would he be here for a bee sting, even if it was fatal? Why would Alex have gotten the crime scene tape out now, after almost everyone had left?

And Detective Reinhart seemed to understand my true question. He nodded toward Alex. "Why don't you fill her in, ask her some more pointed questions, and get that tape up?"

As the detective strode away, Alex's gaze flitted away from me. He wasn't filling me in fast enough, so I pushed. "Alex, what's going on?"

When he looked back at me, his eyes were serious. "It wasn't a bee sting."

I blinked. Then blinked again. "What's that, now?"

He glanced at Detective Reinhart again. When he turned back to me, he said, "When they removed the stinger, it turned out to be a tiny needle, inserted into Candi Banks's rear shoulder, not a bee stinger. I need you to tell me everything you saw here at the park from the moment you arrived until now."

If I'd thought Pastor Jeff looked tired this morning, it was nothing compared to how he looked by the time the police had questioned him, his wife, and the rest of the people left at the park. I felt equally exhausted after rehashing the events of the morning and as the notion started to register with me that what happened to Candi Banks this morning hadn't been an accident. They wouldn't have further information until an autopsy had been performed, but they were clearly treating this as a murder investigation.

Pastor Jeff and his wife, Emily, trudged toward their car with the last of the church supplies. I said goodbye while Alex went over to compare notes with the two detectives. The main section of the park had been cordoned off with police tape, and a forensics team had arrived to comb over the place.

"Thank you again for taking the leftover food, Mallory," Emily said. She shook her head. "The Banks family is going to have a heart-wrenching time ahead of them. I wish there was a way to give them all our extra casseroles, so it could be one less thing for them to worry about."

It just occurred to me now that I hadn't seen any caterers at the wedding. But Mr. Albright had been carrying a fair bit of wine. Perhaps they'd just had a cocktail reception planned. I glanced over at Alex, an idea coming to me. When Detective Reinhart had come over to talk with Alex, I'd heard him ask Alex to run by the Bankses' house while he went to the hospital.

"You know…let me see if I can't make that happen," I said to Emily.

As soon as she left, I strode over to Alex just as he finished speaking with Detective Reinhart. The two detectives headed for their dark blue vehicle. Before I could so much as open my mouth, though, Alex turned a question on me. "Did you happen to see a man named Hector Banks here earlier? Mrs. Winters mentioned him, and we wanted to ask him a few questions."

Drunk Uncle Hector. I'd forgotten all about him when I had relayed my story to Alex. I nodded. "He was here earlier. I think he was the uncle of the bride. If I had to guess, I'd say he'd already had one too many Mai Tais for breakfast."

Alex raised an eyebrow at me. "He was drunk?"

I nodded again. "Candi and her mom had been quite vocal about not wanting him here. Candi's father walked away from where Candi and the church treasurer were arguing to talk to Hector, to make sure he wasn't going to cause a scene. Shortly after that, I'd seen him sneak into the church's bin of supplies. I'd meant to check on what he had been digging for, if there might have been a cash box or something, but only seconds after that, Candi was stung." As soon as I said the words, I recalled it hadn't truly been a bee sting that killed her. "Er...hurt."

Alex flinched on the word "sting" but made a note of everything I told him.

"I asked Emily to check and make sure nothing was missing from the bins, but she was pretty tired, so..."

Alex nodded. "That's okay. Steve Reinhart wants me to head over to the church and track down that treasurer after I go to the Bankses' house, so I'll look into it then."

"Detective Reinhart again, huh?" I asked. The last time Alex had helped in solving a murder, Amber's dad's murder, Detective Reinhart had gotten all of the credit for Alex's work, due to some bad history between Alex's dad and Police Captain Corbett. Alex had been trying for years to get promoted to detective, but seemed to get pushed down at every turn.

Alex nodded, eyeing me as though trying to read into my question. "He's letting me help out with some of the more peripheral interviews. If I can prove myself instrumental in solving this one, you never know what could happen."

I bit my tongue to hold in all my questions about what else they had discovered through their questioning, knowing Alex wouldn't be able to answer them, especially not here, where Detective Reinhart and his partner were still within view.

But now this gave me extra ammunition to ask the question I'd initially had for Alex. "The church pastor's wife, Emily Hawthorne, thought the extra food from the picnic might be helpful to the Banks family in this time of tragedy." I motioned to where the food had been set up earlier. "They're going to be going through an awful time, and it would be one less thing for them to think about. Do you think it would be okay if I followed you over there and offered it to them?"

Alex twisted his lips in thought. "Sure, follow me there, and if Mr. and Mrs. Banks have returned already, I'll ask them if they're interested. But they may just want to be left alone at this point, at least until Steve can get to them to ask a few questions. Steve's just sending me as a precaution in case they've left the hospital."

I nodded and strode back to my Jeep to follow him. But as I got in, started the engine, and then caught up to Alex's police cruiser, I wondered how I had volunteered myself once again to deliver food to a grieving family.

And had Candi's death truly been another murder?

☐

# CHAPTER FIVE

The Banks mansion was no less impressive than the Montrose mansion—Amber's home, which I had seen when I'd helped solve the mystery behind her dad's murder. In fact, while the Montrose mansion included many sculpted shrubs and bushes around the property, as well as sturdy walnut furnishings, the Banks mansion looked more like a property from a movie set, with large white pillars near the front door and a giant fountain in the center of the roundabout driveway. It felt like the difference between old money and new money.

I had planned to wait in the Jeep until Alex called on me, but just sitting in my driver's seat in the roundabout driveway made me feel silly and on display, especially in this hot weather. Without taking the time to ask if it was all right, I followed Alex up the front steps from a few feet back, carrying the potato bacon casserole Amber had made. There was plenty more food in the Jeep, but I'd start with this one so I could be responsible for getting my own casserole dish back.

The doorbell let out a long, varied chime, and we waited in silence for someone to answer. When two voices sounded from within, but the door didn't open, even after a long wait, Alex reached for the bell and rang it again.

After a full minute, the wide white door in front of us swung open. I recognized the teen girl who answered immediately. She was almost as young as Amber, but her blonde hair, which had been curled and half tied back an hour ago, had now been straightened with a flat iron, and she wore a thick layer of eyeliner she hadn't worn earlier.

Lacey Banks, sister of the bride.

Instead of the pink bridesmaid dress, she had changed into a black mini dress that looked both too short and too tight for her frame as it buckled around her stomach.

"My parents are still at the hospital," she said in a bored voice before Alex could open his mouth, as if she'd just said the same thing to twenty other people. The girl forced a fake smile.

"Oh, I see." Alex pulled out a business card and passed it over. "Can you please have them call me as soon as they get in? I'm sure my partner has located them at the hospital, but just in case he missed them."

Lacey took the card, but shrugged noncommittedly.

"And you are...?" Alex asked. It was exactly what I would have started with if someone seemed unhelpful in a murder investigation. While Alex had interviewed me, I had told him about Lacey and the way Candi had snapped at her as she'd fixed her sister's hair. I hoped Alex had put together that this was the same person, but he had conducted several interviews and taken copious notes today.

I hadn't wanted to consider the possibility that Lacey could have killed her own sister, but looking at her detached attitude now, I had to assume she either hadn't heard about her sister's death yet, or she was responsible for it.

"Lacey. Lacey Banks," she said. I waited for her to spell it out like she had for the newspaper photographer, but she didn't bother for Alex.

"And you're Candi's sister?" Alex confirmed.

Lacey scrunched up her face as if it angered her to still be talking to him. "Yes, and if you want to talk to somebody about what happened, you should talk to Troy Offenbach. He was right there fighting with her like he always used to when it happened." She started to close the door, but Alex intercepted the movement with a hand on the door.

"Wait, are you saying she knew Mr. Offenbach?" I asked, something about this suddenly seeming too coincidental.

Lacey rolled her eyes and said, "Uh, yeah," in a way that might as well have been duh. "Back when she pretended she had some kind of halo."

I wanted to know more about this because had loud and angry Candi and the staunch church treasurer been a couple?

"And does a Mr. Hector Banks live here?" Alex tried to get a vantage point inside the house over her shoulder, but she crossed her arms and shifted into his view. "Or do you know where I might find him?"

"He doesn't live here." Again, she tried to close the door on us. This time I said something to stop her.

"I'm sorry about everything that happened at the park today," I said, purposely keeping it vague in the event that she hadn't heard the tragic news about her sister yet. "And we at the Honeysuckle Grove Community Church wanted to offer you some of the food from our picnic today, if it would be helpful." I held out the casserole in my hands.

In less than a second, I knew Lacey's answer. Her face screwed up so tight I thought she might get a cramp. "You want to leave your leftovers here?"

"No, I—they weren't even touched. We couldn't go ahead with the picnic, so..." I trailed off when she shut the door in our faces.

I followed behind Alex toward our vehicles, a bit stunned. "You're not going to ask her anything else?"

Alex shook his head as he reached for his door handle. "It's Steve's case. If he wants to handle the questioning in a certain way, that's up to him. I was only told to see if the parents or Hector Banks were here, and I don't want to get anything wrong."

I knew Alex had to follow protocol if he ever wanted to advance within the department, but it frustrated me to no end that he couldn't follow his gut and press this young girl for some answers.

"Do you know Troy Offenbach?" Alex asked me.

"Not really. He's the church treasurer," I said, even though I was quite certain Alex knew that much. "I didn't know he knew Candi, though. I mean, Candi acted like she blamed Troy for the double-booking right away, but I figured that was because her wedding planner had told her it had been the church treasurer's fault." I thought back to make sure this was true. "Strange, though, if they did know each other, and if they seemed to have had a contentious past, that they both booked the park on the same day. And on the day she died."

"Strange indeed," Alex said. A gleam ignited his green eyes. I got that familiar feeling like we were on a case together again. "I'm headed to the church next. Feel like following? I've been working Sundays for as long as I can remember, so you probably know the staff and members better than I do."

I wasn't sure about that, as I'd only been to church once since Cooper died, but if this was an invitation to help—not to mention find out more about what really happened this morning—I wasn't about to say no.

☐

# CHAPTER SIX

On the drive to the church, I pieced together the little bit of information I knew.

One. It sounded as though Candi's death was the result of a needle someone had purposely stuck into her back. I doubted it could have hit a nerve that killed her. Blood loss couldn't have been the cause, or there would have been a lot of blood on the grass where she'd collapsed. That led me to believe there'd been some kind of poison on the needle. A poison that acted like some kind of allergen, I thought, recalling the hives on her hands.

Two. Troy Offenbach had some kind of a contentious past with Candi, and they'd been arguing right before she died.

Three. There hadn't seemed to have been much love between the Banks sisters, and Lacey had been fiddling with Candi's hair shortly before she died.

Four. And while I had nothing concrete against Drunk Uncle Hector Banks, he was still on my radar if Mrs. Winters had mentioned him, and Alex had been instructed to track him down. I looked forward to finding what had been missing from the church supplies.

I'd always had a lot of respect for Cooper and his ability to piece together murder mystery novels, but maybe I wasn't so bad at it myself. Then again, Cooper always used to say, "It's never the most obvious culprit."

Besides, this was real life, not some carefully-crafted Cooper Beck novel.

On the drive over, I considered what we could ask Troy Offenbach. It seemed Alex might not be willing to ask him anything of consequence, but that didn't mean I had to keep quiet. Maybe I could help get Alex some pertinent answers and, without him, even breaking protocol.

30

First, I'd certainly ask him how long he'd known Candi Banks. Next, if he had known that Candi had planned to get married at Bateman Park today.

I had worried the church might be deserted on a Sunday afternoon, but as I pulled into the parking lot behind Alex, there were a couple of other cars in the lot. One was Pastor Jeff's silver sedan. I hoped the small green car belonged to Troy Offenbach.

As I walked alongside Alex from the church parking lot, I listed off my theories. When I got to Lacey Banks' name, I reminded him, "Candi snapped at Lacey several times right before she collapsed because Lacey had been trying to fix Candi's hair. Candi was angry and acted really disrespectful toward her sister. Plus, why isn't she at the hospital? Do you think her parents have even told her about Candi's death yet?"

Alex twisted his lips as he thought this over. "Fixed her hair from the back?" he finally asked. I nodded. "And you said the two of them weren't getting along very well?"

I shook my head. "Even if you can't conduct the interview, you can deliver all the relevant information to Detective Reinhart before he goes there himself."

"You're right." Alex nodded and nudged my shoulder in what I thought was a thank-you. "I can definitely do that."

Unfortunately, Troy Offenbach wasn't at the church. When we asked for him in the church office, Penny Lismore told us, "I think he went home for the day. He was quite upset about everything that happened at the park."

I glanced at Alex. I supposed any of us could have been so upset by being in close proximity to such a huge commotion that we'd want to take the rest of the day at home, but it certainly seemed to confirm what I'd taken from Lacey's comments: Troy and Candi had some kind of significant history.

Penny was busy sorting through the carnival game pieces and not at her desk, but she didn't seem rattled enough to go home for the day. I looked around for the blue bins, but they hadn't been brought into the office. "Do you happen to know if Troy knew the bride, Candi Banks, from before today at the park?" I asked.

Penny shrugged. Her usual bubbly personality had dissolved in the last couple of hours. "I can't say Troy and I have ever had much in the way of personal conversations."

Alex asked, "Can I please get a contact phone number and address for Troy Offenbach?"

Penny looked up at Alex, and her mouth formed an O for a brief second, as if she hadn't noticed his police uniform until just this second.

"Um, of course, officer," she said.

Penny hurried to her desk a few feet away and jiggled her computer mouse to bring her screen to life. A few seconds later, she had scrawled a phone number and address onto a sticky note. She passed it across the front counter to Alex.

"And is your pastor in?" Alex asked. I had no idea what he planned to ask Pastor Jeff that the detectives hadn't already asked him, but I was just glad he had let me tag along this far. I could already tell this would be one of those situations where I wouldn't be able to think of anything else until we had some answers about what actually happened to Candi Banks.

"He's somewhere in the building." Penny pointed out the office door and toward the worship center. "The twins are here, and last I saw, Sasha was watching them, but you might find them all down near the children's ministry wing."

I'd never ventured down to where the children's ministries took place, but I said, "Come on, I'll show you the way," and led in the direction of the worship center as though I had. "What do you want to ask Pastor Jeff?" I murmured to Alex as we made our way through the giant church lobby. The high ceilings made it feel as though we should be extra quiet.

Alex shrugged. "I got the impression Penny doesn't know Troy well. I figured the pastor probably knows him at least a little better."

That made sense.

At the outside doors to the church lobby, a dozen blue Rubbermaid bins had been stacked. I pointed. "These must be the supplies from the church picnic." Alex headed straight for them, clearly understanding that I was referring to Uncle Hector's covert pilfering. "It was a big blue bin," I added.

Most of the blue bins were only a foot in height. All the taller bins were a light gray—except for one. Alex headed straight for that one and pulled off the three light gray ones that had been stacked on top.

Alex pulled a pair of blue latex gloves from his pocket and slid them on before lifting off the Rubbermaid's lid. He didn't have to dig far before uncovering what Uncle Hector must have been digging for. Or come to think of it, he probably hadn't been digging to find anything. More likely, he'd been digging to stash something. Alex pulled out a quarter-full bottle of whiskey and held it up for me to see.

"I doubt the church staff brought that along," I said with a raised eyebrow.

Alex nodded. "I'll double-check with Pastor Jeff and then pass this along to Detective Reinhart."

On top of one of the Rubbermaid bins, I saw a roll of black garbage bags. I grabbed one and offered it to Alex, motioning to the bottle.

He smiled with one side of his mouth, the way that always reminded me of my seventh-grade crush. "You don't think I should barrel in there with a half-full bottle of whiskey, spouting questions?"

I suppressed my own smile. "I don't think it would be your best tactic, Detective Martinez." It was a title he hadn't been given yet, but he'd earned it as far as I was concerned.

He seemed to appreciate my confidence, but said, "Actually, I'm going to take the whole bin as evidence. They may want to fingerprint it."

He followed me toward the children's ministry wing. As I opened the glass door at the far end of the lobby, I knew I had the right place. Boyish laughter echoed down the hallway. I followed the sounds and told Alex, "Jeff and Emily have twin boys. I think they're six or seven."

We rounded the corner into a wide-open playroom. Bright red bins of toys lined the edges of the room. Ms. Mills and Emily sat on kiddie chairs in the middle of the room, a can of disinfectant wipes between them on a table and the bin of Nerf guns in front of them. One by one, they were wiping down all of the guns—or at least all of the guns not in the hands of Jeff and Emily's twin boys.

The boys had a gun in each hand. They ducked behind standing easels and chalkboards so they could peek around and shoot at each other.

Pastor Jeff was nowhere in sight, but Emily and Ms. Mills were talking in hushed tones about "the awful situation" and "what the family must be going through," and so my best guess was that they were rehashing everything that had happened at the park.

"Any idea where Pastor Jeff is?" I asked. Alex placed the blue bin down, just inside the room.

Emily and Ms. Mills looked up at us. Emily did a once-over of Alex's uniform and stood quickly. "I can go find him."

"It's not urgent," Alex told her, as her voice seemed to hold some sudden tension. "I'd just like to have a word before I leave."

Emily hurried out of the room, no less anxious. Ms. Mills continued cleaning the Nerf guns, and I figured the least I could do was help while we waited. I took a seat in Emily's warm kiddie chair and helped myself to a disinfectant wipe. "How long have you worked for the church?" I asked Ms. Mills as I picked up my first Nerf gun and started wiping.

"Oh, I just volunteer," she said. "Only for the last few months, since Mrs. Latham moved away."

"Mrs. Latham used to run the children's ministry?" I confirmed. Ms. Mills nodded. "So you probably don't know our church treasurer very well."

"Troy? No, not really. It's a big church and I don't usually come in during the week. I'm getting to know everyone in the congregation with kids, though. One day they'll likely be in my class, if they haven't been already, but I don't think Troy has a family yet."

I nodded. Troy did look a little young to have a family. One of the

Hawthorne twins peeked around an easel just then and fired a Nerf bullet right at Alex's chest. He slapped a hand at it melodramatically, let out an "Owww," started to fall, and then at the last second swiped up his own Nerf gun from the floor and fired back. I bit back a smile at seeing the little kid in him.

Alex and the twins were still chasing each other around the big open room and shooting at one another when Emily returned with Pastor Jeff. He cleared his throat, taking everyone's attention except for the twins, who easily ignored their dad and kept playing, no matter how somber his countenance today.

"Oh, Pastor Jeff. Yes." Alex straightened his short-sleeve black police shirt, trying to match the pastor's serious nature. "I stopped by to speak with Troy Offenbach, but I understand he's gone home for the day?"

Pastor Jeff nodded, and when he looked at the floor, his head turned to a shake, as though remembering all that had transpired that afternoon. "He was quite shaken up after the ambulance left the park."

"Oh, he left straight from the park? He didn't come back here?" Alex asked. Pastor Jeff shook his head. "Did he know Candi Banks?"

Pastor Jeff's head snapped up. "Not that I'm aware of. Why?"

"We heard their discussion at the park became heated quickly." Alex tapped a finger on the edge of the Nerf gun in his hand. I suspected he was nervous, either because of interviewing a church pastor or because he had found himself helping in a possible murder investigation. Maybe both.

Pastor Jeff nodded, running a hand through his already messy hair. "She was very upset when she arrived and saw our church congregation scattered across the lawn. Plus, Troy tends to get defensive when he feels any blame has turned on him." Sadness and regret leaked out in the pastor's every word.

"Candi's sister, Lacey Banks, indicated that Candi and Troy had a history of some sort," Alex went on. "You don't know anything about that?"

Pastor Jeff tilted his head, looking genuinely confused. "I'm afraid I don't. Though, to be honest, I haven't spoken to Troy much about personal relationships during the year and a half he's worked part-time for the church. I'm afraid I don't always get as much time as I'd like to discuss our staff's personal lives."

Relationship. My mind hadn't jumped to a full-fledged relationship between the two, but I wondered if it could be true. I'd thought of Troy as a fair bit older than Candi, due to his stoic nature, but maybe I was wrong. And if that was the case, could Troy have still held anger or resentment toward Candi, so much so that he might want her dead on her wedding day?

I thought again of Lacey and her snide comment, urging us to go after Troy. Could there have been sisterly jealousy at play, too? The prettier, skinnier sister was getting married, while her old flame still felt enough passion to enter into a heated argument with her. All this happened while Lacey was being publicly slapped away.

Lost in thought, I missed any other questions Alex asked as he moved on to questioning Emily and Ms. Mills.

Suddenly, Ms. Mills shouted at one of the boys, taking all of our attention. "Bryce! Where did you get that? Bring that here. That's not one of ours!"

We all looked to the little blond boy who held a different-looking kind of plastic gun. This one was purple, one solid color, with none of the fluorescent orange or green trim of the others.

"Come get it!" Bryce said to Ms. Mills and then took off behind a rolling chalkboard.

"Bryce!" Pastor Jeff said. "When Ms. Mills tells you to do something, you do it. Now bring that gun here, right this second!"

But I suspected the boys were feeling the exhaustion of the day, too, because Bryce didn't listen. He and his brother snickered from behind the same chalkboard. A second later, Bryce peered around the edge of the chalkboard, held up the purple gun, aimed it straight at his dad, and fired.

But when the fluorescent yellow Nerf bullet launched from the gun, it simply fell at Bryce's feet. It didn't occur to us until a second later, when Pastor Jeff gasped, that something else had launched full-speed out of the toy gun. And only a moment after that, a bright red splotch of blood seeped around a tiny needle, stuck into Pastor Jeff's lavender shirt.

We all took in a collective gasp.

# CHAPTER SEVEN

Alex and I arrived at the hospital right behind the ambulance. After his son shot him with the needle, Pastor Jeff had quickly yanked it out of his chest and immediately started gasping for air. This time, I hadn't wasted a second calling 911, and because the church was located so close to the hospital, both on the east side of Honeysuckle Grove, Pastor Jeff was still coherent when it arrived.

Tears streaked Emily's face when we found her in the emergency room waiting area.

"Ms. Mills is staying at the church to watch the boys," I told her the moment we found her. Alex had spent an extra minute bagging the toy gun and the needle before we left.

Emily nodded and said between sobs, "They wouldn't let me go in with him, but he couldn't even talk!"

Alex headed toward a set of double doors that read AUTHORIZED PERSONNEL ONLY. "Let me see what I can find out."

Apparently, it paid to have a cop around.

I stood hugging Emily in the ER waiting room for the next several long minutes, assuring her that everything would be okay and that we'd caught it in time.

"But I don't understand." She sniffled. "Why would someone load needles into a toy gun?" Emily Hawthorne was a small, frail lady in her late thirties. She, like her husband, didn't seem to have an untrusting bone in her body. She shook her head in disbelief over the situation as she continued to cry against my shoulder.

What felt like hours later, Alex reappeared through the emergency room doors. He strode straight for us, his gaze squarely on Emily, and my breath caught in my throat.

He took both her hands in his. "He's going to be okay." His words were gentle, but firm.

I let out a gust of air. I wondered how many times in Alex's line of work he'd had to break the news to families that their loved ones would not be okay.

"They have him breathing on a ventilator right now, but the doctor seemed to have some idea of what may have inhibited his breathing and he's trying something now to combat it."

"Was it poison?" The moment the question left my mouth, I realized I shouldn't be asking this in front of Pastor Jeff's wife.

But Alex kept his warm eyes right on Emily and simply said, "We should know more soon."

Still swatting myself for my misstep, I offered, "Hey, why don't I go and get us some coffee?"

They were both quick to take me up on it.

I wove my way through hallways to get to the café in the main hospital lobby, which hopefully promised a better cup than the ER vending machines. The lineup was long, but I didn't care. It gave me time to mentally slap myself again for putting extra worry on Emily's mind.

A tray filled with three coffees in hand, along with a baggie of creamers and sugar, I made my way back through the maze of sterile white hallways toward the ER. As I rounded my second corner, though, I saw a flash of a navy suit with sandy Ken-like coiffed hair. Steve Reinhart was talking with a well-dressed couple, and my knee-jerk reaction was to back up and stay hidden.

Detective Reinhart's baritone voice asked, "And you say she had only known the groom for three months?"

I leaned in closer to the corner, hoping I could catch the conversation. Although I'd only gotten a quick glance, from the looks of things, he was still interviewing Mr. and Mrs. Banks.

"I already explained this to the other officer," Mrs. Banks said. "She loved David Albright with all her heart." She didn't sound as emotional as she had been at the park. Perhaps she was all cried out.

"I thought it was early to get married," Mr. Banks elaborated. "But they were both so eager. David actually proposed after they'd only been dating a couple of weeks. We convinced Candi to at least wait until the end of the summer, so she'd have the wedding she always dreamed of." Mr. Banks choked on the last few words, which made them hard to decipher.

"All right, well, thank you for telling me more about them, and we will certainly speak with the Albrights as well." Detective Reinhart rustled a paper. "And you say I can catch up with your daughter, Laccy, at your house?"

"Can't you leave Lacey for today?" Mrs. Banks asked. "She was here when they told us Candi died, and she'll be an awful mess about losing her sister."

An awful mess? That certainly wasn't what I remembered of Lacey Banks when she'd answered her door in the black mini dress with her hair perfectly straightened. And if what Mrs. Banks was saying was true, Lacey had heard about her sister's death by that time.

"One more question before I go," Detective Reinhart said.

I wondered if this would be about Troy Offenbach and leaned even closer to try and hear every word.

"Is there anyone you know of who would have wanted to bring harm to your daughter?"

A pause—a long one—and then Mr. Banks said, "What are you implying, officer?"

Detective Reinhart cleared his throat. "Nothing for now," he said in the cool, collected voice of someone who had been interviewing prospective witnesses for years. "At this point, we're looking at all angles to get a full picture of this investigation. They're all standard questions after a death that has occurred in a public space."

His words sounded smooth and believable. I wondered how soon he would have to inform Candi's parents that someone had killed her purposely today.

After a longer silence, finally Detective Reinhart nudged. "Did Candi have any enemies, anyone who she didn't get along with perhaps?"

This time Mrs. Banks answered quickly, her voice indignant. "My Candi had a strong personality, and her wedding day had been especially stressful due to the double-booking. She wasn't her best self, so if you're implying she hadn't been kind to someone—"

"I can assure you, Mrs. Banks, I am not implying anything, certainly not about your daughter's character. I'm speaking here of others' characters. Now, you already told me about Troy Offenbach and his argument with her. But was there anyone else?"

I was annoyed at myself for taking so long in the coffee lineup. If I'd been back here sooner, I might have heard the conversation about Troy Offenbach. There were a few seconds of murmuring I couldn't make out, and then Mr. Banks came back with, "Well, those Albrights never cared for Candi, if you ask me. With their natural food choices and making every piece of clothing from hemp or some such thing, I always got the impression they thought of her as superficial because she liked the odd hamburger and enjoyed fashion." He harrumphed to punctuate the statement.

A note page rustled, and then Detective Reinhart confirmed, "That's Brock and Katrina Albright you're talking about? The groom's parents?"

"That's right," Mrs. Banks said. "If you ask us, David was defying his parents by marrying Candi. Might have even been why the boy had been pushing for such a quick wedding."

Or perhaps to get a piece of the Banks' fortune.

"Right. Okay," Detective Reinhart went on. "I'll certainly be interviewing them as well, but what about a Mr. Hector Banks? I heard there was some contention between him and Candi at the park?"

"Hector?" Mr. Banks laughed like the suggestion was ludicrous, but it sounded strained. "Candi's never had an issue with my younger brother. The Banks all get along just fine." He said the words as though there hadn't been at least twenty witnesses who could attest to the opposite.

"All the same," Detective Reinhart went on, undeterred. "Do you know how I can get a hold of Hector? He left the park before my team could speak with him. We're just tying up some loose ends."

"Detective, we'd really like to get back to our Candi before they take her away." Mrs. Banks sniffled, and for the first time, her voice sounded broken.

Detective Reinhart kept his calm. "Absolutely, Mrs. Banks. Just tell me where I can find Hector, and I'll be on my way. If he's your younger brother, you must have an address for him?"

A pause, and then Mr. Banks spoke. "Oh. Yeah. Sure." Mr. Banks rattled off an address.

I quickly placed my tray of coffees on the floor so I could pull out my phone and type in the address.

As I picked up the coffees again, Detective Reinhart thanked the Banks and said goodbye. He was so fast about it, he almost barreled right into me as he rounded the corner away from them.

☐

# CHAPTER EIGHT

"Oh. Um. Hey! Detective Reinhart!" I said, like the smooth-talker I was. His easy smile and warm steadying hand on my arm made me momentarily lose my voice, but I did my best to coax a swallow and then finally some words. "I'm so glad to see you! Alex is here, and he has to speak with you immediately. Come on, this way!"

I led him in the other direction, and once I could see that the Banks were gone, and as soon as I'd calmed my racing heart, I told him more. "Pastor Jeff was just accidentally shot with one of those same tiny needles at the church. It was from a toy gun found within the children's ministry supplies." I held myself back from calling it the "murder weapon" even though it took serious effort to do so. "They have him on a ventilator while they're trying to counteract whatever went into his bloodstream."

"They're not using epinephrine, are they?" Detective Reinhart's sandy eyebrows pulled together when he turned to me.

"I don't think so. I only heard about the ventilator."

I studied him from the side. My first glance was at his ring finger, which was bare. Then I looked up to his face and wondered how long he had worked as a detective—whether Captain Corbett had promoted him, or if he'd found his way into the ranks before the crotchety police captain took over a half dozen years ago. He didn't look much older than Alex. Maybe thirty.

He caught me looking, and I quickly looked away and picked up my pace.

Detective Reinhart was clearly still business-minded. "I hope not because the doctor who treated Candi suggested the EpiPen may have delivered the poison into her lungs faster. We won't know for sure, of course, until we hear from the medical examiner."

I kept pace beside Detective Reinhart in silence as the seriousness of this hit me. Not only had Detective Reinhart confirmed that Pastor Jeff could have died—still could die—he had also just confirmed that it was, indeed, poison that killed Candi Banks, and not some freak accident with some sort of allergen.

Not only that, but if it was poison, it meant beyond any doubt that Candi's death had been intentional. I was quite certain little Bryce Hawthorne hadn't been the mastermind behind the murder of Candi Banks, and he certainly hadn't meant to hurt his dad.

So then who might have attended Candi's wedding or the church picnic to kill her?

My mind kept returning to three people: Troy Offenbach, who had past contention with Candi, had double-booked the park, and most certainly had access to the children's ministry supplies and toy guns. Then there was Lacey Banks, whose emotions over her sister seemed erratic and jealous at best, and was most certainly the closest person to Candi's shoulder right before the poisoning occurred. And I couldn't forget Uncle Hector, who had been drunk and sneaking into the church supplies only moments before Candi had collapsed. The police were clearly interested in him for a reason. Perhaps his whiskey bottle hadn't been the only item he'd been stashing. What if he had been disposing of a purple toy gun?

Detective Reinhart spoke to Alex a mile a minute as soon as he came into view. "Tell me they didn't give the pastor any epinephrine. It may make his condition much worse."

Alex shook his head. "Dr. Khumalo already had a suspicion about possible interactions, and in fact, the pastor is now breathing on his own. They let his wife, Emily, go in."

I looked around, and sure enough, Emily was no longer near any of the waiting room chairs.

"The administering doctor studied in South Africa," Alex went on. "He said the hyperpigmentation that developed on Jeff Hawthorne's chest and back, along with the anaphylactic symptoms, suggested a plant poisoning he had dealt with before."

"Right," Detective Reinhart said. "That's the same doctor who treated Candi and indicated her condition had worsened with the epinephrine."

"Dr. Khumalo knew of a nonthreatening antidote from his days in South Africa," Alex said. "It had been too late for Candi, as her lungs had caused brain hypoxia, but not for Jeff Hawthorne."

I recognized the term brain hypoxia from when I'd helped Cooper with book research, but I couldn't for the life of me remember what it meant. I'd have to look that up in Cooper's medical encyclopedia when I got home.

"They plan to keep him overnight to ensure the plant compound clears his system," Alex said.

What I understood most about Alex and Detective Reinhart's spiel was that Pastor Jeff was likely going to be okay.

Detective Reinhart seemed to have forgotten about my presence and went on to relay his own progress. "They're doing an autopsy on Candi Banks. I'll request they also send a blood sample from Jeff Hawthorne to the lab. I suspect we'll find traces of the same toxin in both of their blood. I don't understand why administering an EpiPen exasperated the problem, but I'm sure we'll find it in their report." After pondering this for a few seconds, he changed topics. "I also interviewed her parents. They confirmed Candi had dated Troy Offenbach for a short time in the spring. She broke up with him when she met David Albright, the groom from this afternoon."

So Candi and Troy had been dating. I reset my brain to try and picture them together. Troy had worked at the church for a year and a half, and Candi, with her brash nature—I just couldn't picture her at church, certainly not at Honeysuckle Grove Community Church.

Detective Reinhart went on about David Albright. "Apparently, the two were madly in love. It was a whirlwind romance, and David proposed within two weeks, but the Bankses encouraged them to wait to marry until at least the end of summer. I'm headed to interview him next. I also have an address for Hector Banks. I planned to head there afterward. Care to join me?"

I wasn't sure where Detective Reinhart's regular partner was, but this sort of investigative work could be a big deal for Alex. As he glanced over at me, I wanted to help in any way I could. "I'll talk to you later," I said to Alex, taking a step away.

Silence followed where Detective Reinhart and Alex looked at each other. It seemed to have just occurred to them that I had been listening to all of their updates.

I quickly took another step back from them, as if I could somehow erase my presence and all the missteps I'd made today. Alex furrowed his brow, but thankfully, neither of them pressed me on why I thought eavesdropping on a police investigation was okay.

Detective Reinhart cleared his throat. "Thank you for all of your help today, Mrs. Beck."

As they turned and left, I couldn't tell whether or not his comment had been sarcastic or simply a dismissal.

☐

# CHAPTER NINE

I felt lonely all the way home, but just inside my front door, I at least gained some feline camaraderie.

Hunch hadn't waited at the door for me since I'd been on the case for the Montrose murder, but somehow, he intuitively knew I had involved myself in an investigation again, and he had dragged his cast all the way from the living room to the front door to reward me with his presence for it.

I had a couple of trips yet to make from the Jeep, hauling in the coolers of leftover food from the picnic, but Hunch waited patiently, sniffing each one as though he'd understand all of the days' proceedings from scent alone.

I, in turn, rewarded his patience with one heck of a story. I started at the beginning and told him everything. By the time I'd described all that happened at the park in detail, as well as the accidental poisoning of Pastor Jeff, Hunch was rubbing his head up against my calf. If I wanted a little affection, apparently all I had to do was involve myself in the latest Honeysuckle Grove murder investigation.

After the day I'd had, plus hauling in the leftover potluck food and squeezing every bit of it into the fridge, I slumped into the nearest kitchen chair, exhausted, to tell him the rest.

Hunch mewled, looking up at me as if he wanted onto my lap. This was new. I was tempted to peek outside and see if the sky was lit up with aliens or flying pigs.

Carefully, I lifted him and then continued to stroke the soft fur on his head. He met my eyes and raised his eye whiskers.

Oh. Right. My cat didn't want to cuddle. He wanted to discuss the case.

"All I can tell you is that it was definitely a poisoned needle that killed

Candi Banks, and another that injured Pastor Jeff. More like a dart, I suppose, as it was rigged to shoot out of a toy gun. Alex is on the case this time, practically officially, so don't worry. He'll figure it out."

I knew before the words were out of my mouth that this answer wouldn't be good enough for Hunch. He growled and dug his front claws into my thigh.

"Ow! Stop! Okay!" As the pain hit me and I was desperate for it to stop, I realized I could at least speculate about a few more details, so Hunch wouldn't feel like I was simply backing away from investigating. Even if I was doing my best to do just that. "As far as I can tell, there are three main suspects: Troy Offenbach, the church treasurer. He was a past boyfriend of Candi's, and apparently, they argued a lot. She dumped him for her groom, David Albright, which must have hurt Troy's ego, if nothing else. He was the one who booked the park, likely knowing Candi was planning a wedding there because it seems like way too much of a coincidence if he didn't. Plus, he had access to all of the church supplies, including the toy guns. That indicates motive and means as far as I'm concerned. He left the picnic before the police could speak to him. Before the incident, Troy had been involved in every aspect of organizing the picnic. I would have expected him to be the last one there, so that spells out avoidance to me."

I reached for one of the madeleines Amber had baked two days ago from the sealable container on my table. "Then there's Candi's sister, Lacey Banks. I'd peg her to have an angry jealous streak—a girl who'd go to almost any length to prove she's as good as her sister and seemed to show absolutely no remorse after she died." I waved a hand. "Anyway, I might have pegged her as our prime suspect because she'd been tinkering with Candi's hair from the back right before she collapsed, and Lacey could have easily inserted a poisoned needle into her shoulder. But that was before we discovered the murder weapon—the toy gun that fired poisoned needle-like darts that I suspect had been aimed at both Candi and Pastor Jeff." I sighed. "Forensics are dusting it for fingerprints, but my guess is that between Pastor Jeff's twin boys, plus Ms. Mills, who grabbed the gun from the kids, there'll be too many prints to decipher anything worthwhile."

Hunch was letting me pet him again and even purred his encouragement, so I went on.

"Then there's Hector Banks, uncle of the bride. Candi clearly hadn't liked him and had just disrespected him in front of a crowd before she collapsed. Plus, he had been digging around in the church's supplies." That was more than likely to stash his whiskey, but I ignored that fact for the moment. "The police are interested in him for some reason." I nibbled my lip at something else that was bothering me. "Then again, I wonder if he would have been too inebriated to have gotten a straight shot into Candi, one she couldn't have simply pulled out on her own." I took a slow breath and let it out as I thought this over. "The police are heading off to question him, clearly thinking he's the prime suspect. My instincts tell me he may have had motive and even opportunity, but not the means because he wasn't sober enough to make an exact shot."

These were the terms Cooper had always used with Hunch, and his ears perked up at them right away.

"So that brings us back to Troy Offenbach, ex-lover and my guess at the prime suspect. Motive and means for sure. Could he have had opportunity in between his arguing with Candi?" I mused aloud. It wasn't as though I had been watching him the whole time. I'd had my attention divided between Ms. Mills and the children, as well as Hector Banks sneaking into the church supplies.

In that moment, Cooper's cat, the one who had never liked me, actually nuzzled the side of his face up against mine. It was the most love and affection I'd received in the last eight and a half months, and I couldn't seem to fight the tears it brought to my eyes.

My phone buzzed from the kitchen table in front of me, thankfully breaking me from the emotion of the moment before Hunch could catch on and roll his little cat eyes at me. He'd never had much patience for sentimentality.

I flipped my phone over to see a new text from Amber.

<Cooking tonight?>

It must've meant her mom was feeling better, or at the very least, her focus was no longer on her daughter. I sighed. I'd love to see Amber, but to be honest, I didn't know if I had the energy to drive across town and pick her up. Of course, I knew better than to let Hunch in on my lame excuse and actually angled my phone away from him in the unlikely event that he could read as well as he seemed to understand spoken English.

But before I could type, as if Amber could read my mind, another text popped up.

<Seth's going out. He can drop me off.>

Seth was Amber's older brother. When I'd first met her, she'd been calling him Danny Jr. after their dad, but after all they'd learned about what their dad had been involved with prior to his death, Amber clearly no longer blamed her brother for going by his middle name of Seth.

<Sure> I typed back, barely taking the time to think about it.

I was too tired to cook, too tired to teach cooking, and there was far too much food in my cluttered fridge already.

However, I'd sooner eat fried worms with gravy than turn down a friend who wanted to come over and keep me company.

# CHAPTER TEN

Amber arrived half an hour later, and it was all I could do not to hug the fifteen-year-old I'd only met three weeks ago. Not only that, but Hunch's allegiance turned on a dime the moment Amber crossed my threshold into my house. He mewled beside her legs in the kitchen until she picked him up and gave him some love. He lapped it up, like he hadn't felt human touch in a year.

Amber looked fresh out of the shower, with less-curly-than-normal damp hair, and a red tank top that read IT'S NOT ME, IT'S YOU.

"How's your mom?" I asked.

Amber shrugged. "Medicated."

I nodded. This was Helen Montrose's approach to grief, which left her two teenage kids mostly fending for themselves. "If you ever need to talk about anything, Amber, you know you don't always have to be strong around me, right?"

Amber shrugged one shoulder, which I thought meant she was too uncomfortable by this subject, but then she said, "Sometimes I have panic attacks, like where I can't breathe."

"Just since your dad died?" I asked. She nodded. "I had them for a while after I lost Cooper. I kept a paper bag with me for months. Have you tried breathing into one? It helps a bit. Or breathing through a straw."

"I'll try that." She looked down at Hunch and continued stroking him. I hated to admit it, but that cranky cat was certainly good for something, or at least someone.

"And you know you can always call me," I added. "Even in the middle of the night."

"So I can talk to your voicemail?" She smirked. She knew I hadn't had a home phone since shortly after Cooper died, but she didn't know how neurotic I still was with my cell phone. I figured it was only fair if I

46

reciprocated in putting myself out there.

"Ever since Cooper died, I can't seem to turn off my phone. I always keep it on, even at night. Even though Cooper died in the middle of the day, I don't know, each night when I get into bed, I put down my phone and think, 'What if something happened to my dad in the night? Or my sister?' Even if you just feel lonely, call me. Okay?"

Amber shrugged, which I was pretty sure meant she was agreeing. But she was done with this soul-bearing conversation. "So that bride is really dead, huh?" she asked, leaning against my kitchen counter. It only occurred to me now how out of the loop Amber was on this. Usually, her quick fifteen-year-old brain kept at least one step ahead of me at every turn. It made me feel strangely uneasy to know I held all the info from today on my own.

"Yeah, not only that, but Pastor Jeff was shot with the same type of needle." Her eyes widened with horror, so I quickly amended, "He's going to be fine. The needle did contain a poison, or what the doctors are calling a 'plant toxin,' but they counteracted it in plenty of time."

"Wait, what?" Amber shook her head as though she had flying insects in her hair. "Somebody shot Pastor Jeff at the park after I left?"

Whoops. I obviously had to backtrack. I waved my hands and said, "No, no, later at the church with the kids and the toys and…"

Amber's horror-stricken face told me I really needed to start at the beginning.

"Okay, listen. Remember when you first arrived at the park and there was an upset between the bride and Troy from the church about a double-booking?"

Amber nodded hesitantly, but at least she was with me now. I led her to two kitchen chairs at the table, opened the cookie container, and went through every detail from the park to the church to the hospital, bit by bit.

Hunch looked just as engaged as he had the last time I'd recounted this story. Except this time, he gave all of his affection to Amber for it.

When I got to the end, about the three suspects I had narrowed it down to, and that the police seemed more interested in Uncle Hector than they did with Troy Offenbach, even though in my opinion, Troy or Lacey were clearly the prime suspects, Amber slumped back into her chair and simply said, "Wow."

"I know, right?" There was only one madeleine left in the cookie container, but all this talk made me want to nibble. I hesitated, knowing I should really leave it for my guest—the person who had baked them, after all. But if I didn't find something to do with my hands soon, I'd be up at the counter cooking off my anxiousness instead. Heaven knew I didn't need any more food. I reached for the cookie.

"What about the Albrights?" Amber asked.

"What's that?" I asked around a mouthful of cookie.

"Troy Offenbach seems too obvious to me. You said the Albrights never liked Candi. I can't remember who said that."

"Mr. and Mrs. Banks," I put in, "but they're both such different families with different affluence. It makes sense if their families aren't exactly besties."

Amber shrugged. "Could be some kind of a family spat, though. I'd look into them before I'd focus on some church treasurer who wasn't hiding his anger and frustration at Candi from anyone that day."

Hmm. What she said made sense. It would be one thing if Troy had gotten so heated and angry that he'd grabbed a rock in the heat of the moment and struck Candi over the head with it or something. But the toy gun, reworked so it could launch toxic needles...that was premeditated. And if Troy had premeditated the murder, why would he have been publicly arguing with Candi only moments before her death? Why would Uncle Hector or Lacey have done that, for that matter? Unless one of them hoped to get caught.

Huh. In all of ten seconds, Amber Montrose had all but exonerated all three of my suspects. Maybe I wasn't so good at this investigative work after all.

"So if it was someone like the Albrights..." Or someone else, entirely, I thought but didn't say. My mind raced through hundreds of people who had flown under my radar at the park Sunday afternoon and who hadn't been cleared by the police. "I suppose I should call Alex and suggest the police look into them."

Hunch growled, which was nothing new, but it seemed by Amber's pursed lips, she didn't think I should hand this suggestion over to the police just yet either.

"You said this Reinhart guy's in charge, right?" Amber asked.

I stupidly felt my cheeks flush at his name, remembering how stupid I'd felt after getting caught eavesdropping on his and Alex's conversation. Amber fiddled with the lid on the cookie container, and I was tempted to apologize for greedily scarfing down the last one. But this conversation was much more important, so I only nodded.

"I don't know if I'm right about the Albrights," Amber said, "and we don't want Alex making bad suggestions if he's trying to win some favor with the local detective squad."

That made a lot of sense. I was glad I had this smart kid in my corner to think of these things. "So what do we do?" I asked.

Amber stood from her chair and paced back and forth in my open kitchen a few times, pondering this. She stopped at the fridge, opened the door wide, and stood in front of it, twisting her lips to the side.

Again, I felt awful for eating the last cookie. I moved behind her to find something I could heat up quickly. Most of the sweets and desserts had been picked up by their church-going owners.

But then Amber asked, "You said the Bankses didn't want any of the food from the picnic?"

I thought back to how offended Lacey Banks had been at even the suggestion. "Nope."

"Well…" Amber looked over her shoulder at me, and the refrigerator light illuminated her face in a way that made her look mischievous. She pulled out a casserole dish and peeked inside. "Maybe the Albrights do."

# CHAPTER ELEVEN

I didn't know if Amber was correct in her suggestions, but with an entire park full of people to investigate, and only two detectives and Alex—who couldn't yet make his own decisions—on the case, I figured anyone we could look into that might slip by the police's immediate notice might help.

Besides, the Bankses and the Albrights couldn't be more different. It wasn't simply a matter of money, either. The Bankses had a superficial consciousness about them, and thinking back to David Albright's mother in her sack-dress and messy braids, she seemed to be the opposite of Mrs. Banks in every way.

After a long discussion about this, and spending some time investigating both families online, Amber spent the night at my place. Her mom had OK'ed it, but one of these days, I suspected Mrs. Montrose would emerge from her fog of grief and want to actually get to know the adult woman who had all but adopted her daughter.

"There's only one Albright in the local directory," Amber said first thing the next morning from the kitchen table, scrolling on her phone.

I finished wiping the counter and came to look over her shoulder. Recognition struck, and I nodded. "That's them, Brock and Katrina Albright. I remember Detective Reinhart mentioning their first names to Alex."

"You're sure?" Amber asked. I nodded.

There had been almost a weekly account of the Banks family in the local paper—everything from the Banks Jewelers locations they owned throughout the state, to Candi's cheerleading accolades from high school two years ago. Last week's online news had spoken of the Banks wedding, but Amber scanned the entire article and didn't see a single instance of the name "Albright."

That got us searching specifically for the Albrights, but they were clearly not newsworthy people. The only instance I could find while googling

"Brock Albright" with "West Virginia" was a building permit from twelve years ago for a free-standing structure.

To be honest, it surprised me that the quiet, keep-to-themselves people were listed in the local phone book, but I was glad to have their address.

Amber stood to check on our casserole in the oven. Even though we had more food in the fridge than two people could eat in a week, we had both decided last night to get up early and make a fresh casserole for the Albrights. This one was vegan and filled with the remainder of fresh vegetables from my fridge. From what Mr. Banks had indicated, the Albrights seemed like a family that lived and ate naturally. When Amber peeked into the oven and saw the vegan cheese sauce bubbling, she turned on the frying pan, ready to crisp up some onions for the top. "Why don't you get ready while I finish this up?"

Sometimes I'd swear Amber was the adult—not to mention the chef—in the house, and I was the teenager. But in an effort to bring the Albrights a wonderfully fresh and warm casserole that might get them talking to us, I followed her instructions and ran up the stairs.

Half an hour later, Amber and I drove to the outskirts of Honeysuckle Grove, following my GPS to a small house that was nestled between two farms. The Albrights' tiny farmhouse sat on a small plot of land, surrounded by a weathered picket fence. Shrubbery was snug up to the right-hand side of the house, while the left side had a large walnut tree, along with about a six-foot-wide "path" of thigh-high grass leading up to a tall fence.

"I wonder if they work on one of the neighboring farms or have some sort of crop on their own out back," I said, surveying the area.

Amber passed me the warm casserole. "Why don't you take it in on your own and ask them? I'll snoop around outside a bit while you have them distracted. See if there's anything out of place."

I nodded, but I was starting to have my doubts about this plan and about the Albrights as serious suspects. This house suited them in every way—from the walnut tree in their front yard to the dreamcatcher hanging over the front porch. They seemed like such simple people who lived a simple life. Sure, they were different from the Bankses, but that didn't make the two families sworn enemies.

Maybe the most we should expect was finding out some intel about who David and Candi spent time with. I hoped we'd even get to speak to David today. He was certainly young enough that he could still live with his parents, and the police had already done their questioning of the groom, so I didn't feel as guilty about looking into him myself.

Still, I had this fresh and warm casserole, constructed specifically for them. The least I could do was deliver it.

Amber and I got out on either side of the Jeep. Amber stayed in a crouch as she moved around the Albright's old beater truck and toward the left side of the house. I took the casserole up the three cement steps to the front door.

The house must have been at least forty years old. The paint looked as though it used to be white, but it was chipped so extensively, it was hard to tell. Even the small patch of lawn in the front yard needed a cut, or more likely a sickle. I wondered what the Albrights spent their time on if they weren't able to keep up on their house and yard.

It seemed the doorbell was broken, so after a long minute of waiting, I knocked. It was Mr. Albright—Brock—who answered. He wore baggy jeans and a plaid short-sleeve shirt. His clothing was worn and looked at least a couple of decades old. His pale forearms and face gave me doubts that he would spend enough time in the sun to work as a farmer.

In his arms, he held a box that was a little bigger than a shoebox. The flaps were folded down over one another, so I couldn't see inside, even when he held it outstretched toward me.

"Mr. Albright?" I asked.

He clued in that the reason I wasn't accepting his outstretched box was because I held a casserole dish in my hands. He looked between the dish and my face several times before pulling the box back toward himself.

Now it was my turn to outstretch the casserole. "Hi!" I said in much too perky and high-pitched of a voice for the reason of my visit. I cleared my throat and dropped my tone. "Um, I'm from Honeysuckle Grove Community Church?" Brock Albright simply furrowed his brow, either not recognizing the name or not understanding why I was bothering him, so I went on. "Our church just felt awful about what happened at your son's wedding yesterday, and we wanted to deliver a casserole." I held the warm dish out another inch toward him.

He pulled the box away and stuffed it under an arm and turned away from me without another word. As he walked away, he called out, "Katrina? The church sent us a casserole."

The lady in braids—Katrina Albright—appeared in the doorway only a moment later. Her blonde braids had loosened and frayed, and I wondered if she hadn't re-braided them since before the wedding yesterday. If not for the yellow collar on her dress, I'd think it was the same beige sack-dress she'd worn to the wedding as well.

"I'm Mallory Beck, from the church that was at the park yesterday," I said, hoping this might make more sense. "We just wanted to do anything we could to make this time easier for everyone involved." I held out the casserole toward her.

Thankfully, Mrs. Albright was quick to don a smile and reach for it. "Oh, isn't that nice." She looked back at the hallway where her husband had disappeared. "That's so nice of them, isn't it, Brock?" she called, but there was no answer. Mrs. Albright accepted the warm casserole from my hands, tilted her head, and said, "Would you like to come in, dear?"

She had to be about forty. Not really old enough that I'd expect her to call me "dear," but I did want to come in.

"Oh, maybe just for a minute," I said.

Katrina Albright lingered, leading me slowly through their entryway to a small living room. There were a dozen photos of a young David along a hearth, each framed in a hand-chiseled frame. Handmade crocheted blankets covered the back of every couch and chair, and the whole place had a homemade feel. Behind the couch, one wall held a large framed painting that looked like it could have been created by a grade-schooler. It was of a family of three—a man and boy with dark hair, and a woman in golden braids. The details were wonky, but not in an abstract sort of way. More like the perspective and depth was attempted by someone not very proficient with a paintbrush.

Katrina sat on the edge of an armchair so I dropped into the couch.

"Is David your only child?" I asked. The more I looked around, the more I saw knickknacks on every surface that looked handmade, and possibly by a child—from the rudimentary metalwork helicopter on the windowsill to the simple wooden shelf on the wall.

"Yes," Katrina said with a beaming smile. "We always wanted more children, but David is what God gave us."

I had never seen the Albrights at Honeysuckle Grove Community Church, which was by far the largest church in town. I wondered if they attended the tiny Seventh Day Adventist Church in town or the Catholic one.

I looked around the room. "Had David already moved in with Candi?" I said her name somberly, as felt natural of the newly deceased.

Katrina's smile didn't decrease any. "Oh, no. Before they were married?" she asked as a rhetorical question. I wasn't sure if I was imagining the edge to her voice. In general, she seemed like such a simple clear-cut lady who wasn't hiding a thing. But maybe there was one thing…

"So he still lives here?" I looked around again, as though David might materialize from somewhere within the small house. He couldn't be much over twenty. It wouldn't be unusual for him to still be living with his parents. Brock hadn't reappeared either, and I wondered where he was hiding, as the house didn't look very large from the outside. I hoped wherever it was, he didn't have a vantage point of Amber sneaking around his backyard.

"Well, not really, not at the moment," Katrina said. She lifted a plate of cookies from the hand-carved coffee table to offer me one. I was a big fan of cookies of any kind and was always curious about other people's recipes.

I helped myself. But after only one bite, I wanted to put it back. The rough texture of it felt and tasted like sawdust.

"Mmm," I said, more in an effort to coax some saliva than to compliment her. "What's in your cookies?"

Katrina beamed and nodded. "Hemp and walnut. All grown right here on our land."

A knock sounded at the front door, and before either Katrina or I could even look in that direction, Brock whisked down the hallway with the same cardboard box and opened it. I could see the hallway, but couldn't quite see him or whoever was on the other side.

A moment later, though, the door closed, and I watched through their front window as Brock walked a young woman about my age who looked a little scruffy in ripped jeans and a black T-shirt back toward the driveway, where a red hatchback was parked. The woman nodded at whatever Brock was telling her as they walked.

I took another bite of my cookie, momentarily forgetting the dryness, and swallowed hard to get it down my throat. At the red car, Brock passed the box to the woman, and she passed him an envelope. If we were somewhere other than nature-ville, I'd swear I was witnessing a drug deal.

Then again, maybe these people ran a grow-op somewhere on their property. I thought of Amber, sneaking around, and willed Brock Albright to keep his focus on his current conversation.

"Another cookie?" Katrina asked, interrupting my thoughts.

That was the last thing I wanted, and so my eyes darted around the room, looking for some way to quickly change the subject. In the corner of the room, I noticed one item that looked out of place from all the homemade knickknacks. It was a bright green lava lamp, definitely store-bought.

"Is that yours?" I asked, pointing. As usual, the words were out of my mouth before I thought of how they might sound. "I mean, it's really pretty." Not much better, considering the cord was dangling nearby, unplugged, not looking all that pretty in its current state.

Katrina sighed. "My mother sends David gifts from England on his birthday each year. I tried to make her understand we preferred homemade items, but that was the closest she seemed to be able to get to the idea." She sighed again.

"So you were mentioning that David doesn't live with you?" I said, fishing. If he'd moved out, why was his lava lamp still here? "What is he, about twenty?"

Katrina's forehead buckled, and she nodded. She was on her third cookie, and I wondered how she swallowed one after another without any water in sight. "He turned eighteen in the spring. He's been moving his things into the new house he planned to share with Candi for weeks. He stayed there last night." She looked down at the floor, and her forehead creased even further.

"It must be awful for him," I said. Eighteen? He was just a kid.

Brock appeared in the entry to the living room and cleared his throat. I hadn't even noticed him return to the house. "We need to water the gardens, sweetheart." His words sounded as though they came through gritted teeth.

Mrs. Albright popped up out of her seat in an instant. "Oh, yes, of course."

It seemed inviting me inside the house had only been a nicety, not one she thought I'd actually accept. I hadn't seen much in the way of kept gardens in the front yard. Amber would know by now if they had one in the back, and if there was anything interesting in their yard.

"Oh. Well. I should be going anyway," I said. An idea came to me, and I said it aloud before I could rethink it. "If David's living at his new place, perhaps I could get the address and deliver a meal to him as well?"

"You told her David wasn't living here?" Brock narrowed his eyes at his wife.

Katrina glanced at her husband, but she responded to me rather than to him. "Oh, that's so nice of you." She wore another smile, but this one looked less genuine. "Why don't you just drop it off here? David should be back soon."

I nibbled the inside of my cheek. Was I just imagining it, or was she trying to keep me from seeing her son? But I couldn't think of any way of pushing the matter, so I stood and headed for the door.

"Yes, okay. I'll do that. I hope you enjoy this one." I didn't know what else to say, and when I got to the door, I saw Amber in the front seat of the Jeep where I'd parked along the road. She was on her phone.

"Oh, I'm sure we will, dear," Katrina said.

"Did you take one to the Bankses yet?" Brock's feelings toward the family were quite clear in his gruff tone as he pronounced their name.

I tilted my head, willing to feed this fire at least a little before I left. "Oh, believe me, I tried. They didn't want any part of what they thought was my charity." I sighed as I watched Brock and Katrina's reaction carefully. "I tried to make them understand that I just wanted to make things easier on them, but..." I looked down and shook my head.

Brock's face deepened into a scowl. "Shoulda probably delivered it to Hector Banks. Told him it was a celebratory casserole."

I put a hand to my chest and faked shock, even though his feelings about the Banks uncle didn't really surprise me. "Oh? Did Hector Banks dislike Candi?"

Brock Albright snickered, and his nostrils flared. "That guy only likes two things—his whiskey and his guns."

55

Brock didn't give me a chance to ask him about this. He disappeared somewhere inside the house again, apparently satisfied that I was leaving.

I pasted on a smile, thanked Katrina for the cookie, and said goodbye. At least I had an invitation to come back, if need be.

☐

# CHAPTER TWELVE

Amber hung up the phone as I got into the Jeep.

"Who were you calling?" I asked as I put the Jeep in drive and headed toward town.

"The municipal office," she said. "Maybe you were right about Troy Offenbach being our prime suspect. Maybe I was looking for something more complicated that wasn't there."

"Why? What did you find out?"

She scrolled through something on her phone as she spoke. "Troy was definitely the person who booked the church picnic at the park, but the lady at the municipal office said he specifically asked for only one shelter, even though the church had always rented both shelters for every picnic they'd had in the past."

I was about to interrupt, to say that didn't automatically make him a murderer, but she had more to tell me.

"The other strange part was that he insisted the bill for the shelter and park rental get mailed to him directly, and not to the church."

"Huh." What amazed me more than this new information was how quickly my allegiance or blame for someone could flip-flop back and forth. But this certainly was something to look into. "I should text Alex and see if the police have tracked Troy down at home to question him."

"You're going to have to," Amber said, clicking off her phone and looking at me. "There are no Offenbachs listed in the online directory, and Penny at the church wouldn't give me his number or address."

"He's unlisted?" Something my dad had said every time we moved to a new town when I was growing up was that people who had nothing to hide listed themselves in the local phone book. I'd thought it was a waste of time for us, as we often didn't end up staying long in each town, but he always insisted. Again, though, I had to remind myself that this wasn't actually proof of guilt. "Anything else?" I asked. I was trying to train myself to get all the facts before convincing myself of my wild theories.

"Nah. I snuck around the back of the Albright's farmhouse, but their entire backyard is taken up by a gigantic greenhouse or something—except it's covered in black plastic."

Maybe I wasn't so far off in my grow-op theory. Still, it certainly didn't make the Albrights murderers. "Brock didn't see you when he went down the driveway with that woman?" I asked.

She shook her head. "No, but funny enough, I'd been trying to figure out a way to get over the tall fence to their backyard because it was locked. Right after the woman drove away, Brock headed straight for the back fence. I had to scramble to get behind a tree so he didn't see me."

My eyes widened. I wondered what a man like Brock might have done if he'd found Amber snooping around, especially if he kept an illegal grow-op back there.

But Amber went on like this was all no big deal. "He was only back there for a minute, but it was long enough for me to jam my gum into the lock so it wouldn't click all the way shut when he came back through it. As soon as he went back into the house, I went for a quick look, but the greenhouse was locked, too." She shrugged. "They could be growing marijuana or coca plants for cocaine, for all we know, but that still wouldn't make them murderers." Exactly my hypothesis. "Anything interesting inside their house?"

"It could have definitely been a drug deal with the red car. None of the neighboring farms would be keeping an eye from their distance away. I doubt he would be on the police's radar way out here in farmland. But like you say, that wouldn't make them murderers." I turned onto Amber's street. "Mr. Albright barely said two words to me until I was leaving, when he told me Hector Banks only liked two things: his whiskey and his guns."

"Guns?" Amber raised her eyebrows. "Even though it was a toy gun, what kind of person would take the time to restructure one to shoot poisoned darts?" She didn't leave me time to answer. "We should check and see if Alex interviewed Hector Banks yet."

I nodded. It was what I planned to do as soon as I got home. "Katrina Albright was nice enough. David is an only child and seems like their pride and joy. Apparently, he's been staying at the house he'd planned to move into with Candi, but they wouldn't tell me where that was."

"So they were evasive?" Amber asked.

"I guess. Mostly I think Brock Albright just wanted me out of their house. He said something about needing to water the plants, so that makes sense if they have some kind of extensive greenhouse in the backyard."

"None of it makes sense if you ask me," Amber said as I pulled up to her house. When we'd been sneaking around together, investigating her dad's murder, I'd always dropped her off and picked her up down the street at the corner. Something about pulling right into her driveway still felt wrong, but I took a deep breath and reminded myself I wasn't doing anything underhanded here.

But then Amber said, "I'll hang out here for a bit, let Mom know I'm around, then I'll sneak out again later. In the meantime, why don't you get the story about Hector Banks from Alex? Also, you should get Troy Offenbach's address out of him."

Sometimes I forgot that Amber was only fifteen. Other times, like now, when she talked about sneaking out of her house and talking a police officer into giving up info about a murder suspect, it was glaringly obvious.

"I'll see what I can do," I told her sarcastically, then waved goodbye before driving home.

I texted Alex, asking him to check in when he had a chance, but didn't get an immediate reply, so I spent the rest of the morning contacting folks from the church about the dishes they'd left behind at the church picnic. Most of them suggested I could go ahead and eat the food and they'd get their dishes back the next Sunday. I hated wasting food, and as I transferred each item to my own dish, I wondered again what I would do with it all. Even if Amber moved in for the week, the two of us wouldn't be able to consume it all, and I didn't think much of it would do well in the freezer.

I was just heading back for the fridge to pull out another armful of potluck dishes when the doorbell rang. Hunch, who hadn't given me the time of day since Amber left, perked up his ears and dragged his cast toward the front door. I made it there before him and opened the door to find Alex on the other side.

"Oh! Hi," I said too enthusiastically. My brain ricocheted to all the information I was supposed to pry out of my cop friend—Hector Banks's story, Troy Offenbach's address, what he'd found out from David Albright—but then I mentally slapped myself for the thoughts. I wasn't in the habit of using people, especially my friends, and besides, Alex's forehead was creased. His eyes looked dark and troubled. "Is everything okay? Come on in," I said instead.

Alex reached down to scratch the fur around Hunch's neck and then followed me to the kitchen. "Whoa!" he said the moment we moved through the doorway. "I wasn't meaning to invite myself for lunch, but..."

"Hey, if you're hungry, you'd be doing me a huge favor to eat some of this up." I had most of the casserole and side dishes out on my counter to figure out what to do with them. I got a microwave-safe plate from the cupboard and passed that, along with a spoon, over to Alex. "Help yourself."

He served himself a heaping plate, and I followed along, filling my own much smaller plate. I wasn't sure if I should ask again, but I couldn't seem to help myself. "So…you didn't answer me. Is everything okay?"

Alex heaved in a big breath and let it out. "I suppose. Just another run-in with Corbett. He found out I'd been assisting with the investigation and gave Reinhart an earful about it." He shook his head at the floor. "The stuff he assigns me is work made for kindergarteners. I shouldn't be surprised. The attribution of work at the station has never been anywhere near even. I should have probably backed out gracefully, or told Corbett I'd wheedled my way into it, something so Reinhart wouldn't take the heat. But I just sat there. Now not only is Corbett trying to keep me away from the detective unit, Reinhart's back to relying on his regular partner, Detective Bernard, who is far too busy to conduct all of the interviews plus deal with forensics."

I slid Alex's full plate into the microwave and set it to heat for a minute. "I don't get it. Why does Corbett have it out for you? You seem like you're trying so hard to get along in the department."

Alex had mentioned it had been his dad, once a cop within the local department, who'd instigated the problem, but he'd never given me any details. I, of anyone, knew how hard it could be to talk about parents and their inadequacies, and I hoped he was learning he could trust me.

He helped himself to his plate from the microwave, and I slid mine in. He dropped into a chair at the table before he spoke again. "My dad, he wasn't the get-along type. He made lots of enemies within the department before he left."

"And Corbett was one of them?" I confirmed, taking my own plate from the microwave and sitting across from him. I already knew this part, but I wanted to keep the conversation going.

Alex shrugged. "For all I know, he's the only one who still has a grudge against him, but Dad was pretty famous for ruffling feathers. Corbett was new in town after our old captain, Ron Salinger, retired. Dad pretty much ran the department himself when Salinger still officially called the shots, so you could say the transition wasn't exactly seamless. Dad and Corbett were both type A personalities. I was fresh out of the academy and trying to work my way up, but it seemed every time Dad had a run-in with Corbett, I found myself on grunt duty or with a mound of extra paperwork. Since Dad transferred out of Honeysuckle Grove, things are better than they were. Just not much room for advancement, you know?"

"Well…did anyone officially tell you that you were off the Candi Banks' murder investigation?"

He shrugged as he finished chewing another big bite. "I guess not, but it's only because I'm waiting to hear back from interview subjects and the medical examiner's office. Reinhart's been running the interviews, Bernard has been balancing his forensics work with his work on another case, and so I was hoping to continue to fill in, but I don't want to be too visible about it or push my luck."

"Well, good," I told Alex. I had yet to take a bite. If Alex was upset, I couldn't think about eating, but I hoped he could see that there might still be a light at the end of the tunnel for him here. "Keep at it quietly then. Does Reinhart know Corbett's problem is really with your dad? And why does Corbett keep hanging your dad's issues over your head if your dad's gone?"

"Everyone knows," Alex said, and then took another big bite. I had to wait for him to chew and then swallow. He clearly had no trouble stomaching food, no matter the amount of stress or emotional upheaval in his life. Finally, he added, "There was a big blowout before Dad left. No one else was there to hear what Corbett actually said, but Dad stormed out, saying he couldn't work with a racist captain and was going to the mayor."

My eyes widened. No wonder Corbett hated the Martinez family, and vice versa.

"Dad couldn't prove anything, and so next thing I knew, he had a job offer down in Charlotte—a good one as chief investigator. I suspect either the mayor or Corbett pulled some strings to get him out of here."

I shook my head and took my first bite, mostly because I didn't know what to say to that. By the time I had swallowed, all I had come up with was, "Too bad you want to stay in Honeysuckle Grove."

"Heh. Yeah, too bad." His response only pointed out how lame my reassurance was.

It seemed like a no-win situation, and so I decided to open up about my own family's no-win situation. "My dad didn't exactly make my life easy, either," I told him. "When I was growing up, my dad got fired so often, I didn't have a chance to get attached to any one town."

Alex tilted his head, like he truly had compassion for me, even in the midst of his much worse turmoil.

"Until now," I said. He stared at me for so long, I looked down and added, "I'm getting pretty attached to Honeysuckle Grove." My cheeks warmed, hoping he wouldn't realize that he was at least half the reason for that. It had been the same in seventh grade.

Alex stood and went to help himself to another plate of food. I was glad he felt comfortable enough to do so. "So if I'm committed to this town, and you're committed to this town," he said, "I guess we just have to find a way to work around any little annoyances."

Little annoyances. I loved how he played down his serious work struggles. "So is that why you came by? To talk about Corbett and Reinhart?"

"Oh. Right. All this food, and I'd momentarily forgotten about the reason for my visit." He smirked over his shoulder at me as he heaped another large spoonful of macaroni and cheese onto his plate. "I wanted to update you on the case."

I scrunched my forehead. "Really?"

"Sure. Well, I mean, I wanted to ask your opinion on something, too."

That didn't clear my confusion up. Again, I had to ask, "Really?" Shouldn't he play it carefully if he wanted to wedge his way into Honeysuckle Grove Police Department's detective unit? And what could he possibly need from me?

"Steve and I finally found Hector Banks late last night. He has a record, and his fingerprints were a match to both the church's Rubbermaid bin and the whiskey bottle. We haven't been able to match a print from the toy gun yet, though."

"A record?"

Alex shrugged. "Just some breaking and entering, petty theft stuff, but Reinhart was familiar with his name as soon as the wedding planner mentioned it. It took us a while to locate him, which tends to happen when someone is hiding in plain sight."

"Oh, yeah? Was he at the address Candi's parents gave to Detective Reinhart?" I wasn't comfortable calling Detective Reinhart Steve yet, but it seemed Alex calling him by his first name was a good sign, a sign there wasn't too much animosity between them.

"Not only was he not there, he moved out the month before. We spoke to his landlord, and get this, his forwarding address was the same as Candi and her parents." Alex sat across from me with his second heaping plate.

"Weird. And so you went back to their house next?" I recalled visiting the house and hearing voices inside before the door opened to a very evasive Lacey Banks.

"We did. We actually ran surveillance for a couple of hours, just watching who came and went, to get a sense of the family, as it seems they're trying to keep some secrets."

"Did you find out anything?" I asked between bites of delicious eggplant parmesan. I made a mental note to look up who had baked it.

"We saw the Bankses arrive home from the hospital, still looking quite broken up about their daughter. That's when Hector appeared out on their front stoop. He wore slippers and held a near-empty liquor bottle, like he'd been inside their house drinking the whole time. They had an animated argument with him. We couldn't hear any of it, but all three of them looked upset. Of course, that was to be expected. We were about to go and get some clear answers out of all of them when we saw the younger daughter, Lacey Banks, sneak out from a side door of the large house."

I'd stopped eating. Even the best eggplant parmesan in the world couldn't take my rapt attention from this story. "None of the other Bankses saw her? Where'd she go?"

He raised his eyebrows. "That's what we wanted to know. We were down the street, watching their house with binoculars. When Lacey snuck along a side path toward a neighbor's house, we decided to back up and follow her. She ended up getting picked up by a group of young people in a convertible. Steve got the plate number, and he's looking into it. We wouldn't have been able to follow them without being noticed, but the strangest part was that Lacey, as well as all the others in the car, were laughing when they left."

"Laughing?" I raised my eyebrows in disbelief. "The day her sister died? Was she still in the black mini dress?"

"Yeah. It seemed almost like a celebration. So that's weird, right?" Alex looked at me with furrowed eyebrows, like his question was a serious one.

"Yeah, that's weird. That's what you wanted to ask me about?" I was beyond confused. Alex wasn't stupid, not by any stretch of the imagination, so why was he asking a stupid question?

He shrugged. "I know you've been hanging around with Amber. She's, what, seventeen?"

I smiled inwardly. Amber would be incredibly pleased to be mistaken for seventeen. "Fifteen," I told him.

"Mm. Okay." He nodded and shrugged. "Lacey Banks is eighteen. I thought you might have some insight into that age group, losing someone close to them, you know, because of Amber."

I took another bite and thought that over. "There's a big difference between fifteen and eighteen, and I suspect a big difference in the girls' personalities as well, so I'm not sure I can be of much help, but I'm quite certain Amber still hasn't been going out with friends and joking around. She spends most evenings over at my house learning how to cook." I hadn't actually thought of that as part of her grieving process for her dad, but it would make sense if it was.

Still, I felt like this comparison would get us nowhere.

"That's all the confirmation I need. I'll definitely look closer at Lacey Banks."

I opened my mouth, then hesitated, wondering if I should nudge him to look into Troy. But maybe Amber was right and nudging him in the wrong direction, before we had any substantial proof, might be bad for Alex's career, especially after everything he told me about his tenuous place in the department. "Did you eventually get to question Hector?"

Alex shook his head. "We went back and banged on the Bankses' door. They insisted Hector wasn't inside and they hadn't seen him. They wouldn't let us in the house, so Steve's requesting a warrant." Alex let out a sigh. "This kind of thing's pointless, though. By the time we get the warrant, Hector Banks will be long gone from their house. All it proves is that the

Bankses clearly have something to hide."

Alex had finished his second full plate of food and returned to the counter for a little more of the eggplant parmesan. He had good taste. He leaned back against the counter, waiting for it to get nuked. Maybe I wouldn't have to worry so much about the surplus of food with Alex around.

After all Alex had told me, and so freely, I felt a little guilty about Amber's idea to look into Troy behind his back, even if we did plan to pass on any information once we found it. The least I could do was tell him what we'd done today.

"Amber and I delivered a casserole to the Albright house this morning."

Alex's eyebrows shot up, but he'd just sat down and taken a large bite of his eggplant parm, so he chewed and swallowed before he asked, "Why'd you do that?"

I shrugged. I wasn't sure if he wanted me to admit that we'd been doing our own investigating, or if he'd reprimand me for it. "We figured they must be grieving, too, and they're not nearly as well off as the Banks family."

Alex nodded. "Steve and I haven't gotten over there yet, but we interviewed their son at the hospital. We didn't learn much, as he was a blubbering mess, clearly upset about the death of his bride. Learn anything interesting from his parents?"

I described the farmhouse with the peeling paint, overgrown grass, and a greenhouse in the back. "Apparently, David had been moving his things into the house he'd planned to share with Candi. His parents figured he was grieving, and he'd be back to live with them shortly, but they didn't seem to want to give me the address of where David was staying."

Alex smirked at me. He knew I'd gone there to investigate.

"I said I wanted to bring David a casserole," I explained. "But Katrina Albright insisted it would be better if I dropped it off with them."

"So David still spends a lot of time at their house, I assume?" Alex asked.

I shrugged. "They didn't seem to be in agreement about that, but I can tell you that their precious son is in every wall hanging and knickknack in that house." I went on to explain how David was Brock and Katrina's only son.

Alex nodded along with my story as he polished off his third plate.

"But the most interesting part of the morning was when Brock Albright started talking about Hector Banks. Said he didn't like Candi and, in fact, only liked two things: his whiskey and his guns."

Alex stopped mid-bite. "His guns?"

I nodded. "I definitely think it's worth tracking down Hector to ask him a few questions."

"Steve and I have talked extensively about whether or not Hector, in his drunken state, had the ability to aim a gun so specifically and be able to conceal the whole event, but you're right. He's worth looking into. Especially if he could have been grossly exaggerating his state of drunkenness."

I thought back. I had been a few mere feet away from Hector Banks shortly before Candi collapsed. He would have had to have been a skilled actor to have faked his drunkenness so well. "I don't think so."

Alex nodded. "Yeah, neither did we. Did you learn anything else from the Albrights?"

"He accompanied a woman out to a red hatchback car in his driveway and handed off a cardboard box while I was there," I said. Alex made a note of this in his ever-present notebook. "Brock was really tight-lipped. He clearly didn't want me there. And neither of them wanted to tell me anything about where I could find David. I know you've already interviewed him, but if you and Detective Reinhart are heading over to interview the parents, that might be a good question to start with."

"We're headed there later this afternoon, actually." He got up with his plate, and I watched to see if he was going to put back a fourth serving, but instead, he rinsed his plate and put it into the dishwasher.

"Let me know if you find out anything I couldn't," I told him, even though it seemed a ridiculous request. He was a police officer on a case, after all, and what was I?

When he turned from the dishes, he looked me over. I'd worn jeans and an argyle sweater this morning, as it had been quite chilly when Amber and I had left the house, but I suspected he wasn't concerned about my choice of wardrobe.

"You know you have to keep everything I've told you to yourself, right?" Alex asked.

I got it. He was trying so hard to get himself promoted within the department. Coming here and spilling everything he and Detective Reinhart had done so far on the Candi Banks murder case was most certainly not an item to be completed on their docket.

But I hoped one day Alex Martinez would trust me enough that he wouldn't have to ask.

"I won't say a word," I told him. "Think of me as a special consultant. And if Amber or I can come up with any other definite leads on who might have killed Candi Banks, you'll be the first to know."

☐

# CHAPTER THIRTEEN

Amber showed up at my door just after two, this time unannounced. I was still repacking leftovers from the picnic and handwashing dishes to return to church members.

She knocked, let herself in without waiting for me to answer, and started talking before she'd even reached the kitchen. "Seth was getting groceries for Mom, so he dropped me off on his way. Said he could pick me up in an hour, but I'll text him if you can drop me off later."

"I can," I told her. It wasn't like I had much else on my agenda.

"Good. Get your shoes on."

I looked down. She hadn't taken hers off. Hunch hadn't wasted any time in dragging his cast over to plant himself at her feet, and he sniffed her shoes as if interested in the unusual practice as well, as Cooper and I hadn't been in a habit of wearing our shoes in our new house.

Then again, my cat was more likely getting a historical account of the entire day solely through the scent of her shoes. But I wasn't a cat with an acute sense of smell and a keen discernment for all things mysterious, so I had to come out and ask. "Where are we going?"

"Honeysuckle Grove Rod and Gun Club. I called to see if Hector Banks was a member."

"And he is?" I asked, slinging the wet dish towel over the oven handle and then heading for the front door.

"Not only is he a member, but he shoots there every afternoon."

~~~

I'd never been much of a fan of guns.

As Amber and I got out of the Jeep and a shot echoed through the nearby air, it made me startle. Amber-the-Fearless grabbed my arm and pulled me toward the cedar pillars that marked the entrance to the gun club.

We entered into a small room that looked like a gun shop. At least a dozen rifles hung on the wall behind a glass counter filled with various types of bullets. Back when I used to help research Cooper's novels, I probably could have told you which bullets were made for which guns, but those sorts of details went in one ear and out the other with me now.

A man with an unkempt red beard, who looked like he belonged on Duck Dynasty, greeted us. "What can I do y'all for?"

I surveyed the small room, looking for the preprepared excuse I should have come in with.

Yet again, Amber was one step ahead of me. "I just need to talk to my Uncle Hector for a minute."

Apparently, Amber wasn't above telling a few lies to get to the greater truth.

Duck Dynasty glanced to a side door, as though that was where Hector could be found, and then looked Amber up and down. "Hector Banks? You Candi's sister?" The man didn't show a hint of sadness, even though he seemed to know Candi, which made me suspect he hadn't heard about her death.

"Yup," Amber said, crossing her arms as though defying him to challenge her on it.

He wasn't the type to be intimidated. "Sure don't look alike, do ya?"

"You know Candi?" I asked, to try and break up this power battle. I turned to Amber. "You didn't tell me your sister comes here, Lacey."

Duck Dynasty looked between us. Then he answered me. "Sure, Candi comes in with Hector every couple weeks to shoot. The boys around here sure like her. If you ask me, she likes the attention."

So this guy definitely didn't know Candi was dead. I wondered, if Hector was here right now, why he wouldn't have told this guy. Then again, maybe Duck Dynasty's macho attitude made the hackles of more than just fifteen-year-old girls prick up.

"So can I go back and see him?" Amber asked.

Duck Dynasty shrugged and pushed a logbook across the counter. "Just need your John Henrys first."

Amber signed "Lacey Banks" in big loopy handwriting. I wasn't sure what to write, but figured writing Mallory Beck wouldn't be the smartest move. The first name I could come up with was a combination of two names currently swimming in my head: Alexis Albright. I scrawled it messily, so it wouldn't be completely readable, and a second later, Duck Dynasty opened a gate that led us to the side door.

Right as we reached for the handle, another gunshot went off, this one louder than the one from the parking lot had been, and it practically made me jump out of my skin.

"Come on," Amber—aka Lacey—told me, as though she knew I needed the push.

Moments later, we were outside again, but now under a long, sheltered overhang, lined with free-standing mini tables that faced a large open field. Hector Banks wasn't hard to spot among the three men spread out along the firing range. The other two had long beards like their Duck Dynasty buddy, and while Hector was by no means clean-shaven, his three- or four-day facial growth looked more lazy than intentional.

Thankfully, the red-bearded man from the front counter hadn't followed us outside. Amber led the way to Hector. He wore the same kind of plaid shirt and dirty jeans he'd worn to his niece's wedding, and he was currently leaning down, trying to line up a shot.

A faded white line marked the area non-shooters were to stand behind. Amber stood right on the line with her arms crossed while Hector took his time lining up the shot. I covered my ears, but nevertheless, as always, when he finally took the shot, the loud bang sent my heart skittering. A paper target fluttered from the bullet half a mile into the field in the distance. I squinted, but couldn't tell from here how accurate Hector's shot had been.

He was no more than two feet in front of us and must have felt our presence because he glanced over his shoulder and then straightened away from the free-standing table he had been lining his gun up on.

"Yeah?" he said. He was quite the opposite, at least in appearance, of his very proper older brother, Candi's dad. "What do ya want?"

"To ask you a few questions. Go ahead and finish up." Amber motioned her chin toward the target in the open field. Her stalling told me she must be nervous, too. Either that, or like me, she thought it might be better for him to have emptied all of his bullets before we started grilling him about his niece's murder.

Then again, we should probably leave the grilling for Alex and Detective Reinhart. We were just here to gather intel, I told myself for the twentieth time.

Hector started to turn away, but then swung back to us, leaving his gun set up where it was. "This about Candi?"

Amber nodded. "Yeah. She was a friend of mine. I just want to know what happened."

Good play, Amber! I wondered if I could pass as Amber's mom, or maybe better to play the aunt—for some sort of "kinship" to Candi's uncle. But Hector barely even glanced my direction and didn't seem to care who I was.

Hector shook his head and looked genuinely in turmoil as he said, "I dunno, but the police are sayin' she wasn't stung by no bee. They're saying they found some kinda needle stuck in her back."

Detective Reinhart must have divulged the ambiguous nature of Candi's death. I couldn't help myself. I glanced at his rifle.

Hector didn't miss the inference. "I didn't poke her with no needle! I woulda never done nothin' to hurt Candi."

The two long-bearded men looked over with raised bushy eyebrows. There wasn't much that intimidated Amber, but Hector's loud and sudden voice did. She took a step back, and I figured it was my turn to ask a question.

"Isn't it true, though, that she didn't want you at her wedding?" My hair was up in a knot, as I'd been packing up food when Amber had come by, so I hoped he wouldn't recognize me from the park, where I'd worn my hair down around my shoulder.

Hector let out a humorless laugh. "What she didn't want was for me and her mom to get into it. If she didn't want anyone there, it was her mother. But a bride can't exactly say that, now can she?"

"And so it had nothing to do with the fact that you showed up drunk?"

I didn't know what I expected. Perhaps for my words to rile Hector up, but they seemed to have the opposite effect. He shrugged and said, "Candi knows—knew—I had to have a couple to be around Tobias and Ella."

I hadn't known the first names of Candi's parents, but now that Hector said them, I could recall Tobias kneeling in panic near Candi's unresponsive body and repeatedly calling his wife, Ella.

Hector grabbed his phone from his front jeans pocket. "You want proof?" he asked. In mere seconds, he had scrolled through his phone and held up a photo of Candi in this exact same shelter, goggles over her eyes, a giant smile enveloping her face. He swiped to another photo of her leaning over a gun, and then several more photos of her grinning in front of the local smoothie shop with a giant purple-and-green cup in her hand.

The other shooters had lost interest in us and had gone back to lining up their own shots. I braced myself for when I might hear another shot.

Hector continued to scroll through more photos. He certainly did seem to have a lot of happy photos of Candi on his phone. And we could question Duck Dynasty at the counter on our way out to see exactly how well Hector and Candi seemed to get along when they came in together.

Amber had another question. "If you didn't stick a poisoned needle into my friend, who did? Did her mom do this to her?" Amber crossed her arms again, her intimidation stance. I wasn't sure if it was actually working on Hector Banks, but he seemed to know how to talk to teens without being patronizing, I'd give him that.

"Nah." Hector shook his head. "The two could scream at each other at home and then vent their anger at either me or Lacey in order to look like the perfect mother/daughter in public. But Ella wouldn't have it in her to kill nobody, no matter how mad she got."

"Speaking of Lacey," I said. "She didn't get on too well with Candi either, huh?"

Hector shrugged. "Lacey's got a chip on her shoulder, thought Candi always got the best of everything. Been that way for years. But she seemed to like David. From what Candi had told me, she was pushing for them to get married."

I squinted, thinking. Was Candi's younger, jealous sister trying to be magnanimous? Or was she planning out a very specific—and very tragic—wedding day for her sister?

"You want to look into somebody?" Hector said. "I'd look at that gold-digger groom of Candi's."

"David?" I asked.

Hector kept his eyes on Amber as he elaborated. "Kid comes from some low-rent family that doesn't want him havin' nothin' they can't grow in their own backyard garden. Made sense he wanted out."

"Well, why not just marry Candi, then?" Amber, as usual, was quick with her smart questions. "I never trusted David," she said, still playing the part of Candi's friend, "but why would he kill his meal ticket out of there? Or at the very least, why wouldn't he wait until after they were married to do it?"

"That I don't know," Hector said. He was definitely soberer here today than he had been at the wedding. I wondered if sobriety was a necessity at a gun range. It would make sense if it was. "But I do know Tobias was trying to talk Candi into a prenup, and she wouldn't take it to David. I also know David's trying to claim squatters rights in that house Tobias had put a down payment on for Candi and David."

Squatters rights? That was why David had been staying there, even though his parents wanted him back home.

"You know where this house of David and Candi's is?" Amber asked, her phone at the ready to take down the address. "I was out of town when they got it."

Even though the lies were getting less believable, Hector shrugged and rattled off an address on Franklin Avenue, not too far from the Bankses' fancy neighborhood.

"And where are you living right now?" I asked Hector.

He studied me for a few long seconds. It didn't make sense why I was asking, and search my brain as I might, I couldn't seem to come up with a reasonable explanation.

But thankfully Amber, as always, could. "Were you living in the same house as Candi when she died?"

Hector didn't hesitate to answer Amber. I got the impression he trusted teenagers a lot more than he trusted adults. "Me 'n Ella can't be in the same room for too long, so when she's around, I've been crashing on friends' couches or in my car sometimes, until I can get back on my feet. Candi was gonna let me move into the basement of her new place, but I don't think David's gonna be so generous."

"Anything else you can tell us about David Albright that we might not know?" Amber asked. "I wanted to go talk to him next." She had relaxed her stance. I could read in her posture that she no longer suspected Hector Banks of being guilty.

Hector chuckled. "Ask him about his parents' secrets. Ask him about their precious greenhouse."

This brought us back to a feud between the Bankses and the Albrights. Perhaps tracking down Troy Offenbach could wait for the moment.

☐

# CHAPTER FOURTEEN

David Albright answered the door to the two-story house he'd been squatting in, holding a game controller in one hand and chomping on a Pop-Tart with the other. I almost had to do a double-take. Was this the same young man who had grown up with Brock and Braidsy Naturalist out in Farmland, USA?

"Hi!" I said. As usual, I hadn't done much to prepare any specific line of questioning, even if Amber and I had chattered on about David for the entire fifteen-minute drive to get here. I nudged her forward and said, "This was a friend of Candi's who just got back into town and heard about the tragedy." Amber was so much better than me at discreet questioning.

"Oh. Uh. Come in," David said around a mouthful of crumbs. His eyes opened wide, and I couldn't tell if he was surprised or trying to hide his grief. He wore sweatpants and a dirty gray T-shirt that looked like it had old tomato sauce smeared on it. His shaggy dark hair stuck up at all angles as though he hadn't seen the inside of a shower yet today, even though it was nearly four in the afternoon.

I couldn't get my head around the fact that Candi had broken up with Troy to date, and even marry, this guy who must be barely out of high school. If Candi was going to rush into getting married, I would've expected it to be with someone who looked like he could hold a job and make a rent payment. Not the guy who couldn't even keep track of his Pop-Tart crumbs.

The inside of David's entryway overflowed with a multitude of boxes. The boxes continued as David led us up the stairs and into what I imagined was supposed to be a living room. This room was a far cry from any typical living room, though. Splayed in the middle of the floor was a mattress covered in messy blankets. If not for the high-tech gaming chair with speakers in the headrest, I would've suspected David to have been in bed all day, which I supposed wouldn't have been an unusual expression of grief. A flat-screen TV with a paused video game encompassed most of the largest wall in the room, but other than that, the room was filled only with more boxes. Most of these ones were either gift-wrapped or partially unwrapped. I wasn't entirely sure why David had led us up here, as it didn't seem there was anywhere other than the gaming chair to sit.

"Looks like you've just moved in," I observed. And had been playing video games nonstop since your wife-to-be was killed. Amber hadn't launched in with any of her astute questions, so I figured I'd might as well open up with the obvious.

"Uh-huh," David said, and then shoved the rest of the Pop-Tart into his mouth.

"Wow, this is a lot of stuff. All yours?" I wasn't sure how else to ask if any of it was Candi's.

David looked almost like a lost child when he shook his head and said, "Most of it was hers. Then my groomsmen, who were really just friends of Candi's, dropped the gifts from the park off here." He rubbed the back of his neck. "Not sure what to do with it all. Don't really want to call her parents."

I wondered if he'd rather not call her parents because they were grieving or because they might find a way to kick him out. This kid didn't seem like much of a brilliant schemer, though.

I looked around again at all the boxes, piles and piles of them against every wall. Maybe he couldn't sue for half of Candi's money because the wedding ceremony hadn't actually happened, but I wondered if all this stuff could have been enough motive for David to kill his bride.

Amber pointed to the gaming chair. "Was that one of the gifts? Or was it Candi's?"

My forehead buckled. Gaming chairs were comfortable, but it seemed a strange wedding gift. Although, now that Amber asked, I was unable to picture such an item in the Albright farmhouse—unless maybe it had been a gift from the same grandmother who had given him the lava lamp.

But David nodded at Amber's question and looked down, as though sadness was momentarily overtaking him. When he looked back up, he pointed across the room at a large gift-wrapped box. "Yeah. That one was supposed to be Candi's. Not sure what to do with that now either."

Who on earth gave matching gaming chairs for a wedding gift? I had to know. "Well, who gave them to you? Maybe they could get a gift receipt."

David shrugged again. "Candi's Uncle Hector bought them. He knew it's what Candi wanted, but he picked 'em up off eBay and dropped 'em off here last week. I doubt he can get his money back. Heard he used his rent money to buy 'em, too. Besides, I don't really want to get rid of Candi's.

They're kind of a pair, you know?" He looked down at his feet again pensively. "Not sure I want to set it up, though, either."

"Understandable." I nodded, wondering if we'd have to track Hector down again to ask him why using rent money to buy the new couple gaming chairs seemed like a good idea. Then again, he'd likely just say that he cared about his niece and wanted to get her whatever her heart desired.

David stared at the unopened gaming chair, pensive for several long seconds. When he spoke again, he turned to Amber and asked, "Were you at the wedding?" Maybe it was too much to hope that none of our questions would raise David's suspicions.

"Yeahhhh." Amber drew out the word and walked over to the front window, I suspected to buy time. She looked down at the driveway where I'd parked the Jeep. There had been no other vehicles in the driveway, and I wondered if David owned a car. I suspected not if he was only eighteen and didn't appear to be made of money. "I was out of town with my parents and arrived a little late, after everything happened." Amber's voice wavered on the word "parents" and I wondered if it was the first time she'd used the word since her dad had died.

"We stopped by your family's farmhouse to drop off a casserole," I told David, mostly to take the focus away from Amber. "I suggested I could drop some food off for you, too, but they said you'd be moving back with them within a few days." If that was the case, did he plan to bring all of these boxes back to the tiny farmhouse? Again, I couldn't picture it.

But David seemed to become energized by my question. He swiped food wrappers off the floor, tossed them toward a wastebasket in the corner, and then fanned the crumpled blanket over the mattress, effectively making up the bed in one quick motion. "I may not be able to stay here forever, but I'm not moving back there. Not ever."

"No? It was that bad?" I looked at Amber. The subject of his parents had him clearly agitated.

David stared at me for a few long seconds and then looked away. "Doesn't matter. I'm not going back." He paced toward the window and gazed outside. "Hopefully, the Bankses'll let me stay here until I can get a job and find somewhere cheaper to live."

"That's some fancy greenhouse they had out back," Amber said, and that's when I remembered Hector mentioning this trigger point for David—not that he seemed to need any more trigger points. "I can't believe they keep a lock on it. They sure keep a lot of plants, huh?"

David scowled, turning from the window. "They showed you the greenhouse?"

Amber shrugged. "Not exactly. But I found it."

David's scowl softened. "Right, well, they don't let anyone inside there, not even me. You want to know what would be so bad about moving back with them? Try being kept on some farmland off the bus routes where you can't go anywhere or see anyone. Try having your parents whisper secrets around your own house and not even let you answer your own front door. If I hadn't met Candi at the farmer's market where my mom had me selling vegetables, if she hadn't been willing to pick me up and take me on our dates, I never woulda gotten outta there!"

I could feel David's embarrassment mixed with anger vibrating throughout the room around us. I hated to do it, but now was the time to strike with the most important question.

"And if anyone wanted Candi dead, who do you think it would be?" My mind was suddenly on David's father, Brock Albright. What did he have locked in that secret black-plastic-covered greenhouse of his? And if he'd been so incredibly strict with his only prized son, what would he have done to someone who interfered with his parenting?

David's eyes shifted back and forth over my face as though it was the daily newspaper. He took a long time to ask, "You think someone did this to Candi on purpose?"

I didn't know how long this information would take to come out as an official statement from the police. If Hector already knew and liked to drink, it likely wouldn't take long to get out, at least unofficially.

I tilted my head and answered David's question with a question. "What if they did?"

David kept his continually shifting eyes on me. His jaw tightened. Then he studied the floor for several long seconds. The delay stretched the tension in the room like a taut rubber band. Finally, he said, "That ex of hers. His name's Troy Offen-somethin'." David kept his eyes narrowed at the floor as he recounted the details he knew about Troy. "When we first pulled up to the park in the limo and Mrs. Winters told us about the double-booking of the park, Candi freaked out. She said, 'If Troy can't have me, he wants to make sure no one can!'" Finally, David looked up at us. "Everybody in the wedding party heard her." He started pacing, raking his hands through his hair, practically frantic.

I looked at Amber. If this was true, the next item on our agenda was clearly to talk a confession out of Troy Offenbach.

"Would you be willing to tell the police what you just told us?" I pulled a notepad and pen from my purse and scrawled Alex's name and number onto it. I passed it to David, even though he still hadn't answered me. "If there was foul play involved with Candi's death, you'd want to know who did this, right?"

Finally, he nodded, but he still looked shell-shocked at the idea of Candi being murdered. David's answers weren't enough to clear his name from suspicion completely, but as far as I was concerned, Amber and I had more promising suspects to investigate.

☐

# CHAPTER FIFTEEN

On the drive to Honeysuckle Grove Community Church, Amber called to check in with her brother, Seth, again. Her mom was medicating herself to get through her grief and might not notice if Amber disappeared for a week, but her brother looked out for her more and more with each passing day, and Amber seemed to appreciate it.

"Yeah, maybe an hour or two," she said into her phone.

Often, the only way I knew what was going on in Amber's overactive head was to eavesdrop in on her phone conversations. If she only planned to be gone another hour or two, it seemed finding and interviewing Troy Offenbach was likely the last item on our agenda today.

"Hey, do you know a girl named Lacey Banks?" she asked into her cell phone. It wouldn't have occurred to me to ask Amber's brother this, but it made sense. They were close to the same age. "Uh-huh. Oh, yeah? What about a guy named David Albright?" I suspected he had been homeschooled and wasn't all that socially connected in Honeysuckle Grove, so it surprised me when Amber said, "Oh, really?" like something had surprised her. I wished she'd put it on speaker, but instead, I tapped my fingers on the steering wheel impatiently until she hung up.

"What did you find out about Lacey?" I hadn't given Amber all of the details Alex had passed along—confidentiality, and all—but I had mentioned Lacey had been spotted laughing with friends.

"She was a year ahead of Seth in school, graduated last year, and he said he only knew her by reputation."

"What kind of reputation?"

Amber laughed. "Apparently she was a bit of a pothead, known for her money and her stupidity. Paid people gobs of money to write all of her essays and even take her exams. She'd been caught more than once, and if rumors were correct, the only reason she graduated was because of the huge donations her parents made to the school's building fund." Amber looked at me with a raised eyebrow. "This doesn't sound like the type of girl who could orchestrate or take part in a very public murder, no matter how much she hated her sister."

She might be right. "And David Albright? Did your brother know him?"

She shook her head. "No, but he knew the last name. Said everyone he knew who bought drugs got them from some guy named Albright."

With only one Albright in the local phone book, I was willing to bet I'd been correct about Brock Albright conducting a grow-op in the greenhouse in his backyard. I didn't have time to think more about this, though, as I pulled into the church parking lot. It was five on the nose, closing time. Penny Lismore was just pulling her key from the office door and turned for the lone car in the parking lot, not noticing my Jeep near the curb of the main sanctuary.

I jumped out of the Jeep on one side, and Amber wasn't far behind me on the other.

"Penny! Penny, can I speak to you for a moment?" I jogged over, glad to have Amber with me, if for no other reason that I often chose sneakers for my footwear when we went out together.

Penny had reached her car already, a small lime-green Datsun that looked striking against her bright orange hair. She stopped and turned my way. "Hi. What can I do for you?" Her question was wary. I got the feeling people asking her for help after hours wasn't exactly an unusual occurrence.

"We were wondering if Troy Offenbach, the church treasurer, was still here?" I motioned to the church office, even though it seemed unlikely, as there were no other cars and the interior lights all appeared to be out.

Penny shook her head. "I'm afraid not." Her tone didn't invite conversation, but thankfully, Amber wasn't deterred.

"But he did come in today, right?"

Penny looked between Amber and me like she didn't know who to answer. She settled her gaze somewhere in between us. "Sure, he was in, but he leaves early on Mondays. He's still working on his degree at the college and has a class at five."

"An accounting class?" I asked.

Penny shrugged. "I suppose so."

"How did he seem today? He was pretty broken up yesterday about the incident at the park, right? I understand he knew the bride?"

Penny nodded and looked down at the pavement in front of her solemnly. "Yes. I still can't believe what happened, but Troy certainly felt it more than the rest of us. He broke down at the copier today, said it was only three months ago that they had been dating. I feel awful for him."

I looked to Amber, a wave of sadness coming over me as well. But she looked as stoic and in control as always. I supposed that was what happened when you found out your dad was murdered by someone you'd have never suspected in a million years. Other people's tragedies probably didn't seem quite as tragic after that.

But my bleeding heart didn't stop with Troy. I had to ask after our wounded pastor as well. "And Pastor Jeff? I don't suppose he was here today, but have you heard if he's out of the hospital?"

Penny sighed and looked up at us, but her countenance didn't appear much brighter. "They're keeping him one more night, just to be sure the toxin has been cleared from his system. I'm headed there now."

"Well, give him our best, will you?" I said, taking a step back so she could go. There was nothing more to learn from Penny Lismore. I was quite certain she wasn't lying about Troy's outburst earlier today, so there were three possible conclusions I could draw from that:

One. Troy Offenbach killed Candi but was a really good actor.

Two. He'd killed Candi and had experienced a deep wave of remorse about it today.

Three. He was innocent and was heartbroken that she'd died.

I wanted to believe the third option, but then again, I tended to want to believe that of everyone.

"Should I take you home?" I asked Amber, but I knew her answer before I'd even asked the question.

"No. You should take me to Honeysuckle Grove Community College. We're going to talk to Troy."

☐

# CHAPTER SIXTEEN

I figured we had lots of time before we could track down Troy, and so I did a drive-thru run on our way over to the community college. Even if Troy's class was only an hour, it wouldn't let out before six.

Amber took a bite of her burger and scowled. "Guess I haven't had fast-food since I've been cooking with you. This is gross."

"You're welcome," I said with a smirk. But I understood what she meant. I wasn't a big fan of fast-food myself, although I found when I was working through a mystery, my brain didn't seem to have room for everything, so food tended to lose its variances—unless something struck me as particularly awesome, like the eggplant parmesan I'd had at lunch.

As I pulled into the college's parking lot, I went over the three possibilities again. "So he's a good actor, he's feeling guilty, or he's innocent. How do we find out which?"

Amber finished chewing and swallowed before answering. "I think we need to start with how to find his classroom." She looked across the sprawling building. The parking lot was about half-full, which meant there were a good number of evening classes going on today.

"Yeah, you're right. I doubt the college office is open after five, but I still want to be ready with some good questions this time."

Amber shrugged, shoving another bite into her mouth. The speed at which she inhaled her burger indicated she couldn't think it was that awful. I took my first nibble, but as usual, I wasn't hungry so much as needing to do something with my hands. Cooking or kneading bread would've been preferable.

Finally, Amber swallowed again and rattled off questions as though they came as naturally to her as breathing. "How'd he and Candi break up? Was he angry about it? Was he angry at her? Why did he only book one shelter at the park for the church? Did he know Candi's wedding was going to be held on the same day at the same park? Why did he have the park mail him the bill directly, instead of to the church?"

When the questions came all in a row like that, they made Troy Offenbach seem guilty. "Maybe I should call Alex," I suggested.

Amber raised her eyebrows and drilled her fifteen-year-old fearless gaze into me. "Maybe I should have brought your cat along instead. He'd have the nerve to do a little fact-checking before we bring the police into it."

She was right. I was scared. What if this was a murderer we were about to confront? Then again, we were in a public place. Chances were good that Troy wouldn't be carrying around a toy gun loaded with poisoned needles to his college classes. And it really would be good to go back to Alex with something more substantial than theories.

"You're right," I told her. I could prove myself at least as helpful as my three-legged ornery cat. "Let's go and see if we can find the accounting wing."

It turned out the community college's board of directions at the front entrance made this part of things easy. Business classes were to the right, in the "E" wing. We headed that way.

"It's pretty nice that the church is letting Troy work as treasurer, even though he hasn't finished his degree," Amber said as we walked. Less than a dozen people passed us as we wove down long hallways and around corners, following other signage toward Wing E. "My career ed. teacher from last year said to break into jobs in business you almost always needed a bachelor's degree or even a master's."

This didn't surprise me if Pastor Jeff had done the hiring. He would most certainly want to help a young person out if it was within his power. "I just hope he didn't throw away a great opportunity," I said, still wanting to believe in Troy's innocence, despite Amber's long list of accusatory questions for him.

I'd barely finished my sentence when Amber threw an arm out in front of my chest to stop me. She pointed two fingers at her wide eyes and then straight ahead, where not fifty feet in front of us, a man who looked like Troy Offenbach, with trim blond hair and long legs, sat alone on a bench with his head between his hands.

Amber and I took about three seconds to look at each other, survey the situation, and then forge ahead.

I still wasn't entirely sure it was him, so when we got about ten feet away and he still hadn't looked up, I said, "Troy?"

Slowly, he lifted his head from his hands to reveal red and swollen eyes behind his wire-rimmed glasses. It was him. He pulled off his glasses to wipe them on his tan-colored dress shirt and then replaced them. I looked around at this empty hallway in Wing E. If he was still acting, I wasn't sure for whose benefit.

"We're sorry to bother you," I said quickly because all of a sudden, I was afraid of Amber taking over with her blunt and badgering questions. "But are you okay?"

Troy looked between me and Amber, and then took a deep breath. "Oh, yes. I'm—" His words started out stoic, like he was putting on a front of having it all together when he recognized us, but his voice broke on the last word, and he looked down at his lap, blinking fast, unable to finish his sentence.

It was my first inclination to slide onto the bench and wrap an arm around him, but Amber spoke up, reminding me of why we were here. "I knew Candi and her sister, Lacey, from school. I just can't even believe what happened. You and Candi used to date, right?" Amber didn't drum up any tears with her words, but she did exude more compassion than I would've expected.

Troy's forehead creased toward Amber. "You were friends with Candi?"

Amber forced a sad smile in way of an answer.

He only nodded. "So you must have been there for the wedding that day?"

"I was at the park when she collapsed, yeah." She impressed me, answering so seamlessly without any out-and-out lies.

"I was surprised to see the church picnic was going to be at the same park. It didn't seem like it would've been big enough."

I was quite certain I didn't imagine Troy's eyes flitting away from me for half a second on that statement. His reaction made me push on with, "Did you know there was a wedding scheduled when you booked the park for the church?"

The bottom rims of his eyes collected water, and again the three options raced through my brain: actor, guilt-ridden, or innocent?

Troy looked down. His answer was barely audible when he said, "I...yeah."

"Were you still in love with Candi?" Amber's question shocked me. It hadn't been on her list, but as usual, my astute young friend seemed to know how to get to the heart of the matter.

Troy nodded down at the floor.

Amber's voice became surprisingly gentle as she said, "And you hoped she wouldn't go through with the wedding if the park wasn't perfect? Or when she saw you there?"

Troy removed his glasses again to wipe his eyes. I felt awful for him. This wasn't the work of an actor, unless he was well beyond Al Pacino in skill and training. He was either severely guilt-ridden or innocent, although now I suspected that even if he was innocent of killing Candi, he still felt guilty for double-booking the park, if that was what led to her death.

"Are you done your class already?" I asked, feeling the need to give both

81

of us a reprieve from these heavy emotions.

Troy heaved in a breath and let it out in a sigh. "I couldn't bring myself to go. This here, this bench, it's where Candi and I met. She was taking a class in cosmetic management. She wanted to own her own spa one day." He choked through the words to get them out.

It was all starting to make sense now. Troy had deeply cared about Candi and was willing to ruin her wedding to show her how much.

"What about David, her groom?" I hated to ask this, but it had to be done. "They must have been madly in love to have such a whirlwind relationship and quick wedding, right?"

Troy's face hardened as he replaced his glasses and looked up at me. "Candi wasn't in love with him. She was in love with her childhood, the lack of responsibility she'd had before her mom forced her to go to college. She dropped out right after she met him, did you know that? She could have been so much more, and David Albright was going to ruin her life!"

"And you would have done anything to stop it?" Amber prodded more bluntly than I would've.

"I would have broken up their wedding, yeah. Her mom would have, too." He popped off the bench, and it made me realize how tall he was as he loomed over us. "I'd never have done anything if I thought she'd get hurt, though." A new round of tears rimmed his eyes. "Not anything," he said.

I wanted to believe him. Amber, however, clearly wasn't there yet. At least her questions were getting gentler as she asked, "Why did you and Candi break up? Was it because of David?"

That seemed obvious to me, from everything Troy had told us so far, but surprisingly, he shook his head. "It was because of the baby." His words were so choked, I could barely make them out.

I had to confirm what he was saying. "Candi Banks was pregnant?" That was certainly something an autopsy could confirm, although I wasn't certain if it would prove anything about her murder, even if it was true.

But Troy shook his head. "It was an accident. She wasn't ready to grow up so fast, but I told her we could handle it. She could finish out the school year, we could get married and save for a home, even if her parents got angry about the pregnancy and wouldn't help us get one. I told her it might be tight, but my job at the church could support us. But within a week, she had aborted it and started dating a lowlife with no aspirations, zero job experience, and she blamed not wanting to see me as the reason she'd dropped out of school. She never did tell anyone about the baby." His bitter words made me realize again how different the two young men were.

"So Mrs. Banks was in on it with you? On breaking up the wedding?" I said to clarify.

He nodded. "First, we teamed up to try and get her back in school, but when that didn't work, I had an idea to double-book the park. Mrs. Banks kept telling Candi she deserved the perfect wedding, and not to accept anything less."

Troy's whole countenance was mixed between anger and hardness and crumpled emotion. Thankfully, Amber seemed to agree that this awful interview was over. She took a step backward.

I wanted to give Troy a hug, but thankfully caught myself, realizing that would be highly inappropriate. "I'm so sorry for your loss." The words—the unhelpful trite ones I swore I'd never say to another person after Cooper's death—launched out of my mouth without my permission.

Thankfully, Amber was much better at this than me. "Anyone could see Candi didn't love David. I'm sure she really loved you, too."

And as Troy Offenbach's countenance morphed into pure gratitude, Amber and I decided to leave him alone.

☐

# CHAPTER SEVENTEEN

I was beat, and from the silence in the Jeep, Amber was, too. Without discussing it, I headed for her family's mansion and pulled into her driveway. I was most certainly not interested in cooking tonight, and besides, Amber had her first day of tenth grade tomorrow. I'd be a cruel excuse for an adult figure if I kept her with me just to fill some insatiable need for company.

"Text me when you're done with school tomorrow," I told her. "Let me know how it goes."

Even though Amber and I had barely spoken about her school life, I'd gotten the impression she wasn't looking forward to it. She didn't seem to have good friends of her own age that she could have a heart-to-heart with about what had happened to her dad.

I was it. And if I were being honest, it made me grateful. She was pretty much it for friends I could talk to about losing Cooper as well.

Amber got out wordlessly and waved on her way to her front door.

I backed out of her driveway and headed away from her house, feeling loneliness overtake me with each yard I moved away from her. There was always Hunch, I told myself. A cat who didn't have an ounce of friendliness toward me was a poor consolation for my bright-eyed teenage friend, but at least it was something.

At the bottom of the hill from Amber's house, though, I was about to pass the local hospital and made a split-second decision to turn in. Penny indicated Pastor Jeff was just being kept overnight as a precaution, but I still couldn't help wanting to see him alive and breathing with my own eyes.

Then again, maybe it was simply that darn insatiable need for company.

Whatever the case, the nurse's station was quick to direct me to his room. Apparently, well-meaning folks from the church had been visiting him all day. I felt bad for being yet another of these folks. But not badly enough to turn around and go home. I knocked with two knuckles on the door I'd been directed to.

Emily's voice called a whispered, "Come in."

I nudged through the door and peeked around the curtain to find a sleeping Pastor Jeff. He normally had such a booming authoritative presence, it was odd to see him lying still and breathing evenly.

I turned to Emily on the chair beside him. Dark skin encircled her eyes. "How's he doing?" I asked softly.

"Good." Despite her obvious exhaustion, she launched out of her chair at seeing me and held out a hand toward it.

There was no way on God's green earth I was going to take her chair after the days she'd had, but I was certain she'd insist, so I waved a hand at the chair and told a half-truth. "I've been sitting all day. Please, you go ahead."

Thankfully, she didn't fight me on it.

"I hear they're keeping him an extra day as a precaution?" I whispered.

She nodded. "They gave him another full dose of the antidote this afternoon." She held up a small silver packet from his tray table, where another dozen silver packets lay. "They thought he should stay here for a full forty-eight hours, just in case it didn't completely clear his symptoms. It's basically just an H2 blocker called Nizatidine combined with a specific antacid—one with magnesium hydroxide. The doctor said it was the first line of defense, and it almost always worked as an antidote if they caught it quickly enough when patients came into the emergency room with symptoms of this particular wild plant poisoning." She looked down at the packet. "They said I could take a few of these home. If we had any concerns, he could just empty a packet under his tongue for quick absorption and then head straight to the hospital."

"Would you mind if I took a packet with me?" I asked. "I don't know if it would help discover anything about Candi's murder, but if the doctor hasn't already passed this antidote along to the forensics lab, I could give it to my police friend, just in case." I was probably reaching, trying to find anything at all helpful to do, but I couldn't seem to stop myself.

Emily Hawthorne grabbed two packets from the table and passed them over. She quirked up a smile with one side of her mouth, like she was too tired to lift both sides. "We'd be grateful if you can find out anything about that horrible tragedy. The family must be going out of their mind."

I opened my mouth to tell them it was Troy that seemed to be going out of his mind about Candi's death, but then I shut it. He could tell them more about his heartache when he was ready.

As I pulled out my phone and sent Alex a quick text, she added, "And thank you, Mallory. I've heard you've been getting in touch with people from the church about their dishes from the potluck. It's so nice to not have to concern ourselves with that."

I couldn't even imagine the church's pastor and his wife worrying about leftover dishes, even if he wasn't in the hospital. But knowing these two and their serving hearts, it seemed quite likely that they normally did do all these things themselves.

As I leaned in to give Emily a hug goodbye and then headed for the door, I vowed to be more helpful to both of them in the future.

Driving for home, I felt just as lonely as I had when I'd dropped Amber at her place. Alex still hadn't texted me back, and I doubted he was still at the police station this late.

Because I didn't want Detective Reinhart to somehow get the credit for turning the antidote into forensics, even if it was only a specific kind of H2 blocker/antacid combo, I was determined to hang onto it until I connected with Alex directly. If he told me they were already two—or more likely ten—steps ahead of me, so be it, but until then, I curled them up and tucked them into the small pen loop of my cell phone case so I wouldn't lose them.

I pulled into my driveway and checked my phone again, but there was still no response. I sighed out a long breath and headed for the house.

Hunch, surprisingly, greeted me at the door. I hated to admit it, but that cat, if only he'd be nice to me, was exactly what I needed right now.

"Wait until I tell you about the day I had investigating," I said, just to keep his attention as I slipped out of my shoes. As I said the words, though, I realized they were true. I did have a lot to tell Hunch. "Come on. Let's go curl up on the couch, and I'll tell you everything."

Shock of my life—Hunch stayed right on my heels as I took a few steps toward the living room. Because he struggled with moving around with his cast, I bent down with my arms out to offer to carry him, and the second shock of my life came when he walked right into them.

Twenty minutes later, I had spelled out most of my afternoon and evening. Hunch knew about Alex coming by at lunch today—at least as well as a cat could know about things in the human world—so instead, I delved into our interview with gun-happy Uncle Hector, David Albright and his matching gaming chairs, Troy Offenbach and his extreme grief over losing a baby, losing Candi to David, and then losing Candi altogether, and then my final stop at the hospital, where I picked up an antidote to pass along to the police.

Hunch sat on my lap, purring and looking me straight in the eye, as if he were hearing and understanding every word. I was petting my cat's soft fur with one hand and studying one of the H2 blocker/antacid packets with the other when my phone rang. Alex Martinez's name appeared on the display, along with the time, which was after 11:00 p.m. I quickly replaced the silver packet and answered.

"Sorry to call so late," he said in way of a hello. "I just got your message now. Steve brought me along on a stakeout for the night so we can discuss the case. It's been a crazy day."

"Oh, yeah? Anything new you can share?"

Alex cleared his throat. "You're on speakerphone. I filled Steve in on what you'd found out at the Albrights'."

I opened my mouth, but I didn't know what to say. Was Detective Reinhart upset that I'd been running around, conducting my own mini-investigation?

But he spoke next and cleared it up for me. "When we went over to question them, Brock Albright didn't even let us in the door. Told us to come back with a warrant."

As Hunch kneaded my lap and mewled, I, with a crazy overestimation of my cat, decided to put my phone on speakerphone as well. "Amber said her brother knew of a drug dealer in town who goes by the name of Albright. Do you think that's why he's so secretive? Is that where you're staking out?"

Alex answered me. "No, the stakeout is for another case. Anyway, we hope to have a warrant and get back there to check out the house and greenhouse by the weekend."

The weekend was still four days away.

"If we can find the time to get over there again," Detective Reinhart put in. "Between finding a few hours to sleep, following up on all the leads on the Hackendale case, and meeting with forensics, it might be next week."

I opened my mouth to offer my help, but closed it before anything could come out. Of course, they wouldn't want, nor would they ever ask for, my help. Instead, I hung on the word "forensics" and asked, "Did they determine a definite cause of death for Candi Banks? Or any matching fingerprints?"

"Yeah," Detective Reinhart told me and again dispelled the myth that I might be prying too hard for information. "The fact that the epinephrine had seemingly compounded the toxin's effect led the ER doctor to suggest possible strychnine poisoning, but that didn't add up when considering how fast-acting it had been. I mentioned that Jeff Hawthorne's managing doctor had suggested a different strain of plant substance it could have been derived from. Something called sciadotenia toxifera, a fast-acting vesicant. Our lab techs weren't familiar, but once we passed along the name from the doctor, they were able to look into the chemical compounds further. A full toxicology report could take weeks, though."

I fiddled with one of the silver packets again. I had wanted to get this information to Alex first, but I couldn't knowingly keep information from the police. "I was just at the hospital, and apparently, Pastor Jeff's treating doctor gave him some H2-blockers combined with an antacid for him to take home in case of furthering symptoms. I took a couple of packets with me in case they could be helpful in your forensics lab."

"Did you hear if they've gotten that yet, Alex?" Detective Reinhart asked.

Papers rustled through the phone, and a few seconds later, Alex said, "Um, I'm not sure…"

Great. My efforts to help Alex look good in the department's eyes had backfired

"Why don't you pick it up from her first thing in the morning when we're done here," Detective Reinhart said, "and drop it off at forensics? Looking at the combination under a microscope may help them understand the molecular structure better, and maybe help us figure out better who might have access to such a toxin."

Alex agreed, and I told him I'd be up early and would be happy to deliver it to him if it was easier.

"Did you get a chance to interview Lacey Banks? Or Hector?" After so much freely given information, I was now spouting my own interrogation questions as though I were part of the police force.

"We still haven't connected with Hector," Detective Reinhart said, "but the Bankses were cooperative when we went over to question Lacey. Mr. Banks assured us that if foul play was involved in Candi's death, they would do anything they could to help bring the guilty parties to justice."

So they had clearly informed Candi's parents of the homicide nature of the case. "And did Lacey's interview reveal anything helpful?"

"Unfortunately, not much beyond her hostile feelings toward her sister. Apparently, Candi always seemed to be favored by everything from teachers to the local press. We had to grill her a little, but we got it out of her that she was excited for the wedding, even while her mother was trying to delay or even stop it because she knew that once Candi was attached to a lowlife like David Albright, the press wouldn't want anything to do with her. In fact, she had expected that her wedding day would have been her last day in the limelight." Detective Reinhart sighed. "Upon questioning Lacey about her sister's death, she simply told us, 'Why would I have killed her? Now she'll be the talk of the town for at least another month.'"

"Wow, pretty coldhearted," I said.

"Yes, but I'm quite certain she's not the sociopath we're looking for in this case."

After Detective Reinhart had been so forthcoming with all of their information, I felt no reason to hide anything I had uncovered, especially if it could help. "Actually, Amber and I tracked down Hector Banks earlier today."

"Really? Where?" Alex and Detective Reinhart asked at the same time.

"We found him at the local gun range. Apparently, he goes there every day." I went on to explain how close he and Candi had been, the photos on his phone, and the time of day they'd be likely to track him down there. Then I told them about our conversation with Troy Offenbach.

"Yes, we got to him earlier today as well, but we hadn't heard about Candi's mother being against the wedding until Lacey told us that part," Detective Reinhart said. "You clearly have a knack for hunting down suspects and asking the right questions, Mallory. It's always helpful to have someone who was on scene of a murder and can give us a better understanding of the events. I'll be sure to mark you down as a special consultant on this one."

I felt myself flush. "Well, any way I can help, I'm happy to, especially when it sounds like your detective unit has too much on its plate."

Detective Reinhart chuckled. "You can say that again."

"So I'll be over first thing," Alex said, "and we'll see if forensics can figure out anything else useful about this South African plant toxin."

After that, we all said goodbye. As I hung up, I was glad to finally have some motivation to go to bed. Otherwise, I'd likely spend the entire night retelling my stories to Hunch in order to keep him by my side.

I picked him up to carry him upstairs to the bedroom. Even on the days he hated me most, he at least kept Cooper's side of the bed warm, but tonight, as I carried him in that direction, he squirmed and pulled to get out of my arms.

"Hunch, it's bedtime!" I told him. Sometimes I thought the cat understood more words in the English language than I did. Other times, like this, I suspected he didn't comprehend a single one.

He dug his claws into my arm, and while I wasn't in the habit of throwing my cast-clad cat, I couldn't help myself. "Ow! What was that for?"

I ran a thumb over my stinging arm, and a streak of blood appeared. Stupid cat! I'd gone out and bought him a second litter box as well as food and water bowls after he'd been fitted for his cast, so he'd never feel imprisoned by the stairs. I always took him upstairs last thing at night and brought him back down first thing in the morning. So what was this cat's problem?

I looked away from my stinging arm to see Hunch nipping at the leaves of my spider plant in the corner. I let out an aggravated sigh and strode toward him. "Come on, Hunch. It's time for bed."

One more try, and I was leaving him down here for the night. I'd taken good care of Cooper's cat since my late husband's death as an honor to Cooper, but Hunch had never drawn blood before.

He looked up and actually growled at me.

I squinted, wondering if my cat had gone rabid in the last two minutes. He'd been so friendly while sitting on my lap and listening to my investigation stories and the conversation with the police officers. He took another nip at the plant and looked back at me. That's when I clued in that he was trying to tell me something.

My thumb had been absently running over the antidote packet alongside my cell phone since I'd hung up from Alex's call. I blinked as a revelation was trying very hard to connect in my brain. The cat. The spider plant. The H2-blocker/antacid antidote.

The spider plant. My cat's unusual reaction to a plant…

All at once, it hit me: the Albright's greenhouse!

If the poison that killed Candi and almost took out Pastor Jeff had come from an unusual plant…where better to look for such a plant than in someone's private locked greenhouse?

☐

# CHAPTER EIGHTEEN

Hunch wouldn't let me go to bed after I finally got "Greenhouse!" out of our cat and mouse (or cat and human, in this case) game of charades. Of course, he wouldn't. But if I were being honest, the adrenaline that rushed through my veins with this new revelation wouldn't have let me sleep regardless.

I googled sciadotenia toxifera under a number of different spellings until I finally found the green-leafed plant with tiny yellow berries. It didn't inform me of much beyond what I already knew: It was a rare wild-growing poisonous plant, native to the forests of South Africa.

I went over all the information I had with Hunch again. I was no longer suspicious of Troy Offenbach or Hector Banks. And it sounded as though Detective Reinhart had cleared Lacey Banks from suspicion.

I clicked over to my phone icon and dialed Alex's number. It rang four times and then went to voicemail. Clearly, they were too busy on their stakeout to answer the phone. I didn't know any details of their other case, but I couldn't help picturing them with guns drawn, rushing into some rundown drug house or back alley, like I'd seen on TV stakeouts.

I nibbled my lip, hoping they were both okay. When Alex's voicemail beeped, I rattled off a message in little more than a whisper, feeling as if someone on the other end might hear me, and I could somehow blow their cover. "Alex! I just thought about it. What if Brock Albright is growing this rare South African toxic plant in his greenhouse? Amber stuck her gum into the lock of the gate yesterday, so I was thinking…if they're thinking you're going to come back with a warrant, maybe someone should look into what's in there before Brock can hide it away? I'm not sure about getting past the greenhouse lock, but I don't know, I feel like someone should get over there and check it out before it's too late. Get back to me when you can and let me know what you think."

Hunch and I both paced my living room for a full fifteen minutes, waiting for Alex to call back. Then a half hour. The words "special consultant" kept rattling around in my brain, egging me on, not to mention my increasingly-agitated feline friend's growls. Finally, I headed upstairs and pulled on a pair of black leggings and my darkest gray hoodie. I was tempted to text Amber and ask her to come along, but I reminded myself again and again that it was her first day of school tomorrow. Besides, I wasn't about to purposely drag a teenager into a dangerous situation.

Not that this was dangerous. I didn't plan to interrupt anyone's life or even let a single person know I was there. It was a fact-finding mission, I told myself for the twentieth time. Nothing more.

If I could get into the backyard and anything inside looked the least bit like the plant I'd found on the Internet, I'd tell Alex right away, and he could put a rush on that search warrant to investigate first thing in the morning—hopefully before the Albrights were any the wiser and could hide any incriminating evidence.

"If there are any signs that the Albrights might still be awake or that they have any kind of alarm system on that greenhouse, I'm out of there," I told Hunch. "No matter what you think."

Thankfully, he didn't growl or argue with me this time. I brought him downstairs to wait for me there, but as I slipped into some black sneakers, he meowed against the edge of the front door.

"You can't come," I told him, even though I kind of did want his company. "You can barely walk."

But when he mewled a frustrated meow at me again, even though I knew it was stupid, I picked the cat up in my arms and headed out the door.

"You can wait in the car," I told him.

I took the Prius, a hybrid that rode much quieter than Cooper's Jeep. Hunch sat with his cast awkwardly stretched out, but nevertheless upright at attention, as was becoming his habit whenever I brought him along on an investigation.

As I drove out of the center of town toward Honeysuckle Grove farmland, the streetlights came fewer and farther between. When I finally turned down Coventry Road, where the Albrights lived, everything seemed dark and quiet. The farm before their house had one light above its barn, but it only illuminated a small circle in front of it. Otherwise, the only light came from the moon as it moved in and out of cloud covering.

I pulled over onto the shoulder a few feet past the lit barn and well before the Albright farmhouse. It would be a bit of a walk to get to the greenhouse, but better too far away than too close.

"You're going to be stuck in here a while," I told Hunch. I was tempted to remind him not to pee in my car, but I realized before it left my mouth that Hunch was either much too responsible to let such an infantile occurrence happen or much too feline to understand my instructions. In eight and a half months, I hadn't discovered which was truer, so what made me think I'd have any real revelations about it tonight?

I picked through the small toolkit I'd brought along, shoving bits and pieces into my hoodie pockets. A tiny screwdriver here, a paperclip and hair clip there. I reached for the glove compartment, flipped it open, and slapped my hand around. My flashlight. Had I left it somewhere while investigating Dan Montrose's death?

No matter, I decided. The flashlight on my phone would work in a pinch, even if it was overly bright. I'd use it sparingly and only when out of view of any of the farmhouse windows. I grabbed my cell phone from the console to get the flashlight app open, but as soon as I flicked it on, I saw Alex had returned my call and left a voicemail, but my phone only had five percent of its battery life left. Usually, it was plugged in beside my bed by this time at night.

I sighed. This was going to be a super fast fact-checking mission after all, and I'd have to call Alex back when I could get back to the phone charger in my car, or I wouldn't have any flashlight at all to work with.

I got out of the Prius and closed the door silently. I'd do my best to navigate my way by moonlight alone as much as possible, only using my phone light when I absolutely needed it. Thankfully, traffic was thin on these farm roads at the best of times, and there were no cars at this time of night, so at least walking the long stretch of road to the Albright farmhouse was a breeze, even in the dark.

Once I could make out the frame of the Albright farmhouse, I decided it was time to leave the easy terrain of the road and wade through the thigh-high grass. I suspected, from the unkempt area, they didn't use this path often. I took each step slowly, ensuring I had solid footing before moving on. Maybe I should've brought one of Hunch's litter boxes in the car, I thought absently as I took another step, because at this rate, getting to the greenhouse and back to the Prius could well take me all night.

I paused and squinted around me, trying to get my bearings, even though a cloud had momentarily shielded the moon and it seemed much darker. The light from the neighboring barn in the distance gave me some sort of spatial awareness. I decided on moving closer to the farmhouse, close enough to run my hand along it. That would help me keep my bearings.

By the time I made it to the farmhouse, my leggings and shoes were soaked from dew. I shivered and told myself I had to be almost at the fence. It was a tiny farmhouse, and Amber had said the greenhouse was right behind it.

Just then, my hand hit something flat in front of me. Running a hand along the worn board, I immediately got a sliver, but I could tell this was definitely the fence in front of me. My hand gently led my way sideways until I found the small latch of the gate. It was a thumb-press latch. It wouldn't press, and I could find the lock above it by feel. But I gave the ten-foot gate a little nudge, and sure enough, Amber's gum must have still been in the strike plate because it moved forward.

I tiptoed through quietly, looking around me in the darkness to make sure nothing and no one had been disturbed. When I got to the back corner of the farmhouse, thankfully the moon had made a reappearance to help me along. Moonlight glinted off the black plastic of the greenhouse, and I could make out its large arched form. In fact, while not quite as tall, the oblong greenhouse seemed to cover much more land than the small farmhouse in front of it. The thing was huge!

I was so caught up in admiring the size of it and tiptoeing toward it, I was being less careful with each of my steps and paused when my foot squished into something soft.

I pulled out my phone, running my hand along its side to find the On button, but that's when I realized the packets of antidote were still curled into the penholder of my phone case. Shoot. I should have left those in the car, or better yet, at home. If I lost it out here in the overgrown grass, Alex would likely have to miss out on any sleep he could get in order to make a special trip to the hospital.

I pulled the packets from the pen loop and went to tuck it into my shoe, but as I flicked my flashlight on, just for a second, the squishy thing I'd stepped on came into view. I jumped back and tried my best to quell my scream with a hand over my mouth.

A dead rat.

It took me several seconds to regain my breath. Flies buzzed around the area, and I wondered if there were other dead—or alive—vermin nearby. Thankfully, I hadn't dropped the little silver packets because there was a zero percent chance I was going to get on my hands and knees in the probably rat-infested thigh-high grass to search for them. In fact, I didn't even want to go anywhere near my shoes again. Instead, I tucked the packets into my hoodie pocket, praying that would be a good enough place to keep it safe.

I was tempted to turn around and quick-step it out of there, but with the one glimpse of light from my phone, I'd caught sight of the greenhouse door, less than three feet in front of me.

I sucked in a deep breath, flicked on my flashlight app for another quick second, and then tiptoed forward. The area in front of the door had been cleared of long grass, and a cleared path led to the back door of the farmhouse, which made sense if the Albrights came in and out to water daily. It took all of my mental strength to put all vermin out of my mind, feel for the padlock on the door, and kneel in front of it so I could get a closer look.

I flicked on my flashlight app again and found it was a simple padlock. That's what I was hoping for. I wouldn't have had a clue where to start if it had been a combination or dial lock of some kind, but back when I helped Cooper research his novels, I'd had to "help" his main character, Marty Sims, pick more than a few simple padlocks. I'd never done it myself, but I'd typed the words about nestling a tension wrench into the top part of the lock and pushing the pins in one by one so many times, it felt like it should be a simple process.

I felt around for my paperclip in the dark, hoping it would work to emulate a tension wrench. Within seconds, I realized one thing: Marty Sims had a lot more skill as a detective than Mallory Beck did. The paperclip didn't have enough tension to move anything within the lock. I grabbed for my tiny flathead screwdriver.

I turned on my flashlight app and held my phone's empty penholder between my teeth so I could get a better look. Maybe this wasn't a job that could be done by a novice lock picker in the dark, after all.

But I was here now. I had to at least try.

The small screwdriver had enough strength that I could tell right away it was going to be more useful than the paperclip. Once I had it fed into the top part of the lock and pulled to the left, which was the direction I was quite sure it should turn, I reached back into my pocket for the paperclip.

Now that I had the lock mechanism held with some tension, I could actually feel the pins on the other end of my paperclip. It wasn't exactly a cinch to push them down, and it was definitely like riding a unicycle through a labyrinth while curling my hair to press them all at once, but I gave it all of my focus and tried again and again until finally I felt a click and the lock turned!

I was so excited, I almost let out a yelp. But just as I turned the lock fully to the other side to unhook it from the greenhouse's latch, my phone died and everything went dark.

"Shoot," I whispered aloud to the air around me. "Now what?"

"Now…" a deep male voice said from behind me, "you'll get up off the ground and tell me what you're doing breaking into my greenhouse."

# CHAPTER NINETEEN

My knees and hands shook as I rose to my feet. Brock Albright was intimidating at the best of times, but now, in the dead of night, he seemed like the Grim Reaper. He shone a flashlight in my face as I turned, blinding me.

"I—I'm sorry," I said. There was no avoiding or explaining away what I might have been doing, breaking and entering into his greenhouse in the dead of night.

Sounds emanated from the greenhouse now. Chattering sounds. Rustling. Screeching. There was more than one animal in there.

"You can tell it to the police," Brock said, roughly grabbing me by the arm.

My eyes had only just started to adjust to the light when Brock yanked me toward the back door of his house. He led me first through a small shed that smelled of vinegar and chemicals. The counters on either side were littered with metal netting, latches, and other building supplies, but I got a flash of one out-of-place object as we passed quickly through the shed and into the house: a bright yellow Nerf dart!

As he hauled me in through the back door, Brock yelled, "Katrina, call the police! We have an intruder."

He pushed me into a tiny kitchen, barely big enough for the two of us, but apparently, this was as far as he planned to take me. A stove light dimly lit a kitchen covered in peeling wallpaper that appeared to be at least three decades old. Brock wore yellow plaid pajama pants and a white T-shirt. His hair was mussed. I had definitely gotten him out of bed. I figured he must have heard me when I stepped on the dead rat and couldn't completely quell my scream.

A moment later, Katrina Albright swept into the small kitchen, and now there truly wasn't room for another person. Brock had me backed up against the stove, while he stood at the counter across from me. Katrina, in her baggy beige nightdress, widened her eyes at me and then looked at her feet when she turned to her husband and murmured, "I'm sorry."

She was sorry for having invited me in two days ago. I had gotten sweet Katrina Albright in trouble with her husband.

Then again, what was a Nerf dart doing in their shed? I'd be willing to bet if I'd had another moment to look around, I'd find more evidence, maybe needle-like darts. For all I knew, these two could've been in it together.

Katrina Albright turned and lifted a phone receiver from the wall. I had seen those kinds of phones in museums before, and I watched in awe as she ran a finger in a circle all the way from the 9 to the top and let the rotary dial click back into its place.

I snapped out of my daze when she dialed the second 1. She really was calling the police on me, which was a good thing, I told myself, even if the only two officers were out of reach for the evening. I'd rather spend the night in jail than with these crazy people.

Katrina started murmuring quietly into the phone. She gave the address of their farmhouse.

"I lost a necklace," I blurted the second the idea came to me. "I thought it might have fallen off in your grass somewhere." It was out of my mouth before I realized that wouldn't explain me trying to break into their greenhouse or even forcing my way into their backyard.

Brock let out a single bitter laugh. "And you didn't think to ask, perhaps when you were here during the daytime?" He laughed again.

"And would you have let me look for it?" I crossed my arms, trying hard to adopt some of Amber's confidence.

Brock raised his eyebrows. Then he grabbed me roughly by the arm again and pulled me out the back door the way we had come. This time, I was a little less in shock and a little more prepared. My eyes darted to every nook and cranny of his small shed as we passed through it.

It was too much to scan in a short amount of time, but as we moved outdoors, I caught sight of scattered straw on the ground. What looked like cat litter strewn on a work shelf. Spray bottles. And that bright yellow dart.

I sucked in a breath as we hit the night air. It still wasn't undeniable proof, but I felt it in my gut. Brock Albright had to be the murderer.

I just somehow had to find undeniable proof before the police arrived.

Brock eyed me as he pocketed the small padlock I had picked, as though I might steal it, and yanked open the sturdy greenhouse door. "Is this what you were looking for?" He shone his flashlight around the greenhouse, lined down one side with garden beds, the wood and soil barely visible for all the green foliage. Then he flipped a loud switch, and a series of what looked like grow lights illuminated one by one along the entire length of the greenhouse. I wondered why he didn't use clear plastic and harness the light from the sun like normal greenhouses.

But then a squeal from the other side of the greenhouse took my attention, and then rustling and more squeals, and I looked to that side to see rows of wire cages, at least a dozen of them, each one housing an individual rat.

I stepped back toward the door, but Brock blocked my path. "Oh, no. You're not going anywhere." He let out a low chuckle.

At least the police would be here soon. I surveyed the rat cages—certainly glad these ones were housed, not like the dead one outside. Halfway along was another worktable, this one metal, and it was covered in test tubes, test tube trays, small clear plastic baggies, and a large plastic bag that appeared to contain dried plants of some kind. My mind went first to marijuana, but only for a second. Then it went to the sciadotenia toxifera plant I had googled earlier. There were also plenty of baggies already packed with the green, dried substance and marked with stickers and names. Was he actually selling lethal plants to other people? The lady in the red car hadn't looked to me like someone out purchasing a murder weapon, but then again, would I think that of anyone?

The rats were all awake now and racing around in their cages. They were hard to turn my back on, but I had to scan the other sides of the greenhouse for the South African plant.

"Wow," I said, trying to buy time to gather as much intel as I could. "You have a real green thumb." Many of the plants were just large leafy ones, but a strain right near the door had smaller leaves and yellow berries. "Do you know where I can buy these sorts of plants or what they're called?"

One glance at Brock's hardened jaw, and I doubted he was going to answer. "Let's cut the ruse, shall we?" He gave me a small shove deeper into the greenhouse, followed me all the way in, and shut the door behind us. The rats went crazy with squealing. Him showing off his greenhouse to me definitely felt more eerie than prideful. "You're here because you think I killed Candi Banks." He said it in such a conversational tone, I would swear we were discussing garden tools or mundane yard work.

I sucked in a breath and let it out slowly before answering. The police were on their way, there was no stopping that. Maybe honesty really was the best approach in talking any new information out of Brock Albright before they arrived. I'd have to let the police cuff me and haul me out in the back of a police cruiser. Then I could tell them to get a hold of Alex, tell him everything I'd discovered.

"Did you?" I asked, trying to match his calmness, but my voice squeaked as high as one of the rats on the second word.

In way of an answer, Brock moved over to one of the nearby plant beds. He ran a hand along the soil under some large green leaves with red-tinged veins. His hand emerged with what looked like a tiny silver spigot, like the kind used to extract maple syrup from maple trees, but much smaller.

"We have plants from all over the world in here, Mallory," he said, and I admit, I was surprised he remembered my name. Although, come to think of it, even when I first brought over the casserole, he had acted as though they seldom had people inside their house. "These plants require constant monitoring of humidity and soil acidity. Some of them are even poisonous." He paused, as if for added effect. "We don't normally allow any outside visitors inside the greenhouse." He explained this as though he were doing me a favor by holding me hostage until the police came.

But there was the Nerf dart and what looked like the same plant Candi and Pastor Jeff were poisoned with. There was a worktable with test tubes. I knew there had to be needle-like darts somewhere on there as well.

He had never wanted his son to marry Candi, even though David had been determined to do so, so he had motive.

"Except for me?" I asked it as a question, wondering if he'd explain why I was given an honor that even his only precious son wasn't.

"Except for you." Brock nodded and smiled. Again, his tone gave me an eerie feeling that made my stomach drop out from within me. He took the tiny silver spigot, moved a step toward the door, lifted some of the small leaves around the yellow berries, and dug the spigot into the stem of the plant, right near the soil.

Was he actually bragging to me about how he'd accomplished a cold-blooded murder while the police were on their way? I glanced toward the door, straining to hear police sirens, but they must not have been close enough yet. If I tried to run, he'd certainly make it to the door before me.

"This one is called a sciacentaria toxifera," he told me conversationally as he pulled the spigot away from the plant and held it up to eye level, so both he and I could see the drops of orange liquid sitting in the groove of it. "African descent," he went on. "The root juices are highly poisonous to humans." He glanced over at me with an easy smile that made my stomach drop even further. "The poison is rare, so it often gets mistaken for strychnine." He took a step toward me.

Strychnine—the poison that was initially suspected to be in Candi's bloodstream.

"Is that what you used to kill Candi?" My throat was parched, so my question came out quieter than I meant to.

One side of his lip turned up as he told me, "The girl wouldn't leave David alone. I forbid him to see her, and still, she kept begging him to sneak out to meet her. She'd come by at all hours of the night. It's why we had the surveillance cameras installed around the property."

It hadn't been my reaction to the rat that had given me away after all. At least not entirely. But I couldn't get over the fact that Brock Albright had just admitted his guilt, and while the police were about to arrive.

"So you had to kill her?" I asked as I took a step backward in the small aisle way between the row of poisonous plants and the row of rats, not really wanting to get closer to either.

He mimicked my move. "I tried threatening her. I tried threatening him. But she was bound and determined to steal our son from us. For a minute there, I thought that with the double-booking of the park, the wedding might fall apart on its own and then everything would be fine. But then my son flashed a shiny key at me and told me that either way, he'd already moved his stuff into a house Mr. Banks had provided for him and their daughter and he wouldn't be back. I had to take care of her. I had to." He tilted his head at me, as though pleading for my understanding.

But I didn't understand. This was murder.

"The truth is, that church treasurer killed her." He said this as though this genuinely uplifted his spirits. "I had no idea about her bee allergy. If not for Mr. Offenbach's administration of the epinephrine, she likely would have made it to the hospital in time for them to help her." He took a breath and sighed it out. "My part was small. I just had to get the toxin into her from a distance. But there were plenty of shrubs and trees around that park to hide behind." He actually chuckled as he reminisced. "Of course, it was only my good fortune that the park had been double-booked and that Candi loved to argue. It gave me just the distraction I needed."

His good fortune? Sure. He sure didn't seem broken up that the EpiPen had sped up Candi's death. "The police should be here soon," I reminded him because the way he held the spigot, along with his creepy smile, felt like a threat.

But my words only made him laugh. "Oh, no. They won't be, my dear," he told me. "That old phone in the kitchen? It hasn't worked in years."

My knees buckled, and the next thing I knew, I fell onto the dirt beneath me.

With a renewed fierceness and confidence in his eyes, Brock Albright and his poison-filled spigot loomed above my head.

☐

# CHAPTER TWENTY

The man with the poison looked so calm and almost cheery, it seemed surreal when suddenly his hand reached out and he pushed me the rest of the way down so I fell face-first on the dirt floor of the greenhouse. It felt as though it took me hours—days—to react, but when I finally attempted to push myself up, his foot was already on my back, forcing me down.

"You won't get away with this!" I told him when I could find my voice.

My mind raced to Alex, who I told I was waiting for his call to discuss coming to the Albright farm. What were the chances he would guess that I had rushed out here on my own? He probably just figured I'd gone to bed for the night, and that was why I hadn't answered my phone. He had planned to drop by my house first thing in the morning. But morning was still hours away.

"Oh, sure I will," Brock told me. I felt a prick in the middle of my back. "In fact, I already have."

A second later, the pressure lifted from my back and I could move, but I didn't have time to worry about Brock. My arms flailed wildly to get at my back because one thing was clear to me: He had just poisoned me with the same type of needle-like dart he'd used on Candi Banks. The only difference was, at this close range, the dart in me hadn't come from a toy gun. Brock had simply dipped it in poison and then pressed it into my skin, like a hot knife through butter.

He knew exactly where to insert it so I wouldn't be able to reach it. I started to push myself up, but I didn't get very far. Suddenly, I wasn't concerned at all about my back or the needle because the toxin hit my bloodstream and I gasped for a breath. My hands flew to my throat, shocked at how fast the poison was affecting me.

"Don't fight it," Brock said in the same smooth voice he'd been using ever since he brought me into his greenhouse/lab.

My world had been turned on its head in the last thirty seconds and focusing on anything at all around me was getting more and more difficult.

His voice wobbled in my head when he added, "If I had some epinephrine on hand, I'd give it to you. It would make the whole process go a lot faster. But don't worry. It'll still be over within a matter of minutes. I know it's probably pointless to tell you this…" He let out a low chuckle that seemed completely out of place in this moment. "But struggling against the process will only make it more painful."

I didn't know whether he was lying or not. Perhaps he wanted me to stop struggling so the poison would have a chance to move seamlessly through my veins. Whatever the case, I did what he said. Somehow, in the depths of my mind, I knew I needed to conserve my energy. I also needed to stop reacting for a few seconds and think.

I kept my hands at my neck, as though that would somehow protect my lungs from the poison that had already infiltrated them, but the second I stopped struggling, Brock turned me over onto my back. I flopped like a rag doll and didn't fight him as he pawed at my hoodie. A second later, my keys jangled in his hand. My car! Hunch! I was doing everything in my power to keep my focus, conserve my energy, and come up with any kind of a plan that could save my life.

"Heh, heh, heh." Brock held a rectangular object right in front of my face, as if teasing me with it. "We wouldn't want you to have this, now would we?"

I blinked until it came into focus. My phone!

I swatted to grab for it. Brock was much quicker than me, though. He stood and pulled it away in plenty of time. Only a second later, I clued in enough to remember it was dead, anyway. It wasn't going to help me. But I couldn't help tracing the form of it with my eyes.

Just before he pocketed my phone, my eyes landed on the little leather pen loop.

My life-saving solution clicked into place in my mind like a bullet in a gun chamber. The revelation made me momentarily forget that my lungs were paralyzed and my mouth attempted to gasp for another breath. My inability to process the breath made my whole body writhe in pain as I struggled against my whole respiratory system.

"I told you," Brock said, backing toward the door with my phone and my keys in his pocket. "Just let it happen. I'll be back when it's over."

For once, Brock's tone, as much as I could concentrate on it, had changed to something less comfortable. The coward, I thought. He was man enough to poison me, but he wasn't man enough to stand around and watch me die?

But the second the door closed behind him, I remembered: I had a plan.

My hand immediately fumbled from my neck down to my right hoodie pocket. But I reached inside, fumbled around, and all I found was the screwdriver, paperclip, and hair clip. Frantically, I tried the other pocket. I hadn't been able to take a breath in what felt like an hour, and black spots filled my vision, but at least I still had feeling in my fingertips.

But the antidote packets weren't in there either!

Had they fallen out of my pocket outside? I slapped every area of my chest and stomach, willing them to appear. What if they'd fallen out when Brock had grabbed my phone?

I pawed the dirt around me and, sure enough, felt one packet, and then the other one, buried half under my side.

I didn't have the energy or the vision to look around to see if Brock had actually left. I tried to steady my hand as I ripped at the top of the packet. The black spots were making me dizzy, and I hoped I wasn't spilling it everywhere.

I'd pulled the packet to my mouth, tipped it back, but my mouth was numb, and I couldn't tell if the antidote made it to my mouth. I recalled what Emily Hawthorne had told me—about Pastor Jeff having been instructed to put it under his tongue to act faster, but I had no idea how to work my tongue anymore. I ripped open the other packet, dumped it into my mouth, and hoped some of it would by chance find its way under my tongue.

And then everything went black.

☐

# CHAPTER TWENTY-ONE

My first breath felt like a knife through my ribs, and I had to wonder if babies felt this kind of pain taking their first breath coming out of the womb. I gripped my chest and gulped for more oxygen. And then more.

My entire body felt achy and sore, but I blinked up and remembered where I was, on the floor of the Albright's greenhouse. And I could see. I could breathe.

There was no time for rejoicing. Brock Albright would be back to bury me or throw me into the river or whatever he planned to do with my dead body, but I didn't intend to be here. I needed to get to the police.

Sitting up took about as much effort as swimming the Atlantic with a tractor-trailer on my back. I turned onto my side. Rested. Pulled up a leg. Took another rest. Got my hands beneath me just in time for my next break. With each motion, I was convinced Brock Albright would return before I could even get myself up off the ground. But I focused and kept working at it anyway, one baby step at a time.

When I'd made it to my hands and knees, that seemed good enough. Why did humans have to walk on two legs anyway? This was much more stable. It certainly took less effort.

I moved on all fours toward the greenhouse door like an overweight hog that hadn't been out of his pen in a year. My muscles shook and ached with the effort of each step. I didn't know if the grow lamps in here were giving off heat or if it was just my own body breaking into a feverish sweat. The rats were no longer squealing, but I felt their eyes on me, like they were waiting for me to keel over so they could break out and feed on me. It felt like I weighed a literal tonne. When I finally made it to the door, I nudged it with my forehead.

It didn't budge.

I used all my effort to reach up and see if there was a knob of some kind to turn, but there was nothing. I pushed harder, this time with both hands and all my weight.

But the door clacked against something on the other side, and in my mind's eye, I could see exactly what was stopping the motion: the padlock I'd picked what felt like hours ago.

I fell back onto my rear, and if I'd had the energy, I would've cried. All this work, all this hope, and I was going to die anyway! How could that be possible?

I gazed around at probably fifty feet of green foliage on one side and two dozen beady eyes on the other. I suspected Brock did work some sort of a drug operation here—one he had kept secret from his son. While David was out hawking the vegetables from their overgrown yard at a farmer's market, likely to just keep him out of the way, his dad was making the real money—harvesting some sort of plant products to sell to local high school students. I didn't see any marijuana plants, so Brock likely dealt in some sort of more exotic drugs.

I supposed this wasn't the worst place to die. At least it was beautiful and earthy. The multitude of shades of green reminded me of Alex, of his eyes. If only Alex were here. I sighed. If only I'd called him back while I still had a phone and some battery life. But as I surveyed the magnificent but deadly plants in front of me, it was Cooper's voice I clearly heard in my head.

Start with what you have.

It's what Cooper always used to say to himself when stuck at some point in one of his mysteries. Hunch would pace alongside him, and before long, he'd stop mid-step, snap his fingers, and smile like the sun had illuminated his mouth.

I looked around again and argued out loud to Cooper. "But what do I have, except a whole lot of plants, most of them probably poisonous, and a dozen rats? Should I poison myself again, huh? Should I let the rats loose to start feeding on my arms and legs?" My voice came out angrier than I expected. It took me aback. Was I angry at Cooper that I'd gotten myself into this situation?

But before I'd even asked myself that question, I knew the answer. No. I was only angry because Cooper had left me. I sighed to myself again. He couldn't have helped that any more than I could have.

In a show of some sort of forgiveness or apology to Cooper's spirit, I dug in my hoodie pockets again, even though I knew my phone and keys were gone. I only had a tiny screwdriver, a hair clip, and a paperclip.

Start with what you have.

I looked at the greenhouse door and sighed. Unfortunately, the padlock was on the outside of the metal door, so these wouldn't do me much good. I dropped them onto the dirt beside me and had a momentary vision of trying to dig my way out of here using my tiny screwdriver.

"That should take, what, about a year?" I asked out loud and then laughed humourlessly. My laugh turned into a sob. I choked and muttered, "Please, God," as though I could actually count on Him to get me out of this.

But then, as though God or Cooper or someone up there was answering my question, a gust of wind rustled the black plastic greenhouse covering.

I blinked. And then blinked again, waiting for a slow-dawning realization to make it into my tired brain.

Plastic. Huh. Maybe I couldn't dig myself out through the dirt floor of the greenhouse, but what if I could dig my way out through the plastic?

The thought had barely formed and I was already lying on the ground, but this time not for a rest. I rolled under the closest plant bed, right up to the edge of the greenhouse, reached for the tiny screwdriver, and punctured it into the plastic.

I guess I expected it to let out a sigh of air, like a balloon slowly popping, but the screwdriver puncturing the plastic was much more innocuous. It didn't matter how it felt, I decided quickly, puncturing another dozen holes around it. It would feel good enough to get out of here and be free.

But it seemed to be three layers of the heavyweight plastic. At this rate, it would take me all night to puncture enough holes through the plastic to even get my arm through.

I rolled out and sat up again, looking around. The tiny bit of success had been enough to fill me with a little extra hope and energy. My eyes roamed the rat cages—and for a second, I wondered if I could somehow convince them that rather than gnawing on me, they might enjoy a meal of black plastic—but then landed on the metal worktable.

The test tubes. Were they glass? They had to be.

I crawled forward and heaved myself up by the bed of the heavyset table. Sure enough, the empty test tubes were made of glass. They were less than an inch around, and there had to be at least twenty of them, but I only needed one. Sharp broken glass would cut plastic a lot easier than a tiny screwdriver would.

The thick plastic took a lot of puncturing and slicing before I could even force an arm through it, and it had as many holes as a screen door by the time I could force my feet and then the rest of my body through. I had effectively ruined about three feet of the Albright's precious greenhouse/lab, and I had to admit, even though it wasn't enough, it still felt pretty satisfying.

Once I had my entire body outside, I took eight or nine deep breaths of the cool night air before I had the energy to move.

"Thank you," I whispered into the night air. I didn't know if I was saying the words to God. But I couldn't say for sure that I wasn't.

Now what? Brock would certainly be coming back for me soon. I didn't have the energy to fight him or even his wife off in my current condition.

Then again, I didn't have car keys or a phone. I hadn't had the strength to pull myself to my feet yet, so how did I expect to walk half a mile down the road to my car? Even if I got there, was teaching Hunch how to hit the unlock button or teaching myself how to hotwire a car a possibility? No and no. So that left the nearest farm, which was even farther.

But it was my only choice, I quickly decided. And regardless of any possible vermin, dead or alive, I figured I had a better chance of making it to a neighboring farm on all fours than I did on two feet.

I took one grueling hog-like step after another around the front of the greenhouse, past the door, past the shed that led to the farmhouse, and into the long grass. It wasn't as though I loved dead rats, so I navigated around the one I knew was there, which kept me closer to the greenhouse, rather than the farmhouse. Even though the greenhouse was lit up like the light of day on the inside, only small cracks of light shone through to the outside. Still, it was easier to see than it had been on my way in, and despite my exhaustion, I quickly made it past the edge of the farmhouse.

As I turned the corner, new lights illuminated my way through the farmhouse windows. The Albrights were clearly still awake inside, probably discussing what to do with my dead body, but they weren't in view through any windows, so I kept low, crawling knee after hand, hand after knee until I reached the gate of the high fence.

Using all my might, I pulled myself up to reach for the handle. When the gate didn't immediately move, for a second, I thought Brock had found and removed Amber's gum. But it turned out it was only my lack of strength holding me back.

I made it all the way past their old truck before I started to breathe a little easier. I looked both ways down the long farm road, only illuminated by the moonlight. That one barn light down past my car was my only beacon of hope. Who knew how far the next farmhouse would be, and could I even make it that far? What if the folks who lived there were friends with the Albrights and called them instead of the cops?

Too many unanswerable questions.

Even though the moonlight seemed at its brightest, I couldn't even make out the shape of my car from here. Part of me wondered if my eyes and brain still weren't working correctly after passing out from lack of oxygen. I swore I could even see black shadows moving on the street in front of me.

I sighed away my questions and confusion and went to take another slow knee-and-hand step toward the pavement, figuring I had to try for the nearest farm. But that's when Brock's voice stopped me.

"How are you still alive?" He sounded astonished as his black form came into focus in front of me on the road.

I groaned inwardly. Even if I had the energy to explain, the last thing I wanted to do was to tip him off that the police had an antidote to his poison before I died.

He jangled some keys, and in an instant, it became clear to me why he was coming from down the road and why I couldn't see my Prius. He had been concealing it, apparently. When he killed me, there would be nothing to lead the police to my being here.

I squinted my eyes shut and then opened them, wondering, if I pooled every single resource inside my body, how far I would be able to stumble away from this crazy man. Could I lift my leg enough to try and kick him in the groin? I sucked in my breath, ready to try.

But as I wobbled to my feet, Brock was quick to grab both of my arms and hold them together in a grip I didn't have a hope of fighting. I already knew he would take me back to his greenhouse/lab and poison me again.

And this time I had no antidote to fight it.

☐

# CHAPTER TWENTY-TWO

I looked up at Brock, but his eyes weren't on me. They were down the farm road. When I followed his gaze, I saw two bright lights coming straight toward us.

These weren't the bright lights of the afterlife I was expecting either. These were the lights of a car barreling full-speed ahead.

Brock yanked me toward the roadside, but the car picked up speed and skidded to a stop at an angle, only ten feet away from the Albright's driveway where Brock had now pulled me. Before he could get any farther, two car doors slammed behind us, and a deep, authoritative voice said, "This is the police! Brock Albright, get your hands in the air!"

I had never been so happy to hear Detective Reinhart's voice. Brock hesitated, but then let me go and raised his hands.

I took a step forward, away from him, but wobbled on my feet. "He did it!" I panted my words out as loudly as I could as I pointed back over my shoulder. "He murdered Candi Banks!"

It was all the energy I had left. I started to collapse forward, and Alex rushed forward from the other side of the car to catch me.

☐

# CHAPTER TWENTY-THREE

I woke up in the back of an ambulance with a large oxygen mask covering the lower half of my face.

"Alex?" I said, trying to pull myself into a sitting position, but I'd been strapped to a gurney. The back doors of the ambulance were wide open, and I could see miles of farmland, now lit up by giant work lights, and the tiny distant light of the neighbor's barn.

A paramedic turned to me from within the ambulance. "Whoa, whoa. You're okay, ma'am. Just relax." He was the same paramedic who had treated me after my near-drowning while tracking down the murderer of Dan Montrose. I wondered if this paramedic thought I just enjoyed this kind of life-threatening adrenaline rush. I wondered if we should be past him calling me "ma'am" by now.

"Alex Martinez?" I asked.

My voice sounded muffled through the oxygen mask, but he must have heard me because he said, "Officer Martinez will check in with you at the hospital. He had to arrange to get some arrests to the station first."

"Arrests?" My hope soared, but the paramedic seemed to realize he'd said too much and patted my shoulder.

"Don't you worry about that. Just get some rest."

I didn't see Alex until I had been poked and prodded a million times at the hospital. Thankfully, I remembered the name of Dr. Khumalo, the doctor who had treated Pastor Jeff, and I asked for him as soon as the paramedics wheeled me through the emergency entrance.

It took some time for the hospital staff to track him down, but as soon as he walked into the ER room they'd parked me in, I started spewing information at him.

110

"I was injected with the same type of toxin as Pastor Jeff Hawthorne. I had the H2-blocker/antacid antidote with me. I swallowed some, and I could breathe again, but my lungs are still working so hard and I'm so tired." I let out a wheeze of air to punctuate the statement.

Dr. Khumalo nodded with his forehead creased. Then he rattled off a slew of instructions to nearby nurses: eight cc's of this, five of that. I was just so tired. I couldn't concentrate on any of it.

Thankfully, whatever Dr. Khumalo prescribed, it allowed me to sleep.

The next time I awoke, I was greeted with a beautiful combination of greens. But these weren't from surrounding poisonous plants that might kill me. These were Alex's warm and worried eyes.

"Did you arrest them?" I asked. My voice croaked, but the oxygen mask had been removed. I must at least be breathing properly on my own now.

"Well, good morning to you, too," he said, smiling with one side of his mouth in a way that made him look a lot like he had in seventh grade. Judging by the dim light around the window curtains, it must have been really early. "And, yes, the Albrights are behind bars. Our forensic scientists have already been able to verify the poisonous species of plants that were responsible for Candi Banks' death."

"There's a shed behind the farmhouse, too," I told him. "You'll find at least one Nerf bullet inside. There's probably more evidence, but I didn't get a chance to look around much."

"Not much?" Alex raised his eyebrows at me. "Just enough to almost get yourself killed. Again," he added. He pulled out a notebook and jotted down everything I told him.

"Did you see his whole drug operation? Was he selling lethal dried plants to other people?" If this was the case, there could be a lot more danger out there.

But Alex shook his head. "We found the setup, yes, but when Steve questioned Brock Albright, he admitted to selling a plant substance that mimics OxyContin. He had recently been fired from Brem Chemical Plant in Martinsburg for suspicion of stealing equipment. Apparently, he had tried to find out about getting FDA approval, but he was out of work and didn't have time or money for the years' long process." Alex shook his head. "I actually got the impression the guy had good intentions—to provide an alternative to a dangerous drug. But where he's going, he won't be supplying anyone for a good long while, with or without FDA approval."

"I guess Amber's brother had it a little off the mark when he thought the Albrights were Honeysuckle Grove's biggest drug dealers," I said.

Alex nodded. "We haven't found a connection to the toy gun that fired any Nerf bullets and needles yet. Our forensics team said it's only available in the UK."

"Katrina Albright's mother sent toys from England each year!" It felt a little like I had the right answer on Jeopardy. Even though the case was solved, more puzzle pieces fitting into place felt very satisfying. Alex made a note of this, too.

"When you're feeling better, I can't wait for you to tell me why you thought it was a good idea to sneak around a murderer's backyard in the middle of the night."

That smile was fighting at the sides of his lips again, and I knew Alex wasn't angry with me. Just worried. And once I explained I'd done it for him—if things had worked out how I had wanted them to, he would've been able to go back to Detective Reinhart and Captain Corbett with a solid case, one only he could take credit for—I knew he'd understand.

"For now, though," he told me, "you'd just better take a few deep breaths and help me get your story straight about why you might have had a reason to be trespassing on the Albright farm because Reinhart and Corbett are on their way in to talk to you."

☐

# CHAPTER TWENTY-FOUR

When I woke up the next time, Detective Reinhart and Captain Corbett loomed above me in their police uniforms. I had no idea how much time had passed since Alex had been by my side, but it looked brighter outside my hospital room window. Even though Alex had been dressed equally formally when he had been here earlier, his appearance had felt a whole lot friendlier. These two men, with their grim faces, looked like they were out for somebody's blood.

Probably mine.

But I took a deep breath—it was getting easier and easier to do that— and said, "Good morning, gentlemen. What can I do for you?"

"We have some questions for you about the incident at the Albright farm last night," Captain Corbett said. Despite his gruff early-morning voice, his authoritative Texan twang still rang through.

"If you're up to it," Detective Reinhart added. He offered a small smile, which earned him a glare from his superior.

"Will Officer Martinez be joining us?" I asked. I already knew he hadn't been invited for this interview, but it didn't mean I wouldn't try.

"Officer Martinez has other obligations within the hospital this morning," Captain Corbett told me. I wished the two men in my room would sit down. They felt intimidating and stress-inducing looming over me. Then again, that was probably their intention. At least Captain Corbett's. "But don't worry, I think Detective Reinhart and I can handle it."

His sarcasm wasn't lost on me, and it was all I could do not to act sarcastic right back and mention how inappropriate his tone was while talking to a victim who had almost died at the hands of a murderer that, as of last night, he hadn't yet caught.

But while Alex and I had discussed my presence at the Albrights' earlier, I had thought this through and had come up with a plan. I opened my mouth to say, "You know, I'd really feel much more comfortable if Officer Martinez was here. He was just so calm and compassionate when I collapsed at the Albright farm." I used my sweetest, most innocent voice to add, "After everything I've been through, I'd just feel better." I sucked in my lips to refrain from spewing all the other things I wanted to say to Alex's bossy, unreasonable captain.

"Officer Martinez is not officially working this case."

I kept my wide eyes right on the police captain. "Well, maybe he should be. After all he's done on this case, should he not at least be in the room to verify any details?" I folded my arms across my chest and waited him out.

He twisted his lips to the side and, after a long pause, offered a single nod to Detective Reinhart—apparently a dismissal. As the detective left the room, he shot me a look with raised eyebrows that I swear was admiration. As soon as the door shut behind him, another miracle happened: Captain Corbett sighed and decided to sit in the only other chair in my room.

"I can't wait to hear how it was y'all were involved so closely in another murder investigation, Mrs. Beck," he told me with a heavy accent on my last name. But it wasn't a direct question, and so I chose not to answer it.

Thankfully, Alex was still in the hospital, and it only took him mere minutes to appear in my stoically silent hospital room.

"Detective Reinhart said you wanted to see me," he said to his boss, and all I wanted in the world was for Alex to finally earn some respect from this man.

"Mrs. Beck has requested for you to sit in on this here interview," Corbett said. He sat back into his chair, relaxed, and had his arms spread out along the windowsill behind him in some sort of power pose. "So why don't you conduct this interview, Officer Martinez. We want to do whatever we can to make Mrs. Beck comfortable."

Again with the sarcasm. In that second, I made it my life's goal to stop focusing on the murderers of Honeysuckle Grove and focus my full attention on driving this bully out of town.

Alex cleared his throat, but we'd already had a practice run at this in the early morning. Alex had already told me, "Captain Corbett will want to ask you this…and then he'll ask you that…" And we had come up with a satisfactory answer for every single question.

I couldn't have asked for better fortune than to have Alex asking the questions. Now I'd be certain to be prepared for each one.

"I had delivered a casserole the day before on behalf of the church," I said to his first question, looking only at Alex. "Something seemed really suspicious about the locked greenhouse they had in the back. They were really evasive, and on my way out the back door, I'd gotten a glimpse of a Nerf bullet." So what if the timeline was off about what I was explaining? It was all still true.

"And you didn't think to call the police with this information rather than investigating yourself?" Corbett demanded.

"Oh, I wasn't out there investigating!" I said, following my preprepared script. "And I did call the police with that information."

"Detective Reinhart was planning to put in a request for a warrant the next morning, sir," Alex told his boss.

Captain Corbett scowled at him for a long moment and then turned back to me. "And so why was it that y'all were out there?"

"I had been getting ready for bed when I realized my locket was missing. It had been a gift from my late husband, and I simply couldn't go to sleep without it. I had the feeling it had fallen off somewhere in the Albrights' long grass when Katrina Albright had been escorting me out, and I simply had to go and find it."

"So y'all were there looking for a necklace in the middle of the night?" Corbett asked, disbelief clear in his every word.

I nodded with wide innocent eyes. So what if he didn't believe me? He couldn't prove I was lying, and it's what had to happen to get to the truth. If he wasn't willing to rework his division of labor on the force, perhaps civilians would have to be out there solving crimes on the regular.

But I held my tongue about all I wanted to say and simply told him, "I was being super quiet, and I found it." I held up my locket, which truly was precious to me. "But I guess somehow Mr. Albright heard me. He thought I was breaking into his greenhouse or something," I said as though that notion had never even crossed my mind.

# CHAPTER TWENTY-FIVE

My cell phone had been retrieved from Brock Albright, but I couldn't charge it until I was released from the hospital and at home the next day. Because I'd swallowed the antidote so quickly after being poisoned, the poison's effects also hadn't been very long-lasting. Still, I went home with a handful of the little packets. When I finally booted up my phone, I had five missed texts and three missed calls, all from Amber.

Oh, no. I immediately felt sick and hoped she was okay.

It was two forty in the afternoon. She should have been just getting out of her last class. I was about to click her contact and dial when my phone rang in my hands.

"Hi!" I said before the name of the caller could register. I just assumed it would be her.

But after a long pause, a deep male voice replied. "Is this Mallory Beck?"

I cleared my throat and quelled my enthusiasm. "Yes, this is she."

"Steve Reinhart here," he said. "I didn't get a chance to speak to you again at the hospital before you were released."

I wondered if he was going to somehow swoop in and take credit for all of Alex's investigative work again. I leaned back into my couch and sighed, waiting for whatever kind of follow-up questions he was going to use to do that. "What can I help you with?" I said in a bland tone that lacked emotion.

"Well, first I wanted to check in on how you were feeling," he said, and his voice really did sound like it held some compassion.

But I couldn't help myself, the snide retort was on the tip of my tongue. "I'd feel a lot better if Alex could finally get some credit for an investigation and get officially promoted to detective work like he deserves."

Detective Reinhart's reply came quickly enough that I figured it had to be truthful. "Actually, I think that's in the works. I wondered if I could take

116

you to dinner one night? We can chat more about it."

I furrowed my brow, wondering if he had talked this over with Alex. But my curiosity wouldn't seem to allow me to decline.

"Okay." I drew out the word.

"Great!" he said, peppier than I'd ever heard the detective. "Tomorrow night? I can pick you up at seven."

I had agreed and hung up the phone, eager to get to Amber, before it occurred to me that this sounded an awful lot like a date. To get my mind off that possibility, I quickly scrolled back to Amber's contact and dialed.

It took her five rings to answer, and when she did, all she said was, "Yeah?" in the same hard tone she'd used when she first tried to convince me her dad had been murdered.

"I'm so sorry I haven't returned your calls," I told her and figured the only thing that might make her soften was the truth. "I've been in the hospital."

A long pause followed. "Oh. How come?" she asked tentatively. She clearly hadn't expected me to have any excuse, let alone such a good one.

I shrugged, trying to get more comfortable without disturbing my sleeping cat. When I'd first sat down over half an hour ago, Hunch had taken all of about thirty seconds to haul his cast up onto my lap, curl up, and promptly fall asleep. After the Albrights had been arrested, Alex had located my car down the road and in the ditch, covered in brush. Hunch had still been locked inside, though I heard he'd clawed some damage into Brock Albright's arm during the process. The poor cat wouldn't admit to being shaken up any sooner than Amber would, but he probably hadn't slept a wink last night.

"I snuck around the Albrights', got caught, got poisoned with a toxic dart, almost died. You know, the usual." I clucked my tongue, and then because I knew Amber would need confirmation, I added, "Check the news. See what it says about the Albright farm."

I waited and could perfectly envision her on the other end of the phone, scrolling on her browser through news headlines. I knew she'd need to see it in black and white with her own eyes before she fully believed I wasn't just shrugging her off. Poor kid needed some sort of adult security in her life. If I had anything to say about it, I planned to give that to her.

"Huh," she said, which in Amber-language meant, Okay, I'll at least half-believe you weren't ditching me. "I called all day, and even called Alex again when I couldn't get a hold of you, but this time he didn't answer."

"Wait. Called Alex again?" I asked. When had she ever called Officer Alex Martinez?

"Yeah, I called him in the night, told him you said you always had your phone on, but it wasn't. I told him I was worried." I knew things like this were hard for Amber to admit, so it didn't surprise me when she rushed on with her words. "He told me everything would be fine, and he'd check up on you. Said he had to go right away, but then when you didn't answer again today, and even he hasn't returned my messages, I thought…"

She called Alex in the night? It hadn't occurred to me before how Alex had known to come and find me at the Albright farm, right when I'd needed him last night. It had been Amber's doing. She had called Alex. Alex had considered my message from earlier and knew me well enough to know that I'd gone running after another murder suspect.

He was going to get tired of saving me. They both were.

But for the moment, I had to reassure Amber I was okay and I wasn't about to desert her. How better to do that than with a cooking lesson?

"How's school been?" I asked, ready to pave the way back to her trusting me. Plus, I felt bad that I hadn't been around for her to decompress about her first day back.

She huffed out a breath. "As expected. Marcy Ralston whispered loud enough that she might as well have had a microphone about how my dad had been murdered. You know. The usual."

"Stupid Marcy Ralston," I said in solidarity, even though I didn't know the girl from anyone else in this town.

"Then all my teachers looked at me with tilted heads like they thought I might break down in tears right in front of them."

"The head tilt of pity. Sounds awful," I told her, knowing how much worse a pity-fest would feel to her than getting pushed or punched or outwardly teased. I had learned enough about Amber Montrose over the last few weeks to know that much. "Feel like cooking?" I asked. I felt bad for lifting Hunch off my lap, but all it took was a positive sigh out of Amber and I was heading for my car keys.

"I could cook," she told me, in way of an answer.

"Wait in front of your school. I'll pick you up."

As I got into the Prius, I envisioned freshly baked bread—something hearty and grainy that would take some serious effort for both of us to knead. Kneading was what we both needed right now. Kneading and trying to figure out if I'd accidentally agreed to date Detective Steve Reinhart.

"I'll be there in ten," I told her, already smelling fresh bread and freedom from all this stress in the air around me. "And I can't wait to tell you everything."

# END OF BOOK 2

# UP NEXT: MURDER AT THE TOWN HALL

An eye witness to a murder, a crush-worthy cop who needs her help, and a cat with a hunch. What could possibly go wrong?

Mallory Beck isn't in the habit of involving herself in local politics, but when she supports a new friend at a meeting to save the local library and the main speaker is found dead on the steps of the town hall, she finds herself deep in the heart of another murder investigation. Her cat, Hunch, who loves a good mystery is thrilled and, as usual, helps her discover a key clue.

Mallory's clever friend and long-ago crush, Alex, is on the case. He was recently promoted to detective within the Honeysuckle Grove Police Department, but when he's paired with a lackadaisical superior who continually botches investigations, Mallory and her famously delicious cooking come to the rescue.

After all, the easiest way to a suspect's truth might just be through their stomach.

## READ ON IN THE SERIES NOW...

# Book Three

# MURDER
## at the Town Hall

DENISE JADEN

# CHAPTER ONE

Everything I knew about dating, I learned from my seventh-grade teacher.

Hang on, that was in the wrong grammatical tense. Everything I was about to know about dating, I was apparently going to learn from my seventh-grade teacher.

I looked at Ms. Sasha Mills with a head tilt as she spoke. I was trying hard to get used to calling my former teacher by her first name, but so far I'd only graduated to using her full name.

"He's very attractive, and he obviously likes you if he asked you out again. Your date couldn't have been that bad." She leaned against the counter across from me as I pulled a batch of chocolate chip cookies from the oven. She wore a purple paisley dress, reminiscent of every day I'd spent in her seventh-grade English class. Her brown hair wisped gray around her face and was cropped to her shoulders rather than halfway down her back now, but otherwise, she looked the same. "Even if you did talk about your friend Alex nonstop."

She was referring to what I couldn't get past calling my "outing" with Detective Steve Reinhart. I'd only gone for dinner with him to discuss Alex's promotion within the police department. I was sure he must have gotten that vibe from my rerouting the conversation back to Alex every three seconds. But Ms. Sasha Mills was right—he had asked me out again. Three times, in fact. My excuses hadn't even been slightly believable— everything from walking my cat to a TV cooking show I simply couldn't miss—and yet he persisted.

"I'm just not sure I'm ready to date," I told my former teacher honestly, offering her a cookie from the rack that had cooled. It had been eleven months since my husband, Cooper, had died. Maybe I should've been ready to date again, but I squirmed like my sweater was made out of spiders every time I considered it. I had planned to spend my entire life with Cooper. How could I switch gears on a dime like that?

An eleven-month dime. But still.

Ms. Mills hummed in appreciation of the cookie while she nodded compassionately. When she finished chewing, she said, "Have you told him that? I'm sure he'd understand."

I was going to have to learn to call her Sasha, at least out loud, if we planned to hang out together outside of children's church. I'd been helping her with the kids on Sunday mornings for the last month. When I'd stayed true to my word and offered Pastor Jeff my help wherever it was needed, he directed me to the most understaffed area of the church and to an overworked Ms. Sasha Mills. She's a sweet lady in her mid-fifties, and after four Sundays together, I was doing my best to treat her like an actual person I could talk to and not just one of my favorite teachers from years past.

I took a deep breath as I reminded myself of all this once again. "I have enough trouble talking to you about Cooper."

I lifted my cooled cookies one by one from the cooling rack into a sealable container, glad they'd turned out nice and gooey, how I liked them. In truth, my fifteen-year-old friend, Amber, was the only person I felt somewhat comfortable reminiscing with about my late husband, perhaps because she was in a similar grieving place, having recently lost her dad.

Whatever the reason, I added, "It's still so hard for me." I choked on the last word, and Ms. Mills reached over to stroke my arm. Maybe I could think of her more like a mother figure than a friend. Then again, that wouldn't help calling her by her first name, and besides, I'd never had much in the mother department, and so I wasn't sure how to navigate that type of relationship either.

"Maybe I could talk to him for you," Ms. Mills said with raised eyebrows, and I had to wonder if we were still in seventh grade.

Right. Of course. I could write him a note. Instead of writing "Do you like me?" with yes/no checkboxes, I could ask "Would you understand if I'm not ready to date yet?" and slip it to him sometime before recess.

"Or you could tell him you're walking your cat again." Ms. Mills chuckled under her breath. It always shocked me when she made jokes. I figured that was part of the transition from seeing her as a teacher to seeing her as a friend. To punctuate this thought, she bent and called, "Here, kitty, kitty."

Hunch sat on his haunches across the kitchen near his food dish, licking his paws and not giving Ms. Mills the time of day. This was the second time she'd been in the house, and tonight was confirmation that he hadn't taken to her the way he had to Alex or especially Amber. He'd barely spared Ms. Mills a glance the two times she'd been here, but he always lurked within hearing distance from us. After being injured by a murder suspect a couple of months ago, he'd finally had his cast removed and should have been enjoying his freedom, but he wasn't about to miss anything if the topic ever changed from my dating inability to something more interesting.

Believe me, Hunch, I tried to tell him telepathically. I'm with you there.

As though my cat and I had conversed aloud, Ms. Mills looked at her watch. "We should probably get going. The meeting starts at seven, and I'm not planning on letting them cut funding to our library the way they did to the drug rehab clinics and our education programs."

I'd offered to accompany her to a town hall meeting tonight. Along with running children's church, Ms. Mills continued to teach seventh-grade English at the local middle school. Apparently, the mayor had proposed a library closure—or rather going to an online-only system—and Ms. Mills was vehemently opposed to the idea. She said many of her students from lower-income families had found a safe haven in getting lost in a good book at the library each day after school. She feared they could so easily fall in with the wrong crowd and get hooked on drugs, and she wanted to do everything she could to protect the sanctuary of the brick-and-mortar library for them. She'd even written to the county superintendent of schools to ask for help in the matter. I couldn't help but offer my support, even if it was only to keep her company for the evening.

We headed for the front door, and no surprise, Hunch didn't bother to follow us. He'd had enough of our boring conversation. Besides, he only liked to go for car rides if Amber was along or if there was some sort of mystery afoot.

Ms. Mills didn't drive. In fact, she had never had her license. She'd made it to my house via bus, but now we got in on either side of my Prius. The smell of freshly baked cookies quickly enveloped the car.

"Are you sure it's not Alex you like?" Ms. Mills asked casually as I backed out of the driveway.

My foot missed the brake pedal, and I nearly backed into a neighbor's car parked along the curb. I found the pedal and slammed it. "Sorry," I said, and as though I hadn't heard her, I added, "What was that?"

Ms. Mills smirked and left the question alone. I wondered if teaching seventh grade had taught her to keep her mouth shut on hot topics and let the internal replay of her words do all the work.

I should have argued that Alex was my friend. I'd simply helped him in his fight against a pigheaded police captain in getting a promotion to detective. I'd even gone out with another detective to make sure it happened. Alex had finally achieved that goal, so who knew if he'd even have any time or need for me anymore, anyway. I hadn't heard from him at all in the last couple of weeks.

I didn't realize how quiet or lost in thought I'd become until I blinked and realized we were already at the town hall. I felt my cheeks flush, knowing how my lack of conversation after a single mention of Alex Martinez must look to Ms. Mills.

Again, she spoke as if she had heard my thoughts out loud. "All I'm saying is that if two of my favorite students found each other interesting, well, that wouldn't be the worst thing in the world."

And as if the universe had made my discomfort its primary mission, my phone sang to life from its dash holster with "There's Nothing Holding Me Back" by Shawn Mendes. I'd originally chosen the song because it had a catchy tune, but now when Alex's name appeared on the screen, my cheeks and neck hit three hundred degrees.

Ms. Mills turned to me with a wink. "How about I meet you in there?"

What was there to do but nod?

I tried to wait out Ms. Mills' exit from the car, but it was as though she was purposely moving in slow motion. I had to pick up before it stopped ringing.

I reached for my phone. "Hi!" As usual, when I tried to be sociable, my voice came out too high and peppy.

This was only emphasized by his somber tone. "Hey, Mallory. I was wondering if I could take you out for a coffee?"

My eyes darted to Ms. Mills' retreating paisley figure, wondering if somehow she'd put Alex up to asking me out. My cheeks had barely lost their flush and it was back again, but thankfully, my brain clued in that the chances of Ms. Mills interfering were slim before I made any such suggestion.

At least I had a ready excuse, so I didn't even have to think about how I felt about this. "Actually, I can't. I'm at a town hall meeting with Ms.—with Sasha Mills. I'm not sure how late these things run. We could go out tomorrow?"

Now why, oh why, did I go and offer that? Being friends was good. He could come over and eat cookies while I baked, like usual. It was all I was ready for. Why did we have to go out together?

But before I could backtrack, he answered. "Yeah, sure." Something in his voice was more than somber, and it was only now that I realized he was most definitely not in that butterfly stage of requesting a first date.

"Is everything okay, Alex?"

He heaved out a sigh. "Yeah, I suppose. It's just stuff here at work."

"At work?" I reached over the seat to grab my container of chocolate chip cookies. Ms. Mills told me I didn't need to bring anything to the meeting, but I hadn't been able to help myself. Social occasions were for cooking or baking, at least in my book. "I thought your promotion had already gone through?"

"Yeah, it did." He paused, and I waited, hoping he would explain. All

Alex Martinez had wanted since he'd graduated the police academy, and from what I could remember of him in seventh grade, was to make detective on the local police force. It hadn't been easy, but he'd finally done it. Could Captain Corbett have somehow taken away the promotion?

Finally, Alex went on to clear things up. "Corbett paired me up with Mickey Bradley."

He let that sit, and I wasn't sure what to make of it. I wondered absently if Mickey was a male or female detective, and then quickly realized I shouldn't care. I couldn't help myself, though. I had to ask something. "And Mickey Bradley is...?"

"Might as well be named Mickey Mouse. On yesterday's case, he didn't even come into the office. I found him in his backyard with a beer in his hand. On last week's missing person's case of an eight-year-old boy, he overlooked the fact that the parents were divorced and the kid had run off to his dad's. If I hadn't completed a follow-up interview, we would have looked like real hacks going back to Corbett with nothing. It's like working with a child." Alex sighed again. "Corbett won't give us any serious cases, and now it's clear why. Mickey knows I won't rat him out for fear of it coming back on me somehow."

"Oh, Alex, I'm so sorry. There's nothing you can do to switch partners?"

I could envision him shaking his head on the other end. I wondered if he was at home. I'd never been to his house, and I wished I could picture him in it. "Not until I prove myself on a worthwhile case. Which could take a while if I'm not assigned a worthwhile case."

"And the two murder investigations you already stumbled into and helped solve didn't prove you as a valuable detective?" I didn't understand how Captain Corbett could ignore Alex's clear abilities.

"Not being part of the detective unit at the time didn't help. I guess all I can hope is that I can stumble into another murder investigation now that the timing is better." He chuckled wryly. "Although, you're usually better at that."

I laughed, too. "I'll see what I can do." It was almost seven, and people were streaming into the town hall in droves. "Listen, I'd better go if I'm going to find Ms.—Sasha before the meeting starts. But how about we go for coffee tomorrow night? We can talk about it more then. Or I can make dinner if you want?" Apparently, my errant mouth was bound and determined to get me ready for dating.

But, no. This was Alex, my friend, and he needed me.

"Thanks, Mallory. I knew I could count on you."

My face flushed again, but this time, it wasn't over any romantic notions. I would be there for Alex to help him in whatever way I could, no matter what Ms. Sasha Mills or anyone else wanted to call it.

But that could wait until tomorrow.

For now, I'd deliver these cookies and figure out how I could help save our local library.

☐

# CHAPTER TWO

I had to admit, as I held out the container of chocolate cookies to the head of catering in the town hall's kitchen, that it felt ominous to be delivering another food item. The last two times I'd delivered food, they had led me to investigate and then discover a murderer.

Although, that could have something to do with how little I left my house without some sort of food offering.

Thankfully, murder wasn't on the docket for tonight's town hall meeting. Only supporting Ms. Mills and her determination to save our local library.

The head of catering was a tall lady in a white chef's jacket and a black apron. She barked orders from her location near a counter where one of her subordinates stood slicing a spongy-looking white cake. In a kitchen, you could always find the boss by his or her voice. That's why I had only ever aspired to sous-chef. I would never have enough volume to be the main boss of any kitchen.

"Excuse me?" I called from the doorway as she finished her rant about keeping all the hot water urns full. It looked like the spread tonight only included cake, cookies, coffee, and tea. I wondered how this irritable lady would fare at providing a full-on dinner.

She turned to where I stood in the doorway, my now-open container of fudgy chocolate chip cookies outstretched toward her. I had to admit, they didn't look all that impressive, but I was certain they'd taste better than the dry-looking sugar cookies one of her catering staff was assembling on a platter.

"What?" She sneered as she glanced down at my cookies.

I swallowed and reminded myself that chefs weren't known for their warm and fuzzy personalities. "I wanted to contribute a plate of cookies to the event."

As the words left my mouth, clarity about the situation struck me. I hadn't known this would be a catered event. I'd thought of it more like a PTA meeting, where parents might all contribute a dish of snacks. I'd clearly had a misguided image, as most of the attendees wore suits and business attire, and a full catering staff was on-site to serve a simple dessert. I wondered if the mayor couldn't trim his catering budget and keep the library.

"I'm sorry?" the catering chef asked, not sounding sorry at all as she walked toward me. Her tone didn't invite further interruption. Her black hair was tied back into a tidy bun, a little too tight judging by the taut skin at her temples, and her nametag read "Talia." She scowled down at my container of cookies again. "We can't serve someone else's food. Are you kidding me? That would be a health violation just waiting for a grievance."

What she said made sense. Again, I tried to realign my image of the type of event I'd walked into. "Oh. I'm sorry. Of course." I couldn't help but want someone to enjoy my cookies, and so I held them out another inch toward her. "Maybe you and your staff would like to enjoy them? You know, when you're not so busy?"

A curvy woman in a white dress shirt and black apron swept by us carrying a tray of cream and sugar. "I'd love one," she said, reaching out her free hand.

But the chef, her boss, actually smacked her hand away. "Listen, Melinda, I know you're new at this, but we don't eat on the job." Talia shook her head and murmured under her breath, "Can you imagine the health code violations."

It had been a long time since I'd worked in a restaurant. Almost a year. In this moment, though, I recalled my last boss's preoccupation with the health inspector. I'd only ever been at a restaurant on one occasion when a health inspector had actually walked through the door and into our kitchen, and if he'd found any violations, I'd never heard about them, but it seemed this overreaction to the possibilities was another common trait of head chefs.

"I'm sorry," Melinda said. She pulled her hand away and turned to her boss. "Do we have more cream somewhere? I didn't see any in the fridge." She was very fidgety, her newness at the job obvious.

Chef Talia flapped her hands up to the skies. "No coffee cream! Are you kidding me?" She marched back into the kitchen with Melinda on her heels, and my cookies and I were all but forgotten.

I decided to try and erase my embarrassment over what had been an honest mistake by tracking down Ms. Sasha Mills. Sasha. I was going to call her Sasha. At the very least, my former teacher could drown her sorrows of a condemned library in gooey sweet chocolatey cookies.

The kitchen was near the back of the hall on the left, with a doorway leading up to the stage and another into the main seating hall. I moved into the main seating hall and surveyed the wide-open space that was filled with probably more than two hundred chairs. Most of them were already occupied, and yet there had to be a few dozen people milling around in aisle ways or around the perimeter of the room with their Styrofoam coffee cups. The cake and cookies, apparently, hadn't been served yet.

Thankfully, Sasha's purple paisley wasn't difficult to spot in the sea of dark suits. At least she fit in, for the most part. I'd opted for a black-and-turquoise polka dot dress, matched with a turquoise headband and shoes—again with the PTA image in my head, but much too casual and peppy for this business meeting. Sasha, thankfully, didn't seem embarrassed and waved me over to where she sat near the center back of the room. Her purse rested on the seat beside her.

"Wow, so busy!" I exclaimed when I moved past a man to the seat she'd saved for me.

She removed her purse so I could sit. "I'm glad to see there are people in this town who actually care about our library. I was at a town hall for education budget cuts last month, and the front three rows were barely full."

I smiled and sat. If this were going to be a night filled with passionate arguments and possibly overturning the mayor's decision, it actually sounded like it could be exciting.

"And look." Sasha pointed over near the kitchen, the direction I'd come from. "Superintendent Garnet must have gotten my letter. I can't believe he's shown up in person to help."

I followed her gaze to a pudgy man in a sky-blue dress shirt and pants that rested under his large belly. He held a Styrofoam cup of coffee, and the armpits of his dress shirt showed arcs of sweat under them. He scowled at the man in a suit who was speaking to him.

I hoped Sasha was right to be so hopeful. He didn't look like the friendliest or the most helpful of gentlemen, even if I was only seeing him from a distance.

"I tried to introduce myself when he first came in, but he was really busy," Sasha said, confirming these thoughts. "He was talking to someone about his speech, so it sounds like he has something prepared for tonight."

Sasha made a show of crossing her fingers, and I crossed mine right back. If that man were our only hope, we would need all the luck we could get.

As we watched, the town's mayor, Tom Lassiter, walked up to the superintendent with an outstretched hand. I'd seen Mayor Lassiter on TV and at a distance before. His gray suit hung comfortably on his robust, powerful frame. He towered over the superintendent. His blond hair and strong jaw made him rather attractive for a man in his forties. He reminded me of Aaron Eckhart's character in the Batman movies who seemed like a boy-next-door type on the outside, but turned out to be the two-faced villain. As I watched the two men, Superintendent Garnet's face morphed into a smile as he shook hands with the mayor.

Oh, no. I had the sudden sickening feeling that the person Sasha had called on for help was on the wrong side of this fight.

A second later, Mayor Lassiter opened the nearby door that led to the stage. He closed it behind the superintendent without following him through. I waited to see Superintendent Garnet appear on the stage, waited to see what he would say, given a chance at the microphone, but a minute passed with no sign of him. Then two minutes.

I turned back toward Mayor Lassiter, who was speaking with a couple of ladies. His winning smile had them grinning right back at him.

I had the feeling this was going to be a bloodbath as far as the local library was concerned. I opened my container and held it out toward Sasha, trying not to show my concern. "Cookie?"

She took one and complimented me on the taste after her first bite, but I couldn't concentrate because Mayor Lassiter had gone through the stage door, and only ten seconds later, he appeared behind a podium in the center of the stage.

"Good evening, ladies and gentlemen," he bellowed in his loud, authoritative voice. "Thank you all so much for coming out tonight."

He went on to introduce council members from around the room. At each introduction, a man or woman around the room raised a hand in recognition. I had the eerie sense that we were surrounded by Mayor Lassiter and his all-powerful team.

The mayor went on to thank the caterers and announce the refreshments would be served at the break.

"And now," he said, placing both hands on the podium in front of him as though it was time to get serious. "Let's move onto the primary discussion topic for tonight: our local library and how to best move forward. I have received several letters from concerned citizens over the matter of changing to an online-only format, and I want to thank you for reaching out to me. Please know that every one of your letters has been carefully read and considered."

He sounded genuine, and yet, deep down, I knew this man was ultimately a politician who kept his own agenda hidden tightly up his sleeve. He said he had carefully considered input from around the town, but I doubted it. I gave a sidelong glance at Sasha, wondering if she was eating up every word he dished out. She kept her eyes straight on the mayor, sitting up tall, as though she still had some sort of confidence.

I held the cookie container tighter, fearing we both might need it.

"I'd like to start the evening by letting our superintendent of schools, Mr. Richard Garnet, say a few words on the matter," Mayor Lassiter said in his cheery voice. It was clear he knew Superintendent Garnet was on his side. An uncomfortably long pause followed, and Mayor Lassiter glanced toward the wings of the stage. He gave a nod to someone hidden by the curtains, but as we all waited, Superintendent Garnet didn't make a move forward onto the stage.

What felt like several long minutes later, Mayor Lassiter strode from his place at the podium to the stage wings. He was only partially visible as he had a hand-flailing conversation with an unseen person. He looked out at the audience, scanned the whole room, and then returned to his backstage hand-flailing conversation. I wondered if Superintendent Garnet, with his sweaty and anxious armpits, had a sudden bout of stage fright.

My insides squeezed with stress. How could Sasha put her hope in this superintendent who wouldn't even take the stage?

Several long seconds later, Mayor Lassiter returned to the microphone. "I'm afraid we're having some trouble locating Superintendent Garnet. In the meantime, is there anyone here who would like to speak for or against moving to an online library system?"

So that was it? Superintendent Garnet had left without a word, was backing out of sticking up for our town's library? I looked at Sasha, but she kept her eyes on our mayor. I had the distinct feeling that she was avoiding my gaze.

But she was passionate about this. She had to say something!

Then again, would this sweet older lady ever actually get up behind the microphone to speak her mind, no matter how passionate she might be?

Murmurs sounded around the town hall, but not a single person stepped forward to speak. I'd never been a great public speaker, but when it came to anything important, I could do it. I'd stood up in front of a church full of Cooper's fans at his memorial and broken down in tears. Nothing could be worse than that. I wondered if the fate of the library was somehow up to me. I'd heard Sasha's arguments about keeping the library. Could I put them into some sort of coherent convincing order? Could I even drum up the confidence to stand up there in front of so many people?

I had to.

But as I stood on shaky legs and took a gulp of a breath, a shriek sounded through the open back doors of the town hall. I turned to where the doorway was plugged with townsfolk. It was standing room only tonight, with people crammed all the way out the door.

There was jostling of the crowd as one lady in a bright blue pantsuit made her way through all the people and into the town hall.

"It's Superintendent Garnet!" she said with a gasp. "He's on the front steps." Mayor Lassiter stepped toward the wings, but only a second later, he stopped in place when the pantsuit lady added, "I think he just jumped to his death!"

☐

# CHAPTER THREE

The whole hall seemed to suck in a collective breath and then move toward the back doors in a clump. I did my best to stick with Sasha. I wasn't sure if it was so I could protect her or so she could protect me from what we were about to see.

We had barely made it into the fresh evening air when I got my first glimpse of Superintendent Garnet. My brain refused to take in the reality of the moment, cataloging small details instead. His body was sprawled across the cement steps, his legs and arms at impossible angles. His empty eyes stared into the night sky, open and unblinking.

Gasps sounded from all around. Muffled crying. Two of the council members stood between the crowd and the body with their arms splayed out, keeping people back, even though I was quite certain no one wanted to get closer. Another man in a suit paced at the bottom of the stairs with a phone to his ear. I hoped he was calling 911. I pulled out my phone to do the same, in case he wasn't, but at the last second, I hit Alex's contact number instead.

Wide-eyed, Sasha had both hands over her open mouth and couldn't seem to tear her gaze from the superintendent. As it turned out, I was clearly the calmer of the two of us in this scenario.

I looked up forty feet to the roof of the town hall. Not much was visible from my vantage point, but it appeared to be a flat roof. A tall cement ledge rimmed the whole thing, but what caught my eye was a white gutter, which, even from this distance, I could tell was dented right above where the superintendent was now sprawled.

Had he jumped? Or possibly slipped?

Alex answered my call, taking my attention. "What's up? I thought you were in a meeting."

"I think you should get down here as soon as possible," I told him. "Someone jumped—er, fell—from the roof. He's dead on the front steps."

The volume of murmurs had risen so much around me, I practically had to yell into my phone. "Can you call it in as an emergency on your way?"

"Sure, but…" He was talking too quietly to hear over all the murmuring around me. Mayor Lassiter had appeared through the doorway and bellowed to the crowd to please calm down and clear some space. Panic tinged his normally level and authoritative voice.

I plugged my other ear and cut Alex off. "Just get to the town hall as soon as possible. I'm going to head up to the roof and make sure no one else is up there."

More quiet questions sounded through the phone. The only words I could make out were, "And make sure no one touches anything," before the line went dead.

I didn't blame him for hanging up on me. It meant he was already in his car, already on his way, and he wanted to call it in. That was exactly what needed to happen, and all the better if this incident could come through the airwaves via the newly promoted Detective Alex Martinez.

As I stared at the awkwardly placed body of the superintendent, I recalled Alex's words to me earlier tonight—about how I seemed to stumble into murder investigations quicker than anyone he knew.

What if the superintendent didn't jump or fall? What if he was pushed?

I didn't realize I'd said the words aloud until Sasha answered them with her own question. "Have you always been this suspicious?"

I shrugged. "I suppose I have."

At least I had all of my adult life, ever since I'd met Cooper and everything either held mystery or could contribute to solving a mystery when it came to his bestselling detective novels. Maybe I was even suspicious before that. From an early age, I'd learned I couldn't believe much of what came out of my dad's mouth.

"Listen…" I turned to her. "I want to check out the roof, make sure no one else is up there making a mess of the scene." And do a little investigating of my own, I added silently. Even though it wasn't my place and I could probably even get into trouble for it, I reasoned that Alex didn't have a decent partner to back him up. I had to do what I could to help. "Keep an eye on things down here, okay?" I asked Sasha, to which I only got a buckled forehead in reply. "Text me if the mayor or anyone else noteworthy heads for the parking lot to leave."

I turned and left her with those instructions before she could question me about them. My mind raced through what I knew of the superintendent and any possibilities of what could have happened, and I couldn't slow down to explain them all. Mayor Lassiter had led Superintendent Garnet through the side stage door only minutes before his death. Was it possible that door also led to the roof?

I was about to find out.

As I marched through the town hall, I took note of the few people who remained inside. A couple of elderly ladies huddled in a back corner, out of view of the open doors. I suspected they didn't want to see what was outside. Others who hadn't quite made it out the crowded doors yet vied for a vantage point to see what was going on. Through the open window into the kitchen, I could see the catering chef moving back and forth through the small space in almost a frenzy. She moved platters of cake from one counter to another and then back again. All of her catering staff had seemingly abandoned her to join the fray and gape at the emergency. A janitor slid one of those big push brooms across the stage, as though he'd already come to terms with the fact that the meeting had unofficially adjourned, and he could possibly go home early tonight.

"Excuse me?" I asked the janitor when I got closer. "Where is the roof access in this building?"

As I suspected, the janitor pointed to the side door of the stage. So Mayor Lassiter had led the superintendent toward the roof and, ultimately, to his death. I wasn't quite certain what that meant yet. I certainly wasn't calling our local mayor a murderer, even in my own mind.

"Thank you," I said to the janitor, a man wearing army green overalls who appeared to be in his seventies, with a full head of gray hair. As I went to turn away for the side door, a red balloon floated down onto the stage, bounced once, and then hit something on the big push broom that made it pop.

The sound in the nearly empty hall made me jolt. When I caught my breath, I moved closer to the stage, which was chest-high for me, and looked up. In the rafters, there appeared to be a whole net of colorful balloons poised and ready to drop—probably a hundred of them.

My forehead furrowed as I looked back to the janitor. The nametag on his overalls read "HANK."

"What are those for?" I pointed up to the balloons.

The elderly janitor looked up and then back at me and shrugged. "Beats me. They weren't there last night."

I nodded, thanked him again, and continued my trek toward the door and the roof access. I was about to pull the green wooden door open when Alex's words about not touching anything returned to me. There was a good chance several people, including Mayor Lassiter and Hank the janitor, had already touched this knob tonight, but I planned to do my part to keep this site of the superintendent's death as clean as possible.

I didn't carry rubber gloves as a habit. I rooted through my purse, but of course, I had nothing rubber or latex with me. I wondered if pulling the sleeve of my cardigan over my hand would be enough.

I wasn't sure, and I most certainly didn't want to tamper with any possible evidence.

I turned back to the nearly empty hall. The crowd had all made their way out the rear doors, and it seemed even the two elderly ladies had worked up the courage to move outside and past the incident. Atop the crowd of people gathered near the open doors, I could see flashing red lights. I let out my breath. At least the ambulance had arrived.

Talia, the catering chef, had seemingly come to terms with the end of the meeting. She moved cake squares from platter to platter and covered them in plastic wrap. Two of her catering staff, a slim man and the curvy lady named Melinda, had reappeared to help.

"Excuse me?" I said from the doorway for the second time tonight. It occurred to me that I'd left my container of chocolate chip cookies on my chair. It seemed a lot of food was going to waste tonight because I wasn't about to take even thirty seconds to go and find it. My words must have shocked the heavier-set caterer because she dropped the platter of cake she had just lifted from the counter. A piece tumbled onto the counter and then to the floor.

"Sorry, sorry!" she said to her boss.

Talia sighed and turned to me. The crease in her forehead made her appear far less bossy than she had been earlier.

"I was wondering if there were any rubber gloves under the sink in here?" I asked.

Surprisingly, rather than snapping at me, Chef Talia appeared thankful at my request, as though she was waiting to be told what to do. She marched to the sink, kneeled down to the cupboards, and reappeared a second later with two bright yellow latex gloves. She passed them over.

"Thank you so much," I told her, and because I did feel bad for all the confusion she must be fighting about the evening, I gave her my two cents' worth. "It looks like no one will be sticking around for coffee or cake. Too bad it's all going to go to waste."

Her two catering staff stood staring at me, the cake already cleaned off the floor, but my words seemed to perk Chef Talia back into some kind of authority about the situation. "Oh, it won't go to waste, believe me. It will be in the care of the local food bank by morning."

I smiled and nodded as though this tiny tidbit made me feel better. And then I headed back for the green wooden door.

As soon as I had the gloves on and opened the door, I saw a long stretch of stairs, illuminated only by a single yellow bulb. I let the door fall shut behind me and trekked up six steps to a platform. Beside a gathered red velvet curtain, I could see the stage where Hank stood sweeping. I moved on, all the way up the thirty or so stairs to a door at the top.

It didn't occur to me until I was at the top that the door could very well be locked. Then again, if it had been, how could Superintendent Garnet have jumped/fallen/been pushed to his death?

I reached out for the silver knob, suddenly nervous about overstepping protocol at a crime scene. But I had to at least make sure no one else was up here.

Sure enough, the knob turned easily between the two pinched fingers of my gloved hand.

The moonlight illuminated the wide-open roof enough to have a decent view of it. It looked bigger than I would have expected from the size of the meeting room downstairs, but perhaps that was only because this area was so empty.

I took a step onto the weathered white surface and gently rested the door closed behind me without clicking it into place. Even though the knob had been unlocked, I had seen too many movies and TV shows where a character got locked up on a roof.

Two square protrusions that looked like heating or cooling units stood in the center of the flat surface, and a cement wall rose up around the perimeter of the roof. Otherwise, there wasn't much to see.

I inched forward across the roof toward the far side where the crowd could be heard down below. As I moved closer, I studied the perimeter further. The ledge only came up to my hip. Even though Superintendent Garnet was on the shorter side, he wouldn't have had a problem scaling the low wall, but at the same time, he couldn't have tripped and fallen over it.

I reached into my purse and rooted around for a flashlight. Ever since being stranded on a stretch of dark farmland with no flashlight and a dead phone, when I'd almost become someone's next murder victim, I'd stocked up with those extra-bright flashlights from the dollar store. I now kept two in each purse, three in the glove compartment of my Prius, and five or six around the house, just in case.

I retrieved a small black one and pointed its beam at the gray, unpainted cement wall. A few black marks marred it. They could have been scuff marks, or it could have been weather marks that had appeared over time.

I wasn't a big fan of heights, but I held my breath and peeked over the ledge. The ambulance had already left, and the superintendent's body was no longer on the steps below, but a police car and Alex's personal car—an early nineties blue Toyota—were parked at messy angles in front of the town hall steps.

It had to be close to four stories down, but even from this distance, I could recognize Steve Reinhart and his partner, Detective Bernard, who seemed to be in a heated argument with Mayor Lassiter. Several other official-looking men wearing gloves and wielding cameras moved around the cement stairs, taking notes and photos of the surrounding area. I scanned the crowd, but I couldn't see Alex anywhere.

The dented gutter caught my eye. As I studied it from this angle, the dent looked clear and obvious. I pulled out my phone and took a few snapshots of it from different angles, wondering if any of it would show up without using my flash, as I didn't want to draw any attention. The fact that the dent didn't seem to have rust in any of its creases suggested to me it had been dented recently. Perhaps tonight.

Steve Reinhart turned toward the building, and I pulled back quickly before the two detectives spotted me up here and wondered what I was doing. I twisted my lips, thinking about the dented gutter. Did Superintendent Garnet step out onto the gutter, thinking it would hold his weight? I doubted it. Could he have been sitting on the ledge and slipped? It was possible.

I just wasn't sure I believed it.

Bending with my flashlight, I inspected the area right before the cement wall where Richard Garnet had likely climbed up. I didn't want to take off my yellow gloves for fear of tampering with the scene, but the coating on the roof felt like it had some give, even through my gloves. It had bumps here and there, but again, because it was fairly weathered, it was tough to say whether any of the bumps were marks from shoes or the coating was only showing general wear.

A creak sounded from the door, and my breath caught in my throat. A second later, Alex stepped through. He clearly hadn't seen as many scary movies as I had because he let the door clack shut before striding toward me.

"Anything interesting?" He didn't wait for my answer, but went on with, "Our forensics expert is downstairs, upset because the body was removed before he got here. His team is documenting the area of the death and will be up here next. Steve and Gerald are downstairs conducting interviews. By first impressions, they seem to think it was an accident, rather than a suicide."

I nodded, running a gloved hand over the roof's surface. "I think this is rubberized," I said the moment it came to me, but then quickly realized that didn't actually help with the investigation.

Alex squatted beside me. He wore dark blue form-fitting gloves. My yellow dishwashing variety looked ridiculously amateurish next to his. He also ran a hand over the roof's surface. "It's an elastomeric roof coating. Generally, it takes a lot of wear and lasts a good decade." He looked around the area and pulled out his own flashlight.

I stood, embarrassed. Sure, I'd been helpful to him on a case or two in the past, but that had clearly been beginner's luck. To cover the fact that I'd been studying the roof's coating for far too long without looking for any real evidence, I decided to point out the one helpful abnormality I had discovered. "Come and look at this gutter. It's dented, and it looks like recently."

Alex stood and moved beside me against the cement ledge. I shone my flashlight at the dent in the gutter, and he nodded. "I'll mention it to the forensics team, but I'd say the dent is consistent with an accidental fall. Perhaps he was resting on the ledge, decided to climb back onto the roof and his foot slipped."

I sighed inwardly. That was what all appearances led to. My overeagerness to help Alex get a leg up in the department had made me call him out here for a simple accident. I looked over his gray sweatpants and navy hoodie, wondering if he had been working out or relaxing at home when I'd called.

"Sorry to have called you out for this," I said.

"Are you kidding me?" He placed a gloved hand on the sleeve of the turquoise cardigan I'd worn over my polka dot dress. "It could have been something. Definitely always call me."

At least he wasn't angry about the imposition. Still, I couldn't shake the feeling that Alex was overly understanding in general. I didn't want to abuse that.

"Why was Reinhart arguing with the mayor?" I asked, looking over the cement ledge. The crowd had thinned considerably over the past five minutes. The center of the stairs had been cordoned off with yellow crime scene tape. Mayor Lassiter was nowhere in sight, and Detectives Reinhart and Bernard were busy speaking and making notes near their police car.

"Mayor Lassiter is the one who told the paramedics to get the body out of here immediately. He wanted to clear the area as quickly as possible, let people go home and get the horrible tragedy out of their heads. It looks as though he got his way." Alex shook his head. "It's procedure to have our forensics expert study the body at the site of death if there's no hope for resuscitation. We're required to gather at least three eyewitness accounts after a public accidental death has occurred, so Steve was arguing to at least make that happen. He's big on procedure." Before I could comment, Alex added, "I heard the two of you have been dating," which stunned me into silence for a few seconds.

"I—uh—no. Not really," I said when I got my voice back. I nibbled my lip, feeling highly embarrassed and I wasn't sure why. I wondered if I should tell him I'd only actually gone out with Steve to make sure Alex's promotion would go through. I didn't know if he'd appreciate that or be bothered by it, so instead, I said, "We went out once. That's all."

Alex raised his eyebrows at me. It looked like he didn't completely believe me. Either that or he was prodding for more.

"I'm not ready to date. You know, after Cooper." My throat got its usual globule in the back of it when I brought up Cooper, and I couldn't say anymore.

Alex studied me. The moonlight glinted off his green eyes, making them look deep and understanding. I wanted to say more. I wanted to tell him that his friendship meant more to me than a date with someone like Steve could ever mean. But when nothing came out of my mouth, he nodded and said, "Right. Of course."

I had to change the subject, get my head together again. "So is that it for this investigation? Are you done here?"

He looked around the expanse of the roof. "The team will be up here with work lights and cameras. I'll rope the place off, come back in the daylight and make sure we haven't missed anything. Of course, we'll talk to his family as well, and I'm sure Steve would have gotten a good indication of the superintendent's mood from the mayor, if nothing else. But, yeah. I think there are only a few outstanding details with this one. Won't take much to tie it up."

He led the way back to the door, and I found myself holding my breath until the knob turned easily in his hand.

We walked down the stairs and through the meeting room, now empty except for the janitor, who was running his big mop broom around the perimeter of the chairs. As we passed, I noticed my cookie container on the floor where I'd been sitting. I quickly grabbed it, opened it, and offered Alex one.

He smirked. "I can always count on you to feed me, can't I?"

I felt myself blush and walked faster until we were outside in the cool air. Less than a dozen people milled around on or below the cement steps. One was the lady in the blue pantsuit, and I pointed her out to Alex.

"If you want to get any eyewitness accounts, that's the lady who first discovered the body. She ran in and announced it to everyone." Her eyes were red-rimmed, and some blonde tendrils had come loose from her half-up hairdo. The evening was wearing on her.

At the side of the building, Chef Talia and all four of her catering staff were busy loading platters of cake and coffee urns into a van marked with a pink logo of a steaming plate of food and the words "MAYBERRY CATERING." I wondered if the catering company bore any relation to Marv and Donna Mayberry, friends of mine and Cooper's from church.

"I should check in with Steve," Alex said, taking my attention from the busy catering crew.

As though he'd heard his name, Steve Reinhart looked over at us. He took off his police cap. His sandy blond hair had grown over the last few weeks. It looked like he was overdue for a cut, but at the same time, his overgrown hair somehow had the effect of making him appear even more attractive. My cheeks burned at the thought, and I mentally slapped myself for it. I'd been doing so well at putting off his date requests. Then again, those hadn't been in person when I had to look him in his blue eyes and perfectly sculpted face.

He held up a hand to me and started to walk toward us.

I backed a few steps away. "I, uh, should probably let you guys do your work," I said to Alex and then scrambled a few more feet down the steps away from Steve as he came up on the other side. The crime scene tape blocked a clear path between us. "But call me tomorrow, okay?" I meant it for Alex, but my voice came out too loud, and I wondered if Steve would take it as an invitation for him.

I took the rest of the steps two at a time to the bottom. Thankfully, Detective Steve Reinhart had work to do and didn't follow me to the parking lot. I hurried there and finally let out my breath when my white Prius came into view. Sasha was perched on a nearby curb.

"I'm so sorry!" I told her. "Have you been waiting long?"

She stood and dusted off her rear. I was glad it at least hadn't been raining. "I could have caught the bus, but you suggested I keep an eye on everyone, so I stayed and did my best."

I had completely forgotten I had made that suggestion before I left her at the scene of the superintendent's death.

"I trailed a few people out to their cars," Sasha said. "Most people seemed to think the superintendent had committed suicide, but the more I thought about it, the more I didn't buy it. Why come here, when he lives two towns over, to jump from a building where he was supposed to be a speaker? Unless someone said something to him and it was a spur of the moment decision." She shook her head like she didn't believe that. It was clear my suspicious nature was rubbing off on her. "And I doubt he was so worried about speaking that he decided to jump. I've seen him speak before. He's very compelling behind a microphone, that's why I wrote to him in the first place." Her last words held a note of somberness, and that's when I remembered she was the one who had invited him to attend the meeting and fight for the library in the first place.

"So what do you think happened?" I asked. "If he didn't jump."

She walked around to the passenger side of my car. "I guess I'd have to side with those who think he slipped."

I hit the unlock button and got in on my side. "It wasn't your fault, you know," I said because if it were me, I would likely be blaming myself.

Then again, Sasha Mills had the kind of wisdom and experience that came with age. She sighed. "I know." And I sensed that she did.

"So those were the two theories?" I said as I started to drive toward her house. I couldn't seem to shake the feeling—or maybe it was the desire—that this was something more than suicide or an accident.

Sasha nodded. "I trailed Mayor Lassiter as he left with his wife. He was worked up about the whole thing, but I got the sense he was more upset about his ruined meeting than he was about someone dying."

"Oh, yeah?" Now that seemed interesting.

I pulled into her driveway as she went on. "Yeah, he told his wife his plan had gone all wrong, and that he had to find a way to fix this, whatever that meant." Sasha shrugged and thanked me for the ride as she got out. "Sorry I dragged you into all this, Mallory," she said before waving and shutting my car door.

But I wasn't sorry at all.

Was this truly more than an unfortunate accident?

# CHAPTER FOUR

My mind was reeling so fast by the time I got home, I almost didn't notice Amber sitting on the edge of my driveway. I slammed on my brakes and gasped before I realized she was actually more on my lawn than on the asphalt where my car had been barreling onto. As I worked at steadying my breathing and pulling my car all the way forward, I tried to recall the entire trip from Sasha's house and couldn't remember even a minute of it.

Thank goodness there hadn't been anyone in my way.

I took a final deep cleansing breath and then stepped out of the driver's seat. Amber stood casually, which seemed wrong, and I had to remind myself again that she hadn't just brushed death.

"Where ya been?" she asked. There was something behind her voice—sadness? rejection?—although she worked hard at hiding those sorts of emotions. Amber was almost sixteen, and her spontaneity of showing up on my doorstep for a cooking lesson at all hours usually made me smile. I felt like I could talk to her more than anyone in my life, perhaps because she didn't get mushy over emotions. I could also count on her for great insight. She was wise beyond her years.

I shook my head, trying to get myself back on track. I probably should apologize for not giving Amber a heads-up that I would be out with Sasha for the evening, as I usually spent my evenings biding my time with Netflix until she came by, but that wasn't as important at the moment as calling Alex. And if I could count on Amber for one thing, it was keeping her priorities in check.

I pulled out my phone and held up my other hand, beckoning for her to follow me inside. Alex picked up on the first ring.

I relayed what Sasha had told me, not making any effort to keep the information from Amber. She had been instrumental in helping us solve two murders in this town, one of which was her dad's, after all. "On the drive home, Sasha Mills told me about different people she had eavesdropped on at the town hall meeting." As I said the words, I realized I was saying them more to give Amber context, plus an explanation of why I hadn't been home, than I was to update Alex. "After Superintendent Garnet was found dead on the steps, the majority of people thought it was suicide, but Sasha sided with those who thought he had slipped and fallen by accident."

Alex started to interrupt, probably to indicate he already knew all of this, but I didn't let him. "She trailed Mayor Lassiter and his wife to their car. The mayor told his wife his plan had gone all wrong, and he had to find a way to fix it."

This time Alex's response didn't come right away. I looked down at Amber, who had wasted no time in kneeling to greet Hunch inside my front door. As she stood with my cat in her arms, she kept her serious eyes trained on me. She was ingesting all of this information. More than likely, even through his purring, Hunch was, too.

"Steve Reinhart's already interviewed Mayor Lassiter," Alex finally said. I had him on speakerphone so Amber could hear everything. "It's officially his case since he was the superior detective on-site. He said he'd submit a report tonight on the whole incident. I guess I should call and stop him."

"Hang on," Amber said, holding up a hand.

I could practically see her brain spinning and bought her a minute to process all of this new information by explaining to Alex, "Amber was at my place when I got home. I was giving her the rundown of what happened, you know, in case we missed anything."

Before Alex could respond, Amber's computer-like speedy brain had done its work. "When you were working on my dad's case, didn't Captain Corbett forbid you to investigate it because you'd already signed off on the report?" she asked Alex.

Alex and I were both quiet. "It was really just a formality to push me around, but I see where you're going with this," he said eventually. "I just don't know if it's completely ethical."

As usual, I was the slowest one on the uptake. "What are you two talking about?"

Amber explained. "If Detective Reinhart signs off on the case, Captain Corbett shouldn't, by his own rules, allow him to continue on the investigation once he's officially signed off on it. Since Detective Martinez was there, too—"

"It might turn into your investigation," I said into the phone, finishing her sentence.

Alex was silent for a few seconds, thinking this over. I grinned at Amber, thankful once again for her quick teenage mind. Today, she wore a black hoodie with white letters that aptly read: I'LL BE NICER IF YOU'LL BE SMARTER.

The truth of the logo made me smile. Except that I didn't need her to be any nicer.

"How about this?" Alex finally said. "I know it sounds stupid, but can you call me again tomorrow morning at nine with this information? I should be at the station by then. I won't have to hide anything or make up stories if others overhear me getting some new information on the case. Can you do that?"

"Of course," I told him.

"Okay, then I'll hopefully get the go-ahead from Corbett to go back and investigate the scene further. I'm certain he'll tell me to get Mickey Mouse to take the reins, but since it's doubtful my lackadaisical partner will even be out of bed, I'm hoping you could join me if you're not busy."

"Sure," I said. "You bet."

Amber raised an eyebrow at the Mickey Mouse reference, but I'd explain that to her later. She said, "And me, too."

"You have school," I told her and checked the time on my phone. It was already almost ten. "And on that note, I should probably get you home."

She rolled her eyes at me. "Okay, Mom." Then she added, clearly into the phone, "I'll be there, too, Detective Martinez." It was her usual mix of teenage respect and disrespect—calling him Detective Martinez, but telling him, rather than asking permission, that she'd unquestionably be at the crime scene.

Alex didn't argue. In fact, I thought I heard him chuckle on the other end of the line before he said goodbye and hung up.

Amber led the way to my kitchen, Hunch purring in her arms. "It's probably easiest if I stay over," she told me, again with the telling rather than the asking. But I'd at least hear her out. "I'll get Seth to tell Mom I went to bed early with a headache. Then Helen Montrose"—she motioned up and down at me with a hand—"can call the school in the morning. Tell them I'm not feeling well and won't be in for the day."

I opened my mouth to argue or at the very least interrupt this crazy underhanded plan she had of me imitating her mother to her school, but she plopped into a kitchen chair and started speaking again before I could get a word out.

"Now tell me everything that happened tonight, and let's make some notes." She placed Hunch down on the floor, and he sat on his haunches at attention, as though he was equally ready to work. She grabbed the notepad from the rear edge of my kitchen table and poised a pen above it. "If we're going to help Detective Martinez, we don't want to miss a single detail."

# CHAPTER FIVE

The next morning, the scent of sizzling bacon woke me. I blinked, feeling disoriented, and then grabbed for my phone, hoping I hadn't slept through my alarm. But it was only seven thirty.

I blinked again and remembered where I was, who was downstairs. It wasn't Cooper making me breakfast as he had on so many Sunday mornings when I had a day shift at the restaurant. I no longer had a husband. In this new life, in this new town, I had friends instead.

I took a deep breath and let it out slowly. This re-remembering had been a daily occurrence last winter. It had been weeks, maybe even months, since I'd woken up and had to remind myself about Cooper's death. I sat up with a final deep breath, deciding I needed to be grateful that even though emerging from my fog of grief wasn't easy, at least it was getting less and less traumatic on my nervous system.

"Smells great," I said as I wandered into the kitchen. I still wore my bathrobe with messy hair. Amber, as usual, already appeared showered and dressed for the day. Not exactly your typical teenager. Today, she wore a pink hoodie that she had left in my guest room, along with a small duffel bag of clothes, for when it was convenient for her to stay over. The hoodie read: ABS ARE COOL BUT HAVE YOU TRIED DONUTS? "What time did you get up?"

She shrugged in my direction and then turned back to a skillet of eggs, multi-colored peppers, and potato chunks. "I dunno. A while ago."

Her words held an edge, which made me wonder if she wasn't sleeping well. Maybe she still woke up and had to remind herself her dad was dead—and had been murdered, no less.

But I knew better than to ask. She'd talk about it when she wanted to.

"What's on the menu?" I asked instead. "Seems like you're getting the hang of this cooking business."

She shrugged again. "I think this needs something." She held up a clean spoon. "Want to taste?"

As if on cue, my stomach let out a loud grumble. I scooped up a large spoonful that included a little of all the ingredients, barely took time to blow on it, and then slipped the whole thing into my mouth. When I'd worked in restaurants, my tongue had built up a tolerance to scalding food.

"Hmm, salt and pepper?" I asked after I finished chewing.

Amber rolled her eyes. "Obviously. But isn't there something else?"

I stirred her concoction and unthinkingly added my own generous amounts of salt and pepper to the dish. I could suggest some oregano, maybe some paprika, but I was trying hard to teach her about building flavors from the bottom up. "Did you start with any type of onion?" I asked. I didn't see any as I mixed.

Her brow furrowed, and she marched for the pantry. "Oh, right." She returned with a yellow onion in one hand and a red onion in the other.

I finished chewing the piece of crispy bacon I'd helped myself to and took the yellow onion. "Reds work better raw, like in salads. You'll like the sweetness of the yellow one in this skillet." I pointed her to the chopping board and instructed her to dice. "Now you'll want to fry these separately, so you don't get any of that raw onion flavor throughout the dish."

She nodded and got to work. Amber was a strange mix of teachable and too smart to be taught. But I sure liked having her around, regardless.

After breakfast, and after I'd called the school to claim Amber was sick, Amber cleaned the kitchen while I cleaned myself up. We were both back at my kitchen table by ten to nine with my phone charged and sitting between us.

"I have no idea why I'm nervous," I said to Amber, tapping my fingers on my phone case.

Hunch purred from her lap as she reread our notes from last night. My cat had taken to sleeping with Amber on the guest bed whenever she stayed over. It didn't seem fair that he could automatically like her so much when I'd been working so hard to get him on my good side for months. But then I reminded myself that she probably wasn't sleeping well. The least I could give her was the company of my cat—who always kept to Cooper's side of my bed anyway.

Amber shrugged. "You're about to come up with some integral information that will launch a possible murder investigation and then call the cops with it. Shouldn't you be nervous?"

I smirked. When she put it like that—forget the fact that Alex was my friend and I'd already spilled any possible clues—if I had been sharing this with the Police, with a capital P, of course I'd be nervous.

Amber tapped a pen on her notes, clearly deep in thought. "So I assume our biggest problem will be getting some honest answers out of Mayor Lassiter. Detective Reinhart already interviewed him and he doesn't sound very cooperative. He's probably not going to listen to the two of us, and I doubt Alex will want to barrel into the mayor's office and pummel him with questions."

I nodded, furrowing my brow. "Do we really think Mayor Lassiter had something to do with the superintendent's death?"

Amber shrugged, letting this idea slide easily around her mind as she did with most things. "Maybe not, but he had some kind of a plan that included the superintendent last night. We need to discover what that was."

"Or maybe we'll find another clue at the town hall," I said hopefully. I turned over my phone. One minute to nine. Navigating to the phone app, my thumb hovered over Alex's contact name, ready to dial.

"It's Quick-Draw McGraw." Amber chuckled at me. I had to admit, I wished I could stay as calm and collected as my fifteen-year-old friend.

When the time clicked over to nine o'clock, I sucked in a deep breath and pressed CALL. I had to remind myself over and over again this was my friend Alex before he finally picked up.

"Detective Martinez," he said in way of an answer. He had never once in the time I'd known him answered a phone call of mine so formally.

Thankfully, the formality kicked me into gear for the purpose of me calling. "Hi there, detective. Last night at the town hall, you suggested I could call you if I thought of anything else I had seen during the terrible incident that took place?"

"Yes, right, of course," he said. "Did you think of something?"

I quickly rattled off the same words I had told him the night before about the mayor and his plans. There was noise in the background—phones ringing, people talking—and I hoped at least one person would take notice that Detective Martinez was receiving a serious tip about a recent case.

"I thought it was worth mentioning," I said.

"Of course," he agreed. "And you said you'd rather not give your name?"

My mind whirred. We hadn't talked about this. Amber, thankfully, was listening in and shook her head vehemently to help me along in my next words. "Um, no. If that's okay?"

Amber scrawled a messy note at the bottom of her paper and turned it toward me.

I spoke the words aloud as soon as I read them. "I'm not trying to bring any accusations against our mayor."

"Right, of course not," Alex said in a calm and authoritative voice I'd never heard out of him. "Well, thank you very much for calling in. We do appreciate every little bit of information, and if you think of anything else, anything at all, please don't hesitate to get a hold of me again."

After we said goodbye and hung up, I finally let out the gust of breath I'd been holding.

"You did good," Amber told me. I didn't know how much I needed to hear her encouragement until she had said it.

"You think?" I asked. I couldn't seem to help myself, but I wasn't normally one to fish for compliments, so I quickly covered with, "So now what?"

She took my phone from the middle of the table and looked at the blank screen. "Now, I guess we wait."

☐

# CHAPTER SIX

The next time Detective Martinez called, he was clearly my friend Alex again, and he seemed to be on the Bluetooth speaker in his car. I could hear passing vehicles in the background.

"It wasn't easy to get Corbett to go for it, and like I suspected, he insisted Mickey Mouse take the lead on it and follow up on the report. But at least I'm officially on the case. Now let's hope there's actually something there to uncover or I'll look like a real schmuck."

I nibbled at my lip. I hadn't thought about that. Then again, Amber always seemed to be aware of how our investigations might affect Alex's career, for better or for worse. I had Alex on speakerphone and had at least some confidence that if she felt this was worth pursuing, there was likely something more to it.

"So what are you going to do about Mickey Mouse?" Amber asked.

I'd explained Alex's partner to her last night. Like when I'd first explained him to her, her voice held a strong edge, as if she didn't find his nickname funny in the least. As always, she was ultimately looking out for Alex, and I felt a little guilty for not having the same kind of immediate protectiveness.

"I told him I was going to drop by his house to discuss a case," Alex told us. "He'd barely gotten out of bed and hadn't even considered coming into the office yet. I'll get him to sign off on the warrant request I've prepared so I can thoroughly follow up on the report on-site at the town hall. I'll tell him it's a formality because I happened to be at the scene, and I don't mind heading over on my own to take care of it. If I know Mickey, he'll take me up on my offer for help and won't rush to get to work."

"Right. So how soon do you think you'll have the warrant?" I asked.

"Should be right away," he said. "With a recent death on the premises of such a public building, I'm certain any judge will want us to quickly get to the truth of the matter and get it open for business again. Can you meet me there at ten?"

Amber popped to her feet and went to pack up the zucchini muffins she'd baked while I was in the shower.

"We'll see you at ten," I told him and then hung up.

My next problem was getting out of the house without Hunch tagging along, especially because it seemed to be two against one today.

"He did help in solving my dad's murder," Amber said. "And I'll bet he would've helped solve the Candi Banks case, too, if he hadn't been stuck at home in a cast."

Truth be told, Hunch had helped me solve the Candi Banks case—directing me pretty specifically to where I should look. But Amber didn't need any more ammunition.

"Fine," I told her as I slipped on a pair of emerald green flats that nicely matched my cable knit sweater. Fall sweater weather was my favorite time of year. "But you're the one that has to explain him to Alex."

We waited across the street in the parking lot of the town hall for nearly fifteen minutes before Alex pulled up beside us in his new unmarked police cruiser. He was alone. All must have gone as planned with Mickey Mouse. His driver's window was open, and after saying hi to me, he looked at Amber. He glanced down at her pink hoodie, smirked, and said, "Donuts, a girl after my own heart," by way of a greeting.

Amber nibbled her lip and quickly looked away.

I wasn't sure what was up with her, as she usually had a smart aleck comeback right on the tip of her tongue.

The parking lot was empty, aside from us, but I asked Alex anyway, "Nothing going on in town hall today?"

Alex got out of his car and shook his head. "Steve told the mayor all events for the rest of the week should be postponed." Alex flipped open a folder and skimmed through a couple of pages of typed notes. "His report said Mayor Lassiter was very agreeable when it came to shutting down the place." He flipped back and forth between two different pages. "I'm not sure what changed when Steve wanted to interview folks who saw what happened, but as far as I can tell, asking people to wait around to be questioned seemed to set the mayor on edge."

"Can you ask the other detective?" Amber asked. Thankfully, Hunch was snuggled up in her arms and not mine—not that snuggling with me was exactly a regular occurrence—so I wouldn't even have to be involved in the discussion about why my cat was here.

But Alex didn't seem to notice Hunch. Either that, or he didn't find him out of place at the site of a police investigation, which, now that I thought about it, seemed the more likely option. I was pretty sure both Amber and my cat would get deputized into the police force before I ever would.

Alex twisted his lips at Amber's question. "I'd rather not go back to Steve or Gerald with any questions until I at least have a solid case to work with. And even then…"

He trailed off, but I understood what he meant. He'd pretty much swooped in and taken the case out from under Steve Reinhart. Steve was one of the most respected detectives in Corbett's books and was usually handed all the best cases. Meanwhile, Alex carried an unfair weight from a dispute between Captain Corbett and his dad. I could see how Alex might feel guilty about going back and questioning the guy who'd given him a leg up in the department on a case where Steve may have missed crucial information.

"Do we need a key?" I asked, trying to get our focus back on the task at hand.

Alex nodded. "I already picked one up at the municipal office when I gave them a copy of the warrant."

Alex started walking for the building, and I followed, but Amber called, "Hang on!" We both turned. She had the container of zucchini muffins outstretched toward Alex. "I baked these this morning." Amber's neck turned pink with her words.

Alex smiled and helped himself to two muffins to take along with him. "These smell amazing!"

The pink in Amber's neck traveled up to her cheeks, and even though Alex seemed oblivious, already marching toward the town hall, I looked back at Amber, furrowing my brow.

She stowed the container in my car and then raced ahead so I couldn't see her face. But I'd seen the blush.

Uh-oh. Did Amber have a crush on Detective Martinez?

I followed them up the cement steps of the town hall, my mind on the possibility. Alex was certainly attractive; I'd give him that. In fact, if I were going to date anyone, it would sooner be him than anyone else in town, certainly sooner than Steve Reinhart, no matter how much the accomplished detective looked like he belonged on a magazine cover. Amber was smart and intuitive in so many ways, but suddenly, I realized she likely hadn't taken the time to do the math on how many years too old Alex Martinez was for her.

I sighed toward her back. She bent down on her hands and knees, studying the cement steps, all business now.

"This must be where he fell," she said. "Was there much blood?" Alex had already passed her a pair of blue gloves, and she ran a gloved hand along the faded patch of cement.

Alex nodded. "A team came in and washed it up last night. The faded area is where we found him."

Both their voices were clearly focused on the case. Now I had to wonder if I had imagined the blush on Amber's face. I shook my head, trying to get back on track. Amber had already let Hunch out of her arms, and he sniffed around the faded patch of cement. He scrunched his nose at whatever kind of solvent had been used to clean up the blood.

"Any word from the coroner?" I asked as Amber stood and Alex led the way up to the heavy front doors.

He shook his head. "Not yet. Hopefully, I'll have a preliminary report by this afternoon. They're doing an autopsy, but I don't expect to find much in the way of a surprise. The paramedics told us his neck appeared to have been broken on impact."

I nodded. As soon as we were through the double entry doors to the town hall, we all fell silent. Light streamed in through a dozen upper windows, but the place seemed somber and quiet without the fluorescent lights or any people occupying the large room.

"So we're mostly concerned with the roof, right?" Amber broke the silence.

Alex led the way across the length of the hall to the side stage door. "Yeah. Unless you see anything out of place down here, I think we need to focus our efforts up there." He pointed upward, and I had the strange urge to put my hands together and pray. After all, in the last investigation I'd been a part of, even I had to admit The Big Guy in the Sky had probably had something to do with me getting out of it alive.

But what would I pray for if I were going to pray? For Alex to nab his first murderer? Should I even be hoping this was somehow a murder investigation, or should I be praying that it would all turn out to be an accident?

My head was upturned when we moved past the stage toward the green wooden door. "Hey, the balloons," I blurted suddenly.

Amber and Alex were both ahead of me, but they stopped and turned. Thanks to my usual lack of graceful explanations, I just pointed. "Hank the janitor said they weren't there two days ago."

I didn't know if they meant anything, of course. Perhaps the hall had been pre-decorated for an upcoming birthday party or some other kind of celebration. But Alex made a note of it in his file before moving toward the door.

As I followed them into the stairwell, Hunch made his way into the hall's kitchen to sniff around. Alex had locked the front doors to the hall, so I placed my purse in the opening of the green door so my cat could follow us up whenever he felt like the main floor had been scrutinized.

The upper door wasn't as easy to prop open, as I didn't have another purse with me, but again, I rested the metal door against the frame and hoped the strength in Hunch's body matched the strength in his mind. If so, he'd have no trouble at all pushing it open.

Even with the overcast sky, the brightness of the roof during the day was quite a contrast to what it had been like the night before. It looked like a completely different roof in the light. Black scuff marks along the white elastomeric roof coating, while they were impossible to decipher beyond any doubt, held a variety of what looked like faded and fresher marks. I bent to study a few right outside the door.

Amber walked straight for the far side of the roof. "Where's this dented gutter you told me about?"

Alex followed her to the ledge and pointed. "Mallory astutely pointed out that there isn't any rust, which the forensics team confirmed. It means the dent is likely recent."

Now I blushed.

"And it's too dented for a bird or anything, right?" she asked, clearly the business-minded one of the two of us.

Alex nodded. "Yeah, I can't think of much in nature that would've dented it that much." He looked around. "There aren't any tree branches anywhere close."

I kept crawling on my gloved hands and knees toward them, pausing to take photos on my phone of any scuff marks that could be noteworthy. The crime scene team should have photos of any noteworthy evidence, but if this were anything like the Montrose murder, I had doubts they did a very thorough job. If Amber and I hadn't been so heavily invested in solving her dad's murder, we both might still be blissfully unaware of how much incompetence ran through the Honeysuckle Grove Police Department.

Then again, Alex was far more competent than either of us, and if any of these marks would actually add anything to the investigation, he would have likely already followed my lead. But I didn't know what else to do, and it felt good to do something.

About halfway across the large roof, a mewling sound from behind me caught my attention. I looked back to the metal door and started to stand, but then I realized Hunch was already through it. I had been analyzing a straight path of roofing from the door to the ledge, but my cat—true to his dog-like nature—was sniffing off to the side, not far away from the door.

I slowly crawled closer on my knees, and even though I couldn't see whatever Hunch was sniffing at, I snapped another photo. Soon he gave up on that spot and took another dozen steps toward the outer cement wall. He stopped with one paw in the air, backed up a couple of steps, and then started sniffing again.

I hated to admit it to Amber, but my cat exuded so much confidence, I was already glad we'd brought him along.

My knees started to ache, but I ignored the pain and quick-stepped on them toward where Hunch was circling—with his nose in the middle. He had clearly found something.

But as I moved closer, the black scuff marks seemed to diminish. "Are you sure there's something here, Hunch?" I asked.

He didn't spare me a glance, just kept sniffing, almost in a frenzy. I turned on the magnifying app on my phone and peered closer with it. A little bit of beige debris came into the view of my camera, but that was it.

I moved even closer, so my nose was almost as close to the roof coating as Hunch's. It didn't look like dirt. As I ran my gloved fingers over the debris, it didn't squish like dirt, either. In fact, it felt almost like the same material as the roof.

"Huh." I sat back, thinking this over. Even if some of the roof coating had come off and gotten discolored, what did that mean? Nothing in the cause of death of Superintendent Garnet, as far as I could tell.

I sighed and was about to tell Hunch not to worry, he'd get the hang of what was important and what wasn't, but Alex's voice took my attention from behind one of the big square heating protrusions.

I stood, glad to get my knees unfolded for a few minutes, and moved toward his voice. Alex was crouched near a white Styrofoam cup that had been placed on a low ledge of the heating unit. It appeared to be half-filled with dark coffee.

"What've you got there?" I asked, bending to his level.

"I suspect Superintendent Garnet was a coffee drinker," he said, motioning to the cup. "But I'll get this into forensics to get a read on it for sure." He stood, shaking his head. "I can't believe they missed this."

I could. After all, they'd never investigated Amber's dad's muddy shoes. "I saw him with a Styrofoam coffee cup before he went through the green door and headed up here," I told Alex.

Hunch hopped up on the ledge of the heating unit and sniffed all around the cup. Alex sucked in his lips, and I could tell he was restraining himself from admonishing my cat away from his evidence. But if this was Superintendent Garnet's cup, out of the three of us, Hunch was the most likely to pick up his scent and figure out where else that scent had been around this building. And I knew Hunch well enough to understand he wouldn't touch the cup.

He did, however, sniff inside it and offer a nose scrunch in response. This didn't mean anything. He regularly did this when I had a pot of coffee brewing at home.

"So if Superintendent Garnet did bring a coffee up here, what does that mean?" I asked, but then answered my own question. "Probably that he wasn't on a mission to kill himself, right?"

"Perhaps," Alex said, standing.

But right then, Hunch hopped down from the ledge to the roof and started sniffing feverishly again. I bent closer and turned on my magnifying app to see. Sure enough, the same type of beige debris was over here behind the heating unit, but here it was concentrated into a tiny arc of about two inches square.

"Huh," I said, and both Alex and Amber kneeled on either side of me.

"What did he find?" Alex asked. I couldn't say for sure, but I thought I detected some admiration in his voice.

"I'm not sure, but it doesn't seem like dirt," I told him. "It feels rubberized. There's more of it over near the door."

Alex nodded and pulled out a baggie. He collected a sample of the beige debris and then used a small file to pick off a lump of the elastomeric roof coating. Out of his file, he pulled a pad of red sticky dots. He took one off and placed it where he'd taken the sample from. "I'll get this analyzed, too. In case it's a match," he said.

"Did you find anything else?" I asked Amber. She had kept mostly to the area that Superintendent Garnet had fallen from.

"No," she said, but as she led the way back around the heating unit, she added, "Only that a broken neck doesn't make a lot of sense if his foot had slipped on the gutter. Broken legs, maybe."

I nodded. "You've got a good point. So if he went headfirst, are we back to suicide?"

Alex shook his head, but he took a long time to answer. "I don't think so. Not if he came up here with a cup of coffee." He took a big breath and let it out slowly. "I could be wrong, but I feel like there's some kind of foul play at work here."

I nodded, feeling it, too. "So what do we do next?"

Alex looked around the empty roof. "I guess we let your bloodhound over there"—he motioned to Hunch—"sniff every inch of this building, inside and out, while the rest of us come up with a way to unobtrusively take a second shot at interviewing the mayor."

# CHAPTER SEVEN

It turned out Hunch had found more of the beige debris in the area right under the ledge where Superintendent Garnet had fallen. My cat also had a preoccupation with the kitchen on our way out, but we hadn't turned up any clues there so he was probably just hungry.

As usual, whenever I helped make the plans, my strongest ideas came down to cooking. Amber, Hunch, and I headed to my place, while Alex took the rubber samples and coffee to the forensics lab to be analyzed.

"If only Superintendent Garnet had been married, it would be a lot easier to tell if he had been suicidal," Amber observed, lifting my large bucket of flour from the pantry. We had decided on the drive home that while good food had the tendency to open the way to getting answers, a casserole or other hot food item would be out of place at the mayor's office. Besides, then we'd have to bring plates and cutlery.

Instead, we'd settled on a blueberry lemon loaf. It would smell and taste amazing, which was the most important part. Plus, it would be easy for the mayor, his secretary, and anyone else who might be in the vicinity to grab a slice with a napkin.

We barely had the flour, baking powder, and salt mixed in one bowl, with the oil, sugar, eggs, vanilla, lemon juice and zest, and sour cream in another when Alex called again. Amber coated the blueberries with a dusting of flour while I wiped off my hands to answer.

"How long are you going to be?" he asked.

I looked down at my recipe. "It'll be a little more than an hour to bake. But it'll be worth it."

This was the plan Amber and I had concocted: We'd drop by the mayor's office to offer a loaf because we felt awful about what had transpired at the town hall meeting the night before, and we hoped they were all doing okay. We'd happen to run into Alex, who would arrive at the same time. We would all clearly know each other, and we'd sit down over a

160

slice of yummy cake to casually talk about the events of the previous night.

This would lay the groundwork before Alex switched to detective mode and demanded clear answers.

He sighed on the other end of the line, and I motioned to Amber to fold the blueberries into the mixture of wet and dry ingredients before I reminded him, "Good food takes time, Alex."

He chuckled. "I know. Okay, how about this?" I heard a paper flip in the background, and I envisioned him sitting in his police cruiser, flipping through his notes. "While you finish up, I'll go back to the municipal office. I'll see who had installed the balloons and follow up on that."

I'd forgotten all about the balloons over the stage. I guess that was one good reason to go to detective school—to learn how to take good notes and then follow up on them.

"Sounds good," I told him and hung up.

An hour later, my house smelled like blueberry-lemon-flavored heaven, and I was about to drizzle the lemon juice and powdered sugar glaze when a knock sounded at my door. I yelled, "Come in," as I finished my drizzle. Hunch was asleep on Amber's lap on the couch.

Seconds later, Alex strode into the kitchen, energy radiating off him like he was hyped up on coffee. He'd added his suit jacket since I saw him last and his attractive and professional appearance made my heart stutter.

I tried to shake the feeling off by asking, "I thought we were meeting at the mayor's office?"

He nodded like a hyperactive Chihuahua. "We were," he said in a rush. "But I had to let you know. I just came from the municipal office, and those balloons? They were put up by the mayor. The mayor's secretary called in two days ago to find a slot of time where she could rig them in time for the town hall meeting."

"Balloons?" I said it as a question. "Why would Mayor Lassiter have wanted balloons rigged for a meeting about the library?"

Alex nodded. "It's all a lot of questions now, isn't it? And it all leads back to Mayor Lassiter. That smells unbelievable, by the way," he said, closing his eyes and taking in a long inhale.

I smiled. "You're right." About all of it, including the smell, but I didn't say that. "But we can't barrel into his office and accuse our local mayor of scheming to commit murder," I said. We'd talked about this a few times since I told Alex about the mayor's words to his wife about his plan getting ruined.

"Yeah, yeah." He nodded, still with the grin. "I know. And I won't. That's why I came here first. To get it out of my system."

Our plan didn't go exactly as envisioned.

We all arrived at the mayor's office lobby, as we had set out to. It was located on the second floor of a large brick building only half a block from the town hall. In fact, I was betting that the window in the mayor's actual office offered a great vantage point of the town's largest meeting hall.

We all pretended it was a chance meeting, as planned, and I shared the blueberry lemon loaf around. But the mayor's secretary, a lady younger than me at maybe twenty-five with blonde hair, a large chest, and a red blouse so tight the top button buckled, informed us that the mayor was out of the office in a council meeting until later this afternoon. The nameplate on her desk read "KELLI" and she had only helped herself to a small corner of the blueberry lemon loaf, but now she went in for a full slice.

"I can pencil you in for four o'clock?" she said in between bites. She looked between all three of us, clearly not knowing who to make the appointment for.

"Sure. That sounds great," Alex said. I nodded, trying to walk the line between being invited to that appointment and not being a part of it. He relaxed onto a corner of her desk. A sour jealousy filled my stomach, and I took a step away to hide my reaction. "Tell me something, Kelli," he went on, leaning a little closer to her. "I saw some balloons rigged above the stage in the town hall, and the municipal office tells me it was your office that put them there. Is that true?"

Kelli let out a huff of a breath and rolled her eyes. "You'd think the mayor's secretary would be a more glamorous job, right?" She laughed a high-pitched grating laugh that made her quite a bit less attractive. "If I'm not filling the soda machine down the hall, then I'm blowing up balloons and climbing ladders in my heels." She held one of her legs up high to show off today's choice of red shiny wedges. I couldn't seem to look away from her slim tanned legs, which protruded from a very short black skirt.

I, for one, had no confusion about why the mayor had hired Kelli. Plus, apparently, she filled soda machines, blew up balloons, and climbed ladders.

Alex, thankfully, didn't seem nearly as caught up in Kelli's gams. "So you rigged the balloons there by yourself?" he confirmed.

She shrugged. "Well, I couldn't do it all by myself, but thankfully Hank, the janitor, was there. He helped hold the ladder for me."

My mind immediately envisioned Hank, the dirty-old-man janitor, kindly holding a ladder for this short-skirted secretary. But only a second later, it rebounded to something else.

Hank had told me specifically that he didn't know how the balloons had gotten there.

"What were the balloons for?" I blurted.

Kelli shrugged again. "Beats me. I do what I'm told." She leaned in, as though to say something conspiratorial to all three of us. In a quieter voice, she said, "But I heard they didn't even get used! All that work!"

"You heard what happened, though, right?" I asked. I couldn't help myself. "With Superintendent Garnet?"

Kelli glanced down the hall toward the mayor's open office door. The light was off, so I doubted anyone was in there. When she turned back to us, her face was much more somber, but she quickly forced a smile. "We're not supposed to talk about that."

I wanted to ask more, to grill this secretary on why, exactly, she'd be told not to talk about the death of a superintendent only eighteen hours ago. But Alex interrupted my racing thoughts.

"Thank you for your help, Kelli," he said. "We'll be back at four."

We'd barely made it out of the building before I told Alex, "Hank, the janitor, was lying. He told me he had no idea how the balloons got up there or what they were for. And why did you rush us out of there? The secretary was told to be quiet about the death? That has to mean something."

Alex nodded. "I want our meeting with the mayor later to go as smoothly as possible. I don't want his secretary warning him that we're all worked up about something he clearly doesn't want talked about."

Hmm. That made sense. Once again, it was clear why I wasn't the lead detective on this case.

"So what about Hank?" Amber asked. "How do we find him?"

Alex sighed. "I guess I'll have to go and bother the municipal office again." He looked down the street at the town hall. "Who else would have known what the mayor was up to last night? I doubt his council members would say much if they've also been told to keep quiet. Plus, it sounds like they're all in a meeting right now. But could there have been anyone else who overheard anything?"

I started to shake my head. My mind skittered over the hundreds of people at the meeting last night. I wouldn't know any of them well enough to track them down and question them about our local mayor. But then I thought of the layout of the building, of Hunch's investigative work this morning and his preoccupation with the kitchen, and my mind thudded to a stop on one specific person.

"Chef Talia!" I said, making Alex and Amber both stop in place even though we were several feet from our cars. "The catering company— Mayberry Catering. It's amazing how much you can overhear in the food business," I explained to them quickly as it started to make sense in my mind. "And the kitchen was situated right near the stage, right near the stairs to the roof. There was at least five catering staff hired to serve cake and coffee. There has to be a chance one of them heard or saw something."

Alex nodded, but I wasn't sure he saw this as a serious avenue of investigation. He didn't know the catering business like I did, though, and how much a person in an apron could overhear. Then again, with Hank's lies, Alex seemed in a hurry to get to the municipal office.

But he said, "Mickey Mouse should be conducting the initial interviews, but since he refuses to exert himself, why don't you see if you can get in touch with Mayberry Catering and any of their workers, and lay the initial groundwork. Then I can have a better idea of where to concentrate on my follow-up questions. In the meantime, I'll check in with the lab and look into Hank the janitor. Then we can meet back here at four."

I had the urge to put a hand in the circle and say, "Ready? Break!" as though we were heading into the fourth quarter of our game and not heading off to investigate a group of food service workers in a quickly developing murder case.

☐

# CHAPTER EIGHT

Mayberry Catering was listed in the local phone book, which made finding them pretty easy. Voicemail picked up when I called, but I decided not to leave a message. Instead, I punched the address into my GPS. If we had to meet up with Alex again in three short hours, we didn't have time to wait around for people to return our phone calls.

My GPS led us to a neighborhood at the outskirts of town made up mostly of tiny houses with white picket fences. It looked more like a retirement community than the hub for a busy catering business.

I found the address and parked along the curb across from it. It was a pale yellow ranch-style house. The street was perfectly quiet, not a single person out in their yard or walking along the street. Again, I only seemed to be able to picture an elderly couple in the tiny house in front of me.

"Do you think this can be right?" I asked Amber.

She had been quietly petting Hunch for the entire drive here. I suspected the wheels in her mind were turning, likely coming up with some new angles I hadn't considered, but she'd tell me when she was ready.

She shrugged. "Why not? I'd guess most small catering companies work out of their houses."

That wasn't what I meant, exactly. "Chef Talia has that bustle about her that goes with a busy kitchen. Try as I might, I'm just having trouble picturing her in this quiet and subdued part of town."

Amber shrugged again. "People live where they have to live." It was an odd statement, especially coming from a girl whose family, as of recently, had very little money, and yet she still lived in a mansion.

Right then, as if the universe wanted to help me along with my inner picture, a white van barreled down the empty road and whipped into the driveway across from us. Sure enough, the pink logo of the steamy food

165

and MAYBERRY CATERING were plastered on the side and rear doors.

A second later, Talia sprung out of the driver's seat, and her long legs took her to her front door before I could blink. She carried a grocery bag in each hand, which made the chore of unlocking her door take an extra second, but she was inside before I could make it out of my car and across the street.

It all happened so fast that Amber had followed my lead without a word. Thankfully, she'd left my cat in the Prius.

I rang the bell, realizing that what I should have been focusing on for the last several minutes wasn't what kind of house suited Chef Talia, but what we planned to ask her when we found her.

But too late for any planning. The door swung open, and she stood on the threshold. Her energy was nearly as electric as it had been the night before. I wondered if she had something on her catering agenda for tonight.

"We're sorry to bother you," I said as she looked between Amber and me with raised eyebrows, clearly waiting for an explanation. "I'm not sure if you remember me, but we met last night. At the town hall meeting?"

She nodded once. "Sure. The cookies. And the rubber gloves."

My face flushed again at the memory of trying to deliver freshly baked cookies to a fully catered event. But this was clearly a lady who didn't have an extra word to spare for anyone. If I planned to get any information out of her, to get her talking, and especially about the speakers last night, I had to get her to relax, at least a little.

I motioned to her van in the driveway. "I noticed your logo on your van. You're not by any chance related to Marv and Donna Mayberry?"

A quick playful eye roll told me I was onto something. "Marv's my brother," she said. "You know him?"

Marv and Donna Mayberry were one of the first couples at Honeysuckle Grove Community Church who had welcomed Cooper and me to town when we'd first moved here. Marv was a bit of a workaholic, and I bit back a smile, quickly seeing a family resemblance, both in looks and hyperactive work ethic.

I nodded. "From church. They've had us over for a few barbecues. Great people," I said. When she looked again between me and Amber, I realized I should clarify who "we" meant. "Oh, it was my late husband and me that they had over."

My words, as always, were followed by the Head Tilt of Pity. But in the matter of a second, I realized this might be the only way to soften this lady and get her to slow down and give us a few minutes.

"Yeah, they invited Cooper and me over when we first moved to town," I went on. "They were some of the most welcoming people we met."

My words seemed to garner a bonus reaction. Not only did they get Talia to soften, apparently, the idea that her brother might be a welcoming force spurred Talia on, perhaps in competitiveness. She swung the door wider and said, "Would you like to come in?"

Amber and I both smiled and quickly took her up on her invitation.

"I'm Mallory Beck," I told her and then introduced Amber in the same way as I had during our last two investigations. "And this is my niece, Amber."

Talia nodded but didn't reply. I guess she assumed we knew who she was, if we'd tracked her down at her home. She led us past a front room, which contained heavily brocaded furniture that looked like it had never been sat on, and down a hallway to a small kitchen. She motioned to two white stools at a marble island that seemed too big for the small kitchen. Amber and I sat, and she proceeded to unpack her grocery bags and wash a variety of cucumber, peppers, and tomatoes.

The idea of her keeping busy in the kitchen while she spoke to us made me feel an immediate kinship toward her.

"I used to cook, too," I blurted, unable to help myself.

Amber screwed up her face and, in typical teenage fashion, contradicted me. "She still does," she told Chef Talia.

I shook my head. "I meant in restaurants. Before I lost my husband, I was working my way up to sous-chef." Something in me lit up inside from seeing Talia's life. I'd never seriously considered catering as a profession, although I'd once briefly daydreamed about owning a food truck. "You must enjoy having your own business." I said the words as they occurred to me.

Talia let out a huff of a laugh. "Sure. Always a barrel of fun." She glanced over her shoulder from the sink. "Believe me, it has its stresses."

"I'll bet," I told her quickly. And it wasn't as though I disagreed. Even from the perspective of working in a restaurant kitchen, that had its stresses. Somehow the stress and bustle gave me a strange sense of nostalgia. I tried not to let myself get caught up in it, though, because this was the opening I had been looking for. "Speaking of stresses, pretty crazy what happened at the meeting last night, huh?"

Talia lifted her cutting board, filled with all of her clean vegetables, from her counter to the island. She shook her head as she started to julienne the vegetables with a deft hand, barely looking at them. "I have to say, I've worked some crazy events, but never one where someone died in the middle of it."

"I couldn't believe it," I said. "Did you know the man who died? I heard he was a school superintendent?"

Talia shook her head. "I saw him once or twice earlier in the evening, but I never spoke with the man."

"What about Mayor Lassiter?" Amber put in. I was glad she was finally finding her voice in this conversation. She always seemed to have the most insightful questions.

Talia shrugged and walked for her oversized stainless steel fridge. "Sure, everyone knows Mayor Lassiter." She returned with a brick of feta cheese, and my mouth started to water. I wondered what she was making.

I forced myself to stay on track. "Did you speak to Mayor Lassiter at all last night?" I asked. Right then, my phone buzzed from my purse. As Talia told me how she hadn't had much time for conversation the night before, I checked my phone display. It was Alex. I doubted he'd disturb me unless it was important.

"Do you mind if I quickly take this?" I asked, standing from my kitchen stool.

Talia motioned down the hallway toward the front room. I nodded and smiled in thanks as I rushed from the room and answered Alex's call. "What's up?"

"Are you still with the catering company?" he asked.

I perched on the edge of the brocaded sofa, but then quickly stood up, remembering how untouched it appeared. "Yes, we're at Chef Talia's house now. Why? What did you find out?"

"I spoke to the janitor on the phone. Apparently, he almost got fired once for jabbering on about a private event he'd cleaned up after. Since then, he makes it a point not to discuss different events, who was there, or what happened." Alex blew out a breath. "As soon as I introduced myself as a police officer, he seemed to have no problem admitting he'd helped the mayor's secretary rig some balloons, but he assured me he had no idea what they were for."

I nodded into the phone. "So that really doesn't help us. We still need to speak to the mayor."

"Right," he said. "But I heard back from forensics and found out something interesting there."

"Oh, yeah? It wasn't coffee in his cup? Was he poisoned?" My heart rate started to ratchet up at the possibility.

But Alex burst my bubble quickly. "No, I'm pretty sure by the smell it was coffee, although they haven't analyzed that yet. But they did get back to me about the beige rubber remnants I collected."

I laughed inwardly. Leave it to Hunch to come up with the one clue that seemed like it might be important. "And? It's not part of the roof coating?"

"No, it's a different substance. Since we found it on the roof, the forensics team suggested it could be part of a non-slip rubberized shoe pad. He suggested that if someone stepped onto the elastomeric coating of the roof with some sort of rubberized soles—especially of the temporary, stick-on variety—it would make sense if they stuck to the roof coating and left some debris behind."

"Huh," I said. I didn't know what this meant as far as our investigation went.

"Forensics is returning to the scene to do a more thorough investigation of it. I also checked with the coroner," he went on. "They haven't finished the autopsy, but he checked Superintendent Garnet's shoes for me, and they had a slick coating."

"So someone else with rubber-soled shoes was on the roof?" I confirmed.

"Possibly with temporarily stick-on rubber pads," he said. "I was thinking of who might where those non-slip pads at a town hall meeting, and my first thought was—"

"The catering staff!" I finished for him.

"Yes." I could hear his smile through the phone. It was funny how people's smiles became audible once you got to know them. "I should really be with you for this, but I made the mistake of checking in with Captain Corbett, and now he has me driving two towns over to interview Superintendent Garnet's neighbors. How do you feel about asking Chef Talia about her footwear?"

"I feel great about it." I grinned now, too. "It's not like it would be the first time I said something to make her think I'd lost my marbles."

I hung up and headed for the kitchen, ready to be known for more than rubber gloves and inappropriate cookie deliveries.

☐

# CHAPTER NINE

"So you don't have any idea if any of your catering staff had spoken to Superintendent Garnet or Mayor Lassiter last night?" Amber was asking as I came back into the kitchen. She sounded much too mature and competent for fifteen. If she did pursue a career in detective work, I had no doubt she would excel at it.

Talia shrugged. "I was much too busy to keep track of who all of my staff had been talking to. But I doubt it. We were all really busy." In the time I was on the phone, Chef Talia had finished assembling a beautiful salad. Apparently, it wasn't for an event later today, as she had divided it into three dishes. Talia and Amber were already eating from theirs.

"Are they all regular employees of yours?" I asked as I perched back onto my stool and reached for the bowl and fork that had been left at my place. "And are you able to get us in touch with them?" I took a bite, and my eyes widened at the blend of flavors. I knew better than to ask a chef for her recipe. But I was tempted to anyway.

Talia placed her bowl on the island across from us. "I suppose I could give you their phone numbers, since you're working with the police." I glanced at Amber, who must have made something up in this regard. I wondered what she'd said, but Talia went on, distracting me. "I usually only have Saundra and Carrie working with me. I'd hired two extra employees for the evening last night because it was my first hire from the municipal office. I wanted to make a good name for Mayberry Catering with them." She shook her head and reached for her bowl again. "Some name. Now they'll probably only remember us as the catering company from the night the man died."

I pulled a pad of paper and pen from my purse and jotted down the names Saundra and Carrie. "And who were the two new employees?" I asked. I had a sixth sense that I'd have an easier time getting newbies to open up than seasoned employees.

"Jarrod Barkman and Melinda Zenky," she told me, looking over at my pad with a scrunched forehead. "Why? Do you think my catering staff did something wrong?"

I had to quickly put her concerns to rest, otherwise she'd clam up before I could even get to my crazy questions about her footwear. "No, no. Not at all. It's just that the kitchen was in such close proximity to the stage entrance and the roof access. We'd like to double-check with everyone in the area to see if they saw or heard anything unusual."

"And you're a special consultant with the police department?" She looked me up and down like maybe she didn't believe this, and truth be told, I wouldn't have believed it either. Even though I had dressed in nice slacks and my favorite cable knit sweater to visit the mayor's office today, I was the lady who had worn polka dots to a business meeting last night and tried to push my baking on her.

But if Amber had given her that story, I would stick with it. "That's right," I told her. "This salad is delicious, by the way."

And Amber, always one step ahead of me, added, "Feel free to check with Detective Martinez if you like. Aunt Mallory can give you his number."

I smiled in agreement, but it seemed this was enough reassurance for Talia. She rattled off Saundra's and Carrie's phone numbers, which she knew by heart, and then scrolled through her phone to find Jarrod's and Melinda's numbers.

"I doubt Melinda will know much," she told me. "Not only was it her first night on the job and she seemed barely able to handle the few tasks I gave her, but we ran out of cream and I sent her to the store to get some more. She didn't even know what was going on when she arrived back at the town hall and people were huddled around the front steps in various states of hysteria. I highly doubt she could have seen or heard anything from anybody."

I nodded, making the note "coffee cream" beside Melinda Zenky's name.

I kept my eyes on my notepad as I worked my way into my next question. "Hey, I noticed your cute black shoes last night," I said, hoping I was correct in remembering them as dark. Or cute. "I always have trouble finding shoes that don't slip in a busy kitchen, and I wondered where you got them?"

I finally felt like I could look up with an interested-but-not-overly-interested look on my face, so I did, carefully avoiding what I was sure would be a confused scowl on Amber's face.

Talia was already walking down the hallway to another room. "Hang on. I'll show you."

While she was gone, I murmured quietly to Amber, "The beige remnants on the roof were likely from non-slip shoe pads."

Her eyes widened in understanding as Talia returned, carrying black pumps with a short heel. "I'd probably be ice skating on these if I didn't have grips on the bottom," she said, flipping them over and showing me a small oval black pad on the bottom of each shoe.

I took one of her shoes from her and ran a thumb over the pad, which had some rubber components, while I thought of how to ask if these came in different colors and if her other staff might have been wearing them as well.

But now that she'd gotten her footing—no pun intended—in this conversation, Amber beat me to it. "Aren't your work shoes more skin-toned, Aunt Mallory?"

I nodded. "That's right. Do you know if these shoe pads come in different colors?" I asked Talia.

Talia nodded, placing her shoes down near the hallway to put away later. "I had to get these ones at the Shoe Shoppe on Eighth, but I'm pretty sure you can get the beige ones at any dollar store. My staff always use those ones."

"They do?" I nodded. "That's great!" And it was. I worked at reining in my enthusiasm. It seemed we had cleared Talia from any suspicion of being on the roof, and we had contact numbers for all of her staff, so we might as well get a move on. "Listen," I said, "thanks so much for all of your help, but we should get going." I piled up my empty bowl with Amber's to help clean up, but Talia held out a hand for them, so I passed them over. "And thank you for the delicious salad."

"My secret ingredient in the dressing is a teaspoon of Dijon," she said with a wink. "From one foodie to another."

I was slightly embarrassed that she'd read my gnawing curiosity about her recipe so easily, and I was also eager to get home and experiment on salad dressings with a hint of Dijon mustard. But that would come later.

For now, we had other catering staff and their shoes to investigate.

□

# CHAPTER TEN

As soon as we were in my Prius, I turned to Amber. "I have a good feeling about this new employee, Jarrod Barkman. Can you do your thing and track him down for us?"

I passed her my notebook with the phone numbers of all the other catering employees, but she was much too busy scratching behind Hunch's ears and cooing to him about how sorry she was that we'd left him alone for so long.

I pulled away from the curb and turned back toward town, so we wouldn't be obviously lurking around this quiet neighborhood.

"You deserve a treat," Amber told my cat, reaching past my notepad of phone numbers to the cat treats she'd brought along from my house.

I resisted the urge to roll my eyes. Yeah, Hunch, you deserve a treat for pestering us into bringing you along and then distracting us from the real objective.

Hunch helped himself to the treat out of Amber's hand, purred up against her neck, and then turned back to the console. He scratched at my notepad.

Okay, better. That was the miniature detective-cat I had come to know and almost love.

Amber picked up the notepad and scanned the list. "You don't think we should start with her regular employees?"

I shrugged. "In my experience, the food business is built on loyalty. If there are any secrets to uncover within Mayberry Catering, I think we'll get them out of the newbies."

"And do you think there are?" she asked. "Any secrets to uncover?"

I wondered if she was stalling because she didn't want to make the phone call. We were getting close to town, though, and I needed to know which way to turn soon.

"Do you want me to do it?" I asked, even though I knew Amber had greater strength in the inconspicuous and unobtrusive questions department.

She shook her head and picked up her phone to dial. A second later, she spoke into it. "Hi, is this Jarrod Barkman?" After a pause, she started speaking in a tone that felt pre-prepared, even though she couldn't have had much time for that. "This is Mallory Beck. I'm working with Detective Martinez of the Honeysuckle Grove Police Department as a special consultant. We have a few follow-up questions about last night's incident at the town hall and I wondered if I might speak to you for a few minutes?"

I glanced away from the road so often, it probably wasn't safe. I hadn't gotten over the fact that she'd introduced herself as me—and "special consultant" rolled off her tongue as though she'd had years of practice at the phrase—when she was talking again.

"That's not a problem. You're there now? I can come to you. Which store are you at?" Amber waved a hand to the left, and in an instant, I threw a look over my shoulder and got into the left-hand turn lane. "No, it's fine," she went on. "Just a few follow-up questions, and they won't take five minutes. I'll meet you near the fountain in, let's say, ten minutes?" Her last words came out in a rush, and she hung up so quickly I doubted Jarrod Barkman had time to answer.

"The fountain?" I asked after such a long silence that I figured she wasn't going to bother filling me in on the phone call.

She nodded. "The one at the mall. He started to sound suspicious about you tracking him down at the mall and not waiting and meeting him at home later, so I hoped if I gave him a time and a place, he'd at least show up to find out if you're legit."

Hunch had snuggled up on her lap, but she was busy punching the other three numbers into her phone to store in her contacts. My cat let out a low growl until she started petting him again.

"If I was legit?" Suddenly, it made sense to me. Amber had laid the groundwork, but she was sending me in alone on this one. I wondered if her voice had sounded enough like mine on the phone that this Jarrod guy wouldn't notice. "Did you get the impression he's already feeling defensive about something?" I asked, my heart rate rising. At least we were meeting in a public place, I reminded myself.

"Maybe," Amber said. She motioned to the right, but I was already changing lanes. I knew how to get to the mall. "Then again, I'd probably act jittery, too, if I'd been at some place where a guy had jumped to his death and then the police were calling me about it. I'm sure he'll relax when he sees you."

I looked down at my slacks and sweater. It was a chilly fall day, but I would do without my overcoat, or maybe sling it over my arm. It might make me appear more approachable.

"So you know Talia's brother from church, huh?" Amber asked, surprising me with the change of subject.

I nodded, but kept my mind on where I was going, on what I planned to ask once I got there.

"I didn't think you were too involved at church, you know, until lately."

"I wasn't...I'm not," bumbled out of my mouth. Then I did my best to clarify. Amber was the one person I could be honest with. "Cooper had been the one who wanted us to find a church when we moved to town," I explained. "He always said that he had to balance out his long days of thinking about deception and murder by focusing on his faith and what he called 'the goodness of God.'" I couldn't seem to help myself from inflecting a note of bitterness into the statement. I rambled on so neither of us could focus on that part. "I liked the idea, but to be honest, I didn't know much about either of those things before Cooper died. And then after he died..." I trailed off, not knowing how to explain it.

As always, Amber had a good handle on the words that escaped me. "You didn't know how to understand a good God that had taken your good husband?" she guessed.

I nodded. I hadn't welled up in a long time, and I certainly didn't want to broach that kind of emotion now, when I was five minutes away from impersonating a special consultant from the police department. I sucked in a slow breath through my nose and let it out with pursed lips.

"Well, I'm glad you're finding your way now," she said with a shrug, as though this was everyday conversation and she was some kind of preacher and I was the runaway prodigal.

But was I even finding my way now? It was true that I'd been helping Sasha with the children's ministry at the church for a few weeks. I'd done my best to tune into the online sermons so I'd be able to converse intelligently about them with anyone I ran into at church. But it seemed my only real encounters with a god I barely knew were during life-threatening circumstances.

It made me wonder, as I pulled into the mall parking lot, whether Cooper had had any last honest moments with God in the burning bank before he died.

"That's him!" Amber snapped me out of my reverie as I pulled into a parking spot, not twenty feet away from the large outdoor mall fountain. The center of the fountain held a weathered statue of our town's founder, Anderson Marshal. While the cement bench that ran the perimeter of the fountain was often busy with children and their mothers during the summer, right now it was deserted—save for a lanky man who paced back and forth beside the cement bench.

I nodded, having trouble getting my voice back with so many deep thoughts swirling in my mind.

"Remember, all you have to ask him about is whether he spoke to either the mayor or Superintendent Garnet last night, or overheard anything they said, and whether or not he wore any non-slip pads on his shoes."

I nodded, but then said, "I don't know if I can do this right now, Amber."

She didn't seem at all bothered by the lack of confidence in myself. "Sure you can," she told me. "God will give you the words."

I studied her, wondering if she really believed that. But then, only a second later, I wondered if the better question was if this smarty-pants fifteen-year-old might be a glowing example of exactly that.

A heartbeat later, I was opening my door, ready to find out more than anything else. If God could give me the words right now, while I was so scattered and emotional, maybe there was something to this faith business Amber was so sure about.

I took long quick steps toward the fountain, not even giving myself a chance to put my first words together in advance. Deep down, I knew this was actually some kind of defiance—or at the very least a dare—toward God, but I didn't care.

"Mr. Barkman?" I asked, striding straight for him and thrusting out a hand. "I'm Mallory Beck." I left off the part about being a special consultant. I didn't have it in me to lie and dare God in the same breath. He shook my hand. "Thanks so much for meeting with me."

"Did you..." His head darted in both directions, as though scanning for who might be within hearing distance. "Did you already speak with my boss, Talia Mayberry?"

I smiled. "Of course. That's how I got your number. She was able to answer most of my questions, but Detective Martinez and I are trying to get a full picture of the evening, so we had a few additional queries." My voice sounded calm and full of authority—more than it ever had before, I had to admit.

Jarrod shrugged. "I don't know what I can tell you. I was there to do my job. It was only my second time working with Mayberry Catering."

Again, he looked from side to side, and I suspected he was more concerned about the idea of losing a new job than anything else. His brown hair was messy, and he wore jeans with holes in the knees and a faded blue flannel shirt. At thirtysomething, I wondered if he was trying to dress young and hip, or if he was too poor to buy better clothing. He was barely recognizable as the put-together guy who'd been in black slacks and a white starched dress shirt the night before.

"Yes, Talia mentioned that. Because the kitchen was in such close proximity to the stairwell that led to both the stage and to the roof access, I wondered whether or not any of the catering staff had had any interaction with either Mayor Lassiter or Superintendent Garnet?"

He shook his head, almost violently. "Oh, no. Melinda and I are both new, so we were tasked with things like filling the hot water stations and cutting up cake. But I heard Talia telling her regular catering crew to make sure the speakers for the evening got coffee and cake."

I looked down at my notepad, confused. Hadn't Talia just told me they were all so busy that she had no idea if any of her staff had time to speak to the mayor or superintendent?

"That's Saundra and Carrie?" I asked to cover my confusion. Only now did I realize I didn't have last names for either of Talia Mayberry's regular employees.

Suddenly, it felt as though the catering chef had been purposely trying to hide something. I wondered if Amber was right, and we should have started with the seasoned employees.

Jarrod nodded. "Yeah, they've been working with her since she started. Around three years ago, I think." It sounded as though Jarrod was relaxing into this conversation.

"So you and Melinda..." I glanced at my notes. "Melinda Zenky. Neither of you had any contact or conversation with either the mayor or superintendent last night?" I confirmed, thinking maybe I could knock off two birds with this one stone.

"That's right," he told me.

"And you didn't overhear them conversing at all?"

He shook his head. His tense posture relaxed, and he rested against the cement fountain bench. "Anything else I can help you with?" I got the feeling he was glad to have the focus anywhere else than on him.

"One more thing," I said, glancing at my notes again, not because I needed them, but only because this seemed like such an odd question to broach. But then, quite suddenly, the words came to me.

I met his eye, undaunted now that I had a clear path. "A bit off topic, but Talia was telling me she wears non-slip shoe pads in the kitchen. Hers, apparently, are expensive, but she was telling me some of her employees got some from the dollar store. Do you wear them? Do you know if they're available here?" I pointed to the dollar store situated a few stores down in the Honeysuckle Grove Mall.

Jarrod dropped onto the cement bench and kicked one of his black, slightly scuffed shoes up sideways over his knee so I could see the bottom. Only now did I recognize that his dress shoes didn't match his torn jeans. He must be too poor to afford multiple pairs of shoes.

But more importantly, the beige oval on the bottom of his right shoe appeared to be smooth along its surface, even if the whole pad seemed to be coming loose at the edges. It didn't look as though it could have left debris behind on a rooftop last night.

"Do you wear them on both shoes?" I blurted as the thought came to me. "Or only one?"

As I hoped, he kicked up the other shoe to show me another new-looking beige oval. "I'd never heard of these, but thankfully, Saundra had extras. She made sure we all had them, but honestly, I'll bet the ones Talia wears are better. One of these cheap ones came off one of the girl's shoes as she was loading the van, and she almost wiped out on the bumper." Jarrod was getting more relaxed and talkative, but I was pretty sure I was done here.

If the two new employees were wearing brand-new non-slip pads, the seasoned employees who possibly had older pads would be next on my list to investigate.

I held out a hand. "Thanks so much for your time, Mr. Barkman. If there's anything else, we'll be in touch."

□

# CHAPTER ELEVEN

"The two regular catering crew, Saundra and Carrie? We need to talk to them," I said as I slid into the driver's seat.

"Okay, good." Amber once again seemed to be spending her energy on making my cat feel loved, but at least she'd been busy since I left. "No answer on Melinda's phone, and I got Carrie's voicemail. But Saundra's at home. I told her we'd be right over."

I liked the sound of "we."

"Besides, her place isn't far from here." Amber scratched Hunch under his chin, and he let out a pleasure-filled growl, as though he appreciated it so much it verged on the point of making him angry. "What did you find out from Barkman?"

I had yet to graduate to referring to our informants by their last names. "Jarrod had brand-new shoe pads, which didn't look as though they could have left any debris behind. He'd gotten them from Saundra."

"And did he speak to or overhear anything from either the mayor or the superintendent?"

I shook my head. "He and Melinda were kept busy with simple tasks like filling hot water and cutting cake." I took a sip of water from my bottle in the console. Impersonating a special consultant made me thirsty. "But get this. Apparently, Chef Talia specifically directed her two regular employees to make sure the speakers for the evening had coffee and cake."

Amber's forehead creased. "She told us they didn't have time for anything like that."

"Exactly," I said, starting up my car. "Sounds like a bold-faced lie to me."

"That's why you want to talk to Saundra and Carrie next?" I nodded, but Amber went on. "But don't you think if she was purposely lying, she'd have already called her two employees to get their stories straight?"

I hadn't thought of that. As I left the mall parking lot and Amber directed me to make a right-hand turn, another thought occurred to me. "But if it wasn't Talia up on the roof, perhaps she already knows she has to cover for one of her long-time employees. She hadn't been expecting us and hadn't had the chance to formulate her words. Given the chance to speak with her employees in person, maybe we can rattle their cages enough to get them to show some sort of incongruity, or better yet, maybe even confess something."

Amber pointed for me to turn again at the next light and then into a small apartment complex on my left. There were less than a dozen units.

"This is where she lives?" I confirmed.

Amber nodded, and thankfully, she delivered the news that Hunch would be staying behind. "We won't be so long this time," she said, holding him at face level and looking him straight in the eye as if he were a person.

When she let him back down, he mewled once and then happily hopped into the back seat. I resisted the urge to scowl at him and his unusually compliant behavior.

Instead, I grabbed my door handle, glad to have Amber along for this one, and said, "Let's go."

Saundra lived on the second floor of the complex, which seemed more like a motel than your standard apartment building. Stairs were situated at either end of the small block of apartments and led to outward-facing doors along an outer corridor. There didn't appear to be a lobby or anywhere we needed to buzz up, so Amber and I headed toward the closest set of stairs.

When we found apartment 204, I stood in front of it, took a deep breath to center myself, and then knocked. I was willing to give this Let-God-Provide-the-Right-Words thing another shot, as it had seemed to work the first time.

I recognized Saundra from the night before the instant her door opened. She was about five-six, around my height, with a short black pixie cut. She wore a comfy-looking burgundy jumpsuit with giant white polka dots. I'd always been a fan of polka dots, and I felt an immediate kinship toward her.

"Hi!" She looked between us. "You're with the police?"

This peppy lady didn't seem like the type of person who had something to hide. Then again, if a person wanted to throw the police off, how would they most likely do it?

Not that we were the police. Or she was necessarily hiding anything.

"That's right," I told her and barreled on with an easy question, so as not to dwell on any of our own falsehoods. "I didn't get your last name from Talia Mayberry. Could I please get that from you?" I poised my pen over my notepad, and when she spelled out "Krzyzewski" I did my best to follow along.

"Right," Amber said, crossing her arms and taking over. "Because the kitchen was so close to the stairs that led to the stage and the roof, we wanted to check with all of the catering staff and see if any of you had had any interactions with either Mayor Lassiter or Superintendent Garnet last night…before the incident."

Saundra turned back to me before answering. I didn't blame her. My fifteen-year-old "niece" could be intimidating when she wanted to be. "No, not that I'm aware of." She shook her head with wide, innocent eyes.

"Did you take notice of who they were?" I asked. "Would you have overheard any of their conversations, or perhaps be able to weigh in on either of their moods last night?"

Even from a distance, I'd been able to recognize the mayor as cheery and welcoming, and the superintendent as grumpy and annoyed, but Saundra only shook her head again at my question.

Leave it to Amber to come in with the big guns. "So Ms. Mayberry didn't instruct you and the other regular caterer, Carrie, to approach the speakers for the evening and offer them coffee and cake?"

Saundra's cheeks immediately flushed, almost the color of her jumpsuit. But she furrowed her brow and said, "I don't think so. Where did you hear that?"

I didn't want to start a war within this small catering company, but at the same time, I needed to get to the bottom of who was lying here. "Jarrod Barkman, one of the new employees, mentioned he'd overheard something of a directive from your boss."

Saundra shook her head again, her forehead creasing even further. "I think he must be mistaken. There was a lot going on last night."

I nibbled my lip, wondering if I could believe either of Talia's employees. At least we had two more to check in with.

Amber, with no thought to any potential discomfort, barreled on with another question. "Jarrod also said you were giving out non-slip pads for everyone's shoes. Can we see what those look like?"

I held my breath as Saundra studied Amber and her unusual question. I'd thought I could count on Amber to be the nonchalant one of the two of us. Apparently, not today.

But then Saundra spun, turned into her apartment, and let the door fall shut behind her. It didn't click shut, so I had at least some hope she planned to return.

It seemed to take her a long time to find the shoes she'd been wearing the night before, and I could picture her inside, calling Talia to go over what we'd asked her and how she'd replied. I gritted my teeth while we waited, wondering if it would even be worth questioning the two other catering employees now.

I gave a couple of knocks on the door. "Excuse me? Ms. Krzyzewski?"

Only seconds later, she swung the door open, looking breathless. She held a pair of black shoes in one hand. She flipped them over to show us the pads on the bottom, and these ones looked even newer and smoother than Jarrod's had.

"This is what you wanted to see?" she asked. "Yeah, the new guy was slipping all over the place as we were unloading, so I offered him a pair from my stash of extras. They really do help in our business." Her tone sounded more clipped than it had when she'd gone to get her shoes.

And suddenly I was torn. Had she taken so long to call Talia, or had she taken a long time because she was sticking on a new pair of non-slip pads? Could she have accomplished both during that amount of time? Would she have somehow even known to replace her shoe pads?

"These ones look so new," Amber commented, clearly thinking the same thing. "These are the same ones you wore for catering last night?"

Saundra shrugged, and the move appeared casual. "Sure. When I gave Jarrod a pair, I figured I might as well replace mine, too. They were getting kind of worn on the bottom, and that always happens before they fall off."

"So you did that at the beginning of the evening?" I asked.

"That's right." She nodded. Her shoulders were more relaxed than they had been, but she wasn't pulling her door open to invite us in or even to let us see her apartment. "As we unloaded the van, probably around six o'clock."

"And did everyone replace their non-slip shoe pads at that point?" I reached out to run a thumb over one of her pads to see if they felt as smooth as they looked. They did. When I looked up at Saundra, her forehead buckled in confusion again. But we were so close to getting the information we needed. And if it hadn't been one of the catering crew up on the roof, where else would we look for someone out of the crowd of hundreds who may have been wearing non-slip shoe pads?

Despite her concern over this line of questioning, Saundra eventually answered. "No, just me and the new guy." I noticed she didn't like calling him by name. I wondered if that was because he'd leaked a secret he shouldn't have. "Carrie doesn't use them and the new girl apparently already had some from her other job."

"Her other job? Do you know where she works?" I glanced at my notes. Her name was Melinda Zenky. Perhaps we could catch her at her other job if Saundra knew where that was. But then my eyes landed on the note beside her name that reminded me she had been out to buy more cream at the time of the incident. She couldn't have been on the roof.

And even if that weren't the case, Saundra shrugged and shook her head as though she had no idea.

"Do you still have your old shoe pads?" Amber asked, which reminded me of our true mission here. Although, if both Jarrod and Saundra had replaced theirs early in the evening, and Melinda hadn't been on the premises during the incident, it was looking more and more like we should focus on finding the other regular caterer, Carrie. Saundra said she didn't use the shoe pads, but all of the regular catering crew seemed to be telling half-truths to protect somebody.

When I clued back in, Saundra was downright scowling. "Of course not. I threw them out at the hall."

"Right, that makes sense." I took a flash of a moment to picture myself searching all the garbage bins at the town hall and then quickly rushed on with one final question. "And the other regular caterer you work with, Carrie? We've been trying to get a hold of her, but she hasn't been picking up. Does she also have another job?"

Saundra twisted her lips, looking hesitant to answer. Finally, she said, "Not that I know of."

It was the loyalty thread that ran so strongly through the food preparation industry, I was sure of it. After working with her for three years, she clearly would have known whether or not Carrie worked another job.

But I couldn't exactly call her on it, so instead, I asked, "Can I at least get Carrie's last name from you?"

Still the twisted lips. But after a brief pause, she told me, "Bowman." This time, she didn't bother to spell it out. In fact, it was quite clear she was done spilling information on her fellow employees. She pushed the door closed an inch and said, "Is that all? I have food cooking, and I should really get back to it."

I didn't know if I believed that, but I thanked her for her help and let her go.

Besides, it was almost four o'clock, and we had an appointment with the mayor.

☐

# CHAPTER TWELVE

Thankfully, we arrived back at the mayor's office five minutes early, so I had time to update Alex about what we had learned from the two catering employees. I had picked up a carton of cookies from Honeysuckle Crumble, a local bakery, on our way, but I felt bad that we no longer had that blueberry lemon cake to pave our way.

"So you think Chef Talia phoned Saundra and told her to lie about having talked to either the mayor or the superintendent?" Alex asked as he led the way from the parking lot to the building.

"That's the feeling we both got. Right?" I asked Amber. We'd talked through a lot of our different theories on the way over, and I wanted to make sure we were on the same page with this.

"Yeah, unless the new employee, Jarrod, was lying to try and either get the focus off of him or get Saundra fired, so he'd find himself in a more permanent job. I was filling Mallory in on the way over about how bad the unemployment situation is in Honeysuckle Grove and the lengths people will go to in order to keep a job."

Alex nodded. "True. Unless you want to work in the coal mines or at one of the chemical plants, it can be hard to make a living in town if you don't have some kind of degree. Even then, people will get hooked on painkillers or send their kids to school sick in order to never miss workdays. I guess it makes sense why anyone in the catering business might lie to keep their job."

Hmm. It didn't help us figure this out if anyone could be lying about anything. I supposed I was pretty fortunate to have gotten on as a line cook at Antonia's when Cooper and I first moved to town. I hadn't been particularly worried, as Cooper's income from his books had become more than enough to support us wherever we decided to settle. Suddenly, I felt a little guilty that I might have been taking a job from someone in town who really needed it.

Not that I'd worked for long in this town anyway.

"Can you get us an address for Carrie Bowman?" Amber asked, snapping me out of my thoughts. "And I don't suppose you can find out if she has another job?"

Right. Carrie. We'd found Melinda Zenky in the local phone book, so if we couldn't track down Carrie, Amber and I planned to go straight to Melinda's house from here. But Carrie, in my mind, was a better bet to approach to get some useful answers.

"Let me put a call in," Alex said and dialed the station as we waited for the elevator. By the time we got to the second floor, he'd hung up and said he should have at least an address by the time we finished our meeting with Mayor Lassiter. "And I spoke with Richard Garnet's neighbors. Neither of them saw him as suicidal or even depressed. I have one more call into the school district, but I already feel fairly convinced we can rule out suicide."

This time, when we walked into the reception area of the mayor's office, I was aware of keeping the box of cookies at my side. I certainly didn't want Kelli the Jack-of-all-trades secretary to think they were all for her.

"Hi!" she said, looking up and recognizing us. "I'll let Mayor Lassiter know you're here." She popped up from her chair, swaggered down the hall to a closed door, and knocked. I admit, it was hard even for me not to survey the legs sprouting from her short tight skirt, but I resisted the urge to look over and see if Alex was watching her, too. I glanced to my other side, though, and Amber's gaze was firmly set on Alex. She was scowling.

Uh-oh. A young crush. A young jealous crush.

Kelli strutted back over, all smiles. "He'll see you now."

I let Alex lead the way, as he was the only person truly in authority here, but as soon as he stepped into the large office and a long uncomfortable silence followed, I realized my place in this.

"Hello, Mayor Lassiter," I said. "Thank you for seeing us. This is Detective Martinez." I motioned to Alex. "I'm Mallory Beck, and this is my niece, Amber." Even though Amber's last name used to have some pull in this town, I was guessing that since her dad's murder case, Montrose might have lost some of its shine. I opened the cookie carton and extended it. "Cookie?"

Mayor Lassiter's face lit up in a smile, and he shook all of our hands before helping himself. When he offered us all seats and rested into his large leather chair, I placed the open cookie box on his side of the desk.

"Now, to what do I owe a visit from the police department?" he asked in his deep authoritative voice, leaning back into his chair.

I hoped my intro had given Alex time to get his footing. After being pushed down within the department for so many years, I understood why he lacked confidence, but he'd have to be able to carry strong interviews with people like our town mayor on his own if he hoped to be taken seriously as a detective.

Thankfully, he quickly cleared his throat and began speaking. "Just a few follow-up questions about the incident at the town hall last night." Mayor Lassiter glanced at me and Amber again. Alex didn't miss this and explained, "Mallory is working with us as a special consultant, as she was on scene during the meeting last night." Rather than try to explain Amber's presence—which would be difficult—he got right back to his questions. "We understand there were balloons rigged up in the rafters above the stage by order of your office?"

Mayor Lassiter shifted in his chair and said, "Yes, that's right," but he reached for another chocolate chip cookie and took a big bite, I suspected so he didn't have to say more.

But I, for one, wasn't going to be deterred that easily. "What were the balloons for, Mayor Lassiter?"

He flipped a page in a fancy leather planner splayed out on his desk, as if he might find the answer in there.

I realized I had been correct. Out his large window, there was a great view of the town hall from here. I fixated on the middle of the upper ledge, where Superintendent Garnet had fallen to his death.

After several seconds of waiting, I had a hard time believing the mayor didn't remember the balloons off the top of his head, so I pushed. "Was it for the meeting about the library? Or were they there for a different event?"

Another long pause followed. Finally, Alex leaned forward in his chair and used a soft but steady voice to say, "It's in your best interest to be open and honest with us about this now. A full investigation has been launched, as it was the death of a public official. If you don't want us suspecting you of being linked to his death somehow, I suggest you tell us everything you know."

Mayor Lassiter's gaze snapped to Alex. "I thought it was ruled as an accident?"

Alex nodded. "That was the initial assumption, but I'm afraid we've uncovered further evidence that indicates foul play."

The room went eerily silent. Wow, Alex was better at this than I thought.

Mayor Lassiter glanced at me, and then Amber, and finally looked back to Alex. His voice held much less authority and almost bordered on meek when he said, "Yes, the balloons were there for the library meeting. We planned to drop them when we announced we were keeping the local library."

Because I knew more about the meeting than Alex did, I inserted myself into the conversation again. "So let me understand this. You knew from the onset of the meeting that you'd be keeping the library? Why even hold a meeting then? And why was Superintendent Garnet even in attendance?"

"It was…" Mayor Lassiter shifted in his chair. "Arranged ahead of time. Superintendent Garnet and I spoke on the phone, and he offered some fair points about keeping the library. Even though he already had me convinced, I decided to hold a town hall about it, as it would give the town something to set their sights on, something to root for. All the focus on the opioid crisis lately has been terrible for the morale of our town."

My mind reeled. Was there someone in Honeysuckle Grove who really didn't want the town to keep its library? Would someone kill to make sure the superintendent didn't get a chance to have his say?

And why had we assumed it would have been one of the catering staff? Suddenly, I felt like we were back to square one of this investigation.

Mayor Lassiter went on to explain. "I thought it would be healthier to let the town feel as though they were part of the decision, to give them something they could fight for, where there could actually be a positive outcome."

"So you lied," I blurted, then raced on with my next words quickly, as my intention hadn't been to put him on the defensive. "Did you ever intend to shut down the local library?"

He pursed his lips and shook his head, which I thought meant no, but then he said, "It was a suggestion at one of the council meetings. They changed to an online-only system in Harper Mills recently to save a little money. When it came out on the agenda to be discussed at the next council meeting, there was an uproar in town about it. People wrote to superintendents and council members, up in arms about losing our library. I knew then that it wouldn't be a wise move for our town, even if it did save a little money. When I spoke further with Richard Garnet about it, he had the suggestion of holding a meeting about it anyway. He knows what Honeysuckle Grove has been going through."

I was glad to hear, at least, that the meeting had been Superintendent Garnet's suggestion. Even so, I could see the guilt on Mayor Lassiter's face about it. This seemed like the reason he'd instructed the staff not to dwell on the tragedy from the night before. He cared too much about his town.

"So the meeting was held predominantly to deflect from the current opioid crisis?" Alex confirmed, making notes.

Mayor Lassiter nodded. "We had a meeting planned to discuss the drug crisis, but the more I spoke to state officials, it seemed I only had bad news about funding cuts that I would be able to offer at this point. After talking to Richard, and coming up with the idea about a library meeting where something in this town could feel like a win, it made sense to hold it as quickly as possible. I hoped to give everyone a little positivity, a favorable outcome from a meeting, plus a few balloons and some cake—I hoped it would help." Mayor Lassiter looked down at his desk and shook his head. I had never seen our mayor in such an emotional and heartbroken state.

"Okay, I think that answers all of our questions for the moment," Alex said, standing. I could tell by his balled fist that he was trying hard to stay professional. Truth be told, all I wanted to do was round Mayor Lassiter's desk and give him a hug. He clearly felt awful about what had transpired the night before.

Amber and I stood and thanked him as well, in a hurry to get out of here.

We had a lot to discuss.

☐

# CHAPTER THIRTEEN

As soon as we left the mayor's office, Alex and I checked our phones, and we both had voicemail messages. Mine was only a message from my sister, Leslie, but I wanted to give Alex some space to check his, so I moved a few feet down the sidewalk and held up my phone, indicating I would be checking mine as well. Amber took my car keys and headed across the street to check on Hunch.

After I punched in my code, my bubbly sister rattled off words into my car at a mile a minute. After a few seconds, I cut off her babbling and hit dial to call her back. I'd be willing to bet her voicemail message was fifteen minutes long, and past experience had taught me I could get her to make her point quicker if I got her on the line.

She picked up after the third ring.

"What's up, Leslie?" I asked when she had barely said hello.

She caught my tone immediately, as sisters could. "What's up with you? Why so busy? Did you get a job?"

Leslie had been trying to convince me for months that getting back to work would help get my mind off my grief. That and meeting a new man. I'd thrown her mostly off the job trail by mentioning my run-in with Alex Martinez—whom she remembered well as my seventh-grade crush—but apparently, she was now back at it.

"Not a regular one, no," I said. "Just helping out a friend."

"Great," she started, but then my sister's hyperactive brain took her where I hoped it wouldn't. "Wait! Is this friend Alex Martinez?" She barely took a breath before she added, "Wait! Is he there now?" She said the words loudly enough that I feared Alex might overhear them from where he stood, phone to his ear and jotting notes, a dozen feet down the sidewalk.

"Shhh!" I said. "No. Well, I mean, yes. But I'm only helping with an investigation." My words came out in a hushed whisper, and before she could go on, as I knew she would, I added, "I haven't got much time here, Leslie. Why did you call?"

As always, using my little sister's name brought her back down to earth. "Oh. Right. I wanted to warn you that you might be hearing from Dad. He lost his job again." She sighed. If any subject could make my sister slow to an exhausted stop, it was this one.

I nodded, even though Leslie couldn't see me. "Okay. Thanks for the heads-up." It wouldn't be the first time Dad had come to me asking for money, not by a long shot, but at least with a little warning, I could make a balanced decision about how much to give him. Before Leslie could return to the topic of Alex, I added, "Listen, Leslie, I do have to go, but I'll call you from home later, okay?"

"If you're not too busy later," she singsonged into the phone, her words filled to the brim with innuendo. "Okay, bye!" she said and hung up.

She'd give me an earful of leading questions later, but I could handle Leslie when I was in my own home, alone. I took a deep breath and headed for Alex, who had just hung up his phone. Amber also crossed the street again, Hunch snuggled up in her arms.

"Forensics got back to me with some interesting information. When they studied the scene further with a focus on the beige rubber remnants, they saw signs of a struggle on the roof."

"A struggle…?" I started, but Alex had more to tell us.

"They also found remnants of the beige rubber in the kitchen. I think you might be right about the catering staff. I'd like to get over and do a follow-up interview with Chef Talia. If she's already giving you mixed information, that warrants investigating. I got an address for Carrie Bowman." Alex ripped off a page from his notepad and passed it over, then he led the way back to our cars. "I couldn't find out about any other employment, but maybe you can try to get in touch with her or the other catering employee at home while I go after Talia Mayberry? It would be best if we can talk to them before they have a chance to confer any more than they already might have."

I nodded. "This is great." I turned to Amber. "Should we phone her again first?"

Amber shook her head. "With all the secrecy going on within that catering company, I think we should show up on her doorstep and take her by surprise."

I tended to agree.

"I'm going by the coroner's office on my way to see if I can put a little pressure on them to give me a report as soon as possible," Alex said when we got to our vehicles. "If there were bruises or other signs of struggle, it could help us make some sense of this."

Alex drove off, and Amber kept busy getting Hunch comfortable on her lap, but I stood beside my car, not getting in yet. My gaze stayed fixed on the town hall, a thought niggling at me, but I couldn't quite put my finger on it.

Amber got back out of the car, cradling Hunch, and that's probably what made me snap out of it and turn her way. But when I did, my eyes settled on another building maybe a block and a half down the road.

Amber followed my eyes. "What are you looking at?"

"The supermarket down the road. They'd have coffee cream, wouldn't they?"

Amber shrugged. "Well, sure, I guess. Why? Do you need..." Her words trailed off, and her eyes widened. We both scanned the short distance between the town hall and the super-mart.

"If Melinda Zenky had to leave the town hall meeting to replenish the stock of cream for Mayberry Catering, how long could that have possibly taken? Could she have possibly missed the entire tragedy?" I figured speaking my suspicions aloud would help us both get to the truth of the matter faster.

"Unless the store was out of cream?" Amber didn't look as though she believed her own words. Hunch was snuggled up to her neck, almost as though he were whispering secrets to her, and a second later, she snapped her fingers like he'd given her the missing piece to our puzzle. I didn't doubt such a thing from my cat. "Or Chef Talia had demanded a certain brand of cream. She seems like the type, doesn't she?"

I felt myself flush slightly because truth be told, I was the type to demand a certain brand of cream or an unusual radish or a particular ripeness of pear for a recipe. Most chefs would, I thought to make myself feel better. But only a second later, I came back to my senses and remembered what this meant.

"She's the type," I told Amber, getting into my car. "I say we figure out where the next closest store is and then figure out where to go from there."

It turned out the next closest store was a good mile away, and they carried three brands of coffee cream. However, talking over the timeline with Amber, now that we were focused on it, there seemed to be a time discrepancy.

"So unless Melinda left the meeting and walked all the way to this store to get cream, I can't see it taking her more than twenty minutes to get to the farther store and back," Amber said, following my rabbit trail.

"Unless she was so stressed out by Chef Talia, she needed a few minutes' break," I suggested. The first time I had worked in a kitchen, I remembered doing that—taking an extra few minutes to breathe when I'd been instructed to take out the garbage. But Amber and I both knew I was only trying to poke holes into what seemed like an abnormality.

"I guess we have a few more questions for Chef Talia then?" Amber asked.

I nodded. "Text them to Alex so he can ask her. Let's do our part and try and track down Carrie as soon as we can. Maybe she can shed more light on Melinda and the cream situation, plus Chef Talia and how much of a bear she may be to work for. They're a tight-knit group," I went on as I followed my GPS toward Carrie Bowman's house. "But this time, I know that going in."

Carrie Bowman's house was a mid-sized rancher not far from the town center. I parked along the curb, and Amber and I stared across the street at it. A lack of cars in the driveway made the place seem deserted, and I held my breath, waiting for Amber to suggest finding a way to break in. It wasn't as though I thought of Amber as a lawbreaker. I also couldn't see her letting us leave here without a little more information.

"Did you see that?" she said suddenly.

I had been zoned out, so I didn't see a thing.

"Right there!" She pointed. "That curtain moved. There's someone inside."

I scrunched my forehead, thinking. We hadn't phoned again, so there was a good chance Carrie Bowman had returned home since the last time we'd called. "But there's no car in the driveway," I told her.

Hunch was the one to answer—with an impatient mewl.

I knew what that mewl meant: He was sick of my stalling. Time to get on with it, Mallory. Letting out a sigh, I reached for the door handle, and without a word, Amber followed suit.

Thirty seconds later, we were at the door, ready to knock, but I held my hand in mid-air, hesitating.

"What?" Amber asked.

"Do you hear that?" I didn't give her time to answer. "Kids. Carrie Bowman has kids in there." I didn't know why that made me feel so much better, but it did. Surely, a mother of young rambunctious kids had too much to worry about to be some kind of accessory in a possible murder.

Even though I knew that wasn't true, I no longer hesitated to knock.

A second later, the door swung open, but it wasn't the fourth member of the catering team who answered—a woman I clearly recalled as a blonde. Instead, a short plump Hispanic lady greeted me. She had to be close to sixty.

"Can I help you?" she asked in smooth English.

My forehead furrowed. "Um, yes. We're looking for Carrie Bowman?"

Behind the short lady, two preschool children were visible, their light brown hair and fair skin a clear contrast to this lady's.

The lady nodded with a smile. "She's at work, but should be home soon."

"Is she working with Chef Talia?" Amber asked, even though we both knew that wasn't true.

This seemed to make the Hispanic nanny relax, though, as we clearly knew Carrie. She let out a laugh and said, "Oh no. Today she's at the yogurt shop." The lady pointed down the street. "Oh, look. There she comes now."

Near the end of their long street, I could make out the form of a blonde lady walking. "She doesn't have a car?" I asked, but then realized that was actually supposed to be my question for the catering employee who had gone for coffee cream. It didn't matter whether or not Carrie Bowman had a vehicle.

The nanny shook her head, but then said, "She shares one with Rico. My son," she added after a second.

My face flushed, and I felt embarrassed that I'd jumped to the conclusion that this was a hired Hispanic nanny. This was Carrie's mother-in-law. "How nice," I said. "And do you live with them?"

The lady nodded and glanced over her shoulder at the children—an older boy and younger girl who were playing nicely together with blocks. "It can be hard to make ends meet. Both Carrie and Rico work two jobs, and I'm finishing up my master's degree virtually, so it makes sense to share a house and the responsibilities of the children."

I was about to open my mouth with niceties about how giving she was to do that for her son and grandchildren, but Amber took over the conversation. "I'm sure Carrie told you about what happened at the town hall last night? It was such a shock."

The lady's smile dimmed, and she nodded. "Yes, Carrie came home quite a mess over the whole thing. She's glad they don't have another catering job until next Saturday. She needs a break to get the memory of it out of her system."

I glanced back down the road to where Carrie was now less than a block away and much easier to make out. She wore a red and white striped apron under a puffy white jacket and held her phone to her ear. But that wasn't what caught my attention. My eyes immediately went to her shoes—big white clunky sneakers. It wasn't until this moment that I recalled what had made this particular catering worker memorable to me. It wasn't her blonde hair or medium build. It was the white sneakers she'd worn with her black and white catering uniform.

Without taking the time to think this through too carefully—because I knew I was right—I spun back to Carrie's mother-in-law. "Does Carrie always wear those same white sneakers to work? I saw her wearing them at the town hall meeting last night."

I glanced at Amber. Her narrowed eyes told me she was with me. Saundra had told us Carrie didn't use non-slip shoe pads, and now I could see why. I had a hard time believing she would need them on her white sneakers.

The lady shook her head and raised an eyebrow. "They are quite the eyesore, aren't they? But Carrie swears by those nursing shoes. Wears them to both of her jobs and says she doesn't care how her feet look. She only cares that she's never lost her balance while carrying a tray of appetizers, and she never leaves work with a sore back."

I was about to ask whether she wore stick-on grips on the bottom of her nursing shoes, just to confirm, but I didn't have a chance. Carrie walked up the driveway and called, "Hi there, can I help you with something?"

Clearly, we could ask her that directly.

"Hi!" I said, realizing we'd never officially introduced ourselves to Carrie's mother-in-law. Apparently, there was a lot to learn in detective school. "We stopped by to talk to you about the meeting at the town hall last night. I'm Mallory Beck." I extended a hand for a shake.

Carrie's mother-in-law looked between Amber and me with a stern look. She had thought we knew Carrie, and I said nothing to lead her to think otherwise.

Carrie reached out tentatively, but before I could say more, she held up her phone with her other hand. "I should return a phone call to my boss. Can you give me a minute to do that first." It didn't sound like a question.

I wondered if that was a warning call from Talia—to let her know what to say or what not to say about serving the mayor and superintendent last night.

Amber must have had the same thought because she jabbed out a hand for a shake, even though it seemed strange for a fifteen-year-old to do so. "I'm Mallory's niece, Amber." Out of politeness, Carrie shook Amber's hand as well. Thankfully, Amber went on because I had no idea how to get Carrie to speak to us before she returned her phone call, short of pulling the "Police's special consultant" card again, and I hoped not to do that. "My aunt and I were at the meeting last night. It was awful what happened to that man."

One of the kids inside the house let out a loud cry, and Carrie's mother-in-law hesitated, but then turned inside to deal with it.

Carrie took a step sideways, an obvious move to make it past us and inside her house as well. She clearly didn't want to talk to us about this.

"Aunt Mallory knows Talia through her brother, right, Auntie?" she asked me with a smile so full of innocence, she might have been a lamb, or a cherub. Thankfully, it was enough to stop Carrie from trying to get into her house. "We were talking to her after the accident, and she said how you had talked to the superintendent right before he died."

Carrie's gaze moved between me and Amber. She didn't say anything at first, so I added, "That must have been awful," in way of a push.

Carrie shook her head, as though trying to shake away the entire experience. "I offered him cake and coffee," she said and then swallowed, like she couldn't help herself from remembering it all over again. "He didn't want cake."

"So you served him a coffee?" I confirmed, offering a caring head tilt.

She nodded. Her eyes started to well up. I had a hard time believing this lady was lying or had done anything she felt she had to lie about.

"And you didn't see him again after that?"

She shook her head, looking down at her shoes.

I took in a big breath and launched into my next line of questioning. "Talia mentioned one of her catering crew slipped loading up her van last night? Was that you?"

The second she called Talia back, she'd know I was lying about all of this, but hopefully, we'd be long gone by then.

Carrie shook her head and seemed grateful for the change of subject. "Are you kidding me? These things wouldn't slip on a butter-coated skating rink." She let out a low chuckle, kicking up one of her shoes to show us. I couldn't quite see the bottom.

"You wear those for catering?" I asked. "Do you wear those non-slip grips on the bottom, too?"

She kicked up her shoe again, this time so I could see the bottom. "Don't need 'em with these. Best catering shoes ever." She put her foot down. I was trying to think of a way to ask to see the bottom of her other shoe when she added, "It was the new girl, Melinda, who slipped. That's what you get for wearing those cheap non-slip pads and trying to make them last a year." She nodded assuredly.

"Right, but wasn't she gone out for cream when you were loading up?" Amber asked. "Isn't that what your friend said, Aunt Mallory?"

Carrie was the one to answer. "No, she went for cream before that. Lucky for her, Melinda missed the whole ordeal because of her trip to the store, but she was back in time to help us load up."

"She missed the whole thing?" I asked. "She must have had to go on quite a drive to find that cream to miss the whole terrible incident."

Carrie furrowed her brow. "Huh. You're right. I wasn't paying much attention, but she walked into the kitchen with two big cartons of cream asking what had happened, so I assumed…"

"Does Talia prefer a certain type of cream?" I asked. Being a long-term employee, Carrie would know this. "Could Melinda have had to go to more than one store to find it?"

Carrie's face tightened further. "Not just for coffee cream, no."

"Talia said Melinda has another job," Amber said, right on the heels of her words. It was starting to feel a little too much like an interrogation, and I had to think of a way to let her know to cool it. "Any idea where she worked?"

Carrie shrugged. "I can't remember. At a shelter or something?" she asked as a question. "I'm pretty sure she said it was a volunteer position."

Huh. Okay. That didn't help much, but I'd file it away.

"I really should get inside and return Talia's call," she said, this time fully sidestepping us to get through her open door.

"Oh, sure," I said. We were done here anyway. "Thanks for talking to us about it, though. My niece was pretty upset and is still processing everything." I felt bad throwing Amber under the bus, as she was pretty much an emotional strongman, but I felt like we needed to provide some excuse for why we'd dropped by.

And good thing, too, because Carrie tilted her head at me and asked, "Hey, aren't you the lady that came and asked Talia for rubber gloves at the end of the night last night?"

"I, uh, yeah," was all I got out before she added, "Sure didn't seem like you knew Talia well."

Amber and I both took a step away from the house in unison.

"Well, it's actually her brother I know better," I said, but my voice had lost its confidence.

"Come on, Auntie," Amber said, trying to paste back on the cherub look, but this time, it didn't look quite as authentic. "We should go."

We definitely should, I decided. Because Carrie had already dialed her phone and was holding it up to her ear.

I only hoped Alex had already gotten Talia talking.

☐

# CHAPTER FOURTEEN

As I drove away from Carrie's house as quickly and safely as possible, my phone buzzed from where I had dropped it into the cupholder of my Prius. I glanced down to see ALEX MARTINEZ flash across the screen.

Uh-oh. If he was calling me, he wasn't with Talia.

I didn't want to pull over while we were in Carrie Bowman's neighborhood, so I asked Amber if she'd pick up. "Put him on speaker," I added.

"Mallory Beck's car phone," she said by way of an answer. "How may we help you?"

"Is this Amber?" Alex's words sounded rushed, almost frantic. "Is Mallory with you?"

"I'm here," I told him. "You're on speaker. Did you already talk to Talia? What's going on?"

"I'm headed there now, but I finally got an answer out of the coroner's office. They're still writing up the official report, but Richard Garnet definitely died from internal bleeding."

I twisted my lips, wondering what that meant. Was it an accident after all? Because of all the lies I'd heard in the last few hours, I found that difficult to believe.

"Technically, a bone from his upper spine splintered off to transect his aorta," Alex went on. "The strike to his largest artery would have killed him instantly upon impact."

I wasn't getting why Alex sounded so jazzed up about this information. Shouldn't his whole investigation be fizzling out?

"But that's not all," he said before I could warn him about Talia.

I held my breath, waiting for him to go on, but my GPS interrupted, instructing me to turn left. I waved a hand at the robotic GPS voice, as if that would shut her up, but a second later, Alex was back on the line.

"The coroner also found a substance called Actiq in his bloodstream."

"A substance?" I asked. "A poison?"

"Noooooo." Alex drew out the word. "A drug. It's a pharmaceutical brand name for Fentanyl."

I didn't know much about opioids, but even I recognized that name. Garnet hadn't struck me as a man who required strong prescription pain medication or who used narcotics recreationally.

I sucked in a breath. "Was it suicide then?" I asked in barely a whisper.

"I don't think so," he said. "In fact, I'm almost positive it wasn't. You see, I was leaving the coroner's office when I got a call from—"

My GPS interrupted him again, and it was all I could do not to throw my robotic directional guide out the window. But chucking her out the window would also effectively end my conversation with Alex.

Thankfully, Amber was on it, thumbs flying over my phone to pause the GPS. We were now a good couple of miles from the Bowman's house, so I pulled over as soon as I found a big enough shoulder, and by that time, Alex was back on the line, rambling on, something about coincidences or lack of coincidences.

"Wait!" I waved a hand at my phone again. "Go back. My GPS cut you off. What were you saying about leaving the coroner's office?"

"Uh…my call from forensics?"

I looked at Amber with wide eyes. I had no idea what this meant, but it felt like a tidbit of information that was going to make or break our case.

"Yeah, that," I said. "Tell us again."

"Forensics called to say they had also found an odd substance in the coffee cup we found on the roof of the town hall."

"Actiq?" I asked at the same time that Amber said, "Fentanyl?"

"Exactly," Alex told me. "The dosage in the cup wasn't lethal, but it was strong, possibly strong enough to knock a man out. But of course, he'd only finished drinking less than half of it."

"So could he have wanted to knock himself out before falling to his death?" I asked the question out loud, even though it didn't make sense in my own mind. If he were passed out, he couldn't have climbed up and over the ledge.

"Actiq is usually delivered in a lozenge form, like a lollipop," Alex went on to tell us. "It seemed there were still slivers of the lozenge stuck around the edges of the cup, that's why they could get the analysis done so quickly. If he was taking Actiq on purpose, why shave it down and insert it into his own coffee?"

"Or did someone else spike his coffee and then send him up to the roof?" Amber put in. "Someone who had actually admitted to serving the man coffee." Amber looked at me with wide eyes, waiting for me to catch on to her line of thinking.

And then it clicked.

"Carrie Bowman!" I said more loudly than necessary in the small car. "We just finished interviewing her and she said she had served Superintendent Garnet a cup of coffee only minutes before his death!"

Amber nodded, but spoke in a much calmer tone as she went on to explain to Alex how we'd conducted the interview as an aunt and niece, not connected to the police, as we thought that would get some true answers.

"That was probably smart," Alex said. "If she's guilty, she would have likely done everything she could to avoid telling me about that cup of coffee. But now that I know about it, I'm pretty sure I can pull it out of her. I'll head over there now and leave questioning Talia Mayberry for later. I'll bring Mickey as backup, but if I know him, he'll be happy to sit in the car and smoke unless she tries to run or something."

"We still have one of the catering crew left to interview," I said, "but maybe we should wait and see what you uncover?"

"No, it's always a good idea to follow all avenues. Maybe that other catering person will be able to shed some light on Carrie Bowman's motive or on the timeline of the murder." His keys jangled, and a second later, I heard his car door slam. "Just do your best to ask smart questions. Call me if you need me."

He said goodbye and hung up, and Amber rerouted my GPS from our current location to Melinda Zenky's house.

"Smart questions," I said out loud. "That sounds like your department."

The second Amber was done programming my phone, Hunch nuzzled his head under her hand. "If only Hunch could talk," she said. "I suspect he'd have the best questions of all."

I didn't doubt it.

We stayed quiet for the rest of the drive, save for GPS robotic lady. I hoped it gave Amber time to get deep in thought about the most targeted questions to ask Melinda and the best order in which to ask them. My GPS directed me to a low-income area I hadn't yet visited since moving to Honeysuckle Grove. It was far enough away from the downtown core that Melinda would have likely needed a car to get to work—I didn't think buses ran this far to the outskirts—which meant her trip to the store for cream shouldn't have taken long.

I turned to Amber and explained my thought process. "So maybe we should start our questioning with the cream and how long she was gone from the town hall?"

Amber nodded and pointed down the street to a dilapidated townhouse with peeling blue paint. "I think that's it."

It sat in the middle of a row of similar peeling blue townhouses. Each townhouse had a tiny square of patchy lawn in front of it, many lawns containing a handful of discarded and broken-looking toys. It made me wonder if Melinda had children as well, even though her lawn was toy-free.

There were no driveways to the townhouses, only street parking, it seemed. The curb contained a smattering of vehicles, all much older than my car. As I pulled into a spot between a beater truck and a nineties-model sedan, my white Prius stood out like a newborn at an old age home.

Amber set Hunch at her feet—he became less objectionable to the process each time she did it—and reached for her door handle. "Start with questions about the cream," she said, and I wasn't sure if it was a reminder for herself or for me.

Most likely me.

We arrived at the front door, which appeared to be missing its screen door from the look of the others, and gave it three strong knocks. We waited. We listened. But it seemed our timing wasn't going to be nearly as fortuitous as it had been at the Bowman house.

"Smart questions, sure," I murmured to myself. "We'll get right on that."

"Come on," Amber said. "Let's look around."

Before I could blink, Amber hopped down the three front steps and moved to the right of the townhouse, where a two-foot-wide cement path separated it from the next townhouse over.

By the time I caught up with her, she was balanced on a crossbeam of a weathered wooden gate and was reaching over top of it.

"What are you—" I stopped speaking as soon as I got my answer. She pulled a threadbare string, and the lock on the other side popped open. She strode through the gate without a second of hesitation. "Amber, wait!" I hissed. "This is private property."

She didn't slow, moving to what only a generous person would call the backyard. In the rear of the townhouse sat a small cement pad, big enough for a tiny patio set or barbecue, but Melinda Zenky's pad sat empty. Shrubs lined the cement, I supposed for privacy, and I thanked my lucky stars for that much. Hopefully, any observant neighbors hadn't already called the police on us.

Amber peered through a dirty window and then moved up a couple of rickety wooden steps toward a sliding glass rear door. She had yet to even respond to me.

When she reached for the handle of the glass door, I had to stop her. "Amber!" I hissed again, as quietly as possible, but loud enough that she had to be able to hear me. "That's breaking and entering!"

She pulled the handle sideways, and it moved—not gracefully, but it did move—to open up a gap big enough for her to squeeze through. She smirked back at me as though what she was doing was everyday fun and not a crime. "No, it's just entering," she said with a shrug.

And a second later, she disappeared inside.

I glanced back at the cement walkway that led to my car, to safety, to lawfulness. I'd always thought of Amber as someone who could almost skip the Police Academy, or Detective School, as I affectionately called it in my head. But maybe not. Maybe she actually needed it more than I did.

She's fifteen and I brought her here, I reminded myself.

And then I rushed up the stairs and through the open door after her.

☐

# CHAPTER FIFTEEN

"Excuse me, Mrs. Zenky?" I heard Amber call the instant I was inside. "Are you home? I wanted to ask you something. Hello?"

Now I wished I'd waited outside. Amber, with her sweet cherub expression, could probably make an ingenious excuse up on the spot and get away with this, even if Melinda Zenky were at home.

But from the lack of response, her house appeared empty. I glanced back toward the open glass door behind me before moving through the small kitchen and farther into the townhouse, following Amber's voice.

I found her in a cozy living room. It had an ancient-looking box TV, a worn orange-and-yellow flowered couch, and a rocking chair. Amber stood across the room at a hearth, which may have once been above a fireplace, but now sat halfway up an empty wall. On the hearth sat a variety of photographs of what looked like Melinda and a man from a distance.

"Looks like she's married," I observed.

"Was married," Amber said, turning to reveal the photo frame in her hands. She angled it so I could see the framed funeral pamphlet, along with a news clipping stuck into the edge, which contained a photo of the same man.

"Oh, that's awful." My heart swelled within me. Losing a husband, and so early in life, was something I could unfortunately understand all too well. I looked closer and exclaimed, "And look at the date. She only lost him this year!"

Amber nodded, replaced the frame on the mantle, seemingly unaffected, and moved on in her explorations. Moving closer, I continued to stare at it, almost in tears. I skimmed the small news clipping that listed those left behind and asked people to make a donation to a local drug rehabilitation shelter in lieu of flowers.

I'd started to read from the top again when Amber called me from another room.

"Hey, Mallory! Come and look at this. I think I found something."

It took little effort to navigate the tiny townhouse and find her, with only the living room, kitchen, a small bathroom, and a bedroom barely big enough to fit a double bed. I found Amber kneeling at the bottom of a single closet.

"What is it?" I asked.

She turned and held up a pair of worn black dress shoes. Before I could ask, she flipped them to show me the bottoms. The surface of the soles was made from some sort of slippery plastic, like you'd find on cheap shoes, but instead, our focus landed on the beige ovals stuck midway along each sole.

One appeared to be half ripped off, and I recalled that one of the girls had lost one of her shoe pads—or at least half of one—while loading the catering van late last night. But what remained of the one and a half ovals looked as though someone had worn them to train for a marathon on gravel for the last few months. Even from a distance, I could see balled up pieces of the rubberized pads that were about to come off. I moved closer to inspect them.

"I'll bet if we took these to Alex's forensics lab, they'd find the rubber matches the stuff we found on the roof of the town hall," Amber said.

"I'll bet you're right," I said from my squatted position beside her. "So what does that mean?"

Amber stood, scanning every inch of the small bedroom for any other possible clues. "It means Melinda Zenky was probably on the roof of the town hall last night. We just need to find out why."

We didn't find anything else of interest in Melinda's townhouse. I debated over whether we should take her shoes as evidence or leave them behind. I finally agreed to let Amber take photos with my phone and rip off a tiny ball of rubber that was about to come free anyway, so we could at least match that up with what they had at the forensics lab.

Then we tiptoed back out the way we came in and around the side of the house.

We emerged in Melinda's small front yard, and I was about to let out a long-held breath when a lady in a loose-fitting flowered dress stepped out of the house beside hers. A little girl of about four played with a toy tractor that had only one wheel on her front lawn.

I froze mid-step when the lady locked eyes with me and scowled. She had been about to sit on a porch chair, but she stood back up, crossing her arms. "What're you all doin' in Melinda's yard?" Her voice was defensive and angry.

Thankfully, Amber piped up. Her smile, once again, exuded cherub-like innocence. "We wondered if she might be out back. I thought she said she'd be home today, didn't she, Aunt Mallory?" Amber looked at me, clearly tossing the baton.

"I...thought so," I said. My ability to come up with reasonable explanations on the spot paled in comparison to Amber's, so I figured the fewer words, the better.

The neighbor lady still looked skeptical. I'd thought she was well into her forties, but now that I was closer, I wondered if this lady was even thirty. "Mel works at the shelter Wednesdays."

"Oh." I looked at Amber. We had heard something about her second job at a shelter from Carrie. That, combined with her late husband's obituary, had it starting to make sense. I wanted to look at the obituary again, but of course, it was too late for that.

It seemed like this lady knew more. It was just a matter of getting it out of her.

"You mean where she volunteers at that shelter up on..." I trailed off and pointed toward town, as if I had simply forgotten the name of the road where the shelter was located. I had no idea about the location of shelters, drug or otherwise, in Honeysuckle Grove, but I guessed any of them would be closer to the town center than way out here. I hoped this neighbor lady would fill in the blank for me.

But her scowl only deepened. I tried to keep my eyes and face honest and innocent as I waited her out.

"What're you two tryin' to pull?" she asked, digging her fists into her waist. Her daughter called, "Mama," from the lawn, but she waved her off. I swallowed and tried to come up with some sort of viable explanation of why we'd been rooting around Melinda Zenky's yard, but the lady cut off my racing thoughts with, "She's at the drug rehab shelter on Fifth, every Wednesday since Austin died. You want to track her down? From now on, I suggest you do it there." Her words didn't leave any room for argument, but at least she didn't whip out a phone to call the police either.

"Right, right!" I said, much too peppy as I headed for the Prius. Amber followed. "On Fifth! Thanks so much!"

I didn't look back to see if any of my words had been believable to this lady because new puzzle pieces were clicking into place in my mind.

I needed to make sense of them with my shrewd teenage co-investigator.

And we needed to get to that drug rehab shelter on Fifth.

☐

# CHAPTER SIXTEEN

"It's starting to make sense." My words tripped over each other as I drove us out of Melinda's neighborhood and back toward town. "Melinda volunteers at a drug rehab shelter. I'll bet if Alex looks into it, we'll find that her husband died of some kind of drug-related problem or overdose. She was angry because the mayor's anti-drug agenda had all but been given up on and taken over by some stupid fake plea to keep the town library."

Amber nodded. For once, Hunch wasn't on her lap, instead pacing back and forth along my back seat. With his enviable nervous system, even when I braked, he barely stumbled.

"I'll bet his overdose was from that same Actiq drug," Amber suggested.

I asked her to dial Alex and put him on speakerphone again, but the call went straight to his voicemail. I gave him a quick overview of what we'd discovered, where we were headed, and I suggested if he was still speaking with Carrie that he ask her who had poured the coffee for Superintendent Garnet.

I was willing to bet Melinda, the new employee, was entrusted with filling cups, adding the appropriate cream or sugar—or, in this case, drug—and passing them off to the more experienced caterers to deliver them to the more notable attendees.

I drove the length of Fifth Street three times before Amber spotted a building that might be a rehab shelter. It was an unmarked brick building with a plaque posted near the glass door, but the small writing wasn't legible from the street. When a tired-looking man lumbered out the door, though, that convinced me to find a nearby parking spot and check it out. Neither of us was certain if the man was a recently rehabilitated drug addict or a tired volunteer, but his worn jeans and red and black plaid shirt, along with his tired appearance, were enough for us to want to check the building out.

After parking, Amber and I jogged across the street to the front door. The plaque became visible as we moved closer. It held a three-column list of names. Otherwise, there was no signage, nothing to tell us if we were in the right building.

"I guess it makes sense that they don't have a sign," Amber told me. "Even though there are a lot of people in town struggling with drug addiction, lots of them prioritize lack of pain so they can keep going to work each day. Employers overlook it because they don't want to lose their good employees. I remember my dad having hushed conversations with my mom about employees at his law firm who he suspected had drug problems. He didn't want to bring it up because he couldn't afford to lose them. It makes a lot of sense that addicts wouldn't want their coworkers or their bosses knowing about it if they were trying to get clean and might have to take a sudden leave of absence."

The dark glass of the door didn't allow us to see inside. I pulled it open and let Amber go in first, as she seemed to know a lot more about this than I did. I wondered if it hit her close to home to have to talk about memories of her dad.

The immediate brightness inside surprised me and took my attention. I blinked a couple of times at the wide cheery-looking turquoise counter that stretched the width of the lobby, blocking our entry.

No one stood on the other side to greet us, although people bustled back and forth through another glass door behind the counter. Amber didn't hesitate to step up to the counter and ring a silver bell that sat atop it.

I wanted to stop her, to tell her to hold on until we'd at least discussed what we should say here, but the bell was already ringing out loudly, and only seconds later, a lady in faded green scrubs pushed through the door to greet us.

"Can I help you?" Her gray frizzy hair was coming loose from her ponytail, and she looked at least as tired as the man we'd seen leaving the building.

"Can we please speak to Melinda Zenky?" Amber asked, full of her usual confidence. When the lady glanced down at the counter and didn't immediately reply, Amber added, "It's about a family emergency."

Good thinking, Amber! Now, to quickly come up with how we knew her family and what the emergency was about...

But before my mind could even start coming up with ideas, the lady answered us. "Could she have already heard about the emergency? She left here about an hour ago, and she seemed pretty upset."

Amber and I glanced at each other. It didn't make any sense. The family emergency was a fabrication, at least as far as we knew. Even if her neighbor had called Melinda to give her a heads-up about us being in her backyard, that would have been no more than twenty minutes ago—

certainly not an hour ago.

"So you have no idea where she was headed?" I confirmed.

The lady tilted her head and shook it at me. "She said she had to go and that she was sorry. Maybe try the hospital?"

"The hospital?" I asked.

When the lady started to answer my question with her own question, I realized she was only riffing off our fake story. "Well...what was the emergency?"

I took a step away and nodded. "Right, yes, the hospital. Good idea."

Amber followed me out the door, not giving the lady any more information, but only offering a quick wave and a thank-you. We raced back to my car as I attempted to get all of my new questions out in some sort of a coherent fashion.

"You made up that family emergency thing, right?" I asked Amber. "Then why was she so upset?"

Amber pulled open the passenger door, looking as calm as ever. "Well, everything we found out today indicates she killed someone last night." Amber shrugged. "Wouldn't that make anyone upset—anyone other than a sociopath? But it sounds as though she left in the middle of her shift. The more important question is where would she go if she's upset? Back home?"

"If she left an hour ago, she would've been there long before we snuck through her sliding glass door." I shook my head, thinking.

Amber reached for Hunch, but he swatted her hand and kept busy pacing the backseat again. Even my cat seemed to know we were close. We had to figure this out.

"I know it sounds stupid," Amber said suddenly, "but the town hall isn't far from here." I squinted at her in confusion, but she only answered my confusion with a question. "Do you think it's open today?"

☐

# CHAPTER SEVENTEEN

On the drive over, Amber let me in on what she was thinking.

"From what we've discovered about Melinda Zenky, she's not a serial killer or some kind of sociopath. She's a hurting woman who recently lost her husband."

I nodded, finally getting it. "So if she did kill Superintendent Garnet, if she did it in an angry rage, and even if she thinks she was justified in doing so, she could very well still feel really guilty about it?"

"It's a thought," Amber said. "And if she's overwhelmed with guilt, where might she go to process that guilt?"

"Somewhere near the town hall," I answered, even though her question sounded rhetorical.

I didn't know if the building was open to the public again today, but searching the grounds around it made more sense than anything else we'd come up with. I expected we'd find Melinda across the street from the meeting hall on the lawn or seated under one of the trees, head in her hands, or looking up and processing all of her regrets.

But as I drove up the street toward the town hall, the streets were nearly empty, most people perhaps having already headed home for dinner. I stopped at the four-way stop a block from the town hall and scanned the entire landscape in front of me. A man walked his dog on the sidewalk to my left. A much older woman was leaving a nail salon on my right. Otherwise, there wasn't another person in sight.

Regardless, I pulled past the stop sign and parked in the next available space I found along the curb. The two lone cars in the town hall's parking lot made me think it couldn't be open for business today. Perhaps Hank was inside cleaning, the forensics team was investigating, or someone else might be setting up for another event.

Or, if we were lucky, Melinda Zenky had gone inside.

For good measure, on our way toward the building, I checked each side of the trees in the small park across the street from the meeting hall. As we gave up on that and crossed toward the large meeting hall, I tried to keep my gaze everywhere except on the front cement steps, where there had been crime scene tape and a dead body less than twenty-four hours ago.

I looked from the post office to the bowling alley and even back toward the mayor's office in an effort to divert my attention. Before we got to the steps, though, Amber cut to the left. "Hang on," she said. "I think I see something!"

Because the town hall appeared to be deserted, I'd let Hunch tag along this time, thinking maybe he could somehow sniff out the whereabouts of Melinda Zenky. Even if he couldn't, it was well time for a bathroom break for my poor cat.

But Hunch didn't seem to have any interest in taking thirty seconds to relieve himself. As Amber raced away from me toward the small driveway to the left of the building, Hunch skipped along inches from her heels. They headed toward the side of the hall where the catering van had been parked last night because of its close proximity to the kitchen door.

By the time I caught up, the two of them had squatted near a small beige object on the pavement. Neither of them touched it. I'd taught them well.

I laughed inwardly at myself, trying to take the credit for their skills. If anything, they were always the ones teaching me.

I didn't even have to bend to make out the object: half an oval of a non-slip shoe pad, clearly torn on one edge.

"This one we can take, right?" Amber asked, looking up at me. "We can get Alex to take it straight to the forensics lab, get them to see if it's a match for the rubber they already tested from the roof? If it's a match, we have definite proof that Melinda Zenky was on the roof, probably last night, because it rained the day before yesterday."

It never ceased to amaze me how quickly her teenage brain worked.

"Do you have a Ziploc or something we can collect it in?" Amber asked.

Strangely, I did have a small sandwich-sized plastic bag in my purse. I hoped to find a way to avoid admitting as much out loud, but for years now, I always kept one with me in case I came across a food item at a party or at a public function that I was bound and determined to emulate.

I rooted in my purse and quickly found the bag. When I passed it over, Amber's satisfaction at me solving her problem was apparently enough to distract her from why I had it in my purse.

She pushed the baggie inside out and then grabbed the shoe pad with the plastic, folding it back around the item as though she was born collecting crime scene samples. She left a small twig in its spot. As she stood, she handed the sealed bag back to me, and I tucked it into my purse.

As I angled toward the front entrance again, trying to avoid looking at those front steps, my eyes drifted up, and I swear I caught movement.

"Did you see that?" I asked. I pointed up to the top ledge of the town hall, but now I wondered if I'd imagined it or if a leaf had blown by my vision.

But only a second later, a swatch of green flashed up above the ledge, catching my eye again.

"Someone's up there!" Amber said.

Someone, indeed. And if it wasn't Amber or Hunch or me, and I highly doubted it was Alex, who was it?

# CHAPTER EIGHTEEN

The front doors to the town hall were locked up tighter than the Kelli-the-secretary's short skirt. I knocked on the heavy wooden doors, but even with all of my effort, my hand only made a quiet thud.

"Come on," Amber said, already racing down the stairs. "The kitchen door."

Right! I followed as quickly as I could manage, but when I'd dressed this morning, I had opted for somewhat professional-looking ballet flats. Teenagers could get away with wearing sneakers and snarky hoodies on a visit to the mayor's office. Unfortunately, mine didn't have non-slip pads on the bottom.

By the time I rounded the corner around the side of the building, Amber and Hunch had already made it up the small set of outside stairs that led to the kitchen. Amber pulled at a door, and it opened.

I kept moving forward as quickly as I could without slipping, as they clearly weren't about to wait for me. By the time I reached the door and moved through it into the town hall's kitchen, they were nowhere in sight.

Hank, however, hovered over the big industrial sink with a scrub brush in hand. He looked over as I entered.

I had no idea what Amber had or had not told him, so I went with, "Did my friend head up those stairs?" I pointed to the green doorway that led to the roof access.

He furrowed his brow, but nodded. I thanked him and raced for the door. Hank's words behind me were slow, too slow for me to stop and respond to them. "You probably shouldn't have a cat in here…"

Whatever else he said was lost when I let the green door fall shut behind me. Let him call the municipal office on me. In fact, it might be better if he did. Amber and I might need the help.

I took the stairs two at a time, blinking at the dimness of the stairwell until I made it to the top. When I pushed open the door that led onto the roof, Amber had already made it halfway across the expanse to the far ledge, where Melinda Zenky stood in a pair of green scrubs. Her hands clutched her chest, as though she were holding her heart in place, and even from this distance, I could tell she was shaking.

"Just come away from the ledge so we can talk to you for a minute," Amber said.

Amber's words, however, made Melinda take a step backward, so her legs pressed right up against the ledge. Like last night, her dark brown hair was in a ponytail, but much of it had come loose at the sides, and now, as if to highlight that fact, she dug her fingers into the edges of her hair, gripped the roots, and pulled.

"I can't," she said, and it sounded more like a whimper or a plea than an argument.

"You should—" Amber started to say, but I'd moved up close to my young friend and placed a hand on her shoulder to stop her.

"Let me," I said gently, and Amber took a step backward, toward the roof's door, her eyes wide and worried. I wasn't sure I'd ever seen Amber like that before. But, truly, a fifteen-year-old shouldn't have the burden of holding someone else's life in her hands.

"Stay back," Melinda said to me, her voice louder and stronger.

"We will," I told her gently. "I will. Just…you stay where you are, too, okay?"

She didn't answer, only glanced over her shoulder. From her vantage point so close to the ledge, she could probably see the ground and even the front steps of the town hall below.

When she turned back, her shaking was worse, almost spastic. "Why are you here?" She didn't leave me time to answer. "Leave me alone."

I nodded. "Okay, yeah, I will," I lied. "I want to talk to you for a second first. You see, I lost my husband less than a year ago. Remember that bank fire last winter? He didn't make it out." It was the most I'd spoken about Cooper's death in a long time, and I couldn't help myself from getting choked up on the words. I took a deep breath, let it out slowly, and then brought the subject back to her. "It seems so unfair, doesn't it?"

She eyed me sideways with squinted eyes. "Were you friends with that superintendent or something?"

I shook my head. "I'd never met him." I let that sit for a few seconds, so she'd know I meant it.

She nodded and kept nodding for an unusually long time. Then she suddenly broke into sobs and covered her face. "I didn't mean to do it," she said from between her hands.

I hadn't seen Hunch since arriving on the roof, but now he edged closer to Melinda, and then closer still, until he nudged his furry body right up against her green scrubs-covered legs.

She jolted, but then looked down and saw it was only a cat. The jolt, though, seemed to be enough to break her from her uncontrolled sobs, and I figured I'd better use this opportunity to get the whole story out of her.

"What did you mean to happen?" I asked in little more than a whisper. I took a small step toward her, and when she didn't react, I took one more. But my second step made her glance over the ledge again.

When she turned back, her jaw jutted out and she balled her fists. Her voice rose when she said, "It's not right, what they're doing, brushing the problem under the carpet when people are dying!"

"Who's they?" I asked, daring one more step closer. "Do you mean the mayor and the superintendent?"

She spoke over me. "They thought some stupid library meeting was more important than all the people in town who are at risk of overdosing? They've shut down almost all the places to help them already! I wanted to show them that anyone could get hooked on the stuff if they were in pain and needed to keep working. Even one of them!"

"So you added some of the drug that killed your husband to the superintendent's coffee?" I confirmed.

I took another step toward her, but she threw out a stop sign of a hand and said, "No! Don't come any closer!"

"I won't." I nodded. "I'll stay here."

"I didn't give him enough to kill him, only enough to knock him out, and if he'd only drank his whole coffee…" She trailed off, shaking her head again.

"What would have happened if he had finished the whole thing?" I pressed, keeping my voice quiet and gentle. The whole story was starting to piece together for me now, though, even before she opened her mouth to explain.

"I was going to go and tell the mayor that the superintendent was passed out on the roof once the meeting had started, so it would be a big public spectacle. Everyone would want to know why, and they would've found the drugs in his system. It would have brought the problem back to light. That's all." She started whimpering again, but I wanted to keep her talking.

"But you came up here and he wasn't passed out—"

"He knew what I'd done! He felt off-kilter from the drugs, and he grabbed me by the collar of my shirt, and he was so much stronger than me. I knew I had to do something before he regained his equilibrium from the drugs. I only had the smallest chance to fight him off. He was so angry, and all I could picture was him pushing me off the roof!"

"And so you pushed him before he could do it to you?" I confirmed, nodding as though I was with her and this whole plan made perfect sense.

It did, in a way, although that would be impossible to explain to law enforcement or a judge. But if I knew Cooper's death could have been prevented, and there were more people in danger because municipal officials weren't willing to take a looming problem seriously, how far might I have gone to make them take notice?

I'd like to think I wouldn't have resorted to murder. But I could see how I might have let myself get pushed off the top of a building to bring some light to what had happened to Cooper.

All she had time to do was nod in response to my question. Then a noise sounded behind me, and I turned to see the door beside Amber fly open. Alex stood in the threshold, decked out in his detective suit.

In about half a second, he took in his surroundings. "Melinda Zenky? Please step away from the ledge." His voice held all the authority mine didn't.

By the time I turned back around, though, I suspected authority wasn't what was needed in this particular situation.

Because Melinda had one leg up on top of the ledge.

☐

# CHAPTER NINETEEN

Several things happened at once.

Amber screamed, "No! Please don't!"

I raced forward, knowing I was too far away to catch her.

And Hunch reached up with one claw and caught her skin inside the pants of the leg that was trailing behind.

The sudden pain of Hunch's claws made her pause for a second to look back. It was the second I needed, and I leaped headfirst toward her leg. I hit my shoulder hard on the cement ledge, but I had her pants and then, a second later, her leg. My shoulder burned with pain, but my next problem was that Melinda was clearly both heavier and stronger than me.

She was going to pull me over!

Thankfully, Alex quickly traversed the distance across the roof, and before she could pull me up onto the ledge, he yanked us both back. Even Amber got in on the action, grabbing hold of Melinda's arm.

We all flopped back onto the floor of the roof in a heap, and I had never been so thankful for elastomeric roof coating. It was a whole lot softer than the bare cement ledge had been.

"No!" Melinda cried from within the pile. "Please just let me die!"

She tried to paw her way to the top of our clump, but I wrapped my arms around her. "Shhh, shhh, shhh," I said into her hair.

Alex and Amber both worked their way out of the pile and into sitting positions, but I continued to lie on the roof holding Melinda.

When she started to calm down, I told her, "If you die, you'll never be able to do any good. If you stay alive, at least you can tell your story. Maybe you can make a difference." I couldn't help but picture her telling her story from a jail cell, as that would likely be the only way she would be able to now.

Then again, maybe that was the best option for her. She clearly felt so

215

guilty about the superintendent's death, she was ready to take her own life. Maybe after the law finished punishing her, and perhaps after some psychological counseling, she'd be able to find better, healthier ways of making a difference.

Eventually, she sat up, and so did I, but she didn't make any sort of move toward the ledge.

In fact, she held her wrists up toward Alex. She knew what was coming. In fact, she was asking for it.

Alex removed his handcuffs from his waistband and said, "You have the right to remain silent..." in the gentlest voice I had ever heard from a police officer.

☐

# CHAPTER TWENTY

Melinda Zenky was facing up to fifteen years in the state penitentiary. Her court-appointed lawyer could probably plead her case down from second-degree murder to voluntary manslaughter or even self-defense, but apparently, Melinda planned to plead guilty and take her punishment without any fight.

When all the details came to light, she admitted that while she hadn't premeditated the murder, she had premeditated the drugging. After applying to work with the catering company, she had grated three of her late husband's Actiq "lollipops" into a small container she kept in the pocket of her black work pants. Then she had stashed two of the catering company's coffee cream containers in her car to give her an excuse to make herself scarce. She hoped that Superintendent Garnet took sweetener in his coffee to hide the flavor of the Actiq, but if not, she had been willing to turn her plan to one of the town council members or even Mayor Lassiter.

I spent the next several days at home alone, but Alex kept me apprised of the details. Amber didn't visit, as exam week had started Monday. I'd never asked her what kind of grades she got in school, but if she was as smart with her academics as she was at detective work, I couldn't imagine her getting less than straight A's.

I expected Alex to be MIA as well since wrapping up a case always entailed a plethora of paperwork, so it surprised me when my phone rang and he wanted to get together on Tuesday.

"Do you have time for a coffee?" he asked when I picked up.

I'd gradually been climbing out of my fog of depression and loneliness, so times when both Alex and Amber had other things to do weren't quite as debilitating as they once had been. I'd even been baking on my own.

"Sure," I told him. "Come on over. I just made a caramel apple cake and it's about to come out of the oven." I wondered if he had some news of his next case to tell me about.

He hesitated, and I heard shifting and fiddling in the background. I suspected he wasn't at his desk. Usually, the atmosphere from the busy precinct made it difficult to hear. "Actually, I thought it might be nice to take you out for something. The café on Tenth has great pastries."

I had been sitting at the kitchen table, petting Hunch while I waited for the oven to ding, but my hand stopped mid-stroke.

This seemed like something else. By the strange nervousness in his voice, I realized this could be a request for a date.

I swallowed hard, and because I had yet to reply, Alex added, "I wanted to, you know, thank you for all your help with the case."

In that instant, he sounded like preteen Xander Martinez—the name he'd gone by when I'd known him in middle school, back when my crush on him had been the spotlight of my existence.

Ah, middle school. Back when a person could have a crush and it didn't have to bring on complicated emotions like guilt and sorrow.

When I didn't answer for a long time, Alex asked, "Mallory? Are you there?"

"I, well...this caramel apple cake is fresh, and...hmm, why don't you just come over here?"

I had no idea why it felt less threatening to have him in my home than it did to be seated across from him at a coffee shop, even without our teenage chaperone, Amber, present. Maybe it was because, at home, I could always escape across the room to the kitchen counter and my recipe books if things got too intense. Seated in a restaurant or coffee shop, where I had no choice but to keep my eyes locked with Alex's...I didn't know if I was ready for that.

"I...sure. That's fine," he said, even though it didn't sound fine. "I'll see you in fifteen."

I hadn't even put my phone down when it buzzed in my hand with a new text. Amber was in class, so I had no idea who it might be. But then Milt Vandewalker flashed across the screen.

Dad. I rolled my eyes before I even clicked on his text.

Dad didn't text, at least not often. In fact, the only time he texted, rather than phoning, was when he was avoiding an issue, but he needed to give me an update. Or a request for money that went far and beyond what he could ask for by voice. In other words, he texted when he knew I'd have an argument, and he didn't want to hear it.

I recalled Leslie's warning. It seemed like a lifetime ago that my sister had told me he'd lost his job.

Finally, I sighed and clicked on his text. I'd have to somehow get whatever it was out of my system before Alex arrived.

&lt;Hi honey! I'm coming through town for a visit. It'll be nice to see you face to face!&gt;

I wasn't sure what to do with the written exuberance from my dad. It had to mean he was covering up something pretty major that he desperately wanted to hide from me.

I swallowed. I used to have to talk Cooper into giving him money, but since Cooper had died, it was as though Dad knew I wouldn't have any reason to say no. He'd asked at least three times this year already. Was this request for money going to be an even bigger one?

I often envied Leslie, who seemed to be able to say no to Dad about anything and everything, and put him out of her mind without a single shred of guilt. I supposed it had something to do with the fact that Leslie and Brad had three highly involved young kids and they didn't have a lot of money to spare.

I sighed and hit reply.

&lt;When are you coming? Will you be here overnight? Should I make up the spare room? Are you sure you don't want to chat on the phone instead?&gt;

When five minutes passed and he hadn't replied, I regretted my words. Chances were good now that if he did phone, it would be right in the middle of my visit with Alex.

Then again, maybe a parental phone call would be another way of keeping things light with Alex. No need to talk about my strange reaction to him inviting me out for coffee if Dad was on the phone.

Or maybe Dad wouldn't call because he was already on his way. I mentally calculated the driving distance from Pittsburgh. It was a little less than three hours, which would put him here around dinner time. At least I had the option of distracting myself from the usual family drama by cooking.

I still hadn't heard back when Alex's knock sounded at the front door. Hunch beat me to the entry and pawed at the door as though he couldn't get it open fast enough. He probably thought it was Amber. It had been almost a week since he'd seen her.

I opened the door, surprised to see Alex in jeans and a navy hoodie. "Oh. Not working today?"

As expected, Hunch took one glance at him, sniffed the air, and headed back for his food bowl in the kitchen. Hunch didn't dislike Alex. He just wasn't Amber.

Alex smirked at my question. "I talked Mickey into filing the rest of the paperwork and giving me a break for once. I'm pretty sure after all the acclaim he's getting for this case, he knew he couldn't exactly say no."

I tilted my head and followed Alex to the kitchen. "Corbett's still not acknowledging your abilities, huh?"

Alex shrugged as he took his usual seat at my small kitchen table. "If we're being honest, it was your abilities that solved this one anyway. Yours and Amber's, so I'm not terribly worried about any misguided credit."

My cheeks warmed as I headed for the coffee pot. I poured a cup for each of us, fixing Alex's up the way I knew he liked it, before bringing it to the table. "Well, I was happy to help in any small way I could."

I was about to sit, but then felt strange about it, like I wasn't ready to be so close to Alex without more than two cups of coffee between us. I headed back to the counter to slice up the caramel apple cake. It was a little too warm inside, and I took in a deep soothing breath of the sweet aroma, waiting for Alex to say something else.

But the silence stretched between us, getting more uncomfortable by the second. Now that I'd cut into it, I didn't want the cake to get cold, but at the same time, I felt an eerie nervousness about bringing it over to him, and I wasn't sure why.

Finally, as I'd arranged two forks and small plates alongside the cake, I couldn't stall any longer. I sucked up my courage and went to the table.

Alex waited me out while I set up a plate and fork in front of both of our places. It had never been this uncomfortable between us before. Had it? Now there was nothing to do but sit.

I kept busy for as long as possible after sliding into my chair. I served Alex a piece of cake and then one for myself. I turned mine on my plate and cut it up into pieces, cringing at myself as I did it because that would release the heat faster and it wouldn't be nearly as tasty cold. I took a small bite, even though I questioned my ability to swallow.

Finally, now that he knew he had me cornered, Alex spoke, but his statement wasn't what I expected. "I guess I thought maybe I could beat him to the punch, but I, um…Well, Steve keeps talking about calling you again this week." Alex had yet to take a bite. He was also separating his cake into tiny cubes, as though he were the nervous one.

I couldn't help myself. I reached out and rested a hand on his arm to stop him from the cake mutilation. I couldn't stand knowing his cake wouldn't be warm when he first tasted it, even if I had done the exact same thing to mine. He looked up at me, and I shook my head. "No. I mean, we only went out once, and I don't plan to go out with him again."

"Oh. You said you weren't ready to date, but then Steve indicated it was turning into a regular thing…"

I shook my head again, resisting the urge to roll my eyes. "I'm really not ready to date again yet. I don't know where Steve got that idea, but the truth is, he's probably just making stuff up in his own head because I can't have an honest conversation with him like I can with you." I finally pulled my hand away from Alex's arm.

"I guess I wondered if you were letting me down easy. Because of

Steve."

"No, definitely not." I nibbled my lip. Even though I much preferred Alex to Steve, I couldn't exactly say that and still give the impression I needed more time. "After Cooper," I started, but my throat choked up on those two words and I couldn't seem to say anymore.

"Oh." He nodded. "Okay, that makes sense." Finally, he took a bite. He chewed and swallowed before adding, "I guess...well, I guess I'm glad. That you weren't just letting me down easy, I mean. I've got plenty of time, if that's what you need." His smile was filled with understanding.

The urge to add more gnawed at me. "In truth, I don't know if I'll ever be ready to date someone else. I expected to grow old with Cooper, you know?" My hoarse voice gave away my wavering emotions.

Alex only nodded. I wanted to ask him if he'd had any serious relationships, if he'd ever imagined growing old with someone. But at the same time, I wasn't sure I wanted to hear about that.

And that's what made me realize what I'd said was untrue, or at the very least a cop-out. But how could I tell him I liked him and at the same time say that I might not be ready for a relationship for a really long time?

I opened my mouth to, at the very least, change this uncomfortable subject, but as I did, my doorbell chimed.

"Sorry about that." I stood, suspecting we could both use the break. I'd go deal with the door-to-door salesman or religious zealot—who else would stop by in the middle of the day?—and then return to have a normal conversation with Alex. We could talk about the case, go over the details. Chat about his next case. We, of all people, shouldn't be stuck for words.

But I swung open my front door and on the other side was my father.

"D-dad!" I said and took a quick glance at the hall clock. He couldn't have possibly made it here in the half hour that had passed since he texted me.

It wasn't until I pulled away from hugging him that I realized he must have texted me from somewhere within West Virginia. He must have been afraid I would have said no if he'd asked me from the onset.

But I'd never said no to him visiting in the past.

I narrowed my eyes at him. "Why didn't you call me earlier?"

He shifted and looked at his feet. My dad, all poufy salt-and-pepper hair and tubby belly that perfectly showed his bachelor eating habits, was nothing if not easy to read—at least when I had him in person. Which was probably why he made sure we usually talked by phone. He could almost always swindle me into his way of thinking using only his salesman voice.

"What, Dad?" I asked, crossing my arms and not immediately inviting him inside. "What are you hiding?"

He gnawed on his lip and then glanced over his shoulder toward the street. That's when I saw the U-Haul, parked along the curb two doors down.

No, no, no, no, no! My eyes widened as they turned back to him. "You got kicked out of your place?"

He shrugged and pushed his way past me into the house. Even when I thought I had the upper hand with him, a simple little move like that reminded me he was the parent.

"That place never suited me. And you know I finished up my job there in Pittsburgh, so there was nothing keeping me in that overrun industrial city."

I happened to know from my sister, Leslie, that "finished" his job actually meant he'd been fired. Again. "And...so...what are you thinking?" My eyes ping-ponged between my dad and his U-Haul. He couldn't be expecting to move in here. Could he?

He shrugged again. He already had his shoes off, and Hunch, the feline investigator, had come to see why there was a new smell in the house. Dad bent to scratch him under the chin, and Hunch, the traitor, lapped up the attention.

"I just need a place to stay until I get my feet on the ground, honey," he said, keeping his eyes on my cat. "You have this whole big house to yourself. You can let your dad stay for a couple of weeks, can't you?"

A couple of weeks?

The truth was, I would have begged for someone to move in and take care of me nine months ago after losing Cooper. But now, I'd barely started getting my life back together. I had Alex now, and Amber, not to mention Sasha Mills and my new friends at the church. Besides, I suspected this would be me taking care of him and not the other way around.

But I was the sister who couldn't say no, and he knew that.

"I— A couple of weeks," I said in my sternest voice. "To be honest, I don't think you'll find work around here anyway. The unemployment rate is really high."

"Oh, yeah?" He stood and raised his eyebrows. "Where are you working then?"

I felt my face flush. If I told Dad I didn't need to work because of Cooper's insurance policy and the ongoing income from his book sales, Dad would be sure to talk me into giving most of it to him. He'd also turn one of the main lectures I'd given to him about laziness back on me.

"I, um, I'm starting a catering business," I said. It was the first thing that came to my mind and popped out of my mouth. "I'm quite busy with it, and I have a young girl helping me. Usually, she's here all the time, and sometimes stays in the guest room, so I'll need my house back soon." I glanced one more time at the U-Haul and then tentatively closed my front door on it.

When I did, Alex called from the kitchen, "Who was it, Mal?"

My face, I swear, hit three hundred degrees. "I—uh, I'll be back in a minute," I called. When I turned back to Dad, his eyebrows were practically one with his hairline.

"Oh!" he said, his voice brimming into a smile. "Is this the fella Leslie told me about?" His loud whisper only gave the illusion of him trying to be respectful and quiet. I was certain Alex would hear it from here. "The one you have a crush on?"

I shook my head as though insects had suddenly infested my hair. "No!" I said in a much quieter whisper. "That was in middle school!" Even though the words were true, I feared my red cheeks might give away my very complicated current feelings.

Dad's smile didn't dim any when he waggled his eyebrows and asked, "Should I come back in a couple of hours?"

Both Dad and Leslie thought that dating again would help me move on from my grief over Cooper. I was tired of assuring them again and again that I wasn't ready. I certainly wasn't about to argue this point in front of Alex.

"Actually, Dad…" I led him back toward the front door. "Why don't you head to the grocery store down the way…" I opened the door and pointed down the road. "Grab a fresh chicken and some veggies, and I'll make you up a nice dinner." I already had a lot of fresh ingredients on hand. Ever since I'd started teaching Amber to cook, I kept my fridge and freezer fairly stocked, but I needed to get him out of here, at least for a few minutes.

"Well, I could, but…" he trailed off, letting my understanding fill in the blank.

He wasn't about to pay for this grocery shopping trip. I raced to my purse in the front closet and, seconds later, pushed a few twenties into his hand.

I could tell by his next words, relaxed and not rushed in the least, that he knew he had the upper hand in this conversation. "You know, I'd rather not take the U-Haul, honey. Parking it at a grocery store might not be easy."

I raced back to my purse and returned with my car keys. "Here. Take my Prius." I pointed to the driveway. "Okay, thanks, Dad!" My voice was much too peppy, but at least he didn't fight me as I started to close the door on him. "Bye!"

I'd have a lot to explain to him later.

But for the moment, I had a man in my kitchen who might have some questions of his own about my middle school crush.

# END OF BOOK 3

# UP NEXT: MURDER IN THE VINEYARD

A heated religious argument. A murder that isn't as obvious as it seems. A first date gone very, very wrong.

Mallory Beck didn't expect to start dating her detective friend and childhood crush, Alex Martinez. At the very least, after her husband's recent death, she didn't expect to date someone she really likes so soon. But it isn't a real date anyway. It's a Bible Study, and she has some questions about God, not to mention the pressing need to escape her recently-freeloading father for an evening. Besides, how heated could things get at a Bible Study?

The heat, it turns out, burns between two other attendees, who can't stop arguing their theology. When one storms out of the meeting early and then later turns up dead, Alex and Mallory find themselves at the heart of another murder investigation.

Can they uncover the secrets simmering through their cozy community town in order to get to the truth?

## READ ON IN THE SERIES NOW…

☐

# Book Four

# MURDER
## in the Vineyard

DENISE JADEN

# CHAPTER ONE

There had to be a better way to purge one's guilt than talking to your late husband's judgmental cat. And yet here I was, babbling on and on to Hunch about how going out with Alex tonight didn't mean I was forgetting about Cooper or that I was ready to date again.

"It's not even a real date," I told my furry accuser as I pulled a purple skirt from the closet and surveyed it. He was curled up on my bed—on Cooper's side, as usual—and watched me with one eye open. "It's a Bible study," I explained. "And Alex only invited me because he knows I have some questions about God. He usually has to work Sundays, so this is kind of like his church."

I laid the purple skirt on my side of the bed. You'd think after nearly a year of mourning Cooper, I'd stop thinking in terms of his side and mine. But it had only been in the last month that I'd let my clothes start to migrate to his empty side of our closet. I'd given an equally wordy explanation to Hunch then, too, justifying that the best way to avoid wrinkles was to space my clothing just a tad across the middle line.

Hunch lifted one paw out from under his chin and placed it a few inches away on my purple skirt. You'd have to know my cat to realize this move, in fact, wasn't him trying to be a helpful and cooperative kitty, coming to my aid in choosing an outfit. This was his way of saying, "If it's not a real date, why have you spent the last forty-five minutes debating what to wear, huh?"

The thing was…my cat was right.

I grabbed for my favorite jeans and orange wool sweater, leaving a mountain of skirts and dresses on my bed. It was too cold for bare legs, anyway.

However, the guilt didn't end with Hunch's side-eye and well-placed paw. I'd barely changed and made my way downstairs when Dad met me at the base of the stairs and whistled.

"Someone looks nice. Hot date tonight?"

My face warmed, which probably only highlighted the fact that I'd applied a little more than my usual lip balm in the way of makeup. "Not a date," I told him. So far I'd only mentioned I had plans outside the house and that he should use the opportunity to make some phone calls about either other housing options or a job. "Actually, I'm going to a Bible study."

Dad raised a thick eyebrow at me. I led the way to my kitchen, already knowing he'd follow and demand more of an explanation. I didn't come from a religious family, and even when I'd attended church regularly with Cooper before he died, I had never mentioned it to my dad. My mother had been the most religious person in our family and used to encourage the rest of us to join her in church. She'd died without any warning when I was eight and Leslie was twelve, leaving us with an irresponsible and loafing dad. We'd written off church as easily as we'd written her off.

"It's not a big deal," I told Dad as I speared a sausage with a fork straight out of the pan and took a bite. "Don't worry. This isn't some big conversion."

Dad leaned back against my counter. His salt-and-pepper hair needed a trim and hadn't been brushed yet today, even though it was six at night. That, apparently, was how serious he was about getting a new job. "Oh, Mallory, believe me, I didn't think you were serious about religion." His words oozed with innuendo.

In truth, I did have questions about God. Big questions that had been plaguing me since Cooper's death. Like why would He take away someone so good, someone who actually searched after all the good in this world, while someone bumbling through life and didn't know what they believed like me got left behind? And why did God keep saving me from life-threatening situations every time I prayed?

I took another bite of my sausage, deciding this train of conversation would only lead to a lengthy debate with my father in which he would pretend to have boatloads of wisdom on such subjects. I likely wouldn't know enough to battle his slick salesman-speak.

So I went with the dating topic. "My friend, Alex, just wants some company. He asked if I'd go. It's a favor." Not entirely true, but Dad didn't need details. I motioned to the pan of sausage and peppers and took another bite. "Help yourself."

Dad had been enjoying my cooking for almost two full weeks now—three meals a day, every day. He'd been promising to look for a job, probably in a bigger city, and at the same time look for another place to live, but I'd seen very little evidence of either.

He took a plate from the cupboard and moved toward the stove, then turned back before he'd served himself anything. "Is this the same Alex you had over the other day? The one you like?"

The day Dad arrived, Alex had been visiting for coffee, and to my humiliation, he had heard Dad and I talking about my middle school crush on him. I didn't need a reminder of that. "No…I mean, yes, it's the same person, but no, I don't like him. Not in that way. Not anymore. Like I told you, we're just friends." I felt like I was twelve years old all over again.

Dad reached for the spatula and served himself three sausages and some pepper slices. I took my last bite, thanking my lucky stars he was finally going to let this conversation go and get something to eat. But just as I did, he motioned with the spatula and said, "So that's why you're all gussied up with your hair and your makeup?"

"I'm in jeans, Dad." I tried to use my most convincing tone, but I didn't address the hair and makeup comment, nor the way my turtleneck and favorite jeans hugged my body. While I usually wore a headband to keep my hair back for cooking, tonight I'd left it down to frame my face. I liked the look, I decided, but my face warmed again as I wondered if Alex would like it, too.

"It's nothing more than two friends going out for an evening." My words sounded less and less convincing by the minute.

"Mm-hmm." Dad chuckled and headed for my small kitchen table with his plate. "But if this guy shows up with chocolates and flowers, I'm going to say, 'I told you so.'"

Now I laughed, too, because Alex would not be showing up with anything but his Bible. The doorbell rang right as I helped myself to a slice of red pepper from the pan. I often snacked while cooking, so I'd had plenty to eat, but these honey-glazed sausages and charred peppers had a tangy, addictive quality that had me coming back for more.

I headed to the door to let Alex in and heard Dad's chair jostle back on the tile kitchen floor as I did. Either he was already headed for seconds, or he planned to check Alex out.

I sighed, knowing exactly which option was true. Forcing a smile, I pulled the door open.

"Hi, Al—" My eyes went from his smiling face to a twelve-inch square gold box in his hands.

He outstretched it toward me. "Hey, Mallory." When I didn't immediately reach for the gift he'd brought me, he went on. "Remember how I told you my mom makes the best chocolates every year for Thanksgiving?" He had mentioned that one of the many times when I wouldn't shut up about the foods I loved most. He outstretched the box an inch more toward me. "She just sent me a box, and of course I had to share them with my favorite foodie."

I let out the breath I'd been unconsciously holding. Right. Good food, from one foodie to another. Nothing more. This wasn't the flowers and chocolate date customs my father had been talking about only moments ago.

But I could hear Dad chuckling under his breath in the kitchen doorway behind me. All in one motion, I took the box from Alex and spun around to face my dad. "Alex brought some of his mom's homemade chocolates to see what I thought of them. That's all." I wondered if Alex would find my phrasing strange. Dad's smile had turned gleeful, and I felt the need to do anything to get him to calm down his overly romanticized thoughts.

So even though my first impulse was not to share my delicious chocolate, I popped open the lid to the box in hopes that him seeing and tasting them might help him back off.

But the second I had the lid open, I couldn't avoid my warming cheeks or my dad's louder chuckle.

Because the homemade chocolates? They had been formed into the shape of flowers.

☐

# CHAPTER TWO

I'd been in Alex's late 90s model Toyota for a full five minutes before I could work up the courage to say something.

"My dad's just…" And then I couldn't come up with the words. Before we'd left my house, my father had said loud and clear, "Flowers and chocolate? Well, as long as this isn't a date."

Alex had laughed uncomfortably and then cleared his throat, only to say nothing. I quickly suggested we should get going. And then the silent car ride followed.

"He's eager for me to get back on the dating horse," I finally finished.

Alex raised his eyebrows and looked over at me for a quick second before setting his eyes back on the road in front of us. "That's what I am, huh?" He smirked.

And then he neighed.

I burst out laughing—so much so, it brought tears to my eyes.

Thankfully, Alex had no problem with this conversation now that I'd started it. "Like I told you, Mallory. I'm not in any rush, even if your dad is. I know how to handle dads. Remember, mine's no picnic, either."

I smiled my thanks over at him for his understanding and grace. Alex wasn't kidding about the problems with his dad. Before moving out of town, his dad had made such a bad name for himself within the police department, Alex still felt the repercussions from his police captain.

"Unless…" Alex started thoughtfully, but I thought I still heard a joke in his tone. "We could go the other way with it. Tell your dad I'm moving in. Maybe that'll get rid of him sooner?"

I laughed. I'd told Alex several times via text how eager I was for my dad to leave. "I doubt it. My dad wouldn't know how to take a hint, even if I spelled it out in multi-colored magnetic letters on the fridge for him." I didn't have a chance to say more, or set my thoughts too much on the idea

233

of Alex moving in, because his cell phone chimed.

He clicked on his aftermarket Bluetooth and said, "Detective Martinez here."

"Well, hello there, detective." The teenage voice through the car speaker was one I recognized, although I'd admittedly never heard it so flirtatious.

"Oh, hey, Amber. What's up?" As usual, Alex seemed clueless to Amber's crush, which I supposed made sense, given their age difference. But I'd been a young girl with crushes once, and so they were likely easier for me to spot.

"Just doing homework. What's up with you?" I got the distinct impression from Amber's words that these phone calls were regular—maybe even daily—occurrences.

"Just headed to my Bible study," he told her. "So I'll have my phone off for a few hours."

I raised my eyebrows. Maybe even more than daily occurrences, from the sounds of things.

"How's your homework going?" Alex shot me an apologetic look, but I held up a hand, encouraging him to go ahead. He did. She talked about math problems she was struggling with, and I was surprised that even over the phone and while driving, he could help with high school algebra.

The more I thought about it, I realized maybe Alex was more astute than I'd given him credit for. So far, he hadn't mentioned my presence, after all.

Now that my humiliation had subsided from my dad's innuendo, I paid attention to the road in front of us for the first time. We were well beyond the streetlights of Honeysuckle Grove, climbing a road on one of the surrounding hills. Alex seemed to know the way without his GPS, so I relaxed back into my seat and listened to algebra talk.

Eventually, Amber was all talked out on the subject, and Alex said, "Listen, I'm almost at the place. I should probably go."

"All right." Amber didn't sound offended. In fact, she sounded almost too casual as she added, "Call me when you're done. You know, if you want."

"You bet." Alex hung up, and a few seconds of silence ensued.

I had to ask. "How long has that been going on?" My voice came out strained, and I wondered if it would sound like jealousy of my fifteen-year-old friend.

Alex shrugged. "She needs a bit of a father figure these days. Not that I have much training in the parenting department, but…"

Alex had a better understanding of the situation than I thought, maybe even better than me. "You should give yourself some credit. You seem to have a pretty good handle on what she needs." In fact, I felt somewhat relieved I wasn't the only adult trying to fill the hole that losing her dad and taking care of her grief-filled mother had created. "How often does she call?"

Rather than give a direct answer, he said, "Don't worry, she knows better than to be a burden." He turned farther up the mountain.

I squinted out the window in front of us. "Where is this Bible study?"

"It's at a local winery."

"Ooh, that sounds fun." It also sounded a little strange. I hadn't grown up in the church, but I'd always had the sense that religious people didn't go to places like wineries or have much in the way of unrestrained excitement in their lives. Of course, I'd been proven wrong about the excitement part more than once in recent months. Solving murders that had taken place in what I thought was a quiet community churchgoing town had been more excitement than I'd been looking for.

"It's somewhere different each week," Alex explained. "Ours is a pretty big group, probably something like fifteen couples. We hold it in a room at the local library if we can't find another big enough space. It makes sense that one of these places up here might have room for us."

"Wait, is it all couples?" My face flushed before the words were out of my mouth.

"No, no. My buddy, Tom, should be there. And Benji. And probably Jennifer."

Jennifer's name was the only one I recognized. Our church gossip, Donna Mayberry, regularly whispered about someone from the church named Jennifer who had been scheduled to speak on TV in Charleston. I wondered if it was the same lady.

Alex flicked his signal to the left when a lit sign near a driveway came into view. It read: SYCAMORE RIDGE WINERY.

Alex turned into the driveway, which led us to an open gravel parking lot. Half a dozen cars were already parked there, but there were no people in sight.

"Wow, it's really pretty." My gaze drifted around at the tiny white lights in the sycamore trees. There were larger, strung lights off to our right, highlighting the vineyard, and a gravel uphill path straight ahead. A wooden sign beside the path pointed to the winery.

"I guess it's that way," Alex said. We got out of the car and walked past the sign.

"It sounds like a bigger Bible study than I was expecting." I kept pace with him. As we stepped onto the path, we were canopied by arching tree branches, which gave it the feeling of walking down the aisle at a country wedding. The tiny white lights sprinkled throughout tree branches led our way. Some had come loose from their arch, and one or both of us found ourselves ducking every so often, so as not to get snagged in the face or the hair.

"What were you expecting?"

I shrugged. "I've never been to a Bible study, so actually, I had no idea. I thought maybe ten people. And food." I lifted the carry tray I'd brought along with a five-cheese dip, crackers, and veggies.

"Well, I know everyone will appreciate your cooking."

I nibbled my lip, wondering if I'd brought enough for such a large crowd.

"So you've never been to a Bible study at all? Even when you lived in Pennsylvania?"

I squirmed my shoulders. Everything about God still felt like a sweater that didn't quite fit. "Cooper was more the churchgoer than me. My family didn't go to church much growing up."

"That's why your dad had that smirk whenever I said the words 'Bible study'?" He said it lightly, completely nonjudgmental, which made it easy to respond.

"That would be why."

The path opened to a grassy area at the top of the hill, and a well-lit two-story cedar building reminiscent of an oversized log cabin came into view. It had been raining earlier today, and I could smell the wood. Once, for about six months, I'd lived with Dad and Leslie in a log cabin in the woods. It had been the cheapest place Dad could find. It only had a fireplace for heat, and he apparently got it for a steal because of the repairs he promised to do. He'd never accomplished any of them, and eventually, we'd been kicked out. Despite that, the scent of cedar and outdoors still held fond memories for me.

Along a top balcony, a couple stood, overlooking the vineyard and sipping from wine glasses. This didn't seem like any kind of Bible study I had ever envisioned. The word "date" in my dad's mocking voice came back to mind, and my cheeks warmed.

Alex held up a hand and waved toward the couple. They waved back.

"Come on." He touched me on the small of my back to lead me toward the cedar structure. "I can't wait for you to meet everyone."

Just inside the front door to the winery, a twentysomething blond man greeted us. "Alex! So glad you could come!"

"Benji! This is your place?" Alex asked, clearly astonished.

"My parents." Benji looked down to where a tiny white Maltese dog rubbed up against his leg. It looked like a little toy. "You two aren't allergic, are you?"

Alex shook his head and started to speak, but I bent to greet the cute little bundle of fur. "This is Mallory. Mallory, this is Benji. I don't know if you two know each other from church…"

I shook my head, placed my box of cheese dip and crackers to the side, and looked up. "Hi, Benji. And who's this little guy?"

The dog left Benji's leg alone to check out my food tray.

"Now, now. That's not for you," I told him. Thankfully, when I started to scratch him behind his ears, he lost interest in the snacks.

"This is my parents' dog, Riesling."

I chuckled at the perfect name for a winery's mascot. "Not allergic," I confirmed. "This is a beautiful place your parents have." I stood and held out the covered tray. The cord for the cheese dip's slow cooker dangled below. "I brought a warm five-cheese dip. Where should I put it?"

Benji motioned over his shoulder toward a long oak bar, where two couples appeared to be arguing—one behind the bar and one in front of it.

Benji didn't seem to notice and smiled at me with one side of his mouth. "That will go great with the wine. Why don't you set it up on the bar and my parents can find you a place to plug it in?"

The couple nearest to me shook their heads at the couple behind the bar and moved away to a quiet table near the back of the large room. The couple behind the bar now wore grins, so the disagreement couldn't have been serious.

I thanked Benji and headed to the bar. Warm cheese dip was a whole different experience than cold and crumbly cheese dip. Alex began to tag along, but then got distracted along the way by another couple he knew. "Go ahead," I told him. "I'll join you in a minute."

After I quickly surveyed the large open room filled with high wooden tables and matching barstools, it seemed that other than Benji, most of the people milling around with coffee cups in hand were indeed couples.

A man in the far corner played background music on his guitar, loud enough that I had to raise my voice to greet the couple behind the bar.

"Hi," I said to Benji's parents, a couple with blondish-white hair. They were busy opening wine bottles and placing clean glasses face down on a black cloth along the bar. "Benji said I might be able to plug this in somewhere over here?" I held the slow cooker out of the carry tray to show them.

"Of course!" The woman reached for my slow cooker, which only had a short cord, and plugged it in on a wooden beam joining the bar to the ceiling. "I'm Marie Tallman, and this is my husband, Don."

"Hi there," the man, Don, said.

Don and Marie. Before my mom left, she used to play music by a brother/sister team named Donny and Marie, so I doubted I would forget this couple's names.

"I'm Mallory." I placed my container of a variety of crackers and veggies near the cheese dip. Along the bar, there was also a store-bought veggie tray, what looked like a tray of store-bought cookies, and two bowls of wrapped chocolates. This didn't seem like much of a homemade food crowd, so hopefully, my cheese dip would be a hit. "How long have you owned the winery?"

Marie smiled at her husband. "We bought the land fifteen years ago, but the vineyard had been neglected by the former owners, so it took us a few years to get a good harvest. We're finally hoping to make it profitable this year. Are you familiar with our wines?"

I shook my head. "To be honest, I don't even know what kinds of wine I like. My late husband, Cooper, used to choose the wine."

Don and Marie both tilted their heads at me. But thankfully, the subject of wine, a subject they clearly loved, quickly snapped them out of the Head Tilt of Pity.

"I think she'll like our Riesling," Marie said to her husband. "Grab it from the cooler for me, hon?"

"I do like your Riesling." I motioned to their dog, but neither of them seemed to get my joke. In truth, I had become more of a cat person, thanks to Cooper's moody feline. Cooper and I used to buy the odd bottle of wine, usually in celebration of a big achievement. I couldn't remember the last time I'd had a glass of wine, but it sounded like a lovely treat.

Don moved to a large cooling fridge behind him and returned seconds later with an uncorked bottle. He poured me a surprisingly large portion and passed it over.

"This is a sweet variety, with notes of apricot and Honeycrisp apple. If you like it, you might also enjoy our pinot blanc. Or if you're a fan of red, you might like our port or our new blackberry wine."

I nodded and tried a sip. Honeycrisp apples were my favorite variety, so I paused and closed my eyes, searching for the flavor, but I felt out of my element on the subject of wine subtleties.

When I opened my eyes, the Tallmans both stared at me in anticipation of my response. Because I had nothing intelligent to say on the subject, I simply offered an "Mmm," followed by a change of subject. "Cute dog, by the way."

"Yup, he's a keeper," Don said. "You'd never know it by his size, but Riese is quite the little watchdog."

Just then, Alex came up behind me. He'd been chatting to several couples since we'd arrived, so I felt some sort of comfort in being able to introduce him to the one couple in the place he didn't know.

"Don and Marie, this is my friend, Alex Martinez. He's a detective with the local police department."

Alex extended his hand and they both shook his, an air of respect noticeable on both of them. Don said, "Thank you for your service in our town."

Alex, being newly promoted to detective, squirmed a little at the acknowledgment, but he said, "Thank you for having us here," just the same.

"Can I get you a glass of something to try?" Marie asked. "Or are you on duty tonight?"

Alex held up a hand. "Not on duty, no, but I'm driving, so I think I'll pass."

"Feel free to grab a plate of snacks and help yourself to somewhere to sit." Marie offered a hand toward the room.

I turned to look around for some empty seats, but when I did, I didn't think I was imagining the hard glares that came at me from almost everyone in the room. The only people who weren't glaring were Benji, the couple he was greeting at the door, and the couple at the back table who had been arguing with the Tallmans at the bar a few minutes ago. That couple now had their heads bowed and appeared to be in prayer.

Marie motioned to a nearby stairwell. "Or head upstairs if you like. There's a beautiful view of the vineyard, and you can enjoy your wine up there."

I tilted my head, recalling the couple with wine glasses on the upper floor. It definitely felt more like a wine tasting event than what I'd imagined of a Bible study, and I wondered if the people on this lower floor weren't too happy about the free-flowing wine.

I had an urge to replace my glass on the counter before taking another sip, but I also didn't want to offend Don and Marie.

Alex reached for a small plate. "I'm definitely trying the cheese dip. This lady…" he nudged me with his elbow. "She can really cook."

A blush warmed my face as Marie took his advice and helped herself to some crackers topped with cheesy goodness. With her first bite, her eyes widened and she said, "I have got to get your recipe!"

I nodded in agreement, but my mind was still on what to do about this full glass of wine. I was about to suggest to Alex that we take a look upstairs when the front door to the winery opened and a woman with black hair and dark angry eyes held out her hands and yelled, "A winery? Are you kidding me?"

☐

# CHAPTER THREE

"Uh-oh," Alex murmured to me. "That's Jennifer Rempel."

I was glad to see her, if for no other reason than she seemed to be the only other single person in the bunch. She looked vaguely familiar—definitely the same Jennifer gossiping Donna Mayberry talked about regularly. Now that I saw her, the last tidbit of gossip Donna had shared came back to me: Jennifer was getting a divorce, which, by Donna's tone, all of the rest of the church ladies were supposed to find scandalous.

But I always found it truly unfortunate when a couple didn't grow old together, as they had once anticipated and hoped for.

If she were divorced, though, this Jennifer certainly looked as though she'd pulled herself together. Her super-shiny black hair was held back with a tiny silver comb on one side and her long bangs covered one eye on the other. The stylish hair matched her chic wardrobe of trendy holey jeans, little black high-heeled booties, and a dark angled poncho that matched the line of her bangs.

Benji hurried over to greet Jennifer, and from our twenty feet away, I couldn't hear what he was saying, but his constant nodding and splayed hands told me he was trying very hard to calm the woman down.

Riesling jumped up and down at Benji's legs, barking as though perturbed by the agitated new visitor. Jennifer didn't actually kick the dog, but she moved one bootie in his direction, which made the dog jump back and shut up, at least momentarily.

"She's a regular?" I whispered to Alex. He'd said so on the drive here, but I had trouble believing it.

The couple from the upstairs balcony came down the stairs, empty wine glasses in hand, and paused at the commotion.

Alex nodded hesitantly. "She wasn't coming for a while, but she's been back again the last few weeks. I think it has something to do with her marriage, but she's always been tight-lipped about her husband."

I opened my mouth, but then closed it again. I wasn't about to spread Donna Mayberry's gossip, no matter how much evidence there was to its truth.

Jennifer Rempel ranted on about her dislike of the location, but her words tumbled out so fast, I couldn't get a firm grasp on why until she pointed a finger into Benji's chest and said, "Ephesians 5:18 tells us 'Do not get drunk on wine, which leads to debauchery!'"

I set my wine glass down and pushed it a few inches away on the bar.

Benji's voice also became louder. "Nobody's getting drunk here, Jennifer."

Don and Marie made their way over. Marie held a tray containing a half-filled wine glass and a bowl of nuts from the counter—a bold move toward someone so angry about the option of drinking, I thought. But they were only a few feet away when Marie spoke and added some understanding.

"We have fruit juices and non-alcoholic wine as well, dear. Would you like some—"

Marie didn't get her full sentence out before Jennifer marched straight at her and swung a hand up toward the tray, knocking it clear out of Marie's hands. Everybody in the room froze at the sound of glass shattering on the dark wood floor.

One silent second passed. Then two.

Benji cleared his throat. "Jennifer, I think it's best if you leave."

"Ha! Sure! Leave you to your debauchery?" She spun on her heel. "I can't get out of here fast enough, and you'd better believe I'll be warning the local police to keep an eye out for any of you on the road tonight." She was about to reach for the door handle but then spun back and pointed an accusing finger right at Alex. "In fact, there's a cop right here! How could you let this happen?"

She didn't wait for an answer but marched out the door and slammed it behind her.

When I looked over, Marie was already down on her hands and knees with a small handheld broom, sweeping up the mess of glass. The attendees for the evening gave her a wide berth.

Don walked over to meet Benji near the door, and I also gravitated closer, wondering how this woman could have gotten so upset so quickly. I must have been missing something.

"You need to go after her, son," Don said. "Make sure she understands we weren't about to serve more than one glass of wine to anyone who's planning to drive. We don't need the cops here. It's bad enough that we already have one."

Benji rolled his eyes, a hardness coming over his face I hadn't seen before. "She's a hardnosed spokesperson for Mothers Against Drunk Drivers. She takes on entire groups who want to lower the drinking age in West Virginia or soften the penalties against drunk drivers. She was on TV just last week. She's not going to listen to me, Dad."

"I guess you should have thought of that before inviting her to our winery for your Bible study. You need to make her listen." Benji's dad held open the door for his son. Apparently, this wasn't up for negotiation. "Our reputation is at stake. Go fix this!" He gave his son a little shove out the door.

Benji shook his head, but went. The guitar player, who had paused when the glass had shattered, resumed his playing now, louder, as if somehow that could erase the tension in the room. As soon as the door closed behind Benji, I turned, mostly to avoid Don's hardened stare, but when I did, Alex strode toward me from a nearby table.

"I did a little asking around, and apparently, Jennifer found out on Monday at a coffee shop that our Bible study would be held at the winery. Her shock was an act." Alex let out a long sigh. "It's not the first cause Jennifer's taken up at our Bible study, not by a long shot, but this is the most passionate I've seen her."

"I overheard that she's a spokesperson for Mothers Against Drunk Drivers." I looked around to find Don and tell Alex about the conversation I'd eavesdropped on, but he seemed to have disappeared somewhere either upstairs or out the back door.

Small groupings of people formed throughout the room, and rather than donning that excitement-inducing look that Donna Mayberry often adopted when something out of the ordinary happened, worry lines creased most of their foreheads. Soon, Marie had cleaned up the broken glass and spilled nuts and stood behind the bar with a forced smile. Nobody would be approaching her for wine, though, that was for sure.

"Is it normal to have wine at a Bible study?" I asked, honestly not knowing.

"No, and to be honest, I'm a little surprised," Alex said. "Most of the group are non-drinkers, as far as I know. Nothing like this has ever happened."

"I guess we'd better get started," a fiftysomething man in wire-rimmed glasses said, coming from the back of the room. It was the man who had been praying with his wife earlier.

"That's Gordon Lam," Alex whispered to me. "He leads the Bible study."

Gordon held a black Bible in his right hand. His wife, a trim older woman who wore jeans and had a short gray pixie cut, followed him toward an empty space of wall without any tables. He spoke to the nearby guitar player, but whatever he said, the guitar player only shook his head in response and continued playing.

Several people left their seats to go and convey their concern to Mr. Lam, taking his attention.

"I'd better help him calm everyone down." Alex touched my arm before heading toward the Bible study leader.

I moved closer to the bar, where Marie was busy cleaning wine glasses and shaking her head every few seconds.

"Would you like some more wine?" she started to hold up the Riesling bottle, but then added, "Oh, or are you driving tonight?"

Jennifer Rempel's outburst had shaken Marie, but not enough to make her refrain from serving their wine.

"I'm not driving, but I'm not a big drinker," I said, wondering if she'd noticed the full wine glass I'd left behind. It was gone now. "It was delicious, though," I added truthfully.

"You should come in for a full tasting sometime, dear," she told me. She seemed glad to have someone calm to converse with, but part of me felt as though I was making enemies with the rest of the room just by my proximity to the bar. "We have twelve varieties in all, from sweet dessert wines to drier varieties. A wine tasting is a nice thing to do on a date night." She motioned her chin in Alex's direction, and I felt my face warm.

Thankfully, my embarrassment didn't last long, as Gordon Lam had gotten everyone to return to their seats.

"I think we should get started," Gordon said, his deep voice full of authority. "I had planned to do a little worship and then continue with our series on Romans, but in light of what has happened, how many of you would prefer to have a thoughtful discussion on what the Bible has to say on the subject of drinking?"

A number of hands went up from around the room, and he opened his Bible. From a dozen feet away, I could tell it was full of highlights, and he flipped pages, apparently looking for somewhere specific to begin. The guitar player stopped playing, but kept his hand on his guitar, as though he might start again at any moment. There had to be twenty-five or thirty people here, and now that everyone had returned to their seats, the room felt full. I swiped a cracker into my barely touched cheese dip and then turned to face Gordon on my barstool. Alex headed over to join me.

But before he could get to me, before Gordon could find the first Bible verse he wanted to start the meeting with, before the cheesy cracker had even made it into my mouth, a shrill woman's scream erupted from outside the cedar building.

# CHAPTER FOUR

For the second time tonight, everyone in the winery froze in silence. Alex made a move for the door, but the second he had it open, Riesling darted out through the opening.

"Riesey!" Marie called. "You get back here!" She rushed toward the door after her dog.

Alex left the door open and rushed forward to see if someone outside was in trouble. By the time I made it to the door, others around the room had stood and pulled on their jackets.

When I got outside, I could see one last glimpse of Alex's brown leather jacket disappearing in between two rows of bushes. I angled in that direction and picked up my pace. The twinkle lights extended down every second row of bushes, adding a pretty ambiance but not much light. As I pulled out my flashlight and got glimpses of either side of the dirt row I headed down, it looked to me like blackberry bushes, not grapevines, as I was expecting.

I shone my light ahead of me enough to see Alex, who had turned on his own much brighter flashlight up ahead. He called out, "Who's out here? Can you hear me? Is everything okay?" The rumbling of a tractor in the distance muffled his words. "Are you all right?"

His flashlight beam was more frantic than mine, and I wondered if he had any idea which direction he should be looking. The scream seemed like it had come from the direction of the vineyard and not the parking lot, but the more I shone my flashlight around in the dark, the bigger the vineyard seemed to become.

As I continued moving forward, slowly catching up to Alex, another sound led my way. The quiet bark of a small dog. That's when I realized I could no longer hear the tractor.

I followed the sound of the dog, as did Alex, but seconds later, he dropped to his hands and knees. Riesling had ducked through a hole in the bushes. I'd almost caught up to Alex when he turned to me and said, "He's down the next row. We'll have to go around."

He sprang to his feet and took doubly large steps toward the end of the row and then around to the next one. I did my best to keep up, but by the time Alex had woven down the next row and then two more after that, I'd fallen a fair way behind.

It felt like Riesling was leading us in circles, or at the very least into a maze of grapevines we'd never find our way out of. I was out of breath, but my eyes had finally started to adjust to the dimness when the dog finally stopped in place, barking much louder. Alex rushed up and stopped not far behind him.

Little Riesling was agitated by something at a T intersection of two grapevine rows, barking and turning in circles. It only took me a second to get around Alex enough to see the object of his agitation.

Jennifer Rempel was faceup on the ground, eyes open, with a corkscrew protruding from her neck.

No sooner had we stopped when Alex talked quietly into his cell phone. He spoke more in numbers than in words, giving the department codes about what had transpired. Riesling was getting close to Jennifer, sniffing at the corkscrew sticking out of her throat. Any second, he'd have her crimson blood marring his bright white fur.

I quickly snatched him up in my arms, ran a hand over his head, and told him, "It's okay," even though everything about this was far from okay. It turned out that it wasn't a T intersection of rows after all. Once my eyes adjusted, I could make out the shrubs on either side, effectively making this row a dead-end.

Alex stayed busy on the phone when the rest of the crowd from the Bible study trickled toward us down the row of grapevines. Many of them were using their phones as flashlights. I cut off their progress before they could get within view of Jennifer's body and held up my hands.

"Folks, there's been an accident out here. Please make your way back to the winery and wait there. Detective Martinez will be back shortly to fill you in."

Couples murmured to one another. Marie, at the front of the brigade, reached for her pup from my arms, and I quickly passed him over.

"Riesey, are you okay?" Her voice trembled with the seriousness of what had gone down, even if she hadn't seen it.

Her eyes moved back and forth over mine, as though she might be able to read in my face what had transpired only a dozen feet behind me. While she paused there, Riesling couldn't contain his agitation and tried to jump from her arms. He seemed to be trying to snap at the nearby twinkle lights, like he knew this was no moment for pretty décor.

"I'd get him back inside if I were you," I told her.

"But…this is our vineyard. What's going on?"

I shook my head, glad I didn't have the authority to tell her. "Alex will be back soon, and he'll talk to you just as soon as he can."

Finally, she turned and hurried off with her little dog. Each of the other Bible study attendees met my eyes for a few seconds before following her lead, and soon Alex and I were alone, or at least as alone as two people could be with a dead body at their feet. He hung up his phone, shining the flashlight around at what clearly had been another murder.

"Could you go back to the winery and make sure nobody leaves before my team can get here and question them? Keep a close eye on the Tallmans—" Alex cut off his words when his flashlight beam landed on a pair of dirty white sneakers. He followed them upward to a stout man in his forties with a few days' facial growth. "What are you doing out here?" Alex asked, clearly taken off guard. "What's your name?"

"I could ask the same thing of y'all." The gruff man had his own flashlight and shone it right into Alex's eyes. "Whatcha all done to this woman?"

"Sir, I'm Detective Martinez from the Honeysuckle Grove Police Department. I'll ask you again, who you are and what is your purpose out here?"

When the man spoke again, his words were much less hostile, more nervous. "I ain't doin' nothin'. I work out here. Just ask the Tallmans."

"Oh, I will," Alex said. "And your name, please, sir?"

"Kristoph," he said. "Kristoph Carter."

"And why were you out here in the dark, Mr. Carter?"

"I was sure I heard the tractor out here." He looked in all directions, as though he might not have noticed a tractor sitting near us.

"Do you live on the property?" I asked.

Kristoph nodded, but couldn't keep his eyes away from the body on the ground. "Who's she? What happened to her?"

"That's what I'm trying to find out." Alex pulled his notepad and pen from his jacket pocket and started scribbling notes. Kristoph bent, as though he was going to reach out and touch the corkscrew in Jennifer's neck. Without looking up from his notes, Alex added, "I'll ask you please not to touch anything."

Kristoph stood back up.

"Are there other workers living here on the property?" Alex asked. "Anyone else who would've been driving a tractor at night?"

Kristoph shook his head.

"Did you see anyone else in the vineyard while looking for the tractor?"

Alex asked.

Kristoph started to shake his head, but then said, "Actually, yeah, but it was a while ago. I knew Benji was having some kinda meeting, so I figured she just got lost out here on her way to the winery. When strangers walk around out here at night, sometimes they kick the rat traps by accident. I was plannin' to do a walk-through, make sure they were all still armed. You don't know what kinda heck rats can cause with the vines."

"No, I'm sure I don't," Alex said. "How long ago was this, that you saw the woman?"

Kristoph shrugged. "Half an hour. Maybe more."

"And what did this woman you saw look like? Are you certain it wasn't the woman here?" He motioned to Jennifer, but he didn't give her name to Kristoph.

Kristoph's forehead creased as his gaze returned to Jennifer. Sirens sounded from the distance, quickly growing louder. "Nah, she was a stocky woman, not skinny like this one, but I didn't see much else. I called out that the winery was thataway and she took off without looking back at me."

"Stocky, and what else can you tell me about this woman?" Alex's pen was poised over his paper.

Kristoph shook his head. "Nothin'. Like I said, I didn't get a good look at her out here in the dark."

"Just the same, I'd like you to meet with our sketch artist and see if you can think of anything else. Where's your house from here?"

Kristoph hesitated, blinking at Alex a few times before he pointed off in the opposite direction from the winery. "Just a loft above the barn. Mr. and Mrs. Tallman put me up there for watching over their place through the night."

Alex nodded. "And you know their son, Benji? You didn't see him out in the vineyard tonight?"

"Nah, he was having some kinda party in the winery." Kristoph stood with his feet apart, fists balled at his sides. A protective stance. I wondered what he was feeling protective of—the winery he took care of? Or the Tallmans?

Alex nodded, and as voices of emergency workers approached, coming to find us, he shone his flashlight in the air and called, "Over here!" Then he turned to me. "Mallory, would you escort Mr. Carter to the winery and be sure no one leaves? I'll update everyone shortly." Alex leaned in and murmured so only I could hear, "See if he recognizes the woman among the people inside. Text me if he does."

I had no idea what I would tell the folks at the Bible study until Alex came back with his update, but if he asked me to do something that would help his investigation, I would be sure to do it.

Besides, it would give me a few minutes to find out a little more about

Jennifer Rempel and why someone might have wanted her dead.

# CHAPTER FIVE

Kristoph Carter followed me silently to the winery, and I could only hope that if he had a corkscrew in his pocket, Alex would hear my scream and get to me before it was too late.

But I didn't get the sense that this man was a killer. Protective over the winery, sure, but he quickly came under Alex's police authority.

It turned out, I didn't have to keep much in the way of secrets by the time I returned to the winery. Someone had gotten a glimpse of Jennifer Rempel, and word had gotten around that she was most certainly dead.

Low whispers sounded from all around the open room. Things like "I can't believe she's dead," and "Who would want to do that to her?" No one sat anymore, but instead, everyone stood in small groupings having hushed conversations.

"Does anyone look familiar as the woman you saw in the vineyard?" I asked Kristoph quietly. "Or is anyone familiar at all?"

He surveyed the room. Benji and his parents stood behind the bar, having their own hushed conversation. "Well, yeah, the Tallmans. But, nah, no one else."

The wine bottles from earlier had all been put away, and no one seemed interested in either coffee or snacks.

Mr. Tallman and Benji, I reminded myself, hadn't been in the open winery room when Jennifer screamed from the vineyard. All three of the Tallmans seemed visibly shaken, moving things hyperactively around behind the bar.

"You're certain you don't see the woman who you saw out in the vineyard earlier?"

Kristoph shook his head. I asked him to have a seat and wait for the police, and then I made a quick announcement, letting everyone know that

Detective Martinez had asked everyone to remain inside the winery until he could get here to talk with them.

Then I headed straight for the bar and used the task of packing up my small warming pot of cheese and crackers as an excuse to stay a few minutes there.

"Is Alex still out there?" Benji asked as soon as I was within earshot.

I nodded. "By now he probably has a whole team scouring the place."

Benji looked to his dad, but Don Tallman kept his gaze on his wife. Then he made a move toward the door. "I should go and help—"

"Actually, Detective Martinez has asked that everyone remain inside for the moment." Did he not hear me the first time? "People moving around throughout the vineyard could easily tamper with any evidence."

"Evidence?" Don said. "What do they think happened? Someone was murdered on our property?"

It struck me as self-serving that the focus for him was immediately on their property and not on the woman who had died.

"I'm afraid I don't know what to tell you, but Detective Martinez will be back with an update soon."

Don looked again at the door, but didn't make any move toward it.

I turned to Benji. "Did you know Jennifer well?"

Benji reached for a coffee cup, but his hand shook as he filled it. He took a sip without adding cream or sugar, and I couldn't help but think black coffee was probably the last thing he needed at the moment.

"We've been attending the same Bible study for probably a year," he finally said, "but she wasn't coming for a while. It's hard to keep track of everyone with such a large group." Benji flailed his hands as he spoke and then motioned to the full room around him.

"I bet," I said. "So those types of arguments weren't common between the two of you?"

His eyes widened at my question, but only for a second. Then he seemed to force calm onto his face. "It wasn't really an argument. I mean, I get why she was upset. She has—er, had—some strong opinions. I probably should have considered that before offering the winery for tonight's Bible study location." Guilt leaked out in his voice.

"It is a beautiful location," I said, leaving off the part I really wanted to say—that just because he offered the space, it didn't mean his parents had to bring out their wine. Looking back on their lengthy explanations about their different varieties, I suspected the whole family had looked at tonight as some sort of publicity push for the winery, rather than just a Bible study.

I couldn't imagine one angry lady intercepting their plan as enough reason to want to kill her, but I still had the feeling the Tallmans were either dishonest or, at the very least, incredibly self-serving.

I decided to try a new tack. "Do you know if Jennifer Rempel had enemies within the group?" I asked Benji. "Anyone who truly disliked her?"

Benji surveyed the room and then leaned closer across the bar, almost conspiratorially. "Dahlia Richards…" He motioned across the room with his chin at a bronze-skinned heavyset woman in a tight black turtleneck and equally tight jeans. "Those two were competitive to the core, always bragging to each other about everything from their diets to their kids."

"They both had kids of the same age?" I confirmed. I had a notebook and pen in my purse, but I held back from retrieving it, not wanting to look like I was asking questions in a professional capacity. I wasn't doing that, after all. Not this time.

Benji nodded. "I hear even their boys have been competing for spots on the primary soccer team. Dahlia's been jealous of Jennifer for a long time. Dahlia always contradicted anything Jennifer had to say about her latest diet, making comments like how it must be nice to be naturally thin. Jennifer often traveled to speak on TV, and Dahlia has been clearly jealous of that, saying it must be nice to have people fly you on vacation all the time."

I studied Dahlia Richards from across the room. She was shaking her head at a man in his fifties, looking just as upset as everyone else in the room. Could she have truly been that jealous of someone within the Bible study? Or was Benji simply trying to get me off his trail? I couldn't recall if I'd seen Dhalia Richards and the older man with her before we'd all headed outside to investigate the scream.

"So you didn't catch up with Jennifer outside?" I asked, not willing to be diverted, at least not for the moment. "I heard your dad had wanted you to go after Jennifer and calm her down."

Don Tallman had moved to the far end of the bar, where he was hunched over a laptop computer. Benji glanced at his dad, but then turned back to me to answer. "I…uh…no. I couldn't find her. I thought she'd already driven off, but her red Honda was still in the parking lot, so I called out, but she never answered. I got distracted, tying back some branches that had come down along the path. Next thing I knew, I heard a scream from the vineyard and came running."

I didn't recall seeing him in the crowd near Jennifer's body, but that didn't necessarily mean anything. However, there still things that didn't add up. Like the length of time he was outside. If he hadn't found her in the parking lot, could he have really been tying back branches for the entire time that Gordon Lam had been calming everyone down and trying to get the meeting started? He must have been looking for her, and where else to look besides the vineyard?

Also, if he claimed not to know her well, how did he know she drove a red Honda?

But before I could ask these questions, the door opened and Alex walked through it, followed by his partner, Detective Mickey Bradley. In private, Alex referred to his partner as Mickey Mouse because of his incompetence. Mickey Mouse didn't have much love for me, ever since one of the senior detectives in the department had offered me a lot of praise for helping Alex solve his last murder case and almost none for Mickey. Not that he'd deserved any.

When Alex and Mickey walked toward the Tallmans, that was my cue to give them some space. I'd offer any of my help to Alex later.

I knew a few others in the room from seeing them around Honeysuckle Grove Community Church, but not well enough that I'd want to chat with them during a crisis. However, there were a lot of people to question here, and in my experience, sometimes people would relax a little more with me than during an official police interview.

I picked up my carry tray filled with the barely touched crackers, veggies, and cheese dip and angled toward Dahlia Richards and her table. There were four of them altogether, but as I approached, one couple took their leave.

"Can I offer you some crackers and cheese dip?"

"Oh, thank you." Dahlia helped herself to two chunks of celery. She ignored the dip.

I angled the cheese dip closer in her direction, but she still ignored it.

The man with her looked old enough to be her father, but at least he wasn't repellent to cheese. He helped himself to a cracker and lopped on a deep scoop of cheesy goodness.

"Do you mind if I sit?" I asked. When I'd come in, everyone in the room had been standing, but since that time, at least half of the people had settled back onto their barstools. I was certain my bold approach seemed odd, as I'd never spoken to Dahlia or her companion before, but I was getting used to seeming odd when it came to prying for answers.

"I'm Mallory Beck," I said, smiling at Dahlia first, who was probably about my age, and then at her companion. He had gray slicked-back hair and was much slimmer than Dahlia, almost too skinny. I was afraid to ask if they were related, in the event that he was actually her date. "I think I've seen you around the church?"

I asked it as a question because this wasn't entirely true. While Dahlia did look familiar, I didn't know whether I actually recognized her from church. For all I knew, she was like Alex and had to work on Sundays, and took part in Bible studies as her only spiritual enrichment. I didn't recognize the older guy at all.

Dahlia rubbed her lips together. Rather than answering my question, she said, "Did you hear what happened? Who did this to Jen?"

Everyone so far had referred to Ms. Rempel as Jennifer. It seemed odd, if this were the deceased's serious adversary, that they'd be going by nicknames.

"I'm afraid I don't know any more than you do," I said.

"Huh. I just saw you talking with Alex earlier." She motioned her chin toward Alex. I hadn't noticed Dahlia in the winery from before Jennifer stormed out or even before we heard the scream. I wished I'd been paying closer attention to who was in the room.

"Alex Martinez is a friend," I told her honestly. "He invited me tonight, as I've been trying to find my place at church since losing my husband."

Dahlia's pursed her lips, as if doubting I was being truthful about this. Part of me wanted to yell at her that losing my husband was the last thing I would want to imagine if it weren't true. I wasn't sure why her presence seemed to be riling me up inside.

Finally, she nodded. "So you don't know how it happened, then."

She didn't ask it as a question, but I felt a strong antagonism for this woman rising up within me. Both she and Jennifer Rempel weren't the type of easygoing ladies I would make an effort to form friendships with. "I hear you and Jen," I put an emphasis on the nickname to see if Dahlia would react. She didn't. "I hear the two of you didn't get along very well."

Dahlia let out a sigh that ended in a chuckle. "I'd say we keep each other sharp."

"Kept," I amended.

"What's that?"

"You kept each other sharp."

Dahlia's eyes widened, and even though I knew this wasn't the case, it seemed as though right at that second was the first time she truly realized that Jennifer Rempel was dead.

As the information settled in on her, she looked down at the floor and nodded solemnly.

"Were you here? When she screamed?" I asked, not ready to be deterred, no matter how sad she suddenly appeared.

Dahlia looked up at me and blinked a couple of times before saying, "Of course. Bart and I arrived a short time before that and I was one of the first people to follow you and Detective Martinez out the door. You didn't see me?"

I let the silence stretch out, willing to let her be bothered by this notion—if I hadn't seen her, and I was one of the closest people to her, who was to say anyone could place her here among the group of people with an alibi, rather than outside killing someone she was wildly jealous of?

But my silence didn't appear to bother her. She only stared at me with raised eyebrows. I decided a change of subject might give me better information.

"Do you know this winery? Have you been here before?"

At my question, Dahlia's companion stood and asked if he could get anyone coffee. We both shook our heads, but he must have wanted some because he headed for the coffee urn at the bar.

I stared back at Dahlia, and she finally answered. "Bart and I aren't really drinkers, so no, I can't say I've been to the property before tonight." Her eyes flitted to the side, making me think she was lying or hiding something.

"You said you and Jennifer have known each other for some time. Do you know if she had enemies? Do you know anyone who might have wanted to hurt her?"

Dahlia's eyebrows pulled together, and she leaned closer across the round wooden table. "Was it definitely murder?"

I didn't like lying, but it seemed Alex and Mickey Mouse were so busy with the Tallmans, they had yet to find time to make an announcement about what had transpired tonight.

"I couldn't tell you that," I told Dahlia. "But if it was? Who would have done it?"

Dahlia nibbled her lip and looked down at the table, thinking this over. "There's that ex-husband of hers. She never out-and-out said he'd gotten physical with her, but we all suspected it."

"You all?"

She nodded. "A group of us moms meets for coffee on Monday mornings after the kids are in school."

Monday. Wasn't that the day someone had met with Jennifer and heard her complaining about the Bible study being held at a winery?

"Was Jennifer with the rest of you ladies for coffee this last Monday?"

"Sure," Dahlia said. "She was running late because of some MADD meeting, and it was only me and Gina this week, but she was there."

"MADD meeting?" I asked, even though I'd heard about Jennifer's involvement with Mothers Against Drunk Drivers. I was poking to see if this was yet another area Dahlia felt some jealousy toward Jennifer.

"Oh, she's always busy with a cause." Dahlia caught herself. "I mean, she used to be."

"And did you talk about the Bible study on Monday?" I asked. "Anything about the location?"

Dahlia's forehead buckled. "Come to think of it, we did. Gina was there, too. Ask her." Dahlia motioned across the room to a lady with red frizzy hair near the windows. "It's strange how she wouldn't have said anything to Gordon earlier if she was so upset."

Strange indeed.

"So she was upset about it being at a winery then?" I asked. "Even on Monday?"

"More like in shock. Gina mentioned it right near the end of our coffee date. Jennifer couldn't believe it, but by the time she walked off, she said it wasn't going to happen if she had anything to say about it."

"So maybe she did approach Gordon Lam and ask him to move the location?"

I recalled how Gordon and his wife had been arguing at the bar when Alex and I arrived. Perhaps he was trying to get the Tallmans to stop serving wine.

I looked over to where the head of the Bible study sat with his wife. They both had their heads bowed and looked like they were quietly praying together again.

Before Dahlia could answer me, Mickey Mouse cleared his throat and spoke loudly from a couple of steps up the stairwell. "Thank you for being patient with us, folks. I'm afraid there's been a tragic occurrence on the property. We'll ask that none of you leave the premises until either me or my partner, Detective Martinez, has had a chance to talk with you."

I guessed Detective Bradley had yet to understand that the people in the room were already fully aware of who the victim had been and that a death had occurred. Once again, I felt sad for Alex. He'd been paired with the worst detective on the force.

As soon as he was done speaking, Mickey Mouse headed straight for Dahlia Richards. Of course. Mickey Mouse figured he'd head for one of the farthest tables away from him, likely just to chase me away from investigating.

I sighed and stood up. "It looks like Detective Bradley is headed your way. Thanks for talking to me and I'm sorry for your loss. For Jennifer." I wasn't sure exactly how to express my condolences, as I seemed to have been given two completely different understandings of Jennifer's and Dahlia's attitudes toward each other.

I supposed I could go and ask Gina from the Monday morning coffee meetings.

But I decided instead to start with the Bible study leader himself.

Mickey Bradley cleared his throat and spoke in a lower, more authoritative voice than usual. "Now, can I please get your name and what brought you to the Sycamore Ridge Winery tonight?" he asked Dahlia, and I wondered if the incompetent detective hadn't even figured out that much yet.

☐

# CHAPTER SIX

"Hi, I'm Mallory." I stepped up to Gordon Lam and his wife.

Gordon stood to greet me. "Gordon. And this is my wife, Lorna. You were out there with Alex. Can you fill us in on anything?"

I shook my head as I set down my cheese platter. I'd brought it along, as it didn't seem like Dahlia planned on having any. "Not really. You already know they found Jennifer out in the vineyard?"

Gordon nodded, looking down at his open hands. "Somebody said she had a corkscrew protruding from her neck." He winced with the words. I could tell how much this man cared about Jennifer, and probably every other member of the Bible study. He seemed on the verge of tears.

"Yeah," I said quietly. "Have you spoken with Alex or Detective Bradley yet?" I knew he hadn't, but I wasn't sure how else to segue into some questions of my own without seeming completely heartless.

"Not yet, no. But as you know, we were all inside when it happened, so I'm not sure what sorts of things they're wanting to know from us."

I could certainly speak in generalizations, if I couldn't perform a formal questioning. "I understand they're usually just looking for background information on a victim—their state of mind, who they may have had squabbles with, that sort of thing. Did Ms. Rempel contact you at all this week, Mr. Lam?"

Gordon Lam looked at his wife, who immediately looked away. He turned back to me. "I'll admit, she tried to contact me. But I work a full-time job at the titles and deeds office during the week. We played phone tag, and finally, I left a voice mail message telling her we'd have to connect tonight. And please, Mallory, call me Gordon."

I nodded. "Did you have any inclination that she might have a problem with the location of the Bible study for tonight?"

A long silence followed. Gordon met his wife's gaze again, but this time she didn't avert hers. After a long moment, she nodded.

"I…suspected she might have," he finally said.

"Because of something you heard or because of her involvement with Mothers Against Drunk Drivers?"

He looked down sheepishly. "Both."

"And so were you avoiding Jennifer Rempel's phone calls this past week?" This was turning into a full-fledged interrogation, but I couldn't help myself with important information so close. Alex was questioning people on the other side of the room, and I didn't think I could trust Mickey Mouse to ask the right questions.

Gordon sucked in his lower lip and nodded, clearly regretting this fact. "When Benji offered up the use of his parents' winery, I understood it was just the space we'd be using, and no wine would be served. I'll admit, I was angry when I first arrived and saw things laid out as they were. I felt I had been tricked into having the Bible study here and started to wonder if Jennifer hadn't been right after all. I spoke with Benji and said we had to be sensitive to everyone's beliefs. He acted like we'd never discussed the logistics and told me I should talk with his parents if I wanted them to put the wine away." Gordon looked at his wife. "They told us they'd only been serving small samples, not enough to even be considered an alcoholic drink. I guess I hoped maybe Jennifer might just decide not to show up tonight. I was still concerned, and so Lorna and I went to the back of the room to pray about whether or not to press the issue with the Tallmans."

That must have been when Alex and I had arrived. One thing I knew for sure, though: Mr. and Mrs. Tallman had most certainly not served me a small sample taster of their wine.

"Do you know anyone who might have wanted to hurt Ms. Rempel?"

Gordon and his wife both shook their heads. "I can't believe anyone from our community would do something like this."

I wasn't surprised at his response. They seemed like trusting people—maybe too much so. "And you know everyone who attended tonight fairly well?"

"It's been the same group for many months. People come and go, of course, but we haven't had a new member in…" He looked to his wife.

"Gina started coming in April."

I glanced to the redhead, who had now been mentioned by two people. Then again, April was seven months ago. That certainly didn't make her new to the group.

But then, to my surprise, Gordon snapped his fingers. "What about that guitar player?" He looked around the room.

I did, too, and couldn't see him anywhere. "You didn't know him?"

Gordon shook his head. "Just met him tonight. Apparently, he'd stopped in for a wine tasting and heard about our Bible study. I saw his guitar and asked if he might want to play." Gordon tilted his head. "It seemed odd, though. He'd been eager to stay for the study, and yet, when I asked him to play a worship song or two to calm everyone down after Jennifer had stormed out, he didn't seem to know any."

That was odd. I wondered if either of the detectives had already questioned the guitar player and let him go. I was about to ask Gordon who he'd heard the gossip from about Jennifer's agitation over the meeting location, but Mickey Mouse interrupted. He couldn't possibly have taken enough time with Dahlia Richards to ask her anything valuable to his investigation.

"I hope Mrs. Beck hasn't been claiming to be a part in this investigation?" Detective Bradley added a chuckle at the end, like his words were a joke, but I knew they were quite serious.

I jumped out of my seat and offered my barstool to the detective. "Not a bit. We were just talking." I nodded to Gordon Lam and his wife and then turned back to the incompetent detective. "I'll leave you to it."

I moved to the side of the bar and lingered there until I caught Alex's eye between interviews.

"I should find you a ride home," he said as he walked over. "I'm so sorry about this."

"It's far from your fault," I said. "And I'm happy to stay until you're done."

He raised an eyebrow. "You know how long this sort of thing can take."

I did. By the time Alex and Mickey Mouse were done interviewing everyone and conferring with the forensics team outside, it would likely be the middle of the night sometime. "I really would like to stay. Besides, I've been chatting with a few people, and I feel like coming in as a Bible study attendee who they don't know very well gives me a different perspective and a reason to ask about things you probably already know and might not question. The way they answer gives me some insight."

"Oh, yeah? Anything interesting so far?"

I motioned inconspicuously to Dahlia Richards. Her elderly companion had rejoined her and brought her a cup of coffee, but they both kept glancing our way. "I understand there was some animosity between Dahlia and Jennifer, but they still met together every Monday for coffee. Apparently, Jennifer definitely knew four days ago that the Bible study was slated to be held here at the winery, she wasn't happy about it, and she had planned to intervene so it didn't happen."

"She must have forgotten or gotten distracted?" Alex guessed.

I shook my head. "She tried to contact Gordon Lam, but he avoided her calls, as he knew she wouldn't be happy about the location. Apparently, he'd discussed refraining from serving wine with Benji, but when he got here, Benji acted like it hadn't been discussed and he sent Gordon to discuss it with his parents. Then Detective Bradley arrived to take over with his own line of questioning." I resisted the urge to roll my eyes.

Alex nodded. "It did seem like Jennifer came in with a plan to derail the Bible study tonight."

"I agree. So would she have simply yelled about it and then headed for the parking lot to leave?" I didn't think so, but I didn't know Jennifer nearly as well as anyone who had been attending Bible study with the woman for many months.

Alex nibbled his lip, thinking. "Benji said he practically jogged to the parking lot, but he didn't see Jennifer on the way or in the parking lot. Her car was still there—it's still there now."

"Do you know what kind of car she drove?"

Alex looked through his notes. "Benji said a red Honda."

"How do you suppose he knew that? How well do you suppose he knew Jennifer Rempel?"

Alex nodded and made a note, but didn't comment.

"What would she have been doing in the vineyard? It's not even in the same direction as the parking lot."

Alex pursed his lips. Clearly, the same question had been bothering him. "Maybe she was looking to try something else that would interrupt the meeting. I feel like Kristoph Carter, the vineyard worker, might have more to tell me when he's done with our sketch artist." Alex motioned to where Kristoph sat across from a uniformed police officer, a sketchpad between them.

Kristoph glanced up in the direction of Dahlia's table, and I wondered if the lady he'd seen in the vineyard looked something like her. But then Dahlia and her companion noticed his glance and angled away, turning their backs to Kristoph.

I sighed, the memory of being interrupted frustrating me again. "Detective Bradley doesn't seem to want to let me talk for any length of time with anyone." I snapped my mouth shut. The last thing I wanted was for Alex to feel like he had to play interference.

"If I had any seniority at all, I'd put a stop to that. You're much more helpful than he is with investigations. But I suspect it's more a matter that he knows you have a better nose for who to ask what questions than him. He's probably trailing you for help. But of course he'd never admit that."

"Which doesn't help us. Hey, did either of you question the guitar player before he left?"

Alex looked through his notes again. "I didn't. I'll have to check with Mickey." He looked around the room. "Was he here when you got back from the vineyard?"

"I'm sorry. I didn't notice." I tried to replay the moment in my mind, but it was all a blur now.

Alex made another note. "I'm going to have a word with Dahlia and Gordon, maybe get a follow-up opinion on Dahlia and Jennifer's ambiguous friendship from Dahlia's husband." He motioned to the old man with Dahlia. "And then I'll check on what the team has found outside. Everyone else in the room was here when the murder occurred and they won't know Jennifer much better than I did, I suspect. So I'll let him clear some of them to leave, and once we have a smaller room of people and some more information from forensics, perhaps the situation will become clearer."

I hoped so, but in my experience, more details could often mean more questions rather than answers. "I'll continue to poke around. Hey, what do you know about Jennifer's ex-husband? Dahlia brought him up as well, thinking he might have been violent. If he followed her out here tonight…"

"He's on my list to investigate, but I'll have to cover everyone here first. I didn't know Dahlia was familiar with Jennifer's ex. I'll certainly ask some questions in that regard."

"And ask Gina." I motioned to the redhead. "Apparently they're both part of a regular Monday morning coffee meeting, where Jennifer used to open up a little."

Alex made a note. "If you change your mind and want a ride home, let me know." This felt like an end to our conversation, and one glance over my shoulder told me why. Detective Bradley was headed our way—either to interrupt our conversation or, if Alex was correct, to see if I might have been onto something.

I wasn't going to stick around to find out. "Let me know if you need anything," I told Alex. "In the meantime, I'll poke around and let you know if I figure anything else out."

☐

# CHAPTER SEVEN

Alex wasn't kidding about it taking all night. It was well after midnight before Detective Bradley cleared most of the room. Alex had re-interviewed those of interest and gone to talk with his forensics team.

I'd spoken to almost all of the Bible study attendees before they left and didn't find out much new, only confirmation that Jennifer regularly took a stand for her strong beliefs, she may have had a rocky marriage, and her ex-husband hadn't attended the Bible study even once. Nobody seemed to know if he was even a Christian, although everyone's guess was that Jennifer would have never married someone if she thought he wasn't a believer.

"She did everything the right way," I'd heard out of more than one person. The impression I'd gotten of Jennifer Rempel was a woman above reproach.

After running out of people to talk to, I'd started texting my teenage BFF, Amber. At first, she'd seemed bothered that I had been at the Bible study with Alex, but once she found out there was another murder investigation in the works, she texted almost faster than I could read.

<I know who she is> Amber texted. <She's been living in Honeysuckle Grove for about three years.>

I texted back: <Is that when she started going to church? Is that how you knew her?>

< She also worked as a crossing guard at the middle school when I was there. A real stick-to-the-rules lady. I don't think she even had a kid at our middle school. Doesn't surprise me that she'd have enemies, but someone who'd want to kill her? Dunno about that>

It was the same feeling I had, and I'd been asking questions about Jennifer Rempel and trying to see her through other peoples' eyes all evening. I supposed it shouldn't surprise me that Amber was automatically so intuitive. It rang true with the three murder investigations she'd helped solve so far.

<Are any Bible study attendees serious suspects?> she asked.

This I didn't know. But I'd tell her what I could. Amber and I were beyond holding back secrets from each other. <One lady was apparently pretty jealous of her, but still met her for coffee every week. She told me that Jennifer already knew and was upset about the winery location on Monday. Dahlia Richards?>

<I know her!> came back right away. <I wouldn't believe anything that lady says. She's on the Honeysuckle Green board with my mom and lies about all the work she's doing just to make herself look good. But she was there with everyone when it happened, right?>

I still wasn't sure about that, and Alex didn't seem to be either, and yet, Mickey Mouse had somehow cleared Dahlia and her much older husband to leave the crime scene. I'd asked three or four people if they'd noticed when the Richards had arrived, and no one seemed to be able to place her inside the winery before Jennifer's scream came from outside.

<Not totally sure yet. Listen, Alex is coming back in. I'll text you in the morning if there's anything else interesting.>

<Text me tonight! And come pick me up before you go investigate the scene tomorrow. I want to help.>

I didn't have time to respond before Alex walked over. It was just like Amber to think she'd of course be invited to help investigate any possible Honeysuckle Grove crime scenes. Then again, Alex had a soft spot for Amber. She'd only have to say the word to him and he'd likely take time away from work to pick her up himself.

"How's everything outside?" I asked. Thankfully, Detective Bradley had headed outside to get his own update, so I had a few minutes to talk without any scrutiny. I stifled a yawn.

"Come on, I'll tell you in the car." He led the way toward the winery door.

Don and Marie Tallman were still behind the bar. They'd been in and around the winery the whole evening, mostly keeping to themselves, cleaning up people's coffee mugs from earlier with forced smiles, but I could feel an edge off them. Don, especially, gave off a strong irritability, and I was quite sure it was because of the rumors that would circulate and the good reputation the winery might lose from having someone die on the property.

Benji had left over an hour ago, after both Alex and Detective Bradley had thoroughly questioned him, but apparently, Mr. and Mrs. Tallman lived in a house behind the winery, so they were here until everyone left and they could close up the front doors.

Alex waved to them on his way out. "I'll be back first thing in the morning. Please make sure your staff knows not to tamper with anything out in the vineyard until we've been able to look over everything in the light."

Don nodded. Marie said, "Thank you so much, Detective." I wasn't entirely sure what she was thanking him for, but I supposed they could have ended up with a much less humane member of the local detective force.

I followed Alex down the pathway toward the parking lot. Our trek was a lot quieter, and certainly any trace of romance from the way up to the winery had vanished long ago. I kept a keen eye on the canopied branches and explained how fixing them had been Benji Tallman's alibi. I didn't find myself ducking as often as I had on the way up.

"Yes, he told me that as well," Alex said in a tired voice.

We reached the parking lot to find four vehicles: Alex's old model Toyota, two police cars, and a red Honda Civic, which belonged to Jennifer Rempel.

"Are they towing her car?" I asked.

"Probably no need for a tow. They found Jennifer's keys on her person. As long as we don't find any evidence as to why she was killed in her car during the daylight, either I or Mickey will likely drive it back to town or have her next of kin come and retrieve it."

It still seemed strange when Alex—whom I'd known since my terrible crush on him in seventh grade—talked in his all-business tone. I knew he was a more than capable detective, but somehow it still shocked me every time.

"I heard you say you'd be out here by nine," I said. "Any chance you'd want some company?" I knew from experience that Detective Bradley rarely rolled out of bed before ten, even if he was supposedly on shift.

Alex offered a tired smirk. "I guess I just assumed I'd be picking you up. And Amber, if she has anything to say about it." He let out a low chuckle, and I suspected after the evening he'd had, it felt good to lighten things up a little.

"Oh, I'm pretty sure Amber will have plenty to say about it." I laughed now, too. "If only our biggest problem was dealing with teenage emotions."

"Right?" As Alex pulled out of the winery parking lot, he glanced over at me to share another smile. "I'm pretty sure if she hangs around long enough, she'll realize I'm a boring old dude who can't focus on much besides my job."

I raised my eyebrows toward the passenger window. I'd been hanging around a fair amount, and that realization wasn't coming quickly to me. Quite the opposite. "She did just lose her dad a couple of months ago," I said to change the subject from one that was making my cheeks warm.

Alex nodded toward the road. "And I'm happy to be an older male figure in her life while she adjusts."

Amber truly couldn't ask for someone better in that regard.

"Plus, I really like the kid. Not to mention her natural ability for investigative work."

"Don't let her hear you say that. She already practically wants to drop out of school to join the police academy."

"I'll have a talk with her. She'll go a lot further if she gets an education first."

I'd never talked to Alex about post-secondary education, but it occurred to me now that while I was off at culinary school, he must have been at a nearby college studying criminology.

"Corbett wouldn't even look at her before she's at least twenty-one with a couple of years of college under her belt. A degree would be better." Alex let out a heavy sigh. "Although, if I'm being honest, I don't think he'll look at her for detective work anyway, no matter how educated and naturally insightful she might be."

"Because she's female?" Despite my exhaustion, outrage rose within me. Sexism had been an obstacle to overcome in the heavily male-dominated realm of cuisine, but I'd doggedly found a few niches to fit into. I wasn't going to stand for Amber being held back in the same way if I had anything to say about it. "What, is Honeysuckle Grove stuck in the 1950s?"

"Not Honeysuckle Grove. Certainly not me. I'd rather take Amber to work with me each day than Mickey Mouse. She'd be a lot more useful." He sighed again. "But Corbett's chauvinism and prejudice are pretty much unmatched."

Again, I made it my life's mission to somehow run Police Captain Corbett out of this town the way he'd run Alex's dad out. Any replacement had to be better than him.

I wasn't sure if Alex was purposely keeping the conversation topic on Amber to avoid telling me details about the investigation, but I was too curious not to bring the conversation back around to that.

"Did the forensics team find anything of interest out in the vineyard? Anything that might prove who had killed Jennifer Rempel?"

Alex's quick answer made me think he'd only neglected to spill his information because of tiredness. "They found a lot. Unfortunately, I'm not sure how to tie any of the details together yet." He rubbed his hands on his steering wheel and turned toward my house, back in town. "Maybe after a good night's sleep, it'll start to make sense."

I was tired, too, but I wanted to know everything. "Did you find anything out about that guitar player?"

Alex shook his head. "Marie Tallman said he came in for a wine tasting around six-thirty. Introduced himself as Gary, apparently from

Morgantown, and asked if he could stick around for the Bible study. He talked to Gordon about playing his guitar. That's all I could find out, but from what I understand, he didn't know anyone in the Bible study or the Tallmans, and he was inside the winery when Jennifer screamed." He went on to tell me about the more useful information he'd found from outside. "There were fresh tractor tracks that wound around the vineyard."

"Right, I heard a tractor when we went outside after Jennifer screamed."

"I suspect the killer came after Jennifer first with a tractor. The medical examiner will let us know if he finds any evidence of her being struck or run over with the tractor, but one thing he did tell me is that the corkscrew in her neck was likely not the cause of her death."

"No? I figured with the blood loss…"

"It didn't hit the jugular, so the blood loss wasn't significant."

"If she wasn't killed with the corkscrew and if it didn't strike her to kill her, why was it there?"

Alex shrugged as he turned onto my street. "It might have been a crime of passion, in the moment, where the killer was throwing anything and everything at his or her disposal at Jennifer to take her out."

It felt like there was a silent "or" at the end of his sentence, so I added it. "Or?"

He pulled into my driveway. "Or it was some kind of a trophy. The killer wanted to leave a mark on her after she was already dead. We may figure out more when we get a full report from the medical examiner, or maybe we'll find something we missed in the light of day."

I just hoped whatever we found led us to answers and not simply more questions.

But for now, I had another light to deal with. I could see from the driveway that the light in my living room was still on and the curtain swished to the side, letting me know Dad was in there, still awake, and likely had a few questions of his own.

I rolled my eyes to myself. I might not be too tired to talk through a murder investigation, but I was definitely too tired to deal with my father's pushy "first date" interrogation.

# CHAPTER EIGHT

"Heh, heh, heh. Awfully late, isn't it?" Dad asked from the living room doorway the second I was inside my house. "That musta been some Bible study."

I pulled off my boot, nearly falling backward onto my butt with my tiredness and the effort. "Dad, it's not what you think. Believe me, it's not."

Dad took a step closer. The entryway light wasn't on, but the front porch light gave enough of a glow through the side panel glass that I could make out the serious look on his face. "He didn't...he didn't hurt you, did he?"

I quelled a laugh, because, really, Dad meant well. He'd always wanted to protect Leslie and me from the big bad dangers of the world. He just often went about it in the wrong way. "No, Dad. Alex would never do that. There was an...occurrence. Out at the winery where the Bible study was held." Just because Alex had allowed me to have more information about the case than I should, didn't mean I was about to share it, even if Dad was family. In fact, that was precisely why Alex could share the information he shared with me.

"What kind of occurrence?"

I should have known Dad would push for more. He was a regular neighborhood busybody. I should have just let him think Alex and I had been making out all night. At least then any further details might have made him uncomfortable.

I pulled at my other boot, annoyed, deciding I could probably tell him as much as the other Bible study attendees knew. It would be on the local news by morning. "A lady was found dead out in the vineyard. It was really upsetting, and even though Alex wasn't officially on duty, as a detective who was there when it happened, he had to take the reins on the case."

At the mention of the word "dead," Hunch, my late husband's mystery-solving cat who lived for a good investigation, peeked his head around the corner from the kitchen. He crept over on soundless paws and then sniffed at the boot I'd already removed.

As I finally got my other boot off and stood back up, Dad touched my shoulder. "It happened while you were there? In the winery? Did you see anything happen?"

I yawned, but Dad looked wide awake at my story. I supposed I'd had almost five hours to get used to the idea that another murder had happened less than a hundred feet away from me. It was a bad sign that this was becoming commonplace.

"I was in the building and this lady was found outside. We heard her scream and then Alex found her out in the vineyard. I'm okay, Dad. Really." I took his hand and squeezed it, meeting his eyes until his softened.

He nodded. "You're sure?"

"I'm sure," I said. "Just really, really tired."

He nodded. "Well, get your rest. I'll be quiet in the morning so you can sleep in."

I already knew I wasn't about to sleep in, but I suspected if I told Dad the truth about why I had to be up early, he'd either argue with me about it or have another million questions to ask.

I told him, "Thanks, Dad," and started up the stairs with Hunch close at my ankles.

The feline member of this household likely wouldn't be so quick to drop the subject of a newly discovered dead body.

I woke up after a few tumultuous hours of sleep with Hunch beside my head, his wide eyes aimed right at my face. He sat up on his haunches, just below my pillow, like he hadn't slept a wink last night.

Then again, cats could sleep all day and were known to be nocturnal. Trying to picture Hunch lazing around all day or night, though, wasn't a vision that came easily. I wouldn't put it past my cat to watch me until I was off in dreamland each night and then instigate some big-scale detective operation of his own during the seven or so hours I usually slept.

I'd fallen asleep last night with Hunch curled into my side, one of his paws resting on my thigh. I'd murmured about everything that had transpired at the winery, and each time I'd nodded off mid-sentence, Hunch had dug his sharp claws into my leg to wake me up. That must have gone on for three or four hours. Hunch had finally let me get some sleep when I got to the part about needing a working brain by eight a.m., but clearly, he had been patiently waiting for anything I might have missed in my story.

He followed me into my adjoining bathroom and waited on the counter while I showered. I was fighting an early morning groggy voice, so I didn't talk to him about the murder or anything else, but by the time I got out of the shower, he was pacing back and forth along the bathroom counter, growling.

"I have to get ready, Hunch. Alex will be here in twenty minutes, and someone kept me awake most of the night, so I'm not moving as quickly as usual."

This excuse only earned me a louder growl.

I ignored him and tiptoed downstairs. Walking quietly into the kitchen, I nearly came out of my skin when a paper rustled. Dad was already up, reading the morning paper at the table.

"What are you doing up?" we both asked at the same time. I wasn't ready for the question and didn't have a prepared answer, so I headed for the coffee pot, which, thankfully, Dad had already set to brew this morning.

"I haven't been sleeping well," he explained. "I know you're not thrilled with having me here, but it's a lot of stress, not knowing where to settle or what to do for work."

I'd have had a little more compassion if I didn't know from experience that this had been his method of living our entire lives. Leslie and I had been uprooted and lied to about the reasons we were moving on so many times, I'd become callous to his sob story. I filled my to-go mug and added some cinnamon and honey. The cinnamon reminded me of a batch of cinnamon buns I'd made yesterday morning. The thought of taking a few along for Alex, Amber, and myself brightened my mood.

But when I looked into the sealable container on the counter, there were only two left.

"How many of these did you eat, Dad?"

He shrugged, flipping a page in the newspaper. "Looking for a job works up your appetite." I could see from here he was enveloped in the sports section and not the Help Wanted pages.

I was about to ask, "And how many jobs, exactly, have you applied for?" but I had little patience for his excuses this morning.

"Well, you'll have to fend for yourself today. There are plenty of ingredients to make yourself some bacon and eggs or a nice stir fry." I knew he wouldn't bother with either of these. I envisioned him sitting on the couch, TV remote in one hand and some peanut butter toast in the other.

"Where are you off to?" It was the first time he'd looked away from the paper for any significant amount of time. "And so early."

Hunch growled from my other side, and I felt like I was going to scream at one of them if I held back many more of my true thoughts. So I blurted out the truth—who cared about the consequences?

"Alex is picking me up. I'm going along as a second set of eyes at the investigation site."

Dad's forehead creased. "Doesn't he have a partner for stuff like that?"

"He should, yes." I didn't feel like getting into it, not when I was already so irritable. I packed the two lone cinnamon buns into a much smaller sealable container and grabbed for my coffee—apparently, the coffee would be my only breakfast today. "I'm helping out today." That was the only explanation I offered as I strode for the front door.

My hair was still damp from the shower, but I didn't have time to blow dry it. If I wasn't ready with my shoes on when Alex pulled up, Dad was likely to give him an earful of questions.

I pulled on my gray sneakers to match my jeans and charcoal cable knit sweater. I'd learned from Amber that comfortable clothing, and especially footwear, were essential when investigating a murder.

Unfortunately, the sports section had lost its appeal, and Dad followed me to the entry. "I don't like this, Mallory. Do you think it's safe out there, playing detective with absolutely no training? I mean, you're a chef, not an experienced investigator."

"If Alex thinks I'll be of help, I'm happy to go along. And I'm twenty-eight years old, Dad. I can take care of myself." My words grew louder as I spoke them.

So did Dad's. "Well, I am still your father, and I'm not about to let you go nosing around some crime scene, even if your new boyfriend thinks this'll be some kind of romantic second date."

There were so many things wrong with that sentence, I didn't know where to start. My blood was boiling, though, so I had to start somewhere.

"Let me?" The two simple words held some of my venom, but certainly not all of it. If I hadn't heard Alex's car in the driveway at that second, there would've been a lot more where that came from. "Listen, Dad, I think it's time for you to find somewhere new to freeload. Today." I reached for the door handle. "I wasn't going to make a big deal of it, but if you can't treat me as the adult I am, you can find yourself a new place to live!"

With that, I yanked open the door and marched toward Alex's vehicle. Today, he'd brought the unmarked dark blue police-issued Cadillac. Amber was already in the front seat, and it wasn't until she opened her door, eyes on the cement behind me, and called out, "Hunchie!" that I realized with Dad standing in my open doorway, my cat thought it was his prerogative to tag along.

"No, Hunch. You can't come." I bent to grab him, but he skirted between my hands and raced into Amber's open arms.

"Hi, baby-boo," she said, already snuggling him into her arms.

From anyone else, Hunch had zero patience for cutesy nicknames. Anyone else would not dare hold Hunch's claws so close to their face, either. But Hunch and Amber had a special relationship, one I was jealous of if I were being honest.

"Can he come?" Amber asked Alex.

"A police car is no place for a—" I started, but Alex was much more understanding and less agitated this morning.

"Ah, it's fine with me," Alex said. "If I'm breaking one rule by bringing the two of you along, I might as well break all the rules."

I suppressed the urge to roll my eyes as I made it to the passenger side of the car "Fine," I said to Amber. "But you're taking care of him."

She let out a squeal and hopped out of the front seat and darted into the back without even being asked. Amber was often trying to prove herself as an adult, especially around Alex, so it surprised me when she so willingly took the "kid" role.

I slid into the passenger seat.

Alex asked, "What's up with your dad?"

My father stood a few feet down the front walkway from the house with his legs apart and fists on his waist, not coming ahead to actually stop me from leaving, but sending me a clear message: If only you were twelve, I would make you stick to my rules again!

I turned to Alex and forced a smile. "He's angry because I finally told him to find somewhere else to freeload. But we have more important things to think about." I motioned to the road, trying to put my dad out of my thoughts for the rest of the day. "Let's get back to the winery and you can fill us in on everything we need to know on the way."

☐

# CHAPTER NINE

There wasn't a lot of new information, but there was some.

When he spoke to the medical examiner first thing this morning, Alex had learned there was evidence of strangulation, which was found once all the blood from the corkscrew in Jennifer's neck had been cleaned up.

"I have an idea of what might have been used, but I want to get back out there and figure out what I can."

"I don't see how you can trust anything at the crime scene today if the Tallmans live there and they're so shady," Amber put in from the backseat.

I looked between the seats at where she was still snuggled up with Hunch like she hadn't seen him in a year, even though she'd been over to make cinnamon buns two nights ago. Her purple hoodie today read: COME BACK WITH A WARRANT.

"I'm not sure if they're shady or just protective over their winery." I turned back toward the front and added, "Except Benji. He disappeared for too long and doesn't seem to have a good excuse for it."

Alex sighed. "You're right. And I'm going to press him with some more questions about that. But even if it doesn't look good that he was outside on his own with virtually no alibi, I've known the guy for years and I just don't think Benji Tallman could have done something like this."

I pursed my lips, wondering if Alex might be too close to the situation to be objective. "How long have you known him? How long has he been coming to Bible study?"

Alex turned up the mountain toward the winery. The view was even more breathtaking during the day, as I could see the rolling hills of the vineyard and the cedar winery structure from a distance. It was autumn, less than a week from Thanksgiving, and colorful orange and red and yellow leaves dangled perilously from surrounding trees.

"I've known Benji for at least five years. We played on a local soccer team together, back when I had time to play soccer. He was actually the person to invite me to the Bible study in the first place."

So definitely not objective, I thought to myself.

"This is where it happened?" Amber asked, highlighting the fact that this was much too beautiful of a location for a murder.

"Just up that way, in the vineyard." I pointed as Alex pulled into the winery's parking lot.

"And so your friend, Benji, was down here hanging out in the parking lot for, like, half an hour, just hoping that Jennifer might show up, and then he heard the scream?" Amber had lost her dad in a terrible murder only a few months ago. I suspected that made her more suspicious and blunter than she had been before, but I had only known her for those few months, so I couldn't say for sure.

Alex took in a breath and let it out slowly. "Benji mentioned several things he had been fixing out here while he waited for Jennifer. He'd also walked down to the road and was nearly back up to the winery when she screamed." Alex parked and then looked over the seat to Amber. "But don't worry, he's still on our suspect list. And we've had a security officer up here putting up crime scene tape and watching that no one steps into our investigation radius through the night. I made sure our forensics team combed over the place pretty carefully last night, too."

"Hmm. Well, let's go look." I still didn't completely trust the Honeysuckle Grove forensics team. They'd missed more than one important clue when it had come to Amber's dad's death—things that the untrained eyes of Amber and I were able to find without much effort.

We got out of the car, and I raised my eyebrows at Amber, still with Hunch in her arms, trying to bring him along. Alex didn't say a word about it. In truth, Hunch had helped in our last couple of investigations—pretty significantly at the one that happened at the town hall—and trying to make him stay in the car at a crime scene might just be asking for unnecessary claw marks and lacerations.

Alex led the way up the path toward the winery, but I was surprised when about twenty feet along, a smaller unpaved path broke off to our right and he took it. I hadn't seen this secondary path on our way up last night. Then again, I'd been fretting and trying not to swoon over my seventh-grade crush at the time.

"You're not going to the winery first to let them know you're here?"

Alex shook his head from in front of us. "I want to make sure all is still secure in the vineyard first and that Officer Krause didn't notice any disturbances through the night."

As we moved along the narrow trail, often ducking from stray overhead branches that hadn't been trimmed, I couldn't help but think of how easy it would have been for Benji Tallman to take a detour up to the vineyard, leave Jennifer Rempel lifeless, and then return to the parking lot, with nobody at the winery any the wiser.

Before long, the path opened up into one of the rows of the vineyard. This row was only about four feet wide, much narrower than the one where we had found Jennifer the night before. Alex caught sight of Officer Krause at the end of the row and walked toward him. While they had a short conversation, I surveyed the bushy blackberry plants on either side, held up by wire fencing and attached to metal poles every few feet. I wondered if the wire fencing could be pulled free to use for strangulation.

By the time Alex returned, I had my bearings of where we were in the vineyard, aided by the sounds of passing cars down on the road.

"It's been quiet out here all night. I told Officer Krause to take a break." Alex headed left, like he knew exactly where we were going. Soon the row turned and opened to a larger row of grapevine bushes, with long slender trunks going into the ground and bush tops that rose above our heads. Many of the leaves had fallen off the plants, leaving them half-bare with dark orange brittle-looking leaves. Because of their bareness, I could see through to the next row in the vineyard and even a little into the one beyond that.

Hunch jumped from Amber's arms and sniffed every inch of the nearby dirt. He stopped and mewled from several feet in front of us.

Alex caught up first and bent down, surveying the ground. Hunch was nothing if not obvious, and he circled around a small section of dirt with his nose in the middle, demonstrating to Alex exactly where he should look.

Alex pulled out his phone and snapped a few photos of the ground. Amber and I caught up to him by the time he opened a folder and pulled out a small white cardboard marker. He wrote the number "5" on it and then stuck it into the ground. I couldn't see much of interest in the area, except maybe some tractor tire tracks.

"What is it?" I asked.

Alex stood and logged something into the papers in his file. "Fresh tractor tracks. Or at least I suspect they're fresh if Hunch felt the need to bring them to my attention."

Hunch had already moved along ahead of us. He mewled again from the corner that led to the next row.

We hurried to catch up. At the corner, Alex marked more tractor tracks with a "5" but also found a deep heel impression in the dirt, and only a couple of feet from that, a small silver metal hair comb. One I recognized.

"That was Jennifer's," I said. "I saw it in her hair when she first walked into the winery."

Alex squatted near the comb to look at it closer.

"Those markers are for all the clues you find?" Amber asked, squatting to look at the latest "5" placeholder. Alex took more photos and placed a "6" marker near the heel print, and a "7" near the comb. Hunch now crept around the ground, sniffing at every angle of the small plastic marker, as if making certain we weren't missing anything.

Alex nodded. "We always leave one when we have to pick up evidence and bring it back for fingerprinting, which will be the case here. I'm going to survey the whole place first, though, before I start bagging evidence. Sometimes seeing items in place offers a more complete picture."

"So this is the sixth most important clue, or what?" Amber still squatted at the marker by the heel print. Hunch moved on from there and sniffed at a marker already in the ground about ten feet away in the middle of the row marked with another "5."

Alex flipped to a photo in his folder. "It's likely the sixth piece of possible evidence they came across. They mark them as they find them, and they give anything similar the same number. All the fresh tractor tracks will have a five, for instance. We'll often denote them later, according to their importance."

I caught up to Alex and looked over his shoulder at the close-up photo of more tractor tracks.

"They found a few of these fresh tracks around various places within the rows of grapevines. Because there was the noise from a tractor right around the time of the murder, we've kept track of the freshest marks. Of course we can't really place them according to time, at least not beyond a few hours, but deeper grooves without footprints marring them, combined with other pieces of evidence we've found nearby…" He pointed to the latest marker with a "5" on it. "We've kept track in case they can help us form a clearer picture."

I nodded and Alex led the rest of the way down the row and onto the next one. "Where do they keep the tractor?" I asked. Alex pointed across the vineyard to where, in the daylight, I could see the top of a barn high above the grapevines. "Is that the same barn where Kristoph lives? Up in the loft?"

Alex nodded. "The same one, yes."

"Wouldn't he have noticed if someone had started up the tractor right underneath his living space?" Amber caught up and joined the conversation.

"That's what I wondered." Alex offered Amber an encouraging smile. "Apparently, if they're not expecting rain, they often leave the tractor out in the vineyard."

"Wouldn't you have heard it from the winery?" she asked.

"We might have, if not for the music," I said. "But I definitely heard it when we came out to find Jennifer."

"A musician from Morgantown was playing some worship songs while we waited for the Bible study to start," Alex explained.

"Actually, Gordon Lam said he asked the musician, Gary, to play a couple of worship songs, but he didn't seem to know any."

"And that wasn't planned?" Amber asked. "The guitar playing?"

Alex checked his notes, but I remembered this part. "He'd come for a wine tasting and asked if he could stay for the Bible study. He had a guitar along and was asked to play. He was inside the winery when Jennifer screamed and seemed to have disappeared before the questioning. All we have is a first name of Gary and his hometown of Morgantown, which is the third largest city in the state."

"He happened to come in last night for the first time and didn't know anybody?" Amber asked.

"It does seem suspicious, but how do we find this guy?" I asked, getting ahead of myself again by accidentally trying to call the shots. I couldn't help it. Something about this seemed too coincidental. The one other stranger last night, other than me, covered up the sounds of a tractor out in the vineyard by playing guitar? "I'd be interested to know if this Gary guy steered the conversation with the Tallmans toward Bible study and orchestrated getting an invite."

"It doesn't change the fact that he was inside the winery, in plain sight of both of us, when Jennifer Rempel was killed," Alex said.

"But," Amber added, "it does prompt the question of whether or not the killer was working alone."

We were silent as we made our way down the next row, which also had a little plastic marker with the number "5" on it.

"Another tractor tire mark." Alex barely paused. Hunch did his usual sniff over the whole area, then quickly caught up to us.

The next row was the last in this area of the vineyard, and I recognized it immediately as the crime scene by the wall of shrubs at the end of the row, cutting it off from all the other rows. Four more markers lay straight ahead, one off to the left and the other three right in the center of the row, where we'd found Jennifer's lifeless body.

Hunch headed straight for marker "4" on the left, and I followed him there. My cat, while not the friendliest feline, had a knack for finding the most important clues. At the plastic marker, while Alex flipped through his folder to read up on the details, I bent down to study the string of twinkle lights that had fallen down from the grapevine. I remembered the little dog, Riesling, snapping at the cord of twinkle lights and wondered if all animals were as insightful as my cat.

Several feet of twinkle lights lay in a haphazard pile—likely the reason this area of the vineyard had been so dark last night. I imagined many killers would want to cover up their crime with darkness, especially if it was committed at night.

"Do you think the murderer yanked down the lights to cover his or her trail?" I asked.

Alex hadn't flipped to the photo of marker "4", but instead, when he showed me the photo he had flipped to, it made me suck in a breath in horror. It was a close-up of Jennifer's neck.

The protrusion from the corkscrew had been cleaned up in the photo, but that wasn't what I was looking at. Around the sides of her neck were indentations of dark purple marks with larger cuts every couple of inches.

I looked between the photo and the string of twinkle lights and said aloud what all of us were thinking. "Jennifer Rempel wasn't killed with a corkscrew or a tractor. She was strangled with a string of white twinkle lights."

# CHAPTER TEN

I didn't have much of a stomach for looking over the other photos of Jennifer's body, but thankfully, Alex could tell us everything we needed to know. The stabbing with the corkscrew occurred in the larynx, better known as the voice box.

"She would have had to scream before being struck with the corkscrew," he explained.

"So why the corkscrew? Why the tractor?" I asked.

"My best guess is that the murderer chased Jennifer up and down the rows of the vineyard on the tractor in order to corner her. Kristoff Carter told us that the vineyard's tractor was top of the line, two hundred and fifty horsepower, and could get up to twenty miles an hour on the road." Alex flipped through pages to confirm this information. "At twenty miles per hour, a person wouldn't be able to outrun it—even on the road or on a running track. In the dark and on this uneven terrain, it would be impossible."

"Plus, she was wearing boots with wedges," I recalled.

"But the murderer didn't run her over," Amber observed. Amber, unlike me, seemed to have no problem staring at the gory photos or talking plainly about the details of a person's recent death. "He or she just backed the victim into this corner and then strangled her?"

I found it interesting that Alex always called Jennifer by name, while Amber seemed more comfortable with calling her "the victim."

"Likely," Alex said. "Chased her, then stabbed her with the corkscrew to quiet her screams. And then finally killed her."

"Where did you find the tractor?" I asked. "Or did the perpetrator leave on it?" Now I was the one using clinical words.

"We found it located down the hill a couple hundred feet. I figure he or

278

she might have been trying to find their way to the parking lot, or maybe even the road, but the layout of the rows of vines doesn't make it easy by tractor. We found the tractor abandoned mid-row, and it was only a short dodge in between grapevines from there to get to the main road."

So that was how the perpetrator escaped. Now we just needed to know who he or she was.

"Kristoph said he saw a woman out here. Was your sketch artist able to get anything useful out of him?"

Alex nodded and flipped pages again. "He sat for an hour and came up with a pretty thorough sketch. It was dark, so he couldn't be sure, but once the seriousness of the situation settled in on him, he wanted to do what he could to help."

I remembered Kristoph looking toward Dahlia's table while he sat with the sketch artist and expected to find a somewhat similar-looking woman in the sketch. But to my surprise, it didn't look one bit like Dahlia Richards. The woman in the sketch had much more angular features and wore a black beanie, hiding most of her hair, except for a few dark wisps around her face and a distinct widow's peak. She wore a dark jacket and jeans and had an unusually long face. Her thick, heavy eyebrows and the dark circles under her eyes made her look devious. I couldn't help but wonder how much of the sketch could have been distorted in Kristoph's dim-light memory, but at least we had something to go on.

"So are we assuming the murderer is this woman?" Amber asked.

"Not assuming, no." Alex led us back down the same row, as even Hunch seemed to agree there wasn't much more to see here. "But she is certainly a serious suspect. Probably the prime suspect at this point."

"If we're ruling out Benji," she said.

Alex kept his eyes averted from the statement. I wanted to find the murderer as much as anybody, but at the same time, my automatic reaction was to ease Alex's discomfort.

"Can we take a look at that tractor before we go?" I asked.

Alex offered a thankful smile. "You bet. This way."

We followed Alex silently up and down rows and eventually found one that led to a lower section of the vineyard. Other than the one path Alex navigated to, that next section was self-contained. A person would need to be familiar with the vineyard to make their way around it efficiently. It would be a bit of a maze for a newcomer, especially in the dark.

"So did the perpetrator know the land, or was he or she taking blind guesses at how to get away quickly in the dark?" I wondered aloud.

"From the haphazard tire tracks, my suspicion is blind guesses." Alex turned another corner, and there sat a shiny green tractor that looked less than a couple years old. "Several of the fresh tractor marks indicated stopping and turning around to go in a new direction."

Hunch had already hopped into the driver's seat—an apt metaphor if I'd ever seen one. I circled the tractor, not knowing what I was looking for, only that there had to be something Alex and his team had missed. I didn't like thinking that way, but I supposed it had become a habit.

The green tractor was tall and narrow—tall enough to reach the tops of the grapevines and narrow enough to make it down each of the rows—even the narrower blackberry ones. I studied the front panel of headlights, all in one plastic molding, but there was no sign of anything hitting the front side of the tractor. I bent to look over each of the tires.

"Does it tow something?" Amber asked from the rear, studying a hitch.

"Kristoph explained the different mechanisms that hook up to the back. He said the power harrow is usually left attached in the fall, but we found it abandoned in the row where Kristoph said he'd left the tractor at the end of his shift yesterday."

"So whoever killed Jennifer knew how to detach a tractor mechanism—" I started, but Amber cut me off.

"Not to mention, he or she knew how to drive the thing."

I got into the cab, understanding the significance of Amber's statement. While there was a key dangling in the ignition, beyond that, I wouldn't have a clue which levers to pull or which pedals to push to make this thing drive—especially down narrow vineyard rows.

Hunch roamed around at my feet, sniffing the pedals. I kept my feet out of his way, giving our most scent-skilled investigator space, and when he wanted back up onto the seat, I cleared out, not having found anything of note.

"And your team dusted the whole thing for prints?" I asked Alex.

He nodded. "There was a fair amount of dirt and dust. Kristoph always wore work gloves when out in the vineyard. We couldn't pick up any clear prints, so we suspect the perpetrator wore gloves as well."

Hunch growled from the tractor seat, so I rounded the side to see if he'd found something. He lay on his belly, his nose tight into the seat back.

"Can I look?" I asked him. Because invading his personal space without asking could make for a painful outcome with Hunch's sharp claws. He pulled up onto his haunches. As usual, Alex had given us blue stretchy gloves when we'd first arrived, so I wiggled a few of my gloved fingers between the seat bottom and the seat back. It didn't seem like much could fit in there, but as I wiggled my fingers back and forth, the edge of a white slip of paper in the crease caught my eye.

Hunch's growl grew louder.

Carefully, I pushed the seat down and tugged gingerly at the swatch of paper. It started to come out, but then ripped. I passed the swatch I had retrieved to Alex. "You don't have anything like tweezers…?"

"I can't say I carry tweezers, no."

Amber appeared at the other side of the tractor. "Will this work?" It was a dried-out twig of grapevine.

I reached for it and used it to push the seat down so I could get my hand in deeper. I was afraid my plan might backfire and send the swatch of paper somewhere into the depth of the seat that would require a mechanic taking it apart to find it.

One thing I was sure about, though: If Hunch sniffed it out as being important, it probably was.

I gently depressed the seat while working my hand into the crease, and after only a few seconds, I had the edge of the swatch pinned between my second and third fingers. Once I had a grip on it, I depressed the seat farther and pulled it out in one piece.

When I turned to hand the swatch to Alex, he was studying the tiny corner. When he put the two pieces together, it only took him a second to have a revelation. "It's an address in Honeysuckle Grove."

I looked over his shoulder. It read: 2388 Meridian Ave. Meridian Avenue wasn't near the center of town, more in the outskirts, near the upscale neighborhood where Amber's family lived. Hunch purred and rubbed against my calves. The strangeness of Hunch giving me affection when Amber was right here made me realize he wanted something.

I bent to pick him up so he could see the note, in the event that he could somehow read it. "So should we go check out this address, or go to the winery and interview the Tallmans again? By the way, where did Don Tallman claim to be when the murder took place?"

"I'm afraid that there is none of your business, young lady," a deep voice said from the base of the row of the vineyard we were in. We all looked over to see Captain Corbett standing in the middle of the open row, feet apart and arms crossed over his police uniform. "A cat and a teenager? I thought surely Mr. Vandewalker had been joking!"

Mr. Vandewalker? My father. He had tattled on me?

Hunch dug his claws into my shoulder, not enough to hurt me, but just enough to say, "Hey, Mallory, I think this is bad news."

And it was. Captain Corbett opened his mouth again to tell Alex in his deep Texan drawl, "Martinez, get back to headquarters. I'll speak to you there, and I'll ask you from now on to leave the civilians and children and felines out of your investigations."

I seethed inwardly. The police captain knew we'd been helping solve crimes in the last few months—crimes that incompetent members of his department couldn't handle on their own—and yet he looked at us as though we'd be the ones to mess this up.

But before we could say a single word in our defense, Captain Corbett turned on his heel and marched purposefully toward the parking lot, clearly expecting us to follow. □

# CHAPTER ELEVEN

The second Corbett marched away from us, Amber let out a harrumph at being dubbed a child.

Alex sucked in a quick breath. "This is bad," he said in barely a whisper. As soon as Captain Corbett had disappeared from sight, Alex was following. "We have to go right away. If he doesn't see me behind him, it could mean my job." He pulled out his phone, dialed, and a second later murmured instructions to Officer Krause about getting back to his post for surveillance.

I shook my head on the walk to the car. We had worked so hard to get Alex's boss to see his worth in the department and earn him some clout, not to mention a promotion to detective. And for what? We'd done our best to fly under Corbett's radar and step in where Alex's incompetent partner couldn't be bothered, but one mistake and Alex might lose it all?

Corbett had his car aimed at the main road by the time we reached the parking lot, but he idled there, likely waiting to make sure Alex obeyed his directive.

We got into Alex's vehicle, and in silent agreement, Amber, Hunch, and I all got into the backseat.

Corbett's police car idled until Alex pulled out of the parking lot. Then he followed us.

"Can I drop you both at Mallory's?" Alex murmured from the front seat.

I wasn't sure if my father would still be there and didn't really want Amber to hear what I had to say to him if he was, but nevertheless, I told Alex, "Of course."

He reached between the seats with the swatch of paper we'd found in the tractor seat in his hand. "Text me a photo of it when you get home. I have a feeling Corbett's going to drown me in paperwork at the office and leave Mickey on the fieldwork for this one. I think we all know how quickly it'll get solved if that happens."

I took the slip of paper, then looked at Amber and then Alex, my forehead creasing. "So what are you saying?"

Alex shook his head. "I'm not saying anything, Mallory. I'm not telling you or Amber to do anything. Okay?"

"How about I'll do the telling then?" Amber said. "We're going to do a little quiet investigative work all on our own. We'll tell you what we find, and we'll do it before Mickey Mouse can waltz in and bumble it all up."

Alex didn't respond, except to offer one solid nod from the front seat.

"We'll update you with anything we find," I reiterated. I felt awful for Alex. He'd been working so hard, and it seemed he could never catch a break with Corbett around. His captain didn't even stay out in the vineyard long enough to see if we'd found anything useful, to see that we'd all actually been helping with the case. Part of me wondered if Corbett already knew what a poor excuse of a detective Mickey Bradley was, but he chose to ignore it just to mess with Alex's pursuits. I bet Corbett was just waiting for the opportunity to pin Mickey Bradley's incompetence on Alex.

"Ridiculous," I said under my breath. Neither Alex nor Amber responded aloud, but I could feel the agreement from both of them.

When Alex pulled into my driveway, Corbett idled across the street like some kind of untrusting parent.

"You don't..." Alex started, then turned in his seat to face me and Amber. "You know I'm not asking you to take over or expecting—"

Amber cut him off. "What we do has nothing to do with you, Detective Martinez." Even though she spoke with unabashed confidence, Amber usually demonstrated her respect by calling Alex Detective Martinez. "Don't worry about it. Your captain needs to show off his testosterone. Doesn't mean he's right, and doesn't mean two smart women can't ask a few questions."

Alex's forehead buckled. "Be safe. Both of you."

I reached for the door handle. "We will," I told him, even though we had little credibility in this area. We'd already almost gotten ourselves killed more than once.

Alex watched us walk up my front path to the door. I waved to make sure he knew he could go, if for no other reason because, if my dad was home, there was most definitely an upcoming conversation Alex didn't need to hear.

As I reached for the door handle, Alex finally backed out. Captain Corbett pulled away from the curb after him, paused, and glared at me and Amber before moving down the street after his insubordinate employee.

I put my key into the lock and was surprised when it turned without effort. It wasn't locked. I surveyed the street—both sides—and the U-Haul was gone.

"What on earth…" I said as I opened the door and walked inside. Sure enough, my father had left not only the front door unlocked, but the window in the kitchen and the patio door wide open. It was freezing in my house.

"Dad?" I called, just for good measure. But I knew this tactic. Dad had done it once when I was in high school and I had gone out without leaving a note. I hadn't been home on time and he'd left the window of my bedroom wide open, even though it had been the middle of winter.

The difference was I hoped and prayed that my father wouldn't be back this time. I wondered if he'd moved onto Leslie's house now that he'd officially worn out his welcome with his pushover daughter.

"Why are all the windows open?" Amber shivered and closed the sliding glass door.

"That's my dad's way of trying to control my life. I mean, his second way. His first way was siccing Captain Corbett on us at the vineyard."

Amber's eyes widened. "That was because of your dad?"

I turned from where I'd shut the kitchen window over the sink. Hunch had already found his food and was hungrily munching on it. I shook my head. "I don't know how Alex will ever forgive me. One thing I'll tell you, though? If I can make up for it by helping with this case, you'd better believe I'm going to do just that."

Amber flopped down onto my couch. "Believe me, Alex is not angry. But I am. Captain Corbett had no right…"

I raised an eyebrow, even though I suspected Amber had trailed off because she knew the truth of the matter. "Captain Corbett could sway anyone to his side on this one. Having civilians and a cat at a crime scene?"

"Even if we shouldn't have been there, and even if he didn't know how much help we'd been on cases before, what kind of a police captain shows up at a crime scene and pulls the lead detective away without even asking about the evidence and if everything would be secure there? One on a power trip, that's what kind," she said, answering her own question. "I think we have a lot of the information we need. You took a photo of the sketch of the woman that Kristoph saw in the vineyard, right?"

I nodded. Alex had encouraged me to take my own photos of everything, just in case he had overlooked any possible connections. I'd print a copy before we left my house, so it would be easier to show around than flashing people my phone.

"So we have a sketch of the woman, and given the new information about the tractor and the strangling, the Tallmans could use another interview. We need to ask them more about that mystery guitar player."

Amber ticked agenda items off on her fingers. "Neither Alex or his partner has had time to get over to question Jennifer's ex-husband, who may have been abusive. Then there's that address from the slip of paper Hunch found. One of those leads has to show some connection to the killer. And if it doesn't, we question Benji some more. In fact, that part might be easier without Detective Martinez."

I moved dishes around my kitchen loudly, nodding and taking in what Amber was saying, but still unsure about how I felt about it all. Dad, of course, had left a tornado of a mess in my kitchen, as he had in my life, and so I continued to bang dishes into the dishwasher and tumble them into the sink, not really caring at this point what got broken.

"I'm going to look up the address from the slip of paper on Google Earth," Amber said. "Can I use your computer?"

I motioned my chin to my laptop on the kitchen table. She'd used it a dozen times before, so she already knew the password, but she never neglected to ask before using it.

She sat at the table and booted it up, and I filled the sink with too-hot water to wash dishes. In the three weeks my dad had lived here, he'd ruined three of my best pans by putting them into the dishwasher. This was yet another good reason to have him gone, and I told myself how thankful I was again and again as I scrubbed burn marks from pots.

The counter was wet from my slinging around of dishes, so when Amber appeared beside me a few minutes later with the laptop open and nowhere to set it, I grabbed for a dish towel and dried a section of counter for her. I'd finally worked off enough angst by scrubbing pots that I could have a conversation.

"I don't get it." She set the laptop down. "It's my old elementary school."

"Seriously?" I dried my hands and turned the laptop so I could see it better. It looked like an average elementary school, nothing unusual. "I don't get it either."

Hunch wove back and forth against my calves again. I bent to pick him up. "See, buddy. It's just the address for a local elementary school. I'm not sure it means anything."

Hunch tried to swat at the screen, and so I put him down. Sometimes my investigative cat seemed incredibly intuitive. Other times, he seemed just plain irritable.

"So if the paper's a bust, are we agreed that next on our list is visiting Jennifer's ex, Mr. Rempel?" Amber asked.

I thought again about Dahlia's words, about the Rempels having problems and the possibility that Jordan Rempel might have been physical with his ex-wife. It didn't make visiting him without a cop—or a warrant—very appealing. I glanced at Amber's hoodie.

And so I replied to Amber's question with the answer I often gave to everyone about everything when I didn't know what else to say.

"For now, I think I need to cook."

# CHAPTER TWELVE

When I checked my phone, there was nothing new from Alex, but I had fifteen missed calls from my sister, Leslie. I didn't have the heart to return them just yet. I knew my dad would have already spun his tale to make himself look like the victim here.

Instead, I tried to ignore my family drama under the guise of making some sort of food gift to deliver to the widower, Jordan Rempel.

While I cooked, Amber looked into Gary from Morgantown on social media.

"There are thirty-five men named Gary in their twenties listed as living in Morgantown." She set up my laptop on the counter again. "Any of them look like the guy playing guitar last night?"

In less than a minute, I'd seen them all and shook my head. "The guy last night had long, dark shaggy hair past his shoulders, and even if these photos were taken a while ago, none of them look like him."

Amber headed back to the table with my laptop. "I'll try the rest of the social media sites."

I had been keeping my frustrations about Dad at bay every time Amber had been over to cook in the last couple of weeks, but today when I said I needed to cook, she seemed to understand things were different and left me to the cooking instruments, eyeing me up every few seconds from the table.

Amber was never this quiet with me, so she understood the seriousness of my mood. If this had been the first time my dad had sold me out because he disagreed with something I was doing or simply because it suited his needs, that would be one thing. This was far from the first time. He'd just never gone to a police captain before. A friend's parent? Sure. Teachers and principals? Absolutely.

"You're baking something?" Amber interrupted my thoughts.

Unthinkingly, I'd pulled out eggs, vanilla, baking soda, and my big bin of

288

flour from the bottom of the pantry. I nodded, wondering if I could have made an entire recipe of something without knowing what it was, if not for Amber bringing me back to my consciousness.

Amber shook her head from the table. "I'm not seeing any different Garys in Morgantown."

"So he's either unlisted or he lied about his name." I held open the fridge and then the freezer, looking for cooking inspiration.

As if she could read my mind, Amber pulled my recipe book from culinary school off the shelf under the counter and started flipping pages. "Are you thinking of cookies or muffins or something savory?"

In truth, I hadn't been thinking at all. But muffins weren't a bad idea. "I'm not sure I can wrap my head around delivering something tasty to someone who beat his wife, or who might have even killed her," I said honestly.

Amber shrugged. "If it helps us get to the truth…"

The girl was far too jaded for fifteen. Which reminded me…her birthday was coming up in December. December was also the one-year anniversary of Cooper's death. I'd much prefer to focus on Amber than wallow in my grief. I'd have to ask Alex if he had any ideas about celebrating. It would be a hard year for her, too, having just lost her dad.

"I'm starting to get why you're so untrusting," Amber said, and for a second, I thought she was reading my thoughts about her. "The way your dad treats you, I mean." She went on when she could see the confusion on my face. "Has he always been like that?"

"Ever since my mom left," I told her, and with the words, something loosened in my chest. As always, talking to Amber about difficult subjects helped calm my emotions more than any kind of meditation or aromatherapy. "I was eight. My sister, Leslie, was twelve."

"So that's where he's gone now? To your sister's?" Amber showed me a recipe for some raspberry explosion muffins, but I scrunched my nose and shook my head at them. Too good for a wife beater.

"Leslie's called about a million times since I left home this morning, so she's obviously heard Dad's side of things, loud and clear."

"Well, your sister grew up with him, too, right? She knows what he's like. Don't you think maybe she's calling to get the real story out of you before her dad arrives on her doorstep?" Amber held out another recipe toward me, this one for a Bundt cake.

I wasn't sure if she meant it this way, but a Bundt cake seemed like the only thing we could give someone like Jordan Rempel. We'd give him a Bundt right back for all he may have done to his wife. And then we'd make sure he went to jail for it.

I focused hard on the recipe to try and let the subject of my dad and my sister go, but it didn't work. Because Amber was right. I had to call Leslie.

Half an hour later, I returned to the kitchen feeling much lighter. Of course Leslie believed every word of my side of things. He had already talked her into letting him stay for the night, but it meant doubling up her kids in bedrooms, which never went well, so she had already set the boundary that he had to be out by tomorrow. I sighed, wishing I could have that strong of boundaries with him from the onset, just once. At the very least, I knew my dad wouldn't have life nearly as easy at Leslie's house, with her strong-minded husband, Brad, who said things like they were, and their three busy, loud children.

I smiled at the thought. Then I took a whiff of the sweet aroma. "You already made it?" I asked Amber.

She shrugged, fighting a smile. Since I'd taught her to cook, it seemed to be the one outlet that gave her a sense of pride and accomplishment, and she was fully capable by this point of making most recipes on her own. I just enjoyed when we did it together.

"You can start on the icing," she said, as though she could read my mind.

I skimmed the recipe and then headed for the pantry for the icing sugar. Amber took this as her break time, rinsed her hands, and reached for Hunch, who had been watching her progress around the kitchen carefully from where he sat perched on a kitchen chair.

She cuddled Hunch onto her lap. "What do you think, Hunchie? A Bundt cake for Bundt-able Mr. Rempel?" She held up his front paws and looked him in the eyes. "Did he do it, Hunchie? Did he kill his ex-wife?"

Hunch squirmed to get down from the human pose Amber had forced him into. He swatted again at the swatch of paper we'd found in the tractor seat, which Amber had taped together and left on the kitchen table.

I blended the sugar, milk, and vanilla with my electric mixer, calling over the noise, "Hunch wants to believe the clue he found is the most important one."

Amber waited until the mixer was off to say, "Still. It couldn't hurt to check it out, right?"

Today was Saturday, so I wasn't sure what we'd find of interest at an elementary school. Then again, what clues to a murder investigation would we find there on a Monday? I couldn't think of a single one, and yet, I said, "Sure."

Maybe I only agreed because I wanted to delay visiting Jordan Rempel. Or maybe it was because I wanted his Bundt cake to be cold by the time we took it to him.

Whatever the reason, as Amber and I cleaned up my kitchen and waited for the Bundt cake to cool enough to add the icing, we discussed whether or not Hunch would be allowed to tag along on this next trip with us.

# CHAPTER THIRTEEN

"You're on speaker," I told Alex the moment my cell phone rang. "Amber's here with me."

"Are you still at your place?" Alex whispered. I wondered if he was crouched in a stairwell or a bathroom stall to have this covert conversation.

"Yes. We've been making a cake to take to Jordan Rempel."

Alex sighed. "I don't know, Mal." He seemed as nervous as I did about us visiting Jennifer's ex-husband.

"Would you rather Mickey handle it?"

It was an honest question, and in this one instance, I wouldn't have been at all offended if he'd said yes. But instead, he told me, "Corbett called Mickey in and told him to get busy on the fieldwork. He proceeded to get a warrant to search the Tallmans' house and the barn behind the winery."

"You really think there's evidence they'd be hiding on the property?" Amber asked.

"No, but Mickey does, and I guess I'd rather have him busy with that than messing up my case by blabbing the details to the wrong person or, worse, arresting Jennifer's ex-husband without cause."

So it was up to us to go there. I eyed the Bundt cake while Amber explained that the address we'd found on the tractor led to her old elementary school.

"Didn't Gina and Dahlia have young kids who went to school with Jennifer's son?" Alex flipped papers in the background. "It might be worth making a couple of quick stops to see if their kids happened to go to that elementary school. There are only a couple in town."

I nodded, feeling much better about this option. "At the same time, we can show them the sketch of the lady Kristoph saw. Maybe they'll recognize her or know something about our missing guitar player. You're okay if we go talk to Dahlia and Gina, then?"

"Absolutely," Alex whispered quieter, as if someone else was coming into his secluded spot. He whispered both of their addresses to us and then added, "Just keep me updated on what you find out."

He hung up without saying goodbye. If I thought of anything else, I'd relay that via text.

Dahlia lived in a rundown neighborhood of Honeysuckle Grove not too far from the elementary school. By her put-together appearance at the Bible study, I would have pegged her as more affluent. She had wanted to meet with us publicly today, at a coffee shop, but when I assured her it wouldn't take five minutes, she didn't seem able to come up with an excuse of why it wouldn't work for us to swing by her townhouse. Seeing her dilapidated unit, I suspected she had been trying to keep up wealthier appearances.

She met us at the door, and when she stepped outside onto her porch to speak with us, a waft of what smelled like pot drifted out the door. But I looked at her eyes, which were clear and alert. She shut the door, and a light breeze quickly pushed the scent from my nose. A second later, I wondered if I'd imagined the smell.

Dahlia had flat ironed her hair and wore tidy jeans and a pretty mustard sweater, which at least made her look the same well-to-do part she had last night, even if it was a complete contrast to the townhouse behind her.

"What's this about?" she said in way of a greeting. "Did Officer Martinez figure out who killed Jen?"

I still wasn't sure how to question her about the nickname, so I went with, "Not yet, no, but he has some good leads. We're just checking up on a few details to help him out."

Dahlia looked over at Amber for the first time, and then to Hunch, who was peaceably curled into Amber's arms. Dahlia looked back at me with a helping of raised eyebrows and an extra-large side of unbelief. "Is that right?"

I nodded. "This is my niece. She's staying with me, so I thought I'd bring her along to help out."

"In a murder investigation?" I couldn't tell by her sarcastic tone if it was an actual question, but I chose to answer it anyway.

"No, no. We're not investigating. Like I said, just helping out with some of the peripheral stuff. Detective Martinez will be doing the heavy lifting." I tried to offer my most disarming smile. Hunch, as if he wanted to help, purred loudly in Dahlia's direction.

But she stepped away, clearly not a fan of felines. "Well, then what can I do for you? What is this peripheral information you think I might know something about?"

I held up the photo of the police sketch I had printed off at home. "Do you recognize this lady?"

Dahlia barely glanced at it. "No."

"Are you sure?" I waved it a little closer to her face.

Dahlia scowled, but then snatched it from my hand and studied it. "Never seen her before in my life."

I slid the picture back into my purse. "And you have kids that went to school with Jennifer's kids?"

She furrowed her brow, still clearly untrusting of us. "My son went to school with Fresco. My daughter's older and is in middle school."

Fresco? I'd never heard the name before, but that must be Jennifer's son's name. "And what school did the boys go to?"

"Honey Littles Elementary. Why?"

I resisted the urge to look at Amber. It was the same school that the address from the tractor seat led to. "Right, okay. And they were in the same grade?"

"Sure. First grade. Mrs. Blakely's class."

My mind raced to think of anything else I could ask about this Mrs. Blakely or how the boys' school could possibly be connected to a murder. I didn't come up with anything, but thankfully, Amber jumped in with a new tack.

"Did you know Jennifer's husband very well?"

"Ex-husband," Dahlia emphasized. "And, no. I'd never met the man."

"If you'd never met him, what gave you the impression he had been abusive with Jennifer?"

Dahlia waved a hand. "We asked to meet him many times, but Jen was so private about him, there had to be hidden problems there. She clammed up every time we talked about him. It's a typical victim response." Dahlia shrugged. "I was just glad she finally left the guy and hoped she'd find someone nicer, like my Bart."

The words sounded caring, and yet there was an undertone that still, even after Jennifer Rempel's death, felt competitive.

"Gina and I even showed up to school early one week and waited in the parking lot to see what he looked, but the guy didn't pull up to the main drop-off area, so we barely got a glimpse of him. He sure didn't look like what we expected from what Jen had told us."

"What had Jennifer told you about her ex?"

Dahlia shrugged. "She never said much without us prodding, but from the way she talked about him, it seemed like she thought she was lucky to have him. I figured he probably had women all over him, some hottie with a nice body. To say I was surprised to see him driving a little smart car, rather than some kind of muscle car, is an understatement."

"I notice you call her Jen, while everyone else calls her Jennifer?" I kept my eyes trained on Dahlia's face, and sure enough, my question made her flinch.

But she shook it off and said, "It was kind of a game with us. She didn't like nicknames, and I didn't like talking about my diet. Whenever she brought up how many calories were in something, I called her by a nickname." Dahlia shrugged. "It happened so often, I guess I never use her full name anymore."

Again, I resisted the urge to look at Amber to see what she thought of this clear animosity between the two women.

I looked forward to hearing what Gina Thomson had to say on the subject.

☐

# CHAPTER FOURTEEN

"Do you really need to come to the door every time?" I asked Hunch from the driver's seat as I parked outside of Gina Thomson's townhouse. "It only makes us seem unprofessional."

Surprisingly, this time, neither Amber nor Hunch fought me on this point. Hunch hopped from Amber's lap to the backseat, where he perched up on his haunches, staring at the red front door of Gina's tidy-looking townhouse.

I followed Amber up the driveway to the front porch and knocked. Not long after, Gina swung the door open, her red hair tied back in an elastic today, and looked between the two of us.

"Oh! Hi!" she said, as though she might actually be happy to see us. When I'd spoken to her for a brief time last night, even in the midst of a murder investigation, she had seemed to be suppressing a naturally bubbly nature. Her voice dropped to almost a whisper. "Is this about Jennifer Rempel? Did they find out anything about who did that to her?"

While these were the same questions Dahlia had asked, they sounded a lot less edgy coming from Gina.

"This is about Ms. Rempel," I said. "But unfortunately we don't have any further details on what happened. Actually, we're looking for a little information." Gina glanced again at Amber, so I made the introductions. "This is my niece, Amber. She's staying with me and offered to come along to help."

This seemed to satisfy Gina, and she opened her door wider. "Would you like to come in?"

Even though Gina was much more welcoming than Dahlia, and with much less of her living space to hide, unfortunately, she couldn't tell us anything beyond what Dahlia had. She also didn't know the woman in the sketch.

"She couldn't have been a parent or a teacher at the elementary school?" Amber asked.

"I helped as a crossing guard most of last year," she told us in her small neatly decorated living room. "So I'm pretty sure I saw all of the teachers and parents come and go, not just the ones in Jesse's class, but for all the grades. That woman doesn't look like anyone I've seen at the school."

"And if she was new this year?" I asked. Both Amber and I sat up straight at the edge of the couch. Neither of us had accepted Gina's offer for coffee or water. We weren't planning to stay long.

"New families are a big subject of talk around Honeysuckle Grove." Gina glanced at my stomach. "You don't have kids in school, I assume."

That was always a hard question for me. Cooper and I had been eager to have a family later this year, if only he'd lived that long. "Um, no..." I started.

Amber, having a knack for saving me from these uncomfortable situations, jumped in with, "A troublemaking niece is enough for Aunt Mallory so far." She elbowed me playfully and winked at Gina.

Gina seemed to think nothing of it and went on about the woman in the sketch. "So you think this woman may have had something to do with Jennifer's death?"

"It's possible," I said. "She was seen in the vineyard yesterday evening. That's why we're trying to find out more about her or the guitar player who left quickly after the incident."

Gina shook her head blankly. We'd forgotten to ask Dahlia about the guitar player, but she'd been sitting even farther away from where he'd been playing, so I doubted she'd had any interactions with the man.

"What about Mr. Tallman? Did you look into him?" she asked.

"Don Tallman? Or do you mean his son, Benji?" It didn't matter which. Alex had questioned them both.

Her forehead furrowed. "I've known Benji a long time, and he's told me more than once that he had to keep secrets from his dad, or his dad would freak out. Plus, well..."

She looked at her lap, and I wondered what she didn't want to share and who she didn't want to hurt.

"Plus, what?" I asked gently. "You can tell us."

She took a breath and looked up. "One of Benji's secrets was about Jennifer. They'd been dating for a few months earlier this year. Benji's dad had wanted him to find himself a woman who had made her way in life, you know, had a good job, and wouldn't be mooching off the Tallmans."

"And Jennifer wasn't that type of person?" I guessed.

Gina shook her head. "She didn't even work. Her husband supported her. That's why I was shocked when she suddenly got divorced, even if she was secretly dating Benji. When I questioned her about it, she said I should wait for a big announcement soon." Gina shook her head in confusion. "Come to think of it, she never did announce anything."

"And she and Benji broke up?" I confirmed.

Gina nodded, her brow still furrowed. "I guess so. She hasn't wanted to talk about him in a while. When he chased after her outside last night, I was hoping they'd be able to work out their problems, but I kind of doubted it, especially with Mr. Tallman already angry over Jennifer's outburst."

As far as I knew, Benji hadn't said a word about this secret relationship to Alex. All of this new information had to mean something. Had Jordan Rempel found out about his wife's affair with Benji? That was certainly a motive to kill her. But even when we questioned Gina further, she didn't seem to know much about either of Jennifer's relationships.

"Did Dahlia Richards know about Jennifer's relationship with Benji?" It would be good to know if Dahlia had been hiding something so important.

But Gina shook her head. "Jennifer never told Dahlia because of how competitive they were. She assured me that after the big announcement, Dahlia and Mr. Tallman and everyone would know. Do you think Mr. Tallman is somehow involved in her murder?" Gina's eyes widened.

"The police have definitely been speaking to the Tallmans," I assured Gina, even though I felt like it might be a good idea to renew them on Alex's radar. I tilted my head and pried a little more into the friendship of the three mothers. "Do you ever refer to her as Jen, rather than Jennifer?"

Gina got a distasteful look on her face, like she'd sucked on a lemon. "Jennifer hated nicknames, so no."

I squinted, wondering if somehow I'd missed something. "But, Dahlia...? She calls—"

Gina interrupted my words with a loud laugh. "Oh, that's not because Jennifer liked it, believe me. That was just another way that Dahlia tried to get back at Jennifer for having it all in life." Gina's countenance softened into a sadder smile and she let out a sigh, but I had to question her wording.

"How she got back at Jennifer?"

Gina must have sensed my serious tone and looked at me with wide eyes. "Oh, no, it was nothing like that! Nothing serious. They just egged each other on, you know? Picked on each other for fun."

For fun? "You don't feel like Dahlia could have had a serious grievance with Jennifer?"

Gina shook her head. "Dahlia had enough to worry about, with Bart and everything."

"With Bart?" I'd gotten the impression Dahlia and Bart, despite their age difference, had a pretty good marriage. "Were things rocky between them?"

"Oh, no, not rocky." Gina looked between me and Amber, waiting for the lightbulb to go on with one of us. When it didn't, she added, "Bart's been really sick for the last six months. Stomach cancer. They're not sure if he'll last the year. She didn't mention it?"

I looked to Amber, wondering if we should pursue this line of questioning. But did I really believe Dahlia Richards had killed Jennifer Rempel over a little friendly competition, especially with a dying husband at home?

No, I didn't think so. Besides, if we had more questions, we knew where these ladies lived, and they didn't seem to be avoiding us. I thought we were done here, but apparently, Amber still had more questions.

"You said you worked as a crossing guard. So you must have seen Jennifer's ex-husband dropping their son off sometimes?"

Gina looked down sheepishly. "Well, sort of."

"Sort of?" Amber pushed, never one to shy away or let people have a moment to compose themselves. It was one thing that made her a better detective than me.

"Well, he always dropped him off across the grocery store parking lot, so I saw him from a distance. Most parents want to drop their kids as close to the school as possible, but I guess Jennifer's ex wasn't like most parents."

"So he made Fresco walk through traffic to get to school?" That seemed odd. First grade seemed awfully young to navigate busy streets, even if there was a crossing guard.

"Oh, the grocery store doesn't open until nine," Gina explained. "It was a smart move on his part. The drop-off circle is crazy busy in the mornings." Under her breath, she added, "Still, I don't know any other parent who would drop their kids that far away."

"So you saw Jordan Rempel from a distance?" Amber forced the conversation back where she wanted it.

Gina squirmed her shoulder again. Finally, she sighed, and said, "Yeah, I did. But it seemed like Jennifer didn't really want anyone to know much about him, and Dahlia was always asking me what he looked like and what I thought of him. I didn't want to get in the middle of it, so I always pretended not to have really seen him."

"Even when Dahlia suggested Jennifer's ex-husband might have been physical with her?" I pressed.

Gina looked down at her lap and nodded. "I knew by the looks of him it probably wasn't true. But Dahlia wouldn't want to hear that." She took in a big breath and let it out slowly. "She wanted to stir up the drama around Jennifer." When Gina looked up again, she asked, "Are you going to tell her about this?"

I couldn't promise that wouldn't be necessary, but for the moment, I could at least say this: "I don't see why we would have to." I tried to offer my most disarming smile.

Amber gave me a single nod and we both stood up. "Thank you so much for your help, Mrs. Thomson."

"Gina," she said, reaching out to shake both of our hands. She led the way to her front door and opened it for us. "If you think of any other way I can help, please let me know. I still can't believe what happened to Jennifer."

I assured her we would, and Amber and I walked to my car at the curb, where Hunch paced back and forth in a frenzy along the backseat. We'd disappeared for nearly fifteen minutes, and he didn't like it one bit.

☐

# CHAPTER FIFTEEN

I looked across my white Prius to the passenger seat, where Amber wore a smug smile. Hunch, on her lap, looked even smugger. After talking through all the details we had discovered from Gina and Dahlia, and updating Alex via text, they were both convinced we'd found our perpetrator.

I still wasn't so sure I one hundred percent believed Jordan had killed his ex-wife, even if he had found out she was cheating on him. What about Benji and his secret relationship with Jennifer? What about Benji's dad? Plus, we still hadn't found out anything about the lady in the sketch. Then again, we were only taking the vineyard employee Kristoph Carter's word on that. Perhaps Mickey Mouse was onto something and we should interview him again.

We stopped by the Honey Littles Elementary School on our way to Jordan Rempel's house, but despite our best efforts, we couldn't find anything that even looked like a clue.

"We should call on Monday and see if the school office knows anything about Jordan Rempel," Amber said.

"Or a Benji or Don Tallman," I suggested. "Or the woman in the sketch."

The Tallmans had quickly fallen off Amber's radar. I wanted to remind her and Hunch that there were still other suspects, and I wanted to interview Kristoph and ask him a few more questions about the woman's exact whereabouts.

"We'll have to go to the elementary school in person. But not until Monday."

Amber wouldn't like—or probably have any patience for—going back to her classes on Monday with the investigation unsolved. I'd been roped into pretending to be her mom and calling to get her out of school once, but I really wasn't comfortable with doing it again.

"Sometimes Hunch gets things wrong, you know," I told her. "The address could have been tucked into that tractor seat for months, maybe even since the Tallmans bought the tractor. I think we were just all determined to find any other possible clues." I felt bad for any time we wasted when Alex was stuck at the station.

Amber shrugged. "We should get over to Jordan Rempel's place before Mickey Mouse decides to head there."

Alex and I had been texting back and forth, ever since Captain Corbett had given him an earful about protocol and then slumped a bin full of paperwork onto his desk to deal with. Alex still felt unsure of us going to Jordan Rempel's house without police, but I'd told him we'd stay outside and eventually talked him into giving over the address.

<I don't know how I feel about Amber going there with you.> Alex texted. <Then again, I don't want you to go by yourself. If I haven't heard back from you in fifteen minutes, I'm heading straight there, no matter what Corbett says.>

I read the text and then started the Prius, clicking start on Jordan Rempel's address in my GPS. It was a ten-minute drive away, so I texted back.

<Don't start the timer yet. Driving…>

A thumbs-up emoji appeared in reply. I got on the road.

"What are we going to ask this guy, you know, after we give him a good Bundt?" It was meant as a joke, but it still bothered me that Amber was asking this question. She was normally the one who knew all the best questions to ask, as though they were being fed into her intravenously.

"Well, I guess I'd like to get a picture of their marriage and when he last saw his ex-wife. Nobody seems to know much about this guy, Jordan Rempel, only that he and Jennifer had been married and split up several months ago. Dahlia and Gina both figured it had been a rocky divorce, as Jennifer hadn't come to Bible study or church or even to their coffee meetings for nearly three months. She'd just started to regularly get back to being social when she died."

"So nobody actually came out and said he beat her up, did they?" Amber asked.

Even though we'd both been interviewing Gina and Dahlia, I was glad Amber confirmed this aloud and brought it back to mind, so we didn't walk up to Jordan starting with the wrong impression.

"That's right," I told her. "Neither of them had ever met Jennifer's husband. They had met her son because their kids regularly played together, but beyond that, they said she was private about her home life. She never even invited them over for a cup of coffee. They didn't know where she lived."

Thanks to Alex, I had both her address and her ex-husband's. An officer had been by Jennifer's apartment late the night before, but when no one answered the door, he went to a neighbor's and found out Jennifer's son would likely be at her ex-husband's place. The officer went from there to Jordan's house, but that was only a quick visit to deliver the news about Jennifer's death. Jordan had been home, in his pajamas, and his son had been asleep in bed. No one had thought of the ex-husband as a serious suspect at that point, so the questioning only included asking for contact information for Jennifer's parents, who lived just outside Morgantown.

Part of the menial work Alex would be busy with today involved speaking with Jennifer's parents when they came into town to identify Jennifer's body. He didn't expect to learn much from them, as Jordan had explained to the officer last night that Jennifer hadn't been close to her parents since she moved out of Morgantown five years ago. Still, the fact they were from Morgantown seemed coincidental, and Alex was eager to describe Gary-the-guitar-player to them and check for any familiarity.

I turned onto Jordan Rempel's street and took in a deep breath as Amber pointed to the house we were looking for.

"So are you my aunt today or are we special consultants from the police department?" Amber asked. Those were both identities we'd hidden behind when questioning suspects in previous murder investigations.

"In light of Captain Corbett's dislike for our interfering, I think we'd better go with niece and aunt."

Amber nodded and reached for the door handle. Without any discussion about it, she placed Hunch down on the pavement. Apparently, he was coming along, and I felt like I had too much on my mind to argue about it.

It was a habit to park along the curb when interviewing suspects, even if there was room in the driveway. More than once, we'd had to make a quick getaway, when a person we were speaking to figured out they may have said too much to us. Only one car sat in Jordan Rempel's driveway—a small black smart car.

As I got out on my side, I shot Alex a quick text: <Going to the door! 15 minutes should be lots.>

Another thumbs-up emoji appeared moments later.

Amber grabbed the Bundt cake from the backseat, and we walked to Jordan Rempel's front door with Hunch trailing behind us.

It was one of the nicer suburban neighborhoods in Honeysuckle Grove, and I wondered what Jordan did for a living to pay for not only the house, but likely child support and Jennifer's living expenses in her apartment across town.

After a long moment with no answer, Amber knocked a second time, much louder. I supposed I should have been glad to have a bold teenager along to give me the push I sometimes needed.

Footsteps sounded and then the door opened in front of us. To say the man on the other side of the door was not what I expected was an understatement. He was shorter than me and couldn't have weighed a hundred and fifty pounds. He wore thick, black-rimmed glasses, and while he had the wrinkles that suggested he was at least in his thirties, I would have guessed him to be a teenager from a distance.

"Are you Jordan Rempel?" I asked doubtfully.

He nodded. "That's me."

"I…um…" I started, but then couldn't seem to form my first question. He was the complete opposite of the tough guy I had expected. In fact, I wasn't sure if this guy could have been physically abusive to someone loud and strong like Jennifer Rempel. I'd have sooner been able to envision her beating him up. In an instant, my pre-prepared questions vanished.

Thankfully, Amber came to my rescue. She passed him the Bundt cake. "My aunt is friends from church with your ex-wife, Jennifer Rempel?" Amber asked it as a question, but then barreled on before he could respond. "We heard something about her, something happened to her, and wanted to come right to the source to check." The crease between Amber's eyes looked like concern, but I knew her well enough to know it was actually undivided attention.

Jordan looked down at the Bundt cake in his hands. "I—yes, what she heard is probably right." He placed the cake inside on a table, neglected to thank us, and pinched the bridge of his nose beneath his glasses.

"So she's—"

"I was supposed to go to Bible study with her last night." I cut Amber off because it sounded like she was treading into an area of bluntness we wouldn't be able to return from. "But I couldn't make it at the last minute."

Jordan shook his head at the ground and murmured to himself, "Maybe that's why she was so angry when she dropped Fresco off." He tilted his head up and said to us, "That's where she died. At the winery where the Bible study was being held."

Something about those last couple of sentences didn't add up for me. It seemed like Jennifer had told Jordan about the winery location, but hadn't let on that this was the reason for her anger. "Is that your son? Fresco?" When he nodded, I went on. "So she dropped your son off before heading to Bible study last night? It sounds like you and Jennifer were on amicable terms."

Jordan shrugged. "Sure. We're…we were friends. I saw her every weekend when she dropped off Fresco. Then I dropped him off at school Monday mornings. Jennifer picked him after coffee with her girlfriends." He looked away from us like the reality of his new normal without Jennifer was hitting him.

So he knew she had coffee with her girlfriends on Monday mornings as well? That seemed friendly enough.

Amber jumped in with another question just as it entered my mind. "You didn't attend Bible study with her?" He shook his head, which instigated her next question. "And I don't think I've seen you around Honeysuckle Grove Community Church?"

He shrugged one shoulder uncomfortably. "Church was more Jennifer's thing."

"And she didn't take your son?" Any Christian woman I knew wanted to have her kids in church on Sunday mornings, but I realized the second the question left my mouth that if I'd indeed been a friend of Jennifer's, I should have known this information.

"Fresco was with me Sundays," he said, not noticing the disparity. It sounded like that meant it was his time and so he wouldn't allow Jennifer to pick him up for church. Maybe this small, young-looking man wasn't physically abusive, but I wondered if he could have been controlling behind closed doors.

"Fresco's an unusual name," Amber observed. "I haven't heard that one before."

Jordan looked over his shoulder, like his son must be inside somewhere. "That one's all Jennifer, I'm afraid. She loved the name—wouldn't let me shorten it or make any nicknames."

Now who sounded like the controlling one? "You had no say at all in naming your son?" I asked.

"Oh, Fresco's not mine," Jordan said, not an ounce of offense or defensiveness in his voice. "He'd already been born when we met." Jordan looked over his shoulder again. "Actually, he's kind of how we met."

"How's that?" I asked, doing the mental math. If Fresco was in first grade, that meant he was about six years old. So Jordan and Jen had met, married, and been divorced sometime in approximately the last five years.

"I'm a software developer," Jordan explained. "I specialize in baby products—baby naming software, baby supply ordering software, that sort of thing. It's easier to be successful in my line of work if you find an untapped niche." He waved a hand, like that wasn't important. "Anyway, I was visiting a local baby store in Morgantown to get them connected on my system when I met Jennifer. We hit it off, and her little guy, even though he was still in a stroller, really took to me, too."

There was the city of Morgantown again. While I could picture Jennifer as a city girl, I still had trouble envisioning the pretty and commanding woman with this scrawny, nerdy guy. Was she truly attracted to him? Or only his money?

"So she gave you visitation rights every weekend, even though Fresco wasn't your son?" I wondered if Fresco's real father could have somehow been involved in Jennifer's murder.

Jordan shrugged, like he didn't see the oddity. "Fresco's dad was a real deadbeat apparently. A drug user who wouldn't even try to get clean to be a role model for his son. He doesn't want anything to do with his own kid. She likes—liked—that I'm good with him and I care about him."

"But the two of you couldn't make it work?" Amber asked. "Even for the sake of the kid?"

This question seemed to strike a nerve with him. He rubbed his hands together uncomfortably, blinked a few times, and finally spoke. "Look, a lot of people think Jennifer just married me for my money, and honestly, she probably did. But I don't care. She was a good friend, and her son is like my own. When she said she wanted to get her own place and share custody of Fresco, I told her it was fine with me because nothing much would change, really."

Nothing much would change if a husband and wife weren't living together? That, for me at least, didn't add up at all. So if Jennifer was really using him for his money, and he seemed completely compliant in this, had they ever even consummated their marriage? But that didn't seem like a question I could ask this man that seemed to be, at the very least, mourning his friend.

"Was she seeing anyone else since the two of you split up?" I watched him carefully, but he didn't flinch.

"Not that I know of, but it wouldn't surprise me. I mean, a beautiful woman like that...and she kept pressing me to hurry the divorce along." His brow furrowed, as though this was the first time he'd considered that notion.

"Did you know much about her involvement with MADD?" I asked. When he tilted his head, I added, "Mothers Against Drunk Drivers?"

"Ah." He nodded. "Jennifer took up a lot of causes and was pretty outspoken about everything she believed. It's why we hit it off so quickly—she loved that I had advocated for a safety rating on each item listed on our baby supply ordering website."

"And she was living in Morgantown at the time? Do you know any of her friends or family from there?"

He shook his head. "She was eager to move to Honeysuckle Grove with me and didn't want to talk at all about that time in her life."

This seemed like confirmation that Gary, or someone else from Morgantown, might have played into her murder.

Before I could come up with another question, a young boy appeared at Jordan's legs. I could barely concentrate on his short dark hair or round dark eyes that matched Jennifer Rempel's because the boy had Hunch snuggled up in his arms.

Jordan saw Hunch at the same time I did. "Oh, Fresco, you shouldn't—
"

I reached out. "I'm so sorry! That's my late husband's cat. Since he died, the cat goes everywhere with me."

Fresco compliantly passed Hunch over, although Hunch didn't seem too excited to be coming to my arms, so I quickly passed him to Amber.

"Can I get a kitty, Uncle Jordan?" the little boy asked.

Jordan tilted his head at the boy and blinked fast a few times, as though holding back tears. "It's something to think about, Fresco. Why don't we talk about it as soon as I'm done visiting with these ladies?"

Fresco nodded, gave Hunch one last look, and then headed back inside. Jordan truly seemed like someone trying to be the best possible uncle to this boy, and so I said, "Cats are actually really easy to take care of," as an encouragement.

Jordan's eyes were still inside his house on where Fresco had disappeared.

In an effort not to lose momentum, I said, "It sounds like Jennifer left some ghosts behind in Morgantown. You said she didn't get along with her parents very well either?"

He rejoined the conversation. "Hasn't talked to them in years. They rarely leave their farm, even to visit their own daughter." He shook his head. "I guess they'll be coming to town now to find out where she was living for the last five years."

I almost opened my mouth to say they would be coming today, but quickly realized if I was just a friend from church, I wouldn't know those details.

"What kind of farm?" Amber asked. "Do they have tractors?"

That hadn't occurred to me. But what was Amber getting at—that Jennifer's parents had killed their own daughter?

Jordan shrugged. "I have no idea. Again, she really didn't talk about her past in Morgantown."

"She kept your last name, though," I observed as a conciliatory point. "Even after the divorce."

He smiled wryly. "Yeah, I think that had more to do with her escaping her past than it did with wanting to keep a piece of me. One time, last month, a news journal published a piece using her maiden name, Gustafson, and she freaked out. She was over here when it came up on her phone, and she called in to the journal's head office right there and then to give them an earful."

That was curious. And suddenly it seemed we could be looking in the wrong pile of suspects. We were only looking into the locals who had known Jennifer for less than five years. What if the killer had been someone from Jennifer's past? Perhaps the guitar player was someone she knew from

Morgantown, maybe even Fresco's dad, but she hadn't been inside the winery long enough to recognize him.

As I pulled out my printed copy of the sketch from the police sketch artist, I couldn't come up with a ready excuse of why I, a friend of Jennifer's from church, would have such an item. But it didn't matter because I had to ask, with or without an excuse. I held up the photo. "Have you ever seen a woman that looks like this around here?"

I didn't know how much I trusted in the abilities of a police sketch artist, especially from a witness who had complained about the dim lighting, until Jordan reached for the printed drawing, his eyebrows buckling.

"Yeah. She was here looking for Jennifer last night. Jennifer had already dropped Fresco off, so I told the woman we were divorced and that my ex lived at a different address, but that I didn't think she'd be home for the evening, as she'd gone out to a Bible study."

"Did the woman say how she knew Jennifer?" I glanced at Amber for a half-second. We were close to getting to the truth now, I could feel it.

Jordan shrugged and passed back the drawing. "Sure. She said her kid went to school with Fresco. She wanted to arrange a playdate or something." Jordan scratched the back of his neck. "Not sure why Jennifer would've given her this address, though."

And why wouldn't Gina or Dahlia have recognized the woman if this were true?

"Did you tell the woman where the Bible study was being held?" I sucked in a breath, but his answer came quickly.

"No. I had no idea where it was being held, not until Officer Krause came here last night and told me what had happened at the winery."

Jordan hadn't known about the winery location. No wonder he hadn't known why she'd been angry when she dropped her son off.

And yet somehow the woman who'd been posing as an elementary school parent, a woman neither Gina nor Dahlia recognized, and a woman who was later seen at the vineyard, figured out exactly where Jennifer had gone for the evening.

☐

# CHAPTER SIXTEEN

Amber and I drove to the nearest donut shop and sat in the parking lot, me with a cup of tea, her with a hot chocolate and an éclair, discussing what we had come up with so far. I texted Alex, letting him know we were done with Jordan, that it went well, and he should call as soon as he had a second away from any listening ears.

"I told you Hunch was onto something with that elementary school," Amber said, scratching him behind his ears the way he only seemed to like from her. "You're a smart little kitten."

Hunch was neither little nor a kitten, but I chose not to debate those points. "We still don't know that for sure." Amber raised an eyebrow at me as I went on. "I'll admit, the fact that the woman in the sketch pretended to be a parent from the school whose address we found on the tractor in the vineyard sounds suspicious."

"Don't forget that when we pressed Mr. Rempel and asked him to go over the conversation as specifically as he could remember it, he said the woman from the sketch had said her son went to school with Fresco, and Jordan had said, 'Oh, your son goes to Honey Littles Elementary as well.' What are the chances that this woman in the sketch is a woman from Jennifer's past in Morgantown, and she was fishing to find out where Jennifer lived, where her kid went to school, and who knows what else, all in order to track her down?"

When she put it like that, the chances seemed pretty strong. "Okay, but how do we find out who this woman is and what she might have had against Jennifer Rempel?"

Amber took a big bite of her éclair and talked with her mouth full. "That sounds like a job for a detective stuck in the office."

309

As if on cue, Alex's name flashed across the screen.

"What's up?" he asked in his same quiet voice.

"First, I think we can clear Jordan as a suspect." I looked to Amber to make sure she was in agreement. She nodded. I even looked to Hunch for approval, but he ignored me in lieu of his affectionate best friend.

"He was pretty broken up about his ex-wife?" Alex asked.

"A little, but that's not why. He didn't seem the type to overtake her physically, and it sounds like they were actually friends. He definitely loves her kid and wouldn't want to do anything to hurt him."

"He's not the father?" Alex asked.

"No, but get this. He recognized the woman from the police sketch. He said she had been by on Friday evening, claiming her kid went to Honey Littles Elementary School with Jennifer's son, Fresco." I rattled on, trying to get all the important details out before he had to go. "He told the woman that Jennifer was at a Bible study."

"Did he tell her its location?"

I shook my head at the phone. "No, he didn't know the location until Officer Krause told him what had happened to Jennifer late last night. He also said Jennifer had a past in Morgantown that she wouldn't even talk about with him."

"Can you search up her past on the police computers?" Amber asked.

"Only if she has a record," Alex said. "But let me look into it. I assume I should be looking under her maiden name, Gustafson, same as her parents?"

"Yes." I explained about the article that had recently really upset Jennifer by printing Gustafson as her last name.

"If she doesn't have any priors, I'll phone the department in Morgantown, just to see if they've come across her or her family in any capacity."

I nodded. "The father of Jennifer's kid is a drug user in Morgantown, but Jordan didn't know his name. Maybe ask if they've come across a user with long straggly hair named Gary?"

Alex agreed. "I guess no one is at the elementary school office until Monday. Checking in to see if they recognize the lady in the sketch might be a task Mickey Mouse can handle."

I wasn't so sure about that, but I wasn't about to argue with Alex when it came to his job. "I thought about dropping by the winery, you know, just to pick up a bottle of that Riesling."

I half-expected Alex to caution me away from there, so it surprised me when he said, "Good idea. It's still under forced closure, but that's a good excuse to poke around with a few more questions about the guitar player and find out what's taking Mickey so long."

If Mickey was still out at the winery, that certainly made me less eager to go.

But this wasn't about what I liked or wanted. This was about solving a murder.

☐

# CHAPTER SEVENTEEN

Today, when we arrived at the winery, the parking lot was empty, and a wooden sign over the directional sign to the winery read: WINERY CLOSED TODAY

"Hmm. Maybe my ruse of going in to buy a bottle of wine isn't going to work after all if they have a sign down here." I slumped back into my seat, but Amber was already reaching for her door handle.

"Still, we drove all the way out here."

Hunch also nosed the door. It was two against one.

"We don't even know if anyone's here," I said as I followed them up the path. "There are no cars."

"I'll bet the Tallmans have a driveway that goes straight to their house. Detective Bradley hasn't reported back in, so unless he went home and crawled back into bed…"

"You say that as if it's unlikely," I mumbled. "What excuse are we going to use to barge in there when they're closed?"

Amber shrugged. "Play dumb. Use the bottle of wine story and say you knew they had to be closed because of the crime scene, but you hoped you could just quickly grab a bottle. From what you told me about the Tallmans, they'd be up for making a sale, no matter what the circumstances."

That was true enough, I supposed. I just hoped we didn't run into Mickey first.

We'd barely made it to the clearing, where the cedar winery came into view, when the other Riesling greeted us.

He rounded the winery, barking like a miniature watchdog. On instinct,

I squatted to the ground and called out, "Shh, shh. It's only us, Riesling."

But the dog didn't stop. It was only when I looked over and saw Hunch with his back arched high and his fur poking stick-straight on all sides that I realized what had the dog so riled up.

"It's okay, Hunch." I reached out a hand to touch him, but he turned, eyes wild, and hissed at me. "Alrighty then." I pulled my hand away.

Apparently, Amber had better instincts than me with animals as well as murder investigations. She ignored Hunch and moved straight for the small dog, scooping him up in less than a second and turning him so Hunch was out of his immediate view.

She mumbled something unintelligible into his fur, and soon his barking subsided. "Get Hunch inside," she said quietly, and I had to assume the directive was for me, even though it was a rare moment when I could make Hunch do anything.

But Hunch, for once, obeyed when I made a large arc around Amber and the dog and called him toward the winery door. Seconds later, we were inside, and Hunch and I let out a collective breath before either of us noticed we weren't alone.

But Mr. and Mrs. Tallman didn't greet us. Their son did.

"I'm sorry, but we're closed today."

"Oh! Benji, hi." I took a moment to even out my breathing. In the meantime, Hunch was completely over his encounter with Riesling and started to sniff at every inch of the floor. "I saw that. I was talking to Alex and heard Detective Bradley was here. I thought I'd stop in and see if he'd figured anything out." The unplanned excuse left my mouth without any planning. Then again, I had planned on encountering Benji's parents.

Benji ran a hand through his blond hair. It stood up, and he didn't bother to fix it. "Yeah, I guess he's searching the house and barn. I have no idea what Detective Bradley's looking for."

By his nervousness, I wasn't sure I believed that. This couldn't have worked out better because I had my own questions for Benji Tallman, ones that even Alex might not want to ask if he were allowed out of the office.

"In a murder investigation, they have to look at all angles and all surroundings," I said. Amber slipped in through the door, but I didn't take the time to introduce her. "Which reminds me. You were gone from the winery around the time of Jennifer's death." He flinched away on my last words, but a doggedness came over me, determined to get the true story one way or another. "Where were you during that time?"

Benji looked at his feet. "As I told Alex—Detective Martinez—I had tried to catch up with her on her way to the parking lot, but she was nowhere in sight. While I waited, I fixed up some of the branches along the path."

"For half an hour?" Amber piped in, her voice full of disbelief.

"What kind of car did Ms. Rempel drive?" I asked, practically on top of Amber's question. As he started to answer, "A Honda—" I spoke over that, too. "How did you know Ms. Rempel's car so well?"

Benji's gaze stayed on his feet, but now he blinked fast, as though he knew we were cornering him.

"Isn't it true that you knew her car because you had been in a relationship with Jennifer Rempel?" I asked.

Benji's gaze darted from me to Amber and, finally, to the door. When he spoke, his words were almost in a whisper. "That was months ago. It wasn't serious."

"Your parents didn't know about the relationship, I assume?" In kindness, I dropped my voice a little as well.

He shook his head. "I...they wouldn't have approved."

I nodded. I already knew that part, thanks to Gina Thompson. "Did you know Jennifer would be bothered by a Bible study being held here at the winery?"

He bit his lip and nodded. "I thought for sure she wouldn't show up. She hadn't been coming regularly for months."

"Ever since you broke up with her?" I guessed. He nodded, looking sheepish about it. "But you offered to have the Bible study here, regardless of how it might bother Jennifer?"

Benji blinked fast again, but now he looked as though he were blinking away tears. "My dad wanted me to, okay?" he suddenly burst out. "I'd been putting him off, but Jennifer had started to come back to Bible studies, so I figured I'd better do it soon, before she got knit into the group again."

"Why did your dad want you to have the Bible study here?" Amber asked as the same thought came to me.

Benji shook his head. "Promotion. They're losing money, month after month, because they can't get people to make the trip this far out of town and see how they've improved the place. They'd been bugging me for months to get my Bible study, my office co-workers, and even my soccer team out here for an event."

That part was all starting to make sense. The part I couldn't get my head around, though, was his secret relationship with Jennifer.

"When Jennifer stormed out of here, you must have felt awful," I said, trying to lead the conversation back in that direction. He nodded, but didn't seem willing to talk on his own, so I pressed. "Are you telling me that you, knowing the property much better than she did, couldn't catch up to her outside?"

He stared at the floor, blinking fast, and clearly full of emotion, but not saying a word.

"Look, Benji. Either the two of you had an awful fight out there, and it ended with you doing something you didn't mean to do—"

314

"No!" He shook his head almost violently. "I didn't kill Jennifer. I didn't!"

"Well, someone did," Amber put in. "And if it wasn't you, don't you feel even a little bit responsible to figure out who did?"

The weight of this statement seemed to settle on Benji, so much so he dropped onto a barstool. Then his face fell into his hands and he started sobbing.

Amber kept opening her mouth to ask him more, but I held up a hand to make her wait, at least for a moment.

Finally, Benji spoke through his tears and his hands, without any prodding. "I lied, okay? I caught up to Jennifer in the parking lot." He looked at me with pained eyes. "I couldn't come back here and face my dad if I didn't, so I blocked her path to her car to make her listen to me and calm down."

"And what did she do when you blocked her path?" I asked gently.

"She told me she was going to shut down the Bible study one way or another. She said she'd find the electrical panel for my parents' precious winery and shut the power down. At first, I felt so guilty that I thought maybe I should just let her. But after a few minutes of stewing, I couldn't just sit around the parking lot and let it all happen. I went up to the electrical panel, but she hadn't found it yet, so I figured I'd guard it until she did and try to talk to her again."

"Where is this electrical panel?" I asked.

He motioned to the back of the winery. "Right around back. It runs all the power to this building and my parents' house."

"Did Jennifer ever show up there, or did anyone see you out there?" I didn't have much hope for this, but it couldn't hurt to ask.

"I saw my dad." He shook his head. "But I stayed out of sight on purpose, so he wouldn't see me." He looked like he perfectly understood how guilty this all made him seem.

But as far as I was concerned, I felt in my gut that he was being truthful for the first time.

"Why did the two of you break up?" Amber asked, always the one with the most insightful questions.

He took in a big breath and let it out in a sigh. "She got way too serious, too fast. She even divorced her husband and said she wanted to marry me, instead." He shook his head again. "I wasn't ready for an instant relationship, especially with a kid. When I finally worked up the courage to tell her that, she freaked out and stopped coming to Bible study for months."

I was about to ask if they'd ever spoken again, if things had smoothed out at all between them, when Don and Marie Tallman burst through the winery door.

"They've arrested Kristoph!" Marie said and burst into her own round of tears.

☐

# CHAPTER EIGHTEEN

"What? What are you talking about?" Benji looked from his emotional mom to his angry dad.

"They found drugs in the barn!" Don Tallman barked. "You better not have known anything about this."

I couldn't tell by the look on Benji's face if he felt guilty over knowing about the drugs in the barn or if this was simply residual guilt from the true circumstances surrounding Jennifer's death.

What truly frustrated me was that Detective Mickey Mouse Bradley had done it again: He'd focused on the wrong part of an investigation and made a quick arrest—two things that Alex was forever complaining about.

I was determined not to let him botch this case, though. "Has Detective Bradley already left?"

Don and Marie Tallman looked at me, noticing me and Amber for what seemed like the first time. Don ran a hand through his graying hair, reminiscent of the way Benji ran one through his. "They just left for the police station."

I motioned to where Hunch was sniffing around where the guitar player had been seated last night. "Let's get going. We'd better give Alex a heads-up."

"Alex? Your detective friend?" Don looked between me and Benji. "Is there any way to keep this quiet? Our winery can't handle all of this bad publicity."

I wasn't certain who the question was for, but I answered it. "I can't tell you that for sure, but I can tell you that if there's anything you've held back from telling the police, your best bet is to call Detective Martinez and come clean about it right away."

I led the way out the door, Amber following behind with Hunch in her arms. We'd tell Alex everything we knew as well, of course, but Captain

Corbett wouldn't be able to deny a detective to take a call from an informant with information on a murder case if they specifically asked for him.

At least I was pretty sure he wouldn't.

We drove back to my house, going over the new information we'd discovered today. We'd tried to call Alex, but when the police receptionist told us he was on the other line, Amber sent him a few overview texts while I drove instead.

"How about a cooking lesson while we wait to hear from Detective Martinez?" Amber said from the passenger seat as soon as we were in my driveway.

I barely thought she needed lessons anymore. She was such a quick learner. She'd picked up many of the most important things I'd learned in culinary school in a matter of months. I supposed I shouldn't be too surprised, as she seemed to pick up detective work nearly as fast.

"Actually, I picked up some jumbo shrimp the other day. Do you like coconut?"

"I love coconut!" Amber exclaimed. This got her quickly out of the car, carrying Hunch to the house. "We're making coconut shrimp?" She let out a little squeal.

I loved how excited she got about food. It reminded me of myself when I'd first gotten into culinary school and hadn't been so jaded by life. "And maybe a mango salsa. What do you think?"

Another squeal. She'd only had the éclair for lunch, and I hadn't felt much like eating. This would be ready in time for dinner, and with any luck, Alex would be released from his tyrant of a boss at some point so he could enjoy them with us while talking over the case.

I filled Hunch's food dish while Amber washed her hands and wiped down the counter with a vinegar and water mixture like I'd taught her. Hunch had no interest in his food and instead hopped up onto a kitchen chair and laid a paw on the swatch of paper on my table—the swatch with the elementary school's address.

"Yes, you were right," I told my cat. I was getting more and more used to talking to him aloud and also calling him my cat. For the longest time, I could only think of him as Cooper's, and I still fell back into that habit once in a while. "Using the elementary school as a connection was how this perpetrator found out from her ex-husband where Jennifer had gone last night. It was most certainly important." I ruffled his fur, but he only growled at me, so I left him alone. "Still, when the woman in the sketch came by, Jordan hadn't known where the Bible study was being held, so he couldn't have told her that part."

I headed for the freezer to get my jumbo shrimp thawing in some cool water and then checked my phone for messages.

I had another voicemail from my sister, Leslie. Clicking in my password, I steeled myself and held it to my ear to listen. "Hey, Mal, it's me. Just wanted to keep you updated. Of course Dad wouldn't admit to any wrongdoing, but after only two hours with his grandchildren, he's talking about moving back to Pennsylvania." She laughed, and the statement was almost enough to make me smile as well. Almost. "But listen, Mallory, Dad's saying you're investigating murders, like, as a regular thing now. That didn't sound like something you'd do, but I just thought I'd check. Aren't you cooking these days? I know you need something to do with your time, but I'd much rather see you making yummy food than prying into the secrets of possible murderers!" She laughed again, but this time her laugh was strained. She rattled on after that about her kids and Brad and what she planned to make for dinner, but all I could think about was what I could tell her when I called her back.

I wasn't about to give up on helping Alex. But admitting that I was, indeed, helping with murder investigations, any way I thought of saying it, seemed like it would only prove my dad's points against me.

When she'd finally talked herself out and hung up, I decided to put her off for a few days with a simple text. <I'll tell you all about it when I have time to chat, but trust me, I'm being safe.>

This murder investigation had to come first. Family drama? I'd deal with that next week.

"So what do you use for the coating?" Amber asked as I walked back into the kitchen. "Coconut and what else?" She already had my pantry open and had fished out a large bag of unsweetened coconut.

"I make my own panko," I told her, reaching for an airy loaf of white bread from the breadbox. "Pan is a Latin-based word that means bread, and ko in Japanese is 'made from.'"

As usual, Amber didn't care for my detailed language lessons. She didn't care about the why, she only cared about the how.

"I actually haven't made this recipe since culinary school. In fact, it's been ages since I've used my deep fryer." I pulled the deep fryer Cooper had given me for my twenty-seventh birthday out from a bottom cupboard and set it on the counter. "You can pan fry these shrimp as well, but the deep fryer gets them extra crispy. I assume we like extra crispy?"

"We love extra crispy." Amber waited at the counter to be told what to do next.

I laid out a cookie sheet and instructed her to cut the crusts off the bread. From there, she fed them into my food processor.

In between pulses of the food processor, she talked through the important information of the case. "So this sketchy lady..." This was what Amber had started calling the woman from the police sketch. "She tricked Mr. Rempel into telling...her where his ex-wife had gone for the night...by

319

using the excuse of her kid's friends from…Honey Littles Elementary School…But he didn't tell her where…the Bible study was being held, right?"

I hadn't focused too much on that part. "The church office was likely already closed for the day by the time she got this information out of Jordan Rempel." I looked down at my notepad, which I'd been filling in with details after each interview, the way I'd seen Alex do on cases. "Jordan said the woman came by just after six in the evening." I motioned to the food processor. "That's enough pulsing. You want the shards of bread big enough to stick nicely and crisp up." From there I instructed her to dump them onto the cookie sheet and spread them out evenly. "We want them to dry out and harden up, but not to brown." I set the oven at 300.

Amber nodded about the breadcrumbs and then started speaking again about the investigation. "So if she heard about the Bible study after six, but didn't know where it was or who was in it and the church was closed, how would she have found out the location to track down Jennifer?"

I twisted my lips and pointed to the mango across the counter. Amber, always in tune with me, grabbed for it. "I have no idea, but tomorrow is Sunday. Maybe we can figure it out at church?"

Amber passed the mango back and forth between her hands, thinking. "So church. That's our next plan? At least until we talk to Detective Martinez."

As if Alex could hear his name, right then my phone buzzed with a new text.

<Corbett's leaving in an hour. I should be able to get away after that. Do you have time to meet and discuss the case?>

I texted back. <You bet! My house. Over coconut shrimp. □ >

"Alex will be here in just over an hour," I told Amber. "That should give us just enough time."

I showed her how to dice up the mango while still in the skin and then scoop out the chunks. Digging my hands into the cold-water bath, I separated the jumbo shrimp so they would thaw faster. When the preheated oven beeped, Amber slid the cookie sheet of breadcrumbs into the oven and I set the timer for five minutes. We proceeded to dice up some red pepper, onion, cilantro, fresh lime, and a little jalapeno to add some heat to our salsa.

By the time we were done making the salsa, the breadcrumbs were crunchy and the jumbo shrimp were thawed. Cooking seemed to give us both some positivity about whatever case we were working on. As I talked through how to make an egg bath and heated the oil in the deep fryer, I told Amber, "It's going to be great. The meal and the investigation. Just wait until Alex gets here. You'll see. It's all going to be great!"

□

# CHAPTER NINETEEN

Great might not have been the correct adjective. When Alex arrived, he slogged through my house from the entryway to the kitchen as though someone had drowned the pathway in molasses.

"Everything okay?" I asked. "You don't look like it is."

He let out a sigh and looked around the kitchen to where Amber was busy cleaning up our mess. On my small round table sat a platter with a mound of fried jumbo coconut shrimp and a side of spicy mango salsa, a spinach and strawberry salad, and a bowl of tropical rice.

He barely seemed to notice the food as he slumped into a chair. "It's fine. I guess I just thought I was past this—Corbett following my every move and getting in my way every time I actually found some momentum on a case. It's been an exhausting day. Smiling through it all has drained every bit of my energy."

"I bet." There was a plate at Alex's place, just waiting for him to serve up some food for himself, but since he hadn't reached for it so far, I decided to do it for him. A good meal could help a person gain a little perspective, in my experience. "The good news is," I told him as I layered a dozen crunchy shrimp onto his plate. "Today some of the work got done anyway, even with Corbett trying to get in your way."

"You mean like Mickey arresting one of my suspects on a completely unrelated charge?" He sighed again. "I hoped he could lay low and ask a few questions, just this once. What if the drug possession is part of a bigger crime? What if he's been trafficking out of the vineyard years and now we'll never be able to connect who he might have been in business with?" He slumped back into his chair. "The guy just doesn't think."

After adding a scoop of rice and salad, I set the plate in front of Alex.

He nodded and dug in, not even thanking me, which was beyond unusual for him. He must be exhausted.

"Hey, didn't Dahlia Richards' house smell like pot when we were there?" Amber finished wiping her hands and came to take the chair in the middle while I sat across from Alex.

I thought I'd smelled it, too, but had quickly dismissed it when we got into our conversation about Jennifer. I flipped through my notes, another tidbit playing at my memory, but I couldn't put my finger on it until my eyes landed on the words. "Dahlia's husband was really sick with stomach cancer. Isn't it possible he was using marijuana for pain relief?"

"Isn't it also possible," Amber said, scooping some shrimp onto her plate, "that the Richards couple was out in the vineyard last night buying pot from that vineyard worker?"

"Kristoph Carter," Alex and I said at the same time. To me, it actually seemed more than possible.

Alex wasn't so sure. "Why wouldn't Bart Richards have just gotten a doctor's prescription and bought from a dispensary?"

Amber knew the answer to this one. "There's only one dispensary in Honeysuckle Grove, and it's right on Main Street. My mom talked about trying pot after my dad died, but she didn't want everyone to see her walking into the dispensary, so she just opted for prescription meds instead."

"If anyone might want to hide her husband's drug use, even if it was for a good reason, I'd think it would be Dahlia Richards."

Alex nodded, but didn't agree or disagree aloud. When we all had food divvied up for ourselves, Amber started relaying the details of our day as she normally would, not taking any extra time or effort to try and cheer Alex up.

"It turns out Mr. Rempel gave the sketchy lady the name of the elementary school where Jennifer's kid went. Neither Gina Thomson or Dahlia Richards recognized the sketch, and they for sure would have if she'd been a parent of a kid at the school. Mr. Rempel also told the sketchy lady that his ex-wife had gone to a Bible study, but he couldn't have told her where because he didn't know where it was until after she was dead." Amber turned to me. "What if the reason she'd written down the address of the elementary school was because she somehow planned to get the Bible study location from one of the school parents?"

I squinted, taking a bite of shrimp. It crackled in my mouth. "I don't see why she would think that, though. What would give her the idea that another kid's parents went to the Bible study or even knew about it?"

"Except that two of them did," Amber replied. She had yet to take a bite, immersed in this conversation. Hunch paced behind my chair, also listening intently to every word. "Gina Thomson and Dahlia Richards were both parents from the school and Bible study attendees. How would the sketchy lady have known that?"

"The sketchy lady?" Alex asked, a hint of a smile on his face. "That's what we're calling her now?"

Amber went on, not entertaining Alex's joking. "Mr. Rempel must have told her. I'll bet she asked if he knew anyone else who went to the Bible study and he told her there were a couple of her coffee buddies from the elementary school PTA or whatever. Somehow she tracked them down and found out about the Bible study location."

"But neither of them recognized the sketch," I reminded Amber.

This clearly stumped her, and she took her first bite. And then her second. Her eyes were intent on the shrimp on her plate, but I could tell her mind was elsewhere. "So she gets the address of the elementary school and drives over there. It's obviously closed on a Friday night, so what? She asks kids in the playground? Or goes knocking door to door?"

"Maybe she saw something posted on a window or a parent's name? A donor of some kind?" Alex put in. "Then she looked up their address, asked some questions to find other people in town who might be churchgoing, and eventually came across someone who knew about the Bible study?"

"That's a lot to do in less than an hour." I shook my head. I wanted to believe we were close, but I just didn't. "This all seems like too much reaching. Take the elementary school address out of the equation, where would she have gone to find out about the Bible study location?"

"The church, which would have been closed," Amber said, shoveling in a mouthful of rice. All of that work on such a beautiful meal, and I doubted any of us were even tasting it. "We already discussed that."

I put down my fork. "Right, but what if she didn't go after elementary school parents? What if she left Jordan Rempel's house and called Pastor Jeff at home? Or asked around town until she found someone who knew about the church and its Bible studies?"

Amber turned to Alex. "We're going to ask people at church tomorrow. Flash the picture of the sketchy lady around, see if anyone has seen her." Amber turned back to me. "I think we should bake cookies or something that will make people come and talk to us on their way into the service."

She had a point. That, or she wanted another cooking lesson tonight.

"This is delicious," Alex said, his voice filled with awe, as though he'd only just noticed what he was eating.

"It really is, isn't it?" Amber said, a glow of pride on her face. I was glad I could help give her that.

"Did you happen to get anywhere on checking up on Jennifer Rempel's past in Morgantown?" I asked. "Or was the medical examiner able to tell you anything?"

Alex shook his head. "The full autopsy results could take up to a month, but I should have a preliminary report by Monday. For the moment, I'm sticking to the idea that the actual cause of death was strangulation with the lighting wires." He took a bite of rice, chewed it, and swallowed while Amber and I both watched him, waiting for more. His multi-shaded green eyes looked like they were getting a little more life to them with every bite he took. "I put a call into Morgantown PD while Corbett stepped out for a few minutes. They're looking into Jennifer Rempel or Jennifer Gustafson, and asking around the station about a long-haired guy named Gary, and will get back to me. Hopefully, when Corbett's not around to intercept."

"It's ridiculous that you have to work around your boss in order to solve a murder," Amber observed. And it was. More than ridiculous, but we'd weathered the storm of helping to get Alex promoted, even when it looked impossible. We would endure this with him, too.

"What about her parents?" I asked. They both looked at me blankly, so I elaborated. "You said Jennifer's parents came in from Morgantown to identify her body and discuss the case. If they're in Morgantown, they must know at least something about Jennifer's past. Perhaps they would even recognize the woman in the sketch." I turned to Amber with a smirk. "The sketchy woman. Or a guitar player named Gary."

Alex nodded, but he didn't look as excited as I did by this revelation. After a long moment of nodding, he explained how Corbett had been hovering and kept taking over the conversation and how Mr. and Mrs. Gustafson weren't exactly helpful when they came in.

"Well, sure. But losing their daughter must have been a shock."

Alex shook his head at me. "That was the odd thing. It didn't seem like it was. Her father, Grant Gustafson, even said something to the tune of, 'Surprised she lasted this long.'"

There was a reason to escape your childhood home, I supposed. I knew all about trying to lose my parents in the rearview of my life—or at the very least, not let my dad keep ruining my opportunities. My mind returned to the Gustafson's farm, their possible ownership of a tractor, and whether or not any parent could purposely kill their child in the way Jennifer was killed in the vineyard.

"Still," Amber said, taking her plate to the dishwasher, "even if they'd had to think about losing their daughter before, even if they weren't surprised she died, shouldn't they be surprised she was murdered? What kind of parents wouldn't want to help find the murderers of their kid if they could?"

I supposed jadedness, to a certain degree, came with age. Alex and I seemed perfectly able to accept that there would be parents in the world like this. But Alex, at least, chose to run with the curiosity that radiated from Amber.

"How about I give them another call first thing in the morning?" Alex said. "I'll go into headquarters before Corbett. If her parents are willing, I can email them a copy of the police sketch to see if they recognize the woman from Jennifer's past."

"And if they don't want to answer right away," Amber said, taking both mine and Alex's empty plates, "you're a police officer. Add some police pressure."

Alex looked down at his phone at that statement, hiding any kind of reaction. Amber was a mix of respectful and sarcastic teenager. Sometimes the two wobbled out of balance.

"You should also interview both Mr. Tallmans again," she went on and told him all about Benji's past secret relationship with Jennifer. "I know you think he didn't do it, and we don't either, but either he or his dad could still be serious suspects. What if the older Mr. Tallman saw his employee selling pot out in the vineyard, maybe even to the lady in the sketch, tried to stop it, and somehow Jennifer got caught in the middle?"

That seemed like a stretch, especially because Don and Marie Tallman had seemed pretty shocked by Kristoph's arrest earlier today, but Amber's theorizing had me at least admitting there were a lot of possibilities we had yet to consider.

Unfortunately, any necessary interviews with the Tallmans would fall to Detective Mickey Bradley.

When my late husband, Cooper, had been drafting one of his mystery novels, he used to say, "Just look for the next step."

"So we have our plans for tomorrow morning," I said to break the strange tension. "Amber and I will go to church and ask around about the sketchy lady. Find out if she approached anyone in the congregation Friday and look into how she might have discovered the location of the Bible study."

"And I'll call the Gustafsons." Alex nodded, seeming more self-assured. "If they won't help me with the information we need, I'll see if I can't get Morgantown PD over there to get some answers. That's the least her parents could do to avenge their daughter's death."

☐

# CHAPTER TWENTY

After Alex left to get a good night's sleep, Amber and I made cookies well into the night. We couldn't stop talking over the details of the case and ways that it might be coming together, and in only a day.

Or these could all be inconsequential details. If there was one thing I'd learned about solving murder cases, it was never as easy as pie to tell the difference.

Speaking of pie, I woke up early with a strong hankering for my special breakfast quiche. I'd made my quiche every Sunday when I worked at Baby Bistro, back when I lived in the first tiny house of my own with Cooper—the man I thought I'd spend the rest of my life with. I hadn't made quiche once, not a single time, since he'd passed, but I still knew the ingredients and measurements by heart.

I crept down the stairs quietly. Amber had spent the night in the guest room, as had been a common occurrence before my father had arrived, but church wasn't for another three hours, so I didn't want to wake her.

Walking into the kitchen with my mind on eggs and cheese and what veggies I had left over in my fridge, I let out a gasp at a sudden movement from the table. Amber was seated in her usual chair, feet kicked up on the chair beside her, with Hunch on her lap.

"Oh, hey," she said, seeing me. "You're up early."

"I could say the same about you." I walked over to ruffle Hunch's fur. I had the urge to do the same to Amber's hair, but she wasn't usually a person who loved to be touched.

Amber squirmed her shoulder at my statement. She hadn't been sleeping well since her dad's death three months ago. She didn't usually want to get into emotional subjects unless she was the one to bring them up, but my tired morning brain made me open my mouth before I remembered that.

"You know, I didn't sleep well for months after Cooper died." I'd told her this before, but I still felt the need to say it to try and open up the conversation. "It was only after I started talking about it with you...I don't know, my nervous system started to calm down. I didn't forget that he had died, of course, but I didn't have to re-remember it each morning. You know?"

She nodded and continued stroking Hunch, not saying a word. I felt her flight response starting to kick in—as though if I opened my mouth with another heartfelt word, she would bolt for the shower or, worse, for home.

So I made sure my next word was the opposite of sentimental, or at least it would be for her.

"Quiche?" I said.

Fifteen minutes later, Amber had a smile on her face. I wasn't sure when she was more in her element, while cooking or while solving crimes, but she was certainly getting good at both.

"The most important part is to precook the veggies," I told her as she stirred the onions and peppers in the frying pan. "We need to get as much moisture out of them as possible, or the quiche will turn out soggy."

"I don't even know if I like quiche." She raised an eyebrow at me. "My mom used to get these little tiny quiches from the wholesale outlet. At least I think they were quiche. But not like this big pie you're making."

I shook my head. "Those were not quiche. You'll see."

Twenty minutes later, I was pleased to have garnered the wide-eyed appreciative look I loved most out of Amber. With her mouth full, she said, "Maybe we should've made enough of this to bring to church."

I laughed, imagining the mess of that. "I think our salted caramel and molasses cookies will do the trick." I winked.

After we both cleaned up and then took our turns in the shower, we loaded up our containers of cookies and headed for the door. Hunch sat on his haunches at attention. He seemed to know the word "church," and so when I told him that's where we were going, he didn't make any effort to join us. I wondered if he had some kind of feline sixth sense that church, for him, would mean a couple of long hours trapped in a car.

"We'll get there early enough to set up a table and catch most people on their way into the worship center," I said to Amber from the driver's seat. This had already been well established, but I tended to babble about information we already knew when I got excited or nervous.

"And then we'll pray, and maybe we'll even listen to a sermon," Amber said, mocking me. Today, she wore a bright yellow hoodie that read: ACTUALLY, I AM A ROCKET SCIENTIST. My wardrobe wasn't nearly as fun as Amber's, but I was starting to wear more polka dots and prints, which felt bold for someone like me, who had always strived to fit in.

Today I wore a knee-length turquoise suede cardigan that dressed up my black chinos and sneakers a little. I'd learned from Amber to always wear sneakers when working on a case.

I pulled into the church parking lot, which held less than a dozen cars so far, and Amber and I each helped ourselves to a cookie from the sealable container in the backseat before heading for the front doors.

The greeters weren't at the doors yet, so we strode inside and surveyed the open lobby for the optimal location for our cookie distribution/sketchy lady questioning. A small square table already sat near the welcome center. I headed there, placed the cookies down, and said to Amber, "I'll find Pastor Jeff and make sure this is all right with him."

Amber nodded, peeking inside the top cookie container, as though she wanted to make sure the scrumptious cookies hadn't evaporated into thin air. "Don't forget to show him the sketch. Who knows? Maybe the lady somehow tracked him down to ask about the Bible study."

I nodded. We had tried to look up Pastor Jeff and his wife, Emily, in the Honeysuckle Grove phone book last night, but they hadn't been listed, which begged the question of how the sketchy lady would have contacted anyone from church if she couldn't find its leader.

Still, if this lady who claimed to be part of the elementary school parentage had wanted to find a local Bible study, who better to go to than the pastor of the church? Perhaps she had a method of finding him we just hadn't thought of.

I found Pastor Jeff speaking with his secretary, Penny, in the church office. Pastor Jeff was a stocky man with a deep, authoritative voice, but you'd only have to listen to a single one of his sermons to realize he was a softie deep down, compassionate to his very core. Penny Lismore had bright orange hair and finally seemed to be getting the hang of her job after nearly a year.

I pushed through the glass door into the office area and waited until they noticed me to speak. "Hi, Pastor Jeff. Hi, Penny." Now that I thought about it, I could kill two birds with one stone. Pastor Jeff and Penny may be the two most likely candidates for an out-of-towner to approach about a church-planned function. When they smiled receptively, I started with, "I'm sure you've heard about the tragic events at Friday night's Bible study at Sycamore Ridge Winery?"

Both their faces fell, showing understanding.

"I understand you were there, Mallory." Pastor Jeff shook his head. "It must have been awful. I'm so sorry."

I used to hate it when people would tell me they were sorry about Cooper's death, but when Pastor Jeff said the words, they oozed with sincerity. It was impossible not to be comforted by them.

But I had to stay focused. "Yes, well, Alex Martinez was there as well," I told him. "He knew Jennifer a lot better than I did. He's investigating her death, and there's some suspicion that the person responsible came from out of town."

Pastor Jeff nodded. "I would hope so. I would hope someone in our little community here couldn't have done this to our Jennifer." Pastor Jeff always spoke of congregation members as part of his fold or his flock. As far as he was concerned, we were all a part of his extended family.

"Yes, well, Alex has a police sketch of a woman who was seen around the vineyard. If she was responsible for Jennifer's death, we're trying to find out why she did it and how she found Jennifer there Friday night."

"Could it have been random?" Penny asked. "Someone in the wrong place at the wrong time? Maybe Jennifer saw this woman doing something she shouldn't have been doing?"

I thought again of a possible drug transaction. Maybe Penny Lismore should go into detective work rather than secretarial pursuits. She seemed to have a natural knack for it. Although, maybe it was because of Jennifer Rempel's strong personality and how many people she rubbed the wrong way, or perhaps it was because all of the murders I had investigated so far having some degree of premeditation involved, but whatever the reason, I still had a strong sense that someone had sought Jennifer out last night to hurt her.

"Tell Detective Martinez to bring by the sketch," Pastor Jeff said. "We can see if anyone on our staff recognizes the woman."

I reached into my purse. "Actually, I can do one better. I have a copy of it right here."

I held up the sketch and Pastor Jeff reached for it. He and Penny studied it for a few seconds, but then they shook their heads.

"I'm afraid she doesn't look familiar to me," Pastor Jeff said.

"Me neither," Penny said.

"Okay, so who within the congregation and staff might have known that the Bible study was being held at the Sycamore Ridge Winery on Friday night?"

Pastor Jeff only considered this for a second before answering. "A lot of people, really. Our staff would have all been aware, and of course all the people in that Bible study. All the other Bible study leaders—they have a special group to cover each other's meetings in prayer."

"How many other Bible studies are there?" I asked in surprise. I didn't know why, but somehow I'd thought the one Alex had brought me to as our community church's one Bible study.

"Five altogether," Pastor Jeff said.

"And Gordon Lam would have been a part of the leaders' get-together?"

"Oh, most definitely. In fact, I heard a couple of them talking about how fortunate Gordon was to have been offered the winery. Some of their biggest frustrations involve finding suitable locations for the bigger groups."

This gave me a thought, and I glanced out toward the worship center. "Do any of the larger groups meet here, Pastor?"

He nodded. "Sure. Bennie's group does, every week lately, as he's been busy moving and hasn't had a chance to seek out other locations."

"And what night does Bennie's group meet?"

It didn't surprise me one bit when Penny gave me the answer I knew was coming. I could feel it in my bones. It was like finding the last puzzle piece to a 3000-piece puzzle. "Friday nights," she said.

I nodded almost hyperactively. "And can one of you get me in touch with this Bennie?" I could see about half of the church lobby through the glass door and I surveyed it. "Is he here yet?"

Pastor Jeff looked to Penny and then to me. "Oh, I'm afraid Bennie Lancaster won't be attending this morning. It's his big moving day."

My hope deflated, but for only a second. They knew this was serious. They'd be able to get me either Bennie Lancaster's new or old address if it came to that. But maybe it wouldn't have to. "Can you tell me who else attends Bennie's Bible study? The one held here at the church?"

Pastor Jeff looked at Penny again. This time, she was the one to answer. "I couldn't say for sure, but there are a lot of them. Bennie's is the biggest group at nearly forty attendees. Don't the Miltons go to that one?" she asked Pastor Jeff.

He nodded. "I think so."

It seemed we were back to cookies. "Listen, Amber Montrose and I brought some cookies to share with the congregants as they arrive. Would you mind if we passed them out and asked folks if they attend Bennie Lancaster's Bible study or recognize the lady in the sketch?"

I knew Pastor Jeff's answer before he gave it, but I was glad to hear it out loud just the same.

"If it'll help Alex figure out who did this to our Jennifer and why? Absolutely."

☐

# CHAPTER TWENTY-ONE

Amber and I touched base with a lot of people who attended Bennie Lancaster's Bible study, but by the time the church service started its live music, we'd had a dozen requests for my cookie recipe, but not a single person who recognized the sketchy lady.

None of the people from the Bible study saw any familiarity, and in fact, when I brought up the tragedy, they all seemed to want to get away from us and our cookies as soon as possible.

Many of the people I'd met at the winery Friday night also walked through the church doors, including Gina Thompson and her husband, but they averted their path away from us, keeping their heads down. Perhaps they'd come to church to try to find some peace after the tragedy, not to talk about the details with me or anyone else.

Dahlia and Bart Richards were noticeably absent, but I had to at least suggest the possibility that their absence was due to sickness when Amber brought it up as suspicious.

Helen Montrose, Amber's mother, rushed into the church lobby just as the worship team finished their first song. She wore her hair in its usual bouffant style, reminiscent of the sixties, and wore a brown wool overcoat that looked a little too warm for the nice November weather we'd been having. She was making a beeline for the worship center doors and didn't see us until Amber called out, "Mom?" surprise clear in her voice.

I was pleased to see Amber's mom back at church, and from the lightness on Amber's face, I suspected she was as well.

Amber held out her container, which now only contained three lone cookies. I had five in mine. "Cookie?"

Helen Montrose headed our way, so I thought she was going to help herself to a taste of our baking, but as soon as she got close, she said, "Oh, I really shouldn't."

Amber placed her container down. The lobby was nearly empty, as everyone had moved into the worship center. "You made it this week," Amber said, stating the obvious. "Seth didn't want to come?"

Amber's brother, Seth, was still having his own ups and downs since his dad's death. He was pretty protective of Amber, though, and regularly texted to check in with her.

Amber's mom shook her head.

"Are you sure you don't want a cookie?" I asked, extending my container. "Amber made them."

Helen Montrose looked between me and the cookies in the container. Amber had mentioned more than once that her mom was always on some kind of diet, and she suspected the diets messed with her mom's anxiety levels more than they actually helped her lose weight.

My suggestion was all the push she needed. She pasted a smile on her face and helped herself to a cookie. "Well, if my daughter made them, I really should, shouldn't I?"

The few times I'd been at Amber's mansion since her dad's death, her mom had been medicated, on the couch, and had barely registered my presence. It was good to see her more coherent.

"It really is nice to see you here, Mrs. Montrose." I offered her a second cookie from my container, as she had already gobbled hers.

"Oh, maybe just one more." She reached for one. "And please, call me Helen." Her smile settled into something more genuine. "I'm really thankful for all the time you've spent teaching my girl to cook." She wrapped an arm around Amber. Amber took the side hug, even if I could sense her discomfort.

Truth be told, I needed Amber around as much, if not more, than she needed me, and a twinge of fear moved through me at her mom recovering from her grief and getting back to church. Would she be ready to parent and want Amber back at home more?

But before the thought could fully form, I knew it was a selfish one. Out of duty, I held up the sketch, even though Helen Montrose, with the time she got out of her house these days, didn't seem like our strongest hope. "You haven't by chance seen a woman that looks like this in the last few days?" I asked.

She studied it for a second and then looked up. "I don't think so. Why?"

"Oh, we're just trying to find her around town." While we had mentioned the words murder investigation to a few other folks to get them to take our question seriously, I feared with Amber's mother, it might cause her to snatch her daughter's help away from me.

Amber, who still seemed a little stunned to see her mother looking so put-together, finally opened her mouth to divert her mother from asking too many more questions. "Are you going in?" Amber motioned her chin toward the worship center. "Do you want me to come and sit with you?"

Helen Montrose looked grateful for the offer, and seconds later, I was alone. But it didn't feel as bad or as scary as I feared. It actually felt warm to see them walk off together arm in arm.

I was tidying up my cookie table and cleaning up crumbs when another late straggling couple rushed through the doors from the parking lot.

"See?" the thirtysomething blonde lady said to her husband. "It's already started."

The man hurried to keep up. They were a good-looking couple, if a little frazzled. "If you hadn't made me move the garbage cans—"

"Excuse me." I intercepted them halfway from the doors to the worship center. I had an instinct that they wouldn't have time or patience for cookies, so I only brought the sketch along with me. "Can I ask you a quick question?" I didn't wait for either of their approval as they looked to one another. I held up the sketch. "Have either of you seen this woman? Do either of you attend a Bible study held at the church here on Friday nights? One run by Bennie Lancaster?"

Every other bit of questioning this morning had been carried on more like a casual conversation. But these folks clearly didn't have time for that, and I didn't want to miss asking anything.

They looked at the sketch. Then they looked at each other. "Didn't a lady come in and ask Bennie something, just after we broke into prayer groups near the beginning?" the lady asked her husband.

The man nodded slowly, looking back at me. "Who is she? Has she done something?"

"Maybe," I said honestly. "But you've been a big help in confirming she might have been here. Do you know if she spoke to anyone else here that night?"

The woman shook her head. "I doubt it. Everyone else was in prayer groups. She marched straight to the front, had a word with Bennie, and then she left. We couldn't hear what she said. Right, honey?"

Her husband shook his head in agreement. It was clear who did most of the talking in this relationship.

I took down their names and cell numbers, just in case I came up with any other questions for them, but it looked as though I'd have to speak to Penny or Pastor Jeff to track down Bennie Lancaster after all.

☐

# CHAPTER TWENTY-TWO

After cleaning up out front and coming to the conclusion that no more stragglers would be arriving, I slipped into the back pew on the right-hand side of the church. It was where I sat every week, whenever I had a week off from helping with the children's ministry.

To my left, I saw the Montrose mother and daughter, absorbed in what Pastor Jeff was saying about faith. Today, Donna Mayberry sat across from the worship center with her husband, Marv. Marv worked a lot and often missed Sunday mornings. Whenever he was gone, Donna sat with what Cooper and I had dubbed her "gossip posse."

Donna and Marv must have come in through the rear doors of the church because I hadn't seen them near our cookie station. Even if Donna didn't attend the Friday evening Bible study, perhaps she could tell me of others who did. Or maybe she knew more about Jennifer Rempel than what we'd discovered so far.

Amber and I had come across about a dozen Bible study attendees while handing out cookies, but none of them, other than the blond couple, had recognized the woman in the sketch. Now I knew why—because they'd all had their heads bowed in prayer.

Still, I wondered if Donna Mayberry's keen nose for news could somehow be helpful for once.

I bided my time through the church service, and sadly, I barely took in a single word of it. The first few times I attended church after Cooper was gone, I couldn't tune in because of my grief. Now that I'd finally started to hear what Pastor Jeff was saying, my mind had been bombarded with a new murder investigation.

The worship team always ended the service with a couple of songs.

During this portion, Amber and her mom skirted up the aisle closest to them, toward the back doors. Helen Montrose most likely wanted to get in and get out before she had to talk with too many people, as I had the first few times I'd been back.

I gave them a second and then headed for the lobby myself. A couple of ladies in their seventies were busy setting up pamphlets in the welcome center, and Helen and Amber stood near the glass front doors, but otherwise, the lobby was empty.

I hung back to give the Montrose ladies a minute to say goodbye. I took in a big breath and let the warmth of the motherly moment fill me. They hugged, and then Helen Montrose pushed out through the door.

Amber watched her go for a few seconds before turning to see me there. "Oh. Hey." She looked a little embarrassed to have been caught in an emotional moment with her mother.

"So guess what?" I was getting almost as good as Amber at breaking uncomfortable moments. "I found a couple who recognized the lady in the sketch."

Amber's face lit up and she hurried toward me. Her eyes stayed on the worship center doors. "Who? Where are they? What could they tell you?"

I shook my head. "Not much, actually. Just a confirmation that she had been here and that she had been talking quietly to Bennie Lancaster during prayer time."

"So we need to track down Mr. Lancaster, after all," Amber said, quickly catching onto the plan.

I was about to go into my thoughts—that Penny Lismore would be a lot easier to catch after the service than Pastor Jeff—when another congregant who obviously wanted to beat the rush snuck out the far worship center door. But this wasn't a regular congregant. This was Jordan Rempel.

I knocked Amber on the shoulder and pointed. Jordan was headed to the children's ministry wing.

We both took one quick look at each other and then rushed in that direction. Since I'd been helping with the children's ministry for the last couple of months, I knew the maze of hallways well. We caught up to Jordan quickly.

"Mr. Rempel?" I called from one end of the second short hallway.

He stopped in place and turned. "Oh. Hi." He didn't look particularly surprised or bothered to see us. Amber and I hurried forward to close the distance.

"I thought you didn't attend church?" Amber asked in all her usual teenage subtlety.

Jordan shrugged. "I normally don't, but I don't know. When you were at my house yesterday, it got me thinking. Maybe Jennifer would've liked it if I did. Maybe she would want her kid to go." He motioned down the hallway to where he must have been headed to pick up Fresco. "I'm not used to making decisions for him. In fact, I don't know what's supposed to happen now."

"Happen?" I asked.

"Well, like, I just don't know if Fresco's mine now or what. I mean, I love the kid a lot, but I work long hours and I'm just not sure about this single parenting thing, you know?"

I nodded. Amber had certainly attached to me in a very strong way after losing her dad. Even though she was a lot older and less needy than a first-grader, a person's perspective could change after losing someone close. Then again, she still had her mom.

"Do you have a minute?" I asked. Before he could answer, I went on to explain. "You see, we think we're starting to put together some details about Friday night, and I wondered if we could go over your conversation with this woman again." I held up the sketch for him to see. "Word for word, as far as you can remember it."

Jordan hesitated, looked back toward the kids' classrooms.

"Don't worry," I said. "I can text Sasha, who's in charge of the children's ministry, and let her know you're with me. Fresco will be well taken care of."

He nodded, and I led the way back out of the children's wing and into a small prayer room just off the lobby. The lighting was purposefully dim in here, and there were three tissue boxes and half a dozen chairs spread around the small room. Amber and I sat as I texted Sasha Mills, letting her know Fresco's uncle was with me for a few minutes. Jordan hesitated, but then eventually took a seat as well.

"You said she came by just after six p.m. on Friday?" Amber said to get him started. I was usually the notetaker of the two of us, but while I was busy texting, she reached into my purse, pulled out my notepad and pen, and poised it on her lap.

"That's right." Jordan pushed up his glasses. He hadn't dressed up for church. He wore jeans and a hoodie, only adding to his adolescent appearance. Nobody, certainly not Dahlia Richards, would have guessed this man to be Jennifer Rempel's ex-husband.

"What was the first thing she said?" Amber prodded.

"She asked if Jennifer Rempel was home."

"That's how she said it?" Amber asked, writing. "First and last name?"

Jordan nodded. "I said that Jennifer and I were divorced and she lived in an apartment over on Third Street now."

I was done texting and could have taken over notetaking, but Amber seemed to be doing a good job.

"The lady turned to leave, but I stopped her, saying Jennifer wouldn't be home tonight. She'd just dropped off her son and was headed to a Bible study." Guilt leaked out in Jordan's voice. As he relayed the details of the conversation, realization seemed to hit that if he hadn't been so forthcoming with the details about Jennifer, she may not have been murdered—at least not so quickly.

"And did she ask you where the Bible study was being held?"

Jordan shook his head. "Not right away. I felt a twinge of unease about how much information I had volunteered. I'd been working on a particularly difficult bit of coding that evening, and my mind wasn't really there," he explained. "But I clued in and asked her how she knew Jennifer. Right then, Fresco came to the door and asked me if he could have some chips from the cupboard. The woman just stared at him in a way that made me uncomfortable. So I told Fresco yes, nudged him back inside the house, and asked her again how she knew Jennifer."

Jordan met my eyes with a serious gaze, as though this entire conversation had new meaning to him. "She held out a hand to where Fresco had been standing, and she said, 'Our boys go to school together.' The statement made me immediately trust her and I said…" He let out a humorless laugh before continuing. "I asked her if her son liked Mrs. Blakely at Honey Littles Elementary as much as Fresco did."

"This was how she found out about the school," I said to Amber, who was still scribbling words furiously. She nodded but didn't respond.

"So you're saying he doesn't," Jordan said. "Her son doesn't go to school with Fresco? He doesn't even go to Honey Littles?"

I tilted my head. "We won't know for sure until we check in with them on Monday morning, but I suspect not. Did she say anything else?"

Jordan twisted his mouth, but he didn't have to think it over long. "She said she had been meaning to start attending a Bible study and asked if I had any idea how to get in touch with Jennifer's. Of course I had no idea, and I told her so." He closed his eyes, took a breath, and then opened them. "But I did tell her I thought it was through the Honeysuckle Grove Community Church." He looked up and around at the small prayer room, wondering what he had done to the ex-wife he still cared very much about.

I knew what it was like to feel guilty and like I should have done something—anything—different the day of Cooper's death. "Listen, Jordan. Even if this woman is responsible for Jennifer's death, the number of lies she told to make that happened were numerous. She's the one truly at fault here. Let's remember that."

He looked like he appreciated my words, even though they didn't seem to absolve him. "Well, I can say for sure that was the whole conversation. I didn't tell her anything else because I didn't know anything else."

"Thank you for talking with us again. I know it can't be easy to rehash it." I turned to Amber. "We should find Penny before she leaves."

We all stood to make our way out of the small prayer room, but before we could go, my phone buzzed from the small table in the center of the room. Alex's name flashed across the screen, so I snatched it up before it could start playing his ringtone.

As was now automatic, I put him immediately on speakerphone.

"I was going to call you," I said in way of an answer. "We're starting to put some things together."

"Before you get to that," Alex said through the line, "I have some news. Hold onto your hat because you were right. Jennifer Gustafson's past in Morgantown wasn't filled with unicorns and rainbows. In fact, she has a police record."

☐

# CHAPTER TWENTY-THREE

"What's he talking about?" Jordan stared at me, and my mouth opened blankly as I realized my mistake.

"Who's there?" Alex asked through the phone line at the same time Jordan asked, "Who is that?"

"Detective Martinez," I said, motioning to my phone, "meet Jordan Rempel, ex-husband of Jennifer Rempel."

"Detective?" Jordan said, his face serious.

"Can I safely assume you have me on speakerphone, Mallory?" I couldn't tell by his tone if Alex was angry with me for my lack of discretion. If he wasn't, he should be.

I gulped. "Yes, you're on speakerphone."

As if to offer full disclosure, Amber said, "Hi, detective."

A small chuckle through the line told me he probably wasn't as angry as he should be. "Hi, Amber."

"What's this about my wife having a record?" Jordan sat back into his chair, suddenly in no hurry to leave. I found it interesting he didn't call her his ex-wife.

"Am I to understand you had no prior knowledge of her arrest back in Morgantown?" Alex asked. In only two seconds, he was proving to be much better at conducting interviews than the way I bumbled through them.

"She wouldn't talk about her past in Morgantown," he said. "We'd only been on a half dozen dates when she moved into my place in Honeysuckle Grove. Soon after that, we were married, and she said she needed to forget everything from before she met me." He swallowed hard. "What was she arrested for?"

"She was charged with vehicular manslaughter. She was inebriated at the time." Alex let that sit for a few seconds and then said, "Do you understand what that means, Mr. Rempel?"

Jordan shook his head. "No, I mean, yeah, I understand it, but it can't be true. It can't be. Jennifer's life mission was to keep drunk people off the roads..." He trailed off, and it seemed to settle in on him that this was why she was so passionate against drunk driving. This was why she wouldn't talk about her past. She was desperately trying to make up for it.

"Okay, but here's the big news," Alex said. "Corbett's out of the office today, so I've had some time to dig around into things. The person Jennifer struck and killed was a ten-year-old child by the name of Brennan Dillon. This was seven years ago, and Jennifer did a year of jail time, but the lawyer hired by her parents pled the case down to a misdemeanor instead of a felony. I looked up a number of newspaper write-ups about the case and I caught sight of the mother of the boy who died in several of the photos."

A knot grew in my stomach, as I was quite certain I knew what Alex was going to say before he said it.

"Her name was Tonya Dillon. And she looks a lot like the woman in our police sketch."

☐

# CHAPTER TWENTY-FOUR

An hour later, Jordan Rempel had left the church with his stepson, Fresco, and a promise for an update as soon as we had one. We had tracked down Penny Lismore and found Bennie Lancaster's new address, but we were no longer in a hurry to locate him there. Alex pulled up to the curb in his old Toyota, and Amber and I rushed outside to get in.

We were making an impromptu trip to Morgantown, West Virginia.

"Sorry it took me so long," Alex said as Amber held the seat forward so I could get into the back. This was the teenager I was used to. "I had to wait until there was a shift change to get away without suspicion."

"And you have an address for this Mrs. Dillon?" I asked.

Alex nodded. "Ms. Dillon. Divorced five years ago."

"And her ex-husband?" I wondered if it would be worth tracking him down to find out exactly how much anger Tonya had still carried toward Jennifer Rempel.

"I can likely find that out from Morgantown PD, but I thought first we'd go in covertly and try to get some real answers before we bombard her with a police attack. I can't be wrong about this."

It was frustrating that Alex felt like he could never make a misstep at work, or he'd immediately be demoted back to a traffic cop, even after all of his hard work. In truth, having Amber and me helping investigate at the vineyard could have been his downfall, as could leaving in the middle of the day to go to Morgantown when he'd been given a boatload of paperwork to complete at the station. But if I knew Alex, the moment we returned from Morgantown, he would be back at his desk, likely working through the night.

"Wait, what about Hunch?" Amber said, suddenly sitting up straight, just as Alex took the entrance onto the highway.

"Hunch will be fine," I told her. "He's a cat."

This was mostly true. If he knew we were on an investigation without him, he would most definitely not be fine about that, but the bigger issue was that I didn't often leave Hunch alone for more than a couple of hours at a time. He would be pacing the front entryway by now like a worried parent. I suspected my cat even had a touch of PTSD from being left for hours in my car when I'd been kidnapped during a previous investigation.

But I wasn't about to get Alex to turn around and go pick up my cat, so I did my best to put Hunch out of my mind.

"How far is it to Morgantown?" Amber asked. Before Alex could answer her, she'd picked up his phone from the console and checked the GPS herself. "Almost two hours? I'd better check in with Seth. Maybe he'd stop by to check in on Hunch. Is there a key under a mat or anything?" she asked me.

I shook my head. I'd never needed to leave a key out for anyone. But it just occurred to me that I was taking a teenager out of town, on a homicide investigation, and without parental permission. Amber had become so helpful to investigations that we barely thought about her age anymore.

"I can double back and drop you off," Alex said, reading my thoughts. "I should probably do that." He changed lanes so he would be ready to exit, but even I knew that wouldn't fly with Amber.

She rolled her eyes. "Seth'll make sure Mom's okay about it. I make excuses for him whenever he wants to escape our house to hit up the video arcade or some other really altruistic purpose." She sat back with a huff.

Alex looked at me in his rearview mirror, as if asking what to do, but a second later, Amber's phone dinged and she said, "It's handled. Seth knows I'm with you for the day, and he's going to order in from that new Greek place for Mom for dinner."

Mmm, Greek food sounded good. Actually, it felt strange to be driving toward a suspect empty-handed—even our cookie containers from church had been emptied long ago.

As Alex drove, he told us everything he knew about Tonya Dillon. "She goes by her maiden name, Dartengel, but she's the only one by that name listed in Morgantown, so I suspect she doesn't have any local family."

"And Jennifer's parents? They're in Morgantown, too, right? Did they recognize the sketch? They must know all about the charges that had been laid against their daughter, especially if they hired the lawyer."

Alex nodded. "I called them, and I'd thought that could be the reason they didn't seem to have a lot of love for their own daughter, even after she'd been murdered." Alex glanced at me in the rearview. "But apparently, they'd been nothing but supportive through the entire court case. Her dad said he hired the best lawyer money could buy."

"Which is probably why it got pled down to a misdemeanor," I suggested.

"Perhaps," Alex agreed. "But the really interesting part was when I asked what turned her life around and they had no idea." Alex paused for dramatic effect. "Apparently, Jennifer's parents had no idea that she had married or that they had a grandson living in Honeysuckle Grove."

"What? You're kidding." I couldn't imagine a young woman—especially one who had just gone through some major life trauma in accidentally killing a kid—keeping something like a pregnancy and then a birth from her own parents.

Alex shook his head. "Apparently her parents took out a second mortgage on their farm in order to finance her legal case. Then, when they got her out of jail after only a year, they thought she would surely turn her life around, but she left home and moved in with a really bad group. More than once, her dad had threatened to call the police on her when he saw her downtown on a street corner, so high she barely recognized him. He didn't know what else to do, as she was clearly self-destructive and suffering from her guilt. After months of this heartache, she suddenly seemed to vanish. When her parents were no longer able to track their daughter down, they felt they had no choice but to accept that she'd probably turn up dead, and there was nothing they could do to stop it."

My heart ached for this couple who I thought had been completely heartless toward their daughter. "And what do they think now?"

"They think they want to meet their grandson."

I sincerely hoped that would be the solution Jordan was looking for, and it wouldn't turn into some kind of awful custody battle. I doubted it would. Jordan only wanted what was best for Fresco. Perhaps some sort of shared custody could be worked out, so they could all get to be a part of his life.

"Huh," Amber said, flashing her phone screen my way, but I couldn't read it. Nor could Alex while he was driving.

"What is it?" I asked.

"Fresco. You said Jennifer insisted on calling him by his full name? His name means new beginnings."

I sat back in my seat, thinking about that. So when she'd had Fresco, Jennifer was determined to start a new beginning for herself and her son. That could be why she had quickly latched onto Jordan Rempel and taken him up on his quick offer for her to move in with him, even if she wasn't in love with him.

It was all starting to make sense. The only things I questioned now were whether or not Tonya Dillon—Dartengel—would be home and if she'd admit to killing Jennifer Rempel.

# CHAPTER TWENTY-FIVE

The first answer came quickly, but unfortunately, it didn't come out in our favor. Tonya Dartengel lived in a rundown apartment complex near the stadium in Morgantown, but there was no answer when we knocked on her apartment door.

"What would it take to get a warrant?" Amber asked.

"In Morgantown?" Alex looked at her. "It would have to be a request from their own department, and they'd have to have some solid proof of wrongdoing. Not just a sketch that had been done by memory of one worker, currently in custody, who'd admitted the lighting was poor."

When Alex put it like that, my hope dwindled. I'd thought we'd been so close. I knocked again, this time much louder.

Tonya Dartengel's door didn't open, but her neighbor's door did. A college-age girl in an oversized blue and gold sports jersey greeted us. She had a vape pen in her hand.

"Get a hint. She's not home!" The girl took a big drag on her pen and let the smoke out in our direction. Alex wore his plainclothes police wear—which I suspected this girl didn't recognize as being anything official.

"You're sure she's not?" I asked.

And then Amber piped in, making stuff up on the spot, as usual. "She told us she'd be here."

While Alex's police training had taught him to always be forthcoming about his police status, especially if questioned, Amber had no such guidelines to move within.

Amber defiantly knocked on Tonya's door again. Loudly.

"Look, you've got to shut up. I'm trying to study. She hasn't been home all weekend, all right? Do I gotta call the manager?"

I had my doubts that the manager would be any more willing to help us, but Tonya being gone all weekend meant something, and Alex, the clearheaded one in this scenario, picked up on that.

"She's been gone since Friday?" Alex asked. "Or before that?"

The girl blinked up at Alex a few times, and her angry face flattened out. It was as if she suddenly knew he was a police officer without any introduction. "Friday sounds about right."

"And she hasn't been back, as far as you know?"

The girl shrugged. "I'm sure I'da heard her."

"Is there anywhere else she might be staying in town?" Alex asked. He'd pulled out his trusty notepad and pen, which added to his police persona. The woman only shrugged, so Alex prodded. "Like with her ex-husband, perhaps?" He raised an eyebrow.

The girl narrowed her eyes, catching on that Alex knew a lot about her neighbor—too much for this to be a few non-threatening questions. "No," she finally blurted out. "No way she'd ever go back to his farm."

"Farm?" Amber asked. "Her ex lives on a farm? Like with a tractor?"

The girl raised an I-think-you're-crazy eyebrow at Amber. Then she turned back to Alex. "Since her kid died, she never goes back to the farm, and she sure wouldn't go back to Gary. That's all I know." She backed into her apartment. "You got more questions? You're gonna have to ask her, because I'm busy." The words were barely out of her mouth before her door shut in our faces.

# CHAPTER TWENTY-SIX

"Gary?" All three of us said his name on the way back to the car. It didn't seem like it could be a coincidence that Tonya's ex-husband had the same first name as our mysterious guitar player.

"We should have asked the neighbor what Gary Dillon looked like." I said the words, but I knew the snotty college girl wouldn't have answered her door again for us, at least not without a warrant.

"I'll see if Morgantown PD will look him up for me." Alex opened his car. As we got in, his cell phone rang. Mickey Bradley flashed across the screen, and Alex held a finger up to his lips to silence us before answering it.

"What's up, Mickey? I'm just out running a few errands for Corbett." Alex's voice seemed overly peppy, but Mickey Mouse didn't seem to notice. For once, I was thankful for his inability as a detective.

"Yeah, well, I just got done at the Richards' townhouse." Mickey's gruff voice came through the speakerphone. "You were right. They said they bought an eighth of marijuana from Kristoph Friday night before their Bible study. I had to pressure them a bunch to answer, but once I told them Kristoph had been arrested and had given them up, they told me the truth."

"Just as I suspected." Alex nodded, but this information was no longer revelatory or even necessary to the case at hand.

Mickey went on, without being prodded. He seemed to like to hear himself talk. "It's why they were late getting into the winery for Bible study. They came in while that guitar player was still playing and before Jennifer screamed. At least that's what they said. They claim it was the first time they'd bought from Kristoph, but I don't know if I believe them. You think

I should bring 'em in?"

"Hmm, if it's a first-time offense, let's leave it for the moment." Mickey tried to interrupt with an objection, but Alex spoke over him. "Besides, I might have a better lead on this murder investigation that I need your help with." I was surprised to hear Alex inviting Mickey Mouse into helping with the murder case, until he said, "I've got an address here for a Bennie Lancaster. Can you go interview him about any interactions he had with the woman in the sketch?"

Right. Alex was only keeping Mickey busy with information we no longer needed.

After I was certain Alex had hung up, I asked, "Is it worth staying over in Morgantown? Staking out Tonya's apartment?" I tried to picture the three of us huddled up in Alex's small car, taking turns sleeping.

Alex shook his head. "If she hasn't been home since Friday, who's to say she would come home tonight? I think I should talk to the local police department. They have a lot more resources and staff than we do in Honeysuckle Grove. Maybe they'll be willing to put someone at her door when I explain what I think has happened."

Alex figured this would be a lot more likely to happen if he paid them a visit in person, so we headed to the Morgantown police department's headquarters.

While Alex went inside the police building, Amber and I took a walk to stretch our legs before the long drive back.

"I hope the Morgantown police are a lot nicer to Alex than his boss in Honeysuckle Grove." Amber led the way into what looked like a busier area of town, as though she'd been here before.

"I hope so, too," I said. "You seem like you know your way around?"

Amber shook her head, looking around as though it just occurred to her to take in her surroundings. "I just feel like we need to do something, you know? Not keep sitting around in a car waiting for this case to get solved."

"We're doing what we can," I said, patting her on the shoulder. "I know. It doesn't feel fast enough."

"It never does." I could tell by the somber look on her face that she was remembering the investigation surrounding her dad's death. That investigation hadn't lasted long, and yet, I knew it had felt like an eternity to her.

"Maybe we should find something to eat?" I suggested. "Our brains might work better if we weren't running solely on salted caramel and molasses cookies, no matter how yummy they were."

We'd actually started the morning with a delicious quiche that had kept us satiated for most of the day. But I figured focusing on food might give us a much-needed break from what felt like a standstill in a very-close-to-being-solved investigation.

We approached a sandwich shop, and I pointed. "Should we get a few sandwiches to go?"

Amber nodded, but her attention wasn't on the sandwich shop sign or on the menu posted in the window. Her attention was rapt on an eight-by-ten black and white photo of a teenager in the window with the word "MISSING" across the top.

I stopped in place and looked with her. "Do you recognize the girl?"

Amber shook her head. "But this Tonya Dartengel is from Morgantown, right?" She looked at me. "Maybe she's hiding out at someone's place in town. Why haven't we been asking around about her while we're here?"

Even though Morgantown had a population of around thirty thousand, she had a point. "Okay. Let's start with the sandwich makers inside."

While two twentysomething cooks made our turkey and Swiss sandwiches, they argued about whether or not they had seen the woman in the sketch. The one who thought she had seen the woman a few days ago in the shop couldn't tell us anything about her, though, or even place the time of day she'd been in.

Amber continued to grill them regardless. I wandered back to the front window, looking at the missing person poster again, this time from the inside. From there, my eyes went to the street, busy with cars, and the far sidewalk, which was bustling with mostly college-age passerby.

A flash of long shaggy hair on a man caught my notice, and a second later, I bolted out the door, not even taking the time to say a word to Amber about where I was going.

In the few seconds it took me to get out the door, the man had turned a corner at the end of the block and was no longer in view. I ran to the corner, thankful for my sneakers, but traffic was too busy to cross. I kept losing sight of the man and was afraid I'd lose him for good.

Without rethinking it, I yelled, "Hey, Gary!" at the top of my lungs.

Several people looked over at me, including the shaggy-haired man. Even from fifty feet away, I was pretty sure it was him. The walk signal sounded, and I raced across the street, but by the time I got there, he had disappeared into the crowd again.

I kept moving, kept searching, but I couldn't see him anywhere. My eyes darted to the shops and bank I passed, but I couldn't see him in any of those buildings either.

By the time I reached the end of the block, I still hadn't found him again. I looked straight ahead, and then to my right and to my left, but he was nowhere. I'd lost him, and I had no idea which direction to go to find the man.

When I returned to Amber outside the sandwich shop, she looked a mix of anxious and perturbed. I called to her from down the street. "I thought I saw that guitar player, Gary. I tried to catch him, but couldn't." I shook my head. "Maybe it wasn't even him."

Amber's frustration showed in the way she kept her eyes down on the sidewalk back toward Alex's car. "This is hopeless."

"I know," I agreed. I wished we'd gotten a police sketch of Gary-the-guitar-player. That seemed like it might be more useful to show around here, but drawing was one skill I had never developed.

"Maybe asking around aimlessly will add more confusion than information. Those people at the sandwich place finally agreed it wasn't even Tonya Dartengel that had been in there the other day."

She might be right. "What do you say we get back to the car and see if Alex is done yet? Hopefully, he'll have had better luck than we've had, and if not, maybe he'll have found out a little more information about Tonya Dartengel or her ex-husband, Gary Dillon, at the very least."

Amber didn't look much like her hope was growing, but she at least followed along. The weather had grown colder and felt like it might rain. I hadn't brought an umbrella, so I hoped the weather would hold out a little longer. When there was no sign of Alex, I unpacked the sandwiches on the hood of his car and passed Amber the first one.

"Come on. You'll feel better once you've eaten."

She rolled her eyes. "Spoken like a true chef."

I smiled. At least she was still making jokes. By the time I had my sandwich unwrapped, Alex walked up, so I passed him that sandwich and reached for the third.

"How did it go?" Amber's mouth was full, so it was up to me to ask.

Alex took his first bite, chewed, and swallowed, leaving us in suspense. "Amazingly well." We stared at him through another bite, waiting for more. "Like, really, really well."

I was tempted to snatch the sandwich back. "Details, detective. We need details!"

He chuckled and unlocked his car. "Let's talk and drive. It's a long way back to Honeysuckle Grove."

"Can we just drive around the block first? I thought I might have seen Gary-the-guitar-player down near the sandwich shop." He agreed and drove around a four-block radius twice before I finally told him, "He's gone. Forget it."

It wasn't the worst thing in the world, though, because the Morgantown captain had pulled up Gary Dillon's address for Alex and sent two of his local officers over to question the man.

"You're sure it was him?" I asked. "The same guitar player from Friday night?"

"It was an old photo they had on file, but yeah, I think it was the same guy."

I still thought Alex should be the one to go and question the man after all the work he'd already put into this investigation, but apparently, that wasn't how it was done.

"You're sure there's nothing more we can do here in Morgantown? Maybe show Tonya Dartengel's picture around and see if anyone has seen her in the last few days?"

Alex headed back for the highway, possibly calmer than I'd ever seen him. "I don't think so. Morgantown PD seems to have it handled." He shook his head. "This must be what it's like working for a police department that doesn't have an egomaniac boss with a whole Rolodex full of personal grievances."

"That good, huh?" I should have been excited right along with Alex. I was excited. But something made me hesitant and I wasn't sure what.

"Better than good, I'm telling you." He finished off his sandwich and I wished I'd bought four. I passed him half of mine, as I had yet to take a bite. Working hard on a case and eating had never mixed particularly well for me. "Thanks. Yeah, I spoke with Detective Ramone, and once I'd explained the situation, he brought his on-duty captain in on it. They both sat and listened, but I hadn't even gotten through the whole story when Captain Jagg called for a detective team to set up a stakeout across the street from Tonya's apartment. He put out an APB on the green Suburban registered in her name. And now he has a second unit paying a visit to her ex-husband."

"That's...incredible," I said, my voice still not holding the weight of gratitude it should.

"He suggested I head back to Honeysuckle Grove and take the sketch into any of our local hotels. Because we only have two, that shouldn't take long, but I also plan to check the local hospital. She could have been hurt during the incident with Jennifer Rempel. Perhaps that's why she hasn't returned home yet."

"Smart," Amber said from the backseat, finally done with her sandwich. I took my first bite. "So we'll go by the Honeysuckle Grove hotels and the hospitals. If those don't turn up anything, what's our next move?" Amber asked in her usual way, as though she expected we were as much a part of this investigation as Alex.

"Well, with any hope, I'll get a call sometime tonight letting me know that Tonya Dartengel has returned home and been taken in for questioning. I should be at my desk by then, trying to wade through the work that was actually assigned to me." He let out a sigh.

Suddenly, I realized why I'd hesitated to be happy about the Morgantown police. When he put it like that, clearly demonstrating the contrast between such a helpful police department and one that blocked Alex at every turn, what were the chances Alex wouldn't have already processed that for himself?

And what were the chances he wouldn't soon desert us for a much more amiable job?

☐

# CHAPTER TWENTY-SEVEN

It was already dark by the time we arrived back in Honeysuckle Grove.

"Should I drop you at your place?" Alex asked Amber, who had willingly taken the backseat after we last stopped for gas.

"No, I'll go to Mallory's." She didn't so much as a glance in my direction to see if it was okay.

"You have school in the morning," I reminded her.

She sighed. "Yes, Mom." Then she changed her tone, back to the helpful investigative assistant. "But I have a feeling we're going to hear something tonight. I won't be able to sleep at home, wondering if I'm missing something. Can't you just drop me off at school in the morning? The high school's closer to your house anyway."

I nibbled my lip to hold in my arguments. If Amber was correct and if we did hear something back from Morgantown PD this evening, I wanted her to be around as well.

"Fine," I said. "But you're not getting out of going to school in the morning, even if we get woken up in the middle of the night with some news."

"Yes, Mom," she said again, but I could hear the smirk in her voice.

Alex dropped us off at my house and seemed eager to get back to the station. It sounded like he had a mound of work to complete.

"You don't even want to come in for a coffee?" I asked.

He shook his head. "I'm sure I'll go through a pot and a half at work, but I really need to get started or I'll have another problem with Corbett in the morning."

"Okay, but let me just grab you something to heat up for a late-night snack at the station," I said. "It'll take two minutes and your brain will work better off of real food than it will off of vending machine junk."

"Spoken like a true chef," Amber mumbled for the second time today. But now that Alex was leaving us for the night, she realized she still had questions about the investigation. "So if Tonya Dartengel shows up at her apartment, will they call you right away? Will you get to go back there and make the arrest?"

I figured Alex would be at least two minutes answering her questions, so I hurried into the house to pack up a large slice of quiche for him.

I'd forgotten all about Hunch, who was just inside the front door, at attention on his haunches when I strode in.

"Hi, Hunch, how was your day?" I quickly strode by him toward the kitchen.

He let out a growl and followed me.

In the kitchen, it took me mere seconds to get the quiche packed up in a to-go container. I decided to just send the rest of the pie along with Alex, as Amber and I could always make another one if we wanted.

Hunch growled again and I told him, "Don't worry, Amber's here. She'll tell you everything."

This seemed to appease him for the moment. I was getting less and less offended that I wasn't Hunch's favorite person. I hadn't been before Cooper died, and it was clear after his death that not much had changed in that department. I was happy Hunch and Amber liked each other. Amber needed Hunch in her life, and I needed Amber in mine. It seemed only logical to quell any jealousy and be glad for what I had.

After Alex had driven off with his quiche, Amber and I headed inside. For once, Amber got a small taste of Hunch's bristly attitude when she tried to snuggle him before spilling all the details of the day.

"Talk first," I told her. "Cuddle later. Trust me."

Amber headed for the kitchen with my irritated cat outstretched in her arms. I filled Hunch's food bowl, while Amber got the notepad out of my purse.

"It's good to go over the whole story, anyway. We should double-check we haven't missed anything," she said.

"You don't think it's clear that Tonya Dartengel had means, opportunity, and the strongest motive of all?"

"Yeah, probably. But what if we're wrong and we just spent the day running on a wild goose chase?" She flipped back through pages.

Hunch ignored his food bowl and hopped up on one of the other kitchen chairs, placing his paws on the table. When Cooper and I had first taken Hunch into our house, I'd gotten mad at him for this sort of thing, telling him tables were for people, but since Cooper's death, I pretty much let him make his own rules. Besides, if he wanted to sit across from me at a meal, that actually felt a lot nicer than eating alone.

"So let's go over the people who were at the vineyard Friday night," she said. As usual, when there was investigative work to go over, my mind worked better when I was cooking. Besides, I'd only eaten that half-sandwich all afternoon, so I was still pretty hungry. I opened the fridge and surveyed its contents as Amber went on. "Don and Marie Tallman, the owners of the winery. Your notes say they were upset with their son after the body was found?"

I pulled a roasting chicken I'd left thawing from the fridge. "They seemed mostly concerned with the reputation of their winery."

Amber made a note. "And Benji saw Don Tallman around the time of the murder, but Benji's whereabouts are unaccounted for? I wonder if Detective Martinez should grill them about their knowledge of Tonya or Gary Dillon. Maybe they were all in on it together."

I set the chicken on the counter and went back to the fridge for some bacon, red pepper, and green onion. I figured I could make a nice stuffing for the chicken while we talked. "Don and Benji both had their reasons for not being in the winery at the time Jennifer was killed. Benji was guarding the electrical panel for the winery in case Jennifer showed up to try and cut the power, and he saw his dad go into his house."

Amber nodded, still making additional notes. "And is his house closer to the vineyard than the winery building or farther away from it?"

"I think it's behind the winery, farther from the vineyard," I said. But if for some reason Tonya Dartengel didn't turn out to be the person responsible for Jennifer Rempel's death, perhaps this was something we'd have to confirm.

"Still, they both seem like weak alibis."

"But let's not forget that Don Tallman had no motive to kill Jennifer Rempel, other than her shunning his wine at a Bible study. He certainly wouldn't have wanted to kill her on his own property."

Amber nodded. "That makes sense. What are you making?"

"I'm stuffing the chicken to roast it." I already had half of the bacon layered on the breast of the chicken, and the other half cut up into small pieces and frying on the stove. I continued chopping a red pepper and green onion to throw in with our leftover panko from this morning.

She watched what I was doing, but didn't offer to get up and help. She was too focused on the investigation at the moment. "Still, both Benji and Don would've known how to operate their own tractor and how to navigate the rows in the vineyard, even at night, right?"

"Sure, but I bet Kristoph Carter was even more proficient with it. And the person who drove it that night didn't seem to know where they were going, with all the stops and turns."

She flipped pages, looking for Kristoph's alibi.

"Kristoph was out in the vineyard because he thought he heard the tractor."

Amber nodded and made another note. "Or he was out there because Bart and Dahlia were meeting him to buy pot. Let's not forget that Tonya and Gary both lived on a farm at one point. So at least six people were in the vicinity, and at least four of them knew how to drive the tractor and were unaccounted for at the time of Ms. Rempel's death." She ticked off names on my notepad. "Benji and Don Tallman, Tonya Dillon, and Kristoph Carter. Gary was inside playing guitar at the time. How long has Mr. Carter worked for the Tallmans?"

"I think for most of the five years they've owned it," I said from memory. I hadn't made a note of that.

"Would Kristoff have had any motivation to kill Jennifer Rempel? Did he know her?"

I shook my head, dumping my diced red pepper into the pan of sizzling bacon. "No, he said they'd never met, and he didn't seem to recognize her when he first came across her body while Alex and I were out there. Remember, he was the one who gave the police sketch of Tonya Dartengel."

"Who we think is Tonya Dartengel," Amber said. "Or could he have been throwing us off his trail by cooperating with the police and helping them come up with a sketch of another suspect?"

This was Amber's way. When we got close in an investigation, she worked hard at poking any possible holes into it. It was another thing that made her a better detective than me. I wondered if it was healthy for her to be so suspicious of everyone though.

"Right. Who we think is Tonya Dartengel, but it seems like a pretty big coincidence that the sketch looks so much like the mother of a kid Jennifer killed seven years ago."

Amber watched as I mixed the stuffing ingredients together and then seasoned them with salt and pepper before wedging it all into the small chicken cavity. Then I slathered the outside of the chicken skin and bacon strips in butter, garlic salt, an Italian seasoning blend I'd made myself, and fresh-ground pepper. I drizzled a little olive oil over the top so it wouldn't burn and slid it into my preheated oven.

"Who else?" I asked from the sink while washing my hands.

Amber flipped pages back and forth. "I think we can safely remove Jordan Rempel from suspicion."

It was a good sign that Amber was willing to remove anyone from suspicion. That part was hard for her. "I agree."

"And neither of us have spoken to Jennifer's parents, but I don't get the feeling they killed their own daughter."

I nodded. "Me neither."

Hunch had finally lost interest in our investigative talk and swatted at a pen on the table.

"I have a good feeling the police in Morgantown are going to catch up with either Tonya or her ex-husband, Gary, tonight." I came to the table and stood across from Amber, but I didn't make any effort to pull out my own chair and sit. I couldn't sit still when I was mentally working through an investigation.

Hunch knocked the pen to the floor. I gave him the evil eye and picked it up, but he paid me no attention. In fact, he was too busy swatting at some of my papers at the back edge of the table. A couple of them fluttered to the floor. I let out a groan as I picked Hunch up off the chair and put him down on the linoleum where he belonged. I swiped up the papers, which include a water bill, an ongoing grocery list, and the swatch of paper with the address of Honey Littles Elementary School.

I stared at the small swatch of paper. "We never did figure out why Tonya had the address of the elementary school written down, if it was indeed her on the tractor."

Amber squinted, pursing her lips. "Maybe it was her backup plan? If she didn't track down Jennifer at the Bible study, she'd track her down Monday when she picked Fresco up from school?"

I nodded. That made sense. "If we haven't heard anything by tomorrow afternoon, I'll pick you up from school. We could swing by the elementary school and talk to the school secretary, see if she's seen a woman that looks like the sketch."

Amber nodded. "Hopefully, we'll have an answer before then. I can't imagine sitting through school all day, still not knowing."

I felt her pain. But just the same, there was no way she was going to talk me out of dropping her off at school in the morning, no matter how much she tried.

I was almost certain of it. □

# CHAPTER TWENTY-EIGHT

It was late by the time we finished eating my chicken and stuffing and the delicious honey-garlic veggie stir fry Amber cooked up using an online recipe.

As we were saying goodnight, a call came in from Alex.

"Did you hear something?" My heart rate ratcheted up as I put him on speakerphone.

"Yeah, the Morgantown PD just called. They caught up with Gary Dillon at his farm when he returned home earlier this evening and have been questioning him ever since."

I checked my watch. It was almost midnight. "If they've been questioning him that long, it must mean he knows something, right?"

I could sense Alex nodding on the other end of the phone, even if I couldn't see it. Amber and I looked at each other with wide, intense eyes, waiting for more.

"He heard from his ex-wife, Tonya, on Friday. Apparently, she rarely spoke to him since their son, Brennan, died, so when she showed up at their farm and told him to get into her vehicle and that it had something to do with Brennan, he didn't hesitate. Tonya talked a blue streak all the way to Honeysuckle Grove about how the woman who had killed Brennan was making herself famous on TV, talking with a complete lack of integrity against drunk drivers and pretending that she would never do such a thing."

Alex took a breath before he went on. Amber and I were holding ours. "He said as far as he knew, Tonya just wanted to tell Jennifer how much it hurt to see the woman who'd killed her son all skinny and happy and on TV, while Tonya had been depressed, gaining weight, and couldn't even hold down a job seven years later. After they stopped by Jordan Rempel's house and Tonya found out Jennifer was divorced, Gary thought this would make Tonya at least feel somewhat better, but she came down the street to where Gary was waiting in Tonya's Suburban, and she became even more driven to find Jennifer and speak her mind. Gary kept trying to calm her down as she ran stoplights all through town, desperate to find Jennifer, and when they finally discovered where she'd be for the night, it seemed to take Tonya mere seconds to come up with a plan: Gary would go into the Bible study, offer to play guitar, and she would intercept Jennifer outside."

"She just happened to have a guitar with her?" Amber asked, interrupting.

"Apparently, that's how Gary and Tonya first met—they were both musicians. Tonya didn't go anywhere without her guitar, and Gary could play, so she decided that would make a good distraction while she went to give Jennifer a piece of her mind."

"He had no idea his wife planned to kill her?"

Alex took another audible breath. "He still doesn't think that's what she intended. He thinks Tonya only meant to yell at her, maybe scare her a little, but then when he heard the scream, and there was a cop there…he panicked. He followed the crowd out toward the vineyard, but then slipped away to where they'd left Tonya's Suburban down the road. But Tonya had taken off on him. He had to hitchhike all the way back to Morgantown, and he hasn't heard from her since."

"Has he seen the news?" I asked. "Did he know Jennifer was dead?"

"Yeah, and he says he was going to come forward to the police, but he wanted to talk to Tonya first, give her the benefit of the doubt. He'd been looking all over Morgantown for her."

"Even though she left him on the side of the road in a different town?" Amber's tone conveyed every bit of her disbelief.

"That's why they've been questioning him all evening, to see if we can get him on an accessory to this murder. We probably still can, as he didn't come forward with what he knew, but to me, it's more important to find out if there's any way he can lead us to Tonya."

"And can he?" Amber and I were at the base of the stairs, neither of us in any hurry to go to bed now. I, for one, would head straight out my front door, even at midnight, if there was something we could do to catch this woman.

But then I heard the defeat in his voice with his first words. "All the people he's gotten me in touch with, friends and relatives, are either in Morgantown and the Morgantown PD has already spoken to them, or they're in Michigan, where she used to live. I'll have to wait until morning to start making those phone calls."

"I don't know. I feel like she's still close." Amber often had good instincts, but sometimes she just wanted to believe in our success so badly that it swayed her. I suspected this was one of those times.

"I'm going to check again at the local hospital on my way home, show them the sketch and make sure they haven't seen anyone that looks like her. Maybe even go back to our two hotels." Alex sounded exhausted.

"Do you think you'll have time for any sleep in there?" I hoped he could tell this was just me caring about him.

"We'll see." Before he hung up, he told us he'd connect with us again in the morning if he found anything useful from calling people in Michigan.

I supposed I should have been concerned for my own sleep as well. I tossed and turned all night, kept awake by my still-stirring questions about the murder investigation, along with the unrelenting stare of my cat from the other side of the bed.

Usually, whenever Amber slept over, Hunch holed up in the guest room with her. I thought it was intuitive on his part, and rather sweet, as Amber hadn't been sleeping well since her dad's death. Hunch seemed to have a sixth sense, though, and somehow knew I would be the one tossing and turning tonight, probably even before I did.

I finally nodded off sometime in the early morning, only to be woken what felt like five minutes later by my alarm clock. I slapped it to turn it off and looked around the bedroom. At some point, I must have been sleeping soundly enough that I didn't notice Hunch slip out because I was alone now.

I could hear the hood fan from the kitchen and figured Amber must be up and cooking something already. I asked her once last week if she had been cooking much at home, but she told me despite the modern amenities of the kitchen in her mansion, she hated cooking there.

"It just feels like you're not supposed to touch anything in our kitchen," Amber had told me. "Maybe it has something to do with growing up with a housekeeper, but at your house, it just feels like everything is here to be used."

I was glad she felt comfortable cooking in my kitchen, even comfortable enough that she would go ahead and do it without me. I decided to head for the shower first and let her complete whatever she'd started on her own. A certain amount of kitchen confidence could only be earned when you made something from start to finish all by yourself. I'd learned that in culinary school.

Before I got in the shower, I texted Alex. <Any new word from Morgantown PD?>

And by the time I got out, he'd responded. <Nothing yet. Mickey checked out our local hotels and the hospital again this morning. No Tonya Dartengel at any of them. I have a call in to the Morgantown captain for an update. He wasn't in yet.>

Fifteen minutes later, I headed down the stairs, my hair still damp. I was feeling refreshed, despite my lack of proper sleep.

"What smells so good?" I asked, entering the kitchen.

Amber shrugged from where she sat at the table, a slice of quiche on a plate in front of her, and the rest still sitting in a pie plate in the oven with the door ajar.

"You made a quiche!" This wasn't the easiest thing to make well, but I could tell just by the look of the slice on her plate that it hadn't come out soggy, which was often the biggest concern.

She shrugged again. Today's choice of hoodie was bright yellow and read: YOU'RE ON MUTE. "You were out of peppers. I put mushrooms in mine."

Mushrooms were even more difficult to incorporate into a quiche because they carried so much natural moisture. Still, I was well aware of Amber's abrasion to compliments, so I didn't go on and on about this. I simply cut myself a slice, poked a fork into each side of it as I brought it to the table, and raised my eyebrows as I said, "Nice."

She bit back a smile and carved off a forkful for herself. Hunch, of course, had followed Amber downstairs and sat at her feet. He had knocked my papers off the table again. Silly cat, always wanting to play—.

That thought stopped midway into my tired, morning brain because it was so obviously incorrect. Hunch, even as a kitten, had never had much patience for playtime.

I tilted my head, looking down at him. The same water bill had fluttered to the floor behind him, but underneath his front paw was the swatch of paper with the elementary school's address on its upturned side. He stared up at me, as if willing me to understand.

"What is it, Hunch?" I asked, leaving the water bill, but reaching for the swatch under his paw. He immediately lifted his paw to let me have it. "Are we missing something here?"

With my question, he stood from his haunches and padded toward my legs. He moved back and forth against my calves, suddenly purring.

"We're missing something," I said, this time as a statement, rather than a question. "Clearly, Tonya Dartengel was responsible for Jennifer Rempel's death. We just have to find her."

"And if she recently killed someone," Amber said, as if continuing my train of thought, "why hang around Honeysuckle Grove? Why take down the address of one of our elementary schools in the first place?"

My mind was on Tonya's visit to Jordan Rempel. She'd gotten the fact that Jennifer was divorced and at a Bible study out of Jordan, but then returned to her own ex-husband more agitated than she already had been. Why?

"She got what she wanted. And then she got more than she might have wanted by killing Jennifer."

As Amber said the words, a new thought occurred to me. "But what if she didn't get what she wanted?" Amber furrowed her brow at my question, so I went on. "What if the revenge wasn't enough? What if what really agitated Tonya was seeing Jennifer's son, Fresco, at the door at Jordan's house?"

Amber started to nod slowly, her eyes moving back and forth over mine as if she were a computer, processing all of these questions. "What if she didn't need the address to the elementary school for the lady who killed her kid?"

My heart rate increased. "Fresco!" I said in revelation, at the same time that Amber said, "What if she's still coming for Jennifer Rempel's son?"

☐

# CHAPTER TWENTY-NINE

All morning, we hadn't been rushed because Amber's school didn't start for another half an hour. But Amber was quite sure the elementary school just down the road from her school started earlier.

"Whenever I go early, I see them walking to school." Without any discussion about it, she led the way to the entry, snatched up her shoes in one hand, and headed for the door without taking the time to put them on. Hunch scampered out after her, and I didn't have the time or the brainpower to argue. I crushed the heels of my own sneakers down and raced for the door.

As soon as we were in my Prius, I told Amber, "Set my GPS. Get me the fastest route to Honey Littles Elementary. Then text Alex."

Amber didn't argue. Hunch let out a low, rumbling growl from the backseat. I was starting to be able to interpret his growls, and this seemed like one that was telling me I was on the right track.

I headed east. I at least had a general idea of where Meridian Avenue was located. The robotic GPS voice interrupted my concentration on the road to tell me our destination was six minutes away. I looked at the clock on the dash, and it said seven forty-five. After texting Alex, Amber searched online for the start time of Honey Littles Elementary, and it came up as eight a.m. I hoped that would be earlier than Jordan Rempel planned to drop off his stepson.

As we got closer, my angst only increased. I depressed my foot on the gas, catching up to the tailgate of the truck in front of me. Each time I stopped, I worked at getting my feet properly into my shoes, but it wasn't enough to distract me from my panic. "There has to be a faster way!"

Amber pulled my phone from the console, searching other routes, but shaking her head. "We're not far now anyway. Alex texted back. He's on his way to the elementary school. Maybe he can get there quicker, coming from the other direction." She put the phone down and pulled on her sneakers, but the time to arrival on my GPS was increasing by the second. Soon we were back at being six minutes away. Then seven. Then eight.

Nobody would get there quickly in this traffic. It was so thick, it was practically at a standstill. "Maybe something has already happened up ahead. Why is everything so slow?" I banged my steering wheel in frustration, but Amber put a hand on my arm.

"This is just drop-off time craziness. Trust me, it's like this every day. When they plan schools, they need to make a better infrastructure for people to easily drop off and pick up their kids." Amber sounded like this was a normal part of life.

"But what if Tonya Dartengel is up ahead in her green Suburban?" I tried to get a vantage point of the road up ahead, but the truck in front of me was too big and, thanks to my impatience, too close. "It would almost be faster to get there on foot."

My words were barely out of my mouth when two things happened at once. My foot hit the brake, and I stopped just in time to avoid hitting the big Ford truck in front of me, and Amber's passenger door flew open.

"You're right," she said. And then she was running.

I kept up my go-go-stop routine with the truck in front of me for the next ten seconds or so, but during that time, my GPS made its way up to ten minutes, and I could only envision Amber running up ahead, seeing a green Suburban, and darting out in front of it, no matter the consequences.

She was fifteen! And I, once again, had brought her into this. Please, God, take care of her!

Without thinking twice, I jammed my car into park, left the car running, and flung open my door.

The second I was on my feet, I could see more of the endless line of cars in front of me, parents waiting to drop off their young kids. But I could also see the elementary school. It would definitely be faster on foot.

I ignored the honks from the cars behind my Prius as I picked up to a run, keeping my eyes peeled for a green Suburban, a teenager on a mission, and a little boy named Fresco.

☐

# CHAPTER THIRTY

As I ran, I tried to think about Tonya Dartengel's plans logically. In a line of nearly stopped cars, she wasn't going to be able to kidnap Fresco or even knock into him very hard with her vehicle. Even without any help, a six-year-old boy would be able to escape that.

But as I grew close enough to see the school sign, the other side of the busy road cut off and it became a one-way. There was only one direction to drop off your kids. And once kids were dropped off, I could see up ahead that the line moved quite quickly. Fast enough that a kid could certainly get injured, if not killed, by someone on a mission.

But I still couldn't see a green Suburban, or now that I thought about it, I also couldn't see the small black smart car that had been in Jordan Rempel's driveway.

I stopped in place, surveying the situation. "I don't understand," I said to myself. "Did we get this all wrong?"

Movement caught my eye, and I turned toward the school to see Amber perched up on the cement base of a flagpole to get a higher vantage point. She looked around for about three seconds, and then she bounded away from the flag, across the crawling traffic, to the next road over.

That was when I remembered Gina Thomson telling me that Jordan Rempel dropped Fresco off from a distance, but from somewhere close enough that she'd been able to see him as a crossing guard.

I bounded after Amber, looking at the two crossing guards near the school, looking at my feet so I didn't trip, and trying not to run into any cars. I caught a glimpse of Amber's bright yellow hoodie and followed it.

I finally got past the two crawling rows of cars, which had to merge to get into the drop-off circle. No wonder they were moving so slowly. As the next street over came into view, I saw two things at once:

One, Fresco stepped out of a black smart car on the far side of a nearly empty grocery store parking lot, and two, a green Suburban idled against the curb along the next much emptier street fifty feet away from them. But it didn't look like anyone was behind the wheel.

Regardless, Amber barreled ahead, her eyes fixated on the Suburban.

I picked up to a run again, straight for Amber. She should not be going after a murderer alone! But when I glanced back to the smart car, Fresco was suddenly nowhere in sight. Had Tonya gotten a hold of him somehow? But no, I was close enough that I would have surely seen her, at least enough to recognize her oblong face and widow's peak from the police sketch.

Had Tonya brought an accomplice? Had the Morgantown police department released her ex-husband in time so he could show up and help her?

But as I looked back and forth between the Suburban and the smart car, Fresco appeared again. He stood from where he'd been crouched behind Jordan's smart car with a bundle of fur in his arms.

Hunch!

Fresco took a step around Jordan's car with his attention rapt on my cat. Even Jordan was momentarily distracted by the cat and called out his window, "They're not going to let you take that into class, bud."

During this distraction, nobody but me noticed a figure sit up behind the wheel of the Suburban, and then it started to move.

"Watch out!" I called to Amber, but at the exact same time, the Suburban revved its engine, drowning out my words.

Amber glanced over her shoulder at me, but couldn't hear me, so she kept barreling forward. I was too far away. If the Suburban launched ahead, Amber would be right in its path. This lady was on a mission. I could make out her dark angled eyebrows and widow's peak from my place down the road. She wasn't going to stop for anybody, even if they weren't her intended target.

The Suburban was going to crush my best friend before it even got to Fresco.

☐

# CHAPTER THIRTY-ONE

Hunch belonged on the police force more than any of us.

When the Suburban's engine revved, he must have dug his claws into Fresco's arm because a second later, Fresco screamed and looked down, dropping my cat. He turned away from the Suburban, away from his stepdad's car, and ran back to the sidewalk to find Hunch. He called, "Bad kitty!" after him.

Jordan put his car in park and got out to go make sure his still-crying stepson was okay. He squatted on the sidewalk to look at Fresco's arm. Unnoticed to them, the Suburban picked up speed straight for them, and I was betting Tonya would be willing to launch right onto the sidewalk and take down Jordan at the same time.

Hunch's distraction had made Amber pause to look at Fresco, only for a second, but it was the second I needed to catch up, grab onto the shoulder of her hoodie, and yank her back from the Suburban's path.

She looked surprised, then angry. Only a second later, the Suburban sailed by us so quickly we could feel its wind. Amber followed my lead. We cupped our hands around our mouths and yelled, "Jordan! Watch out!" at the top of our lungs.

He looked up just in time. The Suburban drove up onto the curb and straight for them. Jordan pushed his stepson behind his car, but Tonya wasn't deterred. She slammed on her brakes and backed up, angled straight toward the smart car. The tiny car would be obliterated by the big Suburban. Not only that, but there was another car not far behind Jordan's in the parking lot. Fresco was going to get crushed between the cars!

Not if I could help it. While Tonya backed up to re-angle, I raced straight for Jordan, who was now behind his car with Fresco. Jordan didn't understand what Tonya was doing—who would purposely try to run people over on a sidewalk?—and stood between the two cars, stunned.

I gave it all my effort, ran straight ahead, and a second later, felt like I'd run straight into a brick wall.

# CHAPTER THIRTY-TWO

The smart car made a crunching sound as it crushed into the sedan behind it. I lay on the cement, shoulder aching. Somehow I'd pushed Fresco and Jordan out of the way and managed to soften the kid's landing on the sidewalk.

I could barely move from the pain, but looking up, I could see the fire in Tonya's eyes as she registered that I'd gotten Fresco out of the way. He was a screaming, crying mess, but Jordan came and grabbed him from me anyway.

As Tonya attempted to back up her Suburban and reset its course yet another time, I yelled to Jordan with everything I had left in me. "Take him! Get him out of here! The lady in the Suburban wants to kill him!"

Only a second later, Jordan was up on his feet, his small stepson in his arms, and he was running toward the school. Unfortunately, the parking lot between Jordan's car and the school drop-off area was a blank slate for possible driving infractions.

Fresco, now a mess of tears, wiggled in Jordan's arms as he zigzagged his path in an attempt to keep Fresco safe from a Suburban.

I finally pushed to my feet by the time Tonya had reversed and re-angled her vehicle, but before she could launch forward, a bang on her window stopped her. Amber had leaped onto the running boards of the Suburban and was banging on Tonya's driver's window.

Seconds felt like minutes, but I looked back to see Jordan and Fresco had nearly made it across the parking lot. Amber only had to buy them a few more seconds.

But then Tonya pushed hard on her driver's door, effectively knocking

Amber off and onto her rear on the pavement.

"No!" I yelled futilely. Jordan had too far to go. The Suburban picked up speed toward them.

But then I heard a glorious sound.

I had never been so thankful to hear police sirens.

As I raced forward to make sure Amber was okay, I prayed the distraction of the sirens would be enough to get Jordan and Fresco safely across the parking lot. Two police cars whipped the wrong way down the other side of the one-way street, trying to get to the parking lot.

Tonya floored the gas in her Suburban. Drivers who had already dropped off their kids tried to let the police cars through, but for a few extended seconds, it was a mess of cars and I wondered if Alex and the police officers were going to be too late.

But before I could blink, one of the police cars got through the brigade of cars and barreled over the curb and right into the grocery store parking lot. It skidded to a stop less than ten feet in front of the Suburban.

For a second, I wondered if this would even be a deterrent for Tonya Dartengel. But when Alex got out of the passenger seat and held up his badge toward her, she finally hit the brakes and collapsed forward against her steering wheel.

As the police officers moved around the Suburban on either side, Jordan got Fresco to the line of drop-off vehicles, through those vehicles, and he finally collapsed with him at the flagpole.

The officers quickly got Tonya out of her Suburban and cuffed her. Amber collapsed back onto her rear on the pavement, obviously spent. God had come through again, this time not only for me, but for those I cared about most. Even Hunch had somehow avoided all the catastrophes and now sniffed around the tires of the Suburban.

I ran to Jordan to make sure they were both all right.

"It's okay, buddy," he said into the kid's dark hair.

Fresco looked up and said, "When we get a kitty, can we pick out a nicer one?"

I smiled down at them, knowing now wasn't the time to brag on my amazing cat. Instead, I turned to Jordan and said, "I think that kid is more yours than you realize."

# CHAPTER THIRTY-THREE

The irony of the matter was that Tonya Dartengel was facing a lot more jail time than Jennifer had ever been sentenced to for killing her child. The difference was intent. Jennifer had never meant to hurt anybody. In fact, when she hit Brennan Dillon, she had only been trying to get a bunch of loudmouth partiers home safely because their "designated driver" had no sense of responsibility and she had been the soberest of the bunch.

Alex found all this out when he followed up with Jennifer's parents to let them know he had caught the person responsible for her death. Jennifer finally found purpose in being a mother, but still couldn't shake her guilt, Alex surmised, and that was likely why she got so involved with Mothers Against Drunk Drivers.

Tonya had admitted to wanting to yell at Jennifer, maybe even scare her, but once Jennifer started screaming, Tonya had to do whatever she could to shut her up. Tonya's ex-husband, Gary, had received reduced charges for helping the police, but he was also likely facing some jail time. Once we explained to him that his ex-wife had found out Jennifer had a son of her own, and she went after him to try to kill him as well, Gary only nodded his head and said, "Ahh," as though her severe retribution was starting to make sense to him.

Even Captain Corbett ended up having to give Alex credit for his detective work and the two arrests, as the Morgantown police captain hadn't stopped showering Alex with praise for his insightful work.

Once the paperwork was filed, Alex had wanted to get together to discuss the details of the case, as we always did. I'd invited him and Amber over the next Saturday, and he'd quickly replied with <It's a date!>, which immediately made me blush.

"Captain Jagg even said that if I ever felt like transferring out of

Honeysuckle Grove, to give him a call," Alex said excitedly the next Saturday from my kitchen table.

That's what I was afraid of. "Who wants cookies?" I asked to change the subject.

Hunch paced alongside the table, as though it wasn't a relaxed weekend of decompressing, and there was still plenty of sleuthing to be done.

"I could always eat one of your cookies. Or maybe more than one," Alex said with a wink.

Amber beat me to the pantry, popping out of her seat in only a second. Alex had given her plenty of praise—and a little admonishment—for going to such lengths to try and stop Tonya from barreling into Fresco, and being the girl who couldn't handle compliments, Amber was eager to get cooking as well.

We discussed more of the details while we measured and mixed flour, sugar, and baking soda to start our dry ingredient mix.

Because the Morgantown police captain had requested Alex's presence to go over the details of the case, he'd been back and forth on the road a lot, while his partner, Mickey Mouse, had been left with the bulk of the paperwork that had originally been piled onto Alex's desk.

Sounded like poetic justice to me.

But even Alex's incompetent partner couldn't bring me down today. It was Saturday, both Alex's and Amber's day off from work and school. We had plenty to celebrate, and no shortage of ingredients in the pantry.

This was the only kind of date I was ready to be on. One with my best friends, my husband's cat, and a whole lot of food.


# END OF BOOK 4.

Honest reviews help bring new books to the attention of other readers. If you enjoyed this book, I would be grateful if you would take five minutes to write a couple of sentences about it. You can find all the books in this series to leave reviews at this link.

Thank you!

# UP NEXT: MURDER AT THE MONTROSE MANSION

There are plenty of things a girl wants to do on her sixteenth birthday. Clearing a family member from suspicion of murder isn't one of them. Amber is finally turning sixteen, and Mallory is determined to make the day perfect, baking her everything from brioche to pink lemonade cupcakes for the party her mom is throwing her. Their favorite Honeysuckle Grove detective, Alex Martinez, will be in attendance, too, at least until he gets called away to investigate a recently discovered death involving possible foul play.

When Amber's last name is the only clue given as to what he might find at the nearby crime scene, Alex and Mallory decide they might have to keep this one quiet or Amber's sixteenth birthday will be anything but sweet.

Order Murder at the Montrose Mansion now!

# JOIN MY COZY MYSTERY READERS' NEWSLETTER TODAY!

Would you like to be among the first to hear about new releases and sales, and receive special excerpts and behind-the-scene bonuses?

Sign up now to get your free copy of Mystery of the Secret Ingredients – A Mallory Beck Cozy Holiday Mystery, where Amber enters a cooking competition and Mallory puts aside her own nagging mystery in order to help her.

You'll also get access to special epilogues to accompany this series—an exclusive bonus for newsletter subscribers. Sign up below and receive your free mystery:

https://www.subscribepage.com/mysteryreaders

# TURN THE PAGE TO FIND A RECIPE FROM MALLORY'S RECIPE BOX...

# From Mallory's Recipe Box: Coconut Shrimp with Mango Salsa

These delectable shrimp are pure crunch-in-the-mouth goodness! Use store-bought panko or try the recipe at the bottom to make your own. The mango salsa adds just the right amount of heat and sweet to complement these tasty treats.

Ingredients

Coconut Shrimp:
- 1 lb. jumbo shrimp, peeled and deveined with tails on
- 1/2 cup all-purpose flour
- Salt to taste
- Ground black pepper to taste
- 1 cup panko bread crumbs (see recipe below to make your own!)
- 1/2 cup shredded sweetened coconut
- 2 large eggs, beaten

Mango Salsa:
- 3 ripe mangos, diced
- 1 red bell pepper, diced
- ½ cup red onion, diced
- ¼ cup packed fresh cilantro leaves, chopped
- 1 jalapeño, seeded and minced
- 1 large lime, juiced (or about ¼ cup lime juice)
- Salt, to taste

Panko:
- 1 loaf of airy white bread, crusts removed

## MANGO SALSA INSTRUCTIONS:

Note: I prepare the mango salsa in advance, so it's ready to eat when the shrimp are hot and fresh.

1. In a processor, combine the prepared mango, bell pepper, onion, cilantro and jalapeño. Drizzle with the juice of one lime.
2. Pulse a couple of times to make the salsa dippable, and then season with salt and stir again.
3. Add to a serving bowl and let the salsa rest for at least ten minutes.

# COCONUT SHRIMP INSTRUCTIONS:

Note: These tasty shrimp can be cooked using a deep fryer, for maximum crispiness, a frying pan with oil, or an air fryer, for a low-fat alternative.

1.      Place three shallow bowls alongside one another. In the first, season flour with salt and pepper. In another shallow bowl, combine panko bread crumbs and coconut. Place beaten eggs in a third shallow bowl.
2.      Working with one at a time, dip shrimp in flour, then eggs, then coconut mixture.
3.      Preheat your deep fryer, air fryer to 400 degrees, or preheat a frying pan coated with coconut oil. When all the shrimp are prepared, space out and place in your deep or air fryer basket, or onto your preheated frying pan. Make sure these shrimp have plenty of room, and don't crown the fryer or the frying pan. Cook until shrimp is golden and cooked through, about 10 to 12 minutes in the air fryer or frying pan (turning once in the frying pan. Work in batches as necessary.

# PANKO INSTRUCTIONS:

1.      Preheat oven to 350 degrees.
2.      Tear into pieces and pulse 1 to 2 times in a food processor.
3.      Place bread shards onto a baking sheet lined with parchment paper.
4.      Bake at 350 degrees for 5-7 minute. Be extra careful not to let the panko brown. Remove breadcrumbs from the oven, let cool, and store in glass jars until you're ready to make your coconut shrimp.

I love to hear from readers after they try out one of Mallory's recipes! Drop me a note at d@denisejaden.com and let me know how you liked this one. Enjoy!

# ACKNOWLEDGEMENTS

Thank you to my ever-helpful team of advance readers and supporters. You are all amazing and I can't thank you enough for helping to get my little books a little notice in the huge and cluttered landscape of new releasing books. I'd like to specifically call out a few people who have really gone above and beyond in supporting me and encouraging me: Marj, Shelly, Betty, Monica, Iris, Chad, and Betsy. If your name is not on that list, please know that I appreciate you just for picking up this book and giving it a chance!

Thank you to my developmental editor, Louise Bates, my copyeditor, Sara Burgess, my cover designer, Steven Novak, and illustrator, Ethan Heyde. Special thanks to the book bloggers and bookstagrammers who have shared about my books, and for anyone who has taken the time to share to their own social media following.

Thank you for joining me, along with Mallory, Amber, Alex, and Hunch on this journey. We're thrilled to have you along on this ride!

# ABOUT THE AUTHOR

Denise Jaden is a co-author of the Rosa Reed Mystery Series by Lee Strauss, the author of several critically-acclaimed young adult novels, as well as the author of several nonfiction books for writers, including the NaNoWriMo-popular guide Fast Fiction. Her new Mallory Beck Cozy Culinary Mystery Series will continue to launch throughout the year, and you can add the first book to your reading list on GoodReads right now. In her spare time, she homeschools her son (a budding filmmaker), acts in TV and movies, and dances with a Polynesian dance troupe. She lives just outside Vancouver, British Columbia, with her husband, son, and one very spoiled cat.

Sign up on Denise's website to receive bonus content as well as updates on her new Cozy Mystery Series. Find out more at www.denisejaden.com

Made in the USA
Monee, IL
24 April 2022

3e54f111-6d33-4ad5-a289-e6d68c6f958dR01